Frank Yerby was born in Augusta, Georgia, in 1916. He studied at Fisk University in Tennessee and at the University of Chicago, where he gained his MA degree. During the war he wrote his first novel and has since had many others published. He now lives in Spain.

Also by Frank Yerby in Pan Books

The Girl from Storyville
Jarrett's Jade
Fairoaks
Captain Rebel
Benton's Row
Griffin's Way

Frank Yerby

THE VOYAGE UNPLANNED

Pan Books in association with
William Heinemann

First published in Great Britain 1974 by William Heinemann Ltd
This edition published 1976 by Pan Books Ltd,
Cavaye Place, London SW10 9PG,
in association with William Heinemann Ltd

ISBN 0 330 24631 3
Made and printed in Great Britain by
Cox & Wyman Ltd, London, Reading and Fakenham

SONNET VII

Down all these sombre roads I now must go
To take a ghostly ship towards some bright land –
That unknown country on whose shores you stand
And call me siren-voiced, although you know
My grave-clogged ears won't hear, and my bark – slow
Clawing off death's own lee shore, spectre manned,
Its Captain blind, charts lost, the voyage unplanned –
Must beat to hopeless windward ever so,
And never reach your heaven from my hell.
Vain pilgrimage, Simone! I can't come back –
And would not if I could – into your life,
To pitch smear with the stains of grief, of strife –
Mere flotsam now – a bed that does not lack
Or need my love. God bless you both. Farewell!

From 'Seven Sonnets for Simone' by Dalton Ross

Prologue

One of the questions a writer is most frequently asked is how he ever thought of the idea for a particular work in the first place. Most of the time, if he's honest, he has to admit that he simply doesn't know. Most novels seem to autodictate themselves by the accumulation of bits and pieces in one's subconscious, where the peculiar kind of minds (?) that novelists have, begin to hook them together without the writer's really being aware of what's going on. Which is tantamount to saying that no *sane* person could ever be a novelist. True. Only one has to be crazy in a very special way.

But this novel – its beginning, anyhow, and the exact physical description of its female protagonist (along with the seed of one other novel he still doesn't *know* the way you have to know a novel in your nerves, your guts, your blood, to even begin writing it) were both handed to this writer upon a silver platter, as it were, the same night, within minutes of each other.

Some twenty-odd years ago, this writer was living in Paris. One night, being rather at loose ends, he went to a party given by some friends of friends in a huge, and mostly empty, apartment on the Left Bank.

The first thing he saw when he got there was the beginning of the novel he has never been able to do, largely because he finds incomprehensible and impenetrable the workings of the French female antagonist's mind. (Though, thinking about it now, she'd have to be the protagonist, wouldn't she? And the novel about how a flaming liberal could retreat – or be beaten down – into, over the years, the type of bone-marrow mean reactionary she had become. You see? Novels really write themselves, any way you figure it!)

That beginning was a cute little Afro-French girl (this writer still, despite all the angry letters, refuses to call a girl the colour of taffy candy, a Black. Abusing language is a stupid way to defend racial pride). She was wearing the first Afro he ever saw.

She didn't know it was an Afro. She simply didn't know where, nor have the money, to get her hair straightened, that was all. And she was crying like a long-lost, lone and motherless child. So this writer went up to her, and asked her – in English, being ignorant enough to assume that all what we could still safely call 'coloured' girls without being threatened with mayhem had to be from the States, or the West Indies, anyhow – what was wrong.

But she glared at him and sniffed: 'Parle pas l'anglais!' So he asked her all over again in his lame, halt, crippled, maimed, and otherwise dismembered French, 'What is it that arrives to you, my little cabbage?' Believe it or not, even in fractured French that sounds good.

So she told him. Her mother, many years repented of a youthful *affaire* with a handsome young Black from the Ivory Coast which had produced this lovely child, was now married to a member of *la haute bourgeoisie*. And, on the day before, having to entertain a group from that class whose continued existence in any country whatsoever has often seemed, to this writer at least, a minor mistake if not a major disaster, had called the pretty little thing upstairs and tried a *maid's uniform* on her – to keep from having to explain the why and how of that lovely little thick-lipped, kinky haired creature to those unmitigated swine. So the forlorn child had left home. And rightly. This writer – or rather his excruciatingly funny French – succeeded in cheering her up after a while. He was seriously entertaining the decidedly appealing idea of taking her home with him to his pavillon out by the Vincennes Gate – she hadn't a sou, nowhere to go, and was as pretty as all get out – when the tall, blond, exceedingly handsome species of a *salaud* she was in love with showed up. And that was that.

So this writer wandered off – Paris can be the lonesomest goddamned town! – until in another corner he spotted another waif. This one was Jewish. And so heartbreakingly beautiful in a very special, very Jewish way, that he halted in midstride, sauntered over – he was sufficiently fortified by eight or nine *fins à l'eau* by then – and asked her to dance. Everybody else was already dancing to what our host proudly called his peek oooop (pick up, or portable phonograph) so it seemed as good a way to break the ice as any. She refused, brusquely. So this writer turned away, said good night to his host, and started to leave. Stupid to fight *that* kind of a night, what?

But she came rushing after him. There were tears in those marvellous green and gold eyes. She said: 'Pardonne-moi, je t'en supplie! Mais—' Then helplessly, wordlessly, she showed him her arm. It had a number tattooed on it. A concentration camp number. She *didn't* show him her other arm. The one with *nur für Offiziere* (only for officers) tattooed on it. Or so he was later told by his host. Whose mouth was no prayer book, so whether that detail was true or not, this writer still doesn't know. She simply whispered: 'Je ne peux pas supporter qu'on me touche! Je ne peux pas!'

This writer sat beside her the rest of the night. Carefully *not* touching her. Talking a little. But mostly not. Just being there. Trying to reach through that terrible solitude somehow. By telepathy, maybe. When the party broke up, she said, meaning it, this writer is pleased to believe: 'Tu es beaucoup trop gentil!' And cried a little. And walked away from there very fast.

Physically, that girl was the Simone Levy of this novel. Very exactly. This writer never saw her again after that night. He hopes with all his heart that she finally found someone she didn't mind touching – and being touched by – a little. That she once more learned to smile. She deserved it. She was something very fine.

The rest? Years of wandering. The stunning impact of Israel – which the writer has visited twice and admires unreservedly. A compassionate girl or two (in Paris mostly, on the Côte, Rome, Istanbul, Athens, Genève, Tangier, Marrakesh, Casablanca, Beirut – who knows? After forty-one countries, the details blur) who supplied the quite exact psychological details: the alternations of mood from hectic gaiety to profound sadness, from fevered loquacity to bottomless silence that all the Holocaust survivors he knew well seemed to have, along with a bitter, if usually well hidden, self-hatred. It was as though they could not forgive themselves for having lived when nearly everyone they'd treasured, loved, had died. There was even a kind of residual, quirky, occasional, antisemitism that was masochism's purest self. And one morning this writer woke up with this novel finished inside his mind.

Except for the historical research, of course. Which brings him to the one slightly ill-humoured, but truly serious thing he has to say. To those people who imagine it is even possible to write reviews – at least of this kind of novel – on the basis of the limited experiences of their sheltered lives (a *good* reviewer would have to be almost as much of a wanderer, an adventurer as any halfway competent novelist always is) and who seem to him excessively fond of words like 'implausible', ignorant of this writer's obsession with getting everything *exactly* right, he hereby states, and takes his most solemn oath, that every major event in this novel actually happened (though not necessarily to the people, or in the places, to whom, and at which, he has, in the legitimate exercise of his chosen profession, assigned them) and in precisely the manner herein described – again with the minor demurrer that the writer has very often felt obliged to reduce the excesses of both heroism and horror involved in the historical circumstances around which this novel was built to a degree that a modern, sophisticated reader (forgetting always that war is neither) would be willing to believe.

As for the events in the modern section of the novel – whose action terminates in October 1972, one need only to have read the newspapers, listened to the radio, watched TV to be aware that everything depicted in this section was commonplace during the period described and, unfortunately, still is.

But the events based upon the activities of the French Resistance, the FFI (French Forces of the Interior), their allies, the British SOE (Special Operations Executive) and the American OSS (Office of Strategic Services) as well as their enemies, the Gestapo (GEheime STAatsPOlizei, the letters capitalized show how the abbreviation was formed) and the Italian OVRA (Opera Vigilanza Repressione Antifascista) during World War II are to a surprising degree unknown to the reading public of the English-speaking countries. Most of the works upon which the writer has drawn were published in France, in French, and nearly all of them still have not been translated into English, which is a pity, since the awful sufferings, and the unequalled heroism of the FFI, as well as their major contribution to the final victory deserve to be better known. The works actually published recently in English about the activities of British Intelligence, and the American OSS, both suffer from what are almost national vices: the British work is filled with smug self-satisfaction (forgetting that for every Nazi spy they 'turned' to their own uses, the Gestapo with all the resources of fiendishly expert torture at their command 'turned' twenty British Intelligence Agents, with the result that literally tons of arms, ammunition, food, medicines, and other supplies intended for the FFI, were dropped almost literally down the chimneys of the Nazi supply depots) while the American work, in pursuit of a light and humorous touch, almost succeeds in the curious attempt to make the OSS appear an organization composed entirely of blithering idiots, to which this writer would like to raise – mildly – the objection that idiots are stupid madmen, while paranoiacs, which is what spy masters and spies generally are, are *brilliant* ones.

The French works – aside from a little natural apologetics and self-serving on their authors' parts – are admirable. For those earnest readers who like to go to a writer's sources for firsthand information (usually to catch him in error, never an impossible task!), herewith a short list: Claude Chambard: *Historie Mondiale Des Maquis*; Paul Dreyfus: *Vercors, Citadelle de la Liberté;* Pierre Tanant: *Vercors, Haut Lieu de France;* Jacques Soustelle: *Envers et Contre Tout*, Vol. Two, and the scholarly French magazines: *Historia* (Normal editions numbers 309 and 313; *hors série* 13, 26 and 27; the writer especially recommends the out of series special numbers 26 and 27 as being beyond all doubt, the best, most superbly detailed histories of the Gestapo's activities in France extant) and *Miroir de L'Historie* number 274, devoted to the invaluable aid provided the Nazi war criminals in escaping by way of Spain, certain segments of the Vatican's hierarchy, and even the OSS/CIA (whom the above magazine accuses – rather convincingly – of having engineered Klaus Barbie's flight to Bolivia in return for certain 'valuable information'). 'Valuable information,' this writer scarcely needs point out, has always been held more important by any intelligence agency whatsoever than human lives.

In any event, the reader can be very sure that this work has been researched exhaustively, and *nothing* has been allowed to happen to a fictional character that an actual historical person has not suffered in far greater measure, nor has any character performed a feat of valour that was not historically – and often far more spectacularly – performed by some actual person under similar circumstances.

Some examples: the Free French air force's bombing of the prison which enables many prisoners, among them the female protagonist, to escape, or to be rescued.

Its historical counterpart: on February 18, 1944, Group Captain P. C. Pickard, holder of no less than *three* DSOs, led De Havilland Mosquito Wing 140 of the Royal Air Force on a low level strike, called in by Resistance radio operators, which blew in the front, and three side walls of the prison at Amiens. Two-hundred-and-fifty prisoners escaped; twenty German guards were killed, eighty wounded. Group Captain Pickard lost his own life in this attack.

The protagonist of the novel is active in sabotaging the German radio installations in Grenoble.

To this there are two historical counterparts: on November 13, 1943, the FFI blew up the munitions dump belonging to the Wehrmacht Artillery Division quartered in Grenoble. Again, on December 2, 1943, the Resistance réseau led by Nal, Bequet, and Sapin, succeeded in enlisting the aid of a Wehrmacht officer, a Pole named Aloyzi Caspicki, who had been recruited into the German army against his will, and passed on to him the explosives with which he totally destroyed La Bonne barracks in the exact centre of Grenoble, killing several hundred Germans. Caspicki escaped alive and unwounded, joined the FFI and fought with them against the Nazis until V-E day.

The battles during the months while the FFI – with the pitifully small and tactically totally misleading aid granted them by the Free French, British and American combat teams parachuted in from time to time – held the Vercors salient against odds ranging from seven to one, up to twenty-five to one – are, as described in this novel, accurate down to the most minute detail. Every action attributed to the protagonists was actually carried out by the nameless men and women fighters of Vercors. Incidentally, one of the Free French officers parachuted in actually was a girl. Of her life and loves, the writer knows *nothing*. Marie Claire is a fictional creation, and the events of her life are fiction.

As for the one remaining item that people who are unaware of the Gestapo's methods are going to find difficult to believe, i.e., that Simone Levy underwent four days of hellish torture and survived it without breaking, this, too, is history. The Gestapo were experts. Since their intention was to extort information from their victims, not to kill them (a matter which the firing squads, or the gas chambers would take care of for them later in any event) they knew how to hurt a person unbelievably, unbearably, while never seriously endangering his life.

When a captive died under torture, as not a few weaker souls did, the torturers were often severely reprimanded by their superiors not, of course, for cruelty, but for clumsiness, inefficiency.

For those reluctant to believe this, the writer concludes with Simone Levy's own words, for he cheerfully admits to having appropriated the name from the heroic French Jewess who actually bore it, during her service with the Resistance, as her *nom de guerre*, mainly as a sincere and humble tribute to her incredible valour. What her real name was, he, of course, does not know. Nor did he ever meet her personally, from which it follows, naturally enough, that none of her personal aspects, either physical, intellectual, or moral, except, of course, her really sublime courage, has been used by him in this work.

These then, are her own words (to which, with the most extreme reluctance, the writer has appended a translation, sinning thus against both their starkness, purity, and style, and his own deep-seated conviction that translations are always distortions, when they aren't actually falsifications) as dictated, some years ago to a reporter from one of France's most serious journals:

'Ils sont vingt, trente. On m'attrape, on me palpe. Je ferme les yeux. On m'enfonce une aiguille dans la bouche, je hurle comme une bête. Ils éclatent de rire, se précipitent tous sur moi. Mes vêtements sont littéralement dechirés: chaque main emporté un lambeau. Je suis nue. Des gifles, des coups pleuvent. Je tombe par terre. On me piétine. Puis on m'installe sur une table médicale, les bras entravés, les jambes ouvertes. La lumière m'aveugle, je ferme les yeux – cauchemar! Je sens qu'ils retiennent leur souffle. Ils s'approchent de la table à pas lents, appuyés. L'un d'eux se détache du groupe et arrive sur moi. Je vais hurler, crier. Aucun son ne sort de ma bouche, mes cris restent à l'intérieur. J'ai la chair de poule, de la pointe des pieds jusqu'à la tête. Il me saisit brutalement les hanches, mon ventre est transpercé, fouillé. Le silence est de plomb. Ils se succèdent, des sauvages. Je suis toujours sans voix. Je me tords de douleur, de peur, d'humiliation. J'ai l'impression que je suis déchirée écartelée.

'Je vomis, je n'arrête plus de vomir. Je sombre, je reviens, je retombe, ils recommencent. Plus rien n'a de nom.

L'eau froide m'apaise. On me lave. Je suis détachée, je me lève.

Plus personne. Des vêtements sont là, je m'habille. Quelqu'un vient me chercher. Mes yeux sont secs.

'J'ai vielli de mille ans.

'Je suis dans un bureau. On m'a mis du pain dans la main et du saucisson. Je mange. Puis je vomis. J'ai mal au coeur. Je vomis encore. Ils sont choqués et m'insultent. Mon nom, on me demande mon nom. Ils le savent, ils savent tout, mais *je* ne dois rien dire. Je ne dois rien dire. Je ne dois pas supporter la douleur, mais m'y enfoncer, m'y couler et disparaître.

'Visages sur moi, ma tête à droite, ma tête à gauche, au rythme des coups, des gifles. Ne rien dire.

'Paoli* s'approche de moi, me frappe très fort. Je m'évanouis. J'ouvre les yeux et je me retrouve dans une cave. La "cave" dont j'ai souvent entendu parler. J'ai froid partout. Une terreur imprécise m'imprègne. Je suis un tas dans un coin. Je sombre dans un demi sommeil.

'Je suis la seule survivante de mon réseau. A l'époque, j'avais quinze ans.'

'They are twenty, thirty. I am trapped. I am felt all over. I shut my eyes. One of them rams a needle through my mouth. I howl like a beast. They burst into laughter, and throw themselves on me. My clothes are literally torn to pieces: each hand rips off a shred. I am naked. Slaps, blows, rain down on me. I fall to the floor. Someone tramples me. Then they install me on a medical table, my arms fettered, my legs wide open. The light blinds me. I close my eyes – nightmare! I sense that they are holding their breaths. They approach the table, their steps slow, held back. One of them separates himself from the group and lands on top of me; I am going to scream, to cry. Not a sound comes from my mouth; my cries remain inside me. I have gooseflesh from the soles of my feet to the top of my head. He seizes me brutally by my hips. My stomach is penetrated, dug into. The silence is leaden. They take turns at me, the savages. I am still without voice. I writhe from pain, from fear, from humiliation. I have the impression that I have been torn to pieces, drawn and quartered.

I vomit, I can't stop vomiting. I pass out, I come back, I faint anew. They start all over again. It is – unspeakable.

*Paoli was a French traitor in the employ of the Gestapo. He had infiltrated the group Simone belonged to, passing as a Maquisard.

Cold water soothes me. I'm being washed. I am released. I get up. There's nobody. Some clothes are there. I dress. Someone comes to look for me. My eyes are dry.

I have aged one thousand years.

I'm in an office. Someone puts bread and sausage in my hands. I eat. Then I vomit. I'm sick to my guts. I go on vomiting. They are shocked and insult me. My name, someone asks my name. They know it, they know everything, but I mustn't say anything. I must not say anything. I mustn't even endure the pain, but plunge myself into it, melt into it, and disappear.

Faces before me. My head jerks right, then left to the rhythm of the blows, the slaps. Say nothing.

Paoli comes to me and hits me very hard. I faint. I open my eyes, and find myself in a cave. The "cave" of which I've so often heard people talk. I'm cold all over. A vague sort of terror invades me. I am a heap in a corner. I sink into a half sleep.

I am the sole survivor of my group. At that time, I was exactly fifteen years old.'

Two afterthoughts: the German poems herein quoted are all from the great German Jewish Romantic Poet, Heinrich Heine, mostly from *Lyrisches Intermezzo*, though one is from *Die Heimkehr*. The writer asks the indulgence of students of the German language and the forgiveness of poets for his verse translations of them.

The free verse poems from *Vers Libres et Libertins* by Dalton Ross, as well as the sonnets from *Seven Sonnets For Simone* by the same poet, should, of course, be blamed upon Dalton Ross himself. Since his shade in Tartarus retains the absolute arrogance the man possessed in life, he will merely shrug and smile.

As will – of it rest assured, reader! – the writer of these lines.

Frank G. Yerby
May 18, 1973

I

It was raining. All over Manhattan and over as many of the other boroughs as attorney John Dalton Farrow could see from the windows of his ebony and teak panelled office on the fifty-first floor of the Dwight-Richardson Tower, the rain came down. By ten forty-five that morning only the nearer half of the bridge as far as Welfare Island was visible. Brooklyn and Queens were blotted out.

'Good riddance,' John Farrow thought. 'Anyhow if this keeps up till quitting time, the air might even be breathable when I hit the street.' Then he realized what his chances of getting a taxi to take him up to Grand Central were going to be. Nil. Every casual passer-by who had even a block to go, but more especially his wife, sister, mother-in-law, and maiden aunt, would be lining the kerbs, screeching and elbowing and jostling one another as if their very lives depended upon getting a cab. Which, he conceded, was absolutely normal metropolitan behaviour or at least it was in New York, that city whose citizens ran a close second to the Parisians in the race for the possession of the worst manners in the whole damned world. Normal, anyhow, every time the lightest drizzle blew in from the harbour. And in a downpour like this one—

'Hell, I'll walk,' he decided; 'need to sweat some of the lard off me anyhow.'

He glanced down at his middle. His paunch wasn't all that bad. But it *was* a paunch. And he was getting bald. And he was fifty-four years old. Over the hill. Downgrade. The quickening slide. Some lines from Byron rose up and went keeing through his mind:

> My life is in the yellow leaf
> The flowers and the fruits of love are gone
> The worm, the canker, and the grief
> Are mine alone . . .

That. Or perhaps Verlaine had said it even better:

> Les sanglots longs
> Des violons

De l'automne
Blessent mon coeur
D'une langueur
Monotone . . .

He grinned at his ghostly reflection in the rain blurred window pane. 'Still belong nowhere, don't I?' he thought. 'Cross-breeding between two races *that* different should be forbidden by law. And to break a kid's mind over the barrier of two such mutually alien cultures, is to insure schizophrenia – or something worse—'

He put his hand into his breast pocket and took his billfold out of it. Flipped it open to the clear plastic partition that had that snapshot in it. It was a miserable snapshot. In the first place, it wasn't even the original that he had taken twenty-eight years ago (the day his life had ended, leaving him to go through the motions of an existence with absolutely no point, meaning, or even any real desire. 'Hell,' he thought, 'they should stamp the IBM trademark on my ass; RUR Rossom's Universal Robots. Ex-human being . . .') but a copy.

Technically speaking, no copy of a photograph can ever be as good as the original. And when the original had been blurred from the outset – not so much out of focus, as spoiled a little by the shake that had got into his hands when he had tried to take it – the copy had to be bad. But when to that fact was added the sadder one that he'd had to piece the original back together again from the fragments Candace had torn it into, using Scotch tape to join each savagely ripped segment to its matching neighbour like a jigsaw puzzle so that the photographer could make a copy, necessarily retouched and air-brushed, the result had to be what it was. Existing in a state of urinal poverty, his iconoclastic mind supplied.

Even so, he was a little shocked to see how bad it was, because he hadn't looked at it in years. He hadn't because one of the things life had taught him was that human existence was bleak enough as it is, without constantly exposing oneself to that kind of gratuitous pain.

Still, it was all he had. Or needed, for that matter: a sort of shorthand, every tingling nerve end in his body could read. A cipher code that memory fleshed out instantly into life. A ghost that stubbornly refused to be laid.

He could see the close-cropped hair, framing her delicate face, and that part of his brain that was branded with her forever restored its colour: a warm soft brown, not quite auburn. Her eyes had been (were? are?) green with little liquified flakes of pure gold in them. Her mouth, her mouth, he tore his gaze away from what wasn't to be borne, not even now, not even after the twenty-eight years that had slid down the chute of time into bleak and bitter hell since then – and looked at that white bulk that was the bandage he, himself, had wrapped around her left hand. He'd thrown up when he'd seen what they'd done to it. She'd explained it to him very calmly: a sort of screw press, like the ones used for printing in Renaissance times, under which they put the victim's fingers, and turned the screw steadily, slowly, until—

But he didn't want to think about that, nor any of the other things they had done to her, the things that in spite of her apparent fragility she had survived. He didn't want to apply high-sounding adjectives to what she had been, and, if she lived, surely still was. He had enough of a language sense – a true and profound feeling for how both of his mother tongues worked ('A part of a heritage very, very likely illegitimate,' he thought bitterly, 'like all the other things that are wrong with me!') – to know that adjectives are a sort of subtraction really. The enemies of the noun. That less is more.

'Especially,' he thought, 'when confronted with a kind of behaviour we nearly always refuse to believe in, largely because we know we aren't capable of it, and comfort ourselves with the thought that nobody else is, either. That makes us sick to the gut. Forces us to reach back for words that usually don't mean anything anymore and embarrass the hell out of us when we say them. The ones with all the shine rubbed off. Worn slick from overuse.'

So he couldn't apply those kinds of words to Simone. He couldn't cheapen what she'd been, and, he hoped, still was, by using terms that had been employed too many times now to praise people not even in the same league with her – that is, if anyone ever was, which he doubted – and to glorify behaviour that wasn't remotely comparable to what she'd done.

All he could do was to put it baldly, flatly, simply; the way it actually had been, and leave the implications to fall where they would:

Simone Levy had been tortured by the Gestapo for four whole days and hadn't given them one name, one fact about the Resistance group she had belonged to. The one he had joined only because she was in it. That he, and his British colleague, Byron Graves had fled south with, after the Vercors debacle – where he, John Farrow, 'Jean le Fou,' as his Free French companions quite accurately called him, had first met her, and being the hopeless romantic he indisputably was, had fallen in love with her on the spur of that same instant – because that was the only direction any of them could go that offered even the remotest chance of staying alive.

And those post-graduate sadists of Sipo Group IV had only stopped beating her and burning and crushing parts of her, and applying electrodes to other, more intimate parts of her, when they saw she was so far gone that they couldn't revive her enough to mumble one more time, 'I don't know anything!' through lips that looked like twin blood puddings by then.

Those four short and simple words that were all they'd got out of her in four days. That they'd realized finally were all they were going to get. That she was perfectly willing to die before saying anything that would do them any good.

Even so, they'd made one last attempt. Had done another thing to her so unspeakable that he had never been able to get out of her what it was.

And, after that too had failed, they had thrown her – stark naked, bleeding, broken, seared, looking a good bit more like something you'd expect to see hung up on a hook in a butcher's shop than a human being – face down on to a heap of filthy straw in an ice-cold cell.

But even before that, two nights before, in fact, while the SS were just beginning to warm up to the task of interrogating Simone, he was already roaring up and down mountain roads in the sidecar of a motor-cycle that Pepe, a Spanish Republican refugee turned Maquisard, had procured for him by the simple expedient of blasting the SS Untersharführer who was driving it clear out of the saddle with his first shot, and killing the SS Haupsturmführer who was riding in the sidecar most completely and satisfactorily dead with his second, and then saved the motorcycle from smashing itself to hell and begone by jumping down off a sheer rockface into the saddle of the bike before it even had time to turn over, just like Douglas Fairbanks Sr in the silent movies, except that John Farrow doubted that the film star would have spent the next hour groaning: '¡Ay, pobre de mi! ¡He aplastado mis cojones!' which quite literally meant: 'Oh, poor me! I've mashed flat my balls!'

And every five kilometres or so, he would order Pepe to stop and the two of them would sling fifteen or twenty metres of bare copper wire up into a tree as high as they could get it to serve as an antenna, and he would squat there crying and cursing and praying and hammer out that raging, half-insane plea to London to send in an RAF strike force to bomb that fortress prison up in the hills behind Cannes where the Gestapo had Simone and more than two hundred other prisoners waiting to be shot or to be sent to places like Auschwitz, Dachau, Buchenwald, Mauthausen, Ravensbrück et al, which, when you came to think of it, was a damned sight worse than the quick and simple business of being shot after all.

Then they would get the hell out of there, carefully packing away that British made radio that weighed thirty-five pounds and used valves, as the British insisted upon calling tubes, and was so damned fragile you couldn't even breathe on it hard without its quitting on you, and used batteries that were always between one half and three quarters dead, and a good bit of the time the whole weird electronic mess wouldn't work at all out of sheer cussedness, so that the first time, twenty-five years later, John Farrow saw an American army communications team using a hand-held transistorized walkie-talkie that weighed less than three pounds and worked all the time he had the damnedest impulse to weep.

Five kilometres farther on, more or less, after zigzagging, doubling back, going on, they'd stop and do it all over again, because if they'd stayed in the same place as long as a half hour, the Gestapo's Funkspiel, with their radio direction finders mounted in closed vans and ambulances and even hearses would lay the three beams like invisible rulers on him, those three beams that were all they needed to pinpoint where he was sending from by triangulation right down to within thirty metres or so, and a very little while after that he and Pepe would both be dead.

And, between times, while they were riding he had to listen to Pepe yelling at him in Spanish which was one of the five languages he spoke by then, the others were English, French, German, and Italian, saying:

'Look, Juanjo, it is impossible, it cannot be done and the English will never come for they are all sons of the Great Whore. And what those Nazi *obscenidades* who never even had mothers, being born of the flyblown shit, are doing to the poor little Simone is not to be supported. So therefore if you who are her lover have not the testicles to shoot her through the window of the cell where they are questioning her allow me to do it, not for the group, because she will die before she will tell them one little word, but for her, *hombre* for her! Are you a man or are you not? Have you balls, or don't you? To permit your woman to suffer like that! I tell you—'

And he saying, 'Shut up, Pepe! Stop this thing I'm going to try again.'

And until the early morning of the day after that fourth night, he'd been almost convinced that Pepe was right, that the British in spite of all Byron Graves had taught him to the contrary, were very likely sons of the Great Whore and legitimate ones at that. In fact, he'd given the RAF up, and started for the back door of the prison all by himself, with twenty-two pounds of gelignite strapped on his back. It was still dark when he got there and cut through the barbed wire with his cutters, and slithered up to the back wall on his belly, and then along it deploying the explosive at the places where he figured the supporting columns had to be, and then lightly all across the back end of the prison, while the German sentries stumbled by sleepily three metres away from where he was so that he had to freeze and hold his breath every time they passed him. But since it was Simone he was doing this for, that was the first, last, and only time in the whole damned war that he wasn't even scared.

Then the sentries had passed him for the third time, and the last that he needed them to because by then he had all ten kilos of the explosive down, so he stood up and took out the grenade. He was just about to pull the pin when he heard the hammering of those motors and looking up, saw through the most exquisitely beautiful daybreak he'd ever seen or ever would see, those eight aircraft, peeling off one by one to come screaming down.

Then he noticed that they were the wrong kind of aircraft and that they were coming from the wrong direction. They weren't De Havilland Mosquitoes or Bristol Beaufighters, as he'd expected them to be, since both of those types were twin-engined fighters or fighter bombers with sufficient range to get this far south from England; but single-engined fighters. And they weren't even the US Eighth Air Force's big bellied P–47s, or sleek Mustangs, both of which types could have made it if you hung dropable belly or wing tanks on to them, being the only single-engined fighters he knew of that had the range to do it. No, they were a type he hadn't seen in a hell of a long time: old, mangey, battle-scarred desert fighters, Curtiss P–40s. Tomahawks, the British called them. And they came from due south.

Then, when the first of them was close enough he saw that the cocades on its wings had the colours hind end to from the way the British painted them, and he realized they were French. Come from Algiers, surely. But Algiers was across the whole damned Mediterranean, nearly six hundred miles due south; and even if a Tomahawk could fly that far, this mission was a suicide mission, because they sure as hell couldn't carry bombs, ammunition for their wing guns, and fuel enough to get back home again.

Which made him feel sick, because he knew the French couldn't afford to sacrifice even the few old creaky fugitives from the scrap pile the American air force had given them, and still less the few incredibly brave, gallant, and skilful fighter pilots that they had left, on the damned fool mission that he, putting aside his emotional stake in the matter, and considering it from the standpoint of cold military logistics, had to admit this one was.

'Poor devils!' he thought; 'poor goddamned brave devils. I wonder how the hell they ever persuaded their high command to let them.'

Then it hit him. The Communist Maquis, all by themselves, almost – except for the one hundred and nine soldiers General Giraud had managed to cram into the submarine *Casablanca*, and the whole artillery battalion, and their field pieces which he had had to split between the two big torpedo boats *Fantasque* and *Terrible* and send across (the submarine two days ahead, on the surface all the way, and so crowded that the Luftwaffe ought to have been able to detect her by the man-stink she made, and the big destroyer-sized torpedo boats foaming hard over at thirty-four knots) from Algiers to aid the Maquis (while General De Gaulle opposed the whole thing, as he – perhaps rightly – opposed any action in which the Communist held the leading role, and the whole Allied high command, except for

Giraud's immediate British superior, sat on their collective and exalted asses and did nothing at all) to which must be added the whole-hearted cooperation of the Italian Occupation Forces in Corsica, who, given a chance to shoot their German allies whom they detested instead of the enemies they rather admired, proved more than brave enough and liberated the island of Corsica completely by October 4, 1943. And Corsica was only a little over a hundred miles south of the Côte. The P–40s had surely re-fuelled there, and could again, going back.

Which was a great relief to him, so he pulled the pin of the grenade, threw it into the gelignite, and was knocked flat on his bony ass by the shock wave of the explosion.

Then he was up and racing through the huge gap those ten kilos of explosives had made in the back wall of the prison and, once inside, from cell to cell until he found the one Simone was in, and blasted the lock off the door with a tiny contact mine about the size of an American half dollar, and dragged her out, just barely alive and mercifully unconscious, jumping over the pile of rubble he had made with the gelignite, holding her in his arms like a broken doll, then cramming her poor pitiful little naked body, which looked like it was made of *viande hachée,* ground meat, into the sidecar of that Nazi motor-cycle that Pepe had miraculously stolen another whole tankful of petrol for, the two of them being saved finally, if not by direct divine intervention of the special god who looks after fools, children, and lovers, at least by the fact that the Curtiss P–40s of the Free French Air Force, blew in the front end of the prison with their bombs not three minutes after he'd blown in the back one, and afterward kept the Gestapo and the Waffen SS so pinned down with their strafing runs that nearly two hundred other prisoners got away as well – at least temporarily – all in fact, whom those French Flyboys' own bombs hadn't killed when they blew in that front wall.

'Proof positive how love can scramble a man's brains,' he thought. 'That was *after* the Normandy landings – and it never even occurred to me to ask when the British could find *one* aircraft that wasn't tied up in the north, to send all the way across France, through flak you could walk on, and all the Nazi fighters, to blast a prison which had no military importance whatsoever, however terrible the prospective fates of the people in it were going to be. Never did find out how the Free French got into the act, except that they already had a couple of fighter squadrons based on Corsica itself by then, waiting for the southern invasion. Maybe London passed my call on to them. Or maybe they accidentally picked it up. And came, God bless them, whatever their reasons were. Probably nothing more altruistic than the itch to splatter a few Krauts; or take advantage of the chance to get a little bombing and strafing practice in – with live targets at that . . . who knows?'

He turned away from the window. The lucid half of him, the French half, perhaps, knew perfectly well that the so-called vacation trip he was going to take tomorrow made absolutely no sense at all. The time when it might have, had long since passed him by.

He was fifty-four years old. The combined gut-ache and anguished dream he had given up as impossible years ago, that is, finding Simone again, had at this late, late date become possible, even probable, when, no more than two weeks ago, life with its usual, hamfisted, insane irony had suddenly reversed itself and served the solution up to him on a silver platter. It was surely the perfect demonstration that the existentialists were one hundred per cent right in their contention that man's fate is, by its very nature, absurd.

'Look at it,' he told himself: '*Now* we meet again. *Now*. A potbellied, balding old wreck, and a poor gone grey and wrinkled patched-up, half-crippled little woman who . . .'

Had taken the middle right out of his life. Had left not a flaming sword between him and his Garden of Eden, but an ice-cold question mark. Had dealt him the wound ('Hell!' he thought, 'be fashionable; call it the trauma!') that had doomed his subsequent relations with other women from the outset. Had, in cold sober fact, wrecked his life.

He thought about the curiously unrealistic mental quirk that makes the western mind reject coincidence, chance, accident, as causative factors in human existence, when, in brutal fact, every damned instant that a man lived – or didn't – depended upon them.

Right down to the criminal irony that two weeks ago, when he'd taken one of the rather faded lovelies he still occasionally dated ('Why?' he asked himself. 'In defence of machismo? To refurbish my image? Prove I'm not gay?') to see a Harold Pinter revival with its original, imported British cast, the first thing he'd seen, when he glanced at the programme, was the director was one Byron Graves. And even the first of the long string of alphabet soup the British print after their names, the DSO, convinced him that this particular Limey had to be the same Byron Graves of *Special Operations Executive* (which was what British Army Intelligence called that absolutely stark-raving mad group of amateur and civilian Scarlet Pimpernels who had organized themselves voluntarily to rescue Jewish scientists and other notables out of Hitler's Germany, after which Intelligence had seen the superb work they were capable of and drafted them into its own ranks) who was the sole survivor of the 'Jedburgh Team' of three liaison officers, one British, one French, and one American, that SOE/RF (Resistance, France), with whom OSS was already working in the closest cooperation by then, had parachuted into the Vercors salient in the spring of 1944. Byron was alive, because he, John Farrow, had saved his life on that occasion. And he, John Farrow, was alive because Byron had returned the compliment on at least three other occasions after that.

By the time the two of them, along with the tattered remnants of Group Merle, the réseau Simone belonged to, had worked their way down the Route Napoléon as far as Gap, he and Byron had stopped even counting which one was ahead at keeping the other alive.

When John had gone backstage after the closing curtain, Byron had jumped up saying: 'My word! If it isn't Jean le Fou, in person! Why my dear old chap! I thought you'd got yours or had been chained to the wall in some booby hatch years ago!'

'Jean le Fou?' John's date had said, 'doesn't that mean—?'

'Crazy John? Oh absolutely, my dear!' Byron said, 'Mad as a hatter, quite! You jolly well must be a brave girl to sally forth with this maniac! Well, well, well, John, old boy, tell me—'

'Later,' John had said. 'How about going pub-crawling with me and this Rag and Bone and Hank of Hair? This is an occasion, Byron!'

'Rag and Bone and *what*?' John's date had shrieked.

'And Hank of Hair,' Byron had supplied blithely. 'That's poetry, my dear. Kipling. Victorian, and a bit out of fashion; but poetry for all that. Don't mind what he says. I told you he was mad—'

'Are you coming?' John said.

'But of course, old boy,' Byron said. 'Jolly good show, seeing *you* again. Let's go!'

And the two of them had talked all night, giving the faded lovely in the fright wig and the shriekingly smart evening dress the sulks because they'd ignored her as though she weren't there.

And of all that night-long conversation, the only thing that had stuck or that mattered, was:

'Simone? Simone Levy? Oh, y'mean that mousey little creature you were more than a bit gone over, John? Damned if I could ever see why—'

John looked at Byron. Or rather glared. Then he saw that Byron was indulging in British humour at his expense. So he said: 'All right, my leg's hereby pulled. Did you hear anything more of her? You know, of course, that she disappeared. Left me flat.'

'People were disappearing with appalling frequency in those days, John. A good many of them, especially if they were Jewish, were simply murdered. The Gestapo's transport systems had all broken down, so there was no way for them to ship their pounds of flesh to Auschwitz, Dachau et al, by then. You'd think that under those conditions they'd have simply let the poor beggars go, wouldn't you?'

'Not bloody likely!' John said.

'No. With the ruddy war collapsing all around them, with every major city in their country being bombed to rubble, they *still* tried to carry out the "Final Solution!" They couldn't get the Jews to the gas chambers? Very well, Hans! Shoot 'em on the spot!'

'And you – you think that something like that happened to – Simone?' John whispered.

'No. As a matter of fact, I don't. For the very simple reason that you left her up at Vence, didn't you? And you and I, old chap, with some slight assistance from the French, British, and American armies, had jolly well cleared Jerry completely from those departments by then. So if the dear little creature disappeared, it was because she *wanted* to. Rough on your ego, I know, my dear old chap; but that's the way it looks to me!'

'And to me. In fact I *know* it was voluntarily, because she left me a note. "John, I am not worthy of you. Good-bye, Simone." Ten words, including the signature.'

'Perhaps,' Byron grinned at him mockingly, 'she'd been indulging in fun and games during your absence, John!'

'No. She couldn't have. I mean that literally, in the exact physical sense. After the Gestapo finished interrogating a woman, Byron, she needed from six months to two years of medical care before sexual relations became possible for her again. Sometimes it even required – surgery . . .'

'That's so? Sorry I can't help you, John; but I never did hear what became of her. One doesn't go to the South of France these days. Too ruddy dear. Brenda and I go to Spain, instead. Much cheaper, and the natives are friendlier. Rum bunch, the French. Oh, I say! I'd forgot that you—'

'Skip it,' John Farrow said. 'I don't know why, but I'd like to see Simone again. If only to find out why she disappeared. Can't think of a thing I'd done to offend her. Except maybe to go on knocking off Krauts after I'd sort of promised her not to—'

'That shouldn't have offended her, not after having been their house guest for four days. Rough show, that, what? The only thing that occurs to me – is that there may have been a certain episode in her past that she didn't want you to know about. That, at that juncture, probably, she just didn't see any hope of keeping you from finding it out any longer.

'Simone,' John said bitterly, 'knew damned well that she could have screwed Adolph Hitler in the middle of the Champs-Elysées with ten thousand spectators cheering 'em on, and that I'd have forgiven her for it. She knew that as far as she was concerned I was helpless. That I simply was incapable of living without her—'

'Yet, you have lived without her,' Byron said. 'And a fairish number of years at that.'

John Farrow looked at Byron. A long time. His gaze was bleaker than hoar frost on highland heather, Byron thought.

'Have I?' he said quietly. 'You could put it that way, I suppose.'

'And how would *you* put it, John?' Byron said.

John stared at his whisky glass. Looked up again, said: 'That I've spent twenty-eight years in hell.'

'John,' Byron said, 'you're a romantic. And at our age romanticism is a luxury a chap just can't afford.'

'I'd say I'm a realist. That I know from having tried – on numerous occasions – to find even a reasonable, an adequate substitute for Simone that there just isn't any. Nowhere in this world.'

'All right,' Byron said. 'I'd say there never is, nor can be, a substitute for a memory idealized out of all possible recognition. I'd promised myself to never tell you this, but it seems to me now that possibly I've been a rather poor friend to you all these years, by not letting you see what the real picture was. You've said that you could have accepted Hitler himself as Simone's former lover. Very well. Could you have accepted – Dalton Ross, John?'

John sat there.

'Oh I say, John!' Byron began, 'I'm deuced sorry! Oh damn and blast this loose tongue of mine! Look, John, old chap I—'

John Farrow smiled then, but his smile was almost infinitely sad.

'Don't be sorry, Byron,' he said. 'Because the answer is yes, I would have accepted even – him.'

'That's a relief!' Byron sighed. 'But, don't you see, that Simone didn't – couldn't know that? I'll wager she never mentioned a word about that episode to you.'

'You'd lose. She actually told me *all* about it – except the man's name. I think she wanted to tell me even that; but I was a young and jealous fool, and wouldn't let her. Couldn't bear hearing it. But what I still don't see is why she should have thought that my knowing she'd slept with that traitorous bastard would have made me go off the deep end.'

'Nor I, really. Except it seems to me she must have known or thought she did, something about Ross's connection with – you – with your family, that you, that I, didn't, and still don't know. God knows I'd never give a poet houseroom, old chap! Strange how often they're such beastly rotters, isn't it? Shelley and Byron come easily enough to mind. Baudelaire among the French. But our times take the prize! Bloody minds saying the nastiest things, with sublime and heavenly grace! Not only your old Gingerbeard in Italy; but Eliot, *chez nous*, though he was yours to start with, wasn't he? And Dalton Ross. I say, John, what precisely *was* his connection with you, with your family? You mentioned something of the sort, but—'

'He,' John Farrow said soberly, 'was always around the house in Paris, when I was a kid. Maman's hobby in those days, collecting literary lions, I mean. In fact, I was named for him. That's what my middle initial stands for, *D* for Dalton. My father insisted upon it. To honour the great man, you know—'

Byron Graves looked at John Farrow out of the corner of one eye. Gave a long slow purring chuckle.

'You'll just have to forgive me, John, old boy,' he said; 'but in that case your governor was a bloody fool!'

'A point that isn't even debatable,' John Farrow thought bleakly now, 'the more so where Maman's subsequent career is taken into consideration.' For Yvette Farrow had been last seen – slim, trim, and looking not a day over thirty, instead of her actual forty-five at the time – on the back seat of a Mercedes-Benz belonging to one of the more elderly of the Wehrmacht's generals, and accompanied by said general, himself, racing for the by then quite illusory security of the Third Reich. She had probably died in the holocaust of Berlin's last days. Before the Russians got there, John fervently hoped.

But even that hurt less than the other item Byron had left twisted in his gut: that Simone might have been Dalton Ross's mistress. He tried that one for size. And it fitted. It fitted as snugly as a rubber glove.

It wasn't, after all, either odd or strange. The Simone he had known had been a normal woman, with no apparent signs of frigidity. At least she had shown him none. And, as he had told Byron, he'd also known Dalton Ross. Well. Much too goddamned well.

The poet – 'that miserable traitorous bastard!' he thought without real anger – had been something more than a 'lady killer' in the quaint, high camp phrase; you could almost call him a classical regency rake. During most of his childhood, John Farrow had watched him operate. Of course, he hadn't understood it then. But, afterwards, looking back from the vantage ground of his own experiences, he had understood it, had realized that Dalton Ross's methods, combined with his rugged good looks, combined with a charm so practised as to be almost honed, combined with an ice-cold contempt for women as people, and an even more glacial one for their husbands, if any, had made him all but infallible.

So he had to move the idea that Simone might well have succumbed to Dalton's almost satanic charm, out of the category of the possible into that of the probable. Even though in the brief time that he, John Farrow, had known her, she had never so much as mentioned Dalton Ross's name. Not once, in spite of the fact that the traitorous bastard was already in full cry by then with those broadcasts he was making for the Nazis' propaganda service. Those subtle insidiously anti-semitic broadcasts, that, from the standpoint of effectiveness, even – since the majority of his listeners had no way of checking his cleverly distorted facts – credibility, were very good indeed. Much better than Lord Haw-Haw's or that ancient crackpot genius' from Italy. No, John Farrow didn't doubt this hurtful thing he hadn't known. He hated it, but he didn't doubt it.

He had been back home again, after his night on the town with Byron Graves, and in his own bed – alone, as usual, because the faded lovely had snapped, 'Find me a taxi, John, will you goddamnit please?' before the night was half over – when it finally hit him what the really important outcome of that unexpected meeting had been:

He could find Simone Levy now. He actually could. At least twenty-five royally fornicated years too late, he could.

All he had to do was to trace Dalton Ross. For up to the time of those broadcasts, Dalton had been famous. And, even though, after them, he had become infamous, tracing him would be a far easier task than searching for one middle-aged, frail, French-Jewish woman with no claim to fame except her courage, would have been. A great poet, people had called Dalton then. Great enough, famous enough to form part of Yvette Farrow's Paris salon. And—

'No,' John Farrow told himself, 'don't go into that. You *know* it's so, but don't. Funny. They don't call him great now. He's all but forgotten, *passé*. His style didn't weather the test of time. *Vers libre*, of course – but too plain. Too clear. Not enough sleek obscurantism to make people believe it meant more than it actually did—

Which wasn't important. The important thing was his certain knowledge that Dalton Ross never lost touch with his victims; retained their half-masochistic worship until they died. Nor was the poet's talent or the lack of it, the question at hand. That question was: now that he had a real chance for the first time in twenty-eight years of finding Simone Levy, why the hell should he? What on earth was there to be gained thereby?

One thing. To free himself of her finally. To remove that question mark that lay athwart his life. To lay the keening ghosts of what might have been. To grant himself, finally, a little peace.

As he turned away from the rainwashed windows, walked back towards his desk, he was working out dismal arithmetical problems in his head. Dalton would be more than seventy-five years old now. And Simone, frozen for ever into the image of gallant girlhood in his memory....

'Let me see,' he calculated, 'she was nineteen years old, then. That'll make her forty-seven now. A grandmother, likely. And I—'

He put out his hand and touched one of the buttons of the inter-communicator on his desk. Betty's voice came cackling over the loudspeaker.

'Yes, sir?' she said.

'Come in here,' John Farrow said. 'Brief me. Tell me what I'm supposed to do today....'

'Right, sir,' Betty said. Then almost at once, with no apparent lapse of time, she was pushing open the door. That was because she had a cubicle of an office of her own next to his, one wall's thickness away. At first she had had a desk in his office; but he'd put an end to that, diplomatically allowing her to believe that he found her physical charms disturbing. Another man might very well have, for Betty actually was decorative to an extreme bordering on both the obscene and the ludicrous. There was nothing subtle about her charms. And the clothes she wore were packaging designed to emphasize their contents. First class marketing technique. Only he would have still given her that little office if she'd looked like home-made sin manufactured by unskilled labour. For the curiously sad truth of the matter was that she had no effect upon him whatsoever. He'd banished her from his office because he valued his solitude. Being alone had become a vice of his finally. Or a necessity.

Now she draped herself into a chair facing his desk, and crossed her long legs under her miniskirt in a position that would have constituted indecent exposure if she hadn't been wearing panty hose, holding her pencil and notebook ready. At the same time she looked at him in a certain way, a way he'd trained himself to disregard in pure self-defence. A long, slow, practised, sidelong glance that could, and probably did, mean many things, among them the suggestion that he, John Dalton

Farrow, attorney at law, could take her out of circulation any time he wanted to, and without half trying at that, despite the handsome and fashionably long-haired young type who was currently dating her. And that word 'dating' probably covers a hell of a lot more activity than it would be prudent to look into, John Farrow added wryly.

He sat there a long moment, bleakly considering all the things that were wrong with that particular proposition. For one thing, she'd seen his house in Westchester County, which had been a piece of pure damned bad luck. By one of those peculiar coincidences that life always seems to arrange in order to fornicate matters dirtily, he'd been laid up as the result of an automobile accident at the precise time that both his partners were out of town on interstate corporation price-fixing cases, so he'd been forced to have her up there twice to take dictation in order to keep things moving. The only good part about the occasion being that he had been encased in enough plaster casts to make even attempted seduction somewhat less than feasible.

She was also aware that his ex-wife, Candace, was married again, for the second time since their divorce, twelve years ago, making her present husband number three – at least legally – on her list; and that this time it looked as though the marriage was going to work, largely because dear Candace had come to a shrewd recognition of the diminishing possibilities that being forty-three years of age entailed.

So Betty knew that not even alimony came out of his more than comfortable income any more. That was the important thing. Less so, but, surprisingly enough actually existing, was the fact that his obvious indifference to her exaggerated and aggressive charms ('silicone injections?' he wondered) had become, combined as it was with daily proximity, both a provocation and a challenge, arousing in her a very real interest in him, that normally wouldn't have occurred at all; since beautiful young women don't usually go for balding middle-aged wrecks old enough to be their fathers. 'Damned if I believe she's got an Electra complex,' he thought; 'even if I were fool enough to buy what would happen when I'm sixty odd and she's still in her early thirties: Candace all over again – marathon screwing all over town.'

'Put down that notebook,' he said. 'No dictation today. You tell *me*. What's happening, Bets?'

'Well,' Betty said; 'for one thing, Hilary Thornton called—'
'Oh Christ!' John Farrow said.
'Wanted to know if you could have lunch with him today. To talk over the Phoenix Pictures contracts. I told him I'd have to consult you first. . . .'
'You've consulted. I can't. Or rather I won't. I'd like to keep my lunch down.'
'Why are you so rough on Hiliary?' Betty said. 'Seems an all right guy to me . . .'
'Writers, for your information, Bets, are *never* all right guys. If they were, they couldn't write. The mixture's eight parts bastardy to one and a half insanity, to one half talent. Believe me, I know. We had one around as a sort of house pet of my mother's during most of my childhood. A poet, which is even worse. Besides Hilary *doesn't* want to talk about those contracts. They're all right, and he knows it. Better than all right, generous even, today's conditions being taken into consideration. The cinema isn't what it used to be, you know. What Hilary wants to do is to pick my brains – again.'
'You lost me two sentences back, Mr Farrow,' Betty said. 'He doesn't write about lawyers – or even whodunits, where maybe a little law would be useful as window dressing. Spy thrillers are his thing – good at it, too – especially the last one—'
'It was. But only because I *let* him pick my brains that time,' John Farrow said. 'Even so, he didn't get it right. He wasn't honest enough to use what I gave him without distorting it. Wish to Christ I'd never told him I was in the OSS. He's been on to me like a leech ever since—'
'You were in the Secret Service?' Betty said. Her tone oddly enough, was disapproving. Then he remembered that after all she belonged to the generation who flatly refused to take well-paying jobs with companies that manufactured stuff like napalm, for instance.
'Yes,' he said, 'you seem surprised—'
'I *am* surprised,' she said. 'Pardon me for speaking out of turn, Mr Farrow, but, well, you just don't look like the type who'd go in for that sort of thing. Espionage is – sort of slimy – isn't it?'
'Worse than slimy. Filthy. Rotten. And a whole new dictionary of other unpleasant terms. But thanks for the implied compliment, anyhow. It so happens you're right. I wasn't the

type. I was crowded into it. They needed a man who spoke French. Really spoke it. Without accent.'

'And you – did? I mean you *do?*'

'I was born in Paris, Bets. My mother was French. I didn't learn to speak English acceptably until I was fifteen years old. My father was with the American embassy. Cultural attaché during the whole of World War I. Afterward we stayed on until he suddenly got the patriotic impulse to send me to Harvard.'

'I see,' Betty said, 'that explains a lot of the interesting things I've noticed about you, sir. Why you're so different. Just loads of savoir faire. Not to mention all that old-world charm—'

'Flattery's bad for my digestion, Bets,' John Farrow said.

'It's not flattery. It's the truth. Understatement, even,' Betty said. 'But what I don't get is why your career in military intelligence makes you dislike Hilary Thornton?'

'It doesn't. My dislike for phonies is inborn. But it does give a yardstick to measure what all that pseudo-realistic school do, or rather don't do. I don't object to the out and out thrillers; in fact I rather like them. You know the kind where the guy gets shot in the stomach seven times at point blank range, is left chained to the wall to bleed to death, slips out of the cuffs, makes it with the girl *first,* and then escapes. That's honest fantasy. But Hilary and company pretend to tell it like it was. They don't. They leave out the main thing.'

'And that main thing is?' Betty said.

John Farrow looked out the window at the rain through the rain. Through the almost palpable element of time. Looked back again. Said:

'Fear.'

'Fear?' Betty said.

'Yes, fear. Terror. But not – panic. That was where the dividing line lay. Between the men and the boys. No. Between the quick and the dead. Because when you panicked, you'd had it. The day, Bets, that those miserable scribblers have their protagonist almost pass out from hunger, not because he has no rations left, but because he hasn't been able to get a crust of bread down in four days, his guts have knotted up on him so, I'll believe them; but not before.'

'That happened to you, sir?' Betty whispered.

'That happened to me. And worse. Far worse. Which closes this subject. For ever. What's next?'

'Your ex called. To remind you to attend your daughter's wedding: Thursday, the thirtieth. I told her you'd be out of town. She was furious. She all but stated I was lying, and ended up by implying you were probably taking me along—'

'She knows better than that. She's had all the proof she needs that I quit disappointing pretty young things horizontally years ago. Oh, damn it all, I'd forgot that! Not the trip, but Cynthia's wedding. Just as well. With all the substitute fathers Candy's supplied the poor kid with since then, my presence at the festivities would only add to the confusion. Buy the young couple something nice for me. A flossy silver tea service, maybe. That's still acceptable, isn't it? And stay under a *G* note, will you? But speaking of the trip, did you—'

'Get your plane tickets? Yes, sir. Here they are. Only the hour is rough, Mr Farrow. Eight o'clock tomorrow morning. Takeoff time, that is. So you'll have to check in at seven—'

'Oh Jesus!' John Farrow said.

'I couldn't do any better, sir,' Betty said. 'You insisted on a direct flight to Nice. Said you didn't want to have to change at Paris or Brussels or Geneva, so—'

'All right. Let me think a minute. Wait, I've got it. Phone Russ at my house and tell him to bring my bags into town in the car. They're already packed. Then phone the airport hotel for an overnight reservation. Russ can pick me up here and drive me out there. Solves both the time and taxi problems. And I'll get a good night's sleep for a change.'

'Don't you usually?' Betty said. Her tone was not entirely mocking. The curiousity in it was real. And what was worse, concerned.

'One of the symptoms of galloping senility is insomnia, Bets. Combined with involuntary, but enforced chastity to make matters worse—'

'Mr Farrow,' Betty said sweetly, 'men only say things like that about themselves when they *know* they aren't going to be believed . . .'

'The credibility of a statement has nothing to do with its truthfulness, Bets,' John Farrow said, 'you've been around a law office long enough to know that. What's next?'

'Oh well, the rest of it's routine. Paper work, mostly. I can handle at least three-quarters of it for you myself. The other quarter I'll dump on to Mr Warren's and Mr Rosenstein's desks. Time they did some work around here anyhow.'

'I agree,' John Farrow said. 'Anything else?'

'Yes, sir. A young fellow was in to see you. Good looking, but – well – grim. Said he'd be back this morning. Wouldn't take no for an answer. Said he was *sure* you'd see him. All but stated you'd *have* to—'

John Farrow thought about that.

'Government type?' he said.

'I – I don't know. If so, he was trying hard *not* to look like one. A little too hard. Cardin suit. Sideburns down to *here*. Hair curling over the back of his collar. Smooth. Only that – grimness kept showing through. Kind of a fellow I *wouldn't* date, good looking as he is. Scary, kind of—'

'You know, Bets, with that figure you've got, half the time I forget how much brains you have. You're a bright girl, baby. When he comes back send him in. I'll cope. Since I'm as pure as the lilies of the field taxwise, politically, and a few other ways I hate to admit even to myself, I can tell Washington what to do in their hats, and the appropriate action to be taken thereafter. Right down over their ears in fact. Now get out of here. You're giving me ideas I'm too old to even think about, let alone accomplish—'

'Oh, I doubt that, sir!' Betty laughed and fled.

Three-quarters of an hour later, she ushered the young man in. And John Farrow saw that she had been right. One hundred per cent right. He sat there, looking at the young man, and not even bothering to hide a distaste that was close to being physical.

'CIA?' he said finally. 'FBI? Treasury?'

The young man smiled. To John Farrow, that even, white-toothed, practised smile seemed both smug and singularly unpleasant. It added up to all the things a man had to have wrong with him to even want to engage in the kind of activities usually classified under the euphemism 'intelligence work'. The auto-hypnotic, self-perpetuating, basically sick activities, founded upon the moral atrocity that the end justifies the means. Even when the means was 'To terminate with extreme prejudice', John Farrow thought.

'I was told you'd be an expert, sir,' the young man said. 'Only you still haven't hit the right department. It's the Federal Narcotics Bureau – though we *do* cooperate with the others on occasion. . . .'

John Farrow sat there. Relaxed a little. What the Narcotics Bureau did was a thing he approved of. Most of the time, that branch of the federal government actually was on the side of the angels.

'Well?' he said.

'You,' the narcotics man said, 'are flying to France tomorrow. The Côte d'Azur. More precisely, Nice. You have reservations at the Hôtel Negresco, on the Promenade des Anglais.'

'In case you missed it, her name's Suzanne. You know, the *poule* from the Rue de la Liberté who will come up to service me around midnight,' John Farrow said.

The young man laughed then. Easily. Pleasantly.

'You wouldn't fly all the way to France for a commodity you can whistle up any time after four o'clock in the afternoon in Times Square,' he said.

'Then why am I going? To cut myself a kilo or two of heroin?' John said.

'Hardly,' the narcotics man said. 'The files on you in Washington are first rate, Mr Farrow. In the CIA's training school, they still lecture about what you did with the French Resistance. Changed the whole route of the southern invasion. Got through to Colonel Zeller who told General Patch—'

'That the way to go was up the Route Napoléon because there weren't any Germans there to speak of. I did. Me and two hundred other guys with the FFI Horse business, son.'

'But Colonel Zeller believed *you*.' He stopped, chuckled a little. 'Some of the old hands in the CIA swear he said that any American who spoke French the way you did and was crazy as you seemed to be had to be telling the truth! So – I insist – thanks to you, sir, to a considerable degree, Task Force Butler and the Thirty-sixth and Forty-fifth Infantry Divisons were in Grenoble two months and twenty-two days ahead of schedule. You were one of the OSS aces, sir. Too bad you didn't decide to stay in.'

'Thanks,' John Farrow said. 'Now let's skip my military intelligence record and get back to this visit. Why are you types after me?'

'But we *aren't*!' the narcotics man said. 'As a matter of fact, we haven't the faintest idea of why you're going to France, and what's more, we don't even care.'

'I thank you kindly,' John Farrow said.

'What we would like, however, is for you to do us – a favour.'

John Farrow looked at him. 'What kind of a favour?' he said.

'You knew a man named Heindrich Kroll once, didn't you?'

John sat there. His mind reconstructed that face. Square as a letter box. The colour of dirty bread dough. The eyes behind those steel-rimmed glasses that had had the exact shade of floe ice. The all but lipless mouth that looked more like a well-healed slash across that square face than anything else. The man who was forever beyond the reach of any sort of punishment or even vengeance because there was nothing anybody could do to him that could come anywhere close to equalling what he had done not once, but hundreds of times to other people. To Maquis, Resistance fighters, French Jews. To kill him would be a joke. To put him in front of a firing squad would be an insult to his victims. And to adopt his own most exquisite methods against him would be to voluntarily resign from the human race, become what he had been. And for that there weren't any words. So, even so, he had won.

'Evil on that level,' John Farrow thought, 'is forever invincible.'

On the level that Schutzstaffeln Obersturmbannführer Heindrich Kroll of the Geheime Staatspolizei had raised it to. Or dropped it to. He tried, mainly to give himself time, to put Kroll's various titles into English – at least into as much English as you could get them into, which wasn't much: constabulary squadrons over assault troops banner leader – or to give its English equivalent rank instead of trying to make all that pompous Nazi nonsense make sense in any way – SS Lieutenant Colonel Heindrich Kroll of the Gestapo. The man who had personally conducted Simone Levy's investigation. After, of course, routinely allowing all those younger members of his staff who so desired to rape her first. 'And thereby saving her life at that point, since the number of those among the SS who could enjoy sex, or reach orgasm by any other means than the practice of sadism upon their female victims was never excessively great,' John Farrow thought.

He was aware that he was staring at the narcotics man's expensive, surely English-made shoes, so he looked up. Said, very softly:

'Yes, I knew him.'

'Good!' the narcotics man said.

'You mean he's into drugs, now?'

'Yes,' the narcotics man said.

That wasn't surprising, John Farrow realized. Ex-Nazis had the Latin American connection sewed up. But for Kroll to operate in southern France, muscle into the Corsican Mafia's territory around Marseilles was incredible. For the ex-SS high priest of sadism, the commander of the Villa Montefleuri at Cannes – along with the two villas next to it, including the Villa Conchita, run by French traitors under Charles Palmieri – to dare to enter France at all called for something there weren't any words for, either.

'Plastic surgery?' John Farrow ventured.

'No. Just age, I'd say. And he doesn't push stuff in France. Neither we, nor the French, have a thing on him. He travels. A tourist. With unlimited funds, it seems. He operates – another thing we can't prove, since the Latin American authorities are so touchy – out of Chile. Safe as in church down there since ITT fouled up things for *any* American agency in that country. But he visits Spain quite often. Rents or owns a villa on the Costa Brava near Barcelona. A mansion in the Moraleja residential section outside Madrid. Lives quietly. Slips into France for two or three days. Rarely as much as a week. Never Nice or Cannes, naturally. But Aix-en-Provence, often. A little hotel called the Black Cat.'

'I know it,' John Farrow said.

'But sometimes Le Roy René, too. That's respectable isn't it?'

'That's the best in Aix,' John Farrow said.

He looked at the narcotics man. 'What do you want me to do, finger him for you?'

'No. Of course not. We *know* him. At least we know the rich German tourist known as Albrecht Holtz, very well. That's the name on his passport. A West German passport which if it isn't legal is the damned best forgery we've ever seen. All we want you to do is to confirm our belief that Albrecht Holtz is Heindrich Kroll. Then we wouldn't even *have* to get anything on him. We could let the French arrest him on all the charges still pending against him. Or the West German authorities themselves. There isn't any statute of limitations as far as that kind of war crime is concerned, you know.'

'Suppose both of them decide it's just too much bother at this late date,' John Farrow said.

The narcotics man smiled.

'Then we'll quietly inform our Israeli friends where the gentleman may be found,' he said.

John Farrow looked at him.

'Even though you can't prove he's pushing narcotics?' he said.

'If he *is* Heindrich Kroll, what difference would that make?' the young agent said.

John Farrow thought about that. Remembered all of it. How after they had unlocked her ankles from the clamps of that professional obstetrician's examination table, being as scientific about rape as they were about murder, they had dumped her into a bathtub filled with cracked ice and water, holding her head under for half minutes at a time, and screaming at her each time they brought her up: '*Parle!* Speak! Or else—'

Then, after that, at intervals during four entire days, beating her with raw beef nerves brought from a local butcher's shop, the toughest and most effective material for making whips that existed. Except for the thin steel rods they'd used next, maybe. And going on to electrodes clamped to her nipples. To the labia. That screw press that had reduced her left hand to something resembling the flipper of a seal. They'd saved her right one so that she could sign her confession. The confession they never got out of her, he thought.

But then he measured all that against her own response to it. He sat there, hurting still, even now, even twenty-eight years later, remembering the nights he had lain in that mountain hut between Sisteron and Digne, with Simone lying naked on top of him, not for sex, which hadn't been even remotely possible after those electrodes, but simply to keep her warm. Because even a blanket would have stuck to her back during those first days. And she lying there with her mouth open and moving on his, whispering:

'Don't kill – not even *them*. Not any more. Don't hurt people, Jean. Don't kill. There's no excuse for it – ever—'

'Not even in self-defence?' he said, humouring her because he was going over in his mind a list of things he was going to do to Kroll and company if the réseau ever managed to capture them, which wasn't bloody likely, he realized sadly.

'Not even that. Better to die. I'm sorry I didn't. And even more that you risked your life to save me. Now I'll never forget – forget—'

'What?' he said.

But that was what she never did tell him. That he'd die not knowing, very likely. The thing that had cost him her, and thereby any chance of a meaningful existence.

Because three weeks after General Alexander Patch and US Army Task Force Butler had swept through, by-passing whole divisions of the Wehrmacht and the SS who, reading the handwriting on the wall, had struck out for the Spanish border, most of them, and after that for home – having found out that the Spanish were going to disarm them and intern them if they crossed it – with every Resistance réseau in that part of France – their members growing hourly as men saw that the invincible German army, could after all be beaten, with a few British officers of the SOE, and he, John Farrow, as the oldest member of the American OSS in terms of actual combat service in southern France by then, among them, hanging on to the German flanks like leeches, harrying them day and night, mining the roads, which was his speciality, ambushing the Boches at every curve until they, those real *cons*, that ragged-assed band of authentic heroes, the men of the Resistance, had liberated that part of France for good, and he could come back to that stone house in Vence where he had left Simone – being able to leave her there by then, by the time of the general uprising, because she was well enough to permit it, but even more because the good people of Vence had taken her to their hearts, and were delighted to feed and care for her while he was out killing Nazis – he had found her gone.

Her note had said, very simply:

I am not worthy of you, Jean.
Good-bye,
Simone

Nobody had seen her go or could give him any idea what direction she had taken. And to snafu things even more royally for him, by late August 1944, all that part of France was filled with would-be lynchers, bent on killing somebody, anybody, to revenge themselves for what they'd suffered during the occupation, most of them having put the FFI armbands on their sleeves only after the last Nazi had hightailed it in the general direction of Deutschland and it was perfectly safe to do so.

He was arrested five times in two days by bloodthirsty idiots who wanted to shoot him out of hand as a spy. But his papers, signed by no less than Colonel Zeller, De Gaulle's own representative, accrediting him as an Allied liaison officer to the Resistance, and, perhaps even more, the high-handed tone he, himself, took – which commenced with asking the *parvenu* heroes where the deep blue hell any of them had been on the day and hour of any of the two dozen pitched battles he personally had taken part in during the last two weeks, and went on from there to a masterly definition of what the two words *crétin* and *lâche* meant, namely types like them, and ending with the suggestion that they *foutez* him the *champ* before he really lost his patience and called in a few honest-to-God Maquisards to put some bullets where they'd do the most good – saved him, so he might have found Simone, after all, if it hadn't been for one man. Except for General Charles de Gaulle.

For when that great man – among the attributes of his real and true and authentic greatness being the possession of sheer guts enough to be absolutely insufferable on all such occasions as demanded treatment sufficiently rough as to keep matters under his full control – arrived in Provence during September and visited the cities of the south, icily refusing to even shake hands with the leaders of the Communist Maquisards who had been the bravest and the best of the Resistance, he found at Toulon two Allied officers at the reception given for him: Byron Graves of the British SOE and John Farrow of the American OSS.

Turning to his escort, the lofty general snapped:

'I want these men out of France within forty-eight hours!'

And they were. For the general's concept of *la grandeur française,* could not permit the risk of the ordinary population's finding out that the Anglo-Saxons – who, especially the British, had parachuted trained officers and arms and explosives and demolition experts and medical supplies and money and radios in to help the Resistance ever since late 1941, and by 1943 were dropping in operational raiding teams of thirty to sixty well-armed men nearly all of whom died along with the Maquis at places like Vercors and a hundred other gallantly, suicidally held hopeless last stands – had anything much to do with the liberation of La Belle France.

And John Farrow's last real chance of finding Simone Levy was gone, though it took him a full five more years to give it up as impossible, finally. But at that very moment, it was gone.

He was aware of how heavy the silence was. Felt the narcotics man's gaze searching his face.

'No,' he said, 'I couldn't.'

'Why not?' the young agent said.

'Hard to say. It would be to – break a promise I made to someone, once. A sacred promise. To a person – sacred to me. I know, I know. Shouldn't say things like that, should I? Sounds phony as old hell, doesn't it?'

'Not the way you said it then,' the Narcotics Bureau agent said. 'And you're entirely within your rights. But if you should change your mind—'

'I won't,' John Farrow said.

The narcotics man stood up, put out his hand.

'Good-bye, sir,' he said, 'Or at least, *au revoir*, anyhow—'

'No, son; it's good-bye,' John Farrow said.

It was very quiet in the office after the young man had gone. John Farrow sat there.

'Oh Christ oh Christ oh Christ,' he said.

2

As he sat there by the window idly watching the big jet pour the ocean backward beneath him, he thought again that a transoceanic flight was one of the dullest ways of getting from one place to another ever invented in the long history of man. To make matters worse, all the things the airlines had thought up to spare their passengers the innate and excruciating boredom were, to any man of reasonably civilized tastes – and he added wryly, overbred nerves – positive irritations, to which simple ennui was actually preferable. For instance, you couldn't even change your position in your seat without having your gaze involuntarily cross the screen on which flickered in full technicolour one of those appalling affronts to human intelligence on its most elementary level that all inflight movies seemed to be. The only partial relief he'd been able to afford his nerves, had been to politely, but firmly refuse the earphones that would have poured the inanities the characters in the picture were saying to one another into his defenceless ears; or granted him, as alternatives, the choice of listening to shatteringly loud hard rock, or syrupy love songs, or the more tired of the classics.

But what really couldn't be managed, he'd found out many, many flights ago was to be let alone; at least not without resorting to a degree of boorishness he simply wasn't capable of. And if Air France's hostesses were not as overpoweringly decorative as the ones on any of the American transatlantic flights, they were much more charming, alert, interesting and well – *mignonnes* – the word that comes out badly and inaccurately in English as 'cute'. But worst of all, from his jaundiced point of view, what they were was efficient.

Ever since he had taken his seat in the first-class section, he had become a challenge to their professionalism, because his lean, ugly, expressive face hadn't looked very happy. It hadn't because he wasn't. Air hostesses, as all the world knows, are supposed to keep their passengers happy. And with John Farrow, they were failing completely. Which distressed them; the more so because – although this time he hadn't even bothered to turn it over to see if it were there – his boarding pass, like his ticket before it, had a tiny, pencilled VIP on the back. He'd earned that rating because of two very minor diplomatic missions he had consented to undertake for Washington during the Kennedy administration, and one during the Johnson; all three of them highly confidential, and negotiated in Paris, itself – while stoutly refusing to become part of the State Department on a permanent basis. 'Can't afford it; pays too bad,' he had said. How this had filtered down to Air France's main office, he didn't know. Perhaps one of the French politicians he'd dealt with leaked the information to the company deliberately. After all, it was government owned. But ever since the first mission he'd been on the French airline's special treatment list.

But what had made him a little more unhappy than he usually was had nothing to do with the amenities of the flight. The actual cause of his renewed depression was the fact that the source he'd been depending upon to give him a lead definite enough to narrow the area he was going to cover in order to lay hands on Dalton Ross to a size that would make finding the old bastard at least possible, had dried up on him, had in fact, no information about the poet-traitor's subsequent fate at all. For John had gone down to Washington, to the CIA's headquarters, whose doors, because of his war time connection with its now defunct predecessor, of OSS, were still open to him, only to be told by Paul Barton, a man he knew well, and trusted, since Barton had been there since OSS days:

'Look, John – put it this way: we weren't exactly told, but it *was* strongly hinted to us to let Ross *stay* lost. Better all around, politically, at the time, I'd say. Or maybe some State Department big wig's wife put the screws on. Afraid of all that dirty linen waving in the breeze, if that bastard were brought to trial. You knew him, so I don't have to tell you what his reputation with women was – other men's women, usually—'

'Yes,' John Farrow said, 'I knew that, Paul.'

'Besides, he's almost surely dead. Hell, he'd be close to eighty, now.'

'Seventy-five. But unless somebody finally shot him, he's alive. Toughest damned hickory limb you ever did see. Type that lives to a hundred and ten, and dies while screwing his twenty-year old nurse in his wheelchair – with her on top, of course—'

'That's Ross, all right. Mind telling me why you're looking for him?'

'Somebody *I* misplaced. And I'm pretty sure that he—'

'Knows where the body's hid? If it had tits on it, you can bet on that, John. That is if the arrogant old swine isn't dead or hiding out in some country where they love us even less than they do in most places, these days—'

'Even that's not necessarily true, Paul. Our relations with Spain are currently excellent, and look at the collection of ex-every goddamned thing – on the rightist side of the spectrum, of course – they've got hiding out there. Hiding, hell. Living it up in grand style. If he's there, it wouldn't even be hard. I could put my hands on Léon Degrelle the day I got there, and on Rudy de Mérode, within a week. Another one – how much would you bet me that that was really Michel Szkolnikoff's corpse they found next to the Madrid-Burgos highway in forty-five?'

'Not a plugged nickel,' Paul Barton said, 'but since neither the Belgians nor the French have ever been able to extradite those bastards in all this time, what makes you think we'd have better luck?'

'Don't want to extradite him. Just a private little chat with him, that's all. Sure you have no idea—?'

'None. Except I'm pretty sure he's *not* in Spain. He'd be too visible there. I'd say he'd choose one of the South American countries where they scream Yanqui imperialism morning, noon, and night, largely to cover their total incompetence, financially, socially, and what have you. People who can mismanage things to the point where *beef* is rationed in Argentina, to give just one example, need a scapegoat, John – and we're it. I wish you luck though. But I wouldn't be too hopeful if I were you. I admit that Dalton Ross was the original hairy-chested writer, long before Hemingway came along; but there were an awful lot of ways of winding up dead in those days, as you should know—'

There damn sure were, John Farrow thought now, and reached out to pick up that book. He'd finally been able to get a copy of it the day after he'd got back from Washington, two days, in fact, before the young Narcotics Bureau agent had increased a little more the profound depression gripping him by reminding him of Heindrich Kroll. 'But even in that there are some grounds for hope,' he thought. 'Swine have great powers for survival. If Heindrich Kroll got away scot free, why not Dalton Ross?'

He had had to go up to Siegal and Hechtfield's offices in person to get that particular book. And even so, it hadn't been easy to pry a copy out of them, even though they were his own publishers, too. For as Ben Siegal put it:

'I know damned well, John, that it's a matter of record that *we* published that son-of-a-bitch first; but people have more or less forgot it. And we'd rather not remind 'em, catch? He's been out of print for years, and we're just as happy to leave him that way—'

'Why?' John Farrow said. 'He was a good poet, wasn't he? Started a number of trends, if I remember right. Of course, I haven't read his stuff in years, and then only scattered examples in magazines; but I honestly don't recall one antisemitic line in any of the things of his I've seen. Which doesn't mean much, does it? I'd have had to have read it all to judge—'

'There wasn't,' Morris Hechtfield said a little sadly, 'and I *have* read it all, John. In fact, I'd have taken my most solemn oath that Dalton hadn't a prejudice to his name—'

'Except against pretty women's husbands,' Ben Siegal said. 'But now you tell me, John: do you think he had any valid excuse to make those broadcasts? Of course he was fool enough to let himself get caught, when the Nazis occupied Vichy's territory in November 1942. But he was Aryan, nordic, blond and all the rest of it. He had absolutely no connection with the Resistance. So the worst they could have done to him was to intern him as an enemy alien and—'

'The Wehrmacht, maybe,' John said then. 'But the Gestapo, Ben? When did they *ever* play by the rules? What they were supposed to do, and what they did do, were always two different things. . . .'

'That's the filthy truth,' Ben Siegal said. 'Look, John, I'm going to let you have a copy of the book, but on the condition that you put a plain brown paper cover over it, if you read it on the plane, as I suspect you're going to. Agreed?'

'Agreed,' John said and smiled. 'Even though that'll only attract more attention to it, not less. Make the other passengers think it's the latest porno hit . . .'

'And you a dirty old man who has to read that kind of stuff to even get it up,' Morris Hechtfield said. 'Let them! Anything at all as long as they don't see Siegal and Hechtfield, Publishers, on the bottom of the cover. I mean that, John!'

'All right, boys, have it your own way,' John Farrow said.

But he hadn't put a brown paper dust-jacket over *Vers Libres et Libertins* by Dalton Ross. Instead he'd done another thing which proved he had the mind of an intelligence agent still; he'd slipped the jacket off one of the smallest of the Agatha Christie murder mysteries and put it on the book of verse. Perfect camouflage: a tired, middle-aged businessman, reading a whodunit. That, he knew, would attract no attention at all.

But, as it turned out, it didn't need to: whatever there was about John Farrow that nearly always struck people, especially women, a sort of Wertheresque *Wehmut*, perhaps, or the indefinable air of distinction he would have sworn he didn't have, had already done the job. The pencilled notation on the back of his boarding pass had been all but superfluous; very probably the inflight first-class cabin crew would have given him special treatment without it. Before he could close his long, sinewy fingers over Dalton Ross's book, one of the *hôtesses de l'air* was there with the champagne – again.

He smiled at her. If you were even ten per cent male, you couldn't help smiling at her. 'And if this were really a male-dominated world, as Woman's Lib claims,' he thought, 'this little creature has got it made.'

'No, thank you,' he said.

'Why not?' she said in that trick accent of hers that was so damned cute he was sure she practised it before the mirror at home. She even said 'ze' and 'zis' for 'the' and 'this' like French maids in American bedroom farces which *proved* she was faking it.

'Can't,' he said, switching into his native French for the first time on the flight. 'Champagne makes me a crisis of the liver all of a sudden—' he snapped his fingers – 'like that!'

At once she was off like a shot, for though the French are sceptical about many things: the good faith of their allies, the fidelity of women, and even, sometimes, the existence of the Good God, their belief in the general maliciousness of the human liver is absolute, as is their certainty that *une crise de foie* is the most terrible thing in this world. But before he could even turn the title page, she was back again with her arms full of bottles containing every damned kind of mineral water that ever bubbled up from the earth in France.

'Vichy?' she began. 'Evian? Vittel?'

'No thanks, my little one,' he said again, and cracked one of the hoariest of French jokes: 'Water rusts the tubes, is it not so?'

'But there must be something—'

'You can do for me?' he said. 'Naturally, there is. But since there is not any privacy on this aeroplane and the other passengers would certainly consider it very shocking, even highly immoral, besides which, at my age, it would surely cost me an *infarctus myocardius* before I could even finish so exquisite an activity, thus making you the most beautiful little murderess in Air France's history, why don't you just run along and let grandfather read his book in peace, *hein*?'

She laughed then, merrily.

'*Tiens!*' she said, 'I was sure you were! *Merci*, m'sieur! You have just caused me to win five hundred francs!'

At first that seemed reasonable enough, for what came to his mind was the early post-war five-hundred-franc note called 'a miserable' in part because it had Victor Hugo's picture on it, but in greater part because its purchasing power actually was miserable; but then he realized she was talking about today's francs which were worth a hell of a lot. So he asked her: 'How, ma'moiselle?'

'I bet Suzanne you were French. *Ma copine,* over there. She said you had to be American because of your clothes—'

'Then,' John Farrow said; 'to be just, you must reduce the amount to two-hundred-and-fifty francs, *ma petite*.'

'Why that, m'sieur?' the *hôtesse* said.

'Because although I well believe that my mother had very pretty legs, she, also, when she was young, they were not as long as yours are. Or perhaps the legs of my father were longer than mine. In any case, he – a young American diplomat in those days – caught up with her, in Paris, in the spring, during the First World War, which is why I am only half French, making it unjust for you to take all of the five hundred francs of Suzanne. But tell me, what made you think I was a compatriot of yours?'

'Because,' she laughed, and blew him a little kiss, 'you are *so* charming, *grand-père*!'

That made him feel good, especially since he was sure she didn't mean that grandfather business at all. But then, abruptly, he stopped feeling good, for he was remembering how many times he'd heard women say, '*Mais il est* si *charmant!*' of Dalton Ross, during the years the poet had practically lived in their flat on the Avenue Kléber, and that nagging doubt that had tugged at the edge of his conscious mind for at least three-quarters of his life was back again. He had never been able to bring himself to actually put it into words, for whatever her other faults, sins, follies, Yvette Farrow had been the sweetest, best, tenderest, the most devoted mother any son could have wished to have. As long as she and his father had continued to live together, she had spoiled him, her only son, outrageously. And he, John Farrow, had loved '*sa petite maman*' as he still thought of her, with his whole being.

'But I *never* loved Papa,' he thought bleakly. 'He was a good man. Kind, gentle. Only he was *so* stupid; and so goddamned dull!'

Which brought on another equally dismal chain of thought. In all his life, no one, not even Candace, had ever accused him of being either stupid or dull. No, Candace's complaint had been that he was much too clever, by far; and the break-up of their marriage had been caused by two things: her all too successful attempts to avenge, by equalling them, the infidelities he hadn't even committed ('Why not?' he thought. 'Because watching a smooth, absolutely heartless bastard like Dalton operate gave me a sort of complex against it? Or because to follow in *his* footsteps would have been tantamount to admitting that what I can't bring myself to accept even yet, was pretty goddamned likely?') and by the fact that nearly all the women they both knew had made scant efforts to hide the effect he had upon them, including those Candace considered close friends, at least two of whom had pursued him openly. Of course her immediate grounds had been cruelty – which he'd handed to her on a silver platter by slapping her clear across the bedroom the day he'd caught her tearing up that snapshot of Simone.

He sat there now, holding the book, and thinking how much of his life had been a linked chain of compensatory behaviour reflexes – negative ones, at that. He'd suppressed his profound desire to write, his inborn gift for language that had made his rare speeches before juries classics of legal eloquence to the extent that Siegal and Hechtfield had finally got his consent to include a collection of them, taken from court-room stenographic records, in a series of university law school textbooks they were publishing. More, he had suppressed the one book he *had* written: a philosophical exposition of the fact that, in human terms, intelligence operations, grand strategy, and war – even victorious war – cost too goddamned much. It was a beautiful book; but he'd suppressed it out of the wry, bitter, and accurate thought: who the hell am *I* to preach?

And, long after the divorce, he'd still kept so tight a rein on the natural gaiety he'd inherited from his mother, along with the native charm that at least probably could have been entirely her legacy to him as well, that most men called him 'dour'. Most men. What most women called him was 'interesting' and in a tone of voice that implied that his air of studied gloom was Heathcliffian; that, moreover, he needed only *her*, each of them inwardly convinced, to free him from the secret sorrow chaining him to the past, which was a notion as completely false as most romantic notions are. He was melancholy because he dared not be gay; dour, because to him charm was an almost Orestian kind of sin.

Orestian, not Oedipal. The difference was vast.

'Don't go into it!' he told himself again; 'don't go into it, you goddamned fool!'

Then once again, he reached down and picked up that book. Started reading it.

But his attention wandered. Dalton Ross's peculiar kind of free verse required only a moderate degree of concentration, once you'd caught the interior, always mocking beat of his curiously subtle rhythms. For one thing, he had never been one of the Imagists, and his meanings had always been almost contemptuously clear. It wasn't an anti-intellectual posture, really; but just one more example of the fact that the poet had given about as much of a damn about the literary mores of his times as he had about the social and sexual ones. Still John Farrow had too many things to think about. Today even Ross's rather facile verses eluded him. He stared at them but he wasn't really reading with comprehension, with thought. In fact, he'd passed the one on page fifty-seven when belatedly something about it struck him. He turned back to it again and saw that it was entitled: 'For Y.F.'

He sat there holding the book and his hands started to shake, but there was no help for it now. He read:

For Y.F.
You call me faithless, but I
have always kept faith
at least with my inner daemon
who lives within me and instructs
me to wisdom, as he did
Sokrates
and other public nuisances
of our sort.
And, after all, neither Byron
nor Shelley
were excessively honourable men.
Not that I compare myself with either
I am,
to put it with becoming modesty,

by far a better poet
than any of your romantic tub thumpers
of metre and rhyme.
Mais, merde, alors!
You've never read the English
poets, have you?
And I have wasted nine precious
lines. No matter. Strike Byron out
and Shelley out and put Rimbaud
and Verlaine in their stead.
Or even Baudelaire, peut-être?
Oh, no; he wouldn't do. He
was a nasty fellow, wasn't he?
A drug addict who also drank
absinthe and died of syphilis
of the brain. Un vrai salaud,
who told the truth about women –
Unpardonable, that; was it not, my dear?
But I stray from the subject,
do I not, ma chère, petite
et si gentille Y?
Which is, as always, my faithlessness . . .
Yes, I am faithless to you.
My love is for woman, for women:
the collective; the plural.
I have no shame of being what I am.
Accept, then,
instead of worthless, faithless me,
these great gifts I leave you:
First, immortality, by having
granted you these lines;
and that one most tender gift we must hold
secret between us—
Soft, secret, tiny and dear:
The best of me, with the best
of you
so gloriously combined,
that you will surely
watching him grow, find him
ainsi intelligent que beau.
How can he help but be both,

Being mine?
And how can you call me
faithless
when I have left ton ventre
swollen and heavy with
my image;
un souvenir vivant de moi
cast in the pliant mould of you,
to keep, to hold, to love
forever?
Is this not enough?
In any case,
Good-bye, my dear!

John Farrow sat there, and what he felt then, at that moment was bad. Although the mocking, insanely arrogant verse only confirmed what he had known all his life and had pushed away from conscious acknowledgement out of a curiously antique kind of filial piety, the pain of that confirmation was almost crippling just the same.

Even now. Even at his age. Even though he had survived far crueller things.

He saw then, finally, that both the air hostesses of the first-class cabin were hurrying towards him, their young faces gone taut with quite genuine concern.

'Are you ill, sir?' the one called Suzanne said.

And the other, the one he'd been flirting with a little: 'Vous êtes malade! Oh, Bon Dieu! Je vais voir s'il y a un médecin à bord!'

'No,' he said solemnly, 'don't go look for a doctor. I am not sick. Just disgusted. And a little angry. It is solely that someone played me a dirty trick. A long time ago. When I was a little kid. No, even before that – and I just found it out.'

'Un sal tour?' they chorused. 'Et ça alors, comment?'

John Farrow smiled at them then. His smile was very gentle and almost infinitely sad.

'They – killed Papa Noël. Hanged him from my first Christmas tree, perhaps. And nobody ever told me up till now,' he said.

He lay – shoes, jacket, tie off, shirt collar unbuttoned, across the huge bed, and stared up at the high ornamented ceiling of his room. Like the Ruhl, down the street, the Negresco dated from Victorian times, when the English tourists had been the lords of the earth, so much so that the niçois had felt obliged to name the seaside boulevard in front of one of the damned rockiest, most miserable, good-for-nothing beaches in the world, after them. The English Promenade, they'd called it. Of course, a few years back when Spanish competition for the hordes of North European tourists had first become serious, the local authorities had tried to combat the spreading knowledge of the really magnificent sandy beaches of Spain by bringing in sand by the tons from North Africa, and had made an almost decent beach. But a little later, when the American Sixth Fleet was in – to the great delight of the legions of whores all the way from Villefranche-sur-Mer to as far as Saint Rafael, that is, three-quarters of the whole Côte – one badly hungover sailor on a refuelling tanker that accompanied the destroyers anchored in front of Nice had not only opened the wrong valve, but had gone to sleep leaving it open, so that a few million gallons of black sticky fuel oil had ruined forever all that nice expensive sand. And after that—

'Oh hell!' he told himself. 'Come off it, John! Why are you remembering total irrelevancies? Get on with it. Face it.

'What right do you have to even be shocked? Weren't you in Germany with them when the divorce was granted Papa; plus, to make the circumstances even more damning, custody of *you*? And, even before that, didn't you stand outside that kitchen door and listen to fat Hilda giving a play by play description of Maman's extra-curricular activities? You're too goddamned old not to accept human nature as it bloody well *is*. Maman was an adulteress. Scarcely a condition of extreme rarity, you know. Nor, when you get right down to cases, as indefensible as you seem to be trying to make it sound. . . .

'So Papa – all right, all right he wasn't, but it's late in the day to stop calling him that now! – was a good and gentle man. But he was also a staid and stolid old stick who would have driven one of the blessed saints to adorning his forehead for him! *Merde, alors!* Have you *ever* met a cuckold who didn't richly deserve what he got? Who hadn't been begging for it for years?'

He sat up then, and grinned wryly at his reflection in one of those horrible gilt-framed mirrors with which the room was adorned. 'Even you, son!' he thought. 'Even one John Dalton Farrow. But before dear Candy got through I needed a prop under my chin to help me hold up all the antlers she'd decorated me with. And why not? Even as a kid I was a solemn little bastard. "My little Huguenot," Maman used to call me . . .'

The grin on the face of his reflection, and on his own faded.

'I wonder if there weren't at least some Huguenots in Maman's family – way back? Since I couldn't, as I've always thought I did, have got that trait from Papa – poor old stick! I must have got it from somewhere. Because I sure as hell didn't inherit being a dull ass from Maman, at least not directly. Nor from *him*. Hell, say it! From Dalton. And, though most people won't believe it, judging all France by Paris and the Côte, the French were, and *are*, as capable of hard-shelled, doctrinaire puritanism as any people on earth. Who *ever* was more rigid than Jean Calvin?

'I,' he thought, 'have always been a puritan at heart, or at least a coward afraid of joy. Have I ever had a love affair I enjoyed? One involving sex, I mean? Yes. Just two. In all my life, two. With Heide von Kressel – and that was ruined for me afterward by what I found out about her; and also by her subsequent fate. And with – Simone. Except for that, "enjoyed" is far too feeble a word. For one brief stretch of time I lived! Knew magic, wonder, perfect happiness. That once – and never again. That once, and surely never more. . . .

'Take my mad career after Candace bowed out of the picture. Jesus! Just one little cheap, round-heeled easy lay after another. And did I feel good afterward? Hell, no; I felt like puking. And all that time, I—' He bent down grunting and shoved his feet back into his shoes, tied them, stood up, picked up his tie.

'Was dreaming of the girl who was for a little time – my life. My whole life. Which she proved when she walked out of it. What have I been since, but one of the walking wounded, the spiritually maimed, the all-but-dead? Dear God, why didn't I, couldn't I, make her pregnant that time? What was wrong with me? Too starved, nerve-shot, broken to jet my life into her. To swell that slender belly. To weight her down with the living anchor that would have held her safe within the harbour of my arms. That is if the child could even have survived what those sadistic swine did to poor Simone—

'Because afterward, sex wasn't even possible. Simone was so broken, seared, hurt – but if we'd made a child, a daughter in her image, please dear God; a girl-child to be the replica of the object of my idolatry! She, or even he, perhaps, would have been glorious. I know that as I know I am alive. And Simone wouldn't have gone away, and I shouldn't be here now, a paunchy, balding, middle-aged old fool, who—'

He finished knotting his tie and slipped into his jacket. Then he went downstairs to the desk, picked up his passport, and asked where the nearest car rental service was.

'Oh, we can do that for you, sir!' the concierge said. 'What make would you like: a Cadillac? A Mercedes? A Bentley? *With* chauffeur, naturally. English-speaking, and—'

There was only one way to stop that kind of nonsense.

'I,' John Farrow said in French, 'would like a Renault Five. Or something even smaller, if you have one. As long as it has sufficient power to climb hills. And I am neither in need of a guide nor in the mood for conversation – in any language. As for your justly celebrated sights, I have seen them all. Many times. Even some that are no longer here – like the old ports of Toulon and Marseilles, for example—

'But I forget! It is no longer chic to speak harshly of your *geliebte und gemütliche* partners in the Common Market, is it?'

The concierge smiled, grimly.

'This is a free country, M'sieur,' he said quietly, 'one may say what one wishes—'

'And what do *you* say, my friend?' John Farrow said.

The concierge leaned forward. His voice came out in a sibilant whisper, between locked teeth.

'That I wish they were all dead and in hell!' Then, in a perfectly normal tone: 'When would you like the Renault, m'sieur?'

'At once,' John Farrow said.

'Would m'sieur be content to wait half an hour? I have to call another agency that is a few streets away from here. The small cars like that, we don't generally—'

'Have much call for from the kind of people who stay at hotels of grand luxury like this one. I know. But would *you* like to drive a Cadillac up to Puget Théniers?'

As soon as he had said that he was ashamed of himself.

It was an old Resistance habit, lying about where you were actually going. But he was alive today because of it. And for some reason, whenever he was in Europe, he found himself doing so constantly and instinctively. 'Conditioned reflex,' he thought. 'I *see* this damned place and—'

'*Non*, m'sieur,' the concierge agreed politely, '*une grosse voiture comme ça* is much too dangerous in the mountains. M'sieur will wait, then?'

'Of course,' John Farrow said, 'I'll go have a drink out on the terrace.'

'If m'sieur will leave his permit to conduct an automobile with me, meantime, it will speed things up,' the concierge said.

Sitting there on the terrace sipping his Pernod, he was remembering the last time he had sat on the Negresco's terrace. No! It had been the Ruhl's. He'd always stopped at the Ruhl before the government closed it because he'd been fond of the barman, Peter Vercelli, an Italian-Swiss who'd been in the Resistance – although John Farrow hadn't met him until after the war – and had a gimpy leg to prove it. Of course, a gimpy leg didn't really prove anything; but that Peter had got the job after the government had thrown out all the men that Michel Szkolnikoff had installed – when he'd bought not only the Ruhl, but the Plaza, the Savoy, the Cercle de la Méditerranée and the Hôtel de France; not to mention the Martínez, the Mirabeau and the Victoria in Cannes, with the loot he'd got out of his deals with the Kriegsmarine, and even with the Gestapo, through its agent SS Hauptsturmführer Fritz Engelke – did.

That was surely one of the sourest smells of history. Because Szkolnikoff had been a Russian Jew. A Jew who not only had been allowed to keep his blonde German mistress Elfrieda, but who'd been on back-slapping, partying terms with Himmler, the head of the Gestapo. The genocide expert who'd almost wiped out his people.

'I hope they did blast his balls off outside of Madrid that time,' John thought, 'but I doubt it. Rats like Szkolnikoff – and my dear illegitimate father – always get away.'

No, the incident he'd started to remember had not occurred on this terrace but on the practically identical one at the Ruhl, down the street. He'd been sitting there with Candace and his daughter, Cynthia. Cynthia was just out of babyhood then, actually, but since they'd never talked baby talk to her, her speech was rapid, clear, shaped into well-formed sentences – and incessant.

'So this is one of the places you won the war in, hero?' Candace had said. Things were already going badly between them by then. 'Against all the *poules* on the coast, I'll bet!'

'The war?' Cynthia had said. 'You were in the war, Papa?'

'Yes, pet,' John had said tiredly.

'Papa, what'd you *do* in the war?' Cynthia piped.

And he'd answered her with the strict literal truth, because his mind had been far away – and sorrowing.

'Made patty-cakes out of horse shit, pet,' he'd said.

'Why, John!' Candace gasped. 'You watch your dirty mouth in front of *my* baby, will you?'

But it *had* been one of the things he'd done. You hid tiny British-made contact mines in mounds of horse droppings. And they blew up the tracks of the first tank that ran over them. Or the wheels of the first truck.

A few kilometres farther along you planted a few more. After that the whole Blitzkrieg column stopped dead every time they came to a place a farmer had led his horse across the road, and broke out the mine detectors. So the column that should have got to the Normandy beach-head, racing up from the south in a couple of days, took two weeks to get there. Especially when you'd also hid gelignite under rock-piles along the road with a low trip wire stretched all the way across in a way that although the first vehicle passing over the trip wire pulled the detonator's pin, it was the second – very often a command car – that caught the blast. And what a pile of small jagged-edged stones and granite slivers could do to a bunch of fat Nazi officers had to be seen to be believed. And to be enjoyed, because he had got to the place he could enjoy it by then.

'It was Simone who induced me to rejoin the human race,' he thought.

Then he saw the concierge coming through the double doors opening out on the terrace with the keys to the little Renault Cinq dangling from his hand.

3

He had first begun to secede from humanity in Paris during the winter of 1942 and the spring of 1943. Nearly all of 1942, through mid-November in fact, he had spent in London as an advance liaison officer with British intelligence from the OSS, his main task being to work on his none too fluent German up to ten hours daily under the tutelage of a young German Jew who had somehow managed to get out in time. England was a good place to be in those days. The Churchillian phrase, 'their finest hour' was very far from being empty rhetoric. The English he met then made him feel humble and grateful and more than a little proud to be a member of the human race.

That he hadn't fallen desperately in love with one of the legions of stunning English girls with their beautiful legs and absolutely marvellous complexions who were all over the place, most of them in the uniforms of the various women's services by then, was due to two factors entirely beyond his control. The SOE's training, designed to keep him alive and functioning at least a reasonable length of time after landing him in occupied France, was so detailed and so thorough that he never really had sufficient leisure to meet one of them socially; and so rough that he was too tired to seriously make the attempt. And, to make matters worse, he was still quite timid, a charmingly youthful trait that had not yet been blasted out of him by the recognition that he could no longer afford timidity or any other wasted motions because time to enjoy life – to eat, drink, screw, and otherwise be merry – was the one thing he could not count on, since the exact minute an allied spy and saboteur set foot upon the soil of *Festung Europa,* was the self-same minute that his future ran out on him. By the records, his chances for survival, for escape were so low that it was statistically impossible to compute them. So that lack of leisure, that bone-marrow deep fatigue, and that youthful timidity were more than enough, to torpedo all his chances.

The one time he had even spoken to an English girl with something between intention and hope, had been during the intermission of a concert at the Albert Hall. In fact, he had been on the point of going home and not sitting through the second half of the programme, out of his acute disappointment at the fact that the man he had gone there to hear, the brilliant young violinist, Anton Rabinowski, hadn't even shown up. He had heard Rabinowski during the Christmas holidays of the last year he'd spent at Harvard, pursuing the LLD degree that would now have to wait until the war was over, if not for ever. Since a love for music was still another of the many good and graceful things that Yvette Farrow had instilled in him, when he had read in *The Times* of London that the French violinist – though it was said that Rabinowski had taken American citizenship now – was to appear, he had shaken off his really crushing weariness to attend.

So at that intermission he was tired, bored, and annoyed. It didn't seem very professional of Rabinowski to simply fail to appear without notice or excuse as apparently the young violinist had done. And it wasn't until two or three nights later that he heard at SOE headquarters what had occurred: when a Pan Am Clipper put in at Lisbon to refuel, discharge some passengers, pick up others, there had been an announced five-hour delay in takeoff time, largely because the weather had turned positively foul. So Anton Rabinowski, who'd never been there before, decided to see a little of the town, and more especially, to hear in person, if he could, a celebrated Fado singer whose records were among the most prized of his extensive collection in New York. And the violinist set out, accompanied by a paid interpreter and guide – and vanished from the face of the earth. After waiting four hours beyond the announced takeoff time the Clipper had had to take off from the choppy waters of the bay without him, for, instead of improving, the weather was getting worse by the minute, and if the big flying boat hadn't broken free of those pounding waves when it did, it and its passengers – most of them very important personages indeed – might have been held in Lisbon by the rising Atlantic gales for weeks.

That much was known. What the SOE suspected and feared, was that even in neutral Portugal, the long arm of AMT IV-B4, Sipo IV's special bureau of Jewish affairs, the *Judenreferat*, had reached out to snatch up so valuable a prize. Because by then, even the Gestapo's leaders were beginning to have serious doubts about the outcome of the war, and Jews of the prominence of France's Léon Blum, and the United States' Anton

Rabinowski must have seemed excellent pawns to be exchanged for their own miserable murderers' lives if – or more likely when – the need for such drastic measures should arise.

But not yet knowing these things, John Farrow, a little put out too by the BBC Symphony Orchestra's lack-lustre performance, had come blindly down the stairs into the lobby and had quite literally collided with the English girl. The ice thus effectively, if somewhat brusquely broken, they had started to chat. She had been both exceedingly lovely and quite friendly in a gentle, subdued way that had an undercurrent of sadness in it. So he'd asked her for a date – after the concert if possible. He proposed to take her nightclubbing and—

But her smile had stopped him cold.

'That's very kind of you, lieutenant,' she said, 'but I'm afraid I can't. You see, I have to go back to my charges—'

'Your charges?' he'd said blankly.

'Over there,' she'd said, and nodded her head towards where five young RAF officers stood quietly chatting and smoking. There weren't any other girls with them, which surprised him because they were obviously fighter pilots, and fighter pilots always got the best. 'And deserve it,' he admitted, humbly. Then something about the way they handled their cigarettes struck him. Looking at them more intently, he realized all five of them were blind. Two of them had faces that told him that they hadn't jumped in time, maybe because the hatches of their Spitfires or Hurricanes had stuck, or because they'd been too low to risk it, or had plain decided to ride their crippled aircraft down. Those two faces were twisted, browless, lashless, flame-seared horrors. But all the rest of them had burn scars, too, mostly around the eyes. He tore his gaze away from them, back to the still softly smiling face of the girl.

'I see,' he stammered, 'and I'm sorry. But some other night? When you're not—'

'All tied up?' she said. 'Thank you again, lieutenant. But that's quite impossible, really. You see – I'm engaged. To – Ted. He's the tallest of my chaps, over there. So I couldn't—'

John had looked again. The tallest of the blind pilots was the one with the worst face of all. John put out his hand to her. She took it, expecting a normal, gentlemanly handshake of good-bye. But he raised it to his lips.

'May I say I'm proud to have met you?' he said. 'No. Honoured is the word.'

And it was then that suddenly, startlingly, she'd cried. He'd stood there like a wooden image, watching her tears brimming on her lashes, breaking free, falling.

'Thank you, lieutenant. That was a lovely thing to say, rather. Now will you please go away? Immediately? This very instant?' she'd said.

And he had gone. That night he got drunker than a skunk and picked up a frizzled cockney tart in one of the blacked-out streets. He wasted his money. He couldn't. He really couldn't. That lovely, tear-wet face kept getting in the way.

Then all his training was done, finally. He'd learned to send messages in code, repair any damned thing that went wrong with a radio, except that thing that *usually* went wrong with them: having all their blessed valves smashed to powdered glass when the SOE's Lysanders or Mosquitoes parachuted them in to you. He'd learned how to kill a man with a knife, or a pistol with a silencer fitted to it, or with his bare hands if need be. He had an exhaustive knowledge of the use of explosives. He'd been thoroughly trained in such elementary tricks for throwing a counter-espionage agent off your trail as starting out from home wearing a soft hat, which you then crushed and stuck under your coat, slipped a beret out of your pocket and put that on when no one was looking, changed from that into a worker's cap, then back to the soft hat again, wore your two-coloured scarf with the red side out a while, then changed it over so the green side was out, threw away an umbrella you knew you were going to need damned badly later on, put folded newspapers inside one shoe to change the characteristics of your walk, and all the rest of a spy's skills.

Among them, how to steal.

That, strangely enough was one of the two things that he, twenty-four-year-old John Farrow, had been best at: stealing. The other, of course, was languages. He was the best pickpocket in the SOE training school's whole history, including a little cockney who had been a professional one. He delighted in his own skill and practised incessantly, until he could and did often go out in the streets of London at night and come back with two or three sidearms stolen right out of British or American officers' holsters. Before the end he could steal a pistol from a cold sober officer instead of the drunken ones he'd picked at first.

This skill was necessary, because in Paris the Germans shot any civilian caught carrying a gun or knife without even bothering to submit him to a drumhead trial. So you went unarmed. But when you needed a weapon you were apt to need it goddamned badly and the only way to get one was to steal it.

He was also quite good at explosives, including the simpler ones that could be manufactured out of materials at hand. One of his first assignments upon reaching Paris was to teach the city's Resistance groups the proper way of making Molotov cocktails. The ones they had been using weren't very effective. To stick a rag wick down the neck of a bottle filled with petrol, and light the wick just before throwing the bottle produced only a small fire that quite often could be put out with one or two squirts from an extinguisher. And even more often the wick went out in mid-air and produced no fire at all. A good Molotov cocktail explodes, and produces a raging holocaust that will gut a restaurant filled with enemy soldiers in minutes. To make them you needed champagne bottles. Champagne bottles, as everyone knows, have a sort of dimple in their bottoms, a sort of depression put there, John Farrow suspected, to cheat the customers out of a few grams of the sparkling stuff. But they were great for Molotov cocktails, because you could seal a little vial of sulphuric acid in that depression with candle wax. Then you filled the bottle with petrol, and slapped a label on to it that had been soaked in potassium chlorate. One of those dropped into the open hatch of a patrolling Tiger tank, burned out that immense and formidable machine and turned it into a mass of useless red-hot iron in three minutes flat. He'd never seen a crewman get out alive from such a blasted tank.

Oh yes, they'd taught him many things. But two of them hadn't stuck: that you couldn't trust anyone at all and expect to stay alive; and the silent, endless, murderously corrosive effect of fear.

He sat in an ice-cold room on the second floor of a dingy building on the Rue Lappe near the Place de la Bastille, one of the best arrondissements in Paris to hide out in since the SS let it alone except for an occasional propaganda drive to induce skilled factory hands to sign up for work in Germany. But the workers of the Eleventh Arrondissement were much too hard nosed to be taken in. Besides, nearly all of them, including the young single men, were exempt from the forced labour requisitions which supplied the Third Reich with slave labour, since all the factories in the Eleventh were theoretically working for the Germans already.

Theoretically. If Jean/John Farrow had been able to smile by then he would have smiled at that. What that work amounted to was the subtlest, best coordinated, most effective sabotage in all modern history.

He knew that, because one of his jobs was to supply the factories with new designs, blueprints, drawings made by the réseau of engineering students and draftsmen of L'Ecole Polytechnique in the Latin Quarter, all of which looked exactly like the originals that the Wehrmacht, Luftwaffe, or Kriegsmarine had given the factory bosses and foremen to work from. Except that they had dozens of dimensions wrong in critical places, essential parts drawn hind end to, whole sections that were mirror images reversed from right to left, so that nothing made from them ever worked. Later they refined the matter even more, turning out drawings for parts that *would* work – for a while. An aircraft part that always failed in mid-air was better than one that merely grounded the plane, for the former very often killed the aircrews as well. And the beauty of it was that the Germans couldn't swear that the mistakes weren't their own, since the very paper was continually being stolen from the Wehrmacht's supply depots, and had all the proper watermarks, and the like. So a foreman could shrug and say:

'But, mon capitaine, we made it exactly the way your drawing called for us to. . . .'

And when the Germans checked, they'd find that he was right.

But even success was no comfort to him now. He was playing everything strictly by the rules, but nothing helped. He had all the documents a Parisian had to carry with him always if he wanted to stay alive and out of the slave factories of the Third Reich: the identity, draft, and labour cards, and the seven kinds of ration cards for meat, wine, bread, butter, canned goods, textiles, and tobacco. And they were the most artistic, perfect forgeries that any crook alive could have dreamed of. What's more, since his father had insisted on his being circumcised soon after his birth, a routine health precaution among middle- and upper-class Americans, he had to carry a Roman Catholic baptismal certificate from the Parish of Rheims, showing that one Jean Claude Dubois had been duly baptized in the cathedral itself on November 13, 1918. Otherwise, if he got caught in one of the SS's strip-to-the-buff raids he would have found himself in a cattle car headed for one of the concentration camps as a Jew. What's more if they phoned the parish rectory, they'd find that his baptism was duly and carefully recorded there. Both the Roman Catholic and the Protestant clergy cooperated to the man with the FFI in this simple and effective ruse to save Resistance people and even many Jews from certain death.

Even his lodgings were tactically sound. His room was neither in the basement nor on the *rez-de-chaussée,* both of which could be cut off front and back by an SS raiding party before he'd have a chance to move. It was on the second floor, high enough for him to hear them come pounding up the stairs and go out of a tiny side window he was thin enough to get through with ease and go down the knotted rope he kept ready into the ancient coachyard of the next house. The only thing that bothered him about that was that he couldn't practise it to time himself. But he was sure he could do it fast enough.

And now it looked like he was going to have to.

He sat there in that ice-cold room and looked at that bowl of lumpy meatless soup he'd heated on his little electric hotplate. But he didn't even pick up his spoon to put a little of it into his mouth. He was shivering all over, and faint with hunger but he knew that one spoonful would make him vomit.

And not because the soup was bad. It *was* bad, of course; but he'd eaten worse things. Three days ago he'd eaten a rabbit stew that Hélène had made for him. He hadn't asked her whether the rabbit had meowed when killed, because he knew damned well it had. By the early spring of 1943, the principal ingredient of Parisian rabbit stew was always alley cat.

Hélène was a member of one of the Left Bank réseaux. She was a university student, and during normal times he was sure she'd been very pretty, maybe even beautiful, but now like every girl or woman in Paris who wasn't a collaborator, which was the exact synonym for a Nazi's whore, she looked like grim death.

Even so, he'd made her his mistress almost from the start, because in his uniquely awful position as liaison courier among all the Resistance réseaux scattered all over town, a little human warmth, and an occasional stolen hour of desperately tender and therefore shattering sex, served to keep him from going quite literally insane. And in almost equal measure, he was sure, it had served to save her from the same fate.

After the war, if they both lived, he was going to marry her. He hadn't the faintest notion whether he loved her or not, but he was going to marry her anyhow, out of pity and simple gratitude. For the risks she took to hold his hand for five minutes, touch his face, nothing more, were absolutely unbelievable. Because there was no doubt that she loved him. And pity and gratitude and a love like Hélène's were more than enough on which to build his life. Her name, of course, was not Hélène, any more than his was Jean Claude. But they'd agreed not to break the rules by revealing their true identities even to each other for fear the SS torturers might wring those names out of them one day. What you didn't know, no degree of pain could force you to say.

He sat there shivering, looking at that soup congealing into sodden lumps again with the cold, and knowing he had to eat it, because he was going to need his strength, but praying: 'Not yet good God not yet for pity – please not yet!'

He couldn't eat that soup because he was cracking up. He hadn't left that room in two whole days. He'd sat there crying and cursing and occasionally babbling in French the childish prayers his mother had taught him when he was a little boy. They were the only prayers he knew. He considered himself an atheist, but he prayed all the same. When you get *that* scared, brother, you pray.

Two days before, after eating that delicious *soupe du chat noir*, he had had a rendezvous with some types who were going to present him to the famous Colonel Roll of the FTP. Now the FTP, the Franc-Tireurs et Partisans Français, were the Communist Maquisards. At first, during that obscene period in which Hitler and Stalin had embraced long enough to carve up Poland's prostrate corpse between them, the Communists had dutifully worshipped at the Nazi shrine, which had made him hate their bloody guts a little more than he always had. But now that Hitler had proved once more that his pledged word wasn't worth the breath he used to utter it and sent his armour clanking into Russia, the Communist Resistance groups were everywhere fighting like tigers.

And because they were the best trained, best disciplined, and most experienced guerrillas in France, they were doing a magnificent job of it. Even though he, Jean Claude/John Farrow agreed one hundred per cent with De Gaulle's expressed belief that they were only fighting to have France fall into their power once the war was won, he could not help but admire them.

Beside he disagreed with De Gaulle's order not to provoke the Nazis because to do so would only cause them to shoot hundreds of innocent hostages in reprisal. He agreed with the Communist position that the Nazis needed no provocation and since they damned well were going to kill, rob, rape, torture and destroy anyhow, the only thing that made sense was to kill them first.

So he'd set up that meeting with Colonel Roll's men, in order to coordinate the efforts of *all* the Resistance groups in Paris. But when he'd got to that dirty bar near the Gare St Lazare, instead of going in, he'd just kept walking on. He couldn't for the life of him have explained why, except that a sudden ice-cold panic had seized him.

But half a block away he looked back and saw the plain-clothes agents of Sip IV clubbing the men he'd gone there to meet into the back seat of a long black Citroën Traction Avant, and he knew that his cover was blown.

So, not knowing what to do, his normally active mind frozen by pure terror, he had gone back to his room and waited there for the SS to come after him. He had a vague notion of killing himself when he heard their feet pounding up the stairs. He knew perfectly well that he wouldn't be able to take what the Gestapo customarily did to their prisoners for as long as five minutes flat, so the only decent thing for him to do was to die, because he was one of only two men in Paris who knew the hideouts and assumed names of the members of practically every non-communist réseau in the city. But even that made no sense, because the Gestapo obviously already had that other man.

Still he sat there, paralysed by pure panic, by sorrow. But not by rage. Because that other man who knew enough about the Resistance réseaux of Paris to wreck that city's forlorn chances of successful revolt for ever was his friend, his almost brother, the man he literally worshipped, that daredevil, hero, near saint of the early Resistance, Alain Roget. And the only other person on this filthy totally corrupt earth who had known the place and the hour of his rendezvous with Colonel Roll's men, besides himself and those men themselves had been Alain Roget.

So now he was going to die messily and badly because he'd broken the first rule: never trust anybody. Not even heroes and saints. Because Sipo IV, the Gestapo, broke heroes and saints in only a little more time than it took them to break ordinary men.

He was sitting like that, shivering and crying, when Hélène came through the door he'd forgot to even lock and stood there looking at him.

'Species of a whore!' he screamed at her. '*Emerdeuse publique!* How many times have I told you *never* to come here twice in the same week? Get out of here, cunt! *Foutez-moi le champ!*'

'Jean,' she whispered then, 'mon pauvre petit, je—'

And his rage was gone, and miraculously even some of his fear.

'Pardon me,' he said, 'I am a swine. And a coward. The only good luck you will have, my love, is that now you'll never have to marry the lump of bad shit that I am. Because my cover is blown. I am a dead man. And I think – *bon petit Jesu, pitié!* – that it was Alain—'

'I know that,' she said. 'They've been parading him from place to place all day like a dog on a leash. He has already betrayed fifty-three people. Good people. The best. So I was told to come to you. By O'Leary. You are ordered to – kill Alain, Jean. Before he can betray us all. Before there is not one réseau left in Paris, except those of the Communists, which he does not know. O'Leary says – that you – can do it – that you know how. That you've been trained especially so that—'

He sat there, staring at her. Then he got up. Put his arms around her. And the fear was gone. All gone.

She went on talking, slowly quietly calmly:

'I have brought you a pistol. Of Belgian fabrication. A Browning. It is my own. I have had it a long time, but since—'

He shook his head, said: 'No, keep it. It might be traced back to you – afterward. I shall procure myself a weapon. One of theirs. From one of them.' He smiled at her then. He felt sad, but he wasn't afraid any more. It came to him that it had been the uncertainty he'd been afraid of. And now that everything had been reduced to absolute certainty, even the hours, minutes, seconds he had left to live, all he felt was sadness, and, curiously, a kind of peace.

He had two most excellent reasons for his sadness: he was going to have to leave Hélène for ever; and he was going to have to kill Alain. He was going to leave this poor, forlorn, starving girl who needed him, and to kill the best friend he'd ever had in this bleak, miserable world. But he could be peaceful about both awful, totally inescapable facts, because he was also going to die himself. That was just as inescapable, and a good bit less awful, because he was sure that under the conditions O'Leary had set up, it was more than probable that he would die very quickly and cleanly; but anyhow he wouldn't have to go on or to remember or to think or to feel.

He ran his fingers through her soft, blonde hair. Kissed it.

'*D'accord*,' he said. 'All right. Tell O'Leary I will do it. But with the most *grand* sadness. For however fast they broke poor Alain, they would have broken me twice as fast. No – three times.' He looked at her, said, 'You realize what this means, do you not, *ma pauvre petite*?'

'Yes,' she said. 'You will die. It is impossible to do this and live. I shall never see you again. Jean—'

'Yes, Hélène?'

'Do not go yet. It is not dark enough. Stay. Make love to me. And – do not – do not use – *une préservative* – this time. Please don't. Give me a baby. *Ton fils. Your* son. Please.'

'Bon petit enfant Jésus!' Jean Dubois/John Farrow said.

When he left her, she was asleep or pretending to be, so he bent down and kissed her very softly, tasting the salt of the tears on her face, and smelling her unwashed sweaty smell. Soap was another thing it was almost impossible to find in Paris in 1943 so that he and everybody else he knew stank like goats, even delicate, refined girls like Hélène.

Then he went out into the night. He walked away from the tall tower of the Bastille Monument, until he came to a little dead-end street that was called the Impasse Primevères, which was what that word *impasse* meant anyhow. Dead end – like his life, now. He walked up to a boarded-up warehouse and entered it by a side door that one of his Resistance experts had made him a key for. The warehouse was empty. It had belonged to a rich Jewish merchant, who, along with his entire family, had been deported. Which meant, although John Farrow wasn't to find it out until the war was over, that the merchant and his family were all dead.

But the warehouse wasn't entirely empty any more. John had his radio there and a supply of Molotov cocktails stacked up in an ordinary wine bottle rack. He sat down and strapped the telegrapher's key to his thigh, plugged the wires from it into the wireless, and started sending. He raised London easily and at once got their promise to send a Westland Lysander, one of those little aircraft that could land on a half-crown and not even spin the stars to pick up him and Hélène on the hidden landing strip twenty kilometres beyond the Vincennes Gate.

Because he had passed from panic to its even more dangerous opposite, that sure sign that a man's brains have cracked, have given way to the never-ending strain, have gone. And as always in such cases, what he suffered was a kind of megalomaniacal paranoia. He felt invincible. He felt braver than a pride of lions. He knew he was going to be able to pull it off, save Hélène, and live.

He was by then, by any clinical criteria, demonstrably insane. And as it turned out afterward – because he was, he did it. All except one small very minor detail – which became to him as a man the most important part – he didn't save Hélène.

When he left the warehouse – realizing again that it was the worst possible matériel depot he could have chosen, because to hide your stuff at the end of a dead-end street was idiotic, and to send wireless messages from it suicidal, because the Funkspiel could bring the SS down on you at any minute, and the only direction you could run was the one they'd be coming from, thus proving he was very lucid, very clear, as all paranoiacs are, which is why that form of madness is so hard to cure – he started walking towards the Place de la Bastille, and from there he took the Rue St Antoine and continued up it past the place where it changes its name and becomes the Rue Rivoli. But when he got to the Place du Palais Royal, he went up the Avenue de l'Opéra. What he was trying to do was to get to the Place Pigalle by the time all the *boîtes* with nude shows closed down and the *poules* started doing a land-office business with the Nazi officers. Because by then most of the Boches would be pretty goddamned drunk, making the task of stealing a sidearm easy enough for an operative who could do it the way he could.

The trouble with that was that the Germans closed down the métro at night, so the only way to get there was to walk, since even the poor devils who made their living pedalling you about in Velo-taxis – a sort of tricycle welded to a two-wheeled basket-shaped affair in which the two passengers sat – didn't stay out very late when it got this cold, and besides damned few people could afford the fare: five francs just to take the 'Libre' sign down, and after that nine francs per kilometre. Even so it was that, the métro, or walk, because only the Nazis, and the big black market operators had *essence* for their cars by then.

But Jean Claude Dubois/John Dalton Farrow would have taken a Velo-taxi tonight, if he could have found one, even at the grave risk of attracting too much attention to himself. There weren't any so he walked. Fast – because from the Place de la Bastille to the Place Pigalle was a hell of a long way. When he got there finally he was dead tired. But he couldn't stop to rest because it had taken him so long to get to Pigalle that it was already the officially decreed closing time for all the clubs, and he had approximately a quarter of an hour to steal himself a pistol before the whores dragged the last of the Nazi officers off, and even the sadistic queers of the SS who stood around sneering at the spectacle, had gone home.

He did it. A fat Wehrmacht Hauptmann was leaning forward, grinding his big belly into a *poule*'s damned skinny one, while he kissed her wetly, noisily, cupping her bony buttocks with his two red beefy hands, having pulled her skirt up around her waist so that her pipestem, slightly bowed thighs showed white, and her panties displayed, even as dark as it was, the fact that she hadn't washed or changed them in three months. It was so goddamned easy that Jean Claude/John almost gave it up as unsporting, but his mad lucidity made him realize in time that he couldn't afford sportsmanship. So he unbuttoned the Wehrmacht captain's holster, slipped the Walther out of it and into his own pocket.

Then and only then did he do a really insane thing. He saw from the grimace on the prostitute's face that that big tub of lard was hurting her. At once he saw why: the ornamental dagger that many Wehrmacht officers wore had slipped around on his belt so that it was between them, and the gross pig was grinding it, scabbard and all, unknowingly of course, into her belly.

So Jean/John stepped in close, slipped his hand between them and adjusted the matter. The captain stopped kissing the whore. Turned, without releasing her, and glared at the intruder.

Blithely Jean Claude Dubois/John Dalton Farrow snapped to attention, and threw the captain the smartest Nazi salute imaginable.

'Es tut mire leid, mein Hauptmann,' he barked, *'aber Sie haben das kleine madchen sehr verletzt mit Ihrem Dolch!'*

'Ach so?' the captain said, and went back to kissing the skinny *poule*. Seeing that it hadn't even occurred to him that there was anything wrong with a dirty, badly dressed Frenchman's saying to him in reasonably fluent German, 'I am sorry, my captain, but you have hurt the little maiden very much with your dagger,' Jean/John stole the dagger too. Which made the whole thing rather sporting after all.

By that time it was five o'clock in the morning, when the métro started running again, so Jean/John was able to ride all the way back to the Place de la Bastille on the underground. He slept all the way, and woke up only when he got to the Bastille métro station, which was another of the things he'd trained himself to do.

He felt a hell of a lot better. He had to go home now, because there was one thing he'd forgot to ask Hélène. He needed to know the name of the last réseau the Gestapo had liquidated with Alain Roget's help. Because knowing how methodical the German mind is, he could easily figure which one they'd hit next.

But again he had one of those premonitions that all Resistance people, and intelligence agents who survived will tell you time and time again saved their lives. He stopped still thinking:

'A sidearm isn't much. There'll be carloads of the bastards. But maybe if I got a chance to throw a Molotov or two into their cars it might liven matters up a bit, mightn't it?'

So first he went back to the warehouse and got two Molotov cocktails, all he could, or dared, carry under his coat, since a litre champagne bottle is big awkward and slippery in the order named and if he dropped one of them on the sidewalk he'd go up in a whoosh of flame before he could even jump out of the way.

His luck up to that point was miraculous, and even beyond that point, except for one thing, except for *sa petite* Hélène. Because by then, one of Colonel Roll's men had broken under torture, and had told the Gestapo whom they'd gone to meet at that bar near the St Lazare train station. And that half-alive, broken, dying on his feet from internal haemorrhages from the thirty-odd terrible beatings they'd given him, ghost that was all Alain Roget was by then, told them where he lived.

So the long black Light Elevens and Fifteens, those famous black front-drive Citroëns that were the Gestapo's favourite mounts, came sliding up to the Rue Lappe just as he got back to it. And he pulled it off.

The first part, anyhow.

He lobbed the first Molotov cocktail into the Citroën where Alain sat. And the fallen hero-saint and the SS men guarding him, rolled out of the blazing car, all of them turned into living torches and tearing the morning apart with their hoarse-voiced, animal screams.

It was then that he made his first mistake. He paused long enough to put a merciful bullet through poor Alain's head, whispering as he fired, *'Pardonne-moi, mon vieux!'* which gave two of the SS men time to get out of the second *Traction-Avant* before he exploded it – and the other three Nazis in it – into another mass of flames.

The two survivors started for him, shooting as they came. He didn't shoot back because he'd been trained that to fire while running was a pure waste of ammunition; better to duck into a doorway, say, steady his arm against the door-frame, and squeeze off his shots with both hands gripping the pistol, shooting slowly, carefully, aiming to kill with at least some hope of doing just that.

But there weren't any doorways available between him and the rooming house he lived in, so he ran for that. What saved him was that they had only handguns – Walther P-38s, and against a pistol, a running, zigzagging man has at least a chance. Which was diminishing fast, for the well-fed, well-trained SS men were gaining on him with every step. They were because both his breath and strength were just about gone. Winning foot races against Gestapo gunmen was not exactly a recommendable pastime for a man who hadn't eaten in two full days. He knew that, but he kept on running until suddenly Hélène, wrapped in his heavy woollen bathrobe, and with not a stitch on under it, he was sure, came out of the front door and shot the Gestapo man closest to him dead.

John whirled to get off a shot at the other one, but he didn't need to, because a German military policeman he hadn't even seen before cut loose with his burpgun from the corner of the Rue de Charon, a full thirty metres away, too goddamned far to hit anything with a burpgun, except that the bastard did. Hélène was dead before she struck the sidewalk, and the Gestapo man took eight bullets before he could throw himself out of the way. But he still had breath enough left in him to bellow:

'Narr! Esel! Dummkopf! Schwein! Ich bin der Sipo Vier und du hast mih getötet!'

And like the automaton all Nazis were at heart, the MP pulled up short. Crept up to where the wounded Sipo IV agent lay. Bent over him.

Jean/John stood there. Then slowly, carefully, holding the Walther with both hands, the way he'd been taught to, his legs wide spread, his body rigid as a tripod, making the perfect firing platform, he squeezed off that one shot that was all he needed, and shot the MP dead. Immediately, not because he was thinking, but because to anyone who did what he did, and had managed to stay alive as long as he had, certain reactions had gone past habit, had become instinctual, he whirled to face the second MP who should have been coming around one of those corners by now. Military policemen *always* worked in pairs.

But there was no second MP. He couldn't believe it. It was impossible. But he was alone in the Rue Lappe except for a sprawl of corpses and two black *Traction-Avants* that were blazing like torches and giving off a smell of hot iron, peeling paint, the stink of burning rubber, and another stench, curiously like that of roasting pork, except that it was rapidly getting overdone. He stood there waiting, but the second MP still didn't come. Having the kind of mind he had, and under other circumstances, it would have delighted him to know why the other Nazi MP didn't appear. The night before, the poor devil had eaten a whole huge sausage in a local bar, so greedily that he hadn't noticed it was slightly spoiled. So this morning he had a full blown case of GI's. At that very moment he was squatting on his heels in one of those French *toilettes* that have no seats and are nothing more than an enamelled platform on the floor, exactly like a shower bath, except that the hole in the middle is much bigger. It was, of course, equipped with a ceiling-high tank and a chain which could be pulled to flush the whole miserable affair, except this being Paris, and the Parisians being as one celebrated writer put it 'the little children of the dung beetle', nobody ever pulled that chain.

So poor Hans balanced there on his heels, holding the seat of his pants as high up off the floor as he could get them, and cursed the French for being seven different varieties of *kotige, unflätige Schweine* (dirty filthy pigs) while trying not to fall over backwards into a ton and a half of human shit. French shit, at that. It was, of course, beyond him to reflect that while the French are not the cleanest people on earth, and while the Germans maybe are, the French don't build gas chambers and the Germans do. In any case no kind of reflection served him for anything before the court martial he faced two days later, or before the firing squad he faced the day after that – especially not the bitter thought that he was one of the few soldiers in history who was executed for the high crime of absolutely having to take a crap.

But John didn't know that. All he did know was that he'd better get the hell out of that unnaturally silent street, so still that the roar of the flames from the two gutted Citroëns seemed to him deafening, before some collaborator, or coward, or spy, telephoned Henri Chamberlin alias Lafont at 93 Rue Lauriston, or Philippe Masay, at 101, Avenue Henri Martin, the two most terrible of the murderous traitors who served the Gestapo, or even Sipo IV itself at 72 Avenue Foch.

He was still functioning by instinct, existing in a curiously lucid state of shock that allowed him to do everything exactly right, proceed with an absolutely inhuman precision, precisely because it didn't permit him to feel at all.

He walked up to where the MP lay atop the Gestapo man. He saw that the MP was gone, and the Gestapo man going fast. Even so, he couldn't take a chance, so he put a bullet between the Gestapo man's eyes. Then he tossed the Walther down beside them and turned back to where Hélène lay.

She lay across the walk. Her face hung down into the gutter. There was a pool of blood a full two metres wide under her. It was incredible that so much blood could have come out of so small a body. His bathrobe was up around her hips, and her bare legs and thighs and even a part of one soft white buttock were exposed to public view. Reverently he bent down and tugged at the bathrobe until she was decently covered to midcalf. Then he walked away very slowly. Nobody stopped him. He mingled with the early morning crowd in the Place de la Bastille. Went down the métro stairs, already lost and safe among them. He took the métro all the way out to La Porte de Vincennes.

Out there, of course, they did stop him. But his papers were in perfect order, and his excuse for requesting a one day's pass for going out into the country very believable.

'I should like to go, *m'sieur capitaine*, out to the country to see if I can buy a little food from the farmers. Some eggs, a little milk. Perhaps even a ham. There is so little to eat in Paris, these days, sir.'

'*Jawohl!*' the hauptmann of the guard said, then winked at him: 'But on the condition, *mein kleiner Franzose*, that you bring *me* back two dozen eggs, and fresh, mind you!'

'With much pleasure, mon capitaine!' John said, and took that slip of paper that saved his life. That, and the fact that out of over-confidence, the SS hunting group he'd wiped out hadn't even notified their headquarters on the Avenue Foch that they were after him. He kept on walking not feeling anything at all, neither the bone-deep weariness gripping him, nor pain, nor even grief, until he got to that beautifully camouflaged flight strip just twenty kilometres beyond the Vincennes Gate.

He lay in a ditch beside it and slept until it was night. Slept deeply, profoundly, without dreams.

That night one of the Lysanders of the National Council of the Resistance's Service d'Atterrissages et Parachutages, picked him up, first landing, then taking off again on that tiny rough airstrip by moonlight only. He didn't open his mouth all the way back to England.

But when he climbed out of the aeroplane he fell flat on his face. He was in the hospital two months. The first one he didn't say anything, but lay on his bed and cried silently day and night until his eyes were swollen completely shut and he hadn't any tears left. During all that time he didn't eat at all and they had to keep him alive by intravenous feedings. The second month he began to eat a little, but also screamed and raved and cursed and threw things at the doctors and nurses, which, curiously enough the British major who was the psychiatrist in charge, said was a sure sign that he was getting better.

They put him under deep sedation for ten whole days. When

he came out of it, he was all right. Practically normal. He begged them to give him another chance to make up for his failure in Paris. They stared at him, not knowing what to say, because they had a full report on his final days in Paris from Lieutenant Commander Pat O'Leary, who naturally enough, wasn't Irish, wasn't a lieutenant commander, and wasn't named Pat O'Leary, but was a Belgian doctor named Albert Guérisse, whose speciality was getting downed Allied airmen out of occupied France. Because of that they were afraid he was crazier than ever, for any man who considered what they now knew he'd done a failure, was, on the face of it, stark raving mad.

But he wasn't a British officer even though he was on loan to SOE. If he had been, they'd have given him a DSO, and a medical discharge with a citation, and enlisted him in something harmless like the Home Guard. But since he was both a ruddy Yank, and a member of the OSS to boot, they called the US Army's Section Eight – Psychological Combat Fatigue and Related Cases.

The American Army sent a qualified psychiatrist. But when his British opposite number suggested the idea of a Silver Star say, a citation, and an honorable medical discharge, the American officer shook his head, took his pipe out of his mouth, and drawled:

'That'll really finish him. He'll sit on his tail and brood and end up nuttier than a fruitcake. You see, he blames himself for this French broad who got it trying to save him. I'd grant his request, if I were you. Some good stiff action – which from this report your Irish friend sent in he seems to be damned good at – will keep him from really cracking up. But – combat, major. Don't hole him up like a rat in some place like Paris. Let him join some FFI mobile strike force in the country. That kind of duty will keep him too busy to brood, and time will clear up what's eating him. Of course, he might get his, too; but, from where I sit, pushing up daisies is a hell of a lot better than cutting out paper dolls . . .'

After they'd got him to translate his slangy American into proper British, they agreed with him. So they parachuted John Farrow into the Vercors Sector in the mountains near Grenoble, late in November 1943.

But they carefully refrained from telling him that the Nazis shot seventy-five innocent people as hostages because of what he'd done. They thought, probably quite rightly, that knowing it, he would really crack up, become incurably mad.

It was Byron Graves who told John Farrow that finally. But by the time Graves informed him of the consequences of the act that had earned him the Croix de la Libération with Palms from the Free French, it had little effect on him at all.

'By then I'd gone beyond even madness,' he thought. 'Seceded from the human race. It was Simone who—'

He slammed the accelerator to the floor, double clutching, and pushed the little Renault on up that mountain road.

4

When John Farrow got to Haut de Cagnes, he locked the little red Renault and left it in the square. Then he started climbing up the twisting narrow streets thinking with mild satisfaction: 'This'll take care of my tub of lard!' until he got to the little flat-topped hill where Jimmy's Bar and Restaurant used to be. In the old days you could eat a fairly decent meal there and dance to recorded music that blared out from loudspeakers hanging from the trees. And it was there that before the war Dalton Ross used to hold court. Intellectuals from all over France dropped in at Jimmy's just to talk to the poet, and Jimmy, if that really were the owner's name, which John Farrow doubted, recognizing what an attraction Dalton was, never presented him with *l'addition* for the food and wine he personally consumed.

'Just as well,' John thought. 'The old scoundrel was always broke. But then aren't poets always penniless? It's a great art, but a hell of a way to make a living—'

Then he stopped short for Jimmy's Bar and Restaurant was no longer there. Another had taken its place. But seedier, more run down, which, considering what a sad joint Jimmy's had been in the first place, was quite a trick. But the new bar succeeded at it.

John Farrow sat down at one of the tables. This was starting badly. He ordered a sandwich of *jambon cru*, which meant only partly cured ham, like Italian prosciutto, and a little red wine. The owner, a Corsican brigand who needed only a knife in his teeth to improve his looks, brought him a glass of red vinegar designed to sear a man's larynx past all speech. John called him back, said pleasantly:

'You will please remove this vinegar and bring me a half bottle of Moulin à Vent? Or Châteauneuf-du-Pape. Or—'

'I am desolate, m'sieur,' the brigand growled, 'but this is the only wine we have.'

'Then bring me some beer. Blonde,' John said.

The beer was drinkable. In fact it was good.

'Tell me, m'sieure patron,' John said. 'What became of Jimmy, who owned this place before? And of his Bar and Restaurant, since I see this construction is new?'

'Died,' the brigand said. 'Closed the place. His son didn't take to the business. Gone up to Paris. I hear he's a *mech*, up there—'

Which was very likely, John realized. Because a *mech* wasn't a mechanic, but was the word the pre-war *maquereau*, 'mackerel' – a pimp, had degenerated into by now.

He didn't ask any more questions. It would be useless and he knew it. He ate part of the sandwich, finding the bread stale, the mustard awful, and the ham slimy. So he left the rest of it, drank the beer, paid the bill and went back to the little car.

'Now what?' he thought. 'Shall I try Tourette-sur-Loup? That's where the old bastard – correction, my beloved father! – correction again, the goddamned old bastard! – used to live. In one of those stone houses down the end of a narrow alley. Damned house always looked like it was going to fall over the edge of the cliff it was hanging on to – and – But the Jerries took him away from there, didn't they? Brought him down to Nice and installed him in the Ruhl in great style. Then every night, they'd take him up to that broadcasting station they had way the hell up on the Grand Corniche above Eze, so they could beam his garbage into Italy, and disaffect our troops there, and across the Mediterranean to confuse the French at Algiers—

'Still, if anybody had a lead on Dalton, it would be some of the older citizens of Tourette. Damned if they didn't love the old son of a bitch up there.' He stopped, smiled. 'He had charm, all right. The kind Candace accused *me* of having. If I did, fat lot of good it ever did me. Still – Hélène. Oh Jesus, Hélène. Go on:

face it. Look at it. Hard. This is my year for laying all my ghosts to rest, isn't it? What exactly did that sad, bad, hurtful episode in my life add up to? That I was in Paris. Occupied Paris. Under circumstances where all I had to do was to chuck my brains at the entrance as I came in, and go on functioning on any level above amoebic to look good. Being scared shitless didn't detract from it at all. Because everybody else was, too. As long as you didn't crack *before* the Gestapo grabbed you, they respected your fear. And if you cracked after Sipo IV, or the French Milice, or those traitorous bastards in the Waffen SS got their hands on you, the Resistance people went on respecting you, because those sub-human obscenities could break anybody who wasn't of the real stuff of heroes – like Simone. Which meant they could break damned near everybody, because heroism, true heroism is the rarest of human qualities. But you weren't even expected to be brave; you were only expected to do your job, somehow, anyhow. And since I did all my screaming on the inside – always have, still do – until my guts were raw and bleeding I looked a little better than most.

'So strike up that offstage mood music: hail the Conquering Hero comes! Striding through that offstage door to go out and die for the cause. Only I didn't stride. I crept, quivered, shook through it. But in a funny way it was true: without the waving flags and heroic gestures, I *was* prepared to die. We all were. What we were fighting had to be stopped, and if getting ours was the only way to stop it, then we accepted, with as much tranquillity as was possible to our individual natures, our deaths. Because that wasn't an ambiguous war. The issues were clear.

'So I was resigned to the idea that tomorrow was a dirty word and today was all I had. Only I lived – and Hélène died. And my guilt cracked me up, because I knew I never loved her. I used her. Used her poor little narrow, insufficiently washed cunt to pour all my desperation into, all my loneliness, all my terror. If she'd lived I'd have made it up to her. But she didn't live. She lay with her face in a stinking gutter, and the rest of her in a two-metre wide pool of blood – for me. Left me to wear the Ancient Mariner's albatross. Her death was noble and useless and absurd, because whether I lived or died at that particular juncture mattered not a good goddamn. My cover was already blown, and hers wasn't. I had to leave Paris or die in Paris and the two things were absolutely equal because I couldn't do what we were all going through daily hell for any more good either way. Remember Sartre's essay on suicide? That was it exactly, absurdity right up to the eyes. But maybe – she – died happy. Escaped what life would have done to her afterward – the slow corrosion, the wearing down. Escaped even finding out that I didn't love her. Or maybe I'd have learned to afterward – who knows?

'And maybe the deal wasn't as rotten as it looked to me then. Maybe I gave her a little shared warmth, two or three grams of distilled tenderness, certain moments of – hell! call it ecstasy! – because maybe an honest to God orgasm wasn't the worst opiate possible against the knowledge that tomorrow and death were synonyms in those days. So – Hélène. *Adieu, ma brave, si gentille, petite Hélène – repose-toi doucement dans ton printemps éternel, amour perdu. . . .*

'But my other ghost? Simone – who left me. Why? Because she was afraid I'd find out she'd been sleeping with – my father? Jesus! It could well be the old swine had told her that. That I was his son. Or enough so that later when she got a chance to put two and two together she realized – what? No matter! And if I *had* found it out, would it have made any difference, really?'

He could answer that question truthfully. 'It would have damned near killed me, but I wouldn't have given her up. I couldn't have by then—'

He got into the car, drove back down to the Bas Corniche, and then at Gros de Cagne took the road up in the direction of Grasse. He had no intention of going to Grasse, that pleasant town afloat in a sea of flowers, which are the source of its wealth, for they are grown for their perfumes, and nearly every important perfume manufacturer has his laboratories there. Before Grasse he was supposed to make a sharp right turn and take a smaller road that would take him up to Tourette-sur-Loup, and also, if he could bear the sight of it to Vence where – he'd lived with poor broken Simone, had nursed her with great tenderness. He remembered suddenly with a sad, wry joy how she'd cried and made him turn his face away because she was so weak that he had to hold her by both shoulders to keep her from falling over, after he'd sat her on the chamber pot to make *pipi*, like a tiny child. But a bedpan was an item not to be had, so each time he'd have to lift her out of the bed and sit her on that pot. Until Madame Toulon, the baker's wife, came in and voluntarily relieved him of that chore.

'Just in time,' he remembered then, 'because she was on the verge of septic intestinal poisoning from refusing to do the other. And I was so worried and so goddamned stupid that it never occurred to me that she hadn't defecated in more than ten days. Good old Madame Toulon! A big fat jolly angel if there ever were one! Strange people the French. Exactly like that little girl with the curl in that nursery rhyme – when they're good, they're very, very good, but when they're bad, they're horrid. No middle ground. They're some of the best people on the face of God's green earth, and – the worst. They're the Resistance heroes who died under torture without opening their mouths, the men who held Vercors and a hundred other places like it almost with pocket knives and their teeth. Who cleared the Boche out of Corsica, practically unaided; who liberated three-fifths of France all by themselves. And they're the people who joined the Milice and the Waffen SS by the thousands, murdered their own heroes, betrayed réseau after réseau to the Gestapo, engaged in the torture of other Frenchmen and women for the benefit of their masters. The people of the Dreyfus case, the country where the leader of the rightist opposition, Xavier Vallat, could stand up on the very floor of the Chamber of Deputies, and insult the president of the Republic, Léon Blum to his face, on the sole basis of his Jewishness, where as late as 1968 the followers of Charles de Gaulle could march up the Champs-Elysées bearing signs which read: 'Cohn Bendit au Dachau!'

'But also the country where a Jew could – hell *can* – be elected president. For after Blum there was Mendès-France. Could *we* elect the finest, kindest, most intelligent Jew alive to the presidency of the United States? And what would happen if we proposed a man like Senator Brooke of Massachusetts – good looking, brilliant, and only a little black for even the *vice* presidency? Blood would flow in the streets, that's what. And George Wallace would become the second man in our history to reach the White House in a wheelchair.

'So remember the *good* French. I have to. If I don't I'm sunk. Because, since one half of my blood belongs to a race of slavers, lynchers, the assassins of Song My, My Lai, the heroes who celebrated their winning of the West by wearing on their hats – as badges of their valour – the torn-out vulvas of the Indian women they'd raped and murdered, it is to Maman's people I must reach back for worth, for value, not ever to that swine Dalton's – swine from a race of bloody swine!

'Which is unfair, too. Americans can be good people – only they're so smug, and so self-satisfied. They're probably the most unlovable people in all of human history. And I include the Germans. Because when they want to be, the Germans can be very winning *gemütlich*, warm. But my father's people? How can you love a race who don't even realize that they're at least the number two sons of bitches on earth today? Who after Hiroshima, Nagasaki, and all the political murders about which the truth was deliberately and carefully suppressed by the highest tribunals of the land, can go right on believing that they're *sans peur, et sans reproche*? Whose highest elected official can deliver himself of such *merde du cheval* as emerging from Vietnam with honour – a quality about as renewable as female virginity is. And as long ago and as totally lost – in pursuit of Manifest Destiny.

'So I grant them a sort of bland and tasteless goodness – carefully limited to the pale of skin, straight of hair, with no slant to their eyes, and whose speech is an acceptable variety of English, and leave them to their hairy, unwashed young to save – through hash, horse, grass and maybe Jesus! And return to the best of my mother's people. The good ones. Who were shot for hiding Jews. Who adopted thousands of Jewish children and gave them good French names, and swore to that murderous army of subhuman technocrats that they were their own. And in spite of their unspeakable coward of a pope, and ranting antisemitic bishops, was there ever *one* Catholic priest or Protestant pastor who betrayed our trust? No – not even one. And those nuns at that cloister near Fayence. The ones Pepe told you about. Who died *singing*, goddamnit, who—'

But he didn't want to think about that, not even now. Because that was one of the bad things, the very bad things, and the memory of the way Pepe had told it made him a little sick, every time it came to mind. So deliberately he went back to thinking about Simone.

'Funny – she didn't mind my bathing her, though. Said Madame Toulon was too horny-handed and too rough. In fact – I'm sure she liked it. . . .' He remembered then her voice whispering: '*Tes mains sont si douces*—' 'Your hands are so –

sweet—' and old as he was now, and as long ago as that had been, all of a sudden he was blind. Which was why he missed that turn, maybe. But there was Grasse before him, where he hadn't meant to go.

'What difference does it make?' he thought. 'The day's shot anyhow. I'll drive through, turn around and come back. Besides I'm still hungry, and—'

He looked at his watch. It was far too late for lunch, and too early for dinner. Unless he wanted to take a chance on another sandwich, he'd have to eat somewhere else. Then he remembered that pleasantly rustic hotel at Gorge-du-Loup, only a few kilometres from Tourette. The Hôtel de la Gorge it was called, if his memory served him. Or simply Hôtel Gorge. One of the two. But the food had been excellent there, the last time – which meant nothing. The last time he'd stopped there had been when he, Candace and Cynthia had been vacationing in France. Cynthia had been six? Seven? And now she was getting married.

But he decided to eat there, and what's more, spend the night. That would give him a whole day to poke about Tourette and the countryside near it, tomorrow. Even taking into account the horrendous standard to which French cuisine had degenerated over the years, he was sure the food would be edible.

He went through Grasse slowly. It was a place that he'd always liked. Then suddenly he slammed down on the brakes, for the sign above a shop on the Rue Droit had caught his eye.

It read Feingold et Fils, Bijoutiers. Feingold and Sons, Jewellers. A man named Feingold had to be a Jew, even in France, so maybe through him he could get a lead on some member of Simone's family. If any of them had survived. Where had Simone been *from*, anyhow? When he'd met her she was already with the Resistance and—

Then it came back to him. She'd once told him that her family had had a villa up at Cimiez, above Nice, which meant they'd been wealthy. He knew she'd at least started studying at the University of Paris, when her father's quite justified fears had forced her to come south again. During the *Sitzkrieg*, the phony war. She'd been lucky. How many Jews had survived the occupation of Paris?

'How many of them survived anywhere,' he thought bleakly. 'Even today most of Europe is still *judenfrei* – free of Jews, to borrow Hitler's own gentle term for it. For the first time in history, genocide had almost succeeded. No – for the second. Because what my North American ancestors did to our so-called Indians fits the definition of that word quite nicely.'

He decided to buy a gift for Cynthia and her husband soon to be. What was that hairy young type's name, anyhow? Oh yes, Jason. Jason what? He'd be blessed if he could remember his future son-in-law's family name.

It didn't matter. What did matter was that the gift or gifts could be used to break the ice, to engage Monsieur Feingold and/or son in a conversation which could be brought around gradually to what he wanted to know. But he'd have to be careful. European Jews had a two-thousand-year accumulation of damned good reasons for being suspicious of strangers even *before* Adolf Hitler came upon the scene.

He locked the car. The Feingolds, *père et fils*, were both there. And Madame Feingold as well. Monsieur et Madame Feingold were both in their fifties. The right age. Feingold, *fils*, was too damned young. Politely he addressed himself to the older man.

The matter of the gift was soon arranged. Solid gold cuff links for his prospective son-in-law. For his daughter Madame Feingold had intervened to suggest a ring.

'Well, if *votre bague* is not too dear—' he'd begun, and they'd brought out a diamond ring that was breathtaking. He'd started to protest, but Monsieur Feingold smiled.

'Frankly, m'sieur, this diamond has a flaw, and the colour is a trifle yellowish,' he said. 'If you will take this *loupe* you may see the flaw – which is invisible to the naked eye. As for the colour, will your daughter or her husband be expert enough to notice it?'

'That no,' he said, 'but suppose they get curious enough to have it appraised?'

'Then m'sieur would be wise to tell madame, his daughter about the flaw, quite frankly, as I am telling you. Honesty is always the best policy, is it not so? And the wisest. Besides, if I know women, your daughter will be so busy amusing herself by making all her girl friends sick with envy that about this little flaw she will say nothing. How does seven hundred and fifty dollars strike you?

It struck him as too damned much for a diamond with a carbon pit as big as the one he could see through the *loupe*; but he decided at once to pay it, and not haggle the price down to the five hundred he knew damned well he could get them to accept – in the interest of good will. Besides, a stone like that on Sixth Avenue with a flaw as bad would cost him over two thousand dollars, so what had he to lose?

'*D'accord*,' he said, 'but could you cut it down for me a bit? I mean the *bague* itself, not the stone. My daughter's fingers are very small.'

That started a discussion as to how small was very small, which was settled by his picking out among the cheaper rings one he was pretty sure was Cynthia's size. And only after that did he venture it:

'M'sieur Feingold, you're Jewish, aren't you? I ask you this only because I am trying to trace a very dear friend of mine, the daughter of M'sieur Ruben Levy who once lived in Nice – in the district known as Cimiez—'

They froze. The air congealed. He stared at them in astonishment.

'I'm sorry,' he said, 'I meant no offence. It is just that his daughter and I were engaged once – during the war—'

'And you, like so many American soldiers, had to move on,' Madame Feingold said, 'an old, old story, m'sieur!'

Her tone said: 'I don't believe a word of it!'

He smiled.

'No, madame,' he said, 'it was the other way around. It was Simone who moved on, not I.'

Monsieur Feingold relaxed. Or pretended to.

'Then,' he said softly, 'she is surely dead. For if the Nazis passed that way—' He spread his hands in a brief, expressive gesture.

'The point, sir,' John said, 'is I don't think so. We'd liberated all this part of France by then. And when I say *we*, I mean the Resistance, not the American army.'

'Ah, so!' Madame Feingold said: 'I knew your French was far too good for you to be an American!'

He let that pass. Explanations could be saved for when they saw that perfectly Anglo-Saxon name on the traveller's cheques he was going to give them for the ring.

'Did you know this family, m'sieur, 'dame?' he said.

'Levy – Ruben Levy?' Monsieur Feingold said. 'It's difficult to say, m'sieur. Levy is such a common name. I have known –

dozens of Levys. Even, perhaps, a Ruben Levy or two. It is as if I were to ask you if you know a man in the States – where you now live, I see from clothes – whatever your origins are – by the name of John Smith.'

'*Touché!*' John Farrow said ruefully. 'It's just that I get to come back to France so seldom now, and—'

'Let me check with friends of mine,' the jeweller said suavely. 'After all, you have to return for the ring, since it must be cut. By the way, when can you come for it, m'sieur?'

'Tomorrow evening if you can have it ready by then. I'm staying at Gorge-du-Loup, tonight, and visiting – friends in Tourette tomorrow. So if you could—'

'Easily,' Monsieur Feingold said. 'You won't be offended if I ask you for *un signal*, will you? After all this *bague* does have a certain value. . . .'

'Not at all,' John said, and counted out five one-hundred-dollar bills. He'd be damned if he was going to go into how a Frenchman, ex-Maquisard, happened to be named John Farrow until he had to. Then he made his second mistake of the evening without knowing he had already made the first one.

'Pardon me for asking so many questions,' he said with a self-deprecative smile, 'but did you ever know a musician named Rabinowski?'

'You mean Anton Rabinowski, the orchestra conductor?' Monsieur Feingold said.

John Farrow thought fast. The names coincided of course. But a symphony orchestra's conductor? Anton might well have decided to give up the violin he had been the absolute master of. On the level of Jascha Heifitz, the critics said. But that was damned unlikely. Yet – another possibility existed. Suppose he'd been forced to – by an injury, say? That, when a man was an active, fighting Maquisard was likely – even probable. You *could* conduct with only one hand, for instance. But to play a violin you needed two hands and all your fingers—

'Yes,' he said, 'that's the one.' He was acutely aware he'd hesitated far too long.

Monsieur Feingold smiled. 'There, I *can* help you. I don't *know* Anton Rabinowski; but I do know where he lives. In Israel. He conducts the Tel Aviv Orchestra. And even, at times, the Israeli National Symphony at Jerusalem. It's odd you didn't know that—'

'I've been out of touch,' John Farrow said. 'My profession's law. And it keeps me so busy that I don't get to go to concerts much these days—'

'A pity. Rabinowski had a great success in your Lincoln Centre last year. I take it that you now hold American citizenship, is it not so?'

'Yes,' John Farrow said, thinking: 'I'd better get out of here. I've blown this one sure as hell so—' He said: *'Merci, mille fois,* M'sieur Feingold – for your patience. I didn't mean to seem too inquisitive, but it is a thing that rankles still. You see, I loved the little Simone very much—'

'I'm sure you did, m'sieur,' the jeweller murmured. 'Wait, don't go yet. I must make you out a receipt for your *signal*—'

'Oh, it isn't necessary,' John Farrow said, too quickly. 'I know an honest man when I see one, m'sieur! Till tomorrow, then?'

And that was mistake number three in the series that afterward he came to consider as being very close to the most serious he had made in all his life, as far as their far-reaching consequences were concerned. In fact, in that regard, only two others exceeded them: his unusual and tragic lack of foresight in not making Hélène go home to her own flat when he left her after that last hour they were ever to spend together, thus giving her a reasonable chance of staying alive, and his monumental idiocy in marrying Candace after a two-year affair that had taught him beyond hope or compassion what she was like. For, try as he would, he could recall no errors at all he had made in his behaviour towards Simone – unless literally worshipping a woman entirely worthy of it be an error – which was one of the reasons that her disappearance hurt so badly.

'Jusqu'à demain, m'sieur,' the jeweller said and took the hand John offered him.

When John Farrow came out into the street, he saw Feingold, *fils,* looking at his car. Particularly at the licence plates. The younger jeweller had neither a pencil nor a pad in his hand, but he had time and to spare to memorize the numbers. 'Not exactly a brilliant tactic,' John Farrow thought, 'for even if the police give him the owner's name, and the car rental service in their turn give him mine, what will he have found out? That I'm American, which I've never denied being, and that I'm staying at the Negresco. Any more details he may want to know will take him so long that I'll have made a round trip to hell and back before he can dig them up. Besides what information does the young fool need? That my money's good, and my cheques won't bounce. Still there's an element in all this that's way off beat. When has the mere fact of asking a man what his religion is been a mortal offence?'

Then he answered that one for himself: 'When the reply to that deceptively simple question could send you to the gas chambers, convert your ass into a bar of soap, your hide into lampshades. Never forget that, John. It's been a long time, but not that long. That memory's burnt into them the way Simone's face, her eyes, the feel of her is branded into you, right down to the bitter bone. In all their lives nobody who's asked them that question has meant them a goddamned bit of good. So why should they believe a French goy in Yankee clothes is the exception? I blew it that time. I really blew it. And I topped it off by not even noticing when it was that this solemn-faced youngster, who's probably got brains hanging out both his ears, left the shop. A hell of an intelligence agent, I'm turning out to be,' he thought. 'These days I couldn't make buck private in the quartermaster's corps!'

But he said, as pleasantly as he could manage, and in English: 'Till tomorrow, Mr Feingold, Junior!'

'Until tomorrow, sir,' the young jeweller said. His accent in English was perfect. Better than perfect: donish Oxonian.

Driving away, John Farrow had that feeling again, for the first time since the war. In those days he had learned to trust it implicitly because it had repeatedly saved his life. A premonition of . . . trouble, even danger, crawled along his nerves. But trouble, danger resulting from a strange, off-beat encounter with a small-town Jewish jeweller, who—?

'But *is* he really?' John thought. 'Either Jewish – or a jeweller? By his features he just as well could be a Slav. Besides, Anti-semites of the World Incorporated to the contrary, there's no such things as Jewish features anyhow. He could very well be – Russian. Or Czech. Or Polish. And that little shop would be the perfect plant if – the Russians, the Czechs, the Poles – or even the Israelis! – don't forget them – they know how to play just as rough as the bigger boys – wanted to—'

'*Merde, alors!*' he told himself, 'Come off it, John! Any of them in their right minds who want to get a fairish deal for their intelligence money would plant Monsieur Feingold, *fils* and all, madame and all, shop and all in Cannes – on the Croisette. Nice, on the Promenade des Anglais – or better still under the arches of the Place Messena. Or in Monte Carlo damn near anywhere. Or in Paris – in any of a thousand streets. But Grasse? Who the devil *ever* comes to Grasse except perfume wholesalers? Or is it, *mon cher* Jean le Fou, Crazy John, that they've discovered a way of making a first-class rocket fuel out of distilled flower petals? Or a nerve-gas out of perfume? Hell, they discovered that years ago. Some of those babes used to come floating into a room wrapped in a cloud of scent that would have you climbing up the wall with your fingernails in no time flat—'

He grinned at his reflection in the rear view mirror.

'Calm down, old fellow,' he told himself, 'my very, very, old fellow – what's the use of entertaining salacious thoughts when to even get it up, you'd probably need a chain hoist or a fork-lift truck?'

In Tourette itself, he went into une parfumerie, and bought himself a safety razor, a brush and some shaving soap. But for toothpaste and a toothbrush he had to enter a pharmacy – as the custom was, is, and will be forever more, in France.

His clothes evoked the usual look of dour hostility until he opened his mouth. It wasn't, he realized, that the French hate Americans; it was rather that the French hate everybody who isn't French. And with good reason, he conceded. With a history like the one they've had, what people wouldn't suffer from galloping xenophobia?

But he didn't remain in Tourette-sur-Loup or even engage anyone in conversation. 'I've asked enough ticklish questions for one day,' he thought, and turned the little car down that steep road to the place where the river Loup runs foaming through the gorge.

The hotel was still there. And the food was as good as he remembered it. But when he asked for a room for the night, things got a bit sticky again.

'M'sieur has no baggage?' madame the concierge said.

'M'sieur has baggage,' John told her, 'but unhappily he left it down at the Hôtel Negresco at Nice where monsieur is staying.' He smiled at her. 'Look, madame, from here to Nice is too far for me to drive tonight as fatigued as I am. So let us consider this razor, this tooth brush *et mes autres petites affaires* – as baggage, *hein*? I have business in Tourette tomorrow, and at my age driving mountain roads is no longer amusing. So give me a very little chamber with a very big soft bed for which I will gladly pay in advance, if that's what's troubling you, madame—'

But she didn't thaw a good goddamn.

'For guests without baggage payment in advance is the rule of the house,' she said.

'Very well,' he sighed, 'how much will the chamber be, *ma chère madame*?'

'With or without bath?' madame said.

'With,' John told her.

She named the price. It was absolutely outrageous, as prices always are in France.

He paid it, began to sign the register.

'One thing more,' madame said severely. 'M'sieur does not think to have *une invitée* in his room, does he?'

John made her a deep and mocking bow.

'I thank you with all my heart, for the compliment, madame! Truly you have made my evening a wild success!'

But she had about as much sense of humour as a Frenchwoman of *la petite bourgeoisie* usually has, which is to say none.

'Does he?' she rapped out.

'If, *chère madame*, a young and pretty woman by some miracle appears in my chamber, you have my pledged word that I shall come running down those stairs screaming for help. And now, with madame's gracious permission I will mount to my chamber – to sleep. That's all I'm fit for now.'

Then only did she flash a brief and wintry smile.

'*Dommage!*' she said. 'All I meant was that it would cost you a little more if you wanted to—'

And got the best of him after all.

'Madame, your amiability moves me to tears!' he said, and went groaning up those stairs.

5

But it took him a long time to go to sleep. And when he did the sound of white water foaming through that gorge was the sound of all the mountain torrents roaring through the hundreds of gorges in that thousand-metre high, arrow-head-shaped mountain plateau that was the Vecors salient. His own voice screaming, woke him up:

'No! Goddamnit, no! Slip your cords, you fools! You're going to land slap dap on Jerry's ass! Oh, Jesus! There they go!'

And the machine guns were stuttering up from the camouflaged German anti-aircraft half-track, so well concealed under the trees, in the thick bush, that even knowing exactly where it was, you had to look hard to see it, white tracers curving dots and dashes through the air, lighting the night with that lethal fireworks display, and the men under those white silk umbrellas, pinned helplessly against the dark by the beam of the half-track's searchlight, jerking in mid-air, sagging, becoming lifeless while they were still two hundred metres high, so that he, John Farrow, not wanting to watch it any more, bent his head, until the voice at his side rasped into his ear:

'They haven't got the third one, Jean. He's faking it. I'll bet my sister's sweet little virgin tail that the minute he hits, he's going to start running this way!'

John Farrow opened his eyes. He was lying in a soft feather bed in the hotel at Gorge-du-Loup, twenty-eight years after that day, and the noise he heard was the river pounding below his window. But that didn't help anything. He was back there again, feeling it, seeing it.

'Shall I knock out that searchlight, Jean?' the voice at his side said.

'No,' he said, 'not yet. Wait till they hit, and a patrol starts out after them. Do it too soon, and the Boches' eyes will accustom themselves to the dark. Now, I go. I am going to flank that patrol. When you hear me open fire – that is if this miserable little piece of worthless English junk from Woolworths—'

'Woolworths?' Pierre said.

'An English *Prix Unique*. A five and ten. For surely that is where our so brilliant friends the English got these from. If, as I said, this toy for children from a Prix Unique will fire at all, then you shoot out that searchlight. And do not miss, Pierre, for if you do, you, I, and that *crapaud* of an Englishman will find ourselves dead. And most of the other *gars*, as well. By now they should be close enough to throw in the grenades—'

'Jean,' Pierre said, 'it is a shame to wreck that half-track. We could put it to good use when they finally decide to leave their warm beds and willing whores and come up here after us, in a serious fashion, I mean—'

'Shit!' Jean hissed at him. 'What will you run it on, Pierre? Piss into the tank?'

'I piss good,' Pierre said. 'In effect, I am a pisser of the first class. And—'

But the chutes were sagging, with no weight under them, then ballooning again, dragging their dead burdens through the grass. In the glare of that searchlight that had followed the parachutists all the way down into that clearing beside which the half-track and its crew had been waiting, having themselves given the coordinates to the pilot of the De Havilland Mosquito that had flown those doomed-from-the-outset poor devils in, using a captured English wireless operator they'd tortured into turning to do it. John could see the one bloody hand come up, and the knife flash, cutting those cords. But even though they had seen it, too, the Germans didn't open fire.

Then he, John Farrow/Jean le Fou, was up and running, that miserable good-for-nothing dime-store Sten gun in his hands. It really wasn't as bad as he swore it was, and after all the work he'd done on it, he could count on it to fire, and to keep on shooting without jamming at least seven times out of ten. Which, of course, wasn't enough, because if it missed or jammed just once tonight he'd be the late John Farrow thirty seconds after that lamentable fact.

When three Germans jumped down out of the half-track, and started towards the wounded man, he was more than ready. He'd figured they would do that. He'd been sure that the only reason one of the three parachutists had got down alive was because the SS wanted him to, so they could play games with him. Such as stretching him out naked on a plank, pouring salt water over him, then running two bare and live electric wires over his hide. Up his nostrils. Into his ears. Into the corners of his eyes. Up his asshole. All over his dong and his testicles.

When they did that you could hear the poor devil screaming from a kilometre and a half away. And John had heard too goddamned much screaming by then.

So he flopped down on his belly, and crossed the three-man patrol's line of march with brief squirting bursts of that 6·3 millimetre pistol ammunition that the baby Sten guns were chambered for. Ammunition was a thing they always had too little of to waste at Vercors, so he was trying to use as few bullets as possible per Jerry. He saw the grotesque dancing steps they made, jerking downward into death, and resisted the temptation to hold the trigger down to prolong matters, to hash them up a bit more, make them dance a second or two longer under the multiple impact of those balls. But if he did, he would run through the twenty-five-shot clip before he had time to think. Or the bloody miserable thing would jam on him. And he and the last of those three poor damned fools who had come piling down the sky right into Jerry's lap would wind up more than a little dead.

He saw the flat, hard-edged beam of the searchlight on the half-track waver, jerk, then come groping around to illuminate the point they thought his fire had come from. So he rolled. Over and over and over, fast. He knew better than to jump up to run. Once you did that, you never got to take three steps before they riddled you.

Then he heard the long, slow, drawn-out board-breaking crack that a rifle in the hands of a sharpshooter like Pierre always seemed to make and the searchlight winked out. In the sudden blackness he was up and running through the scrub of trees. He didn't give a damn how much noise he made doing it because one of the things they'd learned that the sudden loss of sight confuses the hearing too, so Jerry's chances of hitting him were at least poor enough for him to risk them.

Even so he dived behind the first available green moss-slimed boulder one and three-tenths seconds before the Nazis got their 30-millimetre MK108, and their 20-millimetre MK151 anti-aircraft rapid-fire cannon cranked down to dead level, and maybe one second flat before their heavy MG131 13-millimetre machine guns started stuttering. He was lucky they didn't have any 7·9 MG17s mounted on that particular half-track, because those light machine guns would have given him no time at all. But he didn't have to worry about the burpguns every man of the half-track's crew was armed with, because to use them the SS men would have to raise themselves too high above the protection of the light armour the vehicle carried, and those *Schutzstaffeln* men were too battle wary to be that big a bunch of fools.

As it was they were pouring a hail of fire into the exact spot where he'd lain to gun down the patrol they'd sent out to pick up the parachutist, which made him feel as good as a man could feel while his teeth were chattering, his lips turning blue, ice-cold sweat pouring out of him, and feeling the warm wetness in his pants where he had pissed out of fear.

That was the main reason that his comrades in arms called him Jean le Fou, Crazy John. He was obviously one of the scaredest male humans in all of France, and yet his fear never stopped him an instant nor incapacitated him in any way. Instead it seemed to spur him on. He did things that the bravest men, and there were many of the FFI to whom that superlative quite legitimately applied at Vercors, either failed to bring off or died trying to do. But he, Jean le Fou, could succeed every time.

He lay there, shivering, listening to those guns. Listening through those guns for what he was waiting to hear. He heard it: a sudden short sharp hammering explosion. Then another, a trifle longer drawn out. The first, he knew from the sound of it, was an English hand grenade, and the second, a long-handled German one, of the type they called a potato masher, stolen from the Jerries themselves. The gun-fire stopped. In the abrupt silence, he heard a high, clear, almost soprano scream. Then the grenades came lobbing from every direction into the high-walled topless truck bed of the half-track. The explosions lit the night. Then they stopped. The silence pressed down on him like a weight. Nobody was screaming now.

He cupped his hands and roared:

'The cab, Pierre! The driver!' And a dozen dime-store Stens opened up at one. Through them, above them, he heard a frightened boy's voice shrilling:

'*Kamaraden! Ich übergebe mich!*' Which was a waste of breath because if they sometimes did accept the surrender of regular Wehrmacht men when circumstances permitted it, nobody felt the slightest obligation to take an SS man alive, either moral, legal, or military. And that this one was only a boy made no difference; they'd seen black-shirted boys as young, busy with beef-nerve whips, electrodes, and finger crushing screw-presses. Then they stopped shooting, and there was no sound at all, there in the dark, under those trees.

Jean got up and walked through the darkness to where the British parachute team lay. He brought out a small electric torch. Flashed it into the faces of all three. The French and the American officers were dead, bloodily and messily dead, but the Britisher was very much alive. Jedburgh Liaison Teams were always made up of one officer from each of the Allied armies.

He stood there looking at the Englishman. So far as he could see the officer was bleeding heavily from a wound in his forearm, but nowhere else. So he said in English, through clenched and still grinding teeth:

'Can you walk?'

'Yes. Yes, quite. I've only a bit of a scratch. And by the way, old chap, I'd like to express my thanks. Bloody good show, that!'

John Farrow looked at him, up and down, from head to heel; said:

'Fuck you, limey! Now come on!'

Then he started towards the half-track. When he got to it, he laid down the Sten, jumped up high enough to catch the top of the light armour-plated side, drew himself up until he could look into it. Threw one leg across and then the other until he was sitting on the edge, flashed his torch down into that snail of broken, eviscerated, torn, burnt mass of human flesh, into those wide-opened still silently screaming mouths, those dead glassy glittering eyes. Spat. Then he jumped down among them.

He started throwing burpguns out. Extra clips. And the eight ghostly shadows the young English officer could barely distinguish from the surrounding dark started gathering them up. One of them said in French:

'Think-you we could dismount one of the heavy guns, Jean? Or maybe, both? They'd be a gift from the good little God if—'

But Jean shook his head. The words came out between his chattering teeth:

'There's no time. The Boches aren't deaf, Pierre. I'm going to put them out of action. Give me some contact mines, will you?'

They passed him over the flat little mines that looked like

thick silver coins. He slammed back the loading levers of the cannon, jerked the half-fired belts of 20 and 30 millimetre shells out, and rammed the tiny mines into the breeches. Then he said: 'Maybe we could take one of the 13 millimetres out though. . . .'

So they swarmed over the sides, and went to work, completely oblivious to the fact that they were ankle-deep in human entrails. Somebody went around to the cab and, after booting the driver's poor skinny corpse out of it, came back with the half-track's tool kit. In minutes they had the heavy MG131, with its slotted air-cooled barrel dismounted. John draped belts of thirteen-millimetre ammunition all across himself until he looked like a Mexican Pancho Villa bandit. The others did the same thing. Then after they were all out of there, John threw in two more grenades. The explosions set the contact mines off inside the breeches of the anti-aircraft guns and ruined them beyond repair.

One of them saw the English officer stagger, and flashed his torch on him and said:

'Jean, *l'anglais* is bleeding – badly.'

'Impossible,' Jean said, 'all the world knows the English have no blood. They have only tea in their veins, crumpets in their heads, and scones instead of balls.'

'But Jean, *l'anglais* will die if we don't bandage him a little.'

'Let him. Who cares? Oh *merde alors!* Bandage the blighter, if you want to!'

When they'd finished that Captain Byron Graves of the SOE/R-F felt better.

John turned to him and said: 'Come on, you stupid limey bastard! Let's get out of here!'

That afternoon, Byron Graves came back from the town of St Martin where the Vercors Military Hospital was, riding in a captured German truck that was used as an ambulance and for foraging for medicine, surgical supplies and food. It had a diesel motor, and where they got the fuel oil to run it, he never did find out. He'd had his wound expertly dressed by a Dr Fischer. Afterward the doctor took him on a tour of the hospital. He met all the doctors – Ullmann, Ganimède, who was head of the hospital, and very old, and his son, a man in his thirties. There were nine nurses, one of whom was the younger Dr Ganimède's wife.

Being as security conscious as all intelligence agents have to be, Byron was struck by Drs Fischer and Ullmann's obviously German names. But Father Montcheuil, SJ, the hospital's chaplain explained that to him.

'They're Jews,' the Jesuit said. 'Fine doctors. Fine men. We're very lucky to have them.'

But as he jumped down from the truck he saw John sitting off by himself on a fallen tree trunk. He hesitated, then started towards him. When he was very close, he saw that the man who'd saved his life was bent over, shivering like someone with ague, and crying. His tears left pale streaks through the grime on his face.

Byron sat down beside him.

'Fuck off, Limey!' John Farrow said.

Silently Byron took out a pack of cigarettes, and offered them to him.

'Don't smoke,' John said.

'All right,' Byron said, 'but you shouldn't hold my being British against me, old chap. I didn't choose my parents any more than you did. By the way, what *are* you? You talk American, but you don't get it right. Both the accent and the rhythm are a bit off. Believe me, I know. I was an actor before this unholy mess started, and speech patterns are a sort of hobby of mine. You really are French, aren't you?'

'Half,' John Farrow said. 'Mother. Father was a Yank.'

'Then you should speak American better than you do. Why don't you?'

'Don't be so bloody inquisitive!' John flared. Then his anger died. 'Didn't see the States till I was eighteen. We lived here. Paris, anyhow.'

'I see. And that explains it. Jolly good show this morning. Thank you. I mean that sincerely, Jean.'

John Farrow shrugged.

'Nerves a bit shot, what?' Byron said.

'You Limeys don't help them, being so goddamned stupid!'

Byron inhaled deeply, let the smoke trail through his nostrils, said: 'Mind telling me what we're doing wrong now, old boy?'

'Your last Jedburgh Team. No, the one before that. Or maybe it was – hell, I don't remember. My head's not very clear. Anyhow, Jerry captured your radio operator. And turned him. They're damned good at that kind of thing, you know.'

'And?' Byron Graves said.

'He warned you. I heard him. I monitored him on our own wireless. He screwed up his outcall in a way that any jackass would have known something was wrong. But all the same you Limey clowns have dropped tons of food, ammunition, medical supplies that we need goddamned badly right into Jerry's camp. Hell they don't even have to send a patrol out after them. You drop them right down the chimney of their officers' mess. I've called you bastards and called you and you go right on doing it!'

Byron stared at him.

'Sorry, old chap,' he said, 'but d'you know what? We thought *you* were Jerry, trying to bloody things up a bit. I say – what's your name?'

'John. John Farrow. Crazy John. Jean le Fou. I am, you know.'

'You are *what*, John?'

'Nuts. Crackers. Insane.'

'If you are, I hope it's contagious,' Byron said. 'Tell you what, why don't you and I have a try at getting the poor devil out? That wireless operator, I mean.'

'Yeah, and let's steal Hitler's pink silk lacy drawers while we're at it.'

'He *is* a bit of a fruit,' Byron said, 'but not that kind. He likes women, all right. Seems he's deuced rough on them, though. His niece, for instance. He was bedding her – in his own peculiar fashion. Poor thing couldn't stand the gaff. Killed herself. I've seen him a couple of times. And he makes me *sure* we're going to win this one, John. Any people who allow a thing like *that* to come to power, have had it. I don't care how much damage they do in the meantime. In the end we'll take them.'

'Blood, sweat, and tears,' John said, then: 'how'd you happen to see Hitler, Captain Whatever-Your-Name-Is?'

'Graves, Byron Graves. I was in this from the first. SOE *before* it was SOE. We were civilians – and volunteers. First requirement was a decent knowledge of German. I speak it rather well. And being an actor, I get the way they scream and bark and froth at the mouth exactly right. So they sent me in to get this Boffin out. Jewish physicist. Brilliant chap. He *wasn't* being persecuted. They'd made an honorary Aryan out of him. Needed his brains, what? But some relatives of his behind the

Polish lines got the word to him. Don't know if it's true or not, but he believed it. Seems they're exterminating all the Jews in that sector. Execution squads working round the clock. Lime-pits freshly dug – and then they line the poor devils up beside them, men, women, children, babes-in-arms—'

John Farrow stared at him, said: '*I* believe it, Byron.'

'Oh, come now, John. Not even Jerry, impossible chap that he usually is, could pull a stunt like that one!'

'They could,' John Farrow said. 'They could. I was in Paris until last spring. There's nothing they couldn't do.'

They sat there. They didn't say anything for a while. The tears kept stealing out from under John's half-closed eyelids, and running down his face. But he was shivering a great deal less now.

'About that wireless operator—' Byron began.

'Impossible,' John said. 'We might be able to wreck his set, but you clowns would only drop him another one.'

'No, we wouldn't. In the first place, they know my fist in London. Every wireless operator has a touch or two that no one else can duplicate. I've been told my fist – my sending style—'

'I know what fist means,' John said. 'I was trained in London, too, remember.'

'That's so, old chap? I'd assumed you were BACRA, but even so—'

'Wireless training is always SOE's job. BACRA or OSS, we go to your damned school. It's a good one. I grant you that.'

'OSS! I say, John, you don't mean—'

'I don't mean a goddamned thing. Get on with it, Byron.'

'All right. I've been told my fist is the most individual they've ever heard. So when I raise London, they'll have no doubt it's me. Let's wreck the ruddy thing and then I'll put a call through using yours. Straighten the blighters up a bit. No more free gifts to Jerry. All right?'

'All right,' John Farrow said.

'When?' Byron Graves asked.

'Tomorrow night. Because tonight we've got to steal a pig.'

'A pig!' Byron said. 'I say, John, what on earth—'

'To use to trade with Jerry. It always works. They see you with a pig, they don't even ask to see your papers. They bury you in useless occupation francs, and you march right into Grenoble. And if any other patrol stops you, you say regretfully,

'My brother and I came into town to sell our pig, but Hauptmann X – giving the right name, which you make damn sure you get – bought him already.' Then you show the requisition receipt, which Hauptmann X will be only too happy to sign in order to sink a tooth into his little cousin—'

'His little cousin? Oh I say, that's rather good! Carry on, John!'

'And you can go anywhere without showing the proper papers at all.'

'But, John, do we actually have to *steal* the little porker? I have a bag full of francs and—'

John looked at him.

'Who the hell d'you think wants francs, these days, Byron? What can money buy now? If you want to go to *une maison close* while we're there, we'd better steal a couple of chickens while we're at it. A fat poulet will get you the services of the youngest, prettiest girl in the house. Or do you have some chocolate, maybe?'

'Oh, I do. Quite a lot, in fact.'

'Then you can have the *two* prettiest girls. At the same time. Now go over there and ask Pierre Clémont to give you some grenades. You have a knife and a pistol. That's all we'll need. Anything else will slow us down too much.'

'Done,' Byron said. 'Which one is Clémont?'

'The short one. You speak French? Pierre doesn't know English.'

'Rather,' Byron said. 'What time tonight?'

'First dark. The farmers always expect thieves later. So that'll ball them up a bit. Get going, now.'

It was Pierre Clémont who explained to Byron the history of Jean le Fou.

'Il est fou de tristesse, vous savez, mon capitaine,' Pierre said. 'Crazy from sadness. His little mistress died to save his life. In Paris. And he cannot forget that. Therefore, he wishes to die. So, naturally, he bears a charmed life. Have you ever seen a man get killed in combat who wanted to die? It's almost impossible. His body's instincts defeat his will. And being crazy he becomes invincible. I would follow Jean through the front door of hell. His luck is formidable – because, you know, my captain, luck is a dirty bitch who only respects the man who kicks her in the tail. . . .'

'Tell me about him,' Byron said.

'There are men here,' Pierre said, 'who have come down from Paris. Yves Martin, in my squad for one. And he told me what Jean did there. A *grosse affaire* of two carloads of SS and him with only Molotov cocktails—'

'Blast me!' Byron said: 'I *knew* about that! So he's *that* one.'

'Yes. But *la petite Hélène* shot one of the Gestapo men – they machine-gunned her. Cut her almost in half before his eyes. He's been like that ever since. Shaking and crying. But it does not diminish him. When he shoots his hands *stop* shaking. And the Boche he aims at dies.'

'A very rare type, then?'

'*Très rare*. When the Italians were here and not the Boches we had a festival every day. Jean captured the commander of the OVRA, their secret service, in Grenoble itself. Put handcuffs on him, after stripping him naked, then stuck a long fuse like those that dynamiters used to employ up the Italian's ass – and turned him loose to run – after having lit the fuse of course – on the main square. You know that building with two elephants carved on the front?'

'Yes,' Byron said. He did.

'In front of that he kicked him out of the truck with this fuse spluttering and sparking from his asshole. The poor devil thought he'd inserted a detonator as well, but he hadn't. Jean is not cruel. People actually fell down on the *trottoir* from having laughed so much. It was *very* amusing, my Captain. This fat-bellied Italian hopping up and down a metre high each time and trailing smoke and sparks behind him as he ran. . . .'

'It must have been a sight,' Byron chuckled.

'It was. And a couple of nights later, he led twenty of us into town, and captured the Italian officers' special whorehouse. We had ourselves a time! All for free. *Les pauvres filles* were so glad to have *men* for a change. *Les italiens*, you know are *very* fast runners. In the desert – and in bed. For the first time in years *les filles* actually enjoyed themselves. *Mais*, Jean, you know what *he* did?'

'I can imagine,' Byron said.

'No, you cannot, my captain. You cannot possibly. He took a *bath*. Two hours long. With hot water and bath salts. Said he went in there smelling like a goat, and came out smelling like a whore. But as for *les poules*, he would not touch them. Not one. And they were all wild for him. The youngest, prettiest ones.

But he would not. Because of *la petite Hélène, vous savez . . .*'

Byron looked at Pierre and said very quietly:

'*Can* he?'

Pierre bowed his head. Looked up again:

'I do not know. I think not. But the trouble is in his mind, *mon capitaine*, nowhere else. He is all man, and very brave. Of that, you may be sure . . .'

'I am sure,' Byron said, 'but perhaps he will find another girl who will cure him of this sadness that the little Hélène left in him, cause him to find his will to live again . . .'

'*Ça, alors!*' Pierre said, 'that will be his finish, *mon capitaine anglais!* Because, as I told you, luck is a filthy slut who immediately leaves one the minute one starts chasing after her . . .'

Lying in that soft bed in the hotel at Gorge-du-Loup, John Farrow knew that Pierre had been right in the essentials, but wrong in the details. 'Because, like most people,' he thought, 'Pierre considered death the worst possible fate. And it wasn't. It isn't. Life is. Life without meaning. Drained of sweetness. Bereft of savour.'

He looked at his watch.

'Jesus!' he said, 'I'd better get some sleep! I've got to – or else, tomorrow—'

He pounded the pillow with his fist, making a hollow. Burrowed into it groaning. But sleep wouldn't come. It eluded him still. As so many things in his life always had.

And, very probably, always would.

6

He had never listed happiness among the qualities of life that had eluded him, because by the time he'd passed thirty he'd already learned that it was too much to expect. For if the founding fathers had listed the pursuit of happiness as one of the three *sine qua nons* of human existence, neither they nor anyone else had ever promised, or predicted, or even declared feasible the attainment thereof. For, on the face of it, happiness, over any extended period remains a chimera, John Farrow had long since realized, at least to any man intelligent enough to avoid self-delusion. He knew very well that even if he had brought it over his threshold along with Simone, in his arms, it would have escaped him by the window, evaporated into thin air because of some other factor, some disaster small or great, and for ever, and, mockingly, unforeseen.

But it seemed unfair of life to deny him the minor correlative qualities of ordinary contentment, a stoic's peace, which is the acceptance of imperfection, the avoidance of unnecessary pain. If he had no desire to be wildly happy, the desire to stop being profoundly unhappy, to spend his sunset years in a sort of grave measured tranquillity, in order and in peace appeared not unreasonable.

And that, basically, was the motive of this voyage, already out of control, and drifting into deadly shoal waters, though he knew it not. For once that brave and gallant ghost was laid, once he knew why she'd marched out of his life, and how meanly or grandly life had dealt with her thereafter he'd be free—

'For what?' he snarled, pounding his fist into that pillow. 'In the obscene name of absent God, for what?'

But there was no answer to that question, so he lay there, deliberately going over it all in his mind, seeking among the sifted ashes of memory for a clue, for something he had missed before, for—

May 1944, maybe. For the night Byron Graves and he had set out to raid Grenoble.

Of the two raids it looked for a while as if the pig-stealing foray was going to prove the more dangerous. Because that little son of a sow let out a squeal loud enough to wake the dead in the cemetery when John grabbed him, and the farmer came storming out the back door of the farmhouse with an ancient double-barrelled shotgun in his hands. They had a long enough lead – despite the considerable weight of the pig – to get away. But, afterward Byron had had to dig thirteen birdshot out of John's skinny tail with the point of his knife and then dust the wounds with sulfa powder.

'Jesus, I hope my ass doesn't stiffen up on me,' John said.

'Slow me up too much in case we have to run for it . . .'

He looked up at Byron's worried face. 'Goddamnit, Byron, you're too bloody clean!' he said. 'Go get some mud and muck and rub it into your face and hair. Clothes, too. A little cowshit to give you the proper smell. Don't tell me you *shaved*, you ass! Why—'

'No. It's just that my beard's so ruddy blond it takes a week to start to show.'

'Rub a little *merde de vache* into it as well. That'll darken it,' John said. 'Come on now, let's go.'

When, not five minutes after daybreak, they reached the first guard-post at the entrance to Grenoble, Byron saw that 'Operation Porker' was going to work. And work it did – like rendered hog fat, pristine hard, smooth, easy, fast. They were surrounded by German soldiers bidding furiously in bad French and even worse occupation francs for the pig. Not one of them thought to ask to see their papers.

But John held out stubbornly.

'*Mais, messieurs les allemands,*' he repeated time after time, the little pig, he is promised to the *grand chef* at the hôtel Modèrne et des Trois Dauphins. And the chef, him, is a man of very bad character. If I do not deliver the little pig to him as promised, he will break all my bones! I am too poor to pass three months in the hospital. And my wife and my kids will starve!'

The uproar brought the captain of the guard, a Wehrmacht Hauptmann so typical he seemed a caricature. Monocle in his left eye. Ornamental dagger in his belt. Beet-red face. Pot gut. Shaven bullet head. Eagles and crosses and swastikas all over him.

'*Was ist los?*' he bellowed. 'What's going on here?'

The Germans snapped to attention. In a wheedling, whining tone of voice, that almost made Byron strangle on his choked-back laughter, John explained matters.

'Then there is no problem, my good man,' the captain said. 'I will buy your pig. How much do you want for him?'

John made a piteous gesture with his hands. His face showed white with fear beneath all that grime, a tear stole down from his left eye.

'What you will, *mon capitaine,*' he quavered, 'but please your excellency, do not give me all the payment in money. Make me out a requisition slip that I can show to the chef. That way, perhaps he will believe it was not my fault and refrain from beating me into a bloody pulp. He is one terrible tempered man, *le chef!*'

'*Ach, so?*' the Hauptmann said. 'Here take these one hundred thousand francs, and I will make you the slip. *Ganz gut, nicht wahr?* And tell this bad-tempered chef of yours that if he treats you badly he will have to face *me*! Abuse of poor civilians I will not permit! Now wait you *hier*. I will *zurückkommen toute de suite!*'

'So now we're rich!' Byron said as they left the guardpost and entered the city.

'You mean the Vercors' latrine command is,' John said. 'Decent toilet paper is hard to come by these days. That's the only damn thing I can think of that occupation francs are good for. No there's another, sometimes—'

'And that is?' Byron said.

'Lighting fires,' John said. 'If you ever find some with the ink dry enough to let them burn. I'd bet my poor shotgunned ass that they print them five minutes before they give them to you.' He stopped, pushed his hand into the back of his pants, explored his skinny tail gingerly. 'Good thing that type had his cannon loaded for quail. If he'd had buck shot in that thing I'd be a cripple by now . . .'

'Here comes a patrol!' Byron said warningly.

'Look scared,' John said. 'And sullen. And stupid. But for Chrissake don't open your mouth. That Mayfair accent you've got in French would—

'*Bonjour, mon capitaine,*' he went on quietly.

'*Eure papiere!*' the MP sergeant-major snapped.

John looked blank.

'*Eure Ausweise! Ihre urkunden! Dummkopfe! Eure Papiere! Pappeeere! Verstehen Sie nicht?*'

'Ah!' John said, opening his eyes very wide. 'What an actor this chap would make,' Byron thought. '*Nos papiers!* [Our papers!] *Mais oui, mon capitaine, d'accord! Les voila!*'

Then he dug out the Hauptmann's requisition slip.

'*Essel!*' the feldtwebel thundered: '*Das ist nicht—*'

Then he stopped because his gaze had fallen on that signature. He turned to his companion whom normally he outranked for the other was only a sergeant. But instead of being a Wehrmacht sergeant – the German and English words for this rank are identical – he was an Unterscharführer, the equivalent rank in the SS, and though the regular army sergeant major theoretically was his superior officer – by two full grades, he was afraid of him. He also hated his guts, as even non-commissioned officers of the regular army always did their opposite numbers in the Waffen or armed SS, but by the spring of 1944, they dared not risk Himmler's political police's wrath. Even Wehrmacht generals found themselves locked in an empty room with a loaded pistol on the table, and a suicide order – for the honour of the corps! – before them when they offended the SS.

Therefore the sergeant major passed the requisition slip over most respectfully to the mere sergeant.

The SS man read it carefully. Then he said, in very nearly perfect French:

'Are you fellows farmers?'

'But yes, your excellency!' John said.

'And *this* is the only paper you have?'

'But no, your excellency! We have all the papers and they are all in order. Only, my brother here, who is a little backward in the mind since a mule kicked him in the head five years ago, forgot to bring them as I told him. You see, your excellency, we had to bring a pig to the chef of the Hôtel Modèrne et des Trois Dauphins. And since it is so far from here to our farm we had to get up long before daybreak. My brother was sleepy, and so was I, I admit, sir! – so he forgot the *porte-documents*. And I forgot to remind him of it. Besides we had to catch that little swine of a pig! Which wore us out. What a chase! up and down the whole barnyard—'

The SS man was getting a little tired of all the talk. So he said: 'And this famous pig of yours, my boy – where is he?'

'But, *mon capitaine!* It is as this paper says – does it not? The pig he was requisitioned from us by the captain of the Guard!'

The SS man eyed the two of them up and down.

'Suppose I were to telephone the chef at the Three Dolphins?' he said.

John dropped to his knees, his hands folded as in prayer:

'*Oh, mon capitaine, mon colonel, mon général!* Please do not do that! At least until I have had time to explain to the chef what happened! Or else he will *kill* me! As hard as a fat pig is to obtain these days, he will break all my bones! Or cut my throat with his carving knife!'

And a flood of quite genuine tears poured down his cheeks. Whereupon Byron, unable to resist the call of his true profession any longer, got into the act. He rolled his tongue around in his mouth until it was filled with saliva. Let a thick stream of it drool down his chin.

'Dites – dites lui,' he babbled foolishly, *'dites au maréchal qu'il – qu'il doit – qu'il doit téléfoner au – au capitaine!'*

'What *is* this idiot saying?' the SS Unterscharführer said.

'Tiens!' John said, 'he has said an intelligent thing for the first time in five years, your excellency! He says you should ring up the captain of the Guard instead. The one who signed this paper. He will, I am of it sure, confirm every little word I've said!'

The SS sergeant turned to the Wehrmacht sergeant major.

'Kennen Sie Den Hauptmann Reisbrenner?' he rapped out.

'Yes, sir, I know him,' the sergeant major said.

'Well enough to recognize his voice over the telephone?'

'I think so, yes—' the sergeant major said, 'but in any case a Captain Reisbrenner who comes to the phone at Guard Post Five could only be the right one, *nicht wahr, mein Unterscharführer?'*

'True,' the SS sergeant said. 'And this an official Wehrmacht requisition slip. Quite in order, in fact. But these Frenchmen can be damned clever at times. Go into that bar and call Hauptmann Reisbrenner; ask him to confirm, if he can, these dirty fellows' story. Gad, how they stink! Don't the French *ever* wash themselves?'

'Never!' the sergeant major chuckled, 'and their women even less. After one small experience with one of them, I am now being faithful to my wife. Took me three hours to scrub away that smell of spoiled fish!'

'I can well imagine,' the SS sergeant said, and flashed a small tight absolutely mirthless smile. 'Now go call the captain like a good chap, will you please?'

The Feldtwebel came back in less than five minutes.

'Yes, my under-troop-leader,' he said, 'Captain Reisbrenner fully confirms the story. What's more, he graciously invites the two of us to join the Post Five Guard officers' mess tonight – at which the pièce de résistance will be roast pig!'

'Capital!' the SS sergeant laughed, 'it seems that by temporarily detaining these dirty fellows, we have done ourselves a favour!' Then switching back into his excellent French, he said to John:

'Very well, be off with you, you *salauds!* But never let me catch the two of you in town without the proper papers again. If I do, it will go hard with you, of that you may be sure . . .'

'Yes, my captain! Thank you a thousand times, my captain! And now may we go, truly?'

'*Bien sûr. Filez!* March yourselves! And quickly, you dirty French swine!'

'I think,' Byron said out of the corner of his mouth, as they scurried away, 'that Captain Reisbrenner knows which side his scones are buttered on!'

'Yes,' John said, 'the SS has the army crapping its pants these days. Which won't do us any good. Not a mother's son in our upper brass with brains enough to use it.'

'Roger!' Byron said. 'I quite agree, old chap. Now what do we do?'

'We go to Galeries Printemps to buy a clock. An alarm clock.'

Byron didn't even have to ask why. The mechanism of a cheap alarm clock when wired in any of several ways to six or eight ordinary dry cells from an electric torch could, when attached to several kilos of gelignite, or even to a few sticks of ordinary dynamite, blow up half of Grenoble three or four hours after they were safely out of town.

'But the stuff?' he said. 'I brought only what you told me and you—'

'It's already here. Quite a few types in Grenoble love Jerry somewhat less than dearly.'

'Oh I say! That reminds me: what would have happened if that ice-cold bastard of an SS man *had* called the chef at the Three Dolphins?'

'Nothing,' John said, 'he's one of the best men we've got. I put on that act so they *would* call him. Disappointed me though. And you had to go and snafu the whole deal with that business of calling the captain. Good thing he admitted it. Could have denied it, you know—'

'He could have, but he didn't, John. I knew he wouldn't. Old-line Wehrmacht officer, y'know. They're pretty straight-laced. Question of honour, and all that sort of thing—'

'Maybe, but I wouldn't trust any Jerry as far as I could throw him,' John said, 'Now come on!'

Galeries Printemps still had alarm clocks in stock. But the clerk didn't want to take occupation francs for them. Again Captain Reisbrenner's requisition slip saved the day.

'And if I were to tell *le grand capitaine allemand* you refused the money that he, himself, gave me for my little pig?' John said solemnly.

'*C'est vous qui est un petit cochon!*' the clerk shrieked. 'Oh, take it! Fifteen thousand francs, then!'

'Wrap it up,' John said calmly.

The clerk did so. Tears of purest rage showed in her eyes.

'And now what am I to do with this garbage?' she stormed.

John took the package. Then he said, very politely:

'I should suggest that ma'moiselle wipe her little tail with it. Or that she stuff it up another aperture to reduce its size to useful proportions. *Bon soir, ma'moiselle! A bientôt!*'

Then he and Byron marched out together singing:

'*Hola, salope, avec ton 'tite queue mal propre!*' a French folk-song that goes into English very badly indeed, for if the literal translation, 'Hello, slut, with your dirty little tail!' expresses the idea perfectly, it loses both the rhythm and rhyme of that sparkling little ditty. They could still hear the clerk's shrieks of hysterical rage mingled with some very choice French when they'd reached the street.

'I say!' Byron laughed, 'you may be a bit of a silly ass, as you claim, but with you, one enjoys this blinking war!'

But John's face was solemn again.

'Come on,' he said.

This time he led Byron to a watchmaker's shop on a tiny side street. The watchmaker took the *loupe* out of one eye and stared at them fearfully. Then his eyes flared in recognition.

'Jean!' he said. 'Well surely you are crazy to come into Grenoble in daylight!'

'*Tais-toi*, Lucien,' John told him. 'Take this clock. How long will it take you to arrange it a little?'

'The simplest way?' Lucien said.

'No. Some smart type may notice the contacts on the hands. And the wires leading to them. Besides in that fashion it will only blow *ma soupe* at midnight, a quarter to nine, a quarter past three, or half past six. Fix up the alarm itself, Lucien. That way I can choose exactly when I want the stuff to go . . .'

'And it's the *only* way,' Byron said crisply. 'Have you actually ever *tried* that system of having the hands close the circuit when they cross one another, John?'

'No, but it *is* the simplest. And—'

'It's not worth a tinker's damn, old chap. Say it's a little after midday when you set it up? What happens at five minutes after one? That gives you only about an hour to get away. You wait till seven after one to set it up. Then those blinking hands meet and make contact at ten after two. Take the clock and try it. Using the main hands to close the circuit you *never* have more than an hour's grace. Because besides the times you've mentioned, and the ones I've pointed out to you, the hands of a clock cross at twenty minutes after four, five twenty-five, twenty-five minutes to seven, twenty to eight, ten to ten, and five to eleven. You see? *Never* more than an hour. And we'll need *three* to get far enough out of Grenoble not to get caught when the fireworks start. Four would be better.'

John looked at him. His eyes were cold. 'And with that death wish showing in them,' Byron thought.

'Who said we have to leave?' he said: 'If they catch us in a bar, filthy drunk, and feeling up the waitress, they'd likely leave us the hell alone . . .'

'I shouldn't wager tuppence on that, old chap,' Byron said. 'Besides I have a certain fondness for my lordly, aristocratic, very British *gluteus maximus*, y'know!'

Lucien, the watchmaker was staring wonderingly from one to the other of them during the whole of that rapid-fire English exchange.

'What is it, then?' he said to John, 'that *m'sieur l'anglais* says?'

'Mister the Englishman says,' Byron told him in his own quite good, if somewhat accented French, 'that to use the two hands of a clock to set off *la soupe* never gives one more than an hour to get away.'

'M'sieur has it right,' Lucien said, 'but there is another, still simpler way: you remove one hand of the *horloge* and put a little contact anywhere on the face. Then if one wire is led to the hand, and the other to the contact, one may permit oneself twelve full hours of perfect leisure, if one has hidden the package with sufficient care . . .'

They looked at each other. Then they whooped like Indians and pounded Lucien on the back.

'A genius!' Byron said. 'A ruddy Boffin, if there ever was one! It's perfect, John!'

'Taisez-vous, mes enfants!' Lucien gasped: 'Or is it that you wish to bring *les boches* down upon us? I supplicate you both, do not shout so, if you please!'

'How long do you need, Lucien?' John said.

'Can you give me two hours, Jean?' the watchmaker said.

'Take three. There is no hurry. After all, we cannot deliver our little souvenir of love and affection to the Boches until after dark . . .'

'Now what, John?' Byron said, as they left the shop.

'First we go grab a bite to eat and after that we go visit the whorehouse,' John said.

Byron stopped dead.

'Now really, old boy!' he said. 'I enjoy a spot of fun as much as the next chap, but this hardly seems the occasion to—'

'Not fun, business. Monkey business, if you like, but business. We've got plenty of time to eat first though. Jerry never arrives until after dark. Seems that screwing by daylight's *verboten* – or something. What I mean to do is to enlist a couple of the girls in our little endeavour. Get them to parade their well-washed and highly perfumed little anatomies – only women in France who smell good these days, *les poules*, you know, since Jerry treats them to both soap and perfumes – in front of the two patrols of sentries guarding the Funkspiels' garage. Get their minds off duty. That way, Jerry's only human, you know—'

'If,' Byron said, 'they're SS you'd better bring in a pair of pretty boys instead . . .'

'Then I'll use *you* as bait,' John said solemnly. 'That aristocratic British *gluteus maximus* ought to do the trick, oughtn't it?'

'Now see here, old fellow!' Byron began, then he saw that John was grinning at him. 'Oh, devil take you, you silly ass! Let's go grab that bite you mentioned, shall we?'

The restaurant John led him to was very imposing. So much so that Byron halted looking uneasily at their ragged filthy clothing, and their equally filthy faces and hands. Then he saw the two signs. One of them read: *Dieses Restaurant Ist Nur Für Die Herren Offiziere von Der Wehrmacht und Schutzstafeln Des Deutsche Reiches reserviert. Allen Anderen Personen ist Der Eingang streng Verboten*! And the other: *Ce Restaurant est réservé aux Messieurs les Officiers de L'Armée Allemande et SS L'entrée aux Toutes Autres est Expressement Défendue.*

But John headed straight towards it.

'John!' Byron hissed. 'Don't you see those ruddy signs?'

'Yes,' John said. 'Proof positive the food will be good. It always is in joints reserved for Jerry.'

'But I say, old chap—'

'Oh for Chrissake shut up and come on, will you?' John said.

Then at the very last moment, he ducked into a narrow alley, and walked down one side and around the back of the restaurant. Went up a flight of stairs. Byron followed him, thinking: 'Crazy – or just audacious? I'd wager it's the latter. And in this game audacity often wins. Do what they'd never expect you to and—'

But John was knocking on a little door. He knocked with a sharp staccato rhythm that was obviously a code. The door flew open.

'Jean!' a deep voice said. 'Jean le Fou! What is it that passes that is so grave that you must come by daylight?'

'Nothing at all, my dear René,' John said, 'I and my English friend here have a job to do tonight – and one that cannot be done on empty bellies. Prepare us some dinner, will you? We have money. Good money, not occupation garbage—'

'You are my guest,' René said, 'and your friend the Englishman him, also. You vouch for him, of course?'

'For an Englishman? For this son of Perfidious Albion? But of course! They dropped him on us two nights ago. Him and two others. Only the other two arrived in a damaged condition. Somewhat dead, in effect. What is there that one can eat in this *so* patriotic establishment that caters only to *les boches*?'

'What you will, brave idiot! But this job tonight – it is – *importante, hein*?'

'You do not know,' John said. 'I have not told you. Therefore when *les boches* suspend you by fishhooks passed through your balls, while beating *tes grosses fesses avec nerf de boeuf*, you cannot tell *them*, is it not so? *Le menu s'il vous plaît, maître!*'

The food was marvellous. And the wine matched it.

While they ate, John talked. Seriously. Sensibly. Listening to him, Byron was surer than ever that 'Jean le Fou' was an adopted identity, assumed for its protective coloration. A sort of psychological camouflage that served his new friend well.

'Don't believe that business about the Schutzstaffeln being all homosexuals, Byron. In the beginning – when the SS didn't even exist, when they were the Stürmabteilungen, the SA, it was true to a limited extent. But Hitler took care of that when he – I've heard, *personally* – shot Ernst Röhm. Nearly all of the gentlemen of *moeurs douteuses*, as the French so delicately put it, were weeded out then and there. Of course there may be a few left, but they have to keep their tendencies very well hidden if they don't want to face a firing squad. . . .'

'Then why do our chaps *insist* they're all perverts?' Byron said.

'They *are*,' John said. 'But homosexuality isn't the *only* perversion, Byron. Sadism falls under that heading, too, doesn't it?'

'There you have a point, John. Do go on, this is most interesting.'

'Even so they're more perverted than perverts. You get the distinction, don't you? Their leaders convert them to sadism, since – like it or not, use it or not – torture is one of the most effective techniques in this bloody rotten game we're in. I couldn't do it—'

'Nor I,' Byron said.

'And not all of them. I've learned that a fairly high proportion of SS officer candidates crack up in training. But the ones who make it – all the Sipo boys and I'd say the majority of Kripos as well, end up like that sergeant we met this morning: cold as ice and deadly as a serpent. Perverts to the extent that most of them probably do get more of a thrill out of whipping a naked woman to death than having sex with her. But they usually do both. If the culprit's young and attractive, the younger officers all have a go at her first before submitting her to torture—'

'Which is, in itself, a kind of torture,' Byron said grimly.

'Especially if she's from a good family, and has been well brought up. That's the worst of all, at least psychologically. Then she's broken from the outset – her pride of self, some of her identity has been hopelessly destroyed. Or do *you* believe that canard all foreigners seem to accept about the morals of Frenchwomen?'

'You needn't use that belligerent tone, old chap,' Byron said. 'I've lived in France. I know better. Besides, it's jolly well the fault of your own writers, isn't it?'

'Right,' John said soberly; 'speaking as a Frenchman, I'd say our women ought to be allowed to sue the estates of all our writers from Flaubert on down for defamation of character. And speaking as an American, my experience has been that Stateside girls have much rounder heels. About your English girls, I wouldn't know. Never had the time or the energy to try in London—'

'I'd say ours have changed – lately,' Byron said, and his voice was genuinely sad. 'Effects of the war. Tomorrow we die, and all that sort of thing. And, for the first time in history, our women are actually in the front lines – it's an ugly fact that our troops on a good many fronts are actually safer than their wives and sweethearts in England, what with Jerry dropping his calling cards all over—'

'That's just about stopped, hasn't it?'

'Yes – but we've some deuced hard intelligence that Jerry has some new and rather frightful weapons well in hand. Flying bombs – and rockets – long-range rockets – up to several hundred miles – and absolutely impossible to intercept, our Boffins say. So this year – or the next, may be the worst of all.'

He paused, took a sip of wine, and stared off into space.

'So – to tell the unpleasant truth about it, I haven't a girl friend at home just now. Broke with the last one when I joined this Scarlet Pimpernel rot . . . Seemed a bit too much to demand fidelity of a girl who may be splattered all over by a blockbuster any night. Mind you, old chap, I *should* prefer her being faithful to me; but it's rather unsporting to ask that now. To save that little treasure for the brave and absent warrior, when they have to be just as brave, and almost as much warriors themselves. . . .

'Most of them definitely aren't being faithful, at the moment. I finally stopped availing myself of all the delicious little opportunities, when one of them broke down and wept floods all over me the next morning. It seems friend hubby was in Africa facing Rommel's Afrika Corps. She was ashamed of herself, too bloody late, and I felt myself quite the filthiest rotter in recent history . . .'

'Even so, can't say I blame the little dears. Therefore, I stay fancy free for the duration. After the unpleasantness is over, I'll look for one who was a bit too young for fun and games while it was going on—'

John grinned at him wryly.

'Make sure she's got long legs,' he said.

'Long legs? Perhaps it's the wine, but I fail to follow you quite, old boy . . .'

'What's the definition of an English virgin, these days, Byron?'

'Oh, that! Any girl over twelve with legs long enough to outrun a Canadian or a Yank. Bloody truth, rather! But turn about's fair, John, my boy: what are the three things wrong with your Yanks?'

'Beyond being nuts, I wouldn't know.'

'You're overpaid, oversexed, and over *here*. Now, shall we pay a call upon your little dillies? Speaking of which I must confess it's been a damned fairish time since I've enjoyed country comforts. . . .'

'Can do. But *after* we plant the soup, Byron. Rubber legs aren't recommended for running purposes, you know . . .'

But they had gone no more than a couple of blocks when John stopped short.

'Damn my eyes!' he swore. 'I almost forgot!'

'Oh, I quite agree!' Byron quipped, 'damn and blast your bonny brown eyes, John! Now, what have you forgot, *this* time?'

'The soup, Byron, the soup! Now, come on!'

He led the young SOE captain by a long and confusing zigzag through back alleys and small side streets until they came to a fair-sized street called Rue de Lesdignières. John marched up it, swiftly, purposefully until he came to number eighteen. From the matériel displayed in the shop windows, Byron judged that it was a hardware store. Looking up, he saw that he was right, because the sign read: 'Quincaillerie Bouvier – Chichignoud et Allemand.'

'I say, John,' he whispered, 'what about that "and German" business?'

'It's his name, not his nationality,' John said. 'Joseph P. Allemand – or it was. The old boy was from Alsace. And anyhow he's dead, I think. The other owners are fronting for the FTP. This used to be their recruiting station. Or rather, their weeding-out station—'

'Weeding out?'

'Yes. Milice. Those bastards are always trying to infiltrate. But Eugene Chavant used to interrogate all the boys who suddenly became all-fire patriots when the Jerries – aided by Laval – passed the forced labour laws. Strange how the thought of being dragged off to Germany to do slave labour in Jerry's factories and fields reminded so many of how much they loved La Patrie they'd sat on their asses and damned near let die without so much as firing a shot during three long years. But Chavant could tell who those murderous Fascist swine were by the way they answered five questions—'

'What were the questions, John?' Byron said.

'Don't know. That was before I came here, Byron. Now we only use this place for hiding stuff we're going to need later. Damned good place, a *quincaillerie*. You dump a bunch of Stens among axes, saws, hoes and the like, and pile rolls of fence wire on top, and they're almost impossible to spot, whereas in any other kind of store they'd stick out like a sore thumb.'

'I can see how that would be,' Byron said. 'But why don't we go on in?'

'Couple of types in there I don't know. They could be legitimate customers, but we can't take a chance on it. Come on, let's walk on down the street a bit, then turn around and come back. . . .'

'And if they aren't gone by then?'

'We go over to the next street and cut across to the rear entrance of the store by a little alley I know. But I'd rather not do that. Dirty types like us slinking through alleys look too much like thieves. Somebody might call the police. Or some pro-German Vichy type might call the SS. Of course, we've got the police pretty well infiltrated. There are three réseaux among them: Honneur de la Police, Police et Patrie, and Front National de la Police but, Jesus! Byron, there are still a hell of a lot of Vichyites, antisemites, Anglophobes, and pro-Nazis among them as well. So if someone calls the coppers, we'd have to run for it – and take our chances that the ones that answer the call are our boys. Even if the patrol is mixed we'd be done for – because the Maquisards among the police would only blow their own cover by trying to help us. They've orders *never* to do that unless they're *all* réseaux men. What they do do when there's a chance to, is to let us escape from jail. But if it's the SS—'

'I know. Tell me, aren't the FTP Communists?'

'Yes. And men. And heroes. I've never known one of them to be a coward.'

'Oh, I grant you that,' Byron said, 'but are they also – patriots? A man can be a hero for a number of reasons: in defence of an ideology he believes in, rather – or more – than his country. London's quite a bit worried about that aspect of the question . . .'

John looked at him.

'A bridge to be crossed when we come to it, Byron,' he said quietly. 'Right now I'd kiss Satan's own shit-caked ass as long as he's shooting Nazis. And they are. Dead.'

'True. Even Uncle Joe Stalin's "our dear comrade" these days. But all the same, it's a troublesome point, John. Are we going to win the war only to lose the peace? The south's full of Spanish Republican refugees who've formed *réseaux* of their own. Our big boys are a bit *more* afraid of them than they are of the FTP even—'

'Your big boys are horses' asses as usual. The Spaniards are great fighters, and damned fine people. Besides, they aren't Reds – even the ones who *think* they are. What's considered howling radicalism in Spain barely reaches tepid liberalism anywhere else on earth. Which is why their right wingers are so astonishing. Troglodytes, actually. Stone age mentality. People who can take as their slogan: 'Down with Intelligence, Long Live Death" are beyond rational consideration it seems to me. . . .'

'Should we go back now?' Byron said.

'Not yet. I've been watching over my shoulder every twenty seconds or so and they *haven't* come out of there. A trick you'd better learn if you want to stay alive and functioning, Byron. Keep talking. About anything. We're a couple of normally voluble Frenchmen, remember—'

'I say, shouldn't we speak French, John?'

'Street's empty. If you see someone coming, do. But softly so they don't pick up your accent. If we have time, I'll try to rid you of it. You're fluent, and your grammar's good. If it weren't for that *enmerdeur accent de Mayfair* you could pass. Talk damn you! Wave your hands about!'

'Oh all right! How d'you know so much about Spain?'

'Lived there. A year. No eighteen months. In Andalucia. I had this suspicion of a spot on my left lung, and Papa couldn't – or wouldn't – get leave to take me Stateside to Arizona. Besides Maman had no intention of going to the US again. She'd spent her honeymoon there with Papa in 'sixteen, before we got into

World War I, and to say she loathes everything American – up to and including Papa, I strongly suspect – is to put it mildly. So Dalton Ross volunteered to take me to Spain. . . .'

'John! You don't mean—'

'Yes, him. That miserable traitorous son of a bitch. *Mon oncle Dalton!* Fact is, I adored him as a child, Byron. He was so goddamned much fun – and Papa wasn't. So I went with him to Spain. His excuse was that he was going to do a book of poems and a tourist guide. Maybe he was, but what he wanted was for Papa to subsidize his stay. Which, of course, Papa did—'

'And you, what'd you do there?'

'Learned Spanish. Good Spanish. Castilian in fact. Dalton didn't want me to pick up that sing-song Andalucian accent. So he got me a teacher – female, pretty thing about thirty – down from Burgos.'

'How'd she stay awake in the daytime long enough to teach you anything?'

John looked at him.

'I see you know Dalton, Byron,' he said.

'Rather. He was in SOE. We parachuted him into the South of France. Impressed me as being brave as a lion. Never could figure how they turned *him*. . . .'

'The SS can turn the holy martyrs. And the twelve apostles on top of them. Come on, we can't waste any more time. We'll just have to risk that back alley, that's all. . . .'

When they came out of the hardware store, five minutes later – or rather out of the storage room back of it – it was done. *La soupe* – all of twenty kilos of gelignite – would be delivered to the house of a client who lived one street away from the Funkspiel's building and garage, under a pile of gardening tools, and several rolls of wire, which said client hadn't even ordered, but would accept without question since he was an ardent Free Shooter and Partisan man. It would be delivered by pushcart, dragged and shoved along by a teen-aged kid who had no idea what his errand really was, and hence set out whistling gaily.

'Brave little chappie, isn't he?' Byron said. Then: 'Oh I say, John – what would happen to him if a SS patrol should stop him, look into that cart?'

John stared at him.

'He'll die,' he said harshly. 'Badly. Goddamned badly. Screaming his poor stupid guts up because he can't tell them what he doesn't even know.'

'Oh, come now, John! I can't permit this! What we do, knowingly, is on our heads – but a kid like that one, innocent of all—'

John went on looking at him and said very quietly:

'You Limey shit-ass. We've been begging you for months to drop us the arms and the explosives we need so we could sabotage your objectives in France. That way, the lives lost doing it would be very few. And that few, our own. Instead you British and American airborne murderers go right on blasting the guts out of babies. French babies. You kill fifty, a hundred, two hundred *gosses* like that one – and younger, far younger! – in a single night, wasting tons of HE stuff on open fields and the *wrong* towns, because if you could so much as distinguish between your asshole and your appetite you'd know that the bombing plane is *the* most miserably ineffective weapon of warfare ever invented since old grandpapa ape first picked up a rock! We could do it better, but you won't let us. So don't ask me to take into account the life of one kid. Who'll probably deliver this stuff without the slightest trouble. And who – if he's caught, will be dying for France. Which is to say for civilization. Or would you prefer the new dark ages that Hitler and his insane rabble of obedient and scientifically trained technocrats will bring in? I'd give anything to stop that, Byron. My life. Yours. Anybody's—'

'You've proved that, haven't you, John?' Byron said stiffly. 'And I suppose Hélène's death shouldn't be too much on your conscience – since she gave her life voluntarily, for you. But what about those seventy-five hostages the Nazis shot in reprisal for your splendid feat of heroism? I shouldn't like to carry *that* about, y'know—'

He stopped suddenly.

'Oh, I say, John!' he got out. 'That was bloody rotten of me! Do forgive me, old boy! I've a filthy temper and—'

But John was sitting down then, with his head between his knees. He was puking up that magnificent dinner he had eaten; spewing it into the gutter.

Byron sat down beside him. Put his arm across those bony quivering shoulders.

'John,' he all but wept, 'I am sorry! Believe me, I am—'

John looked up at him. Grinned. The tears on his face went right on ploughing white tracks through the grime, but he grinned all the same. It was the most heartbreaking grin Byron Graves had ever had to endure in his whole life, and the most pitiful and the most gallant.

' 'S all right, Byron,' he said. 'I had that one coming I guess. And, anyhow, thanks.'

'Thanks?' Byron said.

'Yes. I'll be faster without all that in my gut to weigh me down. . . . Now, come on—'

When they got to the whorehouse, the spectacle? charade? act? – that greeted them was, Byron's professional instinct told him, either rehearsed, or repeated often enough to have become a ritual. The girl who opened the door said:

'Ahhhhhhh! C'est Jean!'

Afterward Byron tried to write that 'Ahhhhhhh!' – the way it went – in the symbols of poetic scansion. But he couldn't. There weren't any that fitted it. Because it was neither an iamb, or a dactyl, or a trochee, or an anapest, or any other of the poetic measures. It was truly monosyllabic, but drawn out a long, long rising curve so that it sounded like music. Behind her, another girl repeated it.

'Ahhhhhhh! C'est Jean!' ('Ohhhh! It's Jean!')

And John: *'Oui, c'est moi.'* ('Yes, it's me.')

The first girl: *'Et comment va-t-il, ton tout petit frère? Est-il toujours mort?'* ('And how is he, your very small brother? Is he still dead?')

And John, sadly: *'Oui, il est toujours mort.'* ('Yes, he's still dead.')

All the girls, in chorus: *'Ahhhhh le pauvre petit!'* ('Ohhhh, the poor little fellow!')

'That,' Byron thought, 'is just about the saddest sound I've ever heard. But why? If John has a brother who's dead, he jolly well can't resurrect him, can he?'

A tall striking brunette: *'Ça, je ne crois pas, moi! Je vais faire l'épreuve!'* ('That I don't believe! I'm going to try!')

And John: *'Laissez-moi, mes filles, je—'* ('Leave me alone, girls, I—')

But the tall brunette had seized him, wrestled him down across a sofa, and was lying on top of him, kissing his mouth. Without interrupting that kiss ('Positively cannibalistic!' Byron thought) she put her hands inside his sweater, his shirt, and began to run them all over his thin shivering body. John made no move to stop her. He just lay there, taking it.

Then she straightened up, briefly, and shoved her hand beneath his belt and down inside the front of his pants.

'Tu vois, Catherine?' John said, *'il est toujours mort, mon petit frère.'* ('You see, Catherine? He is still dead, my little brother.')

And Catherine, in a tone half-way between sadness and annoyance, if not anger: *'Oh, zut alors, ça!' Mais il faut avoir une façon que –'* (That *'Oh, zut alors, ça!'* Byron reflected, was one of the many, many idiomatic exclamatory phrases in French that have no translation at all in any other language. But the rest of it meant: 'But there must be some way to—')

Byron grinned then.

'Peux-je suggérer un camion avec une grue arrière?' he said. ('May I suggest a truck with a chain hoist on the back of it?')

'Ah, ça! Comme vous êtes mauvais, vous!' a little redhead said. ('Oh that! What a bad boy you are!') But all the others were squealing:

'Un anglais! C'est vraiment un anglais qui parle un français si mignon! Vous êtes une parachutiste, n'est-ce-pas?'

'Yes,' John said, 'he is truly an Englishman who speaks so cute a French. And a parachutist. And a brave type. And, what's more, *his* little brother is far from dead! So now, Catherine, let me up. I have envy to take a bath.'

'You,' Catherine said, 'are an obsessionated of the bathtub. It is your *fétiche*, Jean. But if you have need of a *fétiche*, I will give you a pair of my panties. Black lace. And unwashed so that they will smell like me. Exciting is it not so?'

'*Non*,' John said. 'I do not need excitement, my girl. The Boches provide me with too much of that, as it is. What I need is rest, relaxation. Hot water, good soap, and little bath salts do that—'

'Shall I come up and scrub your back for you?' Catherine said.

'Yes,' John said, 'you and Lucienne also, because there is a thing we must talk about. A thing I want you to do for me. And – for France. It will require courage, *mes filles*; because in a way it is dangerous—'

'You mean we might get – hurt – or killed?' Lucienne whispered.

'Yes, child, I do mean that,' John said.

'Oh zut alors!' Catherine said. 'What's the odds, you cow! I'd just as soon die all at once, than by inches drowning in my own vomit, after having to wallow all night with these dirty Nazi swine! I'll do it, *Jean, mon Jean adoré, mon amour!* For you I will do it – whatever it is!'

'And you, Lucienne?' John said.

'Yes,' Lucienne whispered. 'I, also. Whatever it is.'

When John came back downstairs, he was not only clean, he had shaved and his hair had been trimmed a little. He was wearing one of the girls' quilted bathrobes, because Lucienne had taken his clothes to steam clean over a kettle, and afterward to iron them. Byron was clean again, too. He had only his underwear on because the girls had insisted upon steaming and pressing his clothes as well.

He was dancing with Mirielle, the little redhead, to music coming from a radio. Mirielle was naked except for a pair of panties so brief that they were practically a *cache-sexe,* as the French call a G-string. He wasn't drunk, John saw with relief, but only bemused, and relaxed, and happy. Very happy.

'Ah, Jean!' Mirielle cried, *'il était formidable, ton anglais! Et moi, je croyais toujours que les anglais, eux, sont—'*

'And what is it that you have always believed the English were, my little unfaithful one?' John asked: 'Queers? No, Mirielle, you are wrong. They only act that way to surprise the little girls.'

'Dance with me, Jean,' Catherine said.

'No,' John said: 'Let me rest, Catherine. And you also must rest. This *affaire* tonight will not be at all easy . . .'

'I know. Let's not talk about it. Come sit here – by the radio. And kiss me a little. You do not believe me, and I know it is no great honour to be loved by a whore, but I love you, Jean. Truly. After the war is finished, you must marry me. Make *une femme honnête* of me. Because I am *honnête,* Jean, at heart. I was forced into this dirty business, you know—'

'Catherine, please!' John began, but the radio cut him off.

'And now, my dear boys,' a feminine voice said in English, 'all you tall and handsome GI's over there in Italy, your good friend, the famous American poet, Dalton Ross, has a word to say to you—'

'Shut that bastard off, Catherine!' John snarled.

'Oh, no! Let us hear him, Jean!' the other girls said. 'He is *very* amusing, your Dalton Ross! And now the English will translate for us, so we may see if he says in English the same things he says in French later on—'

'It's the same,' John said. 'In English it's shit. *En français, merde*. But the smell is exactly the same.'

'But you are unfair, Jean!' the girls cried.

'Leave it on, old chap, will you?' Byron said. 'I've never actually heard one of his broadcasts, y'know. We're out of range in England. . . .'

'Not out of range, Byron. It's just that the Nazis beam them. They have much more strength in the direction they want them to go. Italy and Algiers. Oh, hell, if you want to, I can bear up this once. . . .'

'Now look, fellows,' Dalton's voice came over with a purr in it, a sort of suppressed chuckle, 'is it really smart to get your poor tails shot full of holes for Rosenfeldt and his Jew-Deal? What are you doing over there, anyhow? Don't tell me you love those dirty stinking Guinea bastards—'

'John!' Byron said, 'I think he's deliberately sabotaging his own efforts! He must know how many boys of Italian descent you have in that army!'

'I don't know,' John said, 'it seems to me—'

'Of course I can't prove your President's a Hebe,' Dalton went on, 'but with that crowd of kikes he's got surrounding him. Morgenthau, Frankfurter – oh no, boys, I *don't* mean a hot dog; but a dirty Jew! – and all, what can be expected of him? And with what one of your best Washington columnists calls *La Boca Grande* – *do* I have to translate that? Mrs Big Mouth if you please – to cheer him nights, no wonder he's a bit soured, right?'

'Hell, he's not even good at it any more,' John said.

'Or – maybe he's being intentionally bad,' Byron said. 'He really seemed a good enough bloke to me. . . .'

'Translate! Translate!' the girls squealed.

Byron did. Rapidly, accurately.

'I don't like that,' Lucienne said, as she came through the door with John's clothes draped over her arm.

'And why not, Lucienne?' Mirielle said.

'Because – because – *moi, je suis juive*!' Lucienne said, defiantly.

The rest of them stared at her.

'Et moi aussi,' Jean said quietly.

'Ah, it's true!' Catherine said. 'His *tout petit truc* has been cut! Like that! Tell me, Jean, did not the *rabin* cut off too much?'

'Sssh!' another girl said, 'here he goes again!'

'But speaking of Madam Big Mouth,' Dalton went on, his voice dripping amused venom: 'did you fellows hear what happened during Churchill's last visit over there? Well, it seems that old Rosenfeldt's legs aren't the only part of him that're paralysed – and when they were riding up to Hyde Park in a Pullman car—'

'A what, John?' Byron said.

'Sleeping car,' John said. 'Dirty bastard!'

'– old Boca Grande saw her chance? So when Old Blood, Vinegar, Pus and Piss got up to relieve himself during the night, he had to pass by her berth, and she grabbed him.'

The girls let out peals of delighted laughter when Byron translated that.

'But it seems that the sounds of combat awoke dear Franklin. Only, since he's a dirty cripple—'

'Filthy stinking bastard!' John said.

'—there wasn't a damned thing he could do about it. So he lay there patiently until His Majesty's Prime Minister had lost a great deal of sweat, some blood, where Old Big Mouth bit him in her ecstasies, and even some tears. And—'

'Translate! Translate!' the girls cried. All except Lucienne.

'Jean,' she whispered, 'is it true that you – that you—'

'Later, Lucienne,' John said.

'And when the august Prime Minister climbed down out of the berth, the President growled at him: "Now look, Winnie, old boy, I'll have no more of that sort of thing!" '

'And d'you know what the Prime Minister of the now defunct British Empire replied, boys? He groaned: "Nor I, Franklin, old chap, nor I!" '

But when the girls' laughter subsided, Byron looked at John. And he didn't like what he saw. 'If this isn't madness, it's too close to it for comfort,' he thought.

'I say, John, it *is* a jolly good yarn, y'know. Setting aside the man's intentions, as a story it—'

'No,' John said: 'You'd have to know her. And I do. Papa introduced me to them both when I was on my way up to enrol at Harvard. She is – a lady, Byron. A great lady. That ugly face of hers – is beautiful. What she's got inside shows through. So the joke's not funny to me. That's very dirty fighting. Made me change my mind—'

'Change it how?' Byron said.

'I said that when I caught Dalton, for old time's sake, I'd only beat him up. But now—'

'Now?' Byron said.

'Now, I'm going to kill him. Come on, let's go!'

'Look, old chap, it's still too light outside. Let me entertain the girls a bit, will you?'

'All right, Byron,' John said tiredly.

Then Byron did entertain them. He took some charred wood out of the stove. With it, he drew a toothbrush moustache on his upper lip. Then he raked a lock of reddish blond hair down over one eye.

The minute he did that, all the girls squealed: *'Eeet–laire!'*

'Sieg Heil!' Byron said gruffly, and snapped them a sloppy, Chaplinesque salute. Then for the next half hour, he performed with matchless skill. Before he was through, all the girls were rolling on the floor, and hugging one another and weeping helplessly from laughter. What he did was a thing so difficult that until that moment John had believed it impossible. He imitated Adolf Hitler's guttural, all but senseless ravings in French, and made it sound like German.

'That,' John thought, 'is really a stunt! In English it's easy enough to do, because English and German are both Teutonic languages. Hell, they even sound a bit alike, anyhow. But *French*! This type's a comic genius for a fact!'

He sat there listening while Byron/Hitler began by confessing he had already lost the war, and blaming this and all his other misfortunes on: *'Cette toute petite chose de l'Eva!'*

By the time he had finished, he was shrieking, tearing his hair, frothing at the mouth and screaming:

'C'est quand même la faute de cette grosse malpropre chose de l'Eva!'

But still John didn't laugh. He said: 'Can you do that in German, Byron?'

'Of course, John. Even better.'

'Let's hear you. Only a little though. We really have to get started now.'

So Byron started all over again. In German it was absolutely marvellous. One would have sworn it was Hitler himself speaking. But John only let him roar out just once *'Das grosse, schmutzige, kotige, unflätige Ding der Eva!'* before stopping him.

'Good,' he said, 'very good, Byron. Maybe we'll be able to use some of that tonight. Now, Catherine, and Lucienne – go get dressed. Make yourselves very beautiful. You already know what to do—'

'Mais oui, mon amour!' Catherine said. But Lucienne came over to him. Stood there looking up into his eyes. She was crying, very quietly.

'Jean,' she whispered, *'C'est vrai que tu es juif, comme tu as dit? Comme – moi?'*

'Yes,' John said solemnly, 'I am a Jew. But not exactly in the way you are, my dearest. Because I am also a nigger. And a redskin. And a Chinese coolie. And a kid dying of hunger in a gutter in Ceylon. I am all the victims of this world, Lucienne. All the humiliated, offended, starved, tortured, murdered, damned are my brothers, child. In that sense, tonight, and for the duration of this obscenity of a war, I am very much a Jew—'

'Then I am your sister,' Lucienne said. 'You know what happened at the Vél d'Hiver, don't you? In Paris? How they locked up all my people there—'

'And mine,' John said.

'Women, children, old people, babies. The babies died the first day, most of them, before they could even be deported. Because there was no food, no water, and the sanitary facilities were insufficient. All my family were there, *mon Jean.* I only escaped—'

He bent down then, and kissed her very tenderly.

'Ça alors, comme même!' Catherine said. *'Tu vois? Et devant moi! Il est vraiment fou, ce Jean!'* ('Well I like that! You see? And right in front of me! He's really nuts, this John!')

'If he is,' Byron Graves said quietly, 'then madness is a gift from the good God, Catherine. For if this world we live in now be sane – long live madness say I.'

'There you are right, my English!' Catherine said. 'And now, since clearly Jean has deserted me for the little Lucienne, you kiss me. And wish me luck. I'll need it.'

'Il est à moi, vache!' Mirielle shrieked: ('He's mine, you cow!')

'Touch him, and I will pull out your hair! And scratch out your eyes! And cut your throat!'

'Ta gueule, Mirielle,' John said mildly: ('Shut up, Mirielle.') 'Go on, Byron, kiss her. Kiss them all. Who knows? They may be the last women you ever kiss . . .'

'I say, old boy, come off that one, will you?' Byron said.

They crouched behind the chimney of the FTP man's house and looked down into the square where the Funkspiel had its headquarters and its garage. Since Grenoble is at least as hilly as San Francisco is, if not a little more, even the garden of the Communist Maquisard's house was far higher than the roofs of the buildings on that square. Not all of the Funkspiel's vans, and ambulances, and lorries were in the garage; a good many of them were parked all around it in the square – for lack of space, surely, John thought.

He put his hand in his pocket and came out with a ring bearing an assortment of lock-picks of the type a professional burglar uses. As a matter of fact they had been given to him by a professional: the little Cockney who had been his classmate in the SOE sabotage school. For so greatly had that runty little pickpocket, second-story man, safe-cracker, and past master of all the arts of robbery come to admire John Farrow's quite amazing, if acquired skills as a thief that he'd seriously suggested their joining forces and setting up for themselves in London after the war.

Suddenly John touched Byron's arm.

'You see that closed truck down there?' he said softly: 'the good-looking one with what looks an electric trolley harness on top?'

'The six-wheeled job? Black? Very nice finish – much better than anything Jerry ever does?'

'Yes, that's the one. And you're right, it isn't German made. It's Czechoslovakian, a Praga RVR. Great little bus, Byron. Fix its location in mind. In relation to the Funkspiel headquarters, and also in relation to the garage. How many meters would you say it's parked from Headquarters, and how many from the garage?'

Byron squinted. Said: 'I'd say about twelve from headquarters, and somewhat farther from the garage – fifteen very nearly. Why, John?'

'Tell you later. Don't want you scared shitless ahead of time. And nothing may come of it anyhow. Besides I think – yes, there they are! The girls, Byron! Now let's get a move on! Get that lead out of your tail, will you!'

The Germans had been in Grenoble a long time by then. And unlike in Paris, they weren't being picked off every day or so by the FTP's sharpshooters. The Maquis had been able to pull off only one successful sabotage since the Italians, who had held the Alpine regions before the Nazis came, had marched away after the surrender of their country in September 1943. Worst of all, from a military point of view was the fact that all the troops, Luftwaffe, Wehrmacht, and Waffen SS were garrisoned in the city itself. Now troops garrisoned in a pleasant town like Grenoble, in an area where the war had for all intents and purposes stopped, may not, and need not, go entirely soft – their murderous efficiency against Vercors itself within a month was to prove that very well – but they do slacken off a bit. And that, in fact, was what John Farrow was counting on.

He went racing down that street with all twenty kilos of gelignite on his back, having flatly refused to divide those forty-four pounds of lethal explosive with Byron on the score that he was used to handling it and Byron wasn't. He did let Byron carry the clockwork timer that Lucien, the watchmaker, had made from their dime-store alarm clock, which they'd retrieved on their way over, and eight heavy-duty dry cells of the type used for ringing doorbells in rural districts. They moved silently and fast, and without too much effort since their route went downhill all the way. In minutes they were down to the entrance of the square.

John put out his arm and stopped Byron. From where they were in deep shadow under a row of street lights – that somebody in the electric light company's distribution control section had thoughtfully cut not half an hour ago, after having received a call from somebody else, probably one of the owners of the hardware store, who'd said something like: 'There's going to be a damned good play on the radio tonight' – which was enough to anyone who was aware, as all the town réseaux members were that the Germans code word for their direction finder squadrons, Funkspiel, meant literally 'radio play' – they could see Lucienne and Catherine flirting playfully with the two sentries.

But still John didn't move. He waited almost unbreathing

until the other two sentries whose patrol should have met up with this one somewhere behind the building came running around the corner of the garage, burpguns at ready, sure that because the normal contact had not been made, something was *sehr viel Gefickt,* which was the German army's very exact equivalent of the American GI's 'Situation Normal: All Fucked Up!' which they reduced to 'snafued' for gentler ears.

'Les voilà, les héros!' Catherine mocked. *'Je me rends, braves soldats! Je vous en supplie; ne tirez pas s'il vous plaît!'* ('Here they are, the heroes! I give up, brave soldiers! I beg of you, don't shoot, please!')

And Lucienne: *'Est-ce que ce sont des nécrophils, vos copains? Moi, je crois que nous sommes beaucoup plus utiles vivantes, n'est-ce pas?'* ('Are your friends the kind who like to make love to dead bodies? I believe we're much more useful alive, aren't we?')

Sheepishly the other two sentries lowered the muzzles of their burpguns, and joined the group. One of them started protesting in German about their duty, and what they were going to catch from the Oberstürmbannführer, when Catherine interrupted him.

'Comme il est beau, ce garçon! Je vais lui donner un grand baiser!' ('How good looking he is, this boy! I'm going to give him a big kiss!')

As she suited the action to her words, John and Byron were already past and around the side of the building. At the side entrance, John went to work with those lock-picks. It took him the sum total of forty seconds to click that lock open, but to Byron, it seemed closer to forty years.

But once they were inside, he locked the door again.

Byron stared at him, gone beyond speech.

'They always try the doors as they go past,' John whispered. 'Official routine. We leave that one open, and they'd be in here on our asses so damn fast that – oh, hell, come on!'

Next he went to work on the back doors of the biggest van in the garage. They took him a trifle longer, a shade under a full minute. Then they climbed up in the van. The two of them worked together very fast and surely. They hid the gelignite in a huge tool box, removing enough of the tools to make room for it. Byron hooked up the timer. In the silence, its ticking was much too loud.

'I've given us four hours,' Byron said, 'all right?'

'All right,' John said, 'but we've got to smother that damned ticking somehow!'

Byron looked into the driver's seat. As he had expected, there were a pair of heavy leather gloves there. He shoved the clockwork mechanism into one of them. The ticking was barely audible now. They closed the tool box, put it back in place. Hid the tools they'd taken out of it under the seats. Jumped down from the van.

But before John could lock the doors again, Byron said: 'I say, old chap, suppose someone starts sending somewhere hereabouts – and *this* van goes on duty? Could happen, you know. Then we'll have caught up with the Bomber Command as far as killing innocents is concerned. This *soupe* would wreck every house in the street this thing may be passing through when it does—'

'That's a thought,' John said. 'Give me a bunch of those tools, Byron.'

In another two minutes he'd lifted the distributor head and carefully removed the rotor from it. And the breaker points to make doubly sure. Then he cut all the wire leading to the spark plugs a centimetre from their ends, then slipped them back into the rubber protectors so that they seemed to be connected. A plug of wood pressed against the valve of the left front tyre completed the job. The Funkspiel operators always were in a hurry by the very nature of their work. Confronted with a motor that wouldn't start, and a flat tyre, they'd take another van.

'Now what about the wireless of the chap they turned?' Byron said.

'When that *soupe* goes, it'll go, brother!' John said.

'But suppose it isn't here, John?' Byron said.

'Of all the pessimistic sons of – oh, all right! That's surely the storeroom over there. Let's have a look.'

Two minutes more. Closer to three. They were both sweating now. The lock gave finally. And there among all the neat, glistening glossy dialled, chrome and black German radios was a battered old suitcase. They hugged each other. Because the British wireless dropped into Maquis réseaux, saboteurs et al, was always built into this sort of valise. Twenty seconds to get it open. Then John came out with a small flask from the pocket of his pants. He poured it carefully into every opening of the wireless. An acrid smoke drifted up and stung their eyes.

'Acid?' Byron said.

'Sulphuric. *Now* shall we get out of here?'

They waited by that side door, listening. There was no sound. John opened the lock in twenty seconds this time. Locked it again, from the outside, in three. They went up the side alley very fast. Stopped at the corner of the building. Heard the tinkling of soprano laughter. And baritone. And tenor.

John poked his head out. The sentries were having a ball. There already was one empty wine bottle in the gutter. One of the sentries had another raised to his mouth. The girls had been goddamned smart. He hadn't told them to bring wine. It had been their own idea, surely. Lucienne was sitting on the edge of the *trottoir*, between two of the young Germans. She was busily slapping away the hands that both of them were trying to push up between her thighs at the same time. Catherine was kissing the pretty blond boy with considerable relish. His stern Teutonic sense of duty had clearly departed for parts unknown. His companion, between taking great swigs from the wine bottle, was pinching her *derrière* and laughing.

John nodded to Byron. Then in one swift silent rush they were by the frolicking sentries and into the dark street again. But instead of getting the hell away, John made a bee-line for the neat Czech-made truck he'd pointed out before.

The lock-picks did their work. They were inside within one minute.

'Hell!' John said feelingly. 'No keys! We'll have to bridge the contact—'

'But why, John, why?' Byron said.

'Tell you later. Let's get the show on the road, Limey!'

The sentries were so busy that they didn't even notice the RVR roll silently away. John accomplished that by putting the gears in neutral, and releasing the brakes. The downgrade did the rest. Two blocks farther down, they stopped, lifted the hood, bridged the contact so that the starter whirred. That beautiful straight eight caught at once. Then they leaped into the cab, and were off.

'Now, really, John!' Byron said. 'What on earth—'

'This thing's a radio truck. Radio, you Limey, not wireless. Made for on-the-spot-broadcasting: parades, military band concerts, speeches, propaganda. Which means it's got medium and long wave *voice* transmission, not Morse Code. So now what does that suggest to you?'

'I'm afraid I'm a bit dense tonight, old boy. Perhaps you'd better enlighten me . . .'

'Enlighten you, hell! It's the Jerry High Command we're going to enlighten. Don't you think it's time they heard Der Leader's heartbreaking confession of how he lost the war because he couldn't ever get enough of Eva's dirty little thing?'

'Cripes, John! That's the bloodiest idea! But won't the Funkspiel—'

'*Think*, Byron! What does the Funkspiel monitor?'

'By Jove, you're right! Short wave, of course! On the five hundred and two thousand metre bands they can't even hear us!'

'And if by chance they do – harmonics can play some devilish tricks you know – who's going to be standing still waiting for them to lay their beams on us?'

What happened after that was history. In garrisons, offices, bedrooms of their mistresses, all over Grenoble, Wehrmacht, Luftwaffe, and Schutzstafel officers froze, when after the Horst Wessel Lied, that grave, blurry too well-known voice came pouring slowly softly out of the loudspeakers.

'Meinen Herren, Damen, Bürger von das Deutsches Reich, ich habe den Krieg verloren—'

Afterward they found out that a good quarter of the listeners heard Byron's authentic masterpiece all the way through to the end, too petrified to even see the joke. Most of them got at least half-way through it before they realized that even as mad as their Führer indisputably was, he would never say 'The Five-Minute Reich, instead of lasting the five minutes I promised you, has lasted only thirty seconds – and why? Because of – oh shame! – Eva's great big fat dirty *thing*!' Or: 'I tried to make men of you, you slobs! True Aryans: tall as Goebbels, lean as Goering! And as blond as me! *Und so fort!*—'

John was laughing so hard he could scarcely drive, but Byron was putting his heart and soul into his act. He raved, he screamed, he frothed at the mouth, tore his hair, stamped his feet, spewing out an endless stream of bellowed gibberish punctuated at intervals by:

'Das grosse, dicke, schmutzige, Ding der Eva!'

But there must have been one officer at least who caught on

fairly fast. Because just before the end of Byron's speech, they turned into a street that had a rising grade of almost twelve degrees, which was why John didn't see the roadblock, just below the summit on the far side of the hill they were going up in second until they were almost on top of it. John slammed on the brakes, threw the truck into reverse, and rocketed backward down that steep incline, clinging to the steering wheel, and guiding the radio truck by a combination of instinct and feel, because he was lying across the seat, totally unable to see where he was going, for the very simple reason that 6.3 millimetre bullets from the Nazis' burpguns were turning the windshield into powdered glass not thirty centimetres above his head.

Then he felt the left rear wheel hit the kerb, and spun the steering wheel in the opposite direction. The truck heeled over hard, springs and shock-absorbers groaning, tyres screeching like all the damned in hell. Abruptly the linked blow-torch splutter of the burpguns stopped. He raised his head. By miraculous luck he had backed the truck around a blind corner.

He jumped down from the driver's seat, hissing: 'Come on, Limey!' and the two of them went over the hedges into a formal garden. They could hear the snarl of the patrol cars crawling down the hill in second gear, but they lay on their bellies behind the hedges in the dark and didn't move. It was at times like these that the SOE's iron training paid off. If they had panicked, run, they would have been dead men in a shade under two minutes flat. But by keeping still, they stayed alive, at least temporarily.

Because when those patrol cars came around the corner, the first thing they did was to open fire on the truck with everything they had.

'Wehrmacht!' John whispered. 'Come on, follow me!' Then he was off, crawling across the garden on his hands and knees so that at no time were their silhouettes visible above the hedges. On the far side of the garden was a wall. Without hesitation John went up it. Byron followed him. They dropped down to a street considerably higher than the one they'd left.

'Keep going up!' John said, 'even if we get separated. Fugitives always tend to run downhill, because it's easier. What Jerry will expect. So we don't, catch?'

'Roger, old boy,' Byron said.

Down below them the regular army men were still shooting

into the truck. Using the stutter of the machine guns as a guide, John led Byron in the opposite direction. They zigzagged, cut through alleys, went down side streets until they were back in the centre of the town. Three times they saw the light jeeplike patrol cars, the Volkswagen-built KdF 82s, personnel carriers that the troops themselves nick-named Kübelwagens, go screaming through bigger streets a block or two away.

'I say, John, you're a bit of all right at outwitting Jerry, aren't you?'

'Haven't outwitted him yet. We're still in town, and we've got a hell of a way to go, Byron. We got away from that one because those were Wehrmacht troops. Professionals. Did it by the books. Riddle any suspicious vehicle first, *then* go see what you find inside.'

'So they shot up an empty truck, and gave us time to get away?'

'Something like that. The SS would have risked their own skins to take us alive. So that they could play games with us. Electric shocks. Whips. Cracked ice in bathtubs. Bone breakers. To find out *who* sent us, and how many more of our boys are still running loose, and so forth. They *say*. I think they just enjoy it. Girl I knew swears she *saw* one of them shoot off in his pants while he was beating her. Come on.'

'Come on *where*, John?'

'That bar over there. Have two drinks of *vin ordinaire* apiece. Enough to make our breath stink of it. . . . Buy a bottle to take home with us. . . .'

'Jean le Fou!' Byron said.

'Only we don't take it home. We pour it all over each other. Patrol stops us, we're reeling, babbling, filthy drunk. Couple of peasants out on the town. Two reasons: that *enmerdeur* of an accent of yours won't be so noticeable if they think you're drunk, and they'll tend to believe us because, being Jerry, they'll be looking for a couple of dashing movie hero spies, not a couple of dirty drunken farmers.'

'We're not too dirty now, old boy. Your little dillies cleaned us up a bit, remember?'

'Oh, shit!' John said. 'We'll have to remedy that. Mud out of the gutter. If we're lucky we can find a little horse dung in one of the streets—'

'Love that smell, don't you, old chap?' Byron quipped.

'Love *any* smell I can smell,' John said. 'What bugs me are the ones I can't. Like the lilies they put in your hands when they lay you out in that pine box, Byron. Now will you please, for Chrissake, come on?'

'You're going to chance going out by Reisbrenner's post, John?' Byron said.

'Hell, no. We're going out by a way where there isn't even a street, let alone a guard post. Leave us pretty high up, and it'll force us to go across two dozen fences, and too goddamned many people's back yards, but I think we can make it. Poor quarter. Mostly workers. Who *love* the FTP and don't love Jerry, Vichy, the Milice, and the Frenchmen enrolled in the Waffen SS, though not necessarily in the order named. I'm gambling none of them will pick up a phone. Fact is, damned few of them *have* phones. Can't afford it. Let's get going, now.'

Again John Farrow's reasoning proved letter perfect. It was hard going, scrambling over fences, crossing yards, once beating off a damned fierce Alsatian shepherd dog, but nobody stopped them. On the two occasions that people threw open back windows, John sang out quietly:

'FTP! Friends!' and the windows closed again, but not before the people in them had given them the V for victory sign.

Then they were all the way out of town, and safe, with the single reservation that they had to circle at least one third of it to get back to the direction they had to go – one reservation that turned out not only to negate their presumed safety, but came very close to being fatal for both of them, for the Waffen SS weren't really professional military men and their minds tended to work like those of the trained policemen they actually were. Unbemused by such abstractions as strategy, topography, manoeuvres, balance of forces, firepower and the like, they brought to bear a long and concrete experience in the ways of fugitives, a knowledge of all, or nearly all, the tricks a hunted man will use, when fleeing for his life.

They assumed from the outset that their quarry wouldn't make any mistakes, that their flight would be foxlike, wily, never the wild stampede of panic. For the men who'd had nerve enough to steal a radio truck, skill enough to know how to use it, intelligent enough to launch that devastating *reductio ad absurdum* attack upon der Führer, were obviously as professional as they.

So Amt IV of the RSHA, the famous or infamous Sipo IV, called the Gestapo, did at once, the necessary, the absolutely correct thing: they ringed Grenoble round about with motorized patrols circling the city, the first five kilometres out of town, the second ten, and the third fifteen.

So it was that long after Byron and John were sure they were safe, they came slogging wearily around a curve in their narrow mountain road and saw a Kübelwagen with four SS men in it, their burpguns aimed and ready, drawn up across their path, blocking it completely.

'Halt!' the Untersturmführer in command shouted, his voice almost soprano with excitement. *'Hände hoch! Kommen Sie hier!'*

John hesitated the barest fraction of a second. His hands flashed by his belt. Then he raised them high as the SS second lieutenant had ordered him to, but by then he had hand grenades in both of them. Byron ducked behind him a moment, then raised his own hands as lethally full as John's.

'Nahern sie sich! Aber langsam, schmutzige schweinige Franzosen!'

They walked towards the Volkswagen as commanded. Slowly, also as commanded. And, from an SS man's point of view they were a pair of filthy swine indeed, whether French or no.

It was then that it came to Byron Graves that his by-then absolute faith in John Farrow's tactical infallibility was on this occasion badly misplaced. Because while a hand grenade is always thrown with one hand just like a baseball, you need two to make it work. Generally speaking, you hold the damned and damnable thing in your right hand, hook the index finger of your left into the ring attached to the firing pin, yank the ring out and down thus setting a delayed action detonator – with a retardation of from five to ten seconds – in motion, and then you throw.

'But how the bloody hell,' Byron groaned inside his mind, 'does one yank the pin of the bastardy things when one has *both* hands full of them?'

Then John showed him how. His left hand blurred sight flying towards his own mouth. His teeth bit into the ring. His left hand jerked away and the grenade looped across the night – too high, too slow, too short, because the burpguns were all ablaze and stuttering by then. Byron saw John pitch forward like a stone, lie there. Then that grenade hit and blew, throwing a hail of gravel and small stones through the Kübelwagen. The windshield dissolved into splinters of glass. The light side doors buckled under the multiple impact. He could hear the SS men screaming in fear, in pain, in rage, but he had no time. Yanking the pin of the grenade he had in his right hand with his teeth Byron Graves lobbed it underhand in perfect cricketers' bowling style into the Kübelwagen, yelling like a madman:

'Leg before wicket, old chaps! How's that for bowling!'

That first grenade had reduced the Kübelwagen into a mass of junk and its occupants into so much shredded meat. But Byron threw in his anyhow, just in case one of the SS men had strength enough left in him to pull a trigger.

Then he bent over John, heard him groan. So he slung John's thin wiry body over his shoulder and got out of there, not by the road, but through the woods, over the boulders, fallen trees, climbing, going on. Which is what they should have done in the first place after crossing the River Drac. That way the Nazis would never have seen them. Only it would have taken far too long.

He knew what the chances were. He knew that his own would be at least doubled by leaving the unconscious, and probably dying burden he was using up the last of his strength to carry. But it is to his eternal credit, to that of his nation, and his race, to the quaint old-fashioned notions of honour bred into his very bone, that Byron Graves didn't give that idea houseroom for as long as one second flat. He kept on struggling upward until suddenly all the night roared, spoke fire, turned into day.

He looked at his watch in that unearthly glare. Grinned. Said: 'Right on the dot! Hell of a chap, that watchmaker!'

Then, as the night closed back in upon him, he heard the scream of air-cooled motors, the snarl of gears pouring down the road towards Grenoble. He hung there, weak with relief. Because the one unexpected factor had defeated the SS after all: to them that thunderous explosion in almost the centre of the city meant that they'd guessed wrong; that the saboteurs whom they were combing the mountain roads in search of, were still in town, probably in force, planning *der Teufel im Hölle* knew not what!

So he went on plodding upward with John on his back. But daylight caught him still a long, long way from the camp. By the light of the rising sun, he examined John's wound. It was a bullet crease along one side of his skull five centimetres above his left temple, and twelve centimetres long. The wound didn't seem very deep, but the fact that John hadn't regained consciousness in all that time made it impossible to rule out skull fracture, or at least a severe concussion. Wounds like this, Byron knew, often caused blindness, and oftener still, loss of memory.

The main problem was that it was still bleeding sullenly. So Byron dragged out his shirt-tails, cut them into strips with his commando knife, and bandaged John's head. All his thick, dark hair was caked, and wet with blood.

Then, because there was nothing else to do, knowing that if the SS had left one patrol car on that road it would be more than enough, he dumped John's inert form into a little hollow and covered him with brush. Then he crawled in beside him, and pulled more dead limbs and moss over his own head and body. They stayed like that all day without food or drink. But by noon John Farrow came back from wherever his oddball warrior's soul had wandered to. He looked at Byron, snarled:

'You should have left me, you Limey jackass!'

'Oh, do be a good chap, John, and shut up, won't you, please?' Byron said.

They got back to camp at midnight, to be greeted as heroes. The FTP man who had received the explosives at his own house for them again took his own life in his hands, out of his excess of joy. Crossing the whole of Grenoble to a quarter where he was not known, he entered a phone booth in a hotel lobby and phoned the mayor of St Nizier, who in his turn raised his colleague in Villars de Lans, and he sent a messenger on a motorcycle up to the camp. The count was very exact: that twenty kilos of gelignite had destroyed the garage, all the vehicles in it, most of those parked outside it on the street, and set the Funkspiel's headquarters afire as well. But one detail held John Farrow riveted to the spot: the bodies of the four sentries guarding the garage and storehouse had been found – what could be found of them, which wasn't much – up to one hundred metres from the epicentre of the explosion.

John looked at Byron, licked his lips and croaked:

'*Seuls?* Alone? Were there – any girls – killed? I mean – young women – who—'

'No,' Eugene Chavant told him. 'Of course, our informant didn't mention that, but it is a detail he scarcely would have missed, would he, my old one?'

But John had bent his head, and the tears ploughed through the grime and dried blood on his face.

'Take him away, *mon capitaine anglais,*' Chavant said. 'He is overtired. See that he eats something, drinks a whole litre of good wine, that he rests . . .'

And it was that very next morning that Réseau Merle, coming up from the south, from Sisteron, Digne, Gap, joined them. It was led by its commander, Pepe, a Spanish Republican refugee, whose name was already a legend throughout the South of France. He was followed by a tall red-haired young man whom John recognized at once, to his own astonishment, as Anton Rabinowski, the same Anton Rabinowski who was supposed to have been the featured violinist at the Albert Hall, John remembered suddenly, and who had failed to show up, the night the blind ex-fighter pilot's fiancée had cried, but who was here now, unexpectedly and inexplicably, with a rifle instead of a fiddle in his shapely hands, among a band of dirty, ragged villainous-looking Maquis, looking as filthy, bearded, hungry, if a trifle less villainous than they. By the insignia pinned on to his shoulder straps, John saw he was second in command.

But the third officer was a girl. A small, slight, not even especially pretty Jewish girl.

Her name was Simone Levy.

7

When John Farrow did sleep finally, he dreamed. And this time the roar of the white water beneath the window of his hotel room in Gorge-du-Loup became the roar of storm winds sweeping down through the Black Forest from the mountains above it, reminding him of the first time he heard 'The Ride of the Valkeries' from Wagner's opera *Die Walküre*.

He was back again in Germany, one of the two countries he had been especially unhappy in; the other, being, of course, the United States of America, theoretically his own. He was also a little boy not more than seven years old. His Papa had brought him – along with Maman and Oncle Dalton, of course – to Baden-Baden in the Schwartzwald because unhealthy people went there to take the waters and to become healthy. For he, little John Dalton Farrow, was much too delicate a child to suit his father – a sort of Teddy Rooseveltian health fanatic really – and also too delicate to suit his Oncle Dalton, which made him much more unhappy than not pleasing his father did.

But the strangest part about his dream was that two of his avatars inhabited it simultaneously, though one of them from a vantage point outside the space, place, action it embraced, and had, moreover the curious power to move away from it voluntarily along the dimension of subsequently elapsed time. For Attorney John Dalton Farrow, a balding, thickening, almost past middle-aged New Yorker, lay in his bed in the hotel at Gorge-du-Loup, perfectly aware that he was dreaming, caught in the grip of a drugged kind of sleep (though he had taken nothing to induce it) yet unable to break free of its curiously sinister, nightmarish hold. And, despite the half-sensed, half-felt obscure quality of menace in that dream, he, the fifty-four-year-old man (and this, perhaps, was the most dreamlike aspect of an experience having its own poignant life, yet unalive) lay there, and with calm and mature detachment, carefully observed everything seven-year-old John Farrow did.

The wind roared through the great trees, and the lightning rent the night with zigzag spears of awful brightness. Die Walküre rode the sky on great storm horses, screaming through the gale. In some cosmic Götterdammerung, all the gods were dying, if not already dead.

('That's wrong,' John Farrow reasoned from the remove of a thousand miles or so of distance and forty-seven bitter years of time; 'that's absurd. A seven-year-old boy simply does not think in those terms. Besides, I was twelve or more before Maman took me to the Bayreuth festival. I had yet to hear a note of that obscene monster's music in those days.')

The lightning's hard psychedelic glare alternately created out of primordial night the sleeping face of the child – '*Mon petit ange adoré,'* his Maman whispered, kissing him – then annihilated it again into the void. ('I *was* a pretty child,' John Farrow observed dispassionately, 'but looks like all life's possessions are temporary: they go, as all things go, swept down the Lethean river of never halting time—')

He heard, simultaneously, in two pairs of ears, the boy's and the man's, that clap of thunder rock the room. But the man lay still and sorrowing on his lonely bed: while the boy leaped from his and ran, eyes and mouth opened wide, screaming soundlessly towards the door that led to his Oncle Dalton's room.

('Look at it,' John Farrow mused: 'Observe well this curious detail: *in extremis,* the child seeks not the shelter of his father's arms. No, he flies to his stalwart manly *oncle.* Or – did he *know?* Had he realized, young as he was, that – no, again, an absurdity. He'd know that Maman was, had to be, in the other room, down the hall, where Papa was.' 'Turn around, you little ninny. You're going the wrong way. Don't open that door. You hear me, boy? 'Tis hell's portal, *petit Jean.* I forbid you to open it. You must not open it. You goddamned little fool, don't open it. *Je t'en supplie, ne l'ouvre pas!* I ask you, I beg you, please!')

But the child, seven-year-old John Dalton Farrow opened the door. Stood in it, staring into that lightning flashed and flickered room. Saw what he saw. Died the death he died. Received the mortal wound – *be fashionable, you ass, call it the trauma!* that—

(Simone was beginning to heal me of, would surely have healed me of, might still heal me of – *she's dead, you fool, dead!* the appalled and appalling recognition rode in upon him – if it hath healing, if it will not bleed for ever, if unheard screams do not tear your gut more bloodily than mere sound.)

('No,' the sleeping man said, 'this is revisionistic history. This scene never happened. Never at all. I am writing back into my life what I learned on an Air France Boeing 747, thirty thousand feet above the Atlantic, two days ago. It did *not* happen. This dream is Freudian. My mind is shaping images to fit that poem. *What* poem? Why:

> Du bist wie eine Blume,
> So hold und schön und rein:
> Ich schau'dich an und Wehmut
> Schleicht mir ins Herz hinein.

To me like some bright blossom,
So sweet, fair, pure, thou art;
I gaze on thee and sadness
Steals deep into my heart.

'*"So hold und schön und rein!"*' the sleeping man wept. 'So lovely and sweet and pure.')

Pure! And that voice in the alternating dark and unearthly glare whispering, whispering breathlessly:

'Pas comme ça mon Dal-ton! Pas comme ça! Pas si doucement, idiot! Sauvage-moi, gros brute! Fais-moi mal! Fais-moi gémir, crier, hurler! Quoi, donc? Il peut nous écouter? Tant pis! Il m'enmerde, tu sais!' ('This,' John Dalton Farrow thought, 'is one hell of a dream. I want out! *'The subconscious buries deep in the psyche things heard, seen, witnessed, in early childhood, too painful, or too shocking to be borne so that – "Il m'enmerde tu sais!"* – I want out. I – want – out!')

And he, fourteen-year-old John Farrow, coming *down* that *piste* – was it in Switzerland? No. Germany again. St Blasein, just behind Lake Schluch – and daring for the first time to close the back angle of that *chaussé neige*, bringing his skis parallel and together and the trees abruptly blurring with the speed and it, the first curve there below him, and he scared spitless, but caught up in the icy masochistic exhilaration that his own fear always awoke in him, not slowing, not opening up the skis into snowplough position, not digging in the poles, seeing the town down there, five hundred metres, more or less, below him, like a tiny toy Christmas town, so white, and the Benedictine monastery in the middle of it and the church and the Bürgerhaus and beyond them the lake rushing up to meet him, and there was that hairpin turn under his skis so fast that he either had to do what Oncle Dalton had shown him how five hundred times or a thousand, or go over that edge and die. So he did it, leaning far over into the curve, turning his ankles in a murderous twist, so that the edges rather than the flats of the skis dug in and threw a rooster-tail of powdered snow six or seven metres high into the trees, and he was around that curve and bent over in racing position, the ski poles tucked up under his arms and pointing backward and all the world was a blur, so white, so white, so white, and the trees so black and there was another curve and then another in the opposite direction and another split *S-virage* and another *U* and another and another and another, until he was around them all and racing down the straight to jam all that speed sidewise into a dead stop with an absolutely perfect Christie right in front of Oncle Dalton *et* Maman *et aussi* Papa and Oncle Dalton saying quietly:

'Well done, John! Now you've got it!' And the air was like wine and he dizzy from sheer joy until Papa said, drily:

'Well if you'd ever learn to speak comprehensible German, we could at least make a ski instructor of you.'

And ruined it all. As always.

('But I did learn to speak it finally. And English. I learned English because it was Dalton's language too and he spoke it beautifully and – by sheer instinct likely – I adored him. But I was speaking Italian the first month of the year we spent in Rome and Spanish within two, when Dalton took me to Andalucia, while German and English both cost me years and I never got German right and even now my accent comes through in English when I'm tired.')

('I never got German right, I never got—')

He was crouching there in the snow – where—? On Count von Kressel's estate and sighting down the barrel of the rifle. There, the deer broke cover, coming in a magnificent bound over a snow-covered log and shaking its antlers. It was a reddish colour and the most beautiful creature that he, sixteen-year-old John Dalton Farrow, had ever seen. But he had to do it. Or else Papa would be angry at him again and even Oncle Dalton would be ashamed of him, so he shut both eyes and jerked the trigger instead of pulling it slowly, smoothly, the way he'd been taught, hoping that way he would miss. The gun-crash reminded him of another sound he couldn't remember, didn't want to remember by then, perhaps, really did not remember (thunder crashing in a silent room? Two naked bodies obscenely entwined there amid the lightning?)

Then all the air was loud with hurrahs! and bravos! and *Heil*! and Count von Kressel, himself, led him up to the fallen deer – its eyes were wide open and big and brown and soft and pitifully accusing, and the red tongue had lolled out of the side of the beautiful creature's mouth. Count von Kressel bent down and cut the dying animal's throat, and catching the blood (thick, hot, steaming in that wintry landscape) in his slim aristocratic hands, smeared it all over John Farrow's face.

That was the custom. The initiation of the boy into the ranks of manhood.

('Into the ranks of mindless killers!' the sleeping man snarled, 'into the band of murderers!')

And he, sixteen-year-old John Farrow turning, and everything he'd eaten for breakfast, coming up the back of his throat in a vile green-tasting rush and spewing out of his mouth into the snow and he, the boy, knowing he would never be a man if by manhood were meant murdering beautiful creatures like that deer, whirling and running away through the dark twilight under the dark trees, into a darkness greater, more terrible, than they knew, but not before he'd heard son papa's voice rasping:

'Why, you damned little effeminate!'

Dark. So dark. And he burying his face into his pillow so that nobody in the huge, half-timbered hunting lodge – where? In Silesia, wasn't it? Or Prussia? – so that nobody in the hunting lodge could hear him crying. Or whispering even, yet even, at sixteen 'Maman! Maman!'

She wasn't there. She wasn't there. She would never be there again. Because Papa had finally caught her doing that bad, awful, filthy thing that men and women do together (and that he, John Farrow also did, but only by himself, in a locked bathroom because he simply couldn't help it, dreaming of some unknown and lovely face atop some imagined – but vaguely, because the details were still unclear to him, for he'd never seen a girl with less on than a bathing suit – excitingly naked body) with somebody else. *Not* son Oncle Dalton. Oncle Dalton was in Nice. Or Paris. Or maybe London. Or New York.

And he – time shuddering, shifting backward a whole bleak year – going down to the kitchen to get a piece of Apfelstrudel from Hilda the cook – heard through the closed door that kind, jolly, so *gemütlich* voice, hoarse with mockery, with triumph saying:

'*Sie waren nicht einmal in dem Schlafzimmer, sondern in der Halle! Sie taten Ihr Schmutz auf dem Sofa! Die Französin war ganz und gar nackt! Ja, so! Gott hilfe mir! Ich sah ihn so wohl als sie mit meinen zwei Augen! Diese französiche hure hat ihren schlüpfer und Büstenhalter von sich quer über die Halle gewerfen! Und sie hat den Alten Esel nicht gehören als er hinein gekommen ist – und mit funf Offizieren von der*

Luftwaffe! – weil sie so viel Lärm machte! Ihr Schlafkamerad? Ein Junge. Ein sehr schöner blonder Kerl von der SA. Der Führer hat recht! Die Franzosen sind durch Sinnenlust verdorben!'

And he hanging there before that door feeling all the artificial and largely emotional barriers he had erected against all things German crumbling letting meaning through now when he least of all wanted that meaning or could bear to understand what Hilda was saying; but he *did* understand it, and thereafter would always understand German with no more effort than his other languages cost him, except that the meaning came over to him in English, not in French, probably because German and English are at least first cousins while neither of them have any real kinship with the Latin tongues at all. He hung there, shuddering, taking it.

'They weren't even in the bedroom but in the foyer. They were doing their filth on the sofa. The Frenchwoman was stark mother naked. Yes, it's so! God help me if it isn't. I saw him and her both with my two eyes! This French whore had thrown her panties and her bra clear across the foyer. And she didn't hear the old jackass when he came in – and *five* air force officers with him! – because she was making so much noise! Her bedfellow? A youngster. A very handsome, blond boy from the SA. The leader's got them right! These French people are sensual degenerates!'

Dark! He was coming down that *piste* on skis, the world blurring out, lifting that rifle, hot, thick, sticky blood on his face and the green nausea drowning him. His tears drowning him. 'Maman! Maman!' She wasn't here in the hunting lodge, she would never be anywhere he and Papa were again, because der Anwalt stood up in the Gerichtshof and said to the Richter one word or maybe two *'in flagrante'* and Maman was gone on a Lufthansa plane back to Paris and he, John Farrow, was here because Papa had been granted full custody of him and what's more didn't have to pay *pauvre Maman* one *sou* of *pension alimentaire. Sa pauvre petite Maman* who would surely starve!

Dark. So dark. And then, abruptly, light. It was coming towards him, coming towards him slowly, coming towards, becoming the most beautiful light in the world, a candle flame with blonde nineteen-year-old Heide von Kressel's face afloat in its glow, suspended on the dark – '*wie einer blume so hold und süss und* – God!'

And her voice whispering, 'Was gibts bei dir, Johann? Bist du krank?'

And he snarling: 'No, I am not sick! I hate killing things, Heide! So, my father says I'm an effeminate and maybe he's right, because—'

'*Der Vater ist ein Narr. Und ein Esel* – with long, hairy ears. And you, my beautiful, beautiful boy are not an effeminate which I, to you, presently will prove.'

'Prove?' he gasped. 'Prove it, how, Heide?'

'First, we must lock the door. Like this. And then—' She put the candlestick on the bureau and reaching down her slim, suntanned – even in winter – hands, caught at the hem of her nightgown. She swept it up over her head, and pirouetted, posed on tiptoe, her arms curving in an arc above her head, and she laughing, a little tremulously. 'You like me, Johann? *Bin ich schön nackt?*'

And he, unable to speak, staring at all that slim, perfect loveliness, being especially startled by the pale downy tufts in the hollow of her armpits, and the thick, darker blonde thatch, pluming up on to her belly from between her thighs, because he'd never dreamed that creatures so *féerique, angélique* as girls shared any of the characteristics of bestial man, but looking at her with so much awe, reverence, worship (Galahad beholding the Holy Grail!) that she laughed even more merrily, said:

'*Jawohl!* I can see you do. But in the wrong way, *mein engelgleiches Liebling*! So now I must teach you the *right* way. Move over!'

'Move – over?' he gasped.

'Ja. To make room for me. But first you will remove those ugly pyjamas! *Bitte!* Do not be ashamed. You must be naked for me, as I am naked for you. *Bitte* – please! *Ach-so! Wie schön du bist, mein Johann!* Now. *Wir sind jetz zuzammen*. Together. Put your arms around me. *Ach – so! Ganz gut!* Now kiss me *Küss mich! Ah! Noch einmal. Viel mehr. So. Mein Lieber. Mein* beautiful, beautiful *Knabe mit lockigem, schwartzem Harr!*'

He straightened up, sick with shame, wailed:

'Heide!'

'*Was ist los, Liebling?*'

'I – I – I don't know what to do!'

And the tenderness getting into her voice, and she saying softly:

'Ach, Gott! My little love. My angelic, little love. I will teach you. For me a very great happiness is this, you know—'

'What? *Was ist für dich ein sehr grosses Glück, Heide?'*

'That I will be your very first love. That, to me is beautiful. That is *für mich so schön* it makes me cry. So – *küss mich! Ach, mein kleines Liebchen!* Not like that. Do not close thy mouth, not altogether. *Ach, gut. Süss!* So sweet. . . .'

'Und jetz?' he said. 'And now?'

'Not so fast! We have all night. Mein Vater has back to town gone – for two days. So – *küss mich. Aber nicht jetzt auf dem Mund.* But not in the mouth.'

'Then – where?'

'Hier, Liebling – und hier. Du bist mein kleines Kind, nicht wahr? My tiny, little baby boy. So kiss me here and here and here and everywhere! And now – touch me. With the hands. Oh, my little innocent! Give me thy hand, and I will show you where! Ah – so. Ahh sso! Ahhh so! *Und so und so und so und* – halt! Stop it. I am ready now—'

'But Heide—'

'Come into my arms, baby boy. *Ja,* so. On top of me. So. Keep still! I will thee hinein put. Ahhh – *darin* – so! What a *big* boy you are now, *Liebling!'*

The man asleep on the bed, so very far away in time, smiling sadly, tenderly, with amusement saying: 'Poor little fool. He won't last three seconds now—'

And Heide's voice saying: *'Ach! So schnell, Liebling?'*

And the boy, John Farrow, sadly:

'Es tut mir sehr leid, Heide! I am sorry!'

'Why? We still have all night and all day tomorrow and all tomorrow night, for thy father with my father also to town has gone. So now. Turn over. Lie there. Now I will kiss you. And touch you. And play with thy little dead soldier gently, softly, slowly and even kiss him a little bit like this – *süss!* – *Ach,* sweet! And – wonderful! A miracle! See how he stands to attention, *mein kleiner Liebling!'*

'Ah, youth!' the sleeping man said fondly, 'a hair trigger, but what a quick reload!'

'Now – there. Put him – there. Where he wants to go. *Ach,*

there! Inside me. Way, way up inside me. Now! – slowly, *Liebling. Langsam. Slllowly – Laangsam – Sloowlly – Ach! Nicht so langsam*. Not so slowly. Not at all slowly! *Schnell! Sehr schnell! Sehr schnell! Schnell, mein Reiter!* Quickly my horseman, my rider, ride me! Faster! Faster Faster Faster *Ach – Gott! Wunderbar!*'

Dark. And the lights coming up on the stage. And Joan Fontaine in the leading role – what was that play? Oh yes – *Tea and Sympathy* – tugging at the zipper of her skirt and smiling gently, maternally, tenderly at the petrified boy they were calling effeminate, even accusing of overt homosexuality, and he, John Dalton Farrow, attorney at law, touched upon this one warm, wonderful chord of memory, the one good thing he could recall of his sojourn in The Third Reich, letting one lone tear steal down his lean, in-hollowed cheek, and Candace, his wife, saying mockingly:

'Now really, John! It's not *that* good!'

'Must wake up!' John Farrow said. 'I absolutely must wake up! Because when Candace starts getting into my goddamned dreams – it's time!'

He jerked himself upright. Opened his eyes. The sunlight poured into his window.

'*Merde alors!*' he said, 'it must be—' Then: 'What the hell? What's my hurry, anyhow?'

While he was having a leisurely breakfast, he tried to sort the real from the unreal in his dream. But he could not. In retrospect it all seemed real.

'And probably was,' he conceded. 'Very likely it did happen just that way – or close to it. God knows, my love affair with Heide was remarkably exact. Her father smeared blood over my face. But Heide initiated me into the rites of manhood, bless her! Poor Heide. Poor, long-dead murdered Heide – another of my ghosts. . . .'

He drank the scalding coffee slowly.

'Real – and unreal. Real is what you recognize, perceive. Unreal is what you don't. I was *there*. I saw those signs: '*Juden Raus!*' '*Eingang für Juden Verboten!*' And that real cute one: 'Dangerous Curve! Speed twenty kilometres an hour. For Jews, one hundred kilometres an hour!'

'And to me, it was all unreal. Because I didn't *know* a single

Jew. And Papa didn't tell me the house we lived in, in Berlin had been requisitioned from one of them. Nor that he sought the poor devil out and paid him for it, ten thousand dollars cash. The ten thousand that saved his life, because he bribed his way out with the money. Got to France, rejoined his family. Took them to the States, because Papa told him:

' "Don't stay there, sir! Go on to America, to New York, with your family. France will crumble like a house of cards, once Hitler hits her. As he will. As he is going to. I've lived there half my life. I know. France, as a nation, died in World War I. Bled to death. And ghosts make damned poor fighters . . ." '

'Poor old stick!' John Farrow said half-aloud. 'Did he ever do an unfair, a dishonourable thing? No, never. Did my real, if illegitimate, father ever do a fair, an honourable thing? No, never. And he had life eating out of his hands, while nobody ever loved poor Papa, not even me . . .'

'Jesus! What a rough time he had after that episode! Writing letter after letter to the State Department, to the secretary of State, to Roosevelt himself, begging to be relieved, sent elsewhere, allowed to resign. He even told Roosevelt the bitter truth: that his position in Germany had been irrepairably harmed by the scandal and the divorce. As it had been. That story was too rich to keep. Rich hell! Too ripe. That goddamned Brownshirt bastard jumping up with his riding breeches down around his boot ankles, and poor Maman trying to cover her nakedness with the sofa cushions!

'They spread that one all over town. And they weren't even Nazis. Luftwaffe officers of the highest social class. Even Hitler heard it. Dropped a hint to our ambassador that a consul who was as big a fool as Papa really ought to be recalled. But Roosevelt wasn't having any. Papa was a first-class diplomat, and a personal friend of his. So the ambassador got his back up. And the next time one of Von Ribbentrop's lackeys brought the matter up with the snide remark that immorality in the family of a diplomat was an insult to the customs of the German state, the ambassador replied:

'What customs? Incest? It would be difficult to supply Mr Farrow with a Fraulein Raubal.'

'And stopped them cold. The morality of the Master Race! Hitler sleeping with his own niece – Sleeping, hell! Little Geli was being taken care of quite nicely in that department by that ex-convict bodyguard of his – what was the name something French, oh yes, Emil Maurice. And Byron got it wrong – Der Führer was *not* rough with women. Just the contrary. Abject masochism was his thing. Still, Geli Raubal shot herself. Cruelty? There's more than one kind. Having to use your lover's face for a chamber pot, and his naked carcass for a parade ground – in the reglementary spike-heeled shoes of course! must have been discouraging after a time—'

He sat on the terrace, his breakfast finished, looking out over the mountains. He was contemplating bleakly what that thought about the sexual morals of the Third Reich inevitably led to. That life leaves a man nothing. Not even his first joy, his earliest illusion.

'Heide. How was I to know that the Countess von Kressel – correction! – that Bavarian shop girl Kaspar von Kressel married – was a fanatical Nazi? That she shipped poor little Heide off to the Hitler *Jungmaedel* at age ten? Result? *Mein Rose, mein Lilie,* my dove, and my sun! had been screwed by all and sundry *before* age twelve. Brought home by the count from the BDM, the *Bund Deutscher Mädel,* only slightly pregnant at eighteen. A year before I came upon the scene. An abortion is procured. Count von Kressel is damned well *not* going to allow his daughter to repeat his own mistake – especially after having had to obtain a divorce from her mother under circumstances remarkably similar to those that wrecked poor Papa's life.

'So Heide's home again, kept, it would seem, under strictest watch. But *nobody* was watching me. Why should they? A skinny kid, three whole years her junior, whose own father is more than half-convinced he is going to grow up to be a queer?

'So – Heide, who has been laid often enough to learn to like it, is – to be vulgar – hard up. And there *I* am. There's my great, my first, my wondrous love! Hell, I was so damned innocent that I thought *all* the things she did were a normal part of every woman's repertoire—'

He grinned wryly.

'Getting to be, these days. The world's catching up. Still – Heide. And I still bless her, poor, abused darling. She appeared in that doorway at the right time. Confirmed the heterosexual inclinations Papa didn't think I had. Gave me another identity to cling to: man and lover! Showed me I could be both without descending too far down the evolutionary scale. That I damned well could remain above all the killer beasts, and even a hair above both ape and goat, and still function adequately enough as a male.

'Poor Heide! The second of my Bluebeard's harem of female ghosts! Had that – the goddamned horrors of her death thrown into my teeth – by her father. Not that he was blaming me especially. It was just – guilt by association. Didn't like the company we Limeys and Yanks kept. Can't say I blame him. Lord, it took me time to break free of Germany for good! Because there I was again – with Byron. After De Gaulle had pinned the Cross of the Liberation on both of us in London. Even kissed us on both cheeks. It's his way of compensating for the rough deal he gave us in Toulon? I doubt it – Le Grand Charles never felt the slightest need to compensate for anything—

'Last job old Byron and I were ever to do together. Interrogation of prisoners amid the ruins of Hitler's Götterdammerung. No way to get out of that tedious chore, not with German heading the list of languages spoken on both our service records—'

He could remember that as though it were yesterday: he and Byron Graves sitting behind a long desk in a half-ruined Bürgerhaus somewhere in Germany, and the lines shuffling forward and the two of them droning: 'Name, rank, serial number, service record—'

And that haggard, broken man in a Wehrmacht general's uniform staring at him, then suddenly, switching into perfect Oxonian English:

'You're young John Farrow, aren't you? Remember that deer you killed on my estate? You had scant stomach for blood in those days, I recall. This war has taught me that's an admirable trait, rather. Hope this bloody business hasn't changed you.'

'Count von Kressel!' John Farrow said, then to his orderly: 'Bring up a chair for the general, sarge. He's an old, old friend of mine.'

Gratefully, Count von Kressel took the seat. Without even asking him, simply by looking at his insignia, John Farrow called off his name, rank, serial number, unit of command to the enlisted man at the typewriter. But birthplace and dates he had to ask. He, himself, added, without even putting that question to the count: 'Never a member of the Nazi Party. An active opponent of the Hitler regime.'

Byron stared at him. Count von Kressel smiled and said:

'Don't worry, colonel. Captain Farrow happens to be telling the truth. He does know what he is talking about. His father and I were intimate friends for a good many years. By the way, John, how is he?'

'As well as can be expected I suppose. That – divorce business didn't help, you know, sir. But he seems to be bearing up. He's in Genève – our embassy, there. Waiting for me to be demobbed. Then we'll go back to New York. I'm to finish law at Harvard – and then, we'll see. Now it's my turn: How's – Heide?'

Von Kressel looked down. Stared at his dusty boots. Looked up again.

'Dead,' he said harshly. 'She married a young Panzer officer – who came back from Russia with no feet, and only one hand. Frozen. Had to take them off. They were in Berlin – what was left of it – when the Russians arrived. You know how Heide looked. Striking girl. Deuced pretty. I can say that even though she was my own. An honest assessment, what? She was *very* fond of you, my boy. Always swore that if you'd been four years older she'd never have let you get away—'

'Thank you, sir,' John Farrow whispered: 'It was kind of her to say that. And of you to tell me. I – I was quite desperately in love with her, sir. At that age, one—'

'Oh, I knew that! It showed, my boy. A pity you weren't old enough – even to have eloped, I mean. Because now my daughter would be alive instead of—'

'Please, sir!' John said. 'You don't have to talk about that! It's not my business, nor even the army's—'

'I know. But I want it known. I want your army to know it. And your government. You've no connection with the new President, I suppose? Your father and Mr Roosevelt were very close, as I remember.'

'No,' John said. 'I've never even seen President Truman, sir.'

'Still I want it known! See that Foster Dulles hears it, anyhow. So that he can explain to your government what kind of allies you have, at least. Put it fairly. My daughter was only one case. And there were thousands. Girls not yet pubescent. Old women of eighty. The ones too young and too old, died of the abuse. The young and healthy, like my Heide, didn't—'

'But sir! You said—'

'I know. She's dead. But she didn't die – of that. Say rather that she died at the hands of a fool and out of a fool's conception of honour!'

Byron Graves raised his hand, halting the line of men still to be questioned. The sergeant at the typewriter sat there, his boy's mouth and eyes opened wide. The top sergeants who were herding the long, green-clad lines in stopped them at the door, but they themselves eased closer.

'They were Mongols, Tartars,' Von Kressel said. 'Balts, too, maybe. Croats. Serbs. Who knows? About fifty of them. And they all raped her. Some of them twice, and three times. And they made my son-in-law watch.'

'Jesus!' John Farrow said. 'But you said that wasn't the cause—'

'Of Heide's death? It wasn't. My son-in-law shot her – after they had gone. And then, of course, himself. Bungled both jobs, the poor crippled fool! From the evidence, it took them both quite a long time – and considerable pain – to die—'

And he, remembering it, hearing his own youthful voice in that bedroom, in the hunting lodge, whispering into her shell pink ear:

Die Rose, die Lilie, die Taube, die Sonne,
Die liebt' ich einst alle in Liebeswonne.
Ich lieb' sie nicht mehr, ich liebe alleine
Die Kleine, die Feine, die Reine, die Eine,
Sie selber, alle Liebe Bronne,
Ist Rose und Lilie und Taube und Sonne.

The rose, lily and dove, the clear sunlight,
Them loved I all once in love's delight.
I love them no more, now love I alone
The smallest, the finest, the purest, my own;
She, herself, being the fount of all love's delight,
Is rose, lily, and dove, and clear sunlight.

And she turning and kissing him and the world being reborn again and again until it was all too much to be endured, to be borne, and she clinging to him and crying, and babbling damned fool things like: 'I have been purified by thy innocence, *mein Liebling*! Thy love has made me once more clean!' that he didn't understand then, and would not understand until he got back to Berlin, and mentioned her name to Robin Lowell – of the Brookline, Mass., Lowells, the diplomatic corps still being the exclusive preserve of people with names like Lowell, Biddle, Stuyvesant, Van Pensselaer, and Farrow, in those days – who was a classmate of his in the American school that diplomats' and military attachés' children went to, only to be met with: 'Von Kressel's daughter – that little tramp! Where'd you meet *her*? Brother, is *she* ever a hot little number! Only character in Germany who *hasn't* screwed her is Hitler, himself, and he can't even get it up. Did she give *you* any?' And died. Again. This new death being just as ugly, sickening, bad, as the other he'd suffered last year, outside that kitchen door.

'I wonder,' John Farrow thought now with wry amusement, 'if it wasn't *that*, that enlisted me in my personal crusade against Nazism? Or at least against the Brownshirt boys—'

For, pressed for details, Robin Lowell had given them, abundantly. And always, or nearly always, it had been the SA who had shared Heide's girlish revels. 'Last year, her *LandsJahr*, y'know, Farrow – she went on a picnic with *seven* of those Sturmabteilung types. And a good time was had by all, especially by dear Heide. Simple arithmetic, Farrow, old boy: she *had* to have seven times as much fun as any one of them. Stands to reason, doesn't it? Only on that occasion, your new little friend seems to have exaggerated that Kraft Durch Freude business. For the next thing anyone knows is that Count Von Kressel yanked his erring daughter out of the BDM – and she's home again where rumour has it – and rumour, my friend, as far as hanky-panky is concerned, nearly always has it right! – she's busily engaged in tossing up her *pfannküchen* every morning while the count decides what to do. Getting out the family shotgun and making the type do right by our little Nell is definitely out. Even in Hitlerdom, marrying seven prospective fathers at one time is considered bad form. So—'

'So,' John Farrow remembered, 'when Otto, Papa's chauffeur came after me with the car, that same day, I told him I was going to *walk* home from school for a change. Funny. He didn't argue very much. Could he see what a mood I was in, or did the bastard *want* me to learn the hard way what the Third Reich was really like? Because a limousine, like most of the things that too damned much money can buy provides an excellent insulation against life—'

It hadn't been on a tiny side street but on that grand boulevard that runs straight across the heart of Berlin, changing its name at intervals as it goes, because, as in most European capitals, there were more famous men to name streets after than streets to name after them; but specifically on that part of it known as Königstrasse, just before – or just after, depending on which direction you're going – it becomes Unter den Linden, that he, sixteen-year-old (but no longer innocent, thanks to darling Heide!) John Farrow saw it:

Two people, a man and a woman, were scrubbing the sidewalk. Around them a band of teen-aged oafs clad in the brown Sturmabteilung uniform stood. They had taken off their broad leather belts, and were using them to beat the man and the woman across their poor skinny tails. The man and the woman were both above sixty. The woman's white hair had come loose, and was trailing down into the dirty, soapy wetness as she scrubbed.

John Farrow hung frozen. Then one of the SA boys deliberately kicked the poor old woman in the ass so hard that she fell forward, and her face skidded a good metre or so across the sidewalk. When she looked up again, it wasn't a face any more. It was a bloody mess.

And young John Farrow discovered then and there that he wasn't the coward he had believed he was all his life. ('I had my definitions mixed up,' he thought now: 'I thought that to be brave was not to be afraid. But Paris and Vercors and the campaign in Provence taught me better. A brave man is one who overcomes his fear – or at least dominates it enough to function effectively. A coward is the poor bastard who can't. And the type who isn't afraid at all is, in any kind of serious action, two things: a monumental jackass, and shortly thereafter, dead.')

He put his books down on the sidewalk and sailed into eight tall muscular Brownshirts any one of whom was more than a match for him on the best day of his life, screaming:

'Verbrecher! Mörder! Schweinhunde! Hurenshone!' (Criminals! Murderers! Pigdogs! Sons of bitches!) and for five or six minutes gave a little better than he got, probably because astonishment held them in check.

Then, the poor old man, seeing his dark complexion, and

curly black hair said to him, not in Yiddish, because after all Yiddish *is* a form of German, and the SA would have understood it, but in Hebrew: *'Lekh lekha, mein sohn! Lekh lekha, bitte!'* ('Get out of here, my boy! Get out, please!')

And the SA heard him. One of them bawled: *'Ein Jude! Dieser Bastard ist ein Jidd!'*

Then, very seriously, they started to blind, maim, and murder – in the order named – young John Farrow.

And he, not knowing that Otto had been creeping the black Mercedes-Benz along, half a block behind him, was sure that he was going to die. But he didn't run. He stood and fought like a man.

'Or like a cornered cat?' John Farrow asked himself now, sardonically. 'No. Wasn't it rather that I was forming hateful images in my head – bloody, battered, all but broken that it was? Maman snatching up those cushions, clawing them over her nakedness, while that Brownshirt stood there, his breeches about his ankles, and only slowly beginning to lose his erection? Or those seven Brownshirts lining up, while poor Heide, drunk, giggling, skirt above her midriff, pantyless and gapelegged sprawls *auf dem Heidekraut*, waiting? They were trying to kill me. But damn me for an Aryan blond, if I wasn't trying like hell to return the compliment!

'And Otto? He sat there behind the wheel and thoroughly enjoyed the spectacle. Let those thugs beat the shit out of me. It wasn't until they had me down and had started to kick my ribs in that he got out of the car and yelled at them in that half-soprano falsetto bark that nobody who isn't a German officer – except maybe Byron! – can hope to duplicate:

'Halt! Ich bin der Oberstürmbannführer Klutz; und dies ist ein Befehl! Verdammte Tölpel! Horen Sie auf!' ('Halt! I'm Lieutenant-Colonel Klutz, and this is an order! You goddamned oafs! Stop it!')

'Did any one of them ever disobey an order – especially when it was screamed at them in that mad castrate's tone of voice – in all of their history? Almost never. Shout at them to shoot their own mothers, or screw them – and they leap to obey. Wasn't it Franz Josef of Austria who actually had designed a new decoration to be given to a soldier who performed a meritorious service while *disobeying* orders? That should be the highest award in any army on earth. Because the exact difference between a soldier and a man is that a man must ultimately bear the responsibility of his acts, accept their consequences. He has no presidential hand to shove by justice when he's ordered to 'waste' babies and is insane enough or criminal enough to obey. Who else is also wrong is not the point; how high the guilt rises among the top brass is a matter for subsequent judicial action. A man must not be allowed to 'absent himself from humanity awhile' because some dimwit with braid on his cap and salad on his chest has told him to. Even though those babies be Dinks, Slants, Gooks, or what have you.

'Funny. Only the Teutons and their descendants, the Anglo-Saxons, have been in a position historically to carry to its ultimate extreme that sick cancer of racism that blooms forever in the heart of man – and they both tried and nearly succeeded at genocide. But given the position, and the power to act, would any other people behave differently – or better? By the records, no. The Doctrine of Original Sin is the truest estimate of the basic condition of this two-legged, ugly, naked ape, *homo*, often enough at least sexually, but *sapiens*? Oh no, not ever in this world!

'Yet that episode had one value surely: It taught me once and for all that there *are*, after all, men of quality; *hommes san peur et sans reproche*! Yes, Papa – poor old stick! Bumbling, dull, a cuckold, and a fool, the laughing stock of Berlin, maybe – but a man, what's more a gentleman, another of the terms we sneer at now.

'Because he knew, he had to know! that Otto was an SS spy. And that he – or at least his known friendship with Franklin Delano Roosevelt – rated the attention of the best. A full Oberstürmbannführer! But when Otto brought me home – with both eyes blackened and swollen shut, three fractured ribs, my left canine incisor gone, cuts about the face, bruises all over me – after having berated me roundly all the way for interfering in a matter of no concern to me (Am I my brother's keeper? Not when my brother is a member of Die Untermenschen!) and telling me over and over again how furious *mein Vater* was going to be – Papa listened very quietly to Otto's loud, angry, and only slightly distorted telling of my saga, for he was too shrewd an article to stray too far from the truth, he turned to me and said, not in English but in German so that Lt. Col. Otto Klutz of the SS would not fail to understand: 'You behaved well, John. Well and honourably. I'm very proud of you, my boy!'

'And the *next* day we were out of Germany at last: *persona non grata*! Interfering with the internal affairs of the Third Reich. Interfering with – murder. And ineffectually at that, for those Stormtroopers kicked that poor old couple to death, after I had gone. Then, Switzerland for two more years. Then back to the States for my college degree. Then law school for a year. Until Pearl Harbor. Until somebody told Wild Bill Donovan about, quote, my remarkable gift for languages, unquote, and—'

He got into the little red car and drove back up to Tourette-sur-Loup, which took him all of five minutes. He got out of the car and walked up the cobble stoned street much too narrow for any vehicle wider that a motor-cycle to pass through. Came to that house at the end, hanging over the edge of the precipice.

Or where it should have been. For it wasn't there any more.

He looked over the edges, saw the pile of broken stones it had been reduced to, sprawled in a long jumble from about twelve metres below him to all way down to the bottom of the gorge. Say one hundred metres. No, nearer two. Then something caught his eye. A glint of metal. Dull bluish gray. All the way down, sticking out from among the rocks. He couldn't be sure, but it looked like a sort of safe. Or strong-box. Only it seemed too small to be either one. Then the light shifted, a cloud passed over the sun. Stayed there. Ten minutes. A quarter of an hour. When the sun broke through again, it – or rather the earth – had moved enough so that its rays no longer struck the bottom of the gorge. He couldn't see that metallic glint any more.

He stood wondering whether that object really was a box, and if so, whether he should take the considerable risk that climbing down to retrieve it entailed. In the end he decided it wasn't worth it, that breaking his neck for what might well be a baking tin, or the lid of a garbage pail, or even one of those square tins cookies were sometimes sold in, wouldn't help anything.

So he turned around to see an old, old woman staring at him. She was at least ninety, he guessed.

'Bonjour, madame,' he said politely.

'Bonjour, mon fils,' she cackled. *'C'était les boches, qui ont fait ça. Le jour qu'ils l'ont tué.* ('Good day, my son, it was the Nazis who did that. The day they killed him.')

He hung there. Simone's tiny delicate face was there before

him floating in an aureole of light upon the misty air. Her green eyes were gazing upon him sorrowfully. But she was fading fast out of time and mind.

'The day they killed *whom*, grand-mère?' he got out.

'Le poète Le grand poète anglais. Il ètait si beau, tu sais, mon fils. Et si gentil avec tout le monde. Nous l'avons aimé beaucoup, beaucoup—' ('The poet. The great English poet. He was so handsome, you know, son. And so kind with everybody. We loved him very, very much!')

'But how was he *called*, this great English poet of yours, grand-mère? He had a name, did he not?'

The old woman frowned.

'Je n'en souviens plus, fils. Suis vielle, tu sais.' ('I don't remember any more, son. I'm an old woman, you know.')

'Try to remember, grand-mère! Try,' John Farrow said.

But she shook her old white head.

'Je n'en souviens plus,' she said. ('I don't remember any more.')

John Farrow took a deep breath.

'Was it – Ross, grand-mère?' he whispered: 'Dalton Ross?'

Light broke behind those tired, filmy old eyes.

'Oui, fils, c'était bien ça! Dal-ton Ross!' ('Yes, son, that was it! Dalton Ross!') *'Beau, très haut taillé, blond, célèbre. Avant la guerre, les journalistes, ils sont venus et—'* ('Good looking, very tall, blond, famous. Before the war, reporters came and—').

John Farrow bent his head, whispered: 'Merci, mille fois, grand-mère . . .' Then he turned and went back to the square. 'I'll ask someone else,' he thought. 'She's too old. She may be mistaken – mixed up – wrong—'

But he knew she wasn't. He'd flown the whole goddamned Atlantic Ocean for nothing. His last forlorn chance was gone. Then the little Renault came in sight before him and he saw the two gendarmes standing beside it. He walked up to them.

'La voiture, c'est la vôtre, m'sieur?' one of them said. ('Is this your car, mister?')

'Mine, no,' he said, 'that I have rented it, yes.'

Et vous êtes M'sieur Farrow?' ('And you are Mr Farrow?')

'I am,' John Farrow said.

'Will you have the goodness to accompany us to the Commissariat, m'sieur?'

John Farrow stared at them.

'And if I don't have the goodness?' he said.

'That would be regrettable, for in such a case we should be forced to place you under arrest, m'sieur!'

'On what charges, may I ask?'

'If you accompany us voluntarily, none. If not, if you force us to arrest you, there are several most excellent charges we might employ.'

'Such as?'

'Suspicion of acting as an agent of a foreign power to the injury of the sovereignty of France. Suspicion of engaging in terrorism. Suspicion of conspiracy to commit – murder, m'sieur. Are these not enough?'

John Farrow grinned at them suddenly.

'And I also stole the panties off Brigitte Bardot,' he said solemnly, 'and if you will give the telephone number of Catherine Deneuve, I will explain to her the advantages of allowing me to father her next child.'

They looked at him without cracking a smile. The strangest part about it was, that he knew that the French have an excellent sense of humour. Only it seemed not to be in working order since the late great General de Gaulle had come to power. At least not as far as foreigners were concerned.

'This is not a matter for joking, m'sieur!' the gendarme who had been doing all the talking said.

'Very well,' John Farrow sighed, 'I will accompany you. But on the condition that we go in *my* car. Or that at least one of you comes along with me in my pauvre, petite Renault. That way, when m'sieur le commissaire and I have finished our little chat, it will be unnecessary for you to bring me back here to retrieve it. *D'accord?*'

They looked at each other, grim, unsmiling.

'*Voyons, mes gars!*' John Farrow said with not a little exasperation; 'I have not even a pocket-knife on me, as you can easily ascertain. I am old enough to be the father of either of you. And also, I am guilty of absolutely nothing, and am not in the least a fool. You delay me, true, but since I am here on vacation, that is hardly a serious matter. I will not attempt to play either James Bond or the godfather. I have neither the agility nor the strength. And this is becoming a bore. Come, what do you say?'

'*Parole d'honneur* you will not attempt to escape?'

'Word of honour,' John Farrow said.

8

'Il faut que je fasse une mise en accusation après tout,' the commissaire said grimly; *'parce que cette petite espèce d'une Golda Meir qu'ils nous ont envoyé de Paris, n'aura pu arriver jusqu'à demain!'*

John Farrow looked at him. 'Where have I seen that face before?' he thought. He looked at the little sign on the commissaire's desk. 'M le Com. E. Poisson' it read. The name told him nothing. Mister the Commissioner E. Fish, in English. But the face was familiar. 'Too young,' John decided, 'to have fought in World War Two. But – is he? How about that last bunch of Milice we captured at Mougins? Captured, hell! Stopped those Johnny-come-lately types who'd suddenly transformed themselves into Heroes of the Resistance when the last Kraut was out of sight from shooting. Kids. Fourteen to eighteen at the most. And this one – why damn my eyes! – he *was* one of them! That miserable little starved rat's face – a trifle more flesh on it now, but not much. And his pants are dry now, anyhow. When we untied him from that post, they were soaked, and he smelt of shit to high heaven. Can't blame the poor little bastard for that, looking into the muzzles of those twelve rifles will loosen most types' sphincters. Grown men's, not to mention a skinny fifteen-year-old kid. . . .'

He said quietly:

'If you're going to book me, m'sieur le commissaire, you'll have to put your charges in writing. My lawyers will demand the right to see them. So, let's not be hasty, shall we? And why *can't* this little species of a Golda Meir you mentioned get here until tomorrow? Paris–Nice is less than an hour by jet, these days. . . .'

The commissaire stared at him. His little rat's eyes glittered.

'They have it right, the Jews,' he snapped. 'This type is no more an American than I am!'

'You have my passport before you, m'sieur,' John Farrow said.

'A passport – bah! Anyone who so wishes, and has the money and the connections can procure a passport. And one so well forged that he can travel to Moscow and Peking both with it.

But what cannot be arranged M'sieur *le soi-disant* Farrow, *soi-disant américain*, is for any American whatsoever to speak the kind of French you do. That was, shall we say, not at all intelligent of you, my friend. You should have faked an accent, any kind of an accent. So now—'

'So now m'sieur le commissaire will have the goodness to *look* at the passport. Those words 'place of birth' mean '*lieu de naissance*'. Is this not very clear? What are the two words separated by a comma which follow it?'

'*"Lieu de naissance — Paris, France!"*' the commissaire read, aloud. '*Oh, merde!* You're saying that you're French by birth, and American only by naturalization?'

'Not exactly. I am an American, born in France of a French mother and American father. I lived most of my childhood in Paris, and even returned to France for my summer vacations every year after my father – a member of the American diplomatic corps – had been transferred to Berlin. All this is a matter of record. So mister the commissioner of the police of Grasse will have to forgive me if I fail to speak my mother's tongue badly. That is not my fault. She taught me to speak it well.'

'And what was your mother's name?' The commissaire snapped at him. 'Where was *she* born? And—'

John Farrow smiled. Police technique was the same all over the world, mainly because the same kind of people became or drifted into police work, everywhere.

'*Yvette Farrow, née Duclos, à Reims, le douze janvier 1898,*' he said, '*fille d'Henri et Berthe Duclos, professeurs, tour les deux, dans le lycée supérieur de la même ville.* Anything else you'd like to know, m'sieur?'

'Yes. What you are *really* doing in France, and the motives for your asking so many questions about nos bons citoyens juifs' m'sieur!'

'My motives were exactly what I stated to M'sieur Feingold, sir. I was trying to trace an old friend of mine, more precisely a fiancée – during the war at least – who merely happened to be of that religion. I failed then, and I fail now, to see the necessity for making une si grosse affaire of such a simple thing as a question put by an ageing sentimentalist about the whereabouts of the girl – the middle-aged woman now, of course – whom he has never quite managed to forget. Would m'sieur le commissaire care to enlighten me upon this point?'

Monsieur Poisson looked at him out of his little fish's eyes. Thought about that. Shrugged.

'I see no reason not to,' he said slowly. 'It is your legal right to know, and you still will have to prove your innocence en tout cas. Since you have lived in France you know that the basis of our law is—'

'The Code Napoléon which states that the accused is presumed guilty until he can establish his innocence. The exact opposite of Anglo-Saxon law in which the accused is presumed innocent until the state can establish his guilt. I do know it. What's more, the words "attorney at law" next to "profession" on that passport before you mean "*avocat en droit*", m'sieur. Please continue: of what, precisely, am I accused?'

'Of – nothing, as yet, m'sieur. You are detained, temporarily, until you can present us with convincing proofs that you are not an agent of a terrorist organization called—' he paused and peered at John Farrow with narrowed eyes, ridiculously like a commissaire de police in a Simenon movie – '*Septembre Noir.*'

John Farrow threw back his head and laughed aloud.

'Do I look like an Arab to you, m'sieur le commissaire?' he asked.

'Whether you resemble *un bicot* or not is hardly the question, m'sieur Farrow! Would you say that those Japanese at the airport of Jerusalem looked like nord-africains, then, either?'

'There you have a point,' John Farrow said. 'But don't you think that your – and, perhaps M'sieur Feingold's – sensitivity over the question is not at least a trifle exaggerated?'

'No, m'sieur. A month ago, I should have agreed with you. But since then, a foreigner, obviously *pas un bicot*—'

'Let's call them Arabs instead of billy goats, shall we, m'sieur commissaire?' John Farrow said quietly: 'Such an expression is – *raciste*. And racism ill becomes a Frenchman, it seems to me.'

'I don't pretend to love them, m'sieur! Not the Jews either for that matter! I merely uphold the law! In any event, a foreigner, European or American, surely, *not* nord-africain passed through this part of France, and asked questions of an astonishing similarity to those which *you* have asked. He, too, *he said*, was seeking an old Jewish friend. And, thereafter, a number of our good Jewish citizens on the Côte, among them a daughter of M'sieur Feingold, who is married to a well-known jeweller who has his shop in Nice, corner of Rue de Meyerbeer and Rue de France to be exact, received letters posted from Amsterdam *et aussi* from Genève. Need I inform you of *what* was in those letters, M'sieur Farrow?'

'Oh, my God!' John Farrow said. 'And la fille de M'sieur Feingold?'

'Blind. At that she was lucky. Her husband – died. So now you understand that this is a serious matter? All we want of you is proof that you really are Mr John Farrow, attorney at law from New York, and also, even if you are he, that you have no connections with the organization called Black September. Is there no one in this part of France who knew you when you lived in our country? Or even during the war, which I presume you fought in – though hardly as a member of the Resistance, as M'sieur Feingold informs me that you claim?'

'As a member of the Resistance. Third in command of Réseau Merle. Liaison officer from the American OSS to the ill-fated Redoute de Vercors. Holder of la Croix de la Libération, awarded me by no less than the late General De Gaulle, himself. All of which I can prove, but it would take too long. As for people who knew me during my childhood, they would nearly all live in Paris – if they live at all, because by now, they'd be very old. But those who knew me during the war should be somewhat easier to locate'. ('I could reach out and touch one of them this minute' he thought, 'except that would really screw up the deal. For who knows what a cornered rat will do, once the cover that's served him – and goddamned well! – for years is blown? Use his sidearm, likely and write on that blotter "Killed while resisting arrest!"') 'For instance, do any of you know a Madame Toulon, who used to be *la boulangère* at Vence?'

'Dead,' one of the gendarmes said, 'since five years, m'sieur.'

He could hear them thinking: 'This type has done his homework. Names actual people to impress us with his truthfulness, but safely dead so he can't be confronted with them!'

John Farrow considered his next move.

He said finally: 'Is there no one among the older members of the police – men my age, say – and not necessarily here: at Vence, or Cannes or Nice, or Antibes or Juan-les-Pins, who was a member of Honneur de la Police, or Police et Patrie, or Front National de la Police?'

The commissaire and the two gendarmes looked at one another.

'Well—' one of the gendarmes, the younger one, said, 'It seems to me that Roger Herriôt once told me that his old man was in the Resistance. You know him, don't you, sir?'

The last question was directed towards their chief.

'M'sieur le Commissaire at Menton!' The commissaire at Grasse said.

'Yes, sir. That's him,' the gendarme said.

Relief washed over John Farrow. While they'd been talking, he'd been searching his really remarkable memory, no mean asset for a lawyer to have, and had come up with that name.

'Paul André Herriôt?' he said.

And now the commissaire was staring at him in a new way. Among the various things that look expressed were disappointment and disgust. To have captured the terrorist responsible for the letter bombs would have surely meant promotion for him, or even a sizeable cash reward, surely from the very Jews he had admitted he had no love for.

'Oui, c'est le même,' he said grudgingly. 'Or at least the name is the same. . . .'

'Phone him,' John Farrow said. 'I will pay for the call. Ask him if he did not know, and, during the liberation of Nice, itself, fight alongside a French-speaking American OSS officer named John Farrow. And, if that does not ring a bell, ask him if he remembers Jean le Fou, Crazy John. . . .'

The gendarmes looked at the commissaire.

'Well—' he said, then: *'Oh, merde alors!* Make the *sacré* call!'

'Yes,' the older gendarme said. 'M'sieur Herriôt says he recalls very well the young American officer in question. What's more, he says that if we care to bring our suspect down to Menton, he is positive he can identify him even now . . .'

'Then,' John Farrow said, 'what are we waiting for?'

Monsieur le Commissaire glared at all three of them.

'Give me that phone!' he barked. 'Look, Paul,' he said, 'the one we have here has said that – Yes, that's it. It all coincides, does it not? Hence, he must be the same, but – *Quoi! Ah, ça non! A Menton, non.* It's much too far. Besides, we can't leave here. Wait, I will explain it! *Il y a cette Madame Betrand de l'Ambassade Israeli à Paris.* She's going to come down here. It seems she knew the type the Israelis suspect of being the organizer of the whole bloody business – *Ah, non! Pas un bicot! Un européen* – That's why we're holding your supposed friend.

Mais, oui, during her childhood. She was born in France. Une minute, Paul! I do not doubt your word. But don't you see, my old one, that in this case, Madame Betrand's testimony is much more important than yours? Suppose he *is* the same man you knew – twenty-eight years ago, mon vieux! A brave type, *d'accord*! But how many brave types, how many heroes of that war have since murdered people, robbed banks, violated little girls, Paul? That you knew him will help his case immensely, of course. But we also need Madame Betrand's testimony that he is not the man the Israeli government is looking for, in order to turn him loose. . . .

'*Quoi, donc?* You'll come up here, tonight, after closing the Préfecture down there? That's *très aimable de ta part, Paul! Mais oui, mon vieux*, I'll tell him that—'

He hung up the phone, said sourly:

'You heard? He'll come to identify you. But all the same—'

'I must remain under arrest until this Madame Betrand arrives from Paris,' John said. '*D'accord*. I can see the seriousness of the case. But I have grave objections to sleeping in your jail. You have my passport. Keep it until tomorrow. I will take a room in a hotel here – any of the hotels you care to designate. And I give you my word I will appear before you at whatever hour you wish . . .'

Commissioner Poisson gave John his fishiest stare.

'*Comme vous êtes drôle, vous!*' he said. 'You go to a hotel – and disappear. I have your passport – *et quoi*? I cannot charge a passport with murder, m'sieur!'

'When a policeman sets out to be difficult,' John Farrow thought, 'the word takes on new nuances. But when a *French* policeman sets out to be difficult, it actually changes its meaning. Becomes a synonym for impossible. No – insufferable.' He said:

'A double room, then, m'sieur le commissaire – with one of your gars to keep me company. I'll pay for the whole thing.'

'Impossible!' the commissaire snapped.

'Why impossible?' John Farrow said, 'I have committed no crime that I know of. And I have no desire to be removing lice from myself for the next two weeks. . . . When your Mrs Betrand declares I screwed her fore and aft at age six, you may jail me, but not before. Which reminds me: perhaps I had better telephone the American Consul at Nice—'

'*Je m'en fiche de votre négresse!*' the commissaire said.

'That's so,' John Farrow remembered suddenly, 'the current American consul at Nice is a black woman. Part of our widespread and forlorn attempt to demonstrate to the world we aren't the racists that we damned well are. The French have got us beaten there. They've convinced the world that *they* aren't. A country where I've seen Arabs kicked bodily out of shops, and where the segregation maintained in Frejus when the absolutely all black corps – except for their officers, of course! – of Senegalese were training there, could have taught Mississippi how to do it. And the world goes right on believing in their liberalism in racial matters just as though Frantz Fanon had never lived or written a single line. . . .'

'You are,' he said, 'entitled to your prejudices, I suppose. Which is neither here nor there. What is, I suggest, more germane to this case is the fact that the legality of your position is more than a little doubtful . . .' He stopped there, knowing only too well not to pursue that line, for Commissaire Poisson's position under French law was anything but doubtful. 'On a suspicion of conspiracy to commit murder,' John realized bleakly, 'he can hold me without bail until hell freezes over and the devil takes Madame de Pompadour sleigh riding. . . .'

He said: 'But in any case, a little flexibility is never amiss, is it not, m'sieur? I remember that we, of the Resistance, quite often had to exercise it. One case comes specifically to mind. It was at – oh yes, to be certain – Mougins. On September 4, 1944. I recall it as though it were yesterday – Ah, pardon! What is it that passes with you, m'sieur le commissaire—?'

The little fish's face, rat's face, had turned grey.

'*Rien!* Nothing! I don't see the point in all this rigamarole! Why—'

But the younger of the two gendarmes had seen his chief's confusion. And, as John Farrow had guessed, neither of them had profound reasons for loving Mr the Commissioner Fish.

'What happened at Mougins on September 4, 1944, M'sieur Farrow?' he said.

'*Ta gueule,* Renard!' the commissaire thundered.

'Now here we have the whole animal kingdom!' John Farrow thought, 'and Mr the Gendarme Fox lives up to his name. A sly type, aren't you, boy?' He said suavely:

'It is of no importance and since the matter seems to offend your chief—'

'Why should it offend me?' Commissaire Poisson spluttered, 'since I don't even know what you're talking about?'

'Then I shall enlighten you,' John Farrow said. 'Some *soi-distant* Maquisards – of the type m'sieur le commissaire will doubtless recall – *par venus, arrivistes* – those who put on the FFI armbands after the Germans were beyond Lyon, and racing for the Ardennes to escape, were about to "purify" some Milice. And, despite the fact that' – he held the commissaire with his eyes – 'there were no worse traitorous bastards on God's earth than Vichy's Milice, who infiltrated us time and time again, murdered our bravest and our best, raped our women whenever they could, and stole everything not nailed down, this particular purification seemed to me excessive, since it consisted of ventilating *une bande de gosses* no more than fourteen to seventeen years old, with rifle bullets. Oh, they were Milices, all right, and probably as adept at ambush, theft, assassination and violation as their elders. But they were kids – I remember one little fellow who'd both pissed and shitted his pants out of fear – strange, he'd be just about your age now, sir—'

'Enough of this nonsense!' the commissaire said, 'why—'

'But, sir,' Gendarme Renard said, 'we'd like to hear the end of the story. Or is that you already know it, *vous même*, m'sieur le commissaire?'

'Merde!' the commissaire shrieked, 'just what do you mean to imply, Renard?'

'I, sir?' Renard said solemnly. 'Nothing at all, sir! It's just that the matter seems to agitate you a little, sir!'

'Tais-toi, idiot!' his companion warned him sotto voce.

'So,' John Farrow said quietly, 'I stopped them from shooting those kids. Of course we got there too late to save the first three. But the rest of them should appreciate – our flexibility, should they not, m'sieur le commissaire?'

'I still don't know what you're talking about,' the commissaire said: 'But – *d'accord*. You – oh no, not *you*, Renard! You, Bonneval, go out to the Hôtel Bellevue, you know, out on Avenue Riou Blanquet, and engage a room for two persons for tonight. . . .'

Now it was Bonneval's turn to complain.

'But, sir,' he said, 'they won't like it. The guests will think he's a drug runner or something, and the manager will—'

'Not in uniform, idiot! Do as I say!'

'But, sir,' Bonneval tried again, 'Renard, here, isn't married while—'

'*Ta femme* wears the trousers in your house. That, I know. Do her good to believe you spent the night *avec une jolie fille. File, Bonneval!* March, yourself! You, too, Renard! Go chase *les poules et les hippies!*'

The commissaire's handling of the matter was not half bad, John Farrow had to admit. 'So now I'd better make conversation,' he thought, 'not to pacify the bastard, but to find out what I can—' He said:

'Pardon me, m'sieur le commissaire, but this Madame Betrand – what, precisely is her connection with this case?'

'Don't know,' Monsieur Poisson said, 'none, perhaps.' Then he seemed to relent a little, or maybe decided that John Farrow had him over a barrel, so he added: 'The Israelis are looking for some *sale type* – war crimes, I assume. And she's native to this section. Born hereabouts I've heard—'

'But she's Israeli?' John Farrow said.

'*Juive, presque sûrement*; Israeli – not necessarily. They often hire French people of their race to work for them, you know. The point is, I'm told, that she is perhaps the one person alive who can recognize this *type*. Beyond that, I know nothing, M'sieur Farrow. Not even what the bastard's accused of—'

He paused again, went on: 'Her connection with *your* case – if any – is that the Israelis seem to believe that the European who passed through here and apparently made up *une liste noire* for *les billets doux de Septembre Noir* is the same man who operated in these parts during the war, again against *les juifs*, apparently – so since my friend Herriôt is convinced that if you are the John Farrow that he knew, you cannot possibly be the man they're after, Madame Betrand's testimony should clear you completely, shouldn't it?'

'Of course,' John Farrow said, 'but what I don't understand is why she can't get here until tomorrow.'

'*Ça, alors!*' the commissaire said, 'that was our strongest reason for detaining you, M'sieur Farrow. M'sieur Feingold called their ambassade in Paris and told them of the questions you had asked. So this morning Madame Betrand set out on the Paris–Nice Caravelle—'

John Farrow sat bolt upright. A Caravelle is a twin jet short-range aircraft with a top speed of close to 950 kilometres per hour. When the wind was right those beautiful craft quite often made it from Orly or Le Bourget to Nice airport in a shade under forty-five minutes. He stared at the commissaire, got out:

'Mais, m'sieur, vous avez dit demain!'

'And tomorrow it is. She's coming by train. For, M'sieur Farrow, five minutes after that particular avion took off, the tower called it back to Orly once again. A phone call, you comprehend? The usual, a bomb aboard.'

'And was there?' John Farrow said.

'No. But the purpose of the call was accomplished, my friend! Madame Betrand was delayed. Sufficiently in fact, to permit a suspect to get out of France. Only we already had our hands on you. Which, admittedly, may be a mistake. Perhaps by concentrating on you, the real raven will have flown. So, Madame Betrand will arrive tomorrow by train. The Israeli embassy has ordered her *not* to fly just in case. It seems she's well liked there. Secretary to the ambassador, himself. . . .'

That night, John Farrow dined with both commissaires, Poisson and Herriôt. He took them to the restaurant at the Hôtel Beau Soleil on the Boulevard du Crouët. That was policy. The Beau Soleil's restaurant is indisputably the finest in Grasse. It rated three stars, or three forks, or whatever the ratings that the Michelin people used those days. . . .

'Now look, Poisson, *mon ami,*' Paul Herriôt was saying before the end; 'you should just turn this fellow loose, that's all! Brave! I've seen him walk through machine-gun fire as solid as a wall! Why—'

'Please, Paul, *mon vieux,*' John said, 'I was *fou*, remember. *En toute vérité fou.*'

'That you were!' Paul Herriôt said. 'Which reminds me – la petite Simone, did you ever find her?'

'No,' John said sadly, 'but I'm still looking. Only this time, I'm afraid I've reached a dead end. *Voie sans issue. Impasse. Cul de sac—*'

'Et ça, alors, pourquoi?' Paul Herriôt said.

'I was depending upon tracing her through a type I knew before the war. Lived up at Tourette-sur-Loup. A poet. Very famous in those days. You've heard of Dalton Ross, haven't you?'

'But, of course!' Paul Herriôt said.

'Moi, aussi,' Poisson said.

'Only they – correction – one old woman up there told me he's dead. Said les boches did it, though why they should I cannot see. He was on their side. If we'd caught him, he'd have been shot as a traitor. But we didn't catch him. In any case, his house is no longer there. It's tumbled all the way down the Gorge. La vieille says les boches blew it up. . . .'

Herriôt and Poisson looked at each other.

'They did,' Poisson said, 'but Dalton Ross wasn't in it. Les boches had taken him away with them two days before. *C'était comme ça n'est-ce pas,* Paul?'

'Yes,' Paul Herriôt said. 'It seems Ross got away. I for one, am glad, John. I liked him. Brave. And those broadcasts, what did they amount to really? Some clever jokes – propaganda that convinced no one at all, and that he had to do to save his skin – or even someone else's. *Sa 'tite maîtress, peutêtre—'*

John Farrow looked him straight in the eye.

'And his little mistress – who was she, Paul?' he said.

'Ah, ça – cette histoire est très vieille maintenant et—'

'Ancient history or not, I want to know it,' John Farrow said. 'Was she – Simone, Paul?'

Paul Herriôt bent his head. Sighed. Looked up, said:

'Yes, John. But – before your time. She'd left him – for reasons I've never known – before Pepe led Réseau Merle up to Gap, and then to Vercors. Where you met her, didn't you? *C'était une fille splendide, cette Simone! Très femme.* You really couldn't expect her to sit around and wait for you to appear, now could you, my old one? *La virginité!* Bah! What does it matter? What a woman has done before *son vrai homme* arrives upon the scene has little importance. It is her fidelity to him afterward that counts. And la petite Simone was faithful to you, John. Absolutely—'

'Quand même – she left me,' John Farrow said. 'And I'd give anything, up to and including my life, to know why. . . .'

'I'd tell you if I knew, but I don't,' Paul Herriôt said. 'And Poisson here, doesn't either. He was just a snot nose in those days. Pissing his pants when he heard gunfire!'

'No,' John Farrow said, 'he was very brave, *le petit bonhomme* Poisson. He doesn't remember me, but I knew him, too. At a place called Mougins, he stood up and looked death straight in the eye.'

Monsieur le Commissaire Poisson stared at John Farrow. What surprised him most of all was the gentleness of the Franco-American lawyer's tone.

'*Merci pour ça, M'sieur Farrow*,' he said. 'You are too kind. I was scared shitless, as you know only too well. And you, on that occasion, saved my life—' He paused, flashed John Farrow a look. 'Agreement made?' that glance whispered. Imperceptibly, John nodded. '*Donc entre camarades-aux-armes*, I will not place Bonneval over you to guard you. I ask only your *parole d'honneur* that you will return to my office at noon tomorrow, at which time Madame Betrand will be there. . . .'

'You have it,' John Farrow said. 'Besides which, I have to see M'sieur Feingold again to pick up a *bague* I bought from him. I only hope that Madame Betrand will have convinced him by then that I have no wish to blow his head off. . . .'

'*Les pauvres juifs*,' Paul Herriôt said, 'when will people leave them in peace?'

'When will people leave *anybody* in peace?' John Farrow said. 'By the way, why did the Boches blow up the house of Dalton Ross?'

'Oh there was someone in it, all right,' Paul Herriôt said: 'but he wasn't Dalton Ross. A friend of yours, John, *malheureusement* – even of Simone's. One of your réseau – Merle wasn't it called?'

'You know his name?' John Farrow said.

'But of course, old fellow! He was that tall red-haired Jewish boy. Rabin – Rabin – What was it, Emil? You were there, I was told when they marched in . . .'

'And led the bastards to him sure as hell,' John Farrow thought.

'Rabinowski. Anton Rabinowski,' Monsieur le Commissaire Emil Poisson said.

John Farrow opened his mouth. Closed it again. All his warning signals were screaming in his gut. Rabinowski, Feingold had said, was the conductor of the Tel Aviv Orchestra. Had led that ensemble at the Lincoln Centre no more than a year ago. And the two French policemen were saying – that he was dead. Murdered twenty-eight years ago.

His brain had shifted gears, was off, and racing: 'Or were there *two* Anton Rabinowskis? Not bloody likely. The name was too distinctive. Strike that one off.'

His mind downshifted, revved up again: 'Could the man in Tel Aviv be – an impostor?' he followed the thought where it led him: 'Dalton Ross and Anton Rabinowski had looked vaguely alike ('Much more than I resemble Dalton, I who am his son!') They had both been tall and fair, though the poet's hair was more reddish blond than red. Could not that wily old scoundrel, who, after all, did know a hell of a lot about music, have passed himself off, as—

'No.' His growing elation died. 'On that level, no. Ross had a dilettante's knowledge of most of the arts. But any symphony group would have spotted him as a phony the very first day. Besides, the age difference was too great. Anton Rabinowski would be no more than fifty-one or two today, while Dalton—

'Face it, there's no light at the end of the tunnel yet,' John Farrow thought. 'In fact, it's getting darker by the minute.'

As it was. But what he'd forgot is that the darkest hour is always the one that precedes the dawn. . . .

And that dawns are sometimes – glorious.

9

But the third officer was a girl. A small, slight, not even especially pretty Jewish girl.

Her name was Simone Levy.

And all the various Maquis réseaux at Vercors – by then nearly a thousand fighting men – were shouting and laughing and exchanging greetings with the newcomers, the tough, fit, ragged, filthy, members of Réseau Merle, real *durs* to the man, and even embracing them.

And abruptly there was no sound.

And abruptly there were no people.

Except two.

Except Simone and Jean.

For the rest of the world had vanished.

He came towards her, neither slowly nor fast, with his ordinary slouching walk. Stopped, one metre away from her. Stood looking into her face, into her eyes. They were almond shaped. Almost oriental. They were green with flecks of gold in them. He could see them widening as he stared into them. He could see her mouth begin to tremble.

He studied her with great care, almost appraisingly, from head to toe. Saw the brownish stains of sweat at the armpits of her khaki army shirt. The lines of dirt caked into the hollows of her scrawny neck. Registered for ever upon the photographic negative of his memory her soft brown hair, full of dust from the roads Réseau Merle had been marching over for more than a week, her great, heavy brows, whitened with dust, too, the all-but fleshless sculpturing of her face into hollows, planes, angles of an austerity, an ascerticism that her warm, wide-lipped, uncontrollably trembling mouth, contradicted completely, totally belied.

Her nose was too long for beauty and a little hooked. Her features added up to exactly what anti-semites mean when they say a person looks Jewish. She was Sarah, come out of Chaldea with Abraham; she was Rebekah brought by his faithful servant to the house of Isaac; she was Rachel for whom Jacob worked fourteen years; and perhaps even Leah, for whom he worked but seven.

But most of all, she was Ruth, Ruth the faithful, the tender.

('But something of Bathsheba was there, too,' John Farrow thought, now, as he lay remembering, wakeful on still another unfamiliar bed; 'Judith of Holofernes. Delilah. Maybe even – Jezebel. Who knows?')

She had on a pair of sandals cut from old automobile tyres. Her feet were filthy, cracked from marching, calloused, their toenails jagged, black with dirt. Her legs were thorn-torn, stone-scraped, bruised from falls, not quite as filthy as her feet. She had on a pair of French army khaki pants, at least three sizes too big for her, hacked off at the knees into uneven tatters, apparently with a damned dull knife. To keep them from falling off her, and exposing rags of underwear – or none at all, as Jean le Fou quite accurately guessed – she'd bunched them in mammoth folds about her tiny waist, and belted them to her with a piece of rope. She had a Sten gun slung across her back. A duffel bag over one shoulder. A beret perched saucily on the back of her head.

She looked like a beggar. A female clown. A girl Charlot out of *Limelight*.

An angel.

He walked up to her without a word, still wrapped in that quality of recognition that had stopped the world, dumped every other living creature off into some fourth-dimensional void, obliquely tangential to their own private, and peculiar space and time. Bent down and kissed her mouth.

A long time. A very long time. A little age. A small eternity.

But when he drew back, she was with him still, rising on tiptoe, clinging her mouth to his, suspended almost upon his breath, exchanging wonder? magic? joy? through what must have been osmosis.

Then, suddenly the world came back. They heard the booming roars of laughter.

'Regardez, voyez 'ce type de Jean!' ('Look at this character, John!')

'Fou? Comme le Pape à Rome!' ('Crazy? Like the Pope in Rome!')

'Le Pape, mon vieux, n'est pas de tout du genre de Jean. On dirait plus Don Juan ou même Casanova!' ('He's not at all a *pope,* old boy! I'd say Don Juan, rather or Casanova!')

And her green eyes flaring suddenly in shock, in shame. And the anger getting into them. ('What did she think then? That I'd been putting her on? That the whole thing was arranged? Staged to give those horny types a belly laugh?') She brought her right hand whistling around to explode against his face like a pistol shot. She hit him so hard he staggered. The impact of that slap broke the crust that had formed over the bullet furrow along his head. ('I'd taken Byron's shirt tail bandage off by then, and my hair hid the wound, I guess. . . .') A thick, hot stream of blood poured down.

She took a backward step. Her eyes widened in horror.

'Je l'ai tué!' she moaned: *'Mais, pourquoi? Une simple gifle ne peut pas—'* ('I've killed him! But why? A simple slap can't—').

But he had caught her right hand, the one she'd slapped him with, and raised it slowly, reverently to his mouth. Kissed the palm of it, with slow, grave tenderness.

'J'en ai eu assez!' Pepe the Spaniard roared. ('I've had enough!') Then his feeble grasp of French deserting him in his rage: *'Le voy a matar!'* ('I'm going to kill him!')

Jean le Fou turned to him with a dreamy far-off smile, said: *'¿Es tuya, esa mujer?'* ('Is she thine, this woman?')

Pepe stared at him, lowered the muzzle of his Sten, and said wonderingly: '*¡Está loco de remate, ese tío!*' ('He's crazier than hell, this character!')

'*Te he hecho una pregunta, amigo,*' Jean said. '*¿Esa chica, es tuya?*' ('I asked thee a question friend, is this girl thine?')

'No,' Pepe growled. '*¡Pero soy jefe de esa banda y no voy a permitir que un tío loco como tu insultes a nuestra Simone!*' ('No. But I'm chief of the band and I'm not going to let a crazy character like you insult our Simone!')

Jean ignored him. Looked into Anton Rabinowski's eyes. They were black with hurt, with sorrow. But not with rage. A civilized man bows to the inevitable. And he saw how Simone was looking at Jean.

'*Elle est peut-être, la vôtre?*' Jean asked him politely. ('She is perhaps, yours?')

Wordlessly Anton shook his head.

'*Alors, elle est à moi,*' Jean said. '*Viens, donc, ma douce, ma belle, mon ange. Je vais—*' ('Then she's mine. Come, then, my sweet, my beautiful, my angel. I'm going to—')

But Simone stood there. Now she was truly angry.

'*Ecoutez, m'sieur!*' she said, '*Que pensez-vous que je suis? Un animal? Un être sans volonté-propre? Une vache? Une chèvre? Une cochonne?*' ('listen, mister! What do you think I am? An animal? A being with no will of its own? A cow? A she-goat? A sow?')

Jean turned, grinned at her.

'*Ça, oui – tu es ma jolie 'tite cochonne, un peu maigre, mais tu as vraiment l'odeur de cochonne. Peu importe! Je vais te baigner au fleuve, et lorsque tu es encore propre, nous nous marierons.*' ('That yes – you are my pretty little sow, a bit skinny, but you do stink most piggishly. It doesn't matter! I'm going to bathe you in the river, and when you're clean again, we'll get married.')

Simone was so angry by then that she was beside herself. She jerked at the straps of her Sten gun, but Byron Graves's voice stopped her.

'I shouldn't do that, if I were you, my dear,' he said crisply. Then realizing he'd spoken in English, he said it all over again. '*Je ne ferais pas ça, si je fusse vous, ma chérie—*'

'I speak English,' Simone said. 'Now you tell me, mister: why shouldn't I shoot this swine? He's been insulting me ever since I got here and—'

'Not insulting. Wrong word, my dear. Honouring you is more like it. He's the bravest man we have. And the best—'

Jean stood there, waiting. Byron waved him away with a gesture.

'Go away, John. Do be a good chap, and go. It's better that I explain things to your little friend. I'll send her to you once I'm through—'

Jean bent his head, and walked away from them into the grove of trees.

'He – he understands English, too, then?' Simone said.

'Of course. John happens to be American.'

Simone stood there. Her eyes were flooded, blind.

'Ah ça alors! Pas encore!' she wailed. *'Comme je suis malheureuse!'*

'Which means you were in love with a ruddy Yank quite recently, I presume, my dear? I must say they do get about!'

'I hate them!' Simone said, 'they're swine! All of them! And you English are—'

'Billy goats. Bulldogs. Apes. What have you. You can't anger me, my dear. I really do think you should hear me out, though. In the first place, John is only half a Yank—'

'And the other half?' Simone whispered

'French. You've heard how beautifully he speaks your language, haven't you?'

'Yes,' Simone said. 'Perfectly. Like a Parisian.'

'He *is* a Parisian. Born there. Oh I say! Let's go sit down on that log. You must be very tired, my dear—'

'May I come along?' Anton Rabinowski said in English.

'Why of course, old chap! What I am going to tell Ma'moiselle—'

'Levy,' Simone said, 'Simone Levy. And you?'

'Graves. Captain Byron Graves of British Intelligence. I started to say that what I'm going to tell Ma'moiselle Levy is not a secret. You're perfectly welcome to hear it, too.' He looked at Anton inquiringly, said:

'And your name is?'

'Anton Rabinowski.'

'Not the violinist?' Byron said.

'Ex. Maquisard for the duration, friend.'

'I'm delighted to meet you! I heard you once at the Albert Hall and—'

'Oh *zut alors!*' Simone said. 'Music can wait. Tell me about *him*. Is he – mad?'

'Yes. Oh, yes, quite. But he has reason to be. That's why you *must* be kind to him, my dear. You're the first girl he's *looked* at since Hélène died. It's very possible that if you're gentle with him and patient, you might even cure him. I was *so* delighted when he kissed you! You see, I've gone with him to – to—'

'*Une maison close*,' Simone supplied. 'A brothel.'

'Right. Sorry. Please forgive me, Ma'moiselle Levy, but it *is* germane. To a brothel. And all the girls were quite gone over him.'

'I can see why,' Simone whispered. '*Il est très beau. Et – si charmant*. Please go on.'

'He treated them as though they were his sisters. His convent-bred sisters. With great tenderness, and greater respect. One of the reasons, I think, that they adore him. But the – the other – nothing, I assure you, not at all. One of the girls even tried to seduce him. Tried rather desperately. But no. He refused very, very gently. I don't think he's touched a woman since Hélène died—'

'*Sa – femme?*' Simone said. '*Cette Hélène? Elle était sa femme?*'

'No. I don't think so. Say his fiancée—'

'*Sa maîtresse!*' Simone said bitterly.

'Perhaps. I really don't know, Ma'moiselle Levy—'

'Call me Simone. I like you.'

'Oh, I say! That's jolly decent of you, my dear! And you must call me Byron.'

'You,' Anton said, 'like any-damned-body as long as he's not Jewish, Simone.'

'Now, Anton! That's not fair! I like *you*. I really do. Only—'

'You don't love me. *D'accord*. Listen to Captain Graves, will you?'

'All right,' Simone said. 'Tell me about cette Hélène. But I don't think I'm going to like her.'

So Byron did. He'd had the tale from Yves Martin, but he told it with all his actor's skill, as though he himself had witnessed it. Long before he was done, Simone was crying, helplessly.

'Jesus!' Anton Rabinowski said.

'I hate her!' Simone said fiercely. 'She had no right to spoil his life like that! The rest of it, I mean! Now he'll never be free of her, never! Oh why will people do that! Push the burden of their sacrifices off on backs too frail to bear them? I know how it feels! It hurts, goddamn it, it hurts! Don't you see, Anton – it's the same thing? What *he* did to me? No – worse. Because there's no redress possible. No retribution. . . .'

Byron stared at her.

'I don't know how you women think,' he said slowly. 'But if *I* were a girl, I'd wonder what a chappie *has* that makes a woman willing to die for him. And I shouldn't resent the one who died. Bless her, rather. For keeping him alive, say. Until I came along.'

Simone glared at him.

'You call what he is, *alive*?' she grated. 'Why he's a walking ghost!'

Byron studied her. There was a glint of anger in his eyes now. His voice came out evenly, controlled.

'I rather think that that should be your job, Simone,' he said, 'to bring him back to life – into the world of men. Though, I must say you're going at it rather hamfistedly, my dear. Slapping a man with a head wound as bad as the one John has, hard enough to open it again, is scarcely apt to make him less a ghost. Rather more, I'd say.'

'Oh, merde!' Simone said, and jumped to her feet. 'Come on!'

'Come on where?' Anton said.

'To look for him! He's bleeding! He's bleeding like a pig! Only he made me so damned mad that I forgot! He'll bleed to death! We've got to find him – now!'

'No. He won't bleed to death. It will clot again, likely. That's not the point, Simone,' Byron said. 'It's not any physical injury of his I worry about, my dear. Rather I fear – well call them, his internal wounds – the ones that bleed for ever in the human psyche. He responds to you – on the normal plane of man to woman. I call that good. Immensely good. He, I think, needs you. Needs you rather desperately. Because, for all his courage, he is *not* a warrior. He hates war, hates killing with all his soul. He is very lonely – and most terribly afraid. I'm quite sure that if I were as afraid as he seems to be, I couldn't function at all. But he does – always, and magnificently. Strange – there's something – how can I put it? Something rather unearthly about him. Something of the ascetic – of the saint—'

'Et encore plus de sorcier,' Simone whispered. 'He kissed me and – stopped the world. Made it vanish, *pouf*! *Comme ça!* Look Capitan Graves—'

'Byron, please.'

'Byron. But, for the moment, Captain Graves. Because what I have to say is serious. I have had, quite recently, a very bad time. Because of a man. An American. I was his mistress. I am not ashamed of that. He was very good to me – and very gentle. I – I loved him very much.'

'Loved? He's dead then?' Byron said.

'No. It would be much better if he were, but he's not. It's just that I have ceased to love him. He put upon me a burden far too great for me to bear. For any woman to, for that matter. A burden remarkably like the one *cette garce d'une Hélène* placed upon poor Jean—'

'I think you're being unfair to her,' Byron said.

'Moi, je suis jalouse!' Simone said. 'And what jealous woman is ever fair? What arms have I against her, Byron? How can one defeat a ghost who has left her skeletal hands locked about one's lover's heart?'

'Lover!' Anton jeered. 'Presumptuous little piece, aren't you? Just because he kissed you doesn't mean he loves you, Simone. More likely it means he'd like to drag your narrow tail into the sack with him. After you have washed it, anyhow, *'tite cochonne!'*

Simone glared at him.

'When I become prime minister of Israel, *mon cher,*' she said, 'I am going to place a new law before parliament—'

'Knesset,' Anton corrected her.

'You see?' she said to Byron, 'already *ce gros chauvin* is trying to make a Sabra of me!'

'I cannot make Sabra of you, Simone,' Anton said, 'nor even of myself, worse luck! Sabras, my beloved and eternally unfaithful Simone, are *born.* I have told you that a thousand times.'

'So? It doesn't matter. When I become the first female prime minister of Israel, I shall make it legal for any woman to shoot dead a man who says a thing like that to her.'

'And that,' Anton grinned, 'will be the first government in history to begin with an "*oy*!" and end screaming "*gevalt*!" '

'You've lost me, old chap,' Byron said. 'I'm a pretty fair linguist, but—'

'It isn't a language,' Simone said, 'it's only Yiddish. "Oy" means, "Oh my God!" and "Gevalt" – "Help!" Jewish humour.

Don't try to understand it, Byron. For to do that you'd have to understand *us*. And no one does, not even we, ourselves—'

'Bli panika,' Anton teased her, *'lo asson!'*

'Anton, you stop it! Now he's plaguing me in Hebrew, Byron, because he knows I'm *very* bad at it. He says I'm not to panic; and it's not a tragedy. Do you understand that?'

'No,' Byron said.

'Moi, non plus. I agree we shouldn't panic, but it *is* a tragedy to be born Jewish. It always has been. And it always will be.'

'I don't agree,' Byron said. 'Your people have given the world some of history's and culture's great contributions, Simone. Why—'

'Merde!' Simone shrieked, 'my people have given the world an ever-renewable supply of corpses! Only now this murderous Austrian clown is out to end even that. No more corpses, Capitan English Goy! No more Jews. You know what *judenfrei* means?'

'Unfortunately, yes,' Byron said, 'But you shouldn't hold it against me, Simone. I'm English and in my country our Jewish citizens have always been treated well. Why once we even had a prime minister who was born Jewish.'

'One. Benjamin Disraeli, a hundred years ago – No, more. And you had York, 1211, wasn't it, Anton?'

'Yes. But, Simone, that was a hell of a long time ago.'

'No. It's now. Today. Whatever happened in history can happen again. A people who do not learn from their past are condemned to repeat it.'

Byron stared at her. At this thin, nervous, sweaty, dirty, somewhat smelly, holy terror of a girl. And saw, with sudden insight, what John had seen. That she was a person. Real, authentic, whole, and entire. And – marvellous. He said gently:

'What happened at York in 1211, Simone?'

'One of the biggest pogroms in European history. Your ancestors, mon cher Byron, murdered eight hundred and eighty-four of mine in a single day.'

Byron's jaw dropped. Speaking, his voice was genuinely sad.

'By Jove you're one up on me, Simone. I didn't know that – truly. And I'm sorry. Very sorry. I'd thought we were above all that sort of thing.'

Simone laughed suddenly, and reached up and kissed his cheek.

'You're a good boy, Byron!' she said. 'Now shall I lead you off into the woods where we can make one little half-Jew to make up for our losses at York?'

'And have John shoot me?' Byron countered. 'No thank you, my dear!'

'You're afraid I'll give you lice,' she said solemnly. 'Ugh, how I do smell! Haven't had a bath in a month. No privacy. Being the only a woman in a Maquis band – is difficult, Byron.'

'I can see that. But, my dear, it seems to me you were telling me something – something, rather important.'

'Yes. About my lover. The great man. The great goddamned Goy. Who has sunk me, for ever. No, crushed me. Mashed me flat.'

Byron stared at her. Her English was fluent and good. Except that it was American, not English. And not quite that. Her turns of phrase were her own.

'You mean he was unfaithful? That's not so ruddy important, my dear. Everyone slips now and then—'

'No. I don't mean that. Because he wasn't unfaithful. He simply loved me too much. So much that his perspective became distorted. I am a woman, but I am also a soldier. My life is just one life. He had no right – to buy it – at the price he paid for it. It simply is not worth that much—'

'And that price was?' Byron Graves said.

'His – honour,' Simone said slowly. 'Perhaps even – his immortal soul. And – whatever happiness I might have had, both now – and in the future. I am Jewish – *ain brera*! is that right, Anton, dahlink?'

'Yes,' Anton said, 'but you are also *ohev tzarot* and even more *nyet kulturnye*—'

'Oh, for God's sake!' Byron exploded, 'can't you tell a tale straight through without having at each other with your polyglot bickering? Do go on, but translate all that chatter first, will you?'

'Sorry,' Anton said laughing, '*ain brera* means "there's no help for it"; *ohev tzarot* means "a lover of trouble" which my dearest Simone indisputably is. The last one wasn't even Hebrew. It's Russian. It means an ignoramus. And *that*, my dearest darling is – raised to the eleventh power! Especially in Hebrew—'

'*Et tu es un emerdeur publique*,' Simone replied sweetly ('And you are a public defecator'). 'Where was I, Byron?'

'You were saying that this chap of yours had paid too much—'

'For my life. Only he wasn't a chap, Byron. He was quite old. More than fifty, I'd say. But – very sweet. I loved him—'

'You've said that before,' Anton said sourly.

'All right. He paid too much. True – they would have tortured me to death – hideously. I should have been brave for ten minutes – five. Thereafter I should have screamed and prayed and begged for death as all their victims do. *Pas importe!* I should be dead and rotten in the earth, and not have to spend my life bent and crushed – under this shame – this – horror!'

'So?' Byron said.

'I do not know if I can accept the additional burden of your friend Jean. I do not say I could not love him – for, God help me! – I already do. I loved him before I knew him. Since before I was born, perhaps. I walked into this clearing and saw his face – and recognized it – from a million years ago, *tu t'entends ça,* Byron? From before time was. The man I've been waiting for – for ever. Who has been waiting for me. Only it is – spoiled now. He, the other one, spoiled it. Ton Jean is very clean – very pure. *Comme tu as dit, Byron, même un saint, peut-être.* While – the other one – has made of me – a dirty, dirty thing – a thing *d'ordure.* A vileness!'

'Simone, please!' Anton said.

'*Tais-toi,* Anton! I do not mean to survive this war, Capitan Graves. I hope to die in battle – bravely. But if I do survive it, I shall marry Anton here, and become a good and devoted little Jewish wife, give him ten children, and make up to him for all the times I have betrayed him. Betrayed my people and my race for love of some goddamned Goy!'

'You've never betrayed me, Simone,' Anton said quietly. 'You've never belonged to me, so in what does your so-called betrayal consist?'

'That I should have been yours. That I should have chosen among our own. I should have clung to you. I'm not even religious, so I don't even know the words. How do they go? "If I forget thee, Jerusalem! If I hold thee not above me chiefest joy!" Is that right, Anton?'

'Don't ask me. I skipped shul, too.'

She turned back to Byron.

'Is there a place where I can go bathe? He said I was a pig.

He's right. At least I smell like one. So I'm going to bathe. And put on a *dress*. And a bra. And panties—'

Byron stared at her, his eyebrows rising.

'Don't look at me like that!' she flared. 'I have so few underclothes. *Ha' mefaked, Adoni!*' ('My commander, sir!' Anton translated at once) 'that I cannot afford to wear them on the march. They would get so unutterably filthy that I should never get them clean. But now that we are in camp, I shall become quite feminine. And sweet. And charming. Oh if I only had a little perfume!'

'I'll get you some the next time I go down to St Martin,' Byron said. 'That's where the hospital is. They ought to have some left, there.'

'Oh, would you? That's sweet of you, mon capitaine anglais! And after I am clean I shall go find Jean. And kiss him. And hold him in my arms. But nothing more.'

'Why not?' Anton asked her harshly. 'I have no claim on you, Simone!'

'It would not – be right. Or good. Or just. He deserves – far better than une garce like me. *Is* there such a place?'

'Oh, yes. I'll show you *my* waterhole. Well screened by brush. Deuced private. But if you don't mind, Anton and I will come along and stand guard. With our backs to you, of course. Some of these chaps haven't seen a girl in a fairish time. And a naked girl might be a bit too much for their self-control. Right, Anton?'

'Right, Byron,' Anton said. 'You really *are* a good sort, aren't you?'

When she finally found him, Jean was sitting on a fallen tree in the middle of the woods. She tiptoed up behind him and covered his eyes with her hands. Then she jerked them away, and stared at him, wailed: 'Oh, Jean!' and came running around to face him.

He went right on crying.

She dropped to her knees before him, and cupped his face between her slim, non-hard, calloused hands. Knelt there, looking into his eyes. Whispered:

'*Ne pleure pas, mon Jean! Je t'en supplie! Ne pleure pas! Me voici. Je suis à toi, quoi que soit la façon que tu me veux. . . .*' ('Don't cry John. I beg of you, don't cry. Here I am. I am yours, in whatever way that you want me.')

He smiled down at her. His tears bisected the upturned corners of his mouth. He said, *'Donc, comme ma femme. Mais, après—'* ('Then for my wife. But afterward').

'Oh, zut alors! After what?' Simone said.

'La guerre,' Jean said, *'après la guerre.'*

She grinned at him. A gamine's grin, replete with mischief. 'That's going to last a while you know,' she said.

'I know,' Jean said, 'but we must wait. It is not wise to start something we cannot finish.'

'Sage!' Simone exploded. 'Wise! Now look at this blessed John. You want to be *wise*? Why? *I* don't! I want to love you!'

He stretched out his hand and let it rest atop her head.

'Because – I don't want you – dead, Simone,' he said.

She surged up then and wrapped her arms about his neck. Kissed his mouth, angrily, hungrily, her tears mingling with his own. Drew back, grinned at him, her mouth trembling.

'You see? I am *alive*, Jean!'

'I know. But if you love me, you will die. And I could not bear that, Simone. I am mad, now. But only a little. If I caused your death, I should be really mad. Incurably.'

'Then I shall go search you your straitjacket. For if loving you will kill me, I am already dead. *Je t'aime, idiot! Je t'adore! Tu es mon homme, Jesuis à toi. Toujours!'*

'Come, Get up from there. Sit beside me. And never say always. "Always" is a dirty word. "Tomorrow" is another. There is no tomorrow. There is only now.'

'Ça d'accord,' Simone said, and began to unbutton her blouse.

'Stop that!' Jean said sharply.

She stared at him with the face of a child who has been slapped. Whispered: *'Pourquoi, Jean! Tu ne me veux pas?'*

'Yes,' he said sadly. 'But for the rest of my life, Simone. And for my wife, not my whore.'

That made her laugh, merrily.

'Mon Jean!' she giggled. 'Saint John the chaste, the pure! Tell me something: how much money do you have in your pocket, right now?'

He smiled at her, said: *'Pas un sou, Simone.'*

'Alors, tu vois? You *can't* make me your whore, because you can't even pay me!'

He grinned, fell in with her game.

'You'll give me a little on credit?'

'Volontiers!' she said, and started to take off her shirt. He shook his head, said: 'No, Simone. Please – no.'

She stared at him, whispered: 'Why not, John? I want you. I *want* to go to bed with you. Don't be stupid. Tomorrow we could both be dead, you know.'

He bent his head. Looked up again. Faced her. Said: 'To tell the truth, Simone, I don't believe I – can.'

'Oh, so *that's* it! You're wounded – down *there* – are you?'

'No,' he said, 'I am wounded here – and here.' He touched his breast, his head.

'Merde!' Simone said, *'encore ta garce d'une Hélène, n'est-ce pas?'*

His eyes took fire, he said: 'Don't say that, Simone. That's very stupid. You say a thing like that about Hélène just one more time, and I'll slap you winding!'

She slid off the log and knelt beside him, facing away from him. She lay her face against his knee. He could see her thin shoulders shake.

'It's not fair! It's not fair at all! She's dead! She died for you, and now I haven't the slightest chance to—'

'Aucune possibilité de quoi, Simone?' he said.

'To make you see that I love you *more* than she did! More than all the women in the world could love you! Do I have to die for you, too? Then give me your knife ! I'm going to cut my throat! Right now! This minute!'

He put his hands beneath her armpits and raised her up. Sat her upon his knees. She lay against him pillowing her head in the hollow of his throat.

'Jean—' she said.

'Oui, Simone?'

'Donne-moi un baiser.'

He kissed her. She put up her hand and touched his face.

'Jean—'

'*Now* what?'

'Are you going to be like that – always?'

'Comment?' he said, teasing her.

'Impotent.'

He said sadly: 'I don't know, Simone, I hope not.'

'John – I want children, you know.'

'Then, when we're married, I'll let you go on vacations all by yourself. Twice a year. Agreed? And that'll fix things up, quite easily.'

She pounded him in the chest with her fist, hard.

'Oh no! Not that. Because I don't want just children. I want *your* children. Handsome like you. Sweet. Gentle. Good.'

He bent his head.

'Bon Dieu!' she said: 'What have I done *now*?'

'She said that, too, Hélène. The night before she died.'

Simone jumped to her feet. Stood there facing him. Her warm, wonderful mouth was aquiver, her cheeks awash. She put out her hand to him, solemnly.

'Good-bye, Jean,' she said.

'Good-bye?'

'Yes. Because I don't have a chance. She is too strong, for me.'

'Simone,' he said, 'I am going to tell you something I've never told anyone before: I weep for Hélène, because I am ashamed of the way – I – I cheated her. I let her live upon hope, believing that I loved her. I didn't. I have never loved anyone before now. Before – you.'

She stood there searching his face, his eyes. Found what she sought. Conviction. Truth. *Verité.*

She let out a squeal that would have shattered crystal. Hurled herself upon him so hard she knocked him completely off the log. Wrestled him to earth, pinning his arms down, holding him by the wrists, kissing his eyes, his mouth, laughing, babbling, crying:

'I am going to rape you! I am going to violate you! I'm going to make violent love to you! Make you beg for mercy! Oh, how I love you! How I adore you, my John!'

He laughed at her. Said, 'Stop it, Simone. It's quite impossible. That's one of the inequalities between the sexes. A woman can be raped. A man *can't*.'

She turned loose his arms. But she lay there upon him.

'John,' she said.

'No, Simone.'

'Why not, *mon très, très cher? Mon amour, pourquoi pas?* Because you – can't?'

He laughed then, freely, gaily.

'No,' he said, 'I *can* all right!'

She put down her hand and touched him where she shouldn't

have, for which sin or crime her hand should have been cut off by ancient Talmudic law.

'*Voilà!*' she said. 'Let's go!'

'No,' he said, quietly, seriously.

'*Oh, merde alors,*' she said, '*pourquoi pas?*'

'One,' he said, 'it is day. People walk through this wood frequently. Love is not a spectacle to be enjoyed by voyeurs. Especially not our love, Simone. That, I think, is a high and holy thing. Two. I have not a contraceptive to my name. I threw them all away the morning Hélène died—'

'*Zut! Cette Hélène! Elle était, et y reste, très emmerdeuse!*' Simone said.

'I'm going to hit you in a minute,' John said, 'or wash out your mouth with soap. You have one filthy tongue, my girl!'

She laughed, said, 'Forgive me, my love. But it's true! She has cursed my life!'

'I don't want to make you pregnant. Not now. Not until it's reasonably safe. It's true we have a fair hospital in St Martin. But how long we're going to be able to keep it, when those Nazi murderers come up from Grenoble and smoke us out of here, I don't know. Besides, a big belly impedes fast running, and believe me, *bébé*, we're going to have to run!'

'*Oh mer— zut! Comme je suis malheuse!*'

'I'm not,' he said, 'I'm very happy, Simone. I have something to live for now. And – we're going to be happy together, after this war is over. Then you may present me with a baby every year for the next ten years, and—'

But her face was serious suddenly. She got up. Walked away from him and sat on the log. He followed her, sat down beside her, put his arm around her shoulders. She was staring off into space. Her green eyes were smoking, dark with trouble.

'What is it that passes with you, my angel?' he said.

'*Rien.* Nothing. You are right. We cannot make a baby now. They would take it. Put it in a cattle car. Ship it to – a death camp, Jean.'

'No, Simone! You don't really *know*—'

'I *do* know. My Uncle Aaron lived in Poland. In a *shtetl* – a Jewish township. He was a big man. Important. President of the *kahal* – the community board – head of two or three of the *chevras* – the mutual help societies. He escaped into Russia when the Boches invaded Poland. He – God knows how – procured false papers, joined the Soviet Army. He is now a colonel. After the Nazis invaded Russia in June 1941 – they *never* keep their word, Jean, not with anyone – he was able to write us again – a long, round-about way – he wrote to Anton's father in New York. He did not know Anton's father, of course; but he did know Anton's Uncle Yigal. They lived in the same *shtetl.* Yigal Rabinowski was head of another *chevra* so they often had meetings together. For the Rabinowskis were Polish, too, tu sais. Only Anton's father moved to Berlin. But he soon saw that Jewish people were not going to be safe there – not for very long. So he got together all the money he could and sent his family to France. That's why Anton grew up in France, and why he and I have been friends since we were very small. . . .'

'Go on, Simone,' Jean said.

'Only Anton's father couldn't get out himself, because he had no more money. The Nazis had taken his business, his car, and finally his house. You know what *Objeckte* were?'

'Yes,' John said, 'confiscated Jewish properties. I spent a good part of my youth in Germany. Too damned much of it, in fact.'

'But the man they sold M'sieur Casimir Rabinowski's house to was a good Goy. There *are* good Goyim, thank God. Few, but those few deserve every blessing. So he looked for M'sieur Rabinowski, and paid him for the house all over again – paid him an immense sum of money: ten thousand American dollars. Jean! Why are you looking at me like that?'

'Do you know the good gentile's name, Simone?'

'Laisse-moi penser. M'sieur – M'sieur Fah-whoa—!'

John threw back his head and laughed aloud.

'Not Fah-whoa, Simone, Farrow. The same as mine. John Farrow – my father!'

'Ah, non, Jean, ce n'est pas possible!'

'Oui, c'est bien possible. My father told me exactly the same story, except that he didn't mention any names. Simone! Where are you going?'

'To tell Anton, of course! It will make him so happy!'

'No, you don't, idiote! You must finish the story, first. Already you have made un tour du monde. You will never make a writer. Look. The story is *about* your Uncle Aaron, who is a colonel in the Soviet Army, and *what* he wrote Anton's father. The rest is irrelevant.'

'Yes, you are right. You are always right, mon Jean. Even when you are wrong, as in refusing to make love to me. But now, kiss me – or I won't tell you the rest of it. And to give me strength, for the rest of it is very bad.'

He kissed her. She said: *'Hmmmm! M'sieur Doux-baisers! Encore!'*

'No,' he said. 'I won't. You know what that leads to.'

'But I want it to lead to that!' Then she bent her head, whispered. 'No, I don't. Because it is quite impossible, isn't it? Toi et moi – we have no future, have we?'

He stared at her, said, 'Why not?'

'First, the story. Mon Oncle Aaron wrote M'sieur Rabinowski in New York whose address he had of Anton's Oncle Yigal. And he enclosed a letter to be sent back to *my* father in Nice. Because you see, you Yankees – *voilà!* It is as Byron said, *tu es américain, vraiment, n'est-ce pas?'*

'Yes, I am,' John said.

'Tant pis! But I forgive you. It wasn't your fault, was it? Anyhow. Since your government still maintained relations with Vichy in those days we could receive letters from the States. So we got the letter and – oh, Jean!'

'What does "Oh Jean" mean, *mon ange?'*

'That it is too – terrible, mon amour. In the *shtetl* of Oncle Aaron, there is no one left alive. Les boches killed them all. Men, women, old people, babies in their mothers' arms. All, Jean, all! And not only there – they have wiped out every *shtetl* in that part of Poland. Mon oncle estimates that more than seventy thousand Jews have been murdered – and that only up to the time he left there. Ah, no! Don't look at me like that! Suis pas menteuse! It's the truth, I tell you, the truth! And don't tell me that the people of Göethe, of Schiller, of Mozart, of Beethoven, of Hegel, of Kant, of Bach, of – of Herr *Lipschitz* himself, could not do such things! Do not employ le mot civilisé of them. They are *not* civilized! And I am commencing to wonder whether any people is. You Yankees say *you* are civilized, and look what you have done to *vos peaux rouges et vos noirs!'*

He bent his head. Looked up again.

'I wasn't going to say that, Simone,' he said. 'Because they are also the people of Fichte, who first taught the decadence of the Latin races and the Jews, and of the same Hegel you've mentioned – God knows why! – because he taught them that the state must dispense with such sentimental nonsense as ethics and morality, of Von Treitschke who taught them unquestioning obedience, that worst of German vices. Of Nietzsche, who gave them their vocabulary: *Ubermenschen, Untermenschen,* Schopenhauer, who added to it: "*Herrenvolk und Sklavenvolk,*" of Wagner who dramatized for them the blood-swilling blond beasts that he and they call heroes. I don't think that any other people *ever* produced such a collection of totally pernicious thinkers in so short a space of time. And, as if they didn't already have enough loudly braying, pompous native asses of their own, they even managed to import two of the absolutely vilest minds of modern times: Count Joseph Arthur de Gobineau, a *Frenchman,* my sweet! And the *Englishman,* Houston Stewart Chamberlain, who, between them, managed to put that quintessential *merde* of Aryan, Nordic, blond racial superiority into a form simple enough for even an unschooled idiot like Hitler to grasp it.

'So, I grant you your point, Simone. They are not civilized. In fact, they're monsters. And we, *les américains,* are spiritually their children, though we lack any kind of philosophers, even evil ones. But is mindless racism any less evil than a carefully thought-out one? The child is father to the man! Because the fact remains that it was *we,* not they, who first tried to exterminate an entire race. Nearly succeeded at it, too. So we have a long way to go before we reach civilization – if we *ever* do, which I doubt, mon amour.'

'Oh, Jean – pardonne-moi! Je suis cruelle! Ton père était vraiment civilisé et – Oh, Jean! Jean! C'était toi! C'était toi!'

'*What* was me, *petit oiseau fou?*'

'That kid! That kid in Berlin whom the Nazis beat almost to death because he tried to save that old Jewish couple! It was *you!*'

'Yes,' Jean said quietly, 'I suppose it *was* me. Who told *you* that?'

'Anton's father! He wrote my father that your father wrote him from Switzerland that his son was in a very bad way in the hospital because of that. *His* son! You! Let me go! Let me go! I'm going to kiss your hands and your feet!'

'I think that's a few too many fathers and that they've all talked too damned much. Now be still, will you? I only did what I had to. What I couldn't have lived with myself if I hadn't done. Viens, donc, petite hystérique – let's go back to where the others are—'

'No. Not yet. Do not be afraid. I am calm now. Même tranquille. Jean, there is a thing I must say to you.'

He smiled, said gently: 'Say it then.'

'I am not worthy of you. I am a bad girl. *Une garce.*'

'*Voilà!*' he said. 'How many hundreds of thousands of men have you slept with by now, *ma petite drôle d'une garce?*'

'No hundreds of thousands. Just two. The first one was a boy when I was at the Université de Paris. That was curiosity. That's all. Part of my education. That doesn't count.'

'But the other?'

'*Un homme.* A man. Don't ask me to tell you about him. I idolized him, Jean. He was good and sweet and gentle and patient *et – merveilleux au lit* – You see? I must tell the truth! But he did a thing I can never forgive. He saved my life – at the cost of our cause. Never do that for me, Jean. Let me die, first, please!'

'That's an awfully hard thing to ask of me, Simone.'

'Jean, hear me! In most of history – wars haven't been dichotomies, not really—'

'Sorbonne Philosophy Class Number?' he teased.

'I am serious, Jean! Most wars, in the past, have been Hegelian tragedies, my love. You know the term?'

'Yes. The choice between evil and evil. Or between good and good. Where both sides are somewhat right or both are somewhat wrong.'

'Exactly. How wonderful you are! Did I ever tell you how much I love you?'

'Not for a long, long time!' he said and kissed her.

'Mmmmm! More! Another one!'

'No. Go on with your philosophical dissertation, mon ange—'

'But *this* war *is* a dichotomy. The difference between the rightness of the one side and the wrongness of the other is immense. We can say truly, what the writers of the Wasteland generation – you know the works of Eliot, don't you?—'

'Yes, the anti-semitic bastard! As bad as Pound, if not worse. But then all poets are bastards, aren't they?'

She stared at him, whispered: 'Then you *knew*!'

He looked at her blankly. Said: 'Then I knew what?'

She released a huge sigh of pure relief.

'*Rien!* Nothing! I am a very foolish little bird, aren't I? I was going to say that the Wasteland period writers in English, anyhow, sneered at *les gros mots*! The big phrases. The grandiloquent ones. But now I am going to say a big, big phrase that happens to be true: this war *is* in defence of civilization, Jean. If we lose it, a night of barbarism will settle over Europe, over the world. And it will last a thousand years.'

He looked at her, said, '*Çà, d'accord*. I agree.'

'So, if you see that they are about to capture me, please shoot me, Jean. I know I could not stand their tortures. And if they take you, I will shoot you, I promise.'

'And I,' he said quietly.

'But if I am taken, let me die! Even if you *know* it is by torture. Do not risk your life – or the good you can do our cause – our holy cause! Yes I say it! – for me. It is – easy to die, mon Jean. What is difficult is to let other people die. People you love. So I tell you this, I will sacrifice *you*, whom I love more than life, to stop them. To sacrifice me, bah! *C'est rien!* That's nothing. But to be willing to sacrifice your love, mon Jean, is very great. To give other lives than one's own – is a suffering you cannot possibly imagine. You reproach yourself endlessly, you beg God to let you die, remembering—'

'I know, Simone,' he whispered, 'for I have done it.'

'*Ah, non! Ça, non!* Not your Hélène! You did not sacrifice her. She sacrificed herself. And it is precisely that which is unpardonable! You must not die for me, Jean! Promise me.'

He shook his head.

'No,' he said, 'that I will not promise. Besides, you're wrong. I was not speaking of Hélène. I liquidated those SS in Paris, knowing that the Germans were going to shoot thirty-five or forty innocent people to pay for it. But they outdid themselves. They shot seventy-five.'

'*Mon Dieu!*' she murmured. 'How you must have suffered!'

'I went mad. Truly. I was in the psychiatric ward of the London County Clinic – for two months. So they decided to give me the shock treatment. They parachuted me here – into Vercors. Here, I've had only to risk my own life. Which is nothing, as you said. A worthless existence I wanted to be freed of – but now that you've come, it, my life, has also become precious to me. I want to live, Simone! A thousand years or more – at your side, for ever. I want to die in your arms. Be buried beside you—'

'Jean!' she sobbed. 'Oh, Jean, please! Turn away your face! Do not look at me! I cannot bear it if you do . . .'

'You can't bear what, *'tite oiseau?'*

'What I have to tell you. Jean – I cannot marry you. Not ever. I will be *ta 'tite maîtresse,* for the duration if you want me to. But marry you, I cannot!'

He whirled, caught her by both shoulders, said: 'Why not, Simone?'

'Parce que tu – tu n'est pas juif!'

'Oh, merde, alors!' he said.

'I know. It is a foolishness. My Jewishness has never meant anything to me. I am not religious. I am only now beginning to learn Hebrew a little – so that I may go to Israel, afterward, dwell under mine own vine and fig tree in mine own land! But now it does mean something. We are being – exterminated, Jean. I have been a silly slut who slept only with Goyim because Jewish boys were so solemn and bored me stiff! But now to all the betrayals our people have suffered, I can not add one more. Not even one. Because even assimilation is a kind of racial death. We will need *our* children, Jean. Beautiful Jewish children. Sabras to defend the homeland. So now mon Goy – kiss me. And forget me because—'

He grinned at her, said: 'Your – ex-Goy, Simone! How does one become Jewish, little bird?'

She stared at him, speechlessly. Saw that he meant it, meant it absolutely. She wept in a way that was beautiful to see, beautiful as she was beautiful. From the inside out. From the soul.

He put his arms around her and began to say very quietly:

' "Whither thou goest, I will go. Whither thou liest, I will lie—" ' She clung to him sobbing helplessly listening to his voice saying the slow, sonorous words, the truest, most beautiful pledge of love ever written. ' "And thy people, will be my people; And thy God, my God.

' "Whither thou diest, I shall die; and there also will I be buried.

> May Almighty God rain Hell's curses down on me
> And terrors without number,
> If Death, itself, part me from thee!" '

Then they got up and went very quietly, together, back towards where the others were.

10

The one book that Attorney John Farrow of New York City and Westchester County had written bore the deceptively simple title *Pyrrhic Victory: The True Cost of War.* Its theme was that no war in the whole of human history had ever been worth its cost in terms of human anguish; and that not the slightest probability existed that one could ever be. In the end he refrained from publishing it out of the truly mature conviction that the people likely to be impressed by his precisely reasoned arguments were those who already held beliefs very similar to his own; while the others – those who substituted shibboleths, slogans (America: Love it or leave it! God's Country, and the like) syllogisms (War is hell; War must be won; therefore to win war one must employ hellish means) easy dichotomies (they're the bad guys; we – and our allies, including Joseph Stalin – are the good guys; and we stay just as good after having boiled the brains inside baby skulls when we fire-bombed Dresden and Tokyo after having atomized Hiroshima and Nagasaki) simplistic mathematics (that two wrongs, with one committed by the winning side, add up to a right), as well as any and all evasions possible to escape the terrible pain of thought – far from being converted to his point of view would respond with bellows of unthinking rage. It was, he conceded, more than a little stupid to prove at this late date that the biblical injunction: 'Of making of many books there is no end; and much study is a weariness of the flesh' was perfectly correct.

Yet that stillborn work of his did contain several things of value, among them his use of the history of Redoubt Vercors to prove one of his basic contentions: that any man stupid enough to even want to become a professional soldier in the first place, is ipso facto, much too stupid to manage a war.

'In the beginning,' John Farrow wrote, 'it was not a soldier who conceived the master plan for Vercors, but a civilian architect named Pierre Dalloz. Living on a farm near Sassenage within the Vercors salient itself, mountaineer by reason of his simple love for mountains and thereby knowing every inch of that great fortress built by nature herself, Monsieur Dalloz drew up the detailed plan for Operation Montagnards, which, despite the defects that the work of any single man must inevitably contain – products of his misconceptions, his human lack of total knowledge, even of his mental set, his personality, his temperament – was, as a piece of military strategy, very good indeed.

'To appreciate its virtues, one must study the topography of Vercors itself. Three rivers – the Drôme, the Drac, and the Isère – form its boundaries; from their banks, great stone cliffs tower up abruptly, averaging from eight hundred to more than one thousand metres high; within the great paleolithic flint arrowhead they form lies a plateau about six hundred metres high, ringed about by those natural walls far greater than the walls of China.

'There are only seven roads that enter the plateau; roads which due to the ruggedness of the terrain are vulnerable to rock slides, all of which – Pierre Dalloz pointed out – could easily be made hopelessly impassable by a little judicious, and not even difficult mining. There are also not quite two dozen mountaineers' trails leading into Vercors; but they are so narrow, and so winding that the enemy must, perforce, abandon his armoured carriers and attack up them single file. Dalloz was sure that less than a *trentaine* (thirty men) could not only hold each of the more important ones, but could also with impunity inflict such losses upon the foe that he would be forced to beat a quick retreat.

'In all these aspects of the terrain, his analysis was perfectly correct. Yet, in practice, all of them failed. Though mined, not one of the seven roads was ever blown. When storming up the mountaineers' trails no German attack was successfully turned back. The roads were not blown because we at Vercors hoped to use them in our counter-attacks when the airborne paratroopers we were promised came to our aid. On the trails our men slaughtered the Nazis in grisly heaps, but always, after the last bullet from our dime-store Sten guns was gone, the last grenade had been thrown, there were still hundreds of Germans pounding up those trails which Dalloz had been quite correct in believing could be held; except he failed to realize that at the last we would be holding them with rocks.

'Monsieur Dalloz was a Frenchman, a logical son of the world's most logical race, who all through their history have been defeated by their logic. For it was only after this particular cruel war was over that French philosophers came to conclude, and to write that man and his fate rest always in the domain of the ineffectual, the absurd. His plan was perfectly logical, magnificently conceived. It failed totally because it depended upon factors beyond our control, upon men in high places in Algiers and London, the best of whom were sincere, idealistic, high-minded fools, the rest the near morons that the military always seem to be, with – let it be stated frankly – not a few moral cowards among them, and, the events clearly indicate, at least one enemy spy, and/or a traitor or two.

'So be it. As a fortress, or "Redoubt Vercors" as it was called, the salient had only one natural weak point: next to the village of St Nizier to the north, near the point of the arrowhead, there are neither cliffs nor walls but only a long slope leading down to the great city of Grenoble, capital of Dauphiné. But it was here that Dalloz had planned to concentrate his forces, not for defence against the German Panzers, but for attack. For the one great essential of this master plan was that it should be put into action *only after the Allied invasion of Provence from the south* had thrown the Nazis into full retreat, whereupon the Maquis would come swarming down from our fortress to maul and murder them.

'What happened then? Every man in Vercors, this writer among them, was sure that we had heard on the night of June 5, 1944, the signals broadcast from London for us to attack. Of course confusion reigned; June 6 was D-Day in Normandy. By the time London and Algiers got around to correcting what might well have been a mistake born of our eagerness and our tortured nerves, we were in full battle with an enemy force of 27,000 men as against our 3,000.

'What happened is history. The Allied invasion of Provence, striking at Marseilles, Toulon, and by pure error, St Tropez, began on August 15, 1944. But the battle of Vercors had ended July 27, three weeks before the Task Forces Romeo, Rugby, and Rosie hit the beaches of the south, to be followed by Kodak and Butler; and three quarters of the men and women of Vercors, and even *many of their children* were already dead.

'The whys of this senseless tragedy are less well known. First of all, as a non-soldier, Dalloz did not understand the immense difficulties of the logistics needed to support his plan. In sober fact, on one level, sufficient in itself to totally negate the tactical excellence of the plan, medium to heavy weapons supplies, from 12.7 millimetre (fifty calibre) machine guns, through trench mortars, 20 millimetre, 37 millimetre, 40 millimetre, and 75 millimetre cannon, were non-existent. After June 6, 1944, with the Normandy landings in full operation, the Allies simply hadn't a gun and its ammunition in these categories to spare. Another factor was the terrible distances. From Omaha Beach-head to Vercors is all of six hundred miles; from Algiers, an equal distance or more, and the aircraft to drop supplies were, more often than not, badly needed elsewhere.

'But the greatest difficulty was that Dalloz, and the men around him simply did not grasp the immense and terrible stupidity of the military mind.

'For Dalloz's plan contained a fatal flaw; but one, unfortunately, of such a nature that there was no possibility of Chavant, Le Roy, Yves Farge, Jean Moulin, Dalloz himself, or any of the Resistance leaders' detecting it, for to do so they would have needed additional and crucial information they simply did not have, and could not obtain as long as they remained in hiding in occupied France. That flaw was both simple and enormous at the same time: the brutal fact was that at no time during 1943, and even less in 1944 when the actual invasions of the continent were devouring men and material at an unprecedented rate, could the Allies have supplied Vercors with the minimum essentials of medium and heavy weapons necessary to attack armoured Panzer units successfully, not to mention defend the citadel against them if attacked.

'This flaw should have been nothing short of glaring to any half-way competent junior officer in London or Algiers with even a superficial knowledge of what lay to hand as well as what was going to be needed for Omaha Beach in Normandy and Operation Faisçeau in Provence. Yet the fact remains that no office whatsoever to whom the plan was shown – when General Charles Delestraint, moved by the enthusiasm of Jean Moulin, president of the National Council of the Resistance, was flown to London with a copy by the usual Lysander moonlight pick-up flight – seems to have detected it. This in generals of command rank was and remains inexcusable. Their only option in view of this insurmountable problem of supply was to formally and flatly reject Operation Montagnards from the outset as the tactical impossibility that they, with the logistics figures at their fingertips, had no conceivable excuse not to know it was.

'Instead, displaying that monumental incompetence in the exercise of their own profession that is the hallmark of the military mind, they accepted it. And thereby condemned nearly twenty-seven hundred men, women, and not a few children, to unusually horrible deaths. On February 25, 1943, the BBC broadcast the signal 'The mountaineers should continue to scale the heights,' and all Vercors went wild with joy. But it was not until a full eight months had passed, late in November 1943, that the first airdrop of desperately needed supplies was made, and the peasants of the countryside retrieved and kept nearly half of them. The author of this work preceded those supplies, and by the same method, a parachute, to Vercors by one short week.

'In January 1944, the Germans attacked us for the first time. On the twenty-ninth at Malleval, we learned what it was to try to hold off an armoured column with dime-store Stens, pistols and grenades. They burned Malleval to the ground. They caught eight of our men, and several civilians in a farmhouse. With no call for surrender, they hosed it with *Flamenwerfer*. Our people died in agony in the flames.

'The second of their columns was stopped dead. They lost eleven dead and thirteen wounded. Retreated in good order, went back to Grenoble leaving Barraques-en-Vercors a corpse-strewn ruin, and half of Rousset, another village, burned to the ground.

'On March 18 they hit us again; this time at La Matrassière near St Julien. We lost that day Captain Roger Guigou, Lieutenant Marc Oschwold, Lieutenant Simon-Perret, and three enlisted men. They burned all the farmhouses round about St Julien, shot dead Monsieur Borel, a peasant seventy-five years of age before the eyes of his wife and son, burned alive a wounded Maquisard who had hidden in the straw of the barn.

'The first week in April it was the Milice's turn. They stormed into La Chapelle-en-Vercors and into Vassieux, led by the Duke of Bernonville and of D'Agostine. They murdered and tortured, robbed, burned and raped to their hearts content, sent dozens of their own countrymen off to the slave factories of Germany, executed Lieutenant Doucin, and marched away again.

'But late in April we began to hope. A mission from England, Captain Thackthwaite and the men of Group Union parachuted in to us, to learn in detail our needs. We told them: mortars, cannon, heavy machine guns, anti-tank guns, 20, 37, 40 millimetres. We didn't even ask for 75s. We knew better by then. The Lysanders pulled Mission Union out. On May 3 they were in London again. They presented our demands. The officers in charge of supply laughed in their faces. But we didn't know that, then.

'Eugene Chavant flew down to Algiers. They shoved him from office to office, in each of which he had to explain to the military just what we meant to do. He came back to us with an order signed by Jacques Soustelle in the name of General Charles de Gaulle, promising us aid from the air. In Algiers they made Chavant a verbal commitment – how careful they were not to put the details in writing! – to send in four thousand parachute troops. This writer is well aware that Soustelle in his work, *Envers et Contre Tout* flatly states that two groups of regular parachute troops *equipped with heavy arms, including anti-tank guns* (italics the writer!) were sent from Algiers, the first June 29, the second July 8. This writer can only respectfully state that he, personally, had not the privilege of encountering even one of these troops; and as for anti-tank and heavy weapons – well even a great archaeologist like Soustelle must be permitted at times his flights of fantasy!

'In London, Pierre Dalloz was received with great respect on the same day that Chavant landed in Algiers. They asked him to explain his plan. He bristled, said: "Why should I? You've had it in writing for more than six months!"

'They looked at him in astonishment, said: "We *have*? Surely you're mistaken M'sieur Dalloz!" Then they started to look for it. Three days later, the magnificent Operation Montagnards plan was found *one flight above, in the same building*, in the offices of General Koenig, recently appointed commander of the Resistance forces, *unopened*. And Dalloz began to understand at last the monumental limitation of the military mind.

'Fernand Grénier, who, much against the lofty general's will, was minister of Air in De Gaulle's cabinet, rounded up – with extreme reluctance, Jacques Soustelle later wrote (though long before the time he, too, had left the ranks of the double-barred Cross of Lorraine) – twenty-four creaking, patched-up wrecks of transport planes. Old as they were, few as they were, with the Normandy invasion under way, and all the Luftwaffe fighters tied up there, they could have brought us in the men and arms we needed almost with impunity. But Fernand Grénier was a Communist. And Charles de Gaulle, Saviour of France, let Grénier's orders for the airborne relief of Vercors sit on his desk unsigned from June 5 through July 27, 1944.

'Until Vercors was no more. Until the bravest and best of us had died.

'Is it, then, any wonder that Civil Commander Eugene Chavant's last message was: "If you do not send help now, we will agree with the population in saying that you in London and Algiers have understood nothing of our situation here, and we will consider you criminals and cowards. I repeat, criminals and cowards." But the words he used were wrong. Instead of *criminels et lâches,* he should have said, *crétins et idiots. . . .*'

This in part was what John Farrow wrote. What he had no need to write, because it was burned into his very flesh, inscribed for ever along his nerves, etched into his mind, his heart was the memory of his and Simone's two honeymoons. The first of them lasted from June 1 to June 13; the second from June 17 to July 19. The Germans ended both of them; the second one for ever.

Even the first one almost did not take place at all, because of Jean le Fou's antic folly. But finally it did. And this was the manner of it:

They, Simone and Jean, came walking out from under the trees together, their arms about each other's waists.

'Tell me, Simone,' Jean asked her then, 'are you an only child? I am.'

'I wasn't,' she said sadly. 'But I may be now.'

'I don't understand,' Jean said.

'I know you don't,' she told him, 'but that's how it is. Ask Pepe. About his brother Luis – and the nuns at Fayence – and then you'll begin to understand.'

Pepe was sitting with Byron and Anton before a fire. For even though it was the last week in May 1944, in a place as high as Vercors it was still cool in the daytime, and really cold at night. They had finished eating. Thanks to the local farmers at Vercors, food was never in short supply. Anton was telling Byron and Pepe – switching back and forth between English and French to do it – how an FFI réseau of *cheminots*, railway men in civilian life, had dynamited the tracks just beyond Hendaye near the Spanish border in the wild hope of capturing no less than Adolf Hitler, himself, and thus ending the war with one lone, magnificent coup. It seemed they had been informed – or rather misinformed – that Der Führer was having still another meeting there with Generalíssimo Franco, the Caudillo of Spain.

'If it had been so,' Pepe said in his bad French, and not without a certain pride, 'Hitler would have left there without his lacy drawers. Because Franco is a *Gallego*. And if you put a Gallego in a locked room with the Devil and a Jew, the Gallego will come out with the keys to both Jerusalem and Hell. Then what happened, Anton?'

'What happened,' Anton said with a grin, 'was that they had to settle for *me* instead of old Schicklegruber. Because the train that the SS commando group who'd kidnapped me in Lisboa had me on – guarded by four Aryan nordic supermen, the shortest of whom was one metre ninety five (6 feet 4 inches), and the lightest of whom weighed one-hundred-five kilos (230 pounds), hit those torn-up rails about an hour after we'd crossed the frontier between Irun and Hendaye. I'd say we couldn't have been much more than twenty-five kilometres or so inside France when it happened—'

'And?' Byron prompted.

'Those cheminots had themselves a ball, machine-gunning the Nazis as they poured from the wrecked cars. They even got my four supermen who panicked just like ordinary mortals. I stayed where I was. No help for it, since those bastards had me handcuffed to the arm of the train seat. Anyhow, those FFI railroad types came through the cars after the slaughter was over, looking for loot. Guns and ammunition, mostly. And those ruddy handcuffs were the best letter of introduction I could have asked for. They shot them loose from the seat. Got me out of there. Passed me along from réseau to réseau in the general direction of Nice, where I'd asked to be sent, because as you know, I'd spent most of my childhood there, playing hide and seek with Simone, damn her! Finally, when I pass Frejus, I caught up with this one, Réseau Merle.'

'And Simone?' Byron said. 'She was jolly glad to see you again, I assume?'

'You assume dead, damn wrong,' Anton laughed ruefully.

'Hell, she kissed me and cried. Even seemed overjoyed to see me again. But that night, when I tried to profit from the occasion a little, she bent the barrel of her Sten over my head. Opened an eight centimetre long gash in my scalp! And – oh hell, here she comes now with your oddball. What's his name again?'

'John Farrow,' Byron said, 'but here, Jean, Jean Dubois.'

Pepe looked up at the sound of Jean's name. Seeing Jean and Simone coming towards them, he ripped out in Spanish:

'Look, Johnny! If you get Simone pregnant, I won't have any other recourse except to order my men to shoot you. For treason against our cause! A soldier – even a female soldier – with a belly as big as a house isn't worth very much, you know!'

Jean grinned at him, said: 'Don't worry, Pepe. My little brother is like the lifts in Madrid. He *never* rises. When I go out I always take with me one of those signs I brought back from your country; National Manufacture: Out of Order! To keep from disappointing the girls, understand?'

Pepe threw back his head and roared.

Simone stamped her foot.

'I don't like that!' she said. 'What *are* you two saying?' 'It's forbidden to sleep with you,' Pepe said with a grin. His French was awful. 'The Spaniards are the third worst linguists in the world,' Jean thought, 'the first being the English who have spread their language all over the earth by shouting it with ever-increasing loudness at the natives; the second being the North Americans, whose *English* isn't even comprehensible much of the time; but the Spanish are an honourable third. Even if Pepe stays in France till he's eighty, his French will be difficult to understand.'

Simone flashed Pepe an impish grin.

'That's none of your business, Pepe,' she said. 'But anyhow, if the matter interests you so much, you're *already* too late!'

'What a character,' Pepe roared. 'Johnny the speed king!'

But Jean had seen Anton Rabinowski's eyes.

'Don't believe her,' he said in English, 'she's only kidding Pepe. Of course I'm perfectly willing to oblige any dainty little piece whomsoever; but this war has left me somewhat less than able.'

'My gentleman!' Simone mocked: 'My perfect gentleman of the old school! D'you know what, Anton? He takes off his pants most politely. Like that duke. That English duke, and leaves on his tie.'

'Oh I say, now, Simone!' Byron protested, 'that's a bit of too much, isn't it?'

'She's talking about a limerick,' Anton grinned. 'But she *never* gets anything right.'

'Then *you* say it, dahlink!' Simone said.

'Volontiers!' Anton laughed, and began:

'With heaving breast, the duke undressed
The vicar's wife to lie on!
He thought it lewd
To do it nude
So he kept his old school tie on!'

'*¿Qué es eso?*' Pepe said: '*¿Qué han dicho, Juanjo?*'

'Nothing, Pepe,' Jean said in Spanish. 'Poetry. English poetry. Makes no sense even in English. Don't make me translate it.'

He saw another gamine's grin forming itself about the corners of Simone's mouth. So before she could say something else outrageous, he said to Pepe: 'Will you tell me the story of the nuns of Fayence and of your brother Luis and all that?'

Pepe glared at Simone. Then he said, sadly: 'All right. I'll tell it.'

'*En français, s'il-vous plaît!*' Byron said.

'No,' Pepe said. 'My French is too bad. In Spanish. Johnny can translate it for both of you.'

He sat there, looking into the fire. Then he said:

'The nuns at Fayence have an orphanage. And a school. My brother Luis sent his children there to learn French. And they did learn it very quickly and easily.' He paused for Jean to translate; then went on again.

'But the children of my brother don't look French. For one thing, they are very dark; and for another, they are very beautiful. So the Nazis came, and asked, "Are these children Jewish?" And the nuns told them, no, they are Spanish. But one of the Nazis had been in Spain with the Condor Legion, while your great democratic republican nations stood by and let rich reactionaries and pot-bellied generals of an infinity of corruption mount the first successful rebellion in all of history ever directed by the rich against the poor, while Hitler and Mussolini tried out their new aircraft and tanks and cannons with our poor ragged asses as target for tonight – *every* night.

'So he said to the children in Spanish: "*¿Sois españoles, niños?*" And they answered him, "*Si, señor, nosotros somos españoles.*" So he let them alone except to say a thing that neither Luis nor I paid much attention to when the children told us. "Your mother must be very pretty. Is she young?"

'So the kids told him yes their mother was very pretty and oh yes she was young. Then the other Nazis took all the boys out behind the school and made them pull down their pants. Then they brought them all back again, but made the three who had been circumcised stand apart.

'After that, they ordered the three circumcised boys to point out which of the girls were their sisters. Two of them did so at once. But the brother of Simone here—'

Jean whirled upon her, his eyes wild. 'You should have told me this yourself! This is ugly of you, Simone!'

'Not ugly, my Jean,' she whispered. 'Cowardly—'

'—denied he had a sister, there. So they started to beat him. They beat him and beat him and beat him! And the nuns tried to stop them. But they slapped the nuns to the floor of the schoolroom and went on beating the brother of Simone. And then a little girl, a very pretty little girl with blue eyes and golden hair stepped forward. "Moi, je suis sa soeur," she said. And the nuns all cried out, "She is lying; she is not his sister look we will show you the certificates and—" '

'*Cette fille,*' Jean said, '*était-elle ta soeur,* Simone?'

'No,' Simone said, 'my sister – if she lives – is very like me. Same eyes, same hair. Of course she is ten years younger than I am. The two boys, my brothers Ruben and Theodore, came between us. My sister, Rachel, was the youngest of us all. Theodore is the one Pepe's talking about. Or he was. He's dead now of course—'

'But the Nazis took away the three boys and the three girls—' Pepe continued, 'including the little blonde who wasn't Jewish at all, but only the little sweetheart of the brother of Simone. But before that, they looked at the nuns. Two of the nuns were old women, so they took them out back where the outhouses were and shot them in the back of their heads. The other three were young and pretty. So they said to the young pretty ones, "You come with us. Since you have behaved like whores by hiding these filthy degenerate Jewish children you will be treated like whores." Then they put them in the back of the truck with the children and drove away.

'And the same night they drove up to my brother's house. His wife said to him, "Run out the back way. I will talk to them and give you a chance to get away. So my brother Luis who is an intellectual and like all intellectuals somewhat of a coward ran out the back way and my sister-in-law Asunción went to the door. But they weren't after Luis because they didn't even know he was with the Maquis. They were after Asunción herself.

'So they took her and tattooed a number on her left arm and on her right they tattooed *Nur für Offiziere* (Only for Officers) and put her in a field whorehouse. The same field whorehouse they'd already put the three younger nuns into.'

'Jesus!' Byron said, 'is this *true*, Simone? Deuced bad show to put a chap on with a tale like this.'

'Yes, Byron; it's all quite true,' Simone said.

'My brother Luis is very advanced. He has a university education. But it did him no good. That night his advanced ideas all deserted him and he became *simplemente hombre totalmente español y muy macho* which were things I'd accused him of not being, even though he'd made a lot of babies on Asunción. So he took a Sten gun and two Molotov cocktails and went down to the German camp. He had no trouble getting into it, because even the sentries were too busy watching the fun and games to make their rounds properly.

'There were nearly forty young officers, most of them fighter pilots, lined up before the door of the whorehouse. Inside it he could hear the nuns screaming. My sister-in-law wasn't screaming—'

Pepe paused and gave a wicked grin.

'Maybe she was even enjoying herself – who knows? But my poor fool of a brother went crazy at the sound of those screams and used up a whole clip on those horny bastards waiting outside and put in another and used up most of that before somebody shot him. He killed eighteen Nazis outright, and wounded God knows how many more. Seven of the wounded died the next day. Pretty good, eh?'

'Jesus!' Byron said: 'Jesus Jesus Jesus!'

'And while he was lying on the ground gun-shot and bleeding to death, he managed to throw both those Molotov cocktails through the window of the whorehouse. It went up like a torch. And you know what, Juanjo?'

'No,' Jean said. '*No sé absolutamente nade. ¿Que pasó entonces, Pepe?*'

'The nuns stopped screaming. Started to sing: "Gloria! Gloria! Gloree-ah in Excelsis Deo!" They were burning alive, but they went right on singing. Because they were glad. They'd rather be dead than have to lie down for Nazis. For anybody, maybe. And it wasn't even suicide which all those ravens from the caves of ignorance and superstition call a mortal sin, because they hadn't done it themselves. They died singing. Louder and louder and louder and maybe the last of it was more like screaming but even so it was the idea that counted, wasn't it? My sister-in-law outscreamed all three of them put together. But then she was only a woman, not *una religiosa*. I have to admit those *monjas* died well. Almost as though they were *españolas*. Goes to show you, doesn't it?'

'*¿Y que demuestra eso, Pepe?*' Jean said.

'*Que no importa que clase de mierda* one believes, if one believes it truly. Communism. Catholicism. Socialism. Whatever, I'll be *el hijo predilecto de la Gran Puta* if it makes any difference at all. . . .'

He looked at Simone. She was crying very quietly.

'*Mierda!*' he said. '*Juanjo*, take *ese idiota* off into the woods and screw her good. Make her happy. I hate to see her cry.'

'But I didn't,' John Farrow remembered wryly as he lay staring at the ceiling of the room in the Hôtel Bellevue at Grasse. 'Instead, we talked. I asked her questions, and she answered me.'

'Simone – tell me: what happened to your brother – and to that little girl?'

'To her nothing. Her father was a regular army man. Vichy army. So he went to the Wehrmacht commander in that area with his daughter's birth certificate, baptismal certificate *toute genre de documents* – and the Wehrmacht general for once had the guts to outface the SS. The little girl was released. She'll grow up to be a bitter anti-semite, sure as hell.'

'But your brother?'

'He was deported. Which means he's dead.'

'Simone, *ma chérie*, you don't actually know—'

'I do actually know!' she flared. 'He was ten years old. One year older than my little sister. Children that age don't even live to reach the death camps. They die on the trains. In those cattle cars. From the cold. From hunger. From sickness.'

There was nothing to be said to that. So he asked, 'But what were your brothers and sisters doing up in Fayence? Isn't that an awfully long way from Nice?'

'Yes,' she said, 'but I was in Vence. With Papa et Maman. But afterward I got a job. Because I spoke English. With a man in Tourette-sur-Loup.'

She looked at him when she said that. Looked at him hard, in a hateful, sullen way. ('But it didn't register!' John Farrow thought. 'She was trying to tell me, but my head wasn't working; strictly *no Funciona* in those days.')

'But why were any of you there?' he persisted.

'Because of the Italians, bless them!'

He laughed, said: 'They are cowards!'

She said slowly: 'Ils sont des gens très civilisés. Je les aime, beaucoup.'

'Now, Simone!'

'Listen to me, Jean! They are very bad soldiers. They run. Which means that they are sufficiently intelligent to realize that war is an obscenity – and that life is – or ought to be – beautiful. Everywhere they've been – in Africa, in Crete, in Greece, in their own land, they have saved my people. Sometimes at the risk of their own lives. My family was in Vence because the Italian commissioner for Jewish Affairs, Signor Lospinoso sent us and 25,000 other Jews up to Vence and Megève to keep us out of the reach of his so very gentille allies, les allemands! Every Jew who is alive in south-eastern France owes his life to the fact that *les italiens sont des gens civilisés!* They *hate* the Germans, *tu sais!* Give them a chance to shoot Nazis as in Corsica, and look how brave they become!'

'Ça c'est vrai,' Jean said, *'Mais—'*

'But nothing! You have millions of acres of empty land in your country – and before you'll take in one Jewish refugee, you'll let us all die, all, I tell you! *Je me demande qui sont les lâches vraiment, Jean? Les allemands, eux, sont des gens courageux, n'est-ce pas? Un lion est courageux! Un tigre! Toutes les grandes bêtes!* Oh God, give me a man *human* enough to love, pity, and be afraid!'

She turned away from him. She was sobbing convulsively.

'Simone—' he whispered, and put his arms about her shoulders.

'Ne me touche pas!' she screamed at him. *'Tu es un héros! Tout le monde déjà m'a dit!* A hero! So you stink! You stink of blood!'

He took his hand off her shoulder. Stood there, with his head bent.

'Any man who can murder children—' she whispered; 'any race incapable of – of – compassion – anyone who stands by idly and assents to murder – to genocide – those are the cowards, Jean. Not those beautiful Italian boys who throw down their rifles and run because they're young and love life and are afraid. . . .'

She turned her profile towards him, her long, hooked nose, her heavy lips, her utterly Semitic features, her high cheekbones with the tears glistening on them, her utterly unmatched and unique loveliness that halted his breath, his heart, then made them race.

'But people who can do what *they* did at the Vél d'Hiv, while the French stood by with folded hands and let them do – *Moi, je suis juive—*'

('It was a trigger,' John Farrow thought, 'a bolt shot open to dump me back into the past. The words weren't really hers. I had heard them all before. And what hit me in the gut was memory – plunged in deep by – remorse—')

'Lucienne!' he cried aloud: *'Oh bon Dieu! Elle est peut-être morte! Et c'est ma faute! Simone, pardonne-moi! Mais il faut que j'aille—'*

Then he was off and running, sliding, jumping, falling down one of the steepest of the mountaineers' trails.

Simone walked very slowly back to where Byron, Pepe, and Anton were. But Pierre Clemont had joined them. And Yves Martin.

'Byron,' Simone said, *'qui est* – Lucienne?'

'Lucienne?' Byron said; then he remembered. 'Oh—' he said airily, 'a girl. A little girl at Grenoble—'

'Byron, *je t'ai posé une question sérieuse. Lucienne, qui est-elle?'*

Pierre and Yves were grinning at each other. Simone saw that.

'Do *you* know her?' she said to Pierre.

'Yes. Why yes, of course. Not so well as *Jean* does, but all the same—'

'Pierre!' Byron said warningly.

'Do not silence him,' Simone said in English, 'unless you are prepared to tell me the truth. Is she – Jean's mistress?'

Pierre and Yves both got that word. *Mistress* and *maîtresse* are much alike.

'Oh no, daughter,' Pierre said, 'at least no more than she's everybody's mistress. She's a tart. A little whore who—'

Simone turned a stricken face towards Byron.

'A – whore?' she got out, 'he – he left me to – to go to a *whore?*'

'Now see here, Simone!' Byron said, 'I don't know where Jean's gone, but—'

'Elle est trés jolie, cette Lucienne,' Yves said, enjoying the game now. *'Non! Plus que jolie. Elle est belle – vraiment belle, n'est-ce pas, Pierre?'*

'Tais-toi!' Simone screamed at him. 'It is not necessary to make me jealous because I already am! I do not care whether she is pretty as you say, or beautiful or *plus laide que les fesses bleues d'un babouin!*'

Pierre and Yves roared at that. It *was* a good line, Byron conceded that: 'uglier than a baboon's blue ass.'

'What I care about is – does he love her? Does he? Tell me the truth!'

'That, I really couldn't say, my dear,' Byron said, 'for I don't know. What I do know, rather, is that *she* loves him. And the odd part about the matter is that she's Jewish, too.'

'Oh merde!' Simone said.

'I don't believe that,' Anton said a little grimly. 'It's not at all usual to find Jewish girls in whorehouses.'

'Oh don't be a damned chauvinist, Anton!' Simone said angrily. 'It's a matter of luck. By rights *I* should have been in one years ago!'

'That I grant you,' Anton said. 'In fact, you've just delivered yourself of the understatement of the year!'

'Byron – come with me,' Simone said, 'tell me – about her. The truth, not – *comme ces types grossiers* – who only want to plague me.'

'All right,' Byron said, 'excuse us, Anton. *Pardonnez-nous, Pepe, et vous autres—*'

They moved away from the fire.

'She's – a pitiful little thing,' Byron said. 'Truly tragic. I don't think Jean's *ever* slept with her. In fact, I'm sure he hasn't.'

'What makes you so sure?' Simone said sullenly.

'Oh come now, Simone! Even if he has, what difference would it make?'

'If he has – if he does tonight, I'll kill myself.' Simone said.

'Oh cripes!' Byron said. 'Look, Simone, Jean's probably worried about her, that's all. You see she – and another girl – literally risked their lives to help Jean and *me* – pull off a stunt.'

'*Oh merde alors!* Not another one!'

'Like Hélène you mean? No. At least not yet. But if the occasion arose, I'm afraid Lucienne would. She obviously adores him.'

Simone looked at Byron. The tears poured down her face.

'I – I sent him away!' she wailed. 'I told him that he – he stank of blood! I blamed him because the American government won't let Jewish refugees in and—'

'You were in a mood. But I assure you, my dear, that that had nothing to do with Jean's departure. I and he blew up a German warehouse. The sentries guarding it were killed. And Lucienne and Catherine were flirting with those sentries – as Jean had told them to, to keep them out of our way. So Jean's afraid that Lucienne may have been killed – or hurt – through our fault. God knows I hope not! He's burdened himself quite unnecessarily with too much guilt now.'

'You – you're *sure* he doesn't love her?'

'Oh don't be a fool, Simone. As a woman, wife, mate, he loves *you*. That's it. There isn't anybody else. But of course he also loves Lucienne – as a sister, rather. You see she was telling him how she lost all her family at the Vélodrome d'Hiver and—'

'Oh merde!' Simone said: 'Merde! Merde! Merde!'

'Now *really*, my dear!'

'Go on! Tell me what he said! Oh que folle suis-je! Quelle idiote. Quelle bête! Quelle sotte! Quelle—'

'He told her, *he* was a Jew.'

'He *what?*' Simone said.

'Told her he was a Jew. But she didn't believe it, mainly because she could see he wasn't. So he explained it to her: that he was a Jew, and a Chinese coolie, and a pariah boy dying of hunger in India, and a redskin and a Negro – all the – what *was* the Dostoevskian phrase he used? Oh yes! All the humiliated, all the offended, all the damned – all the victims of this world. And then—'

'And then *what?*' Simone said.

'And then, I'm afraid, he kissed her. Didn't mean anything, I'm sure. Just pity—'

'Turn me loose, Byron,' Simone said.

'Now, really, Simone!'

'Don't worry. I – I just need to be alone a while. Do you think he'll come back – tonight?'

'Hardly. It's much too far. Tomorrow night, surely. Let me walk with you to your tent—'

'No. No, thank you, Byron. Don't worry I'm all right.'

He went back to where the others were. Sat down. He looked at Anton, said:

'Anton, how well do you know Simone?'

'Too well,' Anton groaned. 'Why?'

'D'you – d'you think she's capable of – harming herself?'

At once Anton was on his feet.

'Did she say *that*? Make some threat—'

'In a way, yes; but—'

'No buts about it, Byron! Come on!'

They ran towards Simone's tent.

'She's a pure manic-depressive!' Anton said. 'She – she's lost her whole family you know. Father and mother – deported. Both kid brothers. Baby sister's disappeared. Those nuns at Fayence had that kid – pretty little thing, nine years old – but the SS liquidated them for concealing Jewish children – and nobody's seen little Rachel since. What on earth did that fool Jean do or say?'

'A damned fool thing I must admit,' Byron said: 'Seems he suddenly remembered Lucienne – a sweet little commercial bit of goods – not her fault really – and rushed off—'

'Oh Jesus!' Anton said, and reaching down tore open the tent flap.

Simone was kneeling by her bed. She was naked to the waist. Her breasts were small and astonishingly beautiful. She had her tin washbasin on her knees. It had a fairish amount of blood in it. She was pushing a knife into her belly very slowly.

'Isn't this how the Japanese girls do it, Anton?' she said dreamily.

Anton grabbed one wrist, Byron the other one. It was exactly like trying to hold a tigress. She screamed. She swore. She cursed them in English, French, Yiddish and Hebrew. Then Anton slapped her hard. She collapsed into his arms. He yanked the knife out of her slim middle. She'd got over an inch of blade into herself.

'Got a first-aid kit, Byron?' Anton snarled.

'Yes. Why yes, of course! Can you manage her while I'm gone?'

'You bet. She makes a false move and I'll beat the shit out of her! Get going, now.'

Byron was back in two minutes flat. They bandaged the wound after first having dusted it with sulpha powder; put a compress against it. The bleeding didn't stop.

It soaked through the bandage within minutes. They looked at each other.

'Go commandeer Yves' motor-bike, Byron,' Anton said. 'We've got to take her to that hospital. Where'd you say it was? Saint – something—'

'St Martin. All right. Back in a moment, Anton.'

Yves' motor-cycle had a sidecar. Byron drove, while Anton sat in the sidecar, holding Simone in his arms. From where they were, in Camp B-3, near the village of Villars de Lans, to St Martin was just about ten kilometres as the crow flies. But a motor-cycle isn't a crow. They had to go by road. Which meant they had to go almost due west over Route National 531, around some very spectacular curves until they got to les Gorges de la Bourne, and then due south on Route National 518 to St Martin. Like most of his countrymen Byron drove like a maniac.

Anton roared at him through the backward rushing wall of air.

'Slow down! What're you trying to do, oblige her? *I'm* not suffering from a *chagrin d'amour*!'

'Yes, you are, Anton-dahlink,' Simone said. 'You love *me*. Or have you stopped?'

'I,' Anton said grimly, 'would *love* to take off my belt and turn your narrow tail the colour of that baboon's you mentioned!'

'You – should—' Simone said. 'You've always been too – good. Too sweet – too – patient – If you ever – beat me – I—' Then she fainted.

'Step on it!' Anton said. 'Can't you get any more out this wreck than this?'

'Make up your mind, old boy!' Byron said, and blurred the trees into one green-black solid mass with their speed.

Dr Ullmann examined the wound. It was still bleeding sullenly. The doctor looked at the two young men, said: 'Stab wound. Who did it? One of *you*?'

'No,' Anton said, 'she did it herself. Had a fight with her *gar*.'

'*Merde!*' Dr Ullmann said. 'Women!'

'I quite agree, doctor,' Byron said, 'but don't you think you should *do* something about it?'

'Going to. How long has she been bleeding like this?'

'An hour,' Anton said. 'No. An hour and ten minutes.'

'You know her blood type?'

'No,' Anton said.

'She's in shock. Have to give her plasma till we test for her grouping. Damned waste! Need it for people the Boches have shot up, not for sentimental idiots! By the way, she's Jewish, isn't she?'

Byron bristled at that. That question was beginning to get on his nerves. Especially coming from a blond doctor with a noticeable German accent.

'Yes,' he said, 'obviously. Any objections?'

Dr Ullmann glared at him.

'I am Jewish, young man!' he said. 'Now get out of here, both of you. Wait in the hall. I may need blood from either or both of you. After I find out what type she has, and you have. So don't go away!'

Anton's blood didn't match. Byron's did. Anton threw back his head and roared. Said: '*Rassenkunde!*'

'Oh I say, Anton, old boy,' Byron said; then he got it. *Rassenkunde* meant racial science. It was a new word. The Nazis had invented it. By the spring of 1944, the University of Berlin had no less than twenty-five credit-giving courses in this obscene nonsense whose core content could be reduced to one line: 'The German is the author of all good; the Jew, of all evil.' The rector of the university was a veterinarian, and practically – some said totally – illiterate. And the nation that had had the best universities in Europe now had the worst. Except even that statement was misleading. There no longer existed a basis for comparison. German universities weren't universities any longer. They were madhouses. And brothels, where even what little intellect was left in Germany, was being prostituted. And perverted – at one and the same time.

'I say, old chap,' Byron said solemnly, 'aren't you getting your terminology a bit wrong? I'd suggest you try *Mischung* on for size—'

'*Mischung?*' Anton said. Then he put the necessary prefix on to it: *Rassenmischung*. Racial mixing. Miscegenation. 'I still don't get it,' he said.

'Don't you, Anton?' Byron grinned. 'But what is miscegenation essentially if not the mingling of alien bloods? Though I must say I'm hardly enjoying it, at the moment! I'd much rather mingle with Simone in a more normal manner. . . .'

Simone opened one green eye.

'Put you on – my – waiting list, Byron—' she whispered, and fainted again.

But within two hours she was as bright as a new penny. Her self-inflicted wound had been cauterized then stitched, then bandaged. They'd put one of those horrible hospital gowns on her, the kind that open down the back, and are held together with tie strings. But on Simone it didn't look horrible; it looked fetching as all get-out.

'John, old boy, you don't know what you're missing!' Byron said.

'Not missing,' Simone said impishly, 'missed. I cannot marry him now. I have to marry *you mon* Byron. For you have compromised me. You shamelessly took advantage of me while I was helpless. Made a Goy of me. Half, anyhow. So now you must do right by – how is she called, Anton, dahlink? Nelly, no? Nelly with a raisin in her belly?'

'Lord, no! Can't you get anything right? The phrase is "do right by our little Nell." From the Victorian melodramas.'

'So? No matter. You will please both go and arrange to get me out of this *abattoir* – this slaughterhouse? Right now. This minute! And while you're at it, see if you cannot borrow, or steal me, a little perfume!'

To both Byron's and Anton's surprise, getting Simone out of the hospital proved quite easy. Dr Ullmann wanted to keep her at least overnight; but Dr Fischer said angrily, 'Oh let her go!'

And that was that. Afterwards Dr Ganimède told Byron that it was the acute shortage of beds that made them consent to Simone's being taken away even though the wound she had inflicted upon herself was at least serious enough to warrant three or four days of observation. There were already many sick and wounded in Vercors by that time.

But Anton didn't believe it. He said: 'Dr Fischer is a chauvinist. He was truly outraged. Didn't want the French to get the idea that our pure, chaste Jewish girls sometimes behave like ordinary human beings. Took me aside and asked me if I was responsible for Simone's "condition". When I denied being the guilty party, he asked if *you* were. Then it came to me that by "condition" he meant pregnancy. To him it was self-evident that she'd stabbed herself because she was knocked up and her boy friend had skipped. I decided not to waste time trying to explain to him that *nothing* about Simone is self-evident. That she invented contradiction, contrariness, stubbornness and confusion, and holds the original patents on all four. In other words, she's nuts. So's Jean. Maybe that's why they hit it off so well.'

'A rather superior form of insanity, I'd say, Anton.'

'Oh, I agree. They're both so damned sensitive they haven't skins. Go around suffering moral outrage – in, before you remind me! An outrageously immoral world – on their raw and bleeding nerve-ends. So I told Dr Fischer offhandedly that I really couldn't say, that Simone habitually sleeps around. He almost had a stroke. He's Ashkenazic, you know. Pluscumperfecto Orthodox.'

'Orthodox, I follow. Ashkenazic, no.'

'Middle Hebrew for "German." If those types get control of Israel, we'll have had it, Byron. They'll roll up the sidewalks on the Sabbath. And put characters like me in the hoosegow for eating a ham sandwich. With *oy! gevalt!* a glass of milk. Lord, wouldn't I like to have both, right now!'

'I say, Anton – it's really none of my business, of course; but does she?'

'Does she what?' Anton said.

'Sleep around?'

'Simone? No. Of course not. Actually, for modern times, she's quite close to Dr Fischer's ideal of the Jewish maiden. She has had, to my knowledge, one big love affair, with a miserable son of a bitching bastard of a Goy. Again I hasten to add that his being a Goy had nothing to do with his canine ancestry or his, at least spiritual, illegitimacy. Sons of the Great Whore, to quote Pepe's apt term for people like Dalton Ross, come in all sizes, shapes, colours, and religions. You've heard his broadcasts?'

'One. But that one was quite enough, thank you! Anton, do me a favour, will you? *Never* mention this to John. I'm quite sure it would do him immeasurable harm, psychologically and emotionally. Seems that Ross is the *bête noire* of his existence.'

'And of mine. Among other reasons, for the singularly unpleasant one, that to a girl quite, if not totally, inexperienced, as Simone was when she met him, he quickly became – and perhaps even *remains* – the Great God Damn. One of those middle-aged types who take a whole week to get it up, but once up, it *stays* two. A hell of an advantage with a woman, that.'

'I should say it is!' Byron said. 'If I could remake this sorry scheme of things entire, that would be the first thing I'd change – the fact that women are so deuced slow – and that we're so ruddy fast.'

'Me, too,' Anton said. 'Jean back yet?'

'No. I confess I'm a bit worried. By tonight it'll be four days. Doesn't show tonight, I'll have a look-see. Want to come along?'

'Now *that* would be wizard, rather!' Anton mocked. Then soberly, 'Yes. Why, yes, of course. Simpler to find that character than to have to chain Simone to a wall. By the way, have you seen *her*?'

'Yes. She took off for St Nizier this morning in the sidecar of Yves Martin's motor-cycle. With two hundred thousand francs she borrowed from me. Something she wants to buy or rent down there.'

'She'll probably have to spend the whole day fighting Yves off. Damn these Frenchmen, anyhow! Whoever told them they're so great?'

'Jealous, old boy?'

'Of Simone's activities, eternally. I mean to marry her, Byron.'

'Even though – pardon the vulgarity – she should trip down the primrose lane with John?'

'Even that. It would hurt like hell, but I'll bear up. In the end, she'll be mine, and all this will be a fading memory. You see, I have one great advantage, Byron: I'm Jewish and John Farrow's not. Simone, under wartime conditions may stray a bit, but she'll come home eventually. To our vine and fig tree. And once home, she'll stay. . . .'

'I must say that's rather broad-minded of you, Anton.'

'Broad-minded, *merde*! What could I do to stop her? Helplessness is no virtue, God knows. But screaming and grovelling and begging don't help. I'll keep my dignity, thank you. Such as it is – such as it is. . . .'

That night just on the last grey edge of darkness John Farrow came back from Grenoble. He looked like grim death. And his eyes were screaming like the damned souls in the seventh circle of Dante's Hell.

Simone gave him one look and the whole hour-long tirade of marvellously inventive, polyglot invective she had been rehearsing inside her uncommonly weird and wonderful little brain died away into silence, vanished out of time and mind.

She took his hand, said: 'Come with me, *mon Jean*.'

'Lord, Simone!' he protested. 'I'm dead! I'm so tired that—'

She bent and kissed his sweaty, grimy cheek.

'*You* do not have to do anything, mon amour. *I* will do it all,' she said. Then she led him over to where Yves waited with the motor-cycle. She pointed to the sidecar; said: 'Get in, Jean.'

He looked at her wonderingly, then obeyed. She climbed in with him. Draped herself in a long curve on, within, and around him, her two arms encircling his neck. Started to kiss him every place she could reach. By the time they got to St Nizier, Jean didn't feel tired at all.

Before the gate of a house, Yves stopped the motor-cycle. Simone climbed out, put her hand out to Jean. He, too, climbed out, stood there blinking owlishly.

'*Bonne chance, mes enfants!*' Yves said and roared off.

'Now what the devil?' Jean Claude DuBois/John Farrow said.

'This is *our* house. I have rented it for us. Here we shall be *chez-nous*. I left a fire burning in the water heater, I was so sure you would come, tonight. So you may have a hot, hot bath. I also bought you clean underwear and shirts and socks. You may put them on – tomorrow. Tonight, you do not need them. Tonight, they would only get in the way.'

'Simone!' Jean said, 'but I haven't – I still haven't bought—'

'*Les préservative. Tant pis.* We shall make a baby then. Which do you want, Jean? A boy or a girl?'

He turned, looked at her, said:

'A girl. Like you. Exactly like you. With green eyes. With specks of gold in them. And a long nose, crooked like thine. And a big wide mouth. Soft like thine. Sweet like thine, wonderful like thine. All of you all over again. But littler. And I shall chant hosannas all my days as I watch her grow.'

'Oh Jean!' she wept. 'How is that you know, you always know, just what to say?'

She opened the door. Switched on the lights. Strangely enough though the electricity for most of Vercors was generated down in Grenoble itself, the Nazis hadn't cut it off. Nor the telephones. Likely because they had all the lines tapped, and it was more useful to leave them working.

'And now, *mon homme*, you will please go and take a bath – in order to make you smell better and also to remove whatever traces *ta* Lucienne has left upon you, so that I shall not be distressed,' Simone said, a little tartly.

He turned upon her. The dead souls in his eyes were screaming once more. But louder, shriller, now.

'Don't say that, Simone,' he croaked. 'Please don't. Do not – spoil things. *Parce qu'elle est morte, elle aussi, la pauvre Lucienne*. She also – is dead.'

It took Simone a full thirty seconds to control the anguished quiver of her mouth.

'For you? She also? Like Hélène? For you?'

'No,' Jean said, 'it was not for me. They were going to ship her off to an enlisted men's brothel. She and Mirielle and Catherine. You see for the officers they only send women who haven't been whores before. So she killed herself. Cut her throat from ear to ear. I only found it out this morning. Took me all this time to find out where they were.'

'Oh!' Simone said, 'I am sorry, Jean. For her – and for you. You – loved her, didn't you?'

'Yes. Why, yes, of course. *Mais comme une petite soeur. Elle était si douce, si gentille* – Not like I love you. That was not possible. Except with you it will never be again.'

She kissed him very gently.

'Do not distress yourself, my Jean,' she said.

'I am not distressed. I am a little sad, but not distressed. Not for la petite Lucienne. She was very brave and very gallant and she did what she had to do. I am proud of her, Simone. For the others, for Mirielle, and Catherine, I am distressed. Though less; I was never fond of them. Of Lucienne, yes. Very fond. But I am distressed because they put mere living before freedom, before dignity. For life is not worth that much. Especially not life reduced to an obscenity. A vileness.'

'I think you're too hard on them. After all, my crazy love, they were already tarts. Freedom, dignity – that's a laugh!'

'No, they had a little left, in spite of everything. They could still refuse a man they truly didn't like. Most of the time, they could avoid the SS, say – and console themselves with the thought that the Wehrmacht and the Luftwaffe are, after all, soldiers – and some of them fairly decent types. But to be sent to ein Feldtdirnenhaus meant the end of what poor dignity they were clinging to. Lucienne preferred to die. I'm glad. I'm proud of the choice she made.'

'No,' Simone said, 'she had no choice. She was Jewish. Her family all died at the Winger Bicycle Racing Stadium. For her, as for me in like circumstances, choice doesn't exist any more.'

He stared at her. 'Who told you all that? *I* didn't,' he said.

'I'm a witch! Now get out of here. Go bathe, my boy. Meanwhile, I'm going to fix you some supper. To give you strength. The strength you're going to need, I assure you!'

The hot water was wonderfully soothing. He soaped his whole thin, wiry body, then sank down into it gratefully. In a shade under two minutes, he was fast asleep. What woke him was the soft, sweet sighing cling and quiver of her mouth on his. He opened his eyes. She straightened up; her green-gold gaze moving all over his body slowly, becoming tactile, a caress, denying and belying one of the favourite psychological shibboleths of that day, that women are not visual-minded, that the sight of male nakedness – even of the achingly anguished beloved – has no effect upon them. He put up his hand and touched her cheek, let his long fingers stray and worship there. She caught his hand and turned it palm inward to her mouth. Kissed it a long, slow, trembling dead stopped time; bathed and blessed it with her tears.

'Simone!' he said: 'please don't cry! Je t'en supplie! Ne pleure pas!'

'Women cry for all kinds of reasons, Jean. Even – from happiness. It *hurts,* you know. When it is too great. When it is unsupportable – like now.'

He put out his arms to her. But she moved up out of reach; said with her mischievous grin:

'Oh no! Not so fast, my boy! In the first place, you must eat your supper. And afterwards, you must sleep – all night long, because it's apparent that you're too tired!'

'Now, Simone; you aren't going to be a tease, are you?' he said.

'A tease? Yes – certainly. Tomorrow night, I'm going to tease you all night long; but tonight, I'm going to let you sleep.'

He grinned at her, said: 'In your arms, I hope?'

The gamine's grin vanished. A look of – of longing, of a kind of anguish that was unspeakable, maybe even unthinkable, took its place.

'Yes, in my arms. Tonight – and all the other nights that we have left in what remains to both of us of life. If there be any. If God be kind and grant us even one—'

'Simone!' he cried.

'Yes, I know. I'm morbid, aren't I? Pay no attention to me, Jean. And now, hupp! Out of there! I'm going to dry you. When you're dry, you're going to go eat your supper like a good little boy. But alone, because I have to bathe, too. I haven't had time to wash myself in the last four days. Or would you love me better if I stink like a fish-market woman?'

He got out of the tub. Simone picked up the big towel and began to dry him very slowly and carefully and tenderly, like a good and devoted mother drying her baby boy. Which, of course, very quickly got to be too much. He clawed her into his arms, almost broke her mouth. Shoved her away from him, yanked at her blouse, so that the buttons made a shower, dancing all over the bathroom. Then he stopped, staring at those two small miraculous breasts that didn't need a brassière or any other kind of support, and never would. His rage of passion died and was replaced by awe, wonder, tenderness.

She put her arms around his neck, drew him down to them, pillowing his face, his mouth against soft resilience, warmth, life. Whispered:

'That's better. I am your wife, Jean. I don't want you to violate me; I want you to love me.'

After a long embrace, she pushed him away with a laugh that combined woodwinds, and strings, all of them vibrato, saying:

'That's enough, my Jean! Go eat supper. And then to bed. I – I'll visit you a little after I've had my bath. If you're awake, I shall remain. If not – who knows? – I may even wake you up!'

'You'd better!' he growled, and got out of there.

After he had gone (he knew this, because she was forced to tell him later), she drained the tub, ran new water into it. Then going up on tiptoe she looked at her middle in the mirror. The bandage encircled her, a broad belt of white. She took a pair of scissors out of the pocket of her quilted robe and cut through it, then she tugged at it. It stuck to the wound. She took up a bath sponge and wet the bandage. Slowly, carefully, she pulled it loose. The scab was angry, purplish, puckering about the stitches. A drop or two of thick, viscous blood stole out between them. She should have dusted that ugly stab wound at least three times a day with sulfhanilamide powder, but no one had thought to tell her that. And besides no one had any sulfa powder in the camp except Byron, though he would have shared his supply with her gladly and at once, if she had known enough to ask him to.

She shrugged her thin shoulders, peeled off the rest of her clothes, and got into the tub which she had filled only partially so as not to get the wound wet. She lolled in the bathtub for more than an hour, until the water had got so cold that it was uncomfortable to stay any longer. It was not that she shared Jean's sybaritic love for the bath; the truth of the matter was that she was hoping he would fall asleep. That way, she'd be spared for one more night the necessity of explaining that all-too-visible, roughly sewn up hole in her belly, twelve centimetres to the right of her umbilicus. Perhaps tomorrow night, it would be less ugly. Perhaps tomorrow night it would be invisible.

That was what she told herself. And it was true. But it was only part of the truth. The rest of it was that she was suddenly torn and rent with anguished shyness; she was literally trembling with shame, with fear. The last thing on earth she felt like doing was having sex with anyone – and least of all with Jean. And this, oddly enough, because she loved him.

'He is – so gentle!' she wailed inside her mind. 'He cannot

even be a brute – not for long enough at least. And a little of the brute is – necessary. Or is it? How would I know? Dalton – took me. The first day I came to his house – to work, I thought. And, after that, whenever he wanted to. But now whenever I wanted to, which was every minute of the day and night! He – kissed me. Until my mouth was bruised and swollen. Played with – with my body. Played with me – down there. Until I was out of my mind, until he'd forced me to the ultimate surrender, *la dernière lâcheté fémine, la honte plus abjecte.* Until I would slavishly humiliate myself, cry, beg, beseech, implore him to (using that hideously ugly and explicit English word he'd taught me!) ease me. Grovelling before him on my knees in that most hateful, plus honteuse extreme of anguish, before finally, and at long last, he'd laughingly condescend to oblige, to pick me up, toss me on to the bed, mount me, enter me, penetrate me, stoke my mindless, ravenous fury until its own explosion quenched it. For a time. Oh God, for so little time!

'He used me. *Comme un brute!* No, that's not true. He was never brutal. Just – very male. Very sure of himself. Very – no! Most unforgivably expert. Knowing exactly what a woman wants, likes, needs, responds to – from the experience gained upon the ten million and one whorish bitches he'd had before he met me!'

She sat down before the mirror. Picked up the little flask of perfume young Dr Ganimède's wife had given her at the hospital. Began to perfume herself very carefully. Concentrating on the areas that she thought Jean would kiss – or touch.

'Still jealous, Simone? No. Because before the end, I'd won out over all those ten million and one sisters of my shame, my sorrow! For before the end, he'd learned to love me. Me – Simone Levy – a person, living, breathing, dreaming, thinking in the world. Having a mind – of a certain value. Not just – what was that ugly, so very American expression that he used? Not just a piece of tail. Not just a well co-ordinated bundle of hot and willing female flesh, lying there moaning and panting and wiggling for his pleasure!

'And – be honest, Simone! For her own. And for her own!

'He had learned to love me. He, Dalton Ross, the great poet, great man had learned to love – this insignificance – this nothing. This poor scrap of womankind, this ugly little hooked-nosed, skinny-shanked Jewess who – Yet, he loved me. Truly.

He became very gentle, tender, sweet. Told me – and I, God help me! I believe him – that I was the first and only woman in all his life he'd ever wanted to keep, to marry. Ha! How angry he would get in those last days when I'd start in to say all the dirty things that he, himself, had taught me! I was his little plaything of a girl before. It amused him to hear his poupée mignonne, his little doll, talk like a whore. But when I'd become his woman, soulmate, wife, he could not bear mes saletés stupides et crues, d'une pauvre idiote garce!

'He would have – died for me. As – *cette Hélène* died for Jean. Only the SS – *les animaux, les lâches!* – how cruel they are! And how clever in their cruelty! – would not give him that simple, that honourable choice. Nor me the opportunity to cut my throat above his grave – A Polyxena self-sacrificed upon her Achilles' tomb! – as I would have afterwards, I would have! And lie there with him, to guard and keep his mighty shade for ever!

'No – they who know only too well how to ruin everything, spoil everything, smear everything good and true in life with excréments, ordures, vileness! – had to spoil, ruin, dirty that, too – a poor tired, sorrowing and defeated (for all his roars and bluster!) man's autumnal happiness – his last true, pure – yes, yes, pure! – most thoroughly requited love for a silly slip of a girl, for a quaint, grave, erudite, recondite philosophy student already educated far beyond her intelligence! So they – so they—'

In a wild paroxysm of grief, of rage, of bitter, helpless, hopeless self-loathing, she brought her doubled fists up and pounded her naked breasts, striking hard, furiously, cruelly, bruising her tender flesh, mercilessly punishing her slender body for the crime of being alive, for the sin of occupying space, the blasphemy of breathing—

'Oh God!' she moaned, 'I have to die! I have no right to live! Still less to dream of – of happiness. To take – in my arms – un ange comme Jean – He is! He is, I tell you! An angel. One of the hosts of light. No right – no right – to dirty him – salir sa chair angélique avec ma paunteur de femelle, de chienne! – to drag him down to – a thing like me—'

She bent her head and wept – a long time, and terribly. Looked up, faced her image in the mirror. Wailed:

'How ill-favoured I am! Ugly! Hideous! Skinny! A hag! He can't love me! He can't! It isn't even possible!'

She got up very slowly. Put on her quilted robe. Stole on tiptoe to the bedroom. Opened the door with slow, trembling breathless care. It hadn't been oiled in years. The hinges creaked deafeningly.

But Jean didn't move. She sighed – in sorrow? In relief? She did not, would never know. Tiptoed to the edge of the bed, bent over him; saw his eyes were closed, turned – and hung then, blinded by the flood of light as Jean squeezed the little extension switch called *une poire*, a pear, because of its shape, that he had been holding in his hand beneath the pillow all that time.

'Come, Simone. Come, my angel, my beauty,' he murmured, sleepily.

'Oh Jean no, I can't! I don't dare! You're too tired and—'

He stared at her, and his eyes were very dark, suddenly.

'And you – don't really want to,' he said sadly. 'You – never have – have you? It's been all a game to you. Why did you lie to me, Simone? Why did you ever say you loved me?'

She whirled, faced him, her mouth opened and a quaver like an idiot child's, her eyes flooded, blind, her cheeks awash. The tears hung and sparkled on the helpless quiver of her mouth until the very motion shook them free to flash white fire, to fall.

'I don't love you, you say? I who die each instant that I can't see your face, hear your voice? You're right, Jean! I don't love you. I adore you! I idolize you! The day you leave me, that you abandon me, I'll have no need to kill myself. That day I will simply die. Oh no! Not simply. Mad and howling like a beast!'

'In that case, Simone,' he said gently, 'you're going to live for ever. Come.'

'Jean—' she said, 'put out the light—'

'Why?' he said.

'I'm ashamed! I don't want you to see me!'

'Why not? You're very beautiful, you know. You're the most beautiful girl I've known in all my life.'

'Liar!' she said. 'Please, Jean! I beg you!'

'No,' he said. 'I *want* to see you, Simone. We are – man and wife. There can be no shame between us. Thy nakedness is mine – and mine, thine. Viens, laisse-moi te voir. Toute nue et si belle!'

She turned her back to him. Let the quilted robe slide downward over her shoulders, fall to the floor. Turned, facing him –

with her right hand covering that ugly, self-inflicted wound. She was much too thin, of course. In France of 1944, everybody was — except black marketeers, whores, and collaborators. But she was still lovely.

His gaze moved over her lingeringly, recreating her form in reflected light engraving her rather boyish, almost androgyne, figure upon those tissues of his brain where memory has its seat, so until the day that death itself should end him it would glow and tremble there.

She was not as thin as she thought she was; rather she was small, light of bone, and slender. Her long, burnt-honey, dark taffy brown hair (for the SS had not yet hacked it off into that gamine's Peck's-bad-boy cut his only photo of her would show) hung down, part of it in front, between her tiny fierce-tender breasts, whose nipples ached and shamed her, by tautening, quivering, into twin, miniature, but quite visible erections. Her waist was his two hands' span, no more, the whole of her curving just enough to contradict that impression of boyishness for ever. He didn't even gaze at that sudden spray of straight, uncurling brown, not even triangular, a Mohican warrior's scalp-lock, the plume on a Roman's helmet, that broke her belly's whiteness, instead his glance flew, and locked, held upon her oddly placed, awkwardly cupped right hand, then tore free and sought her face.

The shame in her eyes was the only really naked things about her. For the slender, graceful, near perfection of her body's lines had the curious effect of robing and clothing her in light, so that she moved in beauty in the exact sense that Lord Byron meant it.

He said, harshly, sternly, and in English:

'Come here, Simone!' Afterwards he supposed he used his father's, his Uncle Dalton's native tongue, because to him French was the language of love, and he felt far from loving at that moment. He was angry, and hurt; but not cruel enough to scream at her in German, that speech designed, it seemed to him, for senseless rage. (He'd forgot by then, in the sick hatred the Nazis had awakened in him that it was also the language of some of the world's greatest poetry, and the *only* other tongue that Shakespeare can be translated into and lose almost nothing.)

'Yes, Jean,' she whispered, and stumbled forward, crying helplessly; all of her one long unceasing quiver from head to toe. He put out his hand, caught her wrist, pulled her hand away, hung there, staring at that purplish, puckering horror marring her middle.

She heard his breath catch in his throat, heard her own name sound a threnody, a dirge: 'Simone! Oh, Simone!'

And looking down she saw he was crying, openly, bitterly, without shame.

'Ne pleure pas, mon Jean!' she moaned. *'Je t'en supplie, ne pleure pas!* I am not worth one single tear and if you cry for me for this then I must do it again, must finish it, must die! *Tu m'entends, Jean? Je t'ai dit—'*

'Mais pourquoi, Simone? Why?'

'You – you said her name. You said "Lucienne!" and ran off – and left me. I asked Byron who she was, but he wouldn't tell me so they, the others, told me that she – that she was – your love! And that she was *une garce, une poule, une putain!* So I told myself that if you preferred even – even a whore to me what did I want to live for? So I went to my tent. I tricked Byron into leaving me alone although he was terribly worried about me. I thought about what the Japanese do. It is a very bad way to die. But I wanted to die badly. To hurt in a way that would be worse than the way you'd hurt me – only they came back. Byron – and Anton – Jean! Oh Jean, non!'

For he had drawn her to him and was kissing that ugly purplish rent as though he could heal it with his mouth.

It was, she realized suddenly, the only one among the many wounds she was slowly dying of, he couldn't heal that way. She broke gently free of his embrace and lay down beside him – as far away from him as she could possibly get without falling out of bed. And when he put out his arms to her she said in a tone that was harsh, and splinter-full of shame, of terror:

'Ah, non, Jean! Je t'en supplie! Non!'

He stared at her, saw that she meant it. Smiled sadly, gently, said:

'Bonne nuit, Simone!' And turned his back to her.

They lay there like that, without moving for three-quarters of an hour. Jean was thinking that Simone had stumbled upon a form of torture that outdid the SS at their fiendish worst, when he heard her voice.

'Jean!' she wailed. *'Je ne sais pas quoi faire!'*

And he heard his own voice, ten years – ten epochs, aeons, ages – ago, wailing those self-same words, but in German:

'Heide – Ich weiss nicht was tun!'

In almost exactly the same tone of voice.

He turned back over, grinned at her, said:

'I remember a girl once in the woods, who knocked a fellow off a log and proposed to rape, violate and make violent love to him. To make him beg for mercy. Or am I really mad? Did I imagine all that?'

'Non,' she sobbed. 'Non, my Jean – you did not imagine it. And that's *why*, I don't know what to do!'

He propped himself up on one elbow; stared at her. Said:

'Explain *that* to me.'

'That's easy. I – love you. And I *do* know how to be a bitch, how to play the tart, how to have sex. But I don't know how – to make love. Therefore, I'm ashamed! I have this horrible fear of – of disgusting you. I think – with him, I want to be – virgin! Pure! Clean! Spotless. Oh dear God, why couldn't I have waited for you! Why was I so stupid, so moronic, such a bitch, a slut that—'

She turned, faced him, her eyes scalded, blind.

'Oh Jean! Jean! Teach me what to do!'

He hung there lost, thinking: 'How can I? I don't know how to make love either. All my past is filled with Heides of one sort or another. Except – poor Hélène. How does one put the dew back on the rose? Or even find that rose, lily, dove, and sun? Recover lost innocence? For except as ye be as little children are, ye shall nowise enter into the Kingdom of Heaven!

'And yet I have never loved a girl before now. I have had, possessed, taken girls before – mostly in the States, oddly enough. In that puritan land where the girls are far from puritanical. And what was wrong? That I *used* them. And they used me. Reduced my body – and I theirs! – to an instrument for masturbation! Warmer and softer and wetter than the five flying fingers that were my only solace before Heide appeared – but—'

'Jean!' she moaned, 'I want you so badly that I'm dying!'

'So – don't use, have, possess, take – Simone. Love her – cherish, comfort her, and ye twain shall be one flesh! But how – how? Separate this – from all you've done, all you remember! Create the world anew – the first dawn, the first sky – Wake up,

Adam! Feel your side ache! Your rib's gone, old boy – and here she is – the first, the very first woman in all the world!'

He leaped from the bed, laughing; said: '*Viens!* Come!'

Wonderingly she followed him. He sat down in a chair. It was French provençal, and had no arms. Its shape was much the same as a Louis XIV, or XV chair; but it was – God be praised and thanked – much sturdier. He drew her down until she was sitting on his lap, crosswise so that she could face him. Then he reached up, and took her long, soft hair, and drew it around behind his own neck, tied, and knotted it there.

She looked at him, her eyes aglow, whispered:

'Oh Jean, Jean, how marvellous you are!' Then shyly, timidly, 'May I – kiss you?'

'Why yes, girl,' he said, laughing, teasing her. 'But gently – I'm very fragile!'

She bent and found his mouth. Clung hers to his so lightly, gently, tenderly it seemed almost not to touch, until the taste of hers changed, went wet, went salt, so that he drew back said, reproachfully:

'Simone—'

'How I love you, my Jean! How I adore you! Kiss me! Kiss me! A million times! Ten million! Don't stop. Don't stop. Ever!'

He kissed her mouth, her throat, her breasts. She moaned a little. A very little. The absolute minimum she couldn't help. She was thinking with a fear approaching terror: 'He doesn't like wild women – *les filles volupteuses, lascives, les femmes trop ardentes, comme – Dieu me pardonne! Je suis!* Or like – Dalton taught me to be. Trained me like an animal. Like one of the dogs of Pavlov! The swine! No, not a swine. For I – I

'I – I must control myself! Mustn't – mustn't – mustn't – Oh. Oh. Oh. Oh no. Please, no. Please, God, no. Not already! Not – just kissing! Not – Oh! Ohhhhh! – *Oh, merde!* Did he notice? Did he? It was only a little one. Just – *une toute petite orgasme – si mignonne! Presque pas. Presque rien.* Almost nothing. And I didn't – didn't cry out – didn't even move so he couldn't have noticed please God let him not have noticed – let him – not—

'Shall I tell him not to – not to kiss me – there again? That if he so much as touches – *mes mamelles avec ses lévres – je serai perdue?* Lost and more than lost! Off like the rocket of Jules Verne to the moon! To Mars!

'Mais, je n'ose pas! I don't dare! He'll think – he'll think – I know! I'll tell him a fib! I'll – lie to him. Tell him – that – that they're – sore. That my nipples hurt. Ah, God, let me die of such a hurt! So sweet – so sweet – Besides, I can't. I cannot lie to Jean. Not to my – Morning Star, my Winged Angel, my *Chef* of the Hosts of Light—

'Ah, non! Ça, non! Ne me touche pas là-bas! Not down there! Not even the way you touch me – as though I were made of crystal! Of crystal so fine and delicate a high note too long held could shatter me! *This* can shatter me, this will shatter me, thy touch – *ta touche, mon ange me détruira, me fera éclater comme une bombe de mille kilos – une blockbuster!*

'Oh no. Oh no. Oh, please, no. Let me not lose control I might even say all those horrible filthy dirty things that he – that Dalton – taught me. *Oh – non! Aie pitié, Bon Dieu! Aie pitié!'*

He saw, sensed, divined her distress; took his hand away.

'You don't like that, do you?' he said.

'On the contrary,' she whispered, 'I like it too much! But if you make me – get there – too quickly, that way, afterwards I'll be good for absolutely nothing!'

'That, I don't believe!' he laughed. 'And besides, five minutes' rest will—'

'Jean, no – please?'

'Comme tu voudrais, mon amour.'

'Not as I would! It's that I — what miserable luck – am one hot little number!'

He looked at her, said: 'And you hate it, don't you?'

'Yes. It's the thing I detest most in myself. But do you know why?'

'Non. Pourquoi?'

'Because you men can never bring yourselves to believe that a warm girl can be faithful.'

'And, can you?' he said teasing her.

But she answered him with one of those mad bursts of fury of hers that always left him shaken.

'Jean, from now on – from this very hour – if one day I look at another man with desire, I'll heat an iron red hot and plunge it into my eyes! I will, Jean! You've already seen what – for you, for your love – I am capable of!'

He looked at her, said quietly:

'The day you do such a thing, you'll bury me, Simone. For I should die on the spur of that same instant from too much hurt, from too great a pain.'

'Oh, Jean!' she wept, and kissed him. Drew away, said: 'Kiss me. Touch me. Do what you will to me – however you want to. I'm yours. Your lovesick little beast. Your slave.'

But within three minutes, after he had started to kiss and caress her once more, she swooped to him, put her warm wide lips against his ear, let them quiver there, imploringly:

'Jean, I can't bear any more! I simply can't! Shall we go – to bed?'

He said gravely, 'No.'

She stared at him, said: '*Pourquoi pas?*'

He said: 'The bed has too many memories for me. *Et peut-être pour toi, aussi.* Bad. Stupid. Meaningless. I don't want to mix this with them. Not even – slightly. Not even by accident.'

'Nor I,' she said, sadly. 'Then you'll go on – tormenting me?'

He grinned at her, said: 'And why not?'

'Jean, I'll retrogress! Become a bitch all over again. And you wouldn't like that, I'm sure!'

'No,' he said, 'I wouldn't. I love you the way you truly are. Sweet. Gentle. An angel.'

'Oh Jean!' she wept.

'Besides, you've promised me – a daughter. Your image, in miniature. Shall we commence to make her, now?'

'But Jean! How? In this *chair?*'

'*Ici,*' he said. 'Here – in this chair.'

'*Mais ça ce n'est pas possible!*'

'Oh yes, it's perfectly possible.'

'How, Jean? Tell me – how?'

'*A cheval,*' he said. 'Astride – as on horseback. I'm a very strong horse you know, with plenty of wind to run a long, long race. So now swing that long and beautiful left leg of yours across the saddle: but leave the right one where it is. *Tu vois?*'

She laughed freely, gaily, said:

'What a want of delicacy, of decorum!'

Then she stopped laughing, was silent. Stopped being silent. Said: 'Oh!'

'*Je t'ai fait mal?*' he said.

'*Non. Ah non! Jean—*'

'*Quoi, Simone?*'

'I love you, you know. My body also loves you. To feel you there. Inside me. Terribly.'

'Don't talk. Words spoil even the most beautiful things, Simone!'

'Yes, my love! Yes, master! Your slave hears you! And obeys!'

'Shut up, Simone!'

'Then – kiss me! And – and *do* something to me!'

He drew her to him; kissed her mouth. And once begun, it was nothing like anything either of them had experienced before. They were all but motionless. They kissed gently, softly, almost tentatively. Touched, almost not touching, their finger-tips, straying, straying, lighter than a breath. She melted inside to ease and smooth his passage, became wonderfully warm and moist and soft, and trembling, trembling, trembling, moulding and caressing his rigid and penetrant maleness; he was slow and infinitely gentle, waiting with masterly self-control, with exquisite, and absolute patience until he felt her deep internal shudder start, then raced to join it; but seeing her head go back, back, her mouth tearing open in that curiously shocking grimace that is ecstasy's perfect counterfeit of the cruellest anguish, the most insufferable agony – and knowing from bitter experience how thin the line of demarcation was between that kind and degree of pleasure, and murderous pain, especially in people with nerves as wire-fine, singing-taut as Simone's were – he put up his hand and drew her mouth down once more to his own, stifling and absorbing the bitter, sobbing, strangling cries she made, until she wrenched her lips free of his and whispered:

'Jean, I'm – dying! Dying!' and collapsed against him boneless, breath gone, utterly still.

'Simone!' he gasped; and stood, lifted her up, lay her, white, still, motionless upon the bed, and knelt there beside her speechless and paralysed with terror, until he saw her eyelids flutter, saw the great tears steal out from under them – and bent and kissed her mouth.

'Simone! Simone!' he got out, 'how you have frightened me!'

She put her two arms softly, shyly, tenderly around his neck, whispered: 'Jean—'

'Yes, Simone?'

'Thank you.'

'Simone! Don't say that!' he said, a little shocked, a little angry.

'Yes, thank you. A thousand times, thank you. For your sweetness, your tenderness. For having made a woman of me, instead of a bitch. For – you, yourself. So sweet. So good. So kind. So brave! For having honoured me with your love. For now I can die. Happy. Without regrets.'

'Don't talk about that!' he said. 'Don't speak of death!'

She said sadly, slowly, but with a conviction so absolute that it stopped his breath:

'There aren't any other things for us, my Jean. Except those two: love – and death. I mean love followed by death. I know that. I've known it always, since the first time I saw you. Today, love. Tomorrow—'

'Then may today last a thousand years!' he said.

'Oui. Yes. May – it last. Till August comes, anyhow—'

'Till August?' he said. 'Why August, Simone?'

'I don't know. It is – a thing I feel. A dark thing – if we get through August together we will – live. Remain together. Be – happy. If not—'

'If not?' he prompted.

'Who knows? Please, Jean – let's not talk about that now. I feel – rested. And strong. And *très, très amoureuse! Erotique. Sexy*. With a bad case of *les panties chaudes* – "hot pants" you say in English, don't you? That is, if I had on panties, which I don't. *Donc, mon Jean—*'

Then she saw his face. His eyes. She lay there, her eyes going sick, horror getting into them, a shame so abysmal, so abject that he couldn't bear seeing it, and turned away his face. He felt her nails dig into the flesh of his arms, heard her voice moaning:

'Hit me. Beat me. Kill me! But don't look at me like that, John! I beg you, not like that!'

He said, quietly: 'If I ever meet the type – American, wasn't he? – who taught you to say those things, it will be *him*, I'll kill, not you, Simone.'

'Jean!' she sobbed. '*Ah, mon Jean, mon ange adoré, je—*'

'I'm very far from being an angel. There have been other women in my life, women whom I've bedded with, to say it straight out and honestly, Simone. Quite truthfully, they were very few. Suis un type rare, je crois – and besides, they didn't matter. Not one of them. Not even poor Hélène except for the legacy of guilt she left me – for not having cared enough for her, for having failed her. But this type of yours, this one gross type, has marked, and marred you, it seems to me.'

'Jean – you want me to tell you about all that? About him – and me?'

'God, no!' he said; his voice hoarse and shuddering with revulsion. 'Ecoute-moi, Simone! Understand this, now and for ever: I love you. I love you so much that the past doesn't exist for me. Neither that part of it I inhabited, nor the part wherein you dwelt, moved, had your being – and even loved your lover. For me time, creation, life began the hour you walked into our camp and stopped the world. The past is dead, Simone, dead! I ask you only not to drag its stinking corpse into – our house, our bed, our life. There is no yesterday, my love. Nor, perhaps, any tomorrow. There is only – today. There is only now. I ask you only this: don't spoil the only time we have. Don't spoil *now*, Simone!'

She put out her hand, and touched his face, whispered:

'I will try, my Jean. But sometimes, being me, I'll fail. And, when I do, remember this: I'm a *born* bitch, my love! That's nobody's fault, except my own. But, I beg you! find some other way to punish me less cruel than this one is! Don't let me die of desire, with my insides screaming because I want you so – as they are screaming now!'

He looked at her soberly, then he smiled.

'From *that* you'll never die, Simone!' he said.

And kissed her.

II

John Farrow got out of bed, and walked to the window. He drew the curtains open, and looked out. He could see the low, black humps of the mountains above the city of Grasse; and, below him, the streetlights scattered over the hollow like a broken necklace. From behind the hotel, although the sounds actually came from a considerable distance away, he could hear the snort and grumble of truck motors changing their tone and pitch as their drivers shifted up and down gear on National 85, running down to Nice. It was a fine night. The stars were out. He could see them twinkling above the plane trees on the Avenue Riou Blanquet; and, lifting his gaze, through the darker firs and umbrella pines, bordering the Avenue Bellevue.

Idly, he wondered why the Hôtel Bellevue wasn't on the Avenue Bellevue, where, logically, it should have been. Perhaps its builders had decided upon the Avenue Riou Blanquet – he savoured with grave appreciation the provençal word *riou* for river – because it was comparatively level, while the Avenue Bellevue climbed steeply from its intersection with Riou Blanquet through a series of abrupt *virages*, hairpin turns, and split Ss up to the Avenue Antoine de Saint-Exupéry.

So many streets in so many towns he had known before had new names now. Besides the avenue honouring the great aviator-writer (or writer-aviator? he wondered suddenly), Grasse now had an Avenue Général De Gaulle. And in Berlin – his mind made one of its abrupt leaps in space, in time – Unter den Linden no longer ran directly into Königstrasse, after crossing the first bridge on to the island between the two arms of the River Spree. But then, had it before? He didn't remember. He'd never really got to know Berlin, because Papa wouldn't allow him to wander about in that great city alone. Now, in any event, there was Marx-Engelsplatz first, then Rathaustrasse before you got to Alexanderplatz, and then entered Königstrasse, called Neue Königstrasse, New King's Street now. Was it even the same street on which the Brownshirts had beaten him to within an inch of his young life? There was no way to tell. All that part of Berlin, East Berlin, he corrected himself sardonically – had become the world's biggest rubble heap even before the first Russian tanks had come clanking in. The rubble heap in which both Heide von Kressel – and Yvette Farrow (Maman. Ma petite Maman) had died. And even after that, he remembered, they went on changing the street names as the winds from the Kremlin shifted. Stalinallee was Karl-Marxallee now—

'*Merde!*' he told himself, 'why do I do this? Allow my mind to take evasive action, refuse to face what really must be faced, and *now*: that this, as Byron would put it, is a bad show. That I might as well take the next plane back to New York. That my last faint chance of finding Simone is gone. . . .'

He looked at his watch. He hadn't put the lights on, but his watch had a luminous face. 'Three a.m.!' he read; and once more regretted that he hadn't brought – or bought – some sleeping pills. His insomnia was becoming chronic; especially in a country, and more specifically in a region of that country, teeming and haunted with the ghosts of his singularly troubled past.

'Won't do,' he thought, 'to take on Posson et Cie with a head that functions badly or not at all. Because if the practice of law has taught me anything, it is that the mere fact of innocence never saved any poor devil from being hanged. Suppose this Madame Betrand – why do I picture her as a dried-up vinegary old witch, who really didn't need to take either plane or train; since her jet propelled broomstick would have got her here in no time flat? Suppose, this woman I've never seen before in all my life, who surely has never seen me, decides I am, or even look like, the type behind those explosive *billets doux*? It would take me weeks to extricate myself from the whole senseless affair. Probably have to call on Cassière or De La Croix from Paris to identify me. And that would be a *very* bad show indeed. Because I promised both the De Gaullists and Washington to never mention the deal we worked out then to a living soul so long as I was myself above ground. Of course that was John Kennedy's Washington – not this one, times and positions have changed. But still—'

He turned back to the bed; lay down on it. 'Never anticipate trouble, John,' he told himself. 'Does no good. Because trouble, when it comes, is always different in both kind and degree from the usually imaginary type you're worrying about, and kicks the living shit out of you, from the one angle you never thought to watch. As for a prime example, take the time I was eating my bloody guts out over how to find, invent, dream up a kindly, decent way of ridding myself of Candace. A method that wouldn't leave poor Cynthia wrecked (as *I* was wrecked!) by the discovery that sweet, loving motherhood quite often removes its panties and lies down in the wrong places ('Sie waren nicht in dem Schlafzimmer, sondern in der Halle!') with – (Ein Junge. Ein sehr schöner blonder von dem SA) from the legal standpoint, anyhow – the wrong guy. Then dear Candy brought me that book. One of those, How to Screw Effectively in Five Easy Lessons! books. A sex manual, she put it; to – improve our marital relations, she put it; a last chance, she didn't put it, to save the ashes and embers of a fire not merely banked, as she seems to have thought, but out. Out, stone cold, dead.

'Why? Did she really want to patch things up between us at the last minute? Had she already begun to see through the bastard, even then? Wouldn't doubt it. They were separated one year after she'd gone on to marry him, and divorced before eighteen months were out.

'And I – (To humour her? To be polite? The Farrow Groton/Andover/Harvard – schools I never went to, God be praised and thanked, except the last, and it too late to harm me – old school-tie breeding showing through?) took that monumental collection of pure, undiluted *merde* – printed *merde* at that, and started to read it. Got through three chapters of how you should rub this, kiss, lick, suck that, squeeze, pinch, bite the other, before throwing the whole randy collection of pseudo-scientific, pornographic garbage against the wall. And—'

And Candace staring at him with her wide blue eyes and saying: 'Why, John?'

And he: 'Because he doesn't know what he's talking – or rather writing – about. The bastard's a – mechanic, a technocrat. He seems to think that women have ignitions, starters, gear shifts. That love is a branch of – applied physics, say. That it can be reduced to rules, methods of procedure—'

'But, darling,' Candace had laughed, 'he's talking about sex, not love.'

John Farrow (the John Farrow of thirteen years ago, that lean, bitter, burnt forty-one-year-old avatar of what? An idealist? A puritan? A romantic?) stared at his wife.

'Can they be separated?' he mused aloud. 'At least *I* can't separate them. I've never been able to make use of a prostitute in all my life.'

'Doesn't that,' Candace said acidly, 'depend upon your definition of the word "prostitute", darling?'

'To me, no. Not at all. Or perhaps my definition is broad enough to cover a multitude of sins. To me a whore's a woman who's doing it for *reasons*, Candace. For – power say; to pry useful information out of a guy – military, industrial, scientific or what have you, which she then passes on to her superiors; to climb up the social scale; to get even with another person, usually her husband; to hook some poor bastard into marrying her; in short *any* reason, down to, and including, of course, the obvious: a mink coat, jewellery, cash—'

'But would you include,' Candace said, pain breaking through the mockery in her voice, 'a girl who simply, and suddenly gets a plain case of hot pants for a guy? Who looks at a man she doesn't even know, and feels herself getting wet and ready?'

'Unless she stops long enough to get to know him, yes. To find out if he's a type she can talk to after they've resumed a vertical position. A man she can like, respect, even – love. If not, she's using him as most men use women: as a masturbatory device. Or as a scapegoat to vent her fury and her frustrations upon. To make *hate*, Candace, not love. Reminds me of that cartoon I saw in a magazine once: this type is putting his pants back on, and saying to this absolutely gorgeous, mother-naked creature, who's kneeling on a mightily rumpled bed, and facing him: "Babe, you're the greatest!" But, from her back – which he can't see – there's an electric cord protruding that runs down to a wall socket, and is plugged there. And at one point on her spine, just above her splendid, pear-shaped ass, there's a transparent door, through which can be seen a collection of knobs, push-buttons, gauges, dials, and the like, by which, apparently, she can be, or has been, programmed.'

'In other words, the girl is not a girl at all, but a robot?' Candace said.

'Exactly. A robot. A sex machine. What most men want. Not ever anything so difficult, terrifying, marvellous as a woman. A real woman. Of which there are damned few, anyhow – though more, perhaps than there are real men.'

'You're honest, at least,' Candace admitted grudgingly. 'But why do men want robots, sex machines?'

'Because, then, they don't have to really cope. Don't have to be men – by definition, "but little lower than the angels, crowned with glory and honour!" can function on a much lower level, that of the ape, say, of the goat. Get it up, then ram it into her, brother! Simplifies the hell out of things. . . .'

'And that's what's wrong with this book?' Candace said.

'And all such books,' John Farrow said. 'Because the wrong people write them. To get it right, your sexologist would have to be a poet – and once, just once in life – to have been in love. And then, maybe, he couldn't write it. Couldn't blaspheme against her, against love, by producing this sort of manual for emotional castrates, this masturbatory voyeur's view of human love. He couldn't, I believe, so much as put it down on paper, could not so reduce miracles, wonder, joy to these sad and infantile puerilities, the kind of unimaginative sexual fantasies that hard-up adolescents write on lavatory walls. . . .'

Candace was staring at him, bitter eyed; hearing, all too clearly what had got into his voice by then.

'He'd have to have loved – a woman once – who walked into a clearing under the trees and stopped the world. Stopped it dead. Drained time off and poured it down a chute back into something very like the primordial void. Created a silence that rang like all the bells that ever were in all of recorded history, clamouring and clangouring together, making the very air go solid, turn bronze, gold, silver, pealing, tolling, hammering, pounding, until the mind's eardrums have been shattered by the force and fury of that unheard sound. . . .'

Candace looked away from him. Faced him again. Her face was very white; but all the battle signals were there for him to read: the lifted chin, the lips reduced to a taut line; the noticeable flare of shapely, patrician nostrils. She said: 'Go on, John. Please.'

'He'd have to have kissed her mouth and learned once and for ever that ecstasy and anguish are siamese twins, mouth joined, nipple stabbed, groin aching and aflow. He'd have to have discovered that joy's a blade, white hot and glowing, pushed slowly through his gut, followed just as slowly by another one of ice, and that one by a pair of iron claws that reach up through loin, belly, chest, throat to the base of his brain, to the seat of whatever rationality he has, whatever spirit, psyche, mind, id, ego, libido, tongue, palate, larynx, heart, lungs, guts, testicles – down into some obliquely fourth-dimensional cave, set at a tangent to here, to now, where all the black, sulphuric air goes singing threnodies, and flowers grow from the bleached skulls – emptied at last, of dreams, of hope! – of all the martyred lovers. . . .'

'You're saying – that is, if you're saying *anything*, if there's a drop of meaning hidden somewhere in all this flood of words – extravagant, and inflated words, John Farrow! – that love should be sexless?' Candace said. 'And a lover both a romantic, and a fool?'

'No, I'm not saying that. Because, Candace, literary critic extraordinary, he'd also *have* to have lain with her and thereby learned that you simply cannot reduce fusion – of every pore, every breath, every heartbeat; blood, tears, sweat, agony, melted into an incredibly anguished total explosion, disintegrating male and female both into the very stuff of being, then reintegrating them again into one blinding whole – "Ye twin shall be one flesh!" – to what's meant, or at least suggested by a pauper's word like "orgasm" and thereby be constrained – "Oh consummation devoutly to be wished!" – from arguing over such imbecilities as to *where* a woman has them, whether they're clitorial or vaginal – or some such *sacrée merde*!'

'Then where does she?' Candace said, 'I thought I knew, but now you've made me doubt it!'

'A woman – a woman who *is* a woman, and who, being woman, loves you, has them all over, inside and out, from head to heel, and both of you die together and are resurrected into life, into a joy purer than starlight, more blinding than the sun at high noon. Those are a few of the minimum essentials he'd have to know, have to have experienced to write his book, Candace. Those, and at least one other. . . .'

'And that other is, John?' Candace whispered.

'He'd have to have lost her. To spend all his subsequent life – if he can even call that living! – not only absent from felicity the while, but drawing his breath in the most agonizing kind of pain. He'd have to know how it is to walk down a lonely street in any town anywhere, and see someone, anyone, who looks like her only a little, make some small gesture vaguely like one of hers – a trick of tossing heavy hair to one side with a lift of her hand – to find himself leaning back against a wall to keep from falling flat on his ass, absolutely crippled, maimed, murdered in that moment, by memory, reduced, distilled into purest pain. *Then* he could write a book about how to make love, an art on a different plane altogether than the mere physical mechanisms of sex; but then, at the same time, he couldn't write it. Couldn't cast down the only pearl he's ever known before a herd of rutting swine. . . .'

'And your only pearl,' Candace said, 'was your – Simone.'

'Yes,' he said. 'My pearl – my only pearl – was Simone. But

the swine, possessed of all the devils *He* cast into them, were, and are – legion.'

Then he turned his back to her, said:

'Good night, Candace—'

Clicked off the light, and left her, without stirring from their double bed. It was, of course, the very next day he caught her tearing up the one lone, poor and pitiful snapshot he had of Simone.

'The perfect proof,' John Farrow thought now wryly, 'that trouble and even – deliverance, at time – always come from the unexpected quarter. Because when I slapped dear Candy clear across the room for her unpardonable offence, I gave her the quite respectable grounds on which to base her petition of divorce. It was "cruelty" I suppose, for me to hit her; but it wasn't "cruelty" for her to tear up my last, blurred, fading hold on life.

'That snapshot. Taken with a dead man's camera. A Leica Yves Martin lifted off the carcass of an SS Obersturmführer he'd killed. And left to Simone, along with his motor-cycle, by his spoken wish, uttered with his last, his dying breath, when he, too, died that day. Because, upon that conclusive evidence, he loved her, too. Was there a man among us who *didn't* love Simone? Byron. He *says*. And I doubt even that. Anton would have died for her, any minute of the day or night. And the rest of them, less, of course, but still – at St Nizier, that thirteenth of June 1944, we were *all* saved by her. Made into men and heroes by her. And—'

'Jean,' Simone said, 'are you ashamed of me?'

Jean grinned at her; said in English.

'Stop fishing, Simone!'

'Fishing?' Simone said.

'Yes, for compliments.'

She came over to where he sat. He had taken his Sten gun apart, and had the pieces scattered all over the kitchen table. A Sten was very easy to assemble and disassemble. The only thing you really needed for the job was a screwdriver. It had been designed to be as simple as possible, so that guerrilla fighters, such as the FFI, could maintain them with little trouble. But most people who had to use them thought that their simplicity had been overdone. They had the damnedest habit of ripping off a burst when you didn't want them to, and jamming on you when you did.

'Jean—'

'Will you leave me in peace, woman?'

'Tu vois? Tu ne m'aimes plus! Tu es déjà fatigué de moi!'

'Speak English,' he told her. 'You're going to need it when we get to New York.'

'But we are not going to New York,' Simone said. 'We are going to Israel. And you must let your beard grow, and your hair and wear *pelas* and the *cafflin*. And – and a fur hat! Like the *rabbin* in the villages of Poland do. Will you become a rabbi for me, Jean?'

He smiled at her, said:

'For you I'll become anything, my love. Anything at all. But will they let me? I understand that mere converts suffer certain restrictions.'

She pouted, said:

'You've been talking to Anton!'

'Yes, I have. I told him I planned to become a Jew. He didn't seem to like the idea.'

'Of course not, silly! Anton is in love with me. And he was sure that – all – that all – that has happened to our people – would make me so sick of Goyim – that I would end up marrying him. And d'you know what, Jean? He – would have been right, almost surely – if I hadn't met you.'

Jean put down the cocking lever of the Sten. Looked at her, whispered:

'You – you want me to give you up, Simone?'

She bent down to him, kissed him, whispered, with her mouth still on his:

'You want me to die, Jean?'

'Oh, come now, Simone!' he laughed. 'You're a *very* healthy girl, you know!'

'You mean I'm a *garce*. No – *une nymphomane*!'

'Long live nymphomania!' he said.

'Jean, c'est vrai que tu n'as pas honte de moi?'

'No, I am not ashamed of you. Why should I be?'

'Suis – laide. Maigre. Et – mauvaise fille. Nymphomane.'

'You're neither ugly, skinny, a bad girl, nor a nymphomaniac. You're beautiful, slender, a good girl, a very good girl, especially in bed. Would you like for us to go there now? To bed, I mean?'

'*Oui.* Of course. But we mustn't. I must learn to control myself Jean, do you think we've made her yet? *Numéro Deux,* I mean?'

Number Two was what he called their hoped-for daughter: 'Simone, Number Two.'

'Don't know. But just in case we left something off, her left ear say, we'd better—'

'No, Jean.'

'Why not?'

'Don't feel like it. *Suis – triste. Je ne sais pas pourquoi.* But I am. Very sad. I think – I think I'm going – to lose you!'

He put his arm around her waist, drew her down upon his knees, said:

'How – with an axe? Or shall I put the Sten back together again, so you can use that?'

'Don't say such things! They're bad luck! Pierre thinks they're going to attack soon. Says they've been bustling about too much, lately. Do you, mon Jean?'

'Yes, Simone.'

'And then, what?'

'We're going to have to run. Like hell, bébé!'

'Do not call me, bébé! It doesn't sound – nice. Why shall we have to run, *mon ange*? Can't we beat them?'

'With Stens? Pistol ammunition? Against armoured cars and tanks? Oh Christ if we only have one 20 millimetre! Only a little Bofors say, or a Hispano Suiza or—'

'Jean, do not talk about guns like that! As though you *loved* them!'

'No,' he said, 'I hate them with all my soul, Simone. And when this is over, I shall never touch one of the ugly, oily things again.'

'That's better. That's much better! I wonder why I'm – so sad?'

She sat bolt upright.

'Oh, non!' she wailed. *'Pas ça! Pas ça!'*

'Pas quoi?' he said.

'Je pense que je vais tomber du toit! Je suis toujours triste pendant ces jours-ci!'

'You're going to fall off the roof?' he said. 'What on earth?'

She hid her face against his neck, whispered:

'Mes réglés. Ma période.'

'You're sure?' he said.

'Non!' she squealed happily. *'Suis pas sûre. Viens, mon amour!'*

He said, 'If it's time for that, making love won't help it. That's what the Catholic rhythm method is all about. There're only about forty-eight hours in the middle of the month when—'

'I know all that,' she said and grinned at him mischievously. 'All my Catholic girl friends at the University of Paris called it the Vatican roulette. It *never* works. And they were always pregnant, *les pauvres*! So therefore we must try the Catholic method, so that it will fail for us as well, and I shall need a wheelbarrow to push my belly about in, and – and besides you haven't made love to me since last night and—'

And that was another of the good times. The good, fine, wonderful times. But then, for them, all the times were good.

She lay in his arms, warm, glistening with sweat; trembling a little still, with both arms about his neck, and said:

'You are Eros. Love. Like in the Symposium.'

'In the what?' he said.

'The Symposium of Plato. You know I was studying to be a teacher of philosophy, don't you?'

'Plato,' Jean teased her, 'didn't like love. Not this kind, anyhow. He thought it should be platonic.'

'He did *not*! That's a canard! *Un gros canard!* You know what he said? About how Eros – you – were born? And who your mother was?'

'I *know* who my mother was. About *mon père*, I sometimes have my doubts. Maman was, and is, a trifle *frivole*!'

'Good for her! But don't you want to hear the story?'

'Yes,' he said.

'When Aphrodite was born, all the gods had a great feast. And among the invited was Plenty, the son of Cleverness. So all the gods, Zeus, and Hera, and Athena and – well all of them ate their bellies full, and got drunk from nectar, because, you see, wine had not been invented yet. Jean! You're not paying attention, you bad boy, you!'

'I am paying attention – but to these—' he bent and kissed her breasts, 'and to this—'

'Oh no you don't! Not until I have finished my story. And have rested a little. Then we'll see! Where was I?'

'The gods were all drunk. As drunk as – gods. But then, aren't they always?'

'Yes,' Simone said. 'Or – absent. Especially when we need them.'

'Even – Yahweh?' Jean said.

'Oh, Jean, I don't know! I – I'm not religious, really. So many of us, the younger Jews of Europe – weren't. But isn't that – what we're being punished for, maybe? Isn't that what – again, *peut-être* – the death camps – are all about?'

'If he punishes you for your lack of faith, by letting babies die at the Vél d'Hiv – in cattle cars – in the *shtetls* of Poland – he's a bastard. And you can have him, Simone!'

'Jean. No! Don't say that! We – don't know – can't understand—'

'I know Lucienne cut her throat to avoid being branded like *une vache* – and sent to a *Feldtdirnenhaus*. That she's dead. I understand that much, Simone.'

'Jean – you – you *loved* her. You really *loved* her! Oh *comme je suis malheureuse*!'

'Simone – to repeat, to reiterate, I love *you*. Nobody else. I never have. I never will. I have never made loud and hysterical remarks to the effect that I would die without you. But considering the matter calmly, I'm afraid I would. Not necessarily my body. But *me* – who I am. My body might go on existing for a certain number of years – but my heart – my – that quite possibly imaginary and nonexistent quality I am pleased to call my soul, would be *kaput, fini*. I should become a zombie. One of the walking dead.'

'Jean – make love to me some more, now. Please?'

'No. I'm tired. Finish your story.'

'Oh, *zut alors*! Where was I?'

'Wallowing around with a lot of drunken gods.'

'Yes. Why yes. Exactly. Because you see – I am Poverty. Your mother.'

'Now *that's* a new one! Doesn't the Torah say that incest is punishable by death?'

'Oh, don't be so literal-minded! This is an allegory. Poetic. And *I* didn't make it up. Plato did.'

'And—' Jean said.

'And Poverty – me – came begging. Because she – like me – is always hungry. And while she was devouring the scraps the gods had given her, she wandered out into the garden – into, Plato says, the Park of Zeus – and saw Plenty lying in the grass, dead drunk and fast asleep. And she saw he was a beautiful, beautiful old thing – like you. And he didn't have on any clothes, except maybe a *chalmys* – a sort of short cloak, about his shoulders, because people didn't wear clothes much in those days, and especially not to banquets, because banquets always ended in some first-class orgies, and clothes only got in the way.'

He looked at her, groaned: 'Now, Simone!'

'I'm only telling you what Plato says happened! So poor Poverty stood there, looking at fine, beautiful, naked Plenty, and – oh, how can I say it without shocking you? I *always* seem to shock you. And your eyes turn dark. Darker than they are, I mean. And you look so – so hurt. Because instead of *l'ange* you want me to be, I am a *garce. Très garce.* Let me think – let me think. I've got it! So poor Poverty stood there and certain physiological manifestations of her baser instincts took place within her. How's that, Jean?'

'Ganz gut!' he said, 'Very good! *Très bien! Muy bueno! Va bene!* Only what does it *mean*?'

'It means,' Simone hooted, 'that her breasts started to hurt, her belly felt like it had a volcano in it, and – and *sa toute petite chose* – started to melt on the inside and run down her thighs. In other words, she felt *très* sexy. Like I do when I look at you!'

She stopped. Peered at him. Wailed:

'Oh, Jean! You see? You're ashamed of me – *again*!'

'No,' he said. 'No, I'm not. And you don't shock me, Simone. What you do – is remind me – of what I'd rather not be reminded of. . . .'

'That I once belonged to another man? That's *your* fault, Jean!' she said angrily. 'You should have come to me earlier. You would have saved me from so much, so much! But you were a lazy boy, a *bad* lazy boy occupied with your Hélènes and your Luciennes and – and with Tilly Lipschitz, maybe – and did not come until it was too late! So now you have to take me as I am. Flawed, damaged! *Une garce* who—'

'Is not *une garce* at all, but my love,' he said. 'My only love. My *last* love, which is more important than being the first, isn't it? For the first is always – accidental, sort of. But the last is a matter of deliberate, and considered choice. *Et ça, c'est toi* –

mon dernier amour. In whom I'd change nothing – except the mental picture she has of herself. This false, bad distorted mental picture that somebody put there, because he had to maybe—'

'Jean—' she whispered. 'You're wrong, you know!'

'He had to,' Jean went on stubbornly, 'because he wasn't really a man, I think. That's the only kind who debase, degrade women, Simone. The half a testicle eunuch who *has* to cut a girl down to a size, a height that fits him. A man wants a woman. Standing tall. A partner. An equal. Proud. A little fierce at times. But always tender. And he doesn't need to debase – or dominate her. Equals – and *only* equals – mate. The rest is – a kind of necrophilia, isn't it? The use of a dead body for pleasure. For a body without spirit, mind, pride – a degraded, slavish body is dead – even if it remains useful. Retains warmth enough, moisture enough to be fucked. To be screwed. But it's got to have a woman inside of it, Simone, warm, vibrant, tender, fierce, proud, troublesome, and alive for love-making to go on. Because that requires *two* people, my love, trying desperately to *give* themselves to each other. To *give*, never to take. And it must be mutual.'

She stared at him, her green eyes dark and troubled.

'Jean,' she said, 'let me tell you this much – about *that*. I mean. It started out – the way you said. He – wait! I promise you I won't say his name or tell you anything about him! – began, commenced to do what you – described. To debase – to degrade me. And he succeeded. Oh, *how* he succeeded! I was – an innocent. A school girl – with her hair in a bun on the back of her neck, and hideous glasses – I still need them, Jean, do you mind? *Et comme je suis affreuse avec mes lunettes!*'

He smiled at her, said: 'No, I don't mind, *mon ange*. But why don't you wear them now, since you need them?'

'Broke them – ages ago. I only need them for reading – and since there's nothing to read, nor an optician at hand to make me new ones, I do without them. Jean, *mon ange, mon amour*, hear this out. I – I think we'll both feel better if you do.'

'All right,' Jean said, 'tell me, Simone.'

'He set out to – to degrade me. But only because it – amused him, *not* for the motives that you think. He was all man. Too much so, maybe. I was innocent – but not, but not – *vièrge* – a boy at the university had taken care of that chore – already. By that I mean he had hurt me, made me bleed frightfully, gave me no pleasure at all, and enjoyed himself, thoroughly. A real Melvin Lipschitz that one, even though he was a Goy! He never gave me pleasure. Instead he gave me a complex: that sex is messy, painful, no damn fun, and that men are brutes!'

'Unfortunately, that complex is pretty close to the truth in all too many cases,' Jean said.

'Yes. But – the other one – wasn't like that. He was the most masterly, most expert lover any girl could ever dream of. Oh, Jean, Jean, *mon adoré*! Don't look at me like that! Don't you see, realize what an *insult* that was?'

'An insult?' Jean said dully.

'Yes, yes, yes, yes! An insult! For him to be so little perceptive of – of *what* kind of – *avis rara* I was – or as Pepe always says, shaking his head as if the sight of me gives him a headache, '*¡Que bicho más raro!*' Oh Jean, *mon ange* – do help me! I don't know how to say it in English.' She stopped, her green gaze smoky, turned inward. '*Et en français non plus!*' she wailed.

'You're saying,' Jean said quietly, trying to keep the grate, the shake, the rasp of pain out of his voice, 'that this – type – was too dense, too insensitive to perceive, sense, apprehend your quality, your very special quality as a human being. But wasn't that rather too much to expect of him, Simone, since I've already gathered that you weren't exactly fighting him off?'

She bowed her head. Stared at the floor. A long time. A very long time. Looked up again. Made no attempt to hide the streaks of bitter hurt pencilling her face.

'Jean—' she said, 'when you feel that strong an impulse to – to slap me, do it, please! But don't – say things like that to me. They – they hurt – too much!'

'Sorry,' he said. 'Get on with it, Simone!'

'All right! And for your information, Monseigneur le Juge – who has already handed down sentence against me in your mind! – he was neither dense, nor insensitive. He was very – like *you*, in many ways. Astonishingly so, when I come to think of it, now.'

'Jesus!' Jean all but screamed.

'Yes, yes! Very like you, in all but looks. Both sensitive and perceptive. Only, when I first met him he wasn't working at them, very hard. Just as *you* aren't working at them now!'

'All right,' Jean said. 'Right now I'm a dolt. Insensitive. And a murderer. Because if there ever were a bastard on this earth I want to kill, it's—'

She came to her knees; put her slim fingers across his mouth; whispered:

'Please. Please, Jean. Don't say that. Don't even think it. Oh, not because of – of him. Because of you, yourself. *Toi-même.* It destroys – the you, the very special you I love.'

He pulled her hand away, snarled:

'Get on with it, Simone!'

'All right. Even though you're behaving – childishly. And badly, I started to say that he insulted me. He did. Not by assuming he could have sex with me the first time he laid eyes on me. In that he was right. He was – such a beautiful man, Jean! A little tired, a little faded – but weathered so well, with all – autumn's – sadness in him. A little winter at his temples – crinkles about his eyes from gazing steadfastly – with neither fear, nor hope – at his own – decline, his end – at eternity. Where he was wrong – and in this, only because he hadn't even thought about it – was in assuming that he could have meaningless sex with me. That he could add me to his list of – of shove-overs – no, that's wrong; it's pushovers, isn't it? – with impunity! Even his – expertness – was an insult. Any – *vieille putain* – is an expert at mere sex, isn't she?'

'Wouldn't know. I'm no fancier of used goods, Simone! But friends of mine who've had relations with whores, told me that oddly enough, they're not. That they're pretty damned lousy, in fact. It seems they fake passion – and fake it badly. Oh hell, how did we get into this? Go on, since you must, though God knows why!'

'For you, Jean. So you'll understand me. And – start to love me again. For right now, you don't. You're pretty close to hating me, aren't you?'

He looked at her, said flatly:

'Yes.'

'That's all right. In fact it's good. Because the opposite of love isn't hate, as most people think, it's indifference. We *always* hate the people we love – and vice-versa. All right! He was an expert in the same way a champion rider is expert, because he has ridden so many horses that he knows, can sense, just how any particular mount is going to react – to whip, and bit, and spur! Only he – my lover – had ridden so many *women* that he knew *everything* about the human body, female gender, except – the things you said. That it should have – a mind in it. A soul. A person. A loving, tender, fierce, troublesome – no, more than troublesome! – a first-class pain in the ass, like me! – inside. But – *alive*. Wanting to love, to give. To be *loved*, not merely fucked. And he didn't know, realize that, not at first. Largely because, I think, he'd developed the knack of picking out real shoveovers at a glance. Just as he picked *me* out. He wasn't wrong. I *was* a shove – pushover – for him. But he didn't realize all the other things I was, I am. Not at first.'

'But later,' Jean's voice was a croak, a husk of sound, 'he did?'

'Later, he did. Learned that *sa 'tite poupée*, his amusing little doll, *sa drôle de gamine, la pauvre idiote* he'd taught to talk like – *une garce, une putain*, because the contrast between what I *was* and the filthy things he'd taught his so well-trained Pavlovian little bitch to say, diverted him no end – was a woman. A real woman. A true one. Learned in the end to love her. Because I forced him to, I suppose. I've seen him – a man, a mature man, twice your age and more, weep like a child in my arms, because he loved me so! Jean! Just where do you think you're going?'

'Don't know,' Jean said. 'Out. This is – pretty hard to take, Simone!'

'Yet you will take it! As I have had to take *ta Hélène, ta Lucienne!* My past is my own. Just as yours is yours, mon Jean. And neither counts, from this day on – if we love each other. I am nineteen years old. A woman. *Oh merde*, blast and damn! A woman *likes* sex. Needs it! Especially from the man she *loves*, you cretin! You're twenty-six. And, let's face it, Jean! any person in our – terrible times – who reached either age with no sexual experience at all, would have to be – retarded, inhuman, emotionally sick, or a latent homosexual – because the shelter, the paternal vigilance that made virginity until marriage possible – and spoiled a million wedding nights! – just couldn't be exercised under today's conditions, though God knows, *mon Papa* tried! Lord how he tried, the poor old dear! Am I not right, Jean? Think with your head, not your adorable little boy's, oh so childish heart! Am I not *right*?'

'Yes. Yes, you are,' he said ungrudgingly, 'and I apologize. Please go on.'

'Listen to him! To *mon ange! Mon adoré!* Oh Jean, I love you, love you, love you!'

'Stop that!' he said. 'Finish what you started, Simone. Now you've got to. Or leave me – maimed inside. Crippled.'

'Jean – you – you love me *that* much?'

'I love you that much. More than he – or any other old perverse and horny bastard ever could! Now tell me what I want to hear. What I've *got* to hear if you want me to go on living, functioning as a man. That you don't love him *now*. That you've forgotten him!'

Her eyes were green smoke. Gold flaked. Luminous. A little mocking. With more than a touch of the perversity he would have sworn she didn't have in them. The eyes of Jezebel.

'Even – if – I have to lie to you, mon Jean?' she whispered.

He started to leap from the bed. But her hands were claws. Talons. Rapine and fierce. Desperate and tender.

'If you leave me now,' she said quietly, flatly, finally, 'I shall kill myself, *mon Jean*. I will not attempt to live without you. I cannot.'

'But,' he raged, 'you love him still! That's not the past, Simone! That's now, goddamnit! Now!'

'I didn't say that. I didn't say it, because I don't. But neither do I hate him. Nor have I forgotten him. That's too much to ask. I am also entitled to my memories, Jean! I shall never forget him. I don't even want to.'

He stared at her. His face, at that moment, was the face of a man dying, quite literally, under torture.

'You expect me,' he whispered, 'to spend the rest of my life, with his ghost between us in our bed?'

'No,' Simone said, 'because it isn't there. You won't have to support that kind of a memory, *mon Jean*. You'll have quite enough supporting me. A woman who is – if I may borrow your words – maimed on the inside, crippled – but by her *own* sin. The sin of teaching, or forcing him to love me. Wait! I'm going to explain that at once, before you go off like an eighty-eight millimetre shell! I – I taught him to love me to the point that not only would he have died for me, but that he would, and *did* betray his own highest ideals and everything he *knew* I believed in, held most dear – to save my poor, miserable bitch's life! To keep this mangy she-cur's hide unstripped by their whips, unscarred by their hot irons, unmangled by their instruments of torture! I cannot forgive him for *that, mon Jean*. For putting upon me the burden, and the consequences of his weakness. For forcing me to share this awful guilt not my own. I am not worth that much, *mon Jean*. My life is not, nor would my striped, torn, seared flesh have been; my broken bones, my agony. He left me – filled with this sick contempt for him. But also with this lacerating pity. But with neither hate, nor love. Rather – and this most of all – with shame. With shame so great I meant to die, as long as I could die usefully, doing some good for my poor, reviled, tormented, murdered people. Until *you* came, and closed even that door. Because to die would be to leave you, and that, *mon ange adoré, mon amour, ma vie,* is far beyond my strength! So there you have it, Jean. I don't love him any more. I cannot. But do not ask me to forget him, I cannot do that, either.'

'Nor I,' Jean said gravely. 'In fact he – whoever he was, or is – has just entered my private canon of most blessed saints. I'll say a prayer for his health, his happiness, if he still lives, or for the repose of his soul if he is dead, to the God I don't even believe in, every night so long as I shall live.'

'Jean!' she sobbed, 'you mustn't say things like that! You must not! And you mustn't – love me so. I'm not worth it!'

'Ask me not to breathe, Simone,' he said, and kissed her.

'Jean—' she whispered, 'make love to me, now. Please?'

'No,' he said, 'not now, Simone.'

'Why not?'

'Because you – all this you've told me, has made me sad. And love, making love, should always be a happy thing. Playful. Gay. I know! Finish your story. That will cheer me up. The one about all those drunken gods. And Poverty standing there looking at Plenty and—'

'And getting all hot for him!' Simone supplied. 'As I am for you right now. And all the time. All right! So Poverty stood there looking at that great big gorgeous naked man stretched out there on the grass dead drunk and fast asleep, until she couldn't stand it any more. So she snatched off her *chalmys* and her *peplos,* jumped on to him and – and *what,* Jean? What's *not* a dirty word for it? *All* the ones I know are!'

'Had sexual intercourse with him?' Jean suggested.

'*Oh, merde alors!* She did *not*! She screwed him royally! And—'

'Simone, you're not going to lie there on your delectable little tail and tell me that Plato wrote all *this*!'

'He did. He actually did. Only he put it more platonically. His exact words were: "So Poverty, because of her penury made a plan to have a child from Plenty, and lay by his side and conceived Eros—" which is to say – Love. Are you *catholique*, Jean?'

'I was brought up as one. Papa indulged Maman to that extent, out of his considered belief, I found out later, that all religions are nonsense. But it didn't take. I grew up seeing what people do to other people, and came to two conclusions: that either God doesn't give a good goddamn for mankind and all its works, or He isn't there. I like the second conclusion better. It's more – respectful. More religious. I'd rather his being absent than his being a fiendish bastard.'

'Jean, you're a naughty, naughty, naughty boy! Remind me to spank you!'

'I've got a couple of better ideas – as to what you can do to me, I mean.'

'*Ça, d'accord!* But later. To continue. And this is why Eros – Love – *You* – has become the follower and servant of Aphrodite, having been begotten at her birthday party, and at the same time he is by nature a lover busy with beauty because Aphrodite is beautiful—'

He looked at her with wonder, said:

'You're a marvel, Simone! I get used to the idea that you're a hair-brained, scatter-brained, bird-brained little nitwit, and then you stop me cold. You quote Plato word for word – you say things that are not only true, but that have a surprising degree of profundity. Like that remark of yours about the Italian soldiers. You were right, you know. Heroes are beasts. The blond beasts out of the Ring of the Nibelungen. Men, normal men – are afraid. No, please go on with it. Quote some more. It's rather beautiful.'

'All right. "Then, since Love is the son of Plenty and of Poverty, he gets his fortunes from both of them. First, he is always poor, and far from being tender and beautiful, as most people think, he is hard and rough and unshod and homeless, lying always on the ground without bedding, sleeping by the doors and in the streets in the open air, having his mother's nature, always dwelling with want. . . ." '

'But if his father was Plenty,' Jean said, 'didn't he inherit *anything?*'

'Yet,' Simone quoted at once, ' "from his father, again, he has designs upon beautiful and good things—" '

'In other words,' Jean interrupted her, 'upon *you*.'

'*Merci, mon amour!*' Simone said, and kissed him. ' "Being brave and go-ahead and high-strung, a mighty hunter, always weaving devices, and a successful covetor of wisdom, a philosopher all his days, a great wizard, and sorcerer, and sophist." That *mon ange, mon Jean adoré* is what Plato wrote in his Symposium – that very, very perfect description – of *you*!'

'And didn't he describe you at all, Simone?'

'Yes – I think so, yes. Not in the Symposium, though. In the Republic. Book Five. Though, in a way it is rather sad.'

'Say it!' Jean said.

' "So the women of the guardians must strip, since naked they will be clothed in virtue for gowns; they must share in war and in all the guarding of the City, and that shall be their only work. . . ." '

He looked at her, questioningly.

'The City – civilization, as we know it, Simone? War – against the Barbarians – the Hosts of Darkness that would destroy it? And the guardians and their women?'

'You – and me. Who must die, perhaps, mon Jean – that there even *be* a tomorrow. For someone, somewhere. That children may run, skip rope, play ball. That people may – love another – and not hate, not ever hate. Oh Jean!'

'You are clothed in virtue for your gown,' Jean said solemnly, 'as always. . . .'

But her mercurial mood had changed!

'I am clothed in absolutely nothing, at the moment, thank God!' she laughed; 'and now you must command *ton tout petit truc* who has collapsed from exhaustion to stand and deliver! So that we may play *"cache-saucisson"*! And that you may pump me up big as a house with – *Numéro Deux. Oh Jean, comme je t'aime. Vraiment, tu sais. Avec tout mon coeur, mon corps, mon âme!*'

'I'll settle for ton corps at the moment, Simone,' Jean said and kissed her. 'Here will end the philosophy seminar for today.'

'And for tonight,' Simone giggled, '*and* for tomorrow, and—'

But she was wrong. For it was on that tomorrow that the

Germans came. And in that kind of war, a certain amount of philosophy was the only alternative to going mad.

A little before five o'clock that next morning, June 13, 1944, five days after the Allies had stormed ashore in Normandy, Jean le Fou/Crazy John, woke up. He strained his ears, aware that a sound had wakened him. Then he heard it. The rumble of many motors coming on.

'Maybachs!' he told himself; 'and that means – Personnel carriers – Büssing NAG half-tracks, sure as hell! And Jesus, there must be a million of them for me to hear them from so far away! Down below Pariset, I'd say, and—'

He tried to get up, but he couldn't. The reason he couldn't was because Simone was asleep in her customary position, which meant she was atop, around, between, below various parts of him. She had his neck in a half-Nelson. Her left thigh was above his right thigh, but her left calf was below his right calf, and even her toes had a warm prehensile grip on his flesh. Her face was buried in the hollow of his throat. From time to time her lips made lazy kissing motions against his Adam's apple, even though she was fast asleep.

'Swear to God she hasn't any bones!' he thought, 'or is a born contortionist: but I'd better get the hell out of here. Go see – pity to wake her up, but—'

He tried to disentangle himself. Her grip tightened.

'Mon chou,' she murmured, not really awake, *'fais-moi quelque chose!'*

'Not now!' he said sharply. 'I must get up, Simone! I hear motors! Unhand me, woman! I've got to get up!'

Her green eyes flared, flashed. She turned him loose. Sat up. It was already getting light that high up, and he could see her. A stab of tenderness went through him like a crippling blade, seeing her tousle-haired, lithe-limbed, perfect, her face of Nefertiti, leaning forward, sniffing the air for Germans, her small, delicate *pluscumperfecto* – the word he'd invented to describe it – body proving again that she couldn't look awkward or ugly in any position whatsoever, and deranging his orderly thought processes as always by giving off the absolutely maddening smells of perfume, of warm flesh, of healthy sweat, of sex, of young female, all her special fragrances that would linger in his memory for ever. She grinned at him, said,

'Liar!' And started in to kiss him every place she could reach, which took in a considerable amount of territory.

He pulled away from her, listening. But she was right. There wasn't the faintest ghost of a sound. 'Must have been dreaming,' he thought, while he still could think. 'I would have sworn—'

The reason there was no sound was very simple: the German half-tracks, all one hundred of them, each of them seating fifteen men, were already inside the village called Pariset. They, and the Steyr 640s, the six-wheeled *Kommandeurwagens*, command cars, in each of which six officers and their non-com driver rode, had cut their motors. And Pariset was a little too far from St Nizier for the clank of their weapons, and the thud of their boots to carry up to where even ears straining to catch the lightest sound could have heard them. And John Farrow/Jean Claude Dubois was much too busy to have heard the final Trump of Doom by then.

Afterwards, Jean and Simone did not drift off, but fell, plummeting down all seven Dantean levels into sleep. So deep a sleep that they didn't even hear the battle start. What woke them was the ugliest, most brutal alarm clock in this world. A self-propelled 13.7 millimetre machine gun, that is a 50 calibre, the heaviest automatic weapon made, before you get to the 20 millimetre, at which point a machine gun becomes a rapid-fire cannon – mounted as an integral part of an Austro-Daimler ADMK, a little buglike vehicle having both wheels and tracks, but that was not a miniature half-track because its wheels and tracks could only be used alternatively as the terrain demanded, but never together the way true half-tracks always are, came clanking through the trees after having flanked the FFI defence – 250 men against 1,500 Germans – and sat in a little square some thirty metres from, and fifteen metres below, their house.

The gunner cranked the muzzle up the necessary number of degrees. Then he opened up. His helper knelt beside him and supported the belt with his gloved hands as it jumped and bucked into the breech. Beyond the gun, on the other side, the shells showered out of the ejector chute, bounding and clattering on the cobblestones.

A spray of stinging white-hot sleet whined down upon John's and Simone's naked flesh. Their eyes flew open. Both their bodies were covered with powdered glass. Here and there a sliver had dug in and they were bleeding.

They rolled from the bed, like the trained fighters they both were, and crawled across the floor below window height. The machine gun dissolved another window for them. Then the gunner turned his attention to another house.

They stood up, dashed for the clothes closet. But once they were there, Simone muttered something, fiercely, under her breath, and ran back into that powdered glass winterscape of a bedroom again. When she came out, two minutes later, she was wearing panties and a bra. The detail troubled Jean. It meant she feared being killed or hurt, and wanted to preserve, under those extremes, what she could of modesty. Or else, he knew well, she wouldn't have worn them under her uniform, preferring to save them for the times she wore woman's clothing. She came over to the closet and yanked a pair of Jean's American army pants up over her slim flanks. Except for the length, they fitted her a hell of a lot better than the huge ones she had worn into camp. Then she put out her hand towards a flaming red blouse.

'Goddamnit, no!' Jean hissed at her. 'Too visible. You'll be target for tonight. Put on something dark.'

She put on a black turtleneck sweater. Stuck her feet into those old truck-tyre sandals, ran an FFI armband up her left arm. Slapped her beret on to her head, then, being all woman, she paused a long, long moment before the mirror to get the angle of it just right, saucy and jaunty as old hell above her long brown hair. Then she picked up her Sten.

'Oh no you don't!' Jean yelled at her. 'Give me that! I need it! Mine is—'

'In thirty pieces on the kitchen table. I know. So now you just sit down like a good boy and put it back together again. While *ta femme* goes out and shoots Nazis. In the balls. So they won't be able to abuse your extensive harem of whores any more. Ta, ta, *Boy*! *A bientôt!*'

'Simone!' he roared; and made a grab for her. But she was as quick as a cat, and twice as graceful. She ducked under his flailing arms, and was gone through the door.

Somehow, miraculously, his head worked. He paused long enough to slam the 9 millimetre Beretta automatic he'd taken off the fat OVRA officer whose anal sphincter he had fused, into his belt, and grabbed up his sack of grenades. It was a good thing he did, because the ADMK had Simone pinned down below the low stone wall around the house and was showering her with stone dust and granite slivers as its bursts slammed into the wall.

So he had to do it not only right, but perfectly, the first time. Because there wasn't going to be a second time. There wasn't going to be any time at all for either of them if he missed. Fortunately for him, the ugly buglike monster came clanking steadily towards where Simone lay. So he waited, moaning, praying, crying, sweating, pissing his pants a little, hidden just inside the door until it had reduced the thirty metres between it and the house to fifteen. Then he yanked the pin of the grenade, and threw, exposing himself fully, gambling on the fact that they'd cranked the gun down to point blank, to zero elevation, in their attempts to murder one tiny, frail, nineteen-year-old Jewish girl, and now would have to crank it back up again to at least seven degrees in order to get him.

He threw that one grenade like a major league pitcher. Its trajectory was ruler flat, rifle bullet straight. The driver saw it coming, and opened his mouth to shout a warning. He never got his cry out because, freakishly enough, the grenade hit him full in his open mouth, and exploded there. His head vanished. His coal scuttle helmet went soaring end over end higher than the treetops. But his blood, brains, and splinters of what had been his skull, showered and drenched the gunner and his belt feed man, effectively blinding them. Jean lobbed two more grenades underhanded, without haste, in gentle arcs, so that they burst over the self-propelled gun. It sat there, transformed into a slaughterhouse floor, a tripe factory.

'Simone!' Jean screamed, his voice breaking like an adolescent's, 'You get your narrow little ass back into this house! Or, so help me I'm going to kick it so hard that I'll break your back teeth out!'

She grinned at him. Her face was white. She was shaking all over. Her hair was filled with stone dust where the ADMK's bursts had reduced parts of that wall to powder. But she grinned all the same. An infuriating grin. Mule-stubborn. And gallant. As gallant as she was. All the way through, Jean thought, again.

'Listen, cabbage head!' she cried. 'Let me stay here. You go do your homework. Put your play toy back together. We're going to need it, you know!'

He started towards her. Reached down to grab her. But she said quietly, seriously:

'Look, lover – this wall is *stone*. The house is *wood*. They can make hamburger of us inside it. I'm safer here. Go fix your Sten. If any more of them come up this street, I'll shoot their balls off – in memory of *ta Lucienne. D'ac?*'

'D'accord,' he whispered. Bent and kissed her. Went back into the house. Sat down at the kitchen table. Started to put the Sten back together again. Usually he could do it in three minutes flat. But today it took him seven, his hands were shaking so. He slammed a clip into the breech. Gathered up all the clips they both had. Took up his sack of hand grenades, his commando knife, his Beretta. As he started for the door, he heard Simone's Sten start to splutter.

He dived through the doorway, shaking all over, his face white as death, his lips gone blue, moaning, 'Simone! Dear God, please! Simone!'

Then he saw her. She had her Sten propped up across the wall. She was, he could see, having herself one hell of a time. She was squirting the oncoming German patrol like a professional. A burst. Six shots, no more. And a big Wehrmacht trooper collapsed like a punctured balloon. But the other five came rushing towards her. She fanned the Sten. Two down. But the other three were six metres from her now. And one of them had a Schmeisser.

Jean did what he had to. He tore out a grenade. Threw it, praying that none of the splinters would reach Simone. Six metres was much too close for him to risk a grenade. But it was a *risk*. If he didn't knock out those three men, especially the one with the burpgun, what was going to happen next became a certainty. He had a second grenade in mid-air before the first one even burst. It was superfluous, a waste. The first one blew at a point equidistant from the three. Reduced them to bloody rags. The second one did a meat-grinder job on what was left.

He hung there, waiting. There didn't seem to be any more, for the moment, anyhow, in that street. And it was then that, for the first time, that idea hit him. The idea that OSS historians claimed changed, to a considerable degree, the whole course of the war.

'They're slack,' he thought. 'They were ordered to follow that ADMK. Give it close support. And they fell behind. They fell a whole goddamned eight minutes behind! And they're Wehrmacht, not SS! And that means—'

But he didn't have time to figure out what it meant at the

moment. He came damned close to never having the time. He flopped down beside Simone.

'You – get – out of – here!' he grated. 'Go back to Villars de Lans! Tell them—'

'I will not!' she snapped. 'I'm a soldier, Jean. A very good one, as you have seen! Give me a bullet clip. I haven't any more.'

'Simone!' he yelled at her, 'you're nuts, you know! I don't want you to die! Beat it, idiot! Scoot! Fuck off, will you!'

'Why, Jean, you naughty boy!' she said, and put her left arm around his neck. *'Donne-moi un baiser, mon chou?'*

'Oh, Jesus!' Jean said in English. 'Simone, you idiot, I—'

But she stopped his mouth with a long, slow clinging kiss.

He tore his mouth away, moaned: 'Simone—'

'Avec toi, mon ange,' she said. 'With you. Not back there somewhere, going crazy, waiting. Not having to stick a knife in my gut, when they bring you in all – bloody – and horrible – and – dead. Together. *Toi et moi. Dans la vie. Dans la morte. Toujours. D'accord?'*

'Simone!' he wept. 'Oh, God, Simone! Please! We haven't got a chance! I don't want you dead! I don't want—'

'What you want, and what I want matters very little now, Jean,' she said quietly, calmly. 'What we've got to do is all that counts. And that is – to be guardians of our city. Clothed in virtue – even though – even though we're – naked – and afraid. To stop them. To stop these hordes of darkness. D'accord?'

He tried one last way. He poked her slim middle with his finger.

'And Number Two?' he rasped. 'You'd take *her* with you?'

'Oui,' she whispered. 'Better than to leave her alone in the world with her father – dead – and her mother – mad.'

The Germans were reforming down below. When they came up this time, that would be it. There wasn't a hope or a prayer that 250 men – minus the ones already dead – could stop them, hold them off. Jean looked at Simone, said:

'Adieu, mon ange.'

'Adieu, Jean,' Simone whispered. 'It's not hard, you know. To die with you. It's even – sweet.'

Then they saw Huet forming his men into a line, across the entrance to St Nizier.

'Viens, Jean,' Simone said. 'Let's go down there with them.'

'D'accord,' Jean said.

But to do that they had to pass through that street, through

Jean's private tripe factory. Through that sprawl of corpses, most of them dismembered. Through that sticky, stiffening muck of human blood. Simone clung to his arm, retching, shuddering. Her eyes filled with tears.

'Bless you,' Jean said. 'You're still a woman, aren't you?'

'Pas une femme. Ta femme,' Simone said, then bent her head and vomited, noisily, terribly. Looked up again, her eyes twin dancing stars.

'Tu vois!' she exulted, *'C'est la première fois! J'ai vomi! J'ai vomi, Jean! Ça y est! Numéro Deux!'*

'Simone,' Jean said, 'I feel like vomiting, too; and I'll be damned if *I'm* pregnant.'

'But yes! You, too! You shouldn't have let me get on top! As I've done so many times!'

He grinned at her, said tenderly:

'Drôle de fille! If *I'm* pregnant where's the little fellow going to come out?'

She laughed merrily, said:

'From behind!'

'Then,' Jean said solemnly, 'he's sure going to be one poor shitty little bastard! Now come on!'

Afterwards, both Huet and Byron Graves swore Simone won that battle single-handed. The effect of her presence among the men was enough to change that one small piece of history. Hold off disaster. Turn the tide. At first, all of them yelled at her: 'Beat it, Simone! Get out of here, girl! War is a thing for men!'

'Don't see any men!' she yelled back, gaily; laughing. 'I see only little boys! And who can change your drawers for you when you dirty them the minute the Germans start to make some noise, except mama?'

Pierre Clémont took off his beret. Threw it high into the air. *'Vive Simone!'* he roared. *'Vive notre 'tite maman!'*

And all the others, even Byron, taking it up: 'Long live Simone! Long live our little mama!'

Then Yves Martin, whining, in a cracked falsetto: 'Mama! Mama! I'm thirsty! Your little boy's thirsty! Give me a little tit, mama! I'm thirsty!'

And the roars of laughter shaking the ground.

'You're a very, very, very bad boy, Yves!' Simone said. 'I'm going to spank you!'

Then they saw the Germans coming on, and all the laughter died. Strangled in tightened throats. Abruptly.

They lay on their bellies and sprayed the green-clad hordes. Simone fired as coolly as the rest. More coolly than Jean did. He was looking at her most of the time, instead of the men he was shooting at.

Then Yves Martin saw the German officer off to one side, taking pictures of the battle with a Leica. The temptation was too great. Yves raised his Sten. Ripped off a burst. The photographer collapsed. Yves was off like a shot. He reached the dead officer. Tried to yank that beautiful camera free. He couldn't. The neck strap was under the heavy, beefy officer's head. Yves clawed out his commando knife, cut the straps. Lifted the Leica triumphantly. Five metres away a Feldtwebel cut loose with his Schmeisser. Yves went down. They could hear him screaming. The burpgunner didn't finish him off. Looking up, Jean saw why. Simone had already killed him.

Then Jean rolled to his knees. Gave a leap. Another. Was off like a racing greyhound, zigzagging, leaping, falling, rolling, while the German machine guns kept a column of dirt and rocks and sticks three times his height marching along, inches behind him as their bursts ploughed into the exact spots he had been half a second, half a heartbeat before. He got to Yves. Yves was still screaming. He was screaming the way that only a gut-shot man, a down and thrashing horse, or a woman in childbirth scream. Jean bent to him. Dragged Yves' right arm, with the right fist still clenched about the straps of that Leica, up over his own shoulder, straightened his knees, lifting powerfully. Three metres away from them a potato masher grenade went off. Jean took twenty steel slivers in his chest, arms, none of which penetrated deep enough into his flesh, or were big enough to kill him. But that randy old whore, a warrior's fate, stayed true to her nature: what she gave with one hand, she took away with the other. For that grenade had fallen in a little hollow amid some boulders. The great stones broke the blast, caused the heavier case splinters and shrapnel to ricochet *away* from Jean and Yves. But the blast hurled stones high in the air. One of them, falling, caught Jean full on the forehead. It knocked him unconscious. He lay there across poor Yves. Yves was no longer screaming.

No one, not even Anton Rabinowski had thought to hold

Simone. She got to Jean almost before his body had struck the ground. Afterwards, Byron swore that if he'd had a camera, he'd have got the greatest morale-building propaganda picture in the history of warfare; Simone standing wide-legged above her man, shooting into the oncoming Germans, and screaming like a madwoman, a Valkyrie, a tiny fiend, with no cover at all, her small, slim body rock rigid, a perfect target, her finger frozen to the trigger, and the Sten eating up that clip, clattering empty now.

How she lived even thirty seconds was beyond human comprehension.

'To explain it,' Byron declared afterwards, 'you'd have to postulate – God. A loving, caring, tender-hearted God, who occasionally intervenes on behalf of fools, children, and lovers – to all of which categories Simone belonged. And perhaps even to yet another: to that rarest category of all, the truly good – which has little enough to do with sexual morality, and may be mutually exclusive from it. The chaste, being at war with their own natures, are very seldom – kind.'

But even so he, Byron, didn't push the hypothetical tenderloving kindness of the hypothetical god, who at that very moment was sitting on his hypothetical ass and letting nearly six million innocent people be murdered under conditions of total horror, too far. Well within that thirty miraculous seconds, he was up, and racing for her, and Anton behind him and Pierre and Pepe then all of them, 230-odd men – for they already had lost five dead and several wounded by then – charging 1,460 Germans, which was, of course, to subtract the forty enemy soldiers down and apparently dead by that time. It was too much, too incredibly much. The Germans broke, ran. A barrage of grenades rained down upon them.

Byron ran towards Simone. Then he stopped, thinking it was better to leave her alone for the moment. Or, at least, kinder. She was staring at Jean. He was dead white. Blood was coming out of his nose, his mouth. She dropped to her knees. Kissed his bloody mouth. Straightened up. Rammed the very nearly red-hot muzzle of her Sten into her own mouth. Groped for the trigger. Anton screamed an F at least two octaves above high C, and threw himself at her, in flying tackle position, all of him off the ground. But he was no athlete, had never played football in his life. He fell short. The Sten clattered metallically; the firing pin repeatedly slamming into the empty chamber. Simone took the little machine gun's muzzle out of her mouth. Stared at that empty clip. Said: *'Merde!'* Reached for another. But by then, both Byron and Anton had her.

She fought them like a madwoman. Fought them so long, and so hard, that Anton did at last, what he should have done at first. Drew back a closed fist and let her have it. She went down. Lay there. Anton picked her up. He was crying. He bore her back to the barricade.

Byron and the others brought Jean and Yves in. Yves was conscious. Conscious even of the fact that he was dying.

'My motor-bike – and the Leica – for Simone. Understand? For – Simone. I'm very fond of her you know—'

Then he died.

Jean was unconscious. Byron and Pepe felt his head. Ripped off his shirt. His chest was covered with blood. His head didn't seem to be crushed or broken, but there was so much blood on his chest they couldn't tell.

Pepe said: 'He's going to die, Byron. Tie Simone up. With cords. If not she'll kill herself, sure!'

Then Jean opened his eyes; said softly:

'Simone—' Then, his eyes clearing: 'Simone! Byron where is she? Don't tell me she – she's—'

'No, old boy, Simone's quite all right. I'll bring her to you directly.'

'No!' Jean said, 'give me a hand, Byron!'

Wonderingly, Byron did so. Jean caught it in a grip that almost maimed it. Heaved up. Surged up. Took one tottering step, another. Gained strength. Loped away like a bloody, ravenous wolf.

'¡Santa María de los Desamparados!' Pepe said.

And it was at that moment that the two truckloads of Alpine Chasseurs came.

The Germans made one more half-hearted attack. But the blue-clad Alpine Chasseurs, among the finest mountain troops in all the world, beat them off with almost ludicrous ease. The Wehrmacht retreated in good order down to Pariset, bearing with them all of their eighty dead, except the patrol Jean and Simone had liquidated inside St Nizier itself.

And Jean went lurching, loping through the streets like a bloody spectre, searching for Simone. Behind him, at a discreet distance, Byron and Pepe came. 'He's going to fall, Byron!' Pepe insisted. 'He's almost dead. But he doesn't know it. Because he's only thinking of Simone, and not of himself!' So they were there when Jean found her. Or rather when he found Anton bearing her inert form towards the Mairie where the first-aid station was.

'Simone!' he screamed. 'Anton!'

Anton turned, glared at him, rasped: 'Goddamn you, John! Couldn't you even have the decency to *stay* dead?'

'Simone—' Jean croaked. 'Is she – is she—'

'There's nothing the matter with her. I punched her silly face in for her, that's all. Look at her mouth, will you?'

Jean bent over her. Her lips were two enormous blisters.

'Hot Sten muzzle. She was sucking on it as though it was her mother's teat, and trying to pull the trigger. That's why I hit her. She thought you'd bought it. So did I. Don't suppose you'd consider going back down there and letting those beggars finish you off? Be better all round – for everybody.'

Jean grinned at him; said:

'Sorry, Anton; but it so happens that I love her, too.'

'I know. But are you *right* for her, John? Oh, I know, I know! You're willing to convert! Small enough price to pay for Simone, isn't it? And hence, as a conversion, meaningless. There are – centuries between your people and ours. And oceans of blood. You'll never understand anything about us. Never learn to talk as I and Simone do without words – a tone of voice, a nuance, the whole weight of an ancient cultural heritage speaking heart to heart, silently – Oh hell! Why do I waste my breath?'

'I don't think you're wasting it, Anton,' Jean said sadly: 'But I think that Simone has some rights in the matter. Some rights – of choice. Don't you?'

'Hell, no! She's a woman, and women's brains are located between their thighs. Never met one of them yet who didn't think with her cunt instead of her head—'

Simone opened one great green eye, whispered, gleefully:

'But, Anton, my little old thing is *very* intelligent! She knows very well what's good in this world!'

Then she opened them both. And Byron and Pepe saw it. She pushed free of Anton's encircling arms. Took one step towards Jean. Another. Stopped. Her hands came up, tentatively. Fluttered like butterfly wings about his face. Not daring to believe to hope, to touch, they sculptured him anew upon the limpid air.

Her mouth came open. Her huge blistered lips with blood in the corners of them. Quivered, trembled, shook, silently, trying to shape into words what was in her eyes, hope not yet able to be born, the wonder, and worship there.

Pepe turned away.

'I can't,' he snarled. 'I can't look at this, Byron! It would cut off my balls, and make a woman of me! I'll be the favourite son of the Great Whore, if *this* can be borne!'

Byron saw her knees buckle under her. Saw her kneeling there before Jean. Saw Anton turn away his face. Saw Simone take Jean's torn, gunsmoke-soot filled, bloody hands, and turn them palm upward to her wildly quivering mouth.

'Simone—' Jean moaned: 'Not this! Oh my angel, not this! I'm a man, not a god! You must not—'

Her voice came out. It tore free, ashudder with joy, with anguish. Sob-strangled, a laceration in the very flesh of those who heard her.

'You *are* a god. My god. The only one I have, or ever will have. Oh Jean, Jean. I was mad from grief, sadness, pain, and now I'm mad from joy!'

Anton whirled back to face them. He had never been religious, but the war had changed him. Changed him in more ways than the sad, though necessary, transformation from a gentle intellectual, an exceptionally marvellous musician into a tough, competent, and occasionally even cruel fighter. Had made him reach back to his roots, to the ancient atavistic valour of his people. He was a Saul, now, a Gideon. A Joshua. Even a Samson. But he was more. He had found his God again. Found terrible, cruel, unrelenting Yahweh. Who smote the firstborn before the doorpost. Sent plagues, locusts, blood down upon His enemies. Visited the sins of the fathers upon the heads of the children even unto the third and fourth generation. A God of wrath. Of war.

And Anton had become His prophet.

'Simone!' he raged, 'don't blaspheme! You say a thing like that again, and, so help me, I'll slap you blind!'

So naturally, being Simone, she said it again. Coolly, quietly, stubbornly, all of which Anton might have borne. But what he couldn't bear was the fact that she said it with complete conviction, meaning every word of it, believing every monstrous syllable: 'He *is* my god, this Jean. And I idolize him, I worship him. You've heard me well, Anton?'

Then Anton slapped her. He slapped her with all the outrage her words awoke in him, with all the festering hurt her indifference had caused him, with all his thwarted love for her, his furious, though up until now, too well controlled jealousy. He hit her so hard that both her lips burst like ripe plums, and showered her chin with blood. The impact sent her sprawling.

Then, of course, Jean started for Anton. 'Which was a mistake,' John Farrow mused, wryly. 'By then I was in no condition to fight a ninety-year-old cripple in a wheelchair, not to mention a type as strong and as beside himself with rage as Anton Rabinowski was that day. Can't say I blame him really. Simone could be hard to take when she put her mind to it!'

There were only two blows struck. The first was Anton's bony fist, connecting with Jean's face. The second was the back of Jean's head, connecting with the ground.

Then Byron and Pepe grabbed Anton. He struggled furiously until Byron's clipped English voice rasped into his ear:

'I suppose you realize you've probably killed him, Anton? He was damned badly hurt back there. There're at least thirty pieces of shrapnel in his chest – a condition knocking him flat on his arse isn't likely to improve y'know?'

And Pepe: 'Look, you son of a bitch, if you've killed Johnny, *I'll* kill you. Personally. And don't get presumptuous because I made you my second-in-command! Johnny is twice the man you are! Understand? I'll kill you!'

But that wasn't the worst of it. The worst of it was the sight of Simone crawling like a wounded dog to where Jean lay. Getting there, kneeling beside him, staring at him – thrusting her left hand into her own mouth, and biting it as if that kind of pain would help, or cure the other. Biting it so hard that she actually broke the skin, brought blood.

'Turn me loose, Byron,' Anton said, his voice toneless, dull. 'I – I'm all right, now. And I'm sorry. Damned sorry. Simone got me wild, and I lost control. I'm rather fond of John, actually. Let's have a look at him, shall we?'

'*¿Que dice?*' Pepe raged. '*¿Que dice ese hijoputa, Byron? ¡Mierda, Anton! ¿Porque no hables francés, por lo menos?*'

Byron guessed accurately enough at the meaning of Pepe's words; said:

'He says he's sorry he hit Jean. That he lost his temper because of the things Simone said. Turn him loose, Pepe. He doesn't want to do any more harm.'

Pepe did so muttering: 'It's forbidden to kill the only comrade I've got who speaks Spanish, understand?' Anton knelt beside Jean. Took his wrist. Felt his pulse. It beat steadily.

'Seems to be all right,' he said, 'take more than a crack on the jaw to kill him.' Then he pulled open Jean's shirt. Simone's scream split the sky apart. And deafened Anton. 'Stop it!' he said. 'He's only got a few flesh wounds—'

'He's dying!' Simone moaned. 'He's dying, Anton! He's bleeding! Look! See how he's covered with blood! Jean, don't die. Don't leave me alone in the world! I beg you, don't die!'

Anton bent over Jean. Put his arms under him. Lifted.

'Anton!' Simone screamed. *'Qu'est-ce que tu vas faire?'*

'Give me a hand, Byron. *Aidez-moi, Pepe!'*

'Anton!' Simone moaned.

'Look, Simone. We're going to take him in there. Inside the Mairie, where he can be attended to properly. I'm damned sorry I hit him. But you, you stupid little fool, got me wild. And I didn't know he was hurt this badly. So don't stand there glaring at me as though you think I'm going to give him the coup de grâce! Now, come on, boys.'

Simone reached out, and touched his arm, whispered:

'Forgive me, Anton. I – I know I – I'm cruel to you. Without even meaning to be. *Je t'aime bien, tu sais.* But this *affaire de Jean* is – a thing I simply cannot help. I – I'll even grant you it doesn't make much sense, does it? Especially not in this world we live in. But then, you're right. We women do think with our – tails, instead of our heads. With our hearts, anyhow. But, oh God, I do love him so!'

The medical corpsman they had in the Mairie was first rate. And Jean's case was well within his powers. They'd already sent the more seriously wounded down to St Martin, where the hospital and real doctors were. He administered plasma against the shock, and loss of blood, and began busily to dig scrap iron out of Jean's hide. Only one rent was big enough to require a couple of stitches. The rest of them, he simply dumped sulpha powder into, slapped compresses atop, and crisscrossed them with adhesive tape.

Then he looked up, grinning, and said:

'Now I'm going to give him a shot that'll snap him out of it. You're his wife, aren't you?'

'Sa – maîtresse,' Simone said with that painful honesty of hers.

'A moi, c'est égale!' the corpsman said. 'Just don't squeeze for the next few nights, bébé.'

It was only a hundred metres or so from the Mairie to their house. So they walked Jean home, with Anton supporting him on one side and Byron on the other, and Simone scurrying around them in a circle, screaming directions.

'Pepe,' Anton said, 'will you please tie her up? Stuff something in her mouth. Some cow flop, for example?'

Jean grinned at him, weakly.

'Take more than that to shut her up, Anton, as you should know.'

'I do know,' Anton groaned. 'John, please accept my apologies. I'm sorry I hit you. I didn't realize you were so badly hurt. Hell, this idiot got me so wild that I forgot you were hurt at all.'

' 'S all right, Anton,' Jean said. 'No hard feelings. . . .'

The three men lifted him into bed.

'Go make him some *soupe*, Simone,' Byron said. 'A lot of *soupe*. He'll need lots of liquid tonight, and tomorrow. Hope the ruddy Jerrys will give him at least a full day's rest.'

'I think they will,' Jean said suddenly. 'Tell – Huet and Chavant I want to talk to them. Saw something today that could be important. Very important—'

'Oh no you don't, Byron!' Anton said sharply, almost savagely. 'He's got to rest. That's first on the programme for now. Look, John, I've asked Pepe to bring poor Yves' motor-bike up here. If you hear gunfire tomorrow – take this little species of a slut and get out. You've displayed quite enough heroism for now. And even as stupid as Simone is, I think she'd prefer a live husband to a dead jackass. You're in no shape for another fight, you know.'

Jean grinned at him, said:

'Thanks, Anton. Mighty – Jewish – of you, old boy!'

'Goddamn you, John!' Anton began, then: 'Oh hell, I suppose it *is* a good line. I seem to be turning into an awful crab these days, don't I? Not your fault. You didn't make this little idiot fall for you. Good night. And for God's sake, Simone, go sleep in the bathtub, will you? Or as weak as he is, you'll kill him sure!'

But even at that, there was still one more thing to complete that day. After having eaten his *soupe*, Jean fell asleep. More accurately, he dropped through the bottom of the world. But long after midnight, something woke him up. He listened intently, already sure that that something had been a sound. Then he heard those strangling sobs coming from the bathroom. He whirled, clicked on the light, saw at once that not only Simone wasn't on the other side of the bed, but that she hadn't even been there.

He jumped from the bed. Hung there a minute, swaying dizzily. His head cleared at once. He felt much better than he'd even expected to. He made his way to the bathroom. Simone sat on the edge of the tub and stared into the washbasin. She was crying, bitterly.

Then, craning his neck, he saw what was in the washbasin: a pair of quite remarkably bloody panties, floating in water that had already turned a deep pink.

He came up to her, put his arm around her shoulders, said:

'Don't cry, my love.'

She whirled, rammed her tear-wet face into him, about at the general level of his navel, wailed:

'I'm not worth anything, Jean. I'm not even a woman! I can't give you your kid, your daughter! Poor Number Two! My poor little one! She's dead, you know! I've killed her!'

'I think,' he said gently, 'that she didn't even get started. And – in a way, I'm glad. This war is going to be over soon, now. For now, even *they* know they've lost it. Then we can make her properly – and you can bring her into this world safely. That's one thing—'

'And – another?' Simone whispered.

'I think it's probably *my* fault,' he said. 'Lord, Simone, I'm a wreck! I haven't eaten properly or rested enough, or taken the slightest care of myself in years. Hell, it's a wonder I can even get it up!'

She grinned at him now, through her tears, said:

'And on top of that, *I* wear you out! Every night! All night long! So now, boy, you're going to have a rest! A long, long rest. Five whole days. That's how long this – ugh! – business usually lasts—'

She stopped, her face the picture of an almost comical woe.

'But, Jean – what are we going to *do* with all that time?' she wailed.

'Rest. *Talk* to each other for a change. For a starter you can tell me something I've been meaning to ask you for the longest time: who the devil are these Lipschitzes you're always referring to?'

She loosed a peal of silvery laughter.

'They aren't *anybody*! I made them up! You see mon Papa was a – a *fabriqué soi-même* – that's what the English expression means, but I forget how to say it—'

'A self-made man,' Jean supplied.

'Exactly! A self-made man. And they – *mes Lipschitzes imaginaires* – are precisely the kind of – of *grande bourgeoisie juive* – he was hoping I'd marry into! Y'know! The kind that wear mink panties. And diamond rings even around their tits! And paint their left fesse gold, and their right fesse silver. *Riche! Reeche! Très reeeeeche!* The ones who invite forty thousand people to their son's Bar Mitzva! Fifty thousand to their daughter's wedding, under, of course, a *huppah* of velvet! And with the *ketubah* written on illuminated parchment, and with the grand rabbi of Jerusalem imported to officiate! And – and they go across the street to buy the newspaper in their Cadillacs, their Bentleys, their Rolls-Royces! And set sail in their yachts down to the fish market to buy gefilte fish! And—'

Jean bent down and kissed her.

'Y'know, I know a lot of people like that, too,' he said solemnly, 'but they're all Goyim. Now come to bed, will you? At least you can keep me warm.'

And they were happy again. For one more entire day. Which, in the late spring of 1944, was a hell of a long time. Because tomorrow was still a dirty word.

That is, when it was any kind of word at all.

12

The sound of the motors of the aeroplanes woke them both up. Jean looked at his watch. It was three o'clock in the morning. Simone lay there propped up on one elbow listening, and staring at Jean. He grinned at her wearily, said:

'Go back to sleep, angel; they're ours.'

'But,' she protested, 'how can you tell, mon Jean?'

'Take me the rest of the night to explain that; but, for a starter, they're air-cooled motors, a type that for some reason Jerry doesn't use very much. Hear that high-pitched whine? Next, they're twin engined jobs; and both motors are in perfect sync – a trick Jerry never quite seems to manage. If they were going *RRRRR-Rumpf! RRRR K-Rrumpf!* I'd be already running. Because then they'd be Ju 88s; with Jumo liquid-cooled engines. And – oh hell, Simone, take my word for it. They're ours. Probably dropping the heavy stuff that Chavant asked Algiers for. If so, we'll have a chance tomorrow: I mean today. That is, if Jerry attacks again today. Which I doubt. More likely he'll hit us tomorrow with everything but the kitchen sink and throw in three-quarters of his whole damn army to polish us off.'

'Jean—' she whispered, 'are you superstitious?'

'No,' he said, 'I'm not. Why?'

'Today's June thirteenth.'

'Setting aside the fact that you're wrong, that since it's long after midnight, it's already the fourteenth; that's a Goyim superstition, Simone. Based on the idea that there were thirteen people at the Last Supper. So don't mention it in front of Anton. He'll bat you into the middle of next week. And he's already proved that he can whip both of us with one hand tied behind his back. So let's maintain diplomatic relations with him, shall we?'

'Poor Anton,' Simone said. 'Maybe I should marry him, after all—'

'Now see here, young woman!' Jean began.

'Providing I can keep you as *ma 'tite maîtresse* on the side. Would you like to be *ma 'tite maîtresse, mon Jean*?'

'Hell, no! Besides which you're even screwing up the French language now. That you fornicate English is excusable; but not French. The right word is paramour. But there isn't any right word for *une menage à trois* as far as I'm concerned. Nor as far as Anton's concerned either. We'd end up killing each other, which you'd probably enjoy!'

'No, I wouldn't I – love both of you. In different ways. Him – like a brother. You – but there's no way to say that. *How* I love you, I mean I can only demonstrate it. And since at the moment, I cannot even demonstrate it, I—'

'You can shut your angelic, but much too talkative little trap and let me get some sleep, Simone! Now where the devil do you think you're going?'

'To visit Anton. *He'd* let me talk to him in the middle of the night. In fact, he'd be delighted.'

'I wouldn't doubt it. But if you don't haul your narrow little posterior back into this bed both *pronto* and *de suite*, I'm going to take up wife-beating as a pastime. And you wouldn't like that!'

She grinned at him, said: 'Yes, I would, mon chou! Because it would prove that you love me.'

'Simone, don't pull that primitive act on me. You aren't, you know. For even if your personality is split forty-seven different ways, all forty-seven are civilized. Besides, if the day ever comes that you give me serious reasons to beat you, I still wouldn't. I'd just leave you, that's all.'

She stared at him. Whispered:

'Don't you think that beating a woman is kinder than – killing her, Jean? Forcing her to – *se suicider*? Amounts to the same thing, doesn't it?'

'Now, Simone!'

'I would, you know. I'd take a grenade, and hold it against my belly-button with the pin already pulled. So that you would have to *sweep* me up. And scrape me off the ceiling. And—'

'And what, Simone?' he said, grinning at her.

'And you'd have to spend two hours sorting me out. You know, like a picture puzzle. Saying: "Is this her left *fesse*, or her right? Is this her left tit or her—" '

'Right. Goddamnit, Simone; you've got the most morbid sense of humour!'

'And you'd have to go down on your knees to see whether my eyeballs had rolled under the *armoire*. And when you found them, they'd still be crying, and—'

'Oh, Lord!' he groaned. 'Let's get off the subject of interesting ways to kill oneself, shall we? Academic, anyhow. Nothing's going to separate us, not even Jerry's HE stuff. Because, from now on I plan to be the biggest coward in France. And the fastest runner. Which requires a certain degree of strength. *Donc, rest* is indicated. And sleep. And – Simone! You come back to bed!'

'In – a minute, *tête de chou*. Since I must explain *everything* to you, I have to go to the bathroom. To – to change *this*. Sometimes I think that God doesn't like women very much. Or else, why did he give us – the worst part of – everything, Jean? Why did he?'

'Don't think he did – at least not intentionally. Just think that he's a piss-poor engineer. In the plumbing department, anyhow.'

'Jean. You naughty boy! You must not say things like that! Or else he – he will punish you. Punish us – by – oh Jean, let's not take chances, now!'

'All right, Simone, no more chances. Go arrange *ton 'tit truc*, and come back to bed.'

When Colonel Huet, Eugene Chavant and the newcomer, the man they called Faisceau, but who actually was Henri Zeller, De Gaulle's COMAC chief for the South-east (the Military Districts R1 and R2 which extended from Provence to the Jura Mountains), came walking through that street in order to inspect the damage that the long-range artillery barrage the Germans had laid down on the St Nizier area at eight o'clock that morning had done, they found Jean Claude Dubois/John Dalton Farrow sitting on the low stone wall in front of his house, busily drawing something on a large sheet of paper he had thumbtacked to the centre leaf of the dining-room table. Simone stood behind the wall, leaning over it, so that she could put both arms around his neck. Between kissing him, mussing up his hair, and nibbling on his ears, she was busily engaged in criticizing his efforts.

'Mais non, mon chou! Ce n'est pas comme ça! Pas du tout! Saint Trop est beaucoup plus proche à Saint Maxime qu'à Saint Rafael. Et Frejus est ici. Precisement ici!' She pointed with her finger. *'Et voilà, Toulon; et voilà Marseilles et—'*

Colonel Zeller stopped.

'Charmant tableau!' he said.

'That charming picture, *mon cher Faisceau*,' Huet said with a dry chuckle, 'between them accounted for a self-propelled machine gun, its crew, and its supporting patrol. Precisely there. You can still see the blood stains. The young man is an OSS officer, parachuted into us last November. We call him Jean le Fou, because he really is a bit mad.'

'Wish I had a hundred other such madmen,' Eugene Chavant said.

'But – but an American?' Colonel Zeller said. 'He certainly doesn't look it! Appears more French than you or I!'

'Appears – and *is*. Jean, *mon fils, veux-tu venir ici?*'

Jean got up, came towards them. Stopped, saluted. 'A vos ordres, mon colonel!' he said.

'Might I ask what you're drawing, my boy?' Chavant said.

'A map, sir,' Jean said. 'Of the Côte, and of the two ways to get to Grenoble, from there. Because, m'sieur – the military, if left to themselves, will go the *wrong* way. Especially the American Command, who have a great *manque d'expérience* and an even greater dose of Anglo-Saxon over-confidence, so I thought—'

'Spoken like a true Gaulist!' Henri Zeller laughed. 'I take it then that despite that uniform, *you* are not an Anglo-Saxon, my boy?'

'Half, sir. My father. My mother is French—'

'And well did she teach you her native tongue!' Colonel Zeller said.

'Yes, sir. But also, I have lived in France most of my life. Except for a few years in Germany, one in Italy, and one in Spain. Even so, we always came home to France for *les grandes vacances* every year – except for the last three years before – Pearl Harbor, sir. I was in the States, then—'

'Jean,' Huet said, 'is our German expert. He knows what they're going to do next before they do themselves, I'd swear.'

'And what will they do next, lieutenant?' Henri Zeller said.

'Attack. Tomorrow, likely. But that has no importance, sir. It is what they will *not* do that is of an importance capital, mon colonel.'

'And what won't they do, Jean?' Huet said, and added: 'Jean is also our stoutest advocate for the Route Napoléon sweep up from the Côte.'

'They won't *stay* here,' Jean said, 'nor fortify the plateau. Look, mon colonel, I will tell you why. Yesterday, Simone and I had a fight with a machine gun, self-propelled, and its backup patrol—'

'And who is Simone, may I ask?' Henri Zeller said.

'*Simone, c'est moi, mon colonel,*' Simone said. She'd come up to them with that catlike silent tread she was master of.

'And just what do you do, ma fille?' Zeller said.

'I make him happy,' Simone said and put her arm around Jean's waist. 'That is, most of the time.'

'And when you don't?' Zeller said.

'He beats me!' Simone said.

'*Ta gueule*, Simone!' Jean said. 'Look, sir – I'd like to explain this, with your permission, sir—'

But Zeller was staring at Simone's mouth. It was a mess.

'I must say I cannot condone such brutality towards a woman, Lieutenant!' he rapped out. 'Not by an officer under my command! Why—'

'Jean didn't do that, Colonel Faisceau,' Huet said. 'She did it, herself. Our Simone is even madder than Jean is. One of the reasons they get along so splendidly together.' Then he told Colonel Faisceau/Zeller exactly what had happened. Simone hung her head. She looked almost comically like a schoolgirl being reprimanded for getting into mischief. Huet smiled at her, said: '*Simone, ma fille, tu dois me promettre que—*'

Stubbornly she shook her head.

'*Non, mon colonel,*' she said, '*peux pas vivre sans Jean. Moi, je pense qu'on est beaucoup mieux mort que folle. . . .*'

'*Simone, ta gueule!*' Jean said wearily. Then he smiled: 'She's a very good soldier, sir; but a little crazy. And she won't pull an idiotic stunt like that again. I won't let her.

'*Jean—*' Simone said, '*puis-je inviter les grands officiers à casser croûte avec nous? Il y a du vin; et je puis préparer quelque chose vite et—?*'

'And we'll be happy to accept,' Colonel Zeller said and winked at Jean; then added, sotto voce: 'Maybe with her in the kitchen, you can get a word in edgewise!'

'Everyone,' Colonel Zeller said, 'has been telling me the same thing: that the Southern Invasion Task Force should come up the Route Napoléon to Grenoble instead of up National Sept which is a far better road; but no one has given me a convincing reason for it yet! I cannot go to General De Gaulle with "we believe", "we feel", "we think"! But yours, lieutenant, is the wildest excuse yet! We should take this difficult and dangerous mountain route because a Boche patrol was eight minutes behind the gun it was supposed to protect! *Vraiment, jeune homme, vous êtes fou!*'

'*Mais oui, vous avez raison, mon colonel! Suis fou*. But war – is it not, in itself, a thing of total madness? Cannot then, perhaps a madman – *un fou comme moi* – understand it better than those with brains in their heads?'

Colonel Zeller stared at him.

'*Now* you begin to convince me, lieutenant,' he said. 'Explain yourself, clearly please.'

'It is difficult. All I have to go upon is nuance, mon colonel. And a certain understanding of the workings of the German mind. Listen, sir – a patrol – a *Wehrmacht* patrol was eight minutes late. It is a wonder that the sky did not fall! Yesterday, one-thousand-five-hundred first-class troops let two-hundred-fifty men – and two companies of the RCA beat them off. . . .'

'Morale, *hein?*' Zeller said: 'You're saying that they've shot their bolt, Dubois?'

'Not entirely. I'm saying – they're tired, sir. And that a little worm called doubt has begun to gnaw at their guts. I think they are aware they cannot win – especially since the Normandy invasions—'

'So?' Zeller said.

'When the Americans come – they will surrender, or they will run. No matter what the outcome of the battle for Vercors is. Even if we are all dead, they won't stay up here. It is – too cold at night. And there are no whores—'

'Except me!' Simone sang out from the kitchen.

'Simone if you don't stop saying things like that I *will* beat you!' Jean said. 'They won't surrender to us. They don't dare. They – and their friends in the Milice – and the French members of the Waffen SS have done too much to us. They will – wipe us from the face of the earth, unless Algiers and London send us heavy arms. But, even so, even *after* we're dead, they won't stay here. It's too uncomfortable. They'll go back to Grenoble – to Lyon – to Valence – to their warm beds, and willing whores and leave the Route Napoléon wide open. Your invasion forces will have a *défilé* – a parade. On the other hand, if General Patch insists upon mounting National Sept, you will have to fight every centimetre of the way. Oh for God's sake, sir! National Sept is the kind of terrain they *love*. Where they'll hit you *tête-dêfilé!* Where—'

Zeller looked at Chavant, at Huet.

'He's two hundred per cent right, Faisceau!' Huet said. 'All the experience we've had with them so far confirms it!'

'I will tell De Gaulle this, then,' Faisceau said, 'Or would you like to come with me, and tell him yourself, lieutenant?'

'In *this* uniform, sir? And, *mon colonel*, please do not mention to *le général* that anyone – with even a little Anglo-Saxon blood in his veins – had anything to do with this idea. Or else he will not listen to you for thirty seconds. Present it as your own. I beg of you, sir! Or else—'

Colonel Zeller smiled!

'And you'd give up – your Cross of the Liberation and—'

'Sir,' Jean said: 'I only wish to live – and to marry Simone – and to father ten kids—'

'Douze!' Simone said, as she marched in from the kitchen with a tray filled with platters whose smell would have made the mouth of a ghost water, 'Twelve!'

'Why twelve, *ma fille?*' Colonel Zeller said.

Simone bent her head.

'I am Jewish, my colonel,' she whispered. 'And I *had* a father, a mother, two brothers, and a sister. And now I'm alone, except for Jean. Therefore, twelve. With so many it will be difficult to – to kill them all, it is not so, my colonel?'

Henri Zeller Faisceau got up, took the tray from her hands, set it on the table. Then he kissed her, on both cheeks, and on the forehead.

'La voilà, une brave fille!' he said.

The next day, the Germans threw one hundred heavy shells into the St Nizier area. Then they came storming up from Grenoble three full thousand strong. The FFI, and the BCA (Brigade de Chasseurs Alpines) held them off from five that morning of June 15, 1944, until ten o'clock that same morning aided by the fact that among the weapons dropped by the planes Jean and Simone had heard the night before were a few bazookas.

Then François Huet, seeing that it was hopeless, gave the order to disengage and to break up into groups of tens, fives, or even threes, and melt away into the rocky hillsides, into the gorges, ravines, into the trees.

And they did that, all of them who could. Some couldn't, because they were already dead by then. Some, like Sergeant Itier of Compagnie Goderville couldn't, because they were too badly hurt. And in such cases they did what they had to. Sergeant Itier told his men: 'Get out. I'll cover you. I'm too beat up to move.' Then he stayed there, loading and firing his bazooka – a task that normally requires two men – all by himself, with his dog licking his wounds, until they killed him finally. And to demonstrate Teutonic efficiency, or thoroughness, or something, they also killed the dog.

Sergeant Chabal and his Chasseurs Alpines deliberately disobeyed orders and fought on until past noon. Then they dispersed in good order, having lost only one man.

And some simply had bad luck, as was the case of Compagnie Belmont to which Réseau Merle, Pepe's group, had attached itself. And since Simone was a member of Réseau Merle, Jean joined the group, and Byron followed him.

Which meant that they'd attached themselves to the company that took the heaviest losses of all in that second battle for St Nizier. That morning during the whole five-hour fire-fight, Compagnie Belmont and Réseau Merle did all right for themselves. They were still doing all right for themselves, laying down a slanted, toed-in fire across the road in front of them that nothing living could enter and stay alive at 10:25 that morning, when the newcomers came.

They came out of the woods and walked down between the houses slowly, those dirty ragged men with their Stens in their arms. They were obviously French. Probably, the men of Merle and Belmont decided, reinforcements come down from Camps D2 and D3. They looked all right. And there was no time.

So nobody paid them any attention until they spun on their heels and began to cut down the men of Compagnie Belmont, Captain Paul Brissac commanding, at point-blank range.

Simone, who was the member of Réseau Merle closest to them, opened fire. Then she took her finger off the trigger of her Sten. It was impossible to kill the traitors, this band of more than twenty Miliciens disguised as Maquis, without murdering Belmont's men. They were too close together. Intermingled. And you just couldn't do the necessary kind of expert marksman's sharpshooting with a Sten. But one of them had seen her long brown hair flare up in the backwash of the hot gases a Sten used to eject its spent shells. He was upon her with a single bound, grabbing her by the hair, screaming:

'Tail! Cunt! Come on boys! Tail!'

Then he and two other Miliciens dragged Simone, kicking and screaming like a fiend, off into the woods. But before they were half-way across the clearing, Jean was off, slanting at a long diagonal upward and across the street behind the lines and then into a spur of woods that needled almost into the town, so fast that Pepe who had jumped off as soon as he did, was left five metres behind in as many seconds, both of them, ignoring the clatter of Sten fire the Miliciens sprayed in their direction, gambling on any air-cooled submachine gun's notorious inaccuracy at that range, or perhaps not even gambling upon it, not even thinking about it, not even remembering or caring that one lucky burst would have been enough to debowel both of them, simply running hard, head down and plunging, eating space up, leaping, bounding going on.

Jean crossed the Miliciens' line of march and slammed down upon them bodily. The one who had called out first was still screaming obscenities at the resistance Simone was putting up to their consummation of a warrior's oldest privilege, so Jean rammed the muzzle of his Beretta automatic into his open mouth, and held on to the trigger until the heavy Italian sidearm clicked empty. And what seven 9 millimetre bullets fired inside a human mouth do to a man's skull as they mushroom exiting has to be seen to be believed. Then whirling, he smashed the empty pistol into the face of the second Milicien, dragged out his commando knife, which he customarily used for shaving, slammed it into the third Milicien's groin, then ripped upward to the navel before drawing it out, and slashing sidewise at the reeling, stunned man he'd pistol-whipped. The knife opened the Milicien's face from temple to jaw. Opened it so wide that the teeth and gums of both jaws were visible through the rent.

But by then seven of the Miliciens came racing up to join their favourite sport of combining rape with murder only to be met by Pepe charging like a *toro bravo* into the plaza, roaring like all the bulls that ever were in Spain:

'Leave me one, Johnny! At least one! I'm going to cut off their balls and ram them in their mouths! Billy goats! Take this! And this! Sons of bitches! I shit in the bad milk of your sacred whores of mothers!'

Then they heard Byron's voice, saying coolly:

'I say, you chaps! Would you please lie down and get out of the line of fire? Bloody idiotic way to fight a war! Down, Pepe! Down John, down!'

And he and Pepe and Simone melting down and away from the Miliciens, and the whole Réseau Merle, and a goodly part of Compagnie Belmont, which lost eleven good men to the Miliciens' treachery, sighting on that crew of traitorous bastards, that stain on the honour of France, and holding the triggers down until the Stens bucked empty hashing the Miliciens out of existence, tearing them to pieces, to ribbons and rags of bloody flesh.

Then the Germans came surging up from the road below. And it was time to get out now. Time to go.

From the heights above they saw what happened next. The Germans burned St Nizier to the ground. Dragged the corpses of the ten Frenchmen, Yves Martin among them, who had been killed on June 13, out of the mortuary, and threw them into the flames.

Simone had Yves' Leica slung around her neck. But the motorcycle burned in the garage or stable of their house.

'My dresses! My underthings! My bras! Oh shit! They've left me naked!'

Then Jean put out his hand to her.

'We'll buy more in St Martin. Or at Die. Come, Simone—'

But she took a backward step; said, her voice ashudder; but quiet, not even loud:

'Ne me touche pas, Jean. Je t'en supplie; ne me touche pas!'

And he, gazing down at hands and arms, red and thick wet and dripping still, said:

'Sorry, Simone; but I really haven't had time to wash.'

'It's not that, Jean,' she whispered. 'The blood – doesn't matter. I'm used to it. It's you. I think that – I think—'

And he hearing what was in her voice now, divining it, said:

'Say it, Simone!'

'That I can't marry you, Jean. I don't want a – a murderer – for the father of my daughter, of my sons!'

Byron, who was with them, stared at her.

'I say, Simone,' he said. 'Aren't you being a bit unfair? After all Jean saved your life! Saved you from—'

'From rape. I know that, Byron. And in war, one must kill people. I've killed them – too many of them. But one must kill them with – with sadness, with regret – not with joy! One must not savage them! One must be a soldier, not a butcher!'

Jean was staring at her. The pain in his eyes was very great.

'Each time I shoot, I say a prayer: that God pardon them, that He pardon me. That He even forgive those who killed my family: my father, my mother, my brothers, my sister. It's sad not to have any other way except war, to stop them, to save civilization. But that, one doesn't save by joining them, by becoming like them, murderers. Duty is one thing; vengeance, quite another. I'm sorry, Jean; but one doesn't kill people to save *my* hide – nor my tail, for that matter. Neither the one, nor the other is part of French civilization! Therefore—'

He stood there, looking at her. Then he said, quietly, flatly:

'*Adieu, Simone.*'

And walked away from her into the woods, where the trees were very thick. Where it was very dark.

'Simone!' Byron said, angrily. 'Of all the damned rotten, unfair things I've ever heard a person say, this—'

Then he saw how she was crying.

'Now, look, Simone—' he began; but Anton came up to her. Looked into her face, snarled:

'You little bitch! What did you say to John?'

'Leave me, Anton,' she whispered. 'And you, too, Byron. I must go. I want to be alone, and—'

Anton put out his hand.

'Your knife, Simone! Your Sten gun. All the things with which you can—'

'No, Anton. I'm not going to kill myself. That's too easy. May God punish me for having done that to my Jean. May he let me live a hundred years – all alone!'

An hour later, she came through the woods, looking for Jean. She had washed her face and hands, combed her hair. She had put a spray of wildflowers in it. She had left her weapons in the temporary camp. She looked, and even acted, like a bride.

When she found him, she did not say a word. She simply sat on the damp earth beside him, and pillowed her cheek against his knees, staring away from him into the darkness beneath the trees.

She never did say anything. She simply sat like that, crying very quietly, until she felt his bony, blood-crusted hand come out and very gently stroke her hair.

He didn't say anything either. He didn't need to, and he knew it. Between them excuses, pleas for pardon, even words, had become superfluous. They were Jean and Simone. Simone and Jean. Two, who though twain, were made one flesh. So they could sit there, and listen to the silence. Feel the silence. Feel its healing. Until they were very safe, together, very sure.

Then, and only then, did they rise up, and arms about each other's waist, go back to where the others were.

Three days after that, Colonel Zeller Faisceau came up to where Jean sat on a log beyond the camp, with Simone on his knee. Before Jean had even time to jump up to salute the man, who by virtue of the authority vested in him by De Gaulle was really commanding officer over them all, Zeller had saluted *him*.

'Stay where you are, lieutenant!' he said. 'You've earned the right to rest at ease, and even to hold a deuced pretty girl in your arms, it seems to me. You'll get your Cross of the Liberation; I shall make sure of that!'

'Get up, Simone!' Jean hissed at her. 'Haven't you any respect?'

'No!' Simone laughed. 'But all the same, I like the colonel very much. And not because he is a colonel, but because he's truly good looking! Much more than you are!' Then she jumped up, said: 'Give me a kiss, my colonel!' And kissed the astonished – and delighted – Zeller full on the mouth.

'She's crazy, sir!' Jean groaned. 'You'll just have to forgive her, that's all. She—'

'May the world be full of such crazy young and pretty girls, my boy! The point is, you were right. They – *les boches* – were well within our perimeter of defence. One more push and they could have swept this sector clean. But as you predicted that they would, they've gone. Back to Grenoble. Back to their soft and easy barrack life. Strange—'

'What's strange, sir?' Jean said.

'That we professional soldiers – so often forget the *human* side of war. That a man prefers a soft bed, when available, to the hard ground – and a woman beside him in that bed – to sleeping alone. That he will invent all sorts of excuses to tell himself, so that he may remain in the Parises, the Grenobles of this world instead of lumping it in a God-forsaken, dismal place like this Vercors. That's what I credit you with, young sir: that you made me see it. None of the others could—'

'Et pour ça vous allez lui donner La Croix de la Libération, mon colonel?' Simone said.

'Mais oui, ma fille! For that – and also because I think it would look rather pretty on a necklace about your throat; or hanging in your hair!'

They had thereafter one more month, that miraculous month of La République de Vercors. All over the Free World, men sang their praises. Here was the one place in all France where the Tricolor whipped bravely from the flagstaffs, brilliant in the sunlight, proud under the high clear blue free mountain sky.

'And yet,' John Farrow thought, as he lazed in the bathtub in the Hôtel Bellevue in Grasse, Départemente Alpes Maritimes, République de France, on the second of the two days in all his life that afterwards came to mean most to him, the first, being, of course, the day he had met Simone, 'were we not damned and doomed even then? The gods themselves had turned against us. Look what happened when Desmond Longe tried to bring us some heavy stuff in from Algiers. . . .'

For the young English Major Desmond Longe, commander of the mission 'Eucalyptus', had managed to dig up in Algiers a pair of magnificent heavy Vickers machine guns. But on the flight across the Mediterranean, one of the motors of the Lockheed Hudson caught fire. They were less than half-way across; nothing to do but turn back. With the crippled craft losing altitude every minute they had to throw out everything movable – including those machine guns. When Jean heard the story from Major Longe himself, when finally, on the night of June 28–29, Mission Eucalyptus managed to arrive, a cold stab of fear went through him. He was not, as he had told Simone, superstitious, but even luck seemed to have turned against them now.

During that month from the fall of St Nizier to Bastille Day, he and Simone divided their free time between noisy and spectacular quarrels, and making love. The trouble was that it was their love-making itself which was the cause of their quarrels. Because, shortly after St Nizier had gone up in smoke, crashed to the ground, Jean sought out Eugene Chavant, and François Huet. With them was Pierre Tanant, whom of course Jean knew only as Captain Laroche. Not until after the war, when he found on a Seine quay bookstand a copy of Tanant's magnificent eyewitness account of heroic Vercors did he learn who Captain Laroche really was.

And though all of them outranked him, they received him with easy informality. ('In a way,' John Farrow remembered now, fondly, 'Simone and I were the spoiled pets of all Vercors. Everyone loved Simone. She was just lovable, that's all. And I was – a curious freak: an American more French than most of the French themselves. And who – didn't perform badly. And who – belonged to Simone. By that circumstance alone, I had it made!')

So he had put it to them fairly:

'Look, *mes amis* – what chance have we got?'

They looked at each other sadly, then they told him:

'To tell the strict truth, Jean – none. Why, thinking of deserting us, my boy?'

'No. But I'd like to get Simone out.'

'Think she'd go?' Captain Laroche said.

'To get her out of Jean's arms, undrape her from around his neck, you'd have to blast, my dear Laroche,' Huet chuckled. 'And even so, you'd have to use so much HE stuff, that neither of them would be good for much thereafter.'

'Look, mon colonel,' Jean said to François Huet. 'Couldn't you – sort of *order* her to go work in the hospital at St Martin? That's a little farther from the Boches and—'

'Is it, lieutenant?' Huet said. 'There's an awful lot of them in the Drôme Valley – not a half an hour's drive in an armoured car from there. And besides, you know what would happen. She'd defy me. Disobey orders. Whereupon I should have to order her shot. And thereafter I'd have to shoot you, followed by Rabinowski, followed by Graves, followed by Gomez, followed by damned near every young man in Vercors. *Mon Dieu, quelle sorcière!* I don't understand it. She's not even pretty, but she's got Zeller eating out of her hands like a trained poodle. Sweetheart of the whole blessed Free French Forces of the Interior!'

'Maybe it's because she hasn't got much competition up here,' Jean suggested.

'No,' Eugene Chavant said. 'You could bring in a thousand girls, and that thousand the most beautiful in France, and she'd make them all look pale and faded. She has so much vitality, so much élan – and she seems to have cornered the whole *bourse* in charm. You're a lucky man, Dubois!'

'I know that, sir,' Jean said sadly, 'which is why I'm trying to keep her alive.'

'There's only one way to do that, lieutenant,' Huet said soberly, 'and that's for *you* to stay out of battle. You want me to post you to some non-combatant job? There's a lot of them now, you know. Of course I couldn't release you from military service so that Chavant, here, and Yves Farge could put you to work in civil administration – quite a set-up you've got there, mon cher Chavant! – but I could assign you to the Quartermaster Corps, or transport, or guard duty at the stockade we've got the Milice and collaborators in at La Chapelle-en-Vercors – would you like that, mon cher?'

Jean considered that. Said:

'No, *mon colonel*. I'd hate it. If one of my friends – Byron Graves, or Pepe Gomez or even Anton were to die – and I were not there to at least attempt to save them, I'd never sleep another night so long as I should live. And Simone – though she'd deny it if asked – would soon come to despise me. *En tout cas, merci, mes commandants!* I'll figure out something myself.'

What he figured was to hitch a ride down to St Martin, and to Die. In both towns he managed to dig up two dozen contraceptives of the commonest type. And the war *that* started made the threatening German attacks seem a flight of doves of peace by comparison.

'But I want a baby!' Simone yelled. 'I want Number Two. You promised me, Jean!'

'*Ta gueule*, Simone!' Jean said. 'For God's sake, woman! You don't have to inform the whole camp do you?'

'Why not? When I get mad, I yell! And you're getting me awfully mad right now!'

'But, Simone, listen to reason! It's too dangerous right now. We *can't* hold the Boches off! We have, to my certain knowledge, exactly *two* 20-millimetre anti-tank guns, one 13.7-millimetre machine gun and—'

'*Merde!*' Simone shrieked. 'Don't talk to me of guns!' Then, more softly, crying now, crying bitterly: 'Jean, listen to me, my love. If you – if you leave me pregnant, maybe I could live – without you. But if you – you die, and I haven't even your son, your daughter, how do you think I could go on living?'

'Simone,' he said quietly, 'let's look on the bright side of things for a change. Look, when Vercors goes, I'm going to get us *both* out of here alive, I promise you. And from what I've heard from Colonel Zeller, whom you're always flirting with, my sweet—'

'He's good looking,' Simone said. 'Maybe he'd be more – obliging – than *you* are!'

'Simone, I'm going to *hit* you in a minute!'

'Or even Anton. That would please him, wouldn't it, Jean? To knock me up?'

He stopped. Grinned at her. He was used to her tactics by then.

'I take it that all you want is a baby, then?' he said. 'And that *who* the father is doesn't matter? *Alors, va-t'en! Allez-y! File.* Screw the whole damn camp! See if I care!'

She stared at him. Then she said one of her own things, one of the marvellous things he'd never heard any other woman say:

'Jean – if you ever *let* me be unfaithful to you, I'll never forgive you!'

He kissed her then. Said:

'Listen, Simone, Zeller tells me that the Allies are going to attack through Provence very soon now. And Jerry will have had it. So why don't we both try to save *nos derrières* – and leave baby-making for a time and place where poor little Number Two would have a decent chance! Let her be born a Sabra – under her own vine and fig tree. Isn't that what you wanted in the first place?'

'Oh Jean!' she whispered: 'You're too smart for me. You always win out, don't you? All right. We'll wait. . . .'

Which should have settled matters, but it didn't. For in the middle of that same night, she whispered in his ear:

'Jean – I don't like it.'

'Oh Lord!' he said.

'Take it off, Jean. It – feels dead.'

'Mais, Simone—'

'I know! I know. But Jean – this *isn't* making love. It's no good. It's like an old maid using a candle!'

He rose up, grinned at her, said, 'How'd *you* know about that?'

'Tried it once. When I was thirteen years old. It hurt, so I quit. Jean, will you please, please, please take that awful dead feeling thing off so I can enjoy myself?'

'No,' he said.

'Good. Turn me loose. Good night, Jean. I'm going to sleep.'

And she did.

'How many nights did we waste like that?' John Farrow thought now. 'Three – four. Then she gave in. Discovered that if the matter was engaged in a little more vigorously, pleasure, up to and including a relatively decent climax could be managed.

But she was right. Those damned things did spoil love all to hell. Only there weren't any blessed pills in those days. I don't think that even the diaphragm had been invented. Or least *we* hadn't heard of it. Just as well – would have been impossible to procure if it did exist. Even so – it was great. If no longer marvellous, at least great. A little more vigorously, did I say? She damned near killed me, poor little half-starved wreck that I was! And between times, we provided the camp with comic relief. Which was first – the Americans, or Paquebot? The Americans. Boy did I get steamed up that time!'

During the night of June 28–29 they heard the planes. The thunder of their motors was absolutely deafening. Jean caught Simone by the hair just in time to prevent her from dashing out just as she was, which, since, long as her hair was, it was not as abundant as Lady Godiva's would have caused quite an uproar. A few minutes later, both of them decently clad, they went out of their tent and looked up. Four or five giant CR–54's (Douglas DC4s) were circling above the camp. And because they were four-motored transport planes, Jean knew at once that they hadn't come from Algiers, but from England or from Italy. From Algiers a bimotor sufficed. But from England or Italy you needed the biggest aircraft you could find to reach Vercors with any kind of a payload, and still have enough reserve fuel to fly back home.

Then the big craft opened their guts and defecated parachutists across the sky. Followed them with canisters of arms, tools, medical supplies.

('And,' John Farrow thought grimly, 'lifted us into the dangerous euphoria of a hope entirely false. Made us believe that the Allies were finally going to back us up. Still Bob Tuppers and his boys were great types – and so were those British chaps with Longe – even though I thought I was going to have to whip the lot of them single-handed!')

For on the next day, coming back from La-Chapelle-en-Vercors, where Huet had sent him to take a message to Chavant, Jean found Simone surrounded by the twenty-man American combat team, including its Captain Robert Tuppers, and a good many of Major Desmond Longe's British Eucalyptus team as well.

She had finished teaching them to sing 'Alouette, gentille Alouette!' and they were busily teaching her to play 'Spin the bottle.' The idea being that whomever the spun bottle pointed to when it stopped spinning got to kiss Simone.

And Simone, being Simone, was having a whale of a time. It was instantly apparent to Jean that the Anglo-Saxons, with their unshakeable conviction that all French girls come equipped with heels manufactured in a ballbearing factory, were planning to extend the game, or at least await possible developments when night fell. So he marched among them without a word, caught Simone by the shoulder, yanked her out of a huge American's arms, slapped her as hard as he could twice, gave her a shove, said: 'Beat it, Simone! And this time, I'm going to beat you. To death!'

The big Yank growled like a bulldog, and started for Jean, but Simone let out a high despairing wail: 'Oh, no! Please, no! He – he's my – I mean – I – I *belong* to him!'

The big Yank stopped, said:

'Why gawdamnit, Seee-moan! Even if this little jerk of a Frenchie is your old man, I ain't even startin' to let him bat you around!'

'Look, friend,' Jean said then, 'this little jerk of a Frenchie has deballed bigger men than you are, so don't short-fuse my patience, will you? Or else—'

Then Captain Tuppers and Major Longe took over.

'All right, men!' Bob Tuppers barked. 'Stand back; and that's an order!'

'Righto,' Desmond Longe added, 'that goes for British personnel as well!'

'Lieutenant,' Bob Tuppers said, 'just who the ding-dong daddy hell are *you*? And before you even answer, I'm going to tell you *I* don't like guys who go around slapping dames!'

'Captain, sir,' Jean said. 'You can just take what you don't like and shove it, sir! *I* don't like a bunch of hairy apes kissing my girl. But, for the moment, I'm willing to wait and let the Krauts polish you off for me. Don't make me change my mind!'

Captain Tuppers stood there. Studied this thin wire-taut young man before him. Decided that a shavetail with this much pure brass-monkey nerve must have a damned good reason to risk a court martial this way. Then he saw Jean's shoulder patch. And because he and his ranger commando team were on loan to SOE/RF from the US Army, remembered his briefing, especially one specific detail of it: 'You're OSS,' he said slowly.

'One of Wild Bill Donavan's boys. Stark raving crazy, every mother's son of you. And since this *is* Vercors, you must be Farrow, right?'

'Right – sir. John Dalton Farrow, first lieutenant, Office of Strategic Services. And, therefore, *not* under your command – sir. Even if you do outrank me – sir.'

Bob Tuppers grinned, put out his hand.

'Wasn't going to pull rank on you, Farrow. And right now I want to shake the hand of the guy who pulled that Paris stunt. Two car-loads of the bastards. And a skinny little runt like you. Just goes to show you never can tell!'

'Oh, hell!' Jean thought. 'Won't they ever forget that? Or allow me to?' Then slowly he took the captain's hand.

'You surely can't, sir. But there's one detail about that Paris fracas, you don't know. My girl – my best girl – died in that fight. So now, with your permission – or without it, sir! – I'm going to attend to this one. To Simone. Since I mean to marry her as soon as I can, I intend to keep her alive. Which involves educating her. Instructing her as to *who* wears the pants in this family, among other things—'

'You're on your own, Farrow!' Bob Tuppers laughed, 'but just out of simple curiosity, just how do you aim to go about educating the little lady?'

'By applying corrective measures – such as a length of tent rope – to her *derrière* – where women's brains are located anyhow – sir!' John Farrow said, and whirling on his heel, marched away.

When he got back to their tent, Simone was inside it. Her face was swollen. She stared at him sullenly.

'I,' he said, 'am waiting for an explanation, Simone.'

'Oh, *merde*!' she said; then went on, in English: 'Sometimes you – you *bore* me, Jean! And they're very nice boys. And they didn't mean any harm. And – and I *liked* kissing them – so there!'

He went over to the crate with a mirror hung over it that served her as a vanity. Picked up her hairbrush – which along with all her things, he had bought in St Martin to replace the ones burnt up in their house in St Nizier – then turned back to her.

She grinned at him, mockingly, said: 'You wouldn't dare! You're too much a gentleman!'

It came to him that she was right. That he was absolutely incapable of beating her in cold blood, deliberately, now that the initial anger had drained out of him, leaving him sick to the gut, with the taste of nausea in his mouth; hurt more by this quite meaningless folly of hers than he would have been by a more serious offence. 'I,' he thought, 'could understand her – falling in love with someone else. But to hold me – so cheap this way. To disregard me – what I am – what I've meant to her – or at least what I *thought* I meant to her—'

He couldn't form the words. That part of his mind that rejected the sententious wouldn't let him. It seemed too much to say, or even to think the rest of it: 'Is an offence against my dignity as man and lover.'

He put the hairbrush down. Picked up his duffle bag, began to put his things into it: underwear, socks, handkerchiefs, his twin hairbrushes, toilet articles, not ramming them in furiously, but carefully, quietly putting them in, his face grave, expressionless, intent.

He heard the first, deep strangling intake of her breath. Looked up, saw her eyes. They had death in them. The thing itself, not a reflection, an image.

'You – you're leaving me, Jean?' she whispered. 'For that? For such a little thing?'

He stared at her bleakly; said: 'We have different standards of measure, Simone. So now you're forcing me to accept your standards, instead of mine. To – to estimate you at the value you place upon yourself. Cheap goods. Bargain basement material. Anybody's woman. No – everybody's. No, thank you. I'll just bow out of the competition. A woman I have to guard – like a dog snarling over a scrap of meat; a woman who comes back to me with her mouth wet from other men's kisses – the meaningless kisses of men who don't mean anything to her, I simply don't want. I have never shopped at the Prix Unique, my dear.'

'Jean,' she said slowly, quietly; 'I've already told you I'm a slut. That I'm worth nothing. That I despise myself. But I have never despised myself as much as I do right now!'

He had finished packing by then. He really possessed very little. So he picked up the bag, said:

'*Adieu, Simone.*'

Then he went through the tent flap. She caught up with him

less than five metres away. Passed him. Turned, blocking his way. She had his Beretta in her hand. She held it out to him, butt first.

'Take it,' she whispered. 'Kill me. It's less – cruel, Jean.'

He took the automatic from her. Thrust it into his hip pocket.

'No,' he said. 'Live, Simone. Enjoy your life.'

'My life?' she stormed. 'But *you* are my life! I haven't any other! I live in hell, always thinking: "He *can't* love me! I'm too plain, too ugly, too sluttish, too stupid!" and that's why – for that very reason, I did that silly thing! I thought: "Let's see if I can make him jealous." If you'd beaten me, broken my bones, put me in the hospital, I'd be the happiest girl on earth right now! Because I'd be *sure* that you love me. But no! Instead of that, you have to be the gentleman! Saying *words* – to me. Cold, cruel words – and you leave me – you leave me – to go mad – to kill myself – *knowing* that I can't live without you! I can't, Jean! I cannot!'

He put the duffle bag down. Put his arms around her.

'Ah, Simone! Simone!' he said. 'Don't you know I would have come back by daybreak tomorrow?'

'Tomorrow!' she yelped. 'To find me already *dead*? You're crazy, Jean! Craaaazy!'

He grinned at her, said: 'You, too. Bonkers. Crackers. Nuts. Nuttier than a fruit cake. Come, crazy little bird, come. Back to our lunatic asylum!'

But, as he bent to pick up his duffle bag, he saw Pierre Clemont and Pepe standing on a little rise, not three metres behind them. From the way they were grinning, it was evident they had overheard the whole thing. 'Oh Christ!' he thought, 'it'll be all over the whole camp before night!'

But it wasn't. Pepe and Pierre had much better ideas.

Three days after that, Mission Paquebôt arrived.

It was a daylight drop. The five young French officers came floating down the sky, suspended from their parachutes. They flopped over, feet in the air. Got up, braced themselves, tugging against the cords. Pulled the quick release so the the chutes collapsed. Took off their goggles, their crash helmets. And Pepe and Pierre saw the long blonde hair spill out and down about the shoulders of one of them. It was cut in the then fashionable page-boy style. For that particular *lieutenant* was a girl. And as she turned, Pepe Gomez and Pierre Clemont saw that she was a very, very pretty girl indeed.

The two old timber wolves looked at each other. Grinned. They were remembering the scene they had witnessed between Jean and Simone three days before.

'*Eh bien,*' Pierre said, 'and if we sort of arranged it for that little blonde to pass a half an hour alone – with Jean?'

Pepe looked at him.

'And if – also – Simone – just happened to pass that way?'

'*Voilà!*' Pierre said.

'But – without her commando knife, her pistol, or her Sten, Pierre! That little piece of snow-white tail is too cute to end up dead. *D'accord?*'

'*D'accord*. Think we can drag Simone off her while she's still got *both* eyes and some of that pretty blonde hair left?'

'*Ça, alors! Suis pas sûr*. But we can try!'

They went at it as though it were a piece of grand strategy. For the next two days they kept Lieutenant Marie Claire under constant observation.

'Don't think one of those young fellows is her *gar*,' Pepe said, 'but—'

'Leave it to me; I'll find out,' Pierre said.

The first time he saw her alone, Pierre strolled up to the pretty young sous-lieutenant. That in itself was quite a feat. For by then Marie Claire was finding it difficult to go alone to the outhouse behind the quarters assigned to her. There were eight hundred men in the two camps and two girls: Simone and Marie Claire. Which meant, to all practical extents and purposes, there was only one available: Marie Claire.

'Is one of the parachutists your man?' Pierre said with elaborate casualness.

Marie Claire glared at him. Then she saw that Pierre – and Pepe, who had joined him by then – were both in their mid-forties. To her nineteen-year-old eyes, that meant they were a couple of pages out of ancient history. Which was one of the things they were counting on.

'No,' she snapped. 'I'm not crazy. One doesn't get mixed up with the guys one works with!'

'*Voyez, ma fille,*' Pierre said. 'That's all right. Reason why me'n old Pepe, here, came. You reminds us of *our* daughters. So why don't you break bread with us? I mean *all* the time. Sort of put yourself under our protection? That way you could get a rest from having to fight off these horny young fellows all day and all night. Give you time to pick out the *gar* you don't *want* to fight off?'

'That's none of them!' Marie Claire exploded. 'They make me feel like deserting to the Nazis! The English boys aren't so bad, but your Maquis! And those *salauds* of Americans! Whoever told them they were God's gift to women? Or that we French girls are all fairly panting to jump into bed with them?'

'Voyey, ma fille,' Pierre said, 'they're young fellows. Full of piss and vinegar. And you're a pretty little thing for a fact. But there's one young fellow in camp who's different. *Le gar plus gentil* any girl could want to meet. Jean – eh, Pepe? That's him over there talking to your captain.'

'Oh?' Marie Claire said. 'You know, I'd already noticed *him*. Interesting looking. But, since he's the one fellow in camp who pays me no attention at all, instead of undressing me with his eyes, I'd put him down as a queer.'

'The heck you say!' Pepe said. 'He's heavier hung than a bull. And he wears 'em where they ought to be, baby!'

'What's he saying?' Marie Claire said.

'*Que Jean est très homme*. Very man. You'll meet him soon enough. *Alors, ma fille, viens avec nous. A casser croûte. Parler un peu. Reposer. D'accord?*'

'*D'accord*,' Marie Claire said. 'And – thank you. Thank you both. It's – *très gentille de votre* part – to – save me from these howling wolves!'

Pepe grinned at Pierre. Pierre winked at Pepe. Then they led her past the raging American and British boys who were wondering profanely and aloud just how those two old dangling daddies did it, past the young Maquis who sang out: 'Don't believe them, Marie Claire! Those two *vieux salauds* don't have a pot to piss in! Make 'em show you *quelques sous avant que tu fais une bêtise*!' to a place where Jean practically had to pass to go anywhere at all.

When, within ten minutes after they had seated themselves on the grass, and were polishing off great quantities of *jambon cru, fromage du pays, saucisson et vin ordinaire*, Jean did pass that way, they let Marie Claire observe him with care, before giving vent, both of them, to high and mournful sighs.

'*Pauvre Jean!*' Pierre said.

'*¡Ay, pobre Juanjo!*' Pepe echoed.

'*Moi* – I don't see anything poor about *him*,' Lieutenant Marie Claire said. 'He's ugly – but interesting. What makes you call him poor?'

'He's had a hard life,' Pierre said, '*ce pauvre Jean!*'

'*Oui, très dûr!*' Pepe said. '*¡Una vida muy triste!*'

'Tell me about him,' Marie Claire said, 'but don't start off saying he's suffering from a *chagrin d'amour*. I won't believe that. Take him up to Paris, and the girls would eat him alive!'

'*Un chagrin d'amour, oui*,' Pierre said judiciously. 'Or rather *two*. But not because *les pauvres filles* didn't love him. I'd say they loved him, too much, right, Pepe?'

'*Eso, de acuerdo*,' Pepe said. '*Ça, d'accord*.'

Then with a minimum of prodding they proceeded to tell her the story of *la pauvre petite Hélène* who had died trying to save Jean's life. And that of *la pauvre petite Lucienne* who had loved him so terribly that she had killed herself before being forced to betray him by being shipped away to a house of wickedness for the entertainment of Nazi soldiers—

'And now he's alone?' Marie said hopefully.

'*Mais non!*' Pierre said angrily. 'Now he's with a slut who cheats on him! *le pauvre Jean!*'

'She must be crazy,' Marie Claire said with conviction. 'Oh heck! He's come back again! Do you think that—'

'*Jean! Viens ici, mon fils!*' Pierre roared.

Jean came over.

'*Esa chica*,' Pepe told him with a grin, '*quiere conocerte. Ella piensa que eres maraquita, ó tal vez maricon*.'

'*¡Bueno!*' Jean laughed. '*Digala que tiene razón*.'

'*Ah, non!*' Marie Claire protested with a pout that would have melted a stone image, '*Ça, ce n'est pas juste! Parlez français, voulez-vous?*'

'*D'accord*,' Jean said. '*Bonjour, lieutenant! A vos ordres!*' Marie Claire said, 'I order you to sit here beside me. And to tell me what you and this Spanish bandit were talking about.'

'He said,' Jean told her solemnly, 'that you wanted to meet me. And that you think I am a small pederast, or perhaps even a great big pederast.'

That didn't faze Marie Claire at all.

'And which *are* you, lieutenant?' she said.

'Both,' Jean said with a grin, 'depends upon my mood.'

Pierre and Pepe threw back their heads and roared.

'And are you never, lieutenant – lieutenant what?'

'Dubois. Jean Claude Dubois, ma'moiselle.'

'No miss. Not Lieutenant. You – not even – *you. Thou* pleases me, you know.'

This one is an operator, Jean thought. He was amused. He was also – floating. His bones were hollow. Simone had taken very good care of him. This morning. After breakfast. Again.

'Good,' he said. 'We'll use the intimate form of address. Agreed.'

'All the better. Tell me, Jean, are you never in the mood for – girls?'

Jean looked at her. Smiled.

'From time to time,' he said.

'*Et les* – blondes?' she murmured.

'Even – blondes,' he said solemnly, 'but they must be able to pass the flagpole test.'

Pierre and Pepe howled like timber wolves at that one.

'Et qu'est-ce c'est, cette épreuve de la lance de drapeau?'

Then Pepe nudged Pierre.

'Remember that machine gun the colonel told us to tear down? We'd better get at it, Pierre, or the old man will have our hides!'

'This,' Marie Claire said, 'is a trick. *Un truc très bien organisé*. But I *like* it. *Allez-vous-en vous deux! Marchez!*'

They got to their feet.

'Jean,' Pierre said. 'Don't fight *too* hard. One has to lose *everything* sometimes. *Même la virginité!*'

'Grossier!' Marie Claire said. But she was smiling.

When they'd gone, she went to work.

'What's the flagpole test, Jean?' she said.

'That the blondes must climb one. *Sans culottes*. Without panties. To prove they really are. Blondes, I mean.'

'Why you bad boy, you!' Marie Claire said. But she wasn't even starting to get angry or offended. 'Now tell me about you. *All* about you.' But she didn't say vous. She said tu, toi. As in any Latin language, the difference is immense.

And she really was an operator. To his own surprise, Jean found himself doing a thing he almost never did: talking about himself. And – although he wasn't aware of it, he was a good talker. Especially in French, the language he was most at home in. He was, moreover, genuinely modest; had, to boot, an oddball, wry, self-deprecating sense of humour. She dragged out of him tales of his feats of arms he had told nobody, not even Simone; and by his ironic insistence upon how scared he was, that it was all dumb luck, that he was under the protection of the idiots' special God, he was rapidly being transformed in those eyes that were bathing him in an even warmer, softer, more misty sapphire glow into Tristan, Galahad, the Dream Prince come ariding. Even his reticences helped the impression he wasn't even trying to make on her. For when she said softly: 'Tell me – about – your – Hélène?'

His eyes went black with unhealed hurt; and his voice darkened with quite genuine anguish as he said: 'No. About that, no.'

'It – still hurts *that* much, *mon Jean*?' she whispered.

'It still hurts that much,' he said harshly; and his eyes were aglitter suddenly with unashamed tears.

It was then that she put her lily-fingered hands along the slant of his jaw, surged up and clung her soft, warm, open mouth to his. Her timing couldn't possibly have been worse. Because by then Simone was there.

To her right and her left, where they had concealed themselves to watch the fun, after having brought Simone there, telling her only that something was going on they thought she'd better see, Pepe and Pierre got the disappointment of their jokesmith's lives. For neither of them was subtle enough to realize they had engineered a near tragedy. If they had consulted Anton, he would have set them straight, and forced them to call the whole thing off. Because the sad, and now become close to fatal truth of the matter, was that they really didn't know Simone. Didn't even begin to comprehend this strange, fey, elfin, sad and tragic girl who would never learn to love her neighbour as herself, since from the outset she loved him totally, and herself not at all. Who would die under torture for her cause; give her life at any instant in defence of her man; but who was herself defenceless, because the conditions of her life having robbed her of self-love, she could never believe for long that the vast floods of love she poured out of her bleeding, broken heart upon her man, her world, were, or ever could be, returned.

So only Anton could have accurately predicted her reaction.

She dropped to her knees. Thrust her left hand into her mouth, and bit it until blood welled up about her teeth. She remained alive during the next five minutes only because she had come there empty handed, and had no means by which to fatally injure herself.

Afterwards, she realized that those five minutes were the happiest she had ever known, or ever would know again in all her life. For Jean said quietly: 'Thank you very much, Marie Claire; but you're much too kind—'

Marie Claire stared at him, said: 'Then you don't like for me to kiss you?'

'Of course, girl. It's delicious. I am, after all, a man. But I shouldn't like for you to love me. For that has no future at all—'

'Because you have a girl. A woman. That's it, isn't it?'

'No. I haven't a woman. I have – an angel,' Jean said quietly.

'An angel!' Marie Claire exploded, 'a slut who has dishonoured you! Who has horned you!'

'Perhaps,' Jean said with a smile. 'Though I don't believe it. But, let's say it's true; it still makes no difference. Because – I love her.'

'Tu es fou!' Marie Claire said.

'Agreed. I'm crazy. But I'm the happiest madman on earth!'

Marie Claire hung there. Then she whispered: 'She – she must be – beautiful!'

Jean threw back his head and laughed aloud.

'To me, yes,' he said. 'To me she's the most beautiful girl under heaven. You'd find her rather plain. No – ugly, probably. Because, you see, *you* aren't mad. That's the form my madness takes – that I only respond to beauty of the kind Simone has.'

'And what kind is that?'

'Ah, that's the question! Have you ever met a saint?'

'Un saint? Bon Dieu!'

'Yes. There *are* saints, you know. But I don't suppose one can see their halos floating above their heads, not really.'

'Et elle est – une sainte?'

'No. More. Much more. She is an angel. The one genuinely good, undefiled, uncorrupted person I've ever known. With no hate in her. None. She doesn't even hate the Nazis who murdered her entire family. She is *made* of love. All of her. Every pore of her skin breathes love out into the air. So, when I look at her, I see – love. Like a halo; but not just above her head. All around her. Luminous. A glow. A cloud of light. And therefore, she is – beautiful.'

'You know,' Marie Claire said, 'I should like to meet her!'

'Ça c'est très facile,' Simone said softly, *'me voilà!'*

'Simone!' Jean said; then: 'Good Lord! What happened to your hand?'

'Nothing. I bit it. When – she – kissed you. So as not to – scream.'

'I beg your pardon, mademoiselle,' Marie Claire whispered.

'Not miss. Simone. You're beautiful. Very beautiful. I'm not angry. All the girls love my Jean. It's natural. He's very handsome, isn't he?'

'Yes,' Marie Claire got out in a half-strangled voice. 'He's very, very handsome, and you are lucky!'

'Ça oui – et aussi, non. To love him – is a great happiness, Marie Claire. But to live in terror isn't.'

'Terror?' Marie Claire said. *'Pourquoi ça?'*

'That one day – a girl, a beautiful girl like you, will come and take him from me. Knowing that that will be the day I'll die. Because I couldn't live without him. I don't even want to.'

'Then, Simone, *mon ange,*' Jean said, 'you're going to live for ever!'

'And yet,' John Farrow thought bitterly, as he climbed dripping from the tub, in the Hôtel Bellevue at Grasse, twenty-eight years after that day, 'within a month, within a little month she had left me! And I shall go to my grave still not knowing why.'

He was wrong. That very day, at high noon, in the office of Commissaire Poisson, Commissioner Fish, he would at least begin to find out the why.

Of that.

And of something beyond his capacity for dreaming.

13

Jean could feel the sun burning his back and shoulders. It was a good feeling. There was a great glow of heat that lay along his spine and across the trapezoidal muscles of his shoulders, and underneath that glow he could feel the stinging. He lifted the pick and brought it whistling down. It bit in, deep alongside the boulder he was trying to dislodge. Then he rocked the pick back and forth by the handle, not too hard, because you could snap a pick handle that way, until he felt the boulder move a little. He pulled the pick out, and brought it down in another place, close to the first.

In front of him and behind, dozens of men were digging the boulders out with the picks, crowbaring them loose, levering them up; then pushing five and six men against them, rolling them free. It was the twelfth of July, 1944, and that airstrip they'd started to build on the fourth (American Independence Day) damned well wasn't going to be finished for the fourteenth (French Bastille Day) as they'd planned. It wasn't much of an airstrip, only 1,050 metres long by 40 metres wide. But once they'd got the boulders out of it, and filled in the holes they'd left, and covered the whole thing with a layer of small stones, one of dirt well tramped down, and over the dirt, gravel, they'd have an airstrip even a four-motored aircraft could land on, Captain Tournissa, the commander of Mission Paquebot, and Lieutenant Billou, his second-in-command had assured him. Of course the pilot would have to know his business. He'd have to scrape the belly of the aircraft across the top branches of the elms at the far end, bringing the big ship in with full flaps down, in nose-high position, at maybe twenty knots above stalling speed. Once clear of the trees, he'd have to reverse pitch on all four propellers, gun the motors, and stall her in; and pray that the landing gear would take it. It was risky, but it could be done. Bimotors, of course, Dakotas and Hudsons wouldn't have any trouble at all. But then what could Dakotas and Hudsons bring in but small stuff they had too much of now, and were actually giving away to the poor bastards being massacred to the south of them in the Drôme?

Still it felt good to be working, using his muscles, his body, the way a man's body was meant to be used. He was even glad they hadn't any of the bulldozers, scrapers, steam shovels, and crane lifts the engineering corps would have used to make a flight strip like this between eight o'clock in the morning and five o'clock in the afternoon of the same day. With an hour off for lunch at that. Every man on this job was a volunteer, except, of course, Tournissa, Billou, the other two lieutenants whose names he didn't know, and Marie Claire. And they were all working like the illegitimate sons of sin and sorrow, or as Pepe put it, like favourite sons of the Great Whore. Because that airstrip was their only hope. Once done, Algiers would send in those four thousand paratroopers, and the heavy arms that Soustelle had promised Chavant. Until it was done, they couldn't be sent, because although the men could be parachuted in, guns and ammunition above a certain size and weight couldn't. The technique of using three or four circus-tent-sized parachutes to float each 88-millimetre cannon, each 105-millimetre howitzer down hadn't been worked out in those days.

The volunteers were working well and smoothly. They'd quit singing as they worked after the morning of the first day because they found out that first morning that they couldn't spare the breath. They were all happy and full of hope, now. They'd watched the British wireless operator with Mission Eucalyptus raise London with no trouble at all with the new, and vastly improved equipment they brought with them. They'd seen the American radio man using identical equipment – but since they were Americans, they called it radio, not wireless – send messages through for Huet to Algiers as easily as though they had a cable stretched between Vercors and Africa across the Mediterranean sea. And marvel of marvels, they'd stood around and cheered Marie Claire, pinching her delectable derrière to make her swear, as she actually *talked* to the pilots of the aircraft coming in to drop them stuff, over the little miracles Mission Paquebot had brought with them; very high frequency transceivers called S-phones.

They had hope. But he, Jean Claude Dubois/John Dalton Farrow didn't share that hope a good goddamn. The reason he didn't was – Simone.

On the tenth, two days ago, he had volunteered to accompany Tuppers and his boys, to serve as liaison officer and translator between them and Réseau Bourgeois, Company

Eleven of the FFI, led by Officer Candidate Cros, as they set out to stop a German reconnaissance patrol which, they had learned from their lookout in the village of Aspremont, was coming up from the Drôme in the direction of the mountain pass known as Lus la Croix Haute, on National Route 75, itself.

He had been well aware when he had volunteered that the American combat team, with the possible exception of Captain Tuppers, couldn't stand the sight of him. Their reasons ranged from the simple to the complex. First of all, as dutiful sons of the world's greatest matriarchy, they resented the fact that he'd publicly slapped Simone. And they would not have understood his reasons, if he had bothered to give them, which, of course, he didn't: that he'd slapped her not out of any elemental desire to dominate her, but for descending to a level of behaviour far beneath what he knew she was; for letting that built-in testing apparatus for the determination of true masculinity that all normal women come equipped with show – 'Can I make him crazy jealous? Make him fight for me?' – and for using it too crudely. More than that, they resented his monopoly of her, and the fact that she obviously adored him.

From then on, their reasons became complex. If he had been one of *them*, they wouldn't have resented Simone's devotion to him half as much. But what irritated the hell out of them was that this American spoke American English correctly, employed all the Americanisms, and even American slang; but with the *tone*, the inflection, the rhythm of American speech somehow always just a little wrong, and who now and again – when he was very tired, usually – let a marked French accent show through. They found his effortless grace of movement – even his slouching walk was like a ballet dancer's – disturbing. But most of all they disliked his abilities as a linguist. He had not yet learned that all Anglo-Saxon peoples regard the mastery of foreign languages as a blasphemy against their deepest conviction, which, when expressed at all, fit into one classic line: 'Gawddamnit, why don't these here greasy foreigners learn *English*, by God?' Or that they consider anyone who does speak English, but who actually prefers another language, the icy, brilliant clarity of French, for instance, the drum-roll sonority of Spanish, Italian's lovely music, as a presumptuous ass, or even a sort of traitor. That he could chat, and even – when Simone wasn't around – flirt a little with Marie Claire, made it worse. And when he and Byron Graves one day coolly switched a conversation over into German when they became aware of being overheard, they fell back, hopefully, on the conviction that he had to be a spy.

Even Simone was aware that they disliked him. But she hadn't objected to his accompanying them on that mission because of that. She did not believe that they would shoot him in the back – American soldiers had not yet descended to 'fragging' in those days, any more than they were then capable of deliberately murdering children – she was simply obsessed with a premonition that something was going to separate them; and under battle conditions, she couldn't rule out the possibility that that something might be his death.

But he had gone anyhow, climbing aboard that ancient autobus that groaned and clattered up to the Gorge de Menée, with the twenty-four men of Company Eleven and Réseau Bourgeois, plus their commander, Officer Candidate Cros; fifteen of the Americans, including the big one he'd slapped Simone for kissing, plus Captain Robert Tuppers: plus the driver, plus him, Jean Claude DuBois/John Dalton Farrow.

The big Yank leaned forward, said:

'Look, lootie – won't be no girls up here for you to bat around. Only Krauts. Big Krauts. Mean ones. Ain't you on the wrong bus, loot?'

Jean didn't answer him. Bob Tuppers said:

'Shut up, Mike. We've got business up here. Serious business. There's no time for private feuds.'

'Just thought I'd warn the lieutenant, cap'n. That there's a war on. And that the Krauts mean business. Hidin' around in the woods ain't no way to win it.'

'I said shut up, Mike!' Tuppers said, 'and that's an order!'

'Yessir, cap'n!' the big man said.

They got out of the bus. Deployed themselves on both sides of the road. Jean climbed up and away from both groups. Looking down, he saw something he didn't like. Two of the men of Company Eleven, Bourgeois, had gone too far out in the direction of the road. They had a boulder in front of them; but to their left, and behind them they had no cover. Once an enemy patrol had flanked that one big rock, they were dead men. It was a thing that amateurs nearly always did. Put a good high barrier in front of them and they felt as safe as in church. 'Good

God, do they think their asses are armour plated?' Jean thought, and started down to pull them out of there.

But before he could take a step he heard the bellow of Maybach motors and the slap and clatter of tracks. The first half-track was far ahead of the personnel carriers. It was the probe. It was a light armoured half-track, a Sonderkraftfahrzeug, built by Demag. It had a five-man crew, not counting the driver. It was armed with two 13.8-millimetre heavy machine guns, and two 7.9-millimetre light machine guns. Besides, or on top of all that, all five of its crew had Schmeisser 6.3-millimetre machine carbines, the fastest firing submachine guns ever made, which was why the Allied soldiers called them burpguns, because they neither spluttered nor stuttered as Stens or Brens or Thompsons did, but poured out their bursts in one continuous, unbroken belching sound.

'Or a fart,' Jean thought. 'The fart of death. With putrefaction's gases in it.'

He also knew, although he couldn't see them, that they probably had a rack of potato-masher grenades all around the inside of the armoured walls. And side arms. And a Mauser rifle or two stashed away somewhere in case they had to do any sharp-shooting. And all the incestuous, fornicating ammunition in this filthy, excretably, royally sodomized world.

They were enough. By themselves, they were enough. That one light armoured half-track was more than a match for any forty-three infantrymen whatsoever. And when twenty-four of those infantrymen were half-trained (and that half badly, he thought) Maquis; and the other fifteen were green as grass, over-confident Americans who knew even less about guerrilla warfare than the left side of his hindquarters did – '*Mais,*' he could hear Simone's laughter gurgling, '*ta fesse gauche, elle est très intelligente, mon Jean!*') the outcome wasn't even debatable. They were all going to get slaughtered. Then he sat there and held a formal debate with his mind.

'Unless—' his mind said.

'Unless what?' *he* said.

'Unless *you* knock it out, hero.'

'Shit,' he said.

'Glad to oblige. Consider yourself shitted. Up to the eyes.'

'I'll get *killed,*' he said. 'That goddamned thing will kill me. And Simone will go mad!'

'Don't think about Simone. Think about the business at hand. Such as, for instance, whoever told you that obscene mechanical dung beetle down there will politely refrain from killing you if you *don't* knock it out?'

'*Merde!*' he said.

'Likewise in English. And *¡Mierda!* in Spanish. *Und scheisse auf Deutsch.* Still stinks, doesn't it? And you're still buried in it. Up to your eyebrows now.'

He grinned suddenly. 'Tighten up your anal sphincter, old son,' he told himself. Then he started working it out. He was still scared, but he was in control now. It had to be done, and only he knew how, or was even in the right place to do it at the right time. But first, he had to get close. Getting closer was simple. Getting closer was easy. What wasn't easy was getting closer without getting the only hide he had or ever would have ('Such as it is' he thought, 'I'd like it to last a while!') perforated in thirty or forty places.

'Perforated hides are definitely unhealthy,' he told himself. 'Draughty as all get out. Hell, I might even catch cold.'

It was a piss-poor joke, and he knew it; but that was all right. It was better to joke. If he didn't joke, he might start screaming. And that wouldn't help. It wouldn't help a good goddamn.

He marked out a route with his eyes. From this tree to that boulder.

'Do it!' he screamed at himself. And it was done.

From *this* boulder to *that* little hollow down there. Not two metres from those two poor young Maquisards. Those two dead men, who didn't even know they were. At least, not yet. That was close enough. That was pretty close. And the little hollow was beautiful. It was lovely. It was gorgeous. It had all the comforts of home. Boulders fore, boulders aft, boulders port, boulders starboard. And *bâbord* and *tribord,* if you wanted to be French about it. All those beautiful, metre and a half thick granite boulders. He felt an almost sexual appreciation for those boulders. He loved them warmly, tenderly, dearly, hotly, lustfully.

Only he had to get to them. And between where he was and where those boulders were there was no cover at all.

He heard then the stutter of those Stens. Sighed, breathed out:

'Oh, Jesus!' Because those two poor brave gallant idiot fools had opened fire. Had opened fire on an armoured half-track with 6.3-millimetre pistol ammunition. 'Why don't you try pissing on it to see if it will sink?' he thought despairingly and was off.

The half-track's gunners sighted him at once; but before they could crank their guns up to that elevation, he was half-way there, and he preoccupied himself very little about the Schmeissers. He knew that no sub-machine gun can hit the side of a red painted barn at more than five metres range. He also knew that those burpguns could quite easily kill him at any distance up to forty metres – just as one of them had killed Hélène at such an extreme range. But to kill him they had to hit him, and the gamble was good enough.

Down below to Bob Tuppers and his men, he looked very good indeed. He looked great. He looked gigantic. He came down that hillside like the best broken-field runner the greatest football team in history ever had, seeming to know, just as though his half-mad brain were equipped with special radar, just where the burpgun bursts were going to slam rock, plough earth, chew trees, so that he seemed to be playing the game against a team of ghosts, as those 6.3s and the 7.9s that were up to elevation now, threw up spurting columns of dirt, pine needles, twigs, small rocks twice as tall as he was, all around him.

He got to that blessed hollow. Dived into it. Heard as he did so one of the Maquis scream. The other one didn't scream. He couldn't. But the first one went right on screaming.

He thought: 'Oh Christ, make him stop it. Oh bleeding Christ, make him stop it! I've got things to do, and his mucking screaming mucks me. I need a tight asshole right now, and screaming loosens it. Make him stop it, please.'

But the young Frenchman down there couldn't stop it. He had seven 6.3s through the belly at the level of his umbilicus, and that was very bad luck indeed. If they had been heavier stuff, like the 7.9s, the shock would have knocked him out. If they'd been 13.8s they would have killed him almost instantly. But those little pistol balls didn't kill him, didn't knock him out. They just tore his gut all to hell in a way that hurt worse than anybody could possibly imagine hurting, and left him to bleed to death, slowly.

So Jean has to listen to it. And to forget it. Because there was no time. He took out a grenade. Another. Another. Pulled the pin of the first one, let it roll down the slope like a bowling ball. Sent the second one after it. The third. Timing them so that there'd be at most a three-second interval between the explosions.

Heard the first one. The second. The third. Looked over the edge. The grenades had blown one belted track clear off the bogies. The half-track had splewed around. All four machine guns were pointing away from him now.

He stood up, exposing himself fully, and started throwing grenades into the body of the half-track. That was this kind of half-track's great weakness. Though armoured, they were topless. They could always be taken from above. If the Germans had sent a light tank, or even an armoured car to do this probing, they would have been done. He could have wrecked either a tank or an armoured car, but he couldn't have killed the men inside them. And even motionless they would have been too much.

When that last grenade blew, only the driver of the half-track was left alive.

Captain Tuppers turned to the big Yank.

'Mike,' he said, 'how'd you like the job of being Lieutenant Farrow's orderly? Smart fellow like you, who knows so god-damned fuckin' much would be a great help to him it seems to me.'

'Jesus, cap'n!' Mike got out, 'how was I to know that fruity talkin', swishy actin' little Frenchie had *balls*?'

'You should have looked at Simone a little harder,' Tuppers said. 'Dolls like her don't go for guys who haven't. Now shut up! Here they come!'

Jean left his hollow. Got to where the two Maquis were. One of them was man-meat, bullet-hash, dead. Messily dead. But the other one was still screaming. He couldn't survive what he'd got, Jean saw. Only it was going to take him a long time to go. And the going wasn't going to be pleasant. Jean took his Beretta out. Looked into the eyes of the dying Maquisard.

'Oui!' the boy got out: *'Oui, copain! Je vous en supplie!'*

'Turn your head a little, son,' Jean whispered. 'Good. That's enough. Like that. Good-bye, my brave one. May God receive you—'

Then quickly, surely, with aching tenderness, he shot the boy through the head.

He put the automatic back into its holster. Sat there a long moment, all gone nerveless, spent, his eyes scalded, blind.

'Merde!' he whispered. 'All the varieties of it. In all the languages of the world! If only there could be no more wars. If only nobody would ever kill any body anymore for any reason whatsoever. Because there aren't any good reasons for it. None. If only the filthy power mad old bastards who run the world would let boys like this poor little snot-nose live to grow up, and to drink good red wine and eat their bellies full and screw their girls. That much, anyhow. Is it too much to ask?'

Then he picked up their Sten guns and bullet clips and got back to his hollow.

He was just in time. The Germans were pouring out of the personnel carriers, the heavy Büssing NAG Maybach powered half-tracks which had canvas convertible tops, weren't armoured at all, had no mounted weapons, and seated fifteen infantry men each. They were good for what they were intended for: to get the largest possible number of men from one place to another in the shortest possible time; but if enemy artillery, or aircraft, or even ordinary troops caught them on the road, they were death traps, and the Germans knew it. So one of the things they did best and fastest was to get out of those Sd Kfzle's when they had to.

The first fifteen out of the first carrier formed up into two six-man patrols, each with a Feldwebel at its head. They left the fifteenth man behind with the driver to guard the half-track. That blessedly lucky fifteenth man. One of the patrols came probing up the road, ran into crossfire from the Americans and the French and was pinned down there. The second started up that hill after Jean. They had seen what he had done to the light armoured Demag. And that he was alone. They were boiling mad. They should have taken a breather to cool off. Instead they quickly learned that Teutonic berserkers weren't worth a good goddamn in this kind of a war.

They started up that hill on the double, all bunched together, not spread out.

Jean looked at them in wonder. Even if they were SS, and not Wehrmacht, they should have known better than that. The German army was definitely deteriorating. Only green troops, or damned fools stormed up a hill in a compact mass. He started bowling again. He sent one grenade after another rolling down that slope. Seeing them coming, the patrol broke, ran. It did them no good. Shrapnel penetrates the human back as easily as it does the chest and belly. And there was absolutely no cover in front of that rock nest Jean had found, wherein he'd installed himself. There were five shredded corpses on that slope before him now, blackening and stiffening in the sun, amid the rocks and brush, under that pitiless sky.

Thereafter, he held off the other patrols who tried it, with his Sten. Before it was over he had used up all his clips, and was down to half of the last one of those he had got from the two dead Maquis. He was contemplating with gloomy satisfaction this perfect demonstration of his dearest theory: that, granting from the outset that perfection is beyond attainment in any human activity, war, being as it is, utterly insane, precludes the attainment of even mediocrity, because nobody who wasn't a spavined, windbroken, blind, utterly idiotic jackass would ever choose soldiering as a profession anyhow. The proofs of that were evident, ex-generals led the list of the worst presidents of the United States: ex-military men were notoriously bad businessmen, failures in any profession where even a little imagination, human warmth, intelligence were required; and all the countries – usually Spanish or Portuguese speaking – governed by military juntas were without exception unmitigated political disasters.

There was no perfect strategy, he realized as he lay there contemplating the one defect of his perfect natural fortress: that you could never walk out of it. Or even crawl out of it. You could only be lifted out of it. Dead.

He pulled out the Beretta and looked at it.

'Let us,' he thought, 'be not hasty. One is dead a long time. And there's Simone. And you still have half a clip. And – oh *merde*! Which art in *merde*. Hallowed be thy *merde*! For here they come!'

But then he heard those Maybachs barking into life. And looking up, he saw that what he'd heard before was the patrol he'd held pinned down behind the lowest rocks with his fire, racing for the half-tracks.

He lifted the Sten. Lowered it again; said: 'No. Let them live. Drink *bier*. Wallow with buxom blondes. In Deutschland. Till they grow old. Till their bellies hang over their Lederhosen. Till they learn that this life is all a man's got and he's entitled to it,

Herren, Sklaven, Über, Unter. But *Menschen*. But *alle Menschen* everywhere. Poor bastard *Menschen*. Let them live. No, not them. Us. But in Us including them. All of us together. Let us live, God, let us live.'

Then wearily, clumsily, jerkily, trembling all over – the reaction hitting him now, the after-killing sickness – he got out of his perfect hole that had almost become his perfect grave, and went back to the others.

On the long ride back to Vassieux, they all stared at him in awe. But they didn't say anything to him at all. Because he sat there shivering and shaking with his jaws clenched shut, his lips blue, and tears ploughing white streaks through the dirt on his face. Finally Bob Tuppers leaned forward with an open pack of Camels extended.

'Don't smoke,' Jean grated.

'Those – two boys,' Captain Tuppers said gently, 'friends of yours?'

'No. Didn't even know them. Just hate – killing people, captain – sir! Even Nazis. Got bad nerves. Leave me alone, please. Be all right in a little while.'

'All right,' Bob Tuppers said. 'But I hope those kind of bad nerves are catching. Damned if I wouldn't inoculate my whole company with them!'

He was all right by the time they got to Vassieux. Perfectly normal – at least to those who didn't know him well. But as he started towards his tent, Byron, Pepe and Anton – seeing how it was with him – seeing how drained he was, how gut sick, nerve tortured, utterly down, lost, beaten, sad with that bad sadness that comes upon a man who, being no killer, yet is forced to kill, the worst of the walking wounded, a combat fatigue case with no hope of being pulled out, withdrawn – gathered around him supporting him by his arms to keep him from falling, he was stumbling so.

He mumbled his thanks, and entered his tent. But before they were two metres away, they heard him scream.

Anton, of course, got there first. His blue eyes were madman's eyes, blazing wild.

'Simone!' he grated. 'Oh dear God, Simone!'

She was on the dirt floor of the tent. She lay with one side of her face in a sticky mess of her own vomit. Her hair was matted with it. The sour smell was overwhelming in that little tent.

Anton stood there. He couldn't move. Jean knelt beside her, shivering and shaking like a spastic, tears dripping off his chin.

So Pepe and Byron had to pick her up. Pepe shoved a rough hand inside her blouse; growled to Jean:

'She isn't dead. She's just fainted, Johnny. Do you hear me? She's fainted.'

'Yes, Pepe,' Jean whispered. 'I hear you. She's fainted, but *why*? Tell me – why?'

'Man!' Pepe grinned at him, 'hasn't anybody ever told you what has to happen when you screw your woman all night long every night in the week?'

'Oh, Jesus!' Jean said.

'You bastard!' Anton said, 'you blind, dumb, stupid bastard! To get her pregnant now! Of all the miserable, selfish, unfeeling—'

'Anton,' Jean said, 'I – we – took precautions. Always. Always. Anton.'

'Condoms?' Anton said.

'Yes,' Jean said.

'Maybe they were too old, rotten. Didn't any of them – break?'

'No. Not that I know of.'

'Then I don't understand it! Sure you didn't skip even once? Once is enough, y'know. . . .'

'Not once,' Jean said.

'All right. Didn't think you were that kind of a heartless bastard. And it's none of my business, anyhow—'

'You're jolly right it isn't!' Byron said angrily. 'Now let's take her outside, give her air. And you might fetch us a pail of water, Anton, instead of wasting time berating John!'

But when they'd brought her around, she told them, told all of them, so that Jean could never swear it was his own imagination:

'You went down the hill. To – to get those two boys. Who were hurt. Only they were dead when you got there. And you couldn't get out. So you stayed there – and you fought the whole German army all by yourself. I could see it. I could see it in my head, Jean! I kept watching it. Hearing those bullets slamming into the rocks in front of you. Until I couldn't stand it any more. Until I knew how they were going to feel when they tore into you. Then I started to throw up. And after that I fainted. I kept trying to come back, but I couldn't. Because – my heart kept telling me you weren't dead.'

Pepe looked at Jean.

'*¿C'est juste, Juanjo?*' he said. '*¿Es exacto lo que ha dicho la Simone?*'

'Yes,' Jean whispered. 'She's got it exactly right. That's how it was.'

'Do you have gypsy blood, Johnny? You or her? No matter which one. Do you have gypsy blood?'

'No,' Jean said. 'No. Neither I, nor she.'

'*¡Entonces no lo comprendo!*' Pepe said.

'I do,' Jean whispered, 'it's because – we aren't two people any more. We're – just one.'

But the whole incident had had at least one good effect. Simone consented without argument to stay abed for the next two or three days. He brought her food when he was not working on the airstrip. Or Anton did. Voluntarily. He realized it was a little cruel to allow Anton to do this, because he knew Anton loved her as much as he did. But to deny him the privilege seemed small minded. He wasn't jealous of Anton. He wasn't jealous of anyone. By then he had the warm, comforting feeling that he had no need to be; nor ever would again. He believed in Simone the way, as a small child, he'd believed in God. And he loved her in a way, and to a degree that was past both belief and bearing.

So now, on the twelfth of July, he was working in the sun, and, physically, anyhow, feeling good all over. He would have been able to feel good inside himself, inside his mind, his heart, his belly, if he could have been sure that Simone was wrong when last night, she turned to him and said: 'Love me. Love me *now*. I know I'm sick; but we haven't any time, Jean. It's run out on us. There isn't any future for us. At least not together. That's what's so – odd. So strange. Because – inside my mind, where I *see* things now, I don't see us dead. Neither you – nor me.'

'If you see me without you, you see me dead, Simone!' he said, 'because nothing else could part us. Not even *that*. Because, even if I get mine, and you marry Anton, I'll sneak past the Devil, out the gates of hell, and come back to earth to give poor old Anton paralysis of the balls. So he can't. Because you're mine, goddamnit, mine! And you're always going to be!'

But he had refused to make love to her, all the same. He figured she needed the rest. And so did he. Besides Pepe's mocking words had made him a little ashamed. *Every* night was overdoing it, after all.

He dug the pick in, once again. Then he felt a hand on his naked back. A slim, soft, feminine hand that wasn't Simone's. He didn't even have to look to know that. He knew very perfectly and surely and lovingly and achingly and tenderly how every millimetre of Simone felt. He looked up with an expression of annoyance.

Marie Claire took her hand away. She looked like she had been crying. And she was trying not to cry now.

'What's the matter, Marie Claire?' he said.

'You. You're what's the matter with me.' Then her blue eyes widened. She was staring at the pinkish white whorls and puckers and rents with which his chest was covered. He'd got them on the day he'd tried to save Yves Martin. One month ago to the day. Before St Nizier. Ex–St Nizier. The town that didn't exist now.

She said in a hushed, choked voice: 'Turn around, I want to see your back again.'

He turned.

'Not one,' she whispered. 'Not one sole scar on your back. Therefore – a hero. Oh Jean, I detest you! You're detestable! Hateful! Cruel!'

'*Alors*, Marie Claire,' Anton's deep, harsh voice came over to them suddenly, 'why are you crying?'

'*Parce que* – because they told me what he did – the other day. And Byron – Captain Graves told me he's *always* doing things like that. And because – because I'm so in love with him, I'm *sick*. In love with him without even the *right* to cry all night. The way I do for fear they'll bring him in shot to bloody rags! Because he doesn't love me in return! Instead he's mad over that ugly long-nosed little Jewish bitch who—'

Anton stiffened.

'*I* am Jewish, Marie Claire,' he said.

'I know. *Suis pas antisémite; crois-moi*. I didn't use the word as an epithet, M'sieur Rabinowski! I've nothing against Simone.

Except that she's got him. And I can't even understand it! She's not at all pretty, and I am. Or perhaps I'm wrong! Do *you* find me pretty, M'sieur Rabinowski? Am I?'

'More than pretty,' Anton said, 'you're truly beautiful. But you're falling into your sex's commonest error; that *men* fall in love with a lovely face, a shapely body. We don't, you know. Only *boys* do. Of course some stay boys an awfully long time. But grown men soon learn not to judge the goods by how prettily it's gift-wrapped. . . .'

Marie Claire stared at him.

'*Oh zut alors!*' she said. 'But, then, what else could *you* say? Everybody knows you're in love with her, too!'

'I am,' Anton said calmly, 'and so is Pepe, and Byron, and Pierre, and every manjack of Réseau Merle. And Colonel Faisceau. And I suspect Laroche and Huet and Chavant and Farges and everything in pants who knows Simone, even a little. Except maybe the Americans. They *never* grow up. And even they like her. Because, you see, my dear, Simone is lovable.'

'And I'm *not?*' Marie Claire said. Her voice sounded appalled.

'You're not,' Anton said gravely, 'or at least very little. You could get to be, if you worked at it a little. If you stopped thinking of life in terms of first person singular. Concentrated a bit – as Simone *always* does – on what you can *give*, instead of what you can get. I'd even suggest that you let your face and your body off with a good bit less attention. All they'll ever get you is into bed with a man. They won't get you into his heart. You call Simone ugly. Until you reach the place where you can see she's one of the most beautiful girls Almighty God ever blew the breath of life into, because she has no ugliness in her, no pettiness, spite, malice, envy, jealousy, or hate, you won't even understand what I mean.'

'Thank you, Anton,' Simone's voice came from a little way behind them, 'but that's not true. Not all of it, anyhow. I am jealous. I'm jealous of *her*. But you're right. I don't hate her. I don't know how to hate. I wish I did. I wish I were an ancient Schopenhauer Jew.'

'Lord God!' Jean said. 'Simone, I told you to stay in bed! Look at you! You look like a ghost, and—'

'I'm sick,' Simone said, 'the same sickness you've caught, Marie Claire. Sick from being in love with him. From waiting,

waiting for them to – to bring him in – or to come tell me there's not even enough left of him to bring in. Or—'

'Now, Simone!' Jean said.

Simone walked over to Marie Claire.

'I like you,' she said. 'Tu es une brave fille. And – and douce – I think. I cannot hate you for loving Jean. That merely shows you've got good judgment. And good taste. If – if I die, I'll leave him to you. Will you – be good to him? Faithful? And – give him lots of babies?'

'Bon Dieu!' Marie Claire got out, 'the things one has to hear!'

'And I, if I die,' Jean said suddenly, 'I leave you to Anton. Agreed? That way, maybe I could die in peace, knowing you'd stay alive.'

'But you *wouldn't* know it,' Simone said. 'I like Anton very much. I probably even love him more than I think I do, but what has that to do with the fact that I'll just drop dead when they bring you in, or come to tell me that you're scattered all over some hillside in a million bloody pieces?'

'Simone, stop it!' Jean said.

'It's stopped,' Simone said. *'Ton esclave t'écoute et t'obéit.'*

'She's mad!' Marie Claire said, 'she's stark raving mad!'

'I think it's the other way around – that she and Jean are sane,' Anton said slowly, 'and that the world we live in is mad. A world where people – murder children. Massacre old women, grandfathers, babes in arms. Firebomb cities. Jean and Simone are the two kindest people I've ever known. And they're both dying of that kindness – in a world where one has to be cruel to even survive. Simone—'

'Yes, Anton?'

'What the devil is an ancient Schopenhauer Jew? From all I've ever read Schopenhauer didn't like *anybody* very much; but Jews even less!'

'Then listen to what he said, Anton: "When the Jews were a conquering people—" that's a bad translation, *mon cher*; what he actually said was *Herrenvolk*, "a master race".'

'You mean he actually conceded that we *were* a master race once?' Anton said.

'Of course! He wasn't stupid. And look who's *nyet kulturnye* now!'

'Go on, Simone,' Jean said, 'I love to hear you quote.'

'And I just love you, period,' Simone said. 'Everything you say or do or feel or think or imagine. *Tu es ma vie, tu sais.*'

'Likewise,' Jean said. 'Now finish quoting Schopenhauer will you?'

'*D'ac.* "When the Jews were a conquering people, they too called good all things that were hardy, manly, warlike, perfidious and cruel. But once they had become a conquered people—" That's bad again; he said *Sklavenvolk*; a race of slaves – "they introduced the weak and stupid slave virtues of the Good, the True, and the Beautiful—" There's more; but that's the important thing – and the reason I'd like to be an ancient Schopenhauer Jew is then I could sneak into Marie Claire's tent tonight and – and do things to her!'

Marie Claire looked at her a little fearfully.

'What kind of things, Simone?' she said.

'Well,' Simone said judiciously, 'first I should rub some rich merde de vache on your pretty little nose to make it grow long like mine. And some urine *de cochon* into your hair to turn it dark—'

'That wouldn't work,' Anton said. 'What an idiot you are! Urine is a bleach. It would only make it lighter.'

'Well – shoe polish then. Black shoe polish. And – and what would make her lips thick? Tell me that, Anton?'

Anton considered the matter. Bent down and observed Marie Claire's mouth at close range.

'Kissing them,' he said.

'Why, Anton!' Simone grasped. 'You – you're falling for her! You're being unfaithful to me! In your mind!'

In spite of herself, Marie Claire had to laugh.

'You can be unfaithful to An— to M'sieur Rabinowski,' she said, 'but *he* cannot be unfaithful to you, Simone?'

'Of course not! Anton has belonged to me all his life, and he knows it! I will not permit him to – to me *faire un sal tour!*'

'But – after you're married to – to Jean?' Marie Claire said.

'Oh Jean is very liberal – *très large d'esprit.* He will allow me to put him the very little horns with Anton once in a while, won't you, *mon amour?*'

'I will break every bone in your delightful little body,' Jean said, 'starting from your south end and working north. Besides which violinists like Anton are born once every two or three hundred years. I refuse to be placed in a position where I should be forced to remove such genius from the world.'

Anton made him a deep mocking bow.

'I thank you, John,' he said, 'but the other way around the idea has been, and remains awfully tempting!'

Marie Claire was staring at Anton now.

'You – you're *that* Anton Rabinowski?' she said; then: 'But of course! I knew you seemed familiar. I've heard you play at least three times in Paris, and—'

'Oh merde!' Simone said. *'Now* look what I've done!'

'I'd suggest,' Jean said with a grin, 'that you go back to bed. And let Anton and Marie Claire get to know each other a little better. Besides if you don't rest a great deal more, and eat enough, you'll continue to look like something the cat vomited up on the parlour rug. And even *I* will get a yen to change my luck!'

'Change your luck? *Qu'est-ce c'est ça Jean? Changer to chance?'*

'It's a thing the Negroes in the States say. It means to go to bed with somebody else.'

'Oh Jean!' Simone wailed.

'Go home, woman! Scat! I've got work to do!'

'No! And anyhow I came out here to see *her*. To see Marie Claire.'

'To see – *me?*' Marie Claire said.

'Yes. Day after tomorrow's Bastille Day. And Colonel Faisceau has told me there are going to be parades and celebrations at Die, at St Martin – and in the Forest of Lente. That's the one I want to go to, Jean: the one in the forest. Because – they're going to have a Memorial Mass for – for our dead. I want to say a prayer for poor Yves. Will they let me, Marie Claire? Or is there some law that says I can't?'

'They'll throw him out of heaven sure as hell,' Anton said sardonically. 'The minute a Jewish prayer floats up there to besmirch his Christian soul, they'll—'

'Stop it, Anton! – I mean M'sieur Rabinowski!' Marie Claire said sharply. 'Of course you can, *ma chérie!* It – it's very sweet of you to want to. Is *that* what you wanted to ask me?'

'No. Another thing. Would you – would you – arrange my hair? Yours – is so neat. So well coiffé! And mine's a mess. Of course it was born a mess; but—'

'Why, of course!' Marie Claire said. 'You'll have to come over to my place, though. I have all *mes toiletteries* – over there and—'

'Wait,' Simone said, 'that's only part of it. Jean, do you have any money? Or will I have to borrow from Byron again?'

'Some,' Jean said, 'not much, but—'

'I've some,' Anton said.

'And I,' Marie Claire said. 'Perhaps between us all we can – but what is it you want to do?'

'Rent a room at the Hôtel Beylier in La-Chapelle-en-Vercors – for Jean et moi – the night before. Not – not to make love in. Oh *zut*! Not *just* to make love in. But to take a *bath*. In a bathtub. with hot water and bathsalts. And me *raser les aisselles et les jambes et*—'

'*Halte!*' Jean grinned. 'The armpits and the legs are quite enough to shave, Simone! You leave the rest alone!'

'Oh what a naughty boy you are, mon Jean! I wasn't going to say that. I was going to say perfume myself, that's all.'

'Oh what a heavenly idea!' Marie Claire said. 'You men can't possibly imagine what it is to be a woman in a camp full of men.'

'Should be fun,' Anton said.

'It isn't though, An— M'sieur Rabinowski.'

'Please call him Anton,' Simone said. 'I don't mind.'

'Nor I,' Anton said. 'Please do, my dear.'

'It's no fun at all. Those swine of Americans have made two dozen holes in my tent to spy on me as I wash myself. And I need a guard detail to escort me to the outhouse and—'

'You see? That's what you get for being *too* spectacular, Marie Claire,' Anton said.

'Can't be done,' Jean said then soberly. 'The hotel, I mean.'

'Why not?' Simone said, 'if we can get together enough money, I don't see—'

'Not the money. This is neither Paris nor the Côte, Simone. And we are not married. They wouldn't rent us the room. We'd have to present our documents, you know.'

Marie Claire stared at him in astonishment. Then she looked at Anton.

'He's right,' Anton said, 'these provincial towns are astonishingly puritanical. The French are essentially a puritanical people. Your average Frenchman, and more especially, your

Frenchwoman is far closer to the Swiss in such matters, than he or she is to that small and noisy set from Paris, Cannes, Nice, St Tropez and the like. And even they *talk* a hell of a lot more love-making than they do—'

'I've got it!' Marie Claire said. 'We rent *two* rooms. And you and I, Simone, sleep together, while Anton et Jean—'

'Bon!' Simone said, *'ça me plaira! Comme Jean a dit, je vais changer ma chance! Tu es très belle, Marie Claire. On essaye faire les lesbiennes, alors?'*

'Pay her no attention,' Anton groaned. 'If she couldn't say something outrageous every five minutes, she'd die!'

So it was arranged. But it didn't work out as arranged. Nothing in life ever does. ('But just that one time, a little *better* than as planned,' John Farrow thought, and smiled to himself, remembering it.)

A little after midnight, Anton heard that light, rapid knocking on the door. He looked at Jean who was fast asleep in the other bed. Then with a groan of pure certitude, he got up, slipped on his robe, and opened the door.

Simone stood there. She was radiant: her hair had been washed, set, and arranged in a coiffure that was wonderfully becoming. She had on a nightgown that was like a morning mist. That Anton could see through it as though it were not there troubled Simone not at all. She fairly floated in a cloud of perfume; her eyes were alight with love, laughter, and pure mischief in about equal measure. Then they clouded.

'Oh merde!' she wailed, *'il dort!'*

'Wake him up,' Anton said harshly. 'I'll go take a walk. But make it a quickie, damnit! I don't plan to stroll around all night!'

'I didn't come – for that—' Simone began, then she stopped, bowed her head. 'You're right,' she whispered, 'I *did* come for that. To make love. I – I *need* him, Anton. And there's so little time!'

Anton went down the corridor, swearing under his breath.

'Gallant, aren't you?' he told himself. 'Gallant ass? Gallant jackass! *Merde*! She loves him and—'

He stopped. His breath stopped. His heart.

Because the door he was passing swung open, and Marie Claire stood there. Her hair was coiffed in the same way that Simone's was. She wore the same perfume. Her nightgown was just as transparent, or a little more so. The only difference was that she was crying.

'Come in, Anton,' she said.

He stood there.

'I said come in!' she said.

'Vengeance, Marie Claire?' he said, sadly.

'No. Loneliness, And – and *zut alors*. Anton! Do I have to analyse it for you? I – I want to be – to be held – to be kissed, to be made love to! What's wrong with that?'

'That – it's meaningless,' Anton said.

She took a step forward. Put those soft, milk-white, delicately perfumed arms about his neck. Went up on tiptoe and clung her mouth to his. A long time. A very long time. Drew back. Smiled through her tears.

'Is it meaningless, Anton?' she whispered. 'Is it?'

'Maybe it is,' Anton thought, 'maybe it isn't. But who the double-dyed, deep-blue hell cares now!'

'Oh zut!' Simone said, *'il faut que je m'en aille!'*

'Why?' Jean said.

'I left poor Anton strolling around in the corridor! Hours and hours ago! Look it's getting light! And – and I need *another* bath now. Phew! I stink! I smell like *une maison close* after a busy night and—'

'Well, it was a busy night, wasn't it?' Jean teased.

'Yes. But not busy enough. Not long enough. But I must go and bathe. Oh, my hair's a mess, again! Marie Claire's going to be angry with me! She took so much pain with it, and—'

'All right,' Jean said. 'Scoot! I'm going back to sleep. Wake me up in time to catch the bus. . . .'

But two minutes later, she was back. Jean stared at her, then leaped out of bed and caught her in his arms.

'Oh Jean! Oh Jean!' she wept. *'Ils – nous ont cocus!'*

'Whaaat?' he said, then it hit him. He threw back his head and roared. It was characteristic of Simone that she didn't even see the humour in her words. 'They've cheated on us!'

'Viens!' she sobbed. *'Viens voir!'*

Jean slipped on his robe. Tiptoed down the hall with her. She pushed open the door, gently, quietly.

Marie Claire and Anton were fast asleep. Lovingly entwined. It struck Jean with a great wave of real tenderness that together the tableau they presented was truly beautiful. Harmonious of line. Glowing in the morning light. With a plasticity that Rodin at his best might have got close to, maybe. But only close. Because those two naked bodies were living miracles.

He said whispering the words:

'This I find very moving, Simone. Enormously. It is – so right. So beautiful!'

She stared at him. Then her warm wide lips trembled into a smile.

'You're right, mon Jean! Come now – let's leave them there. . . .'

There was one awkward moment when Marie Claire and Anton joined them for breakfast. Marie Claire had her again beautifully coiffured head held a little too high; and except for the rouge on her cheeks, her face was much too white. Anton fairly slunk in behind her, his eyes fixed upon her smart high heels. But Simone said, in the most natural tone in the world:

'My hair's a mess again, Marie Claire. Could you – arrange it – even a little, after breakfast? The bus doesn't leave for another hour and—'

But Jean was grinning at Anton.

'So,' he said, 'according to Simone, and I quote, 'You two have been cheating on *us*!''

Anton looked at Marie Claire. Anton and Marie Claire looked at Simone and Jean. Saw that the two of them were almost bursting with suppressed laughter. Then all four of them let it out. They quite literally laughed till they cried.

Simone got up and put her arms around Marie Claire. Kissed her with grave tenderness.

'Now you're my sister,' she said. 'I love you very much, you know!'

And that was that. Or it would have been, if there had been no such thing as war. Or mankind's criminal folly.

The Bastille Day ceremonies were singularly beautiful and moving. General Koenig's message from London was read aloud:

'Fighters of the French Forces of the Interior and of Vercors! For three long years you have been preparing in Vercors for the difficult struggle as Maquis!

'On D-Day, you have picked up your arms, and heroically resisting all the attacks of the enemy, you have set the Tricolour waving as our proof of liberation over a piece of French earth!

'To you, fighters of the French Forces of the Interior, and to the valiant people of Vercors who help you, I extend my warmest felicitations, and the wish to see your success extended rapidly to the entire territory of France!'

The cheers at the conclusion of that were deafening.

At the Memorial Mass for the St Nizier dead, men and women alike wept without shame.

At the banquet that followed, everybody got just a little drunk. Which too was right, was fitting.

And it was the same at St Martin, in Vercors, and in Die. For the first time in four long years, Frenchmen celebrated Bastille Day in freedom. It came very close to being the last. It *was* the last for several hundred men, women, and children.

Afterwards, of course, a good many young couples wandered deeper into the woods. So many of them, in fact, that being alone, got to be a problem. An almost insoluble problem. But Anton and Marie Claire, having only last night rediscovered that God – or whoever, or whatever, was responsible – had had one first-class idea when 'male and female created He them,' managed it, after a while.

And so did Simone and Jean.

'Are you sure there's nobody?' Simone whispered.

'Very sure,' Jean said: 'Why, little bird?'

'Because I want us to be entirely naked. I want our bodies to – to kiss. All along themselves. I want us to be so much alone that nothing can ever separate us again. Not – even death, *mon* Jean.'

'Simone! *Parle pas de malheur!*'

'I must speak of it. Jean – one of us is going to die. A – a long time before the other does. Which means – it's going to be *me*. It has to be. Because if you die first, I should die at once, immediately.'

'Simone!' he rasped, 'for the love of God, don't speak of that! You – you seem to invite it!'

'No' she said, quietly, seriously. 'I do not invite it, mon Jean. But I accept it. I *know* that's the way it's going to be. . . .'

'Then you have gypsy blood, as Pepe said?' he said, trying to break through this mood of hers.

'No. But I have the blood of my people, the Jews. And Jews

have always been – prophets, Jean. Please – unbutton me. While I take my hair loose.'

'Why?' he said. 'I like it that way. It's beautiful.'

'I know. I do, too. But I want it loose, so you can tie it behind your neck. Like the first time.'

'Oh God!' he got out. 'Simone, I—'

'Don't talk. If this is going to be the last time, we must put into it all the times we are never going to have. You must love me so much today that I can die serenely and beautifully and happily. And so much that you can live with me always with you. Always. I am going to make an – an etching of myself – with my tears, my sweat – as acids. As very strong acids that will burn me into you so deep that my image will be scarred all along your flesh. I am going to – to ruin – the rest of your life, mon Jean! That is cruel of me, selfish of me, but I cannot help it!'

'Simone!' he wept.

'For any woman who sees you naked like this, will see my ghostly presence glowing on you like this! Like this! So that you will smell of me forever like this! And taste of me like this! And your eyes will be full of me – and your mouth will be bruised with me, swollen with me, broken and bloody with me, like this, like this, like *this*!'

'Simone!' he moaned. (Or mourned?)

'Don't talk. Now let our bodies talk. Like this, like this, so slowly like this, so sweetly, like this, tenderly like this, fiercely like this! Let my breasts stab into you like this, flatten against you like this, and my belly melt into thine like this and you and me together and one like this and there is no death my Jean and we are immortal you and I, immortal though I die. Now make me die a little like the first time, be not gentle with me, *mon* Jean, be hard and strong and furious and cruel and destroy me so that the other will be as nothing when it comes and—'

'No,' he said. 'No. Cruel with you, no. Never. Gentle with you always. Tender. Like this. Slow and sweet and tender, like this, so that—'

But she surged up and her mouth was on his like a brand; and all of her was so tight pressed to all of him, so co-joined, inseparable, one, fused, melted together, locked mouth to mouth yet keening, mourning, flagellant, tortured and torturing, with so much desperation, despair, loss, and longing, that it was a death at the end, and no small death, a bursting together, a destruction, so utter, multiple, prolonged, unbelievable, murderously sweet and continuous a dying, that they had been lying inert, unmoving, unbreathing, suspended outside of time for an indeterminate and indeterminable time, when they were blasted back into life, again, into being, thinking, pain; by the hammering, bellowing, pounding, gut-quivering thunder of the planes.

They came over the Forest of Lent so low that the trees rocked backward with the air gone solid from their propellers; big black bimotors that were shaped like sharks, with glassed-in nose cones for the bombardiers, and machine guns protruding from the blister turrets, and goggled faces grinning down so clear that if you had known them before you could have identified them, distinguished Otto from Karl and Manfred from Wilhelm.

He leaped to his feet, stark naked as he was, and shook his puny, helpless fist at them, a pygmy defying the gods of death, because there was nothing on earth he hated more than bombers. Nothing else was so wantonly, senselessly, randomly cruel. No other weapon except perhaps long-range artillery – and even that to a much lesser extent – permitted men to commit such utter horrors of pure bestial criminality, and escape from even seeing what they had done.

'All of them!' Jean screamed inside his mind, 'should be forced to bathe in blood and entrails! Should have blasted-out brains of babies ground into their faces! Should have their heads plunged into the torn open bellies of pregnant women! *All* of them – theirs and ours! Theirs and ours!'

Then he heard Simone's voice saying:

'Put on your clothes, my love, for we must go.'

When they were still six kilometres from La-Chapelle-en-Vercors, they could see it burning, see those obscene black monsters, Heinkel IIIs, and Junkers Ju 88s, diving into the flame and smoke. Hear those bombs thump and thunder, making the ground shake so that they could feel it through the floor of the autobus.

When they got there, there was nothing really they could do. The town was past saving. Even the people they managed to drag out of the flaming houses were mostly dying or so badly burnt that they begged the coup de grâce. Many of the Maquis were shooting at the bombers; but without true flak guns, fast firing multiple mounted 20, 37 or 40 millimetre shell firing cannon, or at least heavy machine guns, power driven to track, they were wasting ammunition and Jean knew it. So he and Simone, black as minstrel-show Negroes, burnt and bleeding, their clothes in sooty rags, tore into the collapsed and burning houses with crowbars, shovels, any tools that lay to hand. Anton and Marie Claire helped them, as burnt and blackened and reduced to rags as they. Many of the other returning couples did the same.

Then it happened: a row of single-engined fighter planes, Messerschmitt 109s, peeled off and came screaming through the main street of La Chapelle, lower than the tree tops, strafing everything that moved. And, as they barrel-rolled upwards into beautiful Immelmann turns, they cut loose with small bombs that made very little noise, a soft plop, like thrown mud pies, and a column of flame, snow white, blue white stabbed the heavens where each bomb had fallen.

'White phosphorus!' Anton gasped. 'Nothing will put it out, Jean! Nothing!'

And, at that very moment, they all saw the child. A little girl, nine or ten years old, running through that street, trailing a solid sheet of pure white fire a full metre behind her as she ran. They couldn't hear her screaming. But they could see her pitiful little mouth was opened wide. And that the flesh was blistering and peeling off her in strips as she came towards them.

Anton dropped his shovel. Yanked his captured Mauser rifle up and over. Took long slow careful aim.

'Do not miss, Anton,' Simone said.

The rifle barked, slammed back against his shoulder. There was a little rapidly blackening mound in the middle of the street now. With those white flames standing up from it. Standing tall. And Anton was leaning on his rifle and crying like a woman and vomiting his guts up, and Marie Claire had both her arms around him, and dragging his head down against her burnt, blistered, sooty breasts. And Jean was gone from there and was kneeling in the street with his Sten, his absolutely useless and impotent Sten slanting up in the direction the fighters were again coming from now, and the spurting dust columns from the three MG 15, 20-millimetre cannons those 109 Gs were armed with, one shooting through the prop spinner itself, mounted through the hollow prop shaft, and the other two under the wings, and the two synchronized 13-millimetre machine guns, mounted beneath the engine cowling, and firing through the propeller, being camgear timed not to hit the blades, were all around him ploughing, leaping, snaking furrows along that street, and the spent shells from the ejector chutes showering down to bounce and glitter on the road, and he shooting back at them with that goddamned useless and worse than useless 6.3-millimetre pistol ammunition that couldn't even pierce the light plate armour that they bore, felt something, a soft, warm, human body, strike him, knock him down, lie across him, then all the world burst apart in thunder, shook, stank of heat, of chemical stenches, of burning, went silent, and the planes were gone.

He struggled out from under, snarled: 'Goddamnit, Simone!'

Then he saw how she was bleeding.

He bent, picked her up. Started running down the street with her, his mouth wide open, and screaming worse than the white-phosphorous scarred and dying girl child had screamed, screaming his absolute agony, his maddened hate against God, fate, a universe that could or would do a thing like this to his Simone, screaming in a way that was absolutely not to be borne.

Anton stopped throwing up. Like that. Abruptly. Raced after him. And Marie Claire after Anton. And Pepe, and Byron, who were down below, in the direction he was running, came towards him on a long slant, bent on intercepting him, tackling him, throwing him down, for it was very clear that he was utterly mad with grief, clinically insane. All four of them got to him within seconds of one another.

They had to knock him unconscious before they could tear Simone from his arms.

She had a piece of bomb casing in the small of her back. It wasn't in very deep. But that wasn't where all that blood was coming from. Another bomb splinter had gone across her back, just below her shoulder blades and had made a huge shallow rent, a full thirty-eight centimetres long. Through it they could see the bluish-red, striated back muscles showing through.

'*¡Menos mal!*' Pepe got out: 'But this of the bleeding must be stopped now and at once, or—'

He picked her up. Raced with her in his arms, with Byron on one side of him and Anton on the other and Marie Claire behind them. Strangely enough it was Anton who thought of it.

'Marie Claire!' he said. 'Go back to Jean! Get that Beretta

away from him before he comes to! Bring it here – or else!'

'Bon!' Marie Claire whispered: *'J'y vais!'*

They brought Simone into the first-aid station in the bomb-wrecked Mairie. The medical corpsman simply sewed her up like a torn sack, dusted the two wounds with sulpha powder, rammed a needle big enough to gut an elephant into her arm, attached a tube from a plasma bottle to the needle, adjusted the drip of the plasma with a little stop-cock, hung the bottle from a stand attached to the cot itself, nodded to his helpers to roll her cot the hell out of the way, and growled: 'Next!'

They converted the autobus into an ambulance on the spot. Started out for St Martin where the hospital was. Most of the wounded on the bus didn't make it.

But Simone did. Apart from the loss of blood, neither of her wounds was really bad. Two days later she was sitting up in bed and smiling at Jean when he came to visit her. Smiling at him. And almost, once more, daring to – hope.

She had a full thirteen days, from July 14, to July 27 to recover from her wounds; or more precisely from July 14 through July 21, when the hospital was evacuated. She spent the next six days with eight more of the walking wounded, hiding in the woods where Doctors Ganimède, Fischer and Ullmann had sent them. They had little water and no food to speak of. But even so they were better off than the other patients, and the hospital staff were. For on the day the hospital at St Martin was evacuated they had all started out to go to Die, only to find that the Germans had reached that town before them. So, as had been previously agreed upon at the conference of the Vercors chiefs of staff, they bore the stretcher cases to the cave at La Luire, accompanied by the walking wounded. En route, they sent the nine – including Simone – whom they thought strong enough to survive, off into the forest, giving them what food they could spare. The rest went on until they reached the cave.

And there, on July 27, 1944, the Germans found them.

Inside Vercors, from July 19 on, all was horror. And among the countless tragedies of heroic Vercors, there was one that was achingly personal: the one that happened to Anton Rabinowski and his Marie Claire.

The Germans brought in professional mountain troops from the 157th Division, commanded by General Pflaum. Then they hit Vercors from every direction at once, and there was no stopping them. The more so when it was discovered that all the southern roads and trails had had their obstacles torn down, their mines *removed* by orders of a coward and/or traitor named Alain, whose real name was Pierre Raynaud.

Those fast, tough mountain troops tore into the northern sector, near the point of the arrowhead, pouring through ruined St Nizier without even slowing down. Split their column into two pinchers; struck out for Autrans over the Croix Perrin pass with one. Dived for the heart of Villard de Lans with the other.

While the BCA and the Maquis were doing their best to even slow them down a little, the chiefs of staff called an urgent meeting in Lente Forest to consider what to do. Those present were Faisceau (Colonel Henri Zeller), Laroche (Captain Pierre Tenant), Colonel François Huet, Civil Governor Eugene Chavant, Civil Administrator Yves Farges, and the Allied officers, Major Desmond Longe and Captain Robert Tuppers.

And this last circumstance, the inclusion of the British and the American commanders in the conference, had a very direct bearing upon Simone's fate; for having been in occupied France long enough by then for the inadequacy of their spoken French to have been forceably demonstrated to them, Major Longe brought along Captain Byron Graves; and Captain Tuppers, Lieutenant John Farrow, as their personal interpreters.

At that conference three solutions to their more than desperate military situation were discussed:

First, to try to break out through the enemy lines. But, with their own forces spread out over two hundred square kilometres, there was neither the time to regroup them for the kind of massive spearhead attack that might – miraculously work, nor the heavy weapons to support it.

Second, to try to break out in little groups. This was, everyone agreed, a one line definition of suicide.

Third, to keep fighting as long as possible, then melt away by twos, by threes, by fives, at the most, into the forest, the gorges, up the peaks, over and away, creating a vacuum before the enemy, a silence leaving martyred Vercors to an enemy to whom it had no military value, and who, they were sure, didn't even want it. Who would abandon it, as soon as they found there were no longer any Maquis there – and thus turn their defeat into potential victory when the southern invasion came – *if* Faisceau could persuade De Gaulle, persuade General Patch to strike through the mountains, up National 75, up the Route Napoléon.

This third solution was decided upon. Agreed to by unanimous vote. It and one thing more: that the hospital at St Martin-en-Vercors should be evacuated and consolidated with the civil one at Die. But, if German troop movements made this operation impossible, the forty-odd wounded and the staff should be installed in the huge cave of La Luire.

Byron looked at Jean when he heard that. They were too far apart to talk, but they nodded solemnly. And that was why, in the end, they knew just where to find Simone.

The next morning at Vassieux, Jean suddenly had explained to him a thing that had been tugging at the edges of his mind for the last week: the Heinkels and Junkers had bombed Vassieux without mercy on Bastille Day, just as they had La Chapelle-en-Vercors. And yet not one single bomb had fallen on their half-completed airstrip. He knew damned well that the Germans knew it was there; because a Fiesler Storch, that ugly, ungainly aircraft that looked something like a Piper Cub – except that it was twice the size of a Cub, and could fly so slowly it seemed to be standing still in the air, as well as land on an outhouse roof if the wind was right – had floated over them while they were working at least three times – and each time had been driven away with small-arms fire.

But the Luftwaffe had made no attempt to destroy that strip – a thing they could have done in *one* strafing, bombing run. Which made no sense. No sense at all. Had, moreover, given them time to finish it. So now, on July 21, it was ready—

'For troops and guns that will never be sent, never come!' Jean had snarled to all who would listen to him.

At nine-thirty that morning, Pierre Clémont stuck his head inside Jean's tent.

'They're coming, Jean!' he roared. 'They're coming! The planes from Algiers! All of them towing gliders! Enormous gliders! You were wrong, old fellow! You were wrong!'

Jean leaped from his bunk. Dashed out of the tent. Looked southward above the oaks, the elms. And saw them: nearly twenty transport planes, towing troop-carrying gliders behind them. He started to turn, to shake hands with Pierre. To embrace him. Then he stopped. Looked at those planes again.

'Why,' his mind demanded, 'have they extended their landing

gear that far up, and that far away? Makes no sense. At the speed you're down to when you're dragging those big, heavy bastards behind you, to put down your gear could make you stall. Hell, no pilot in his right mind would crank his retractable gear down and create that much additional wind resistance until *after* he'd cut the gliders loose. That's one thing and – and another is—

'That son of a bitching bastardized unmentionable third propeller in the *nose* of those planes! Trimotors! A type we haven't built since Ford got out of the aviation business. A lousy arrangement, because even if you reverse the direction of rotation of one outboard motor you've still got *two* turning in the same direction to pile up so much torque that to get the damned things down without their ground-looping on you calls for the muscles of a mule, and no nerves at all. And *who*, my friend, *still* builds trimotors? The Italians with their Savoia-Marchetti which is sleek and fast and has retractable landing gear. And—

'The Germans. The Junker Ju 52/3 M troop transport, and/or glider tug. A low-wing trimotor with *fixed* landing gear. Which is what those utter obscenities, towing behind them those thrice befouled great floating turds of quintessential *merde* of DFS 230 *Nazi* gliders up there are!'

He turned to Pierre, said quietly, sadly:

'Pierre – round up every man you can. Every gun. We have been screwed. Up our poor shitty ass-holes. Those planes – are German.'

'But – Jean! You cannot be sure! And some of them have already landed and—'

And it was then that they heard the heavy fire. Coming from down below. Where the airstrip was.

By the time Jean got to the edge of the landing strip, fully one hundred Maquis were already dead. They had been gunned down as they rushed to greet what they thought were their saviours.

Jean saw young Jacques Descour, son of Colonel Descour, dead over his heavy belt-fed Vickers. Booted his poor pitiful corpse out of the way, flopped down behind the heavy machine gun and opened fire. With no one to feed the belt in smoothly, it jammed after the seventh shot. While he was clearing it, he saw Aviation Corporal Victor Vermonil, firing the 13.8 millimetre he and Pierre had taken from the half-track the day Byron Graves arrived. Vermonil had already accounted for two gliders full of SS. But they kept on coming. *Ten* gliders were safely down on that airstrip now. *Four hundred* SS. He saw Tournissa crawling away, badly wounded. François Billiou bleeding from three wounds but still fighting. Vermonil reeled away from his gun, a bullet through his shoulder. Picked up a Sten and fired it left handed.

More gliders. Three were down in Jossalux, behind them. Two in La Mure. Two on the castle above them. Two in Chaux.

They were, Jean realized, already surrounded. This time the debate he had with his mind was short. In fact, it wasn't even a debate.

'Nous sommes foutus,' he told his mind. *'Jodidos.* Fucked. *Sehr viel und sehr kötigliche geficktet!* Do y'know what all that means?'

'That your ass-hole's sore. And your tail's dragging. Haul it out of here, boy!'

'Tiens!' he said, 'so we aren't going to be *un héros aujourd'hui?'*

'You don't get us both out of here right now, what we're going to be is dead! Get moving, Jean! In the general direction of St Martin. Where Simone is!'

'Now, we're in perfect agreement,' he told his mind.

But before he'd got half-way through the camp, he halted. And what stopped him made him sick to the gut. He hadn't even thought of it. It hadn't so much as occurred to him. But under the given circumstances, its probability was so strong that it had to be considered. As it was evident. Anton had already considered it; was, it appeared, about to take appropriate action. And what brought the green taste of nausea to the back of Jean's throat was the realization that Anton was, had to be, right.

Marie Claire was leaning back against a tree, a fairish distance from Anton. Say – three metres, give or take a few centimetres. Her face was very white. She had both hands crossed behind her, between her and the tree trunk. She was trembling, very, very little; the exact minimum she could manage. But she was crying in a sick, whipped, pitiful way that was hurtful to see, that emasculated a man to look at.

And Anton was pointing a Browning automatic at her, with a wildly shaking hand and roaring in German:

'What's your name, Miss Nazi? *Please,* tell me! What's your name?'

'She came with the others,' Jean thought slowly, painfully, 'with Mission Paquebot. To show us how to build that airstrip. For the SS to land their gliders on. To – to murder us!'

'You're going to kill me, Anton?' she said in French. Her control was remarkable. There was only the slightest tremor in her voice.

'Of course!' Anton grated. 'What do you think?'

'Then come closer, your hand is trembling. I shouldn't like to be butchered – torn . . .'

Anton stared at her.

'You aren't going to beg for your life?' he said harshly.

'No, Anton. If you believe of me the things you've said, life means very little to me.'

'And you're not – afraid?' he whispered.

'That, yes – terribly.'

He hung there, staring at her.

'But – only – of the moment itself. Of being – badly hurt. Of not being able to bear the pain. And – of dying. Why not? It's always – overwhelming – death is, you know. But it's quickly done, isn't it? So come – closer. One shot from your pistol, well aimed. Here – in this idiot heart, already broken. But – I beg of you – don't riddle me, don't make me die badly – crying, screaming, whimpering. Let me die with – with a little dignity. The dignity you've already robbed me of in life.'

Which was a little too much. And, because it was, it forced him, Jean le Fou, to remember at last all the things he should have remembered at first. In two swift strides he was there between them, between Marie Claire and the muzzle of the gun.

'Put that goddamned thing up, Anton,' he said, 'it's dangerous. It might go off. Kill somebody.'

'You're goddamned right it will, Jean!' Anton snarled. 'In fact, it's going to! One filthy little treacherous Nazi bitch who—'

'Anton,' Jean said, waving his index finger from side to side, as schoolteachers do to naughty and rather stupid boys: '*now*, Anton!'

'You're going to tell me she *isn't*?' Anton rasped. 'Look at her! Hell, she looks like Hitler and Goebbels designed her between them! The perfect, Aryan, nordic blonde! Goddamnit, Jean, get out of the way! I—'

'Her blondeness didn't offend you a little while back, grand rabbi of the synagogue,' Jean grinned at him. 'Come on, Anton, put that incestuous mother-gripping sidearm up before you do something you'll be sorry for. I know, I know! The Nazis sent them here – in *American aircraft* with French markings from Algiers – to suck us in to building the airstrip for their gliders. Then explain this, great brain! Didn't – or couldn't that big black buzzard of a Fiesler Storch that was always up there peering down the back of our necks while we worked have had something to do with it? Could not that Nazi spotter pilot have gone home and said, "Boys, they're building an airstrip! Let's use it?"'

'Well—' Anton said.

'Well, *merde*! I just left Captain Tournissa – who *commanded* Mission Paquebot, my friend! – crawling away from that strip looking like a piece of Gruyère cheese! And Billiou already had three Schmeisser bullets through his hide and is *still* shooting Nazis. The other two members of Paquebot are *dead*. So now you tell *me*; just what do you plan to kill Marie Claire *for*?'

He turned, put out his hand to her.

'Come, my sweet, my lovely,' he said. 'Anton's a moron, an idiot. Love has scrambled his brains. You must forgive him.'

'I must thank you, mustn't I, Jean?' Marie Claire said quietly, slowly. 'All right, I do. I thank you for having saved my life. One is very attached to it, isn't one? To this crazy life, by – by pure animal instinct, the instinct of – a beast. To this life that's worth nothing, now. That I don't want at all. But – one must live, mustn't one? Perhaps one day somebody will explain to me for *what* – and even for – *whom*. . . .'

She said all that with enormous dignity. She was, Jean saw, exactly what the Spanish mean when they say '*¡Mucha mujer!*' Much woman. *Très femme*. As much as Simone was, maybe, though in a different way. Anton was staring at her. His heart was in his eyes. And it was breaking, there.

'Oh Christ!' he said. 'Look, Marie Claire, I—'

She looked at him, but she didn't see him. Her eyes were absolutely blind.

'Good-bye, Anton,' she whispered. 'I've loved you – very much. Perhaps – too much. I even thought that we – that we could make – a life – together. But if Jean has saved you from killing me, from killing my body, he hasn't been able to save you from a crime even more – painful – from having assassinated my spirit, having – riddled – my feminine pride. I shan't forget you easily. No – that's not well said. It's not even true. I shall *never* forget you.'

Then very quietly she turned and walked away towards the forest.

'Go after her, you fool!' Jean said.

But Anton shook his head.

'No, John,' he croaked, 'that's finished. I've been a fool. An utter blithering ass. But it's finished – through my fault...'

'But what in God's name did you say to her?'

'Too many things At least one of them, I suspect close enough to the truth to hurt too much: that she only dragged me into bed with her, because she couldn't have *you*. But the rest of them – cruel. Unfair and cruel. That she was a born whore. That she'd proved that to me the first night by being *too* good at it. Then I went on from there to outdo all previous records in bastardy: told her, among other things that I was going to cut it off. Castrate myself for ever having shoved it up a filthy Nazi cunt. That I'd never be clean again, after having soiled my flesh with one of the daughters of the murderers of my people. And quite a few other things of the same eloquent style. Y'know, I think she – she meant that. That she really *wanted* to die, because I'd hurt her so badly.'

'She did. You have to handle women, gently, Anton. Real ones anyhow. And Marie Claire *is*. Now come on!'

What they – Jean, Anton, Byron, Pepe and Pierre at the head of as many members of Réseau Merle as they could find – travelled through outdid Dante, as the real, the true, beggars the imagination every time.

Vassieux, where everyone of the hamlet's sixty-four inhabitants were now dead. Shot. Bayoneted. Burnt. Tortured to death.

Seesawed. That was a beauty. '¡Eso es de una ingenuidad sorprendente!' Pepe said. Of a surprising ingeniousness. They built a seesaw – just like the ones children played on. Only they built it high. So high that the two beaten, burnt, all but flayed, bastards they hung by their necks on loops of piano wire from both ends of it, could barely touch the ground with the tips of their toes. The piano wire had slip knots, not the heavy handyman's knots that break the neck. So the victims struggled. The one who got his feet on the ground, strangled the other. And he, strangling, jerked his comrade off the ground, and so on alternately until ten, twelve, twenty minutes later, both were dead. And the innocent gentle SS hadn't killed them. They'd killed each other.

They, Réseau Merle, carried with them on their backs, Suzanne Berthet, eight years old, daughter of the mayor of Vassieux (dead now – shot). Alice Giraud, ten years old, and Lucien Emery, four. Suzanne had grenade fragments in her foot, Alice in her back, and little Lucien's hand was torn off. The Germans had found them hiding behind a rock and threw grenades at them. Madame Bonthoux, seventy years old, came out to plead for the children. They shot her dead on the spot.

So it was throughout Vercors. People locked in their houses and then hosed with *Flamenwerfer*. Clubbed to death with gun butts. Riddled merely for being visible, being there. Until they were wondering if another 'Final Solution' was not perhaps so unthinkable after all. If vengeance down to the third and fourth generation was not a simple necessity. If Europe and the world would ever be safe as long as one blond, Aryan, nordic Ubermensch was left alive to breed, to procreate, to perpetuate through the very genes of his children the idea that certain men, of certain physical, racial types, have all the rights, and others, the darker, alien breeds without the law, have none, not even the simple right to live.

They got down to St Martin finally. It took them one whole week. For one thing they could only travel at night most of the time. For another they lost hours, days crouched in gorges, caves, waiting for the Nazi armour to finish rumbling and clanking by. For another thing they were sorely burdened with the wounded children, with their arms, with the wireless Byron had insisted on bringing along.

'We get down to the Côte, old boy,' he said, 'I want to be able to call Algiers, Italy, Gibraltar. Somebody to send a submarine or a plane to pull one tired Limey *out*. Namely me. I've had it, John!'

But the first thing they learned upon reaching St Martin was that the hospital had already been evacuated. So they started out for Die. Before they got there, they found the hospital's abandoned vehicles under the trees a little way off the road.

Which meant that the hospital staff and the wounded had never even got to Die. And that in its turn meant that they were, they had to be, hiding out in the cave of La Luire.

But there was the problem of the children. Despite their best efforts the little ones were weakening; if they didn't get them into trained hands soon, they'd die. Pepe examined the ambulances, the trucks. Found one he was able to start. Roared off in it with the children to Die.

The rest of them started for the cave, after having agreed to come back to where the vehicles were, after they had found – or had not found, someone most of them thought of, but were too fond of Jean to say – Simone.

When they reached the cave at last, what they found there would have turned the stomach of a goat. There were twenty-six bodies scattered below the mouth of the cave, and in the public square of the hamlet of Rousset. Of the forty-odd wounded in Vercors Military Hospital the Germans had spared four wounded Nazi prisoners whom the doctors and the nursing staff had cared for as tenderly as if they were their own people, Second Lieutenant Chester Meyers, of the American combat team, whose American army uniform, dogtag, and identification papers forced them to treat him as a prisoner of war, two women wounded in the Bastille Day air raids and a nurse wounded at the same time, who was able to convince them somehow that she was a civilian like the other two.

All the others had been shot. The more seriously wounded at the cave itself, and their bodies rolled down the slope. Those who could hobble, in the public square. Among them Lieutenant François Billiou of Mission Paquebot. Despite his regular French Army papers, and his uniform. To the Nazis, France no longer existed. Uniform or not, papers or not, Billiou was a 'terrorist'. And as a 'terrorist' he died.

Among the civilian staff, they released the Doctors Ganimède, father and son, and their wives. But they sent the seven nurses to Ravensbrück, in comparison to which a firing squad was the tenderest of all tender mercies. Of their fates, no further trace has ever been found. Perhaps they died in the decompression chambers, designed to test how little atmospheric pressure the human lungs can stand before they burst. Or in the surgical operations, grafting tests, organ transplants and the like, performed always without anaesthesia. Or of pneumonia, after their warm young naked bodies had been used to warm, to thaw out the all-but-dead bodies of Russians, Poles, Balts, Jews, or whatever sub-human species lay to hand for the 'master race's' purposes, recently removed from barrels of cracked ice and water placed outside in the snow; or in the comparison tests of which type of crucifixion was most effective, that supposedly performed upon our (supposed) Lord or that said to have been performed upon St Peter, that is, suspended from the cross head down.

And in the square they shot Drs Fischer and Ullmann, and Padre De Montcheuil, SJ, the chaplain. 'The first two,' Pierre Tanant wrote in his eye-witness account of heroic Vercors, 'for being of Christ's race; the third, for being his apostle.'

They, Byron Graves, Anton Rabinowski, and John Farrow were standing there with what was left of Réseau Merle, looking at those bloating blackening heaps of what had been human beings, covering their nostrils with whatever parts of their own clothing they could spare against the utterly unbearable stench of putrefaction, when Simone Levy came tottering out of the woods leading the eight other walking wounded whom Ullmann and Fischer had sent away to save their lives.

She stood there with her arm about John Farrow's waist, crying very quietly. Then she said:

'We must – bury them, Jean. So that they may rest – in dignity, in decency, if not in peace. . . .'

'But, Simone,' Jean protested, 'there's no time!'

'We must bury them. You know what he—' she pointed to Dr Fischer's distended corpse, 'said to me? Do you know mon Jean?'

'Non, mon ange,' Jean said.

' "Go, daughter! You who have the map of every Pale, every ghetto written on your face – every pogrom sorrowing in your eyes! Go – live. We'll need your children!" So if you do not bury him, I will stay and do it. With my hands, if need be. But I ask you, my husband, in God's sight, if not in man's, to grant them this. That we bury them, Jean! That we bury them!'

'That we bury them,' Jean said. 'Yes. I will give the orders now.'

They started southward down the Route Napoléon, riding in the truck that Pepe had salvaged. They had filled the tank by siphoning the gasoline out of the other vehicles with surgical tubing, the kind used to drain wounds, make transfusions, drip plasma and the like, that they'd found among the medical supplies in the abandoned hospital vehicles. They kept the tubing in case they had to steal more gasoline, which was just about the only way to get some now. And in the even more likely case they ran into Germans and would have to fight they brought all the sulphanilomide, bandages, and plasma.

They had more than enough gasoline to get past Gap, perhaps even past Sisteron. Or so they thought. But twenty full kilometres before they reached Gap, the truck's motor coughed and quit. The gasoline gauge hadn't been working from the outset, so they had had no warning.

Swearing, Pepe climbed down from the cab and lifted the hood. There was nothing wrong with the motor that he could see. Nor that Byron could see, nor that Jean could see, nor Pierre, all of them first-class mechanics.

It was Byron who thought of it first.

'Could we be out of petrol, old boy?' he said to Jean.

'*¿Y la gasolina, Pepe?*' Jean said.

'Man we've got enough to get to Cannes with luck!'

'But without luck, Pepe,' Jean said. 'Such as, for instance – a tank that leaks?'

'*¡Valgame Dios!*' Pepe said. 'I never thought of that!' He crawled under the back of the truck. Came out again, said:

'Bullet hole. *One*. I shit in the milk of Hitler's mother! One goddamned bullet and we are fucked!'

'Can't the hole be plugged?' Byron asked.

'Yes,' Jean said, 'a plug of green wood with a rag around it hammered into the hole will do that nicely. Only—' Then he looked at Pepe. Said in Spanish: 'To Gap and back, walking – you and I? With two jerry cans? And the tubes. And the possibility of borrowing a little gasoline from the Nazis? Speak of it.'

Pepe looked at the sky.

'Too soon. It must be timed so that we arrive after dark. Well after dark. Say midnight. No. Later. The stealing of the *gasolina* is less than bad. Within the gravity, it is possible. The return with the heavy jerry cans – bad. But not impossible. We will do it. Thou and I. No one else. *We* can do it. It calls for a certain quickness, and also for the possession of the two attributes of masculinity, well placed. Therefore thou and I. Agreed?'

Simone had climbed down from the truck. She stood there looking at Pepe. She said:

'No. Please, Pepe, no! Not Jean! He's had too much luck up until now. Therefore he has very little left! Not Jean!'

'But, Simone,' Pepe said. 'You understand the Spanish not. How is it that now you have understood it?'

'Now,' Simone whispered, 'I have – another eye. I have a wound in my heart, Pepe, that hurts horribly – and through which I see the future! Please do not take my Jean!'

'I'll come back, Simone,' Jean said. 'I promise you. . . .'

'Concentrate, gypsy!' Pepe said seriously. 'Concentrate! *Can* Johnny and I do it? Tell me! Can we?'

Simone closed her eyes. Her face went grey. She looked ugly suddenly. Ugly and old. Then she sighed.

'Yes,' she whispered, 'you can do it. You can do it with no trouble at all. You can steal the gasoline and come back safely. *That's* not where the trouble lies—'

'Then where does it, *mon ange*?' Jean said.

She put her arms about his neck. Kissed him. Said: 'I do not know, my Jean. Sometimes the eye closes, sleeps. Or its own tears blind it. But no matter. *You* will be safe. I'm sure of that.'

'And she was right,' John Farrow thought. 'We had no trouble at all. The Wehrmacht garrison at Gap hadn't had to fire a gun in anger since they got there in November 1943. They'd slackened off, become fat, sleepy. Found the kind of girls to whom any soldier is irresistible. The ones whose heads we shaved later on. . . .'

No trouble. He and Pepe had stolen the gasoline with that mocking, deceptive ease with which most things in life are accomplished just before they turn on you, go bad, become impossible to accomplish at all. It was, in the wry phrase not yet even coined: 'the build-up before the terrific let-down'. They siphoned the gasoline off into the jerry cans, out of the tanks parked in the garrison's parking place, while the sentries who should have been guarding the trucks slept soundly, stretched out in two widely separated trucks' cabs. They got out of town with it with that same, mocking deceptive ease.

Got back to the place where they'd left the others. It was full daylight by then. But the others weren't there. Only the truck was. Its windshield had been reduced to powdered glass by machine-gun fire. Water dripped sullenly from a dozen holes in its radiator. They stood there, looking at it, and they didn't say anything. They didn't, because there really wasn't anything to be said.

Then Pierre came out of the woods leading the others. Two of them were supporting Byron Graves between them. He was bleeding from a bullet wound in the left shoulder. Another one brought out that precious wireless. But without even counting, Jean could see that there were four missing. And that two of that four were Anton and Simone.

'The SS,' Pierre said. 'We lost two, Jean. The Mathieu brothers. Philippe and Emil. They're back there. In the woods. When we've patched Byron up, we'll go back and – and bury them—'

'Simone?' Jean said, hearing his own voice come up flat, still, unshaking, calm. 'Anton?'

'They took them alive, John,' Byron whispered. 'They took them alive – deliberately. I don't know why. They had them dead to rights. Just as they had the Mathieus. But they shot Philippe and Emil at once. I think – I think—'

'Bandage him!' Jean said then, 'they didn't take our stuff out of the truck did they?'

Pierre went and looked. 'No,' he said. Then he came back with the medical supplies. Byron had been lucky. The ball, a 7.9, had gone clear through. And it hadn't hit bone and mushroomed. The entry and the exit wounds were the same size. Barring torn ligaments, or a severed nerve, he'd be all right. What was luckiest of all for him, they wouldn't have to probe for that slug, because they hadn't any anaesthesia, and digging a bullet out of a man's living flesh hurt. In fact, it hurt like hell.

Jean stood waiting while they bandaged Byron. He was conscious of an extraordinary heightening of all his perceptions. That mountain sky was the highest, the clearest he had ever seen. The morning breeze was the freshest, the coolest. He could count every needle in the umbrella pine a hundred metres away. He could hear the wild doves cooing deep in the woods.

And all the time he was holding on to his own insides with delicate fingers, holding them still, suspended and quiescent, so that they could not move, holding them the way a gutshot man, his company cut off and surrounded in the dark, holds his middle quietly, softly, knowing that the slightest movement will bring the pain.

There were times you couldn't afford to scream, and this was one of them. You needed all of yourself, ripped apart and bleeding though it was, to even start to do what you had to do. You needed the guts that were threatening every second to crawl up through your chest like bloody snakes, and force you to spew them up, slimy and dripping with quite intolerable anguish, there on the road. You needed the testicles that were trying to retreat back up into your belly, perform an autocastration on you, to leave you a thing, at the exact instant when you needed everything that manhood implies, needed the ancient atavistic juices of antique valour, needed above all, to remain in control.

So he stood there, holding himself in, perfectly, quietly, enormously alive, perceptive, alert, not even knowing what he'd have to do next, but knowing that whatever it was he could and would do it, thinking, because only Spanish, that sonorous tongue of unreconstructed, unaltered, even unselfconscious maleness, too primitive to ever be chauvinistic about it, could say it:

'*¡Aquí estoy yo!*' ('Here I am!') Implying the willingness and the capability both; having no need to say them, mouth them over; himself, being present on this occasion, ready, and in full control.

'I think—' Byron said then again.

'What do you think, Byron?' he said then quietly.

'That they recognized Anton. And thought that Simone was his wife.'

'And?' Jean said.

'Anton's – big game, John. They – know they've had it. So – hostages. To ransom their miserable murderers' hides with. One of the world's greatest violinists and—'

'Where?' Jean said. 'Did you get any idea?'

'No. Heard them talking, though. They were SS despite the fact that one of them was an educated, even a cultured man. Spoke the purest Hochdeutsch. Prussian accent. Even got his name. They called him Kroll. The Oberstürmbannführer Kroll – Heindrich Kroll. His opposite number – same rank – kept saying, 'Aber mein lieber Heindrich!'

'Mother of my soul!' Pepe got out. 'Did he say Kroll? Heindrich Kroll?'

'Yes. You know him, Pepe?'

'Do I know him! He's the first and favourite son of the Great Whore, and Satan is his father!'

'Which,' John Farrow thought, 'turned out to be the understatement of the century. But we were – or soon reached after we'd plugged fourteen holes in the radiator of that truck with wooden plugs – on Pepe's old territory. Where he was a legend. So – we could get that gelignite from the stuff Algiers was dropping to the southern Maquis for use when the invasion started. And Pepe ambushed that beautiful Nazi motor-bike – '*Aplastando sus cojones*' in the process. And Byron had hung on to that thrice-blessed wireless like grim death. And those planes came up from Corsica and bombed that prison on request. My luck was nothing short of miraculous. *Everything* worked. Except that we found no trace of Anton. But, according to Monsieur Feingold of Feingold et Fils, that worked, too. Though according to Herriot and Poisson, it didn't. I believe Feingold. His data is more recent; and damned easy to check. In fact, I will check it. Tomorrow, maybe. But the brutal truth of the matter was that what had happened to Anton mattered less than a damn to me by then. Nothing did, except Simone. And that worked. It really worked. I saved her.

'Only to have her leave me.'

He looked at his face in the mirror. His eyes were very tired, very old.

'So now we have come full circle. That's all I know. And all I'll ever know, probably. . .'

He looked at his watch It was time to go. He had a rendezvous with Mister the Commissioner Fish. With the much-delayed Madame Betrand.

And – with a pair of ghosts. A pair of restless, singularly unquiet ghosts, waiting to speak to him from beyond the grave. As, be it granted, such ghosts quite often do.

The catch, of course, is to hear them.

14

On the way down from the Hôtel Bellevue to the Commissariat John Farrow got lost, which was a tribute to Grasse's age, rather than to its size. As in any city of Europe dating back to the Middle Ages, the streets in the older sections progressed by whim, fantasy, 'and, at times, sheer cussedness,' he thought. He had gone down the Avenue Riou Blanquet, entered the curving Avenue E. Caremil, but finding it was taking him too far east, turned off it in a southerly direction, crossed the Place Martelly, and the Place du Patti, coming out on the Rue Amiral de Grasse. So far, he had been comfortably sure he was going in the right direction. But shortly after crossing the Place Aux Aires, the Rue Amiral de Grasse proceeded to bend itself into a complete U and start straight back in the direction he had been coming from.

He sat behind the wheel of the little red Renault and swore freely. In a very little while, he was going to be late, and he wouldn't put it past Monsieur le Commissaire Poisson to send out at least a departmental, if not a national alarm to have him picked up. And before five full minutes had passed by at that.

Then, to his great relief, he saw a blue-clad agent de police directing the traffic that was coming out of the Rue de l'Oratoire. So he drove up to him and asked him how to get to the Commissariat. Whereupon the traffic cop looked at him as if he were trying to determine exactly what kind of rock a Frenchman who knew so little about Grasse had crawled out from under. And he wouldn't have been one whit more amiable with an authentic tourist, John Farrow was sure. Less, probably.

'There isn't any,' he said.

'Then where, one permits oneself to ask, does one go when one has an *affaire* that concerns itself with the police?' John Farrow said.

'Préfecture, Avenue Général De Gaulle,' Monsieur l'Agent said.

John Farrow sat there. He knew that wasn't right. Because the Commissariat damned well hadn't been on the Avenue Général De Gaulle, but on the Boulevard something-or-other. Because when the two young gendarmes had taken him there, they'd—

He stopped short. Gendarmes! But of course! And the sign over the building hadn't said 'Commissariat.' It hadn't for the very simple reason that the Commissariat was only an office inside the building itself and not a real Commissariat of a district or a zone as in a large city. Besides which, it came to him at last, Commissaire Poisson's uniform had been khaki, not blue. Which meant of course that he was a commissaire of gendarmes, and not of city police.

'Is there, perhaps, a gendarmerie in Grasse, Mister the Agent?' he said.

'But yes. Boulevard du Jeu de Ballon,' Mister the Agent said.

So John Farrow got there finally, with exactly two minutes to spare. And saw that his guess had been right; that this was the building where he'd been before.

When he walked into the office, he saw that Madame Betrand had been punctual, this time, for she was already there before him. She sat with her back to the door so that he couldn't see her face. But that wasn't all to the bad, he realized. To any trained intelligence operator, a few seconds to study a person who is unaware of one's presence can be priceless. In fact, he knew of cases where such an opportunity had actually saved an OSS man's life.

The first thing he saw about her was that she wasn't young. Her hair was almost entirely white. And it hadn't been dyed or bleached that colour for here and there amid the clean, beautifully cut and shaped whiteness – a career woman's coiffure that needed only a touch of a comb, a pat of the hand to fall effortlessly into place – he could make out a darker strand or two of what must have been its original shade: a soft, not quite golden, burnt taffy colour. That, at once, told him something about her: a woman who refused to dye, tint, or otherwise disguise the only immediately discernable evidence of her actual age possessed considerable force of character, he was abruptly sure.

And, as he passed a warmly appreciative gaze over the rest of her, he was surer of that fact. For her figure was a hymn to the virtues of auto-discipline, of self-control. White-haired Madame Betrand had a body that any girl of twenty might well have envied, and that most of them would have died of both starvation and despair trying to attain. There wasn't a surplus gram on any of the parts of her that he could see. Her lines sang.

She was as taut as a three-year-old racing filly, and her exquisite bones carried that almost angular, sculptured flesh and matchless grace. Her clothes also confirmed his first impression; they were so nakedly simple that only a woman absolutely sure of herself, of the flawless rightness of her taste, would have been attracted by them in the first place, or would have dared wear them in the second. Even the few women who would have known how good that simple linen summer dress of blue and white that she wore actually was would have hesitated before buying it out of the consideration that it would be wasted on nine out of ten onlookers; since it required the onlooker – male, at least – to be possessed of a taste at least approximately as discerning as her own.

'Deductions?' John Farrow asked himself: 'that Madame Betrand is her *own* woman. And that Monsieur Betrand – even if the face I can't see is ugly – is one goddamned lucky man! Age? Forty at the very least. But less than forty-five. Though I can't be sure until I see her face.'

He stood there, watching as she chatted easily with Monsieur le Commissaire Poisson and also with the gendarmes Bonneval and Renard. Her French was Parisian. More than Parisian; it was Sorbonne and Université de Paris; but not 'Toute Paris' for it had none of those oh-so-chic, shriekingly smart turns of phrase that changed every week or so, as the 'ins' became the 'outs' and the 'outs' the 'ins'. She, he was sure, would have regarded those gaudy fools with cool contempt. Would stay away from both St Trop. and first nights at the Olympia deliberately. And probably from the benefit ball for the Red Cross at Monte Carlo as well.

But what was beginning to get over to him by then was the feeling that he knew her. That not merely something about her was familiar; but that everything was. So familiar that only one phrase fitted a sense of recognition so visceral:

'I,' he thought with complete conviction, 'have shared a bed with that woman there!'

'Mais, non!' she was saying, *'il ne peut pas être mon homme, M'sieur Commissaire. La description que vous m'avez donnée, ce n'est pas du tout la même – Nous cherchons un gross blond. Très germanique. Et ce M'sieur Farrow, vous m'avez dit est–'*

'Ici. Présent!' John Farrow said.

She whirled in her chair.

And he hung there, death in him, his paralysed lungs fighting for air, found it at last, dragged it in, held it long enough to shape it into sound; to make of it an organ chord, vibrant with twenty-eight miserable years' accumulation of pain, longing, loss. He opened his mouth, said:

'Simone!'

She stood up then, crossed the room, stopped before him, a little less than a metre away. The only reason he did not claw her into his arms, proceed to almost break her mouth was because he quite literally hadn't the strength. Standing up was as much as he could manage at the moment. He hung there, visibly trembling, fighting for control, sure now that he was neither mad nor dreaming, because that face was there before him still; those great green eyes with flecks of gold in them stared at him in astonished wonder, the nostrils of that beautifully too long, exquisitely hooked nose flared a little, that wide, warm, wonderful mouth that he could taste still, was moving, shaping words.

Then he heard them. They came over to him in that clipped, much too perfect British English that no Englishman, no matter how high his rank, his social position ever speaks; that too precise precision of enunciation and pronunciation both, nothing slurred, dropped, swallowed, drawled, every vowel, every consonant breath-etched and clear, that is the hallmark of the highly cultured, linguistically gifted foreigner.

'And who, Mr Farrow, might I ask, is – Simone?' she said.

He bowed his head; stared at the floor. At her slim feet in chic, yet comfortable, summer shoes. At toenails tinted a faint rose instead of a fashionable violent shade. Looked up again, faced her. Saw her push her heavy white hair aside, with her left hand. With a slim, perfect left hand that no SS torturer's screw press had ever touched. Looked into that face that couldn't possibly be forty-seven years old. That looked precisely like the Simone's he remembered, because she was so much younger than Simone would be now.

Her hair's wintry colouring was premature, he saw now. Her age could be anywhere from a minimum of twenty-eight to a maximum of thirty-two. But no older. He'd stake his life on that.

'I hardly think that matters at the moment, madame,' he said; and his voice, speaking, was quite the saddest sound that she had ever heard.

She stared at him out of those eyes that were the same, made a wry, amused grimace with that mouth that was the same, then said in that English that was *not* the same, being at least two or three hundred per cent better than the droll and delightful version of it that Simone had largely improvised as she went along:

'I can't say I agree with you, Mr Farrow. For to judge by your reaction at seeing me for the first time, you have either grossly insulted me, or paid me the most profound compliment I've ever had from a man in all my life. And I should dearly like to know which it was.'

He smiled at her then. He was beginning to recover a little, now.

'Then why don't you ask Mister the Commissioner Fish—'

She loosed a little gurgle of curiously girlish laughter at that, laughter that was to him – achingly, and terribly – Simone's own.

'—to release me to your custody, Madame Betrand? Then we might go into the matter, if you like.'

'But of course. Jolly good idea, Mr Farrow.' She turned to Monsieur le Commissaire Poisson, said:

'Ce gentilhomme n'est pas le type que nous cherchons. Il est, comme il a dit, Mr John Dalton Farrow de New York, avocat en droit. Si vous avez encore les questions ou même les doutes, je suis autorisée à vous référer aux Messieurs Jacques Cassière et Raoul de la Croix, tous les deux sous-secrétaires au Ministère des Affaires Estrangères à Paris. Ils connaisent Monsieur Farrow très, très bien. En effect, ils l'ont connu depuis les jours quand il était envoyé special du Président des Etats Unis. . . .'

Monsieur le Commissaire Poisson gazed at John Farrow in awe. Launched into a series of apologies and regrets for the inconveniences caused that required cutting off.

'Think nothing of it, M'sieur Commissaire,' John told him. 'In fact it is I who stand eternally in your debt. For all such inconveniences are overcompensated for a thousand times by the privilege I have gained through you: that of meeting the *si belle et si charmante Madame Betrand*!'

She lifted one eyebrow at that in a gesture that was mockery's self, said: 'I'll permit you that one out of gallant ignorance. Yours, of course. For every man to date who has come to know me well has agreed that I'm something of a holy terror.'

He shook hands with Monsieur le Commissaire Poisson. Said good-bye to Bonneval and Renard. Offered Madame Betrand his arm. Once they were outside, and walking towards the little red Renault – she apparently had arrived by taxi, for no other car was parked before the Gendarmerie – he said to her:

'Does M'sieur Betrand agree with that verdict?'

'That I'm a perfect terror? Oh, quite. Or rather he did. What he thinks now, would be rather difficult to ascertain, I'm afraid. We have not a hot line or red telephone connection with hell, that's sure. And, for your information, it's Madame la Veuve Betrand, Attorney Farrow.'

John held open the door of the Renault Cinq; admired the expert skirtcraft with which she doubled and slid into the diminutive car without exposing one millimetre more of lissome thigh than she wanted to. Then he went around to the driver's side, and eased himself under the wheel. As he turned the key in the ignition, he said:

'Did *you* shoot him, or hire it done?'

She threw back her head and laughed freely, gaily.

'Neither. Though that I didn't proves I was a monument of patience in those days,' she said. 'As a matter of fact, we were divorced ages ago. But he did die rather badly, the poor old boy. He went out to Lod Airport to meet his latest light of love, on the wrong day. The day three young Japanese with machine guns demonstrated the exact degree of sanity possessed by the world we live in by murdering, among others, fifteen Puerto Rican Catholics, because the Arabs hate the Jews. . . .'

'Oh, I say,' John Farrow said, 'I am sorry!'

'Are you? I'll be blessed if I can see why. *I'm* not. At least they saved that poor little fool he was out there to meet from a miserable life. My dear ex was a bit of a bastard, y'know. No, more than a bit.'

'Might I suggest that I *still* don't know whether he was or not?' John said quietly. 'In a court of law, you'd be considered a prejudiced witness and the jury instructed to disregard and discount your testimony.'

'Touché!' she said cheerfully. 'Of course I'm prejudiced. He made me quite dreadfully unhappy at an age when a girl still believes in happiness. I was only twenty when I married him.'

'And how old are you now?' He put that question to her like

that directly, knowing damned well it is the one question one *never* asks a woman, because even the way she evaded answering it would tell him a good many things he wanted to know about her. But she answered it at once, and directly without the slightest hesitation, or taking thought, and, he realized, told the unvarnished truth, because she gave a figure five full years older than he had guessed she was.

'I'm thirty-seven,' she said. 'Why?'

'No reason. No, that's not true. I wanted to see how big a lie you'd tell me. And you've told me the truth. I'd put your age at thirty-two.'

'Now that's *very* sweet of you, Mr Farrow!' she said. 'By the way, where *are* you taking me?'

'Type I know in the white slave racket,' John said solemnly. 'When he sees *you*, I've got my fortune made.'

'Oh I say! You really do know how to put a girl on, don't you! And I'm truly flattered! You're the first chap I've *ever* met who thought I'd make a decent *poule*. And d'you know what? I *would*. Only no one's ever been willing to give me a chance before. How'll we work it? Will you be my *souteneur*, and take a cut of my earnings?'

He threw back his head and laughed aloud.

'You win!' he said, 'you're far, far ahead of me. The dull truth is I'm a trifle hungry. How does La Bonne Auberge strike you?'

'It doesn't,' she said at once. 'It's much too dear; and the food's too rich for me. Oh, no! Not what you're thinking – I'm not a weight watcher. I can eat absolutely anything and never gain an ounce. It's just that all the pomp and circumstance turns me off. I actually prefer far simpler foods. Grilled brook trout, for instance. Oh I say, why don't we drive down to Vence? The food at la Farigoule is plenty good enough for me. And you *need* to watch your weight a bit, my dear sir!'

'No,' he said, and his voice made her turn and look at him, really look at him. 'Not Vence. Not with *you*. Anywhere but Vence. Do you mind?'

'Why not *Vence*, John?' she said quietly, seriously. 'And especially why not with *me*?'

'I spent the last ten days I ever was to spend – with Simone, there. I couldn't bear going there with you. You look exactly like her. It – would crack me up, I might even behave badly. Cry into my brandy snifter – or something.'

He could feel her eyes on him now.

'When was it that you spent those last ten days with – this Simone, John?' she said very quietly.

'Between August fourth and fifteenth, 1944,' he said.

'And you – *still* – feel this way about her?' she whispered. '*Still*, after twenty-eight long years?'

'Yes,' he said. 'I know, I know. I'm a romantic, a condition unbecoming to my years. Mentally retarded. A fool. I've heard it all before – what do I call you, anyhow?'

'Gabrielle. Gabby to you. Suits me. I *do* talk too ruddy much!'

'Gabby. *D'accord*. Let's go down to Cros de Cagnes. To Du Vieux Moulin. The seafood's great there. Fish broiled in hickory embers. Would you like that?'

'As far from Vence as possible, *hein*? Oh, all right! John please tell me about her. D'you mean the poor little thing *actually* looked like me? That's what I call overdoing heaven's ill favour, rather! One mug like this one was quite enough, thank you!'

His voice came over to her, hard and taut with anger.

'That's quite enough, Gabrielle. Please stop it now,' he said.

'Oh!' she said. 'Have I offended you? If so, I'm dreadfully sorry, John! But I'll be blessed if I *know* what I did to bring *this* on! *Do* tell me, so that I shan't do it again, ever. You – you're rather frightening when you're angry, y'know!'

'Sorry,' he said. 'It's just that, to me, Simone – was the most beautiful girl into whom Almighty God ever blew the breath of life. Beauty lay upon her like – like an extra presence, an aureole. It emanated from her every pore. Because she *was* beautiful. All the way through. Beautiful and good. From the inside out. From the soul. That's it. That's your cue to tell me what a sententious old fool I am. Go ahead – with my leave, milady! It happens to be true. I am. And a sentimentalist too, I suppose.'

'No,' she said, 'you're neither. You're something else – something rarer. And you still – insist that *I* look like her?'

'Exactly. And are – at least physically – just as beautiful. Perhaps even a little more so.'

He felt her hand rest on his arm.

'John,' she said quietly, 'don't – go too fast, will you please? Don't – fall in love with me. Especially not for this so *very* wrong reason. That I look like her, I mean. I'd disappoint you rather cruelly. I am surely not – nor even anything like – except, as you have said, perhaps physically – your Simone.'

He said, harshly:

'I don't mean to, Gabrielle. As unflattering as that sounds. At fifty-four, a man has scant desire to turn his life up on beam ends. And that's what you would do to mine. I don't want a living breathing replica of Simone to shock me speechless thrice daily by doing or saying something utterly foreign to her nature. I shall probably *never* marry again – I've been divorced, too, you might as well know – but if I ever do, it will be someone who doesn't even remind me of Simone. Now, let's change this subject, shall we?'

'Not yet, I have been given two weeks' vacation – after the rather pleasant task of proving you are not the murderer we're after. Shall we – spend them together? I'd like that, very much! Oh, no! Oh, please no! Don't misunderstand me, I didn't mean *that* much together. Or are you of the super-macho school who is offended by the very idea that a man and woman need *not* be lovers, can be, and remain – good friends?'

He looked at her sombrely, said:

'Offended? Of course not. But neither do I believe it, Gabrielle. It's a good thought. Only, like so many good thoughts, it usually doesn't work. Especially not between two people who have struck as many sparks off one another as you and I have in the scant half-hour since we met—'

'Oh!' she said, and her voice, speaking, was genuinely sad. 'Well that settles *that*. I confess I'm more than a little disappointed, John. I was – looking forward to getting to know you better. You are, kind sir, a most unusual, and a most interesting man!'

'Then I won't disappoint you. We'll spend the next two weeks together – though it won't be all vacation, for me. I still have a thing or two to do. And you hereby have my solemn promise that I'll keep my lecherous paws off you – difficult as that's going to be. For you, fair lady, are one fetching little piece, if I ever saw one!'

She lifted her face, and loosed that purring, gurgling laughter that butchered him internally, it was so much like Simone's.

'God, but you're good for my morale, John!' she said. 'You cannot possibly imagine what it does for a woman crowding forty to be told she's a fetching little piece!'

'Hasn't any man told you that before?' he said.

Her face darkened abruptly.

'Yes,' she said. 'Several. But always the wrong men; at the wrong time, place – and when – both my mood – and the general ambience were also wrong. Or worse still – acted upon the thought. Or tried to. Coming from them – it was an insult. From *you* – it's a compliment.'

'Now it's my turn to thank you. Tell me something, Gabrielle: how long have you been divorced?'

She turned to stare at him; and her green eyes were bleak, suddenly. She said:

'All of thirteen years. Now, go on. *Do*, please. Ask me the rest of it!'

'The rest of what?' he said.

'About the men in my life since. How many there have been. How much I've slept around.'

'No,' he said. Like that, flatly.

She stared at him, a long slow time before she whispered: 'Why not, John?'

'Because I don't want to know.'

She went on looking at him; and her voice became softer still:

'Same question, John: why – not? Meaning, this time: why don't you want to know?'

'One: it's absolutely none of my business. Your past is entirely your own. Two: I should find the knowledge – burdensome. It might even – hurt. . . .'

'Because I look like her?'

'No. Not at all. Because you, yourself, are something very fine. It's strange the way we were thrown together, Gabrielle; and it probably – no, surely – has no future at all; on my side, largely, perhaps *only* – because you wear Simone's face. We've agreed upon two weeks. Two weeks to substitute for what quite possibly ought to be a lifetime. So, I ask you; don't spoil them from the outset. *Je t'en supplie*. I beg you. Please—'

'John – stop the car.'

'Lord, Gabrielle – why?'

'Because if I hurl myself upon you like a hungry she-wolf, you'd probably wreck it, and on this miserable road we'd be killed. I don't want to die. Not now. Not after you've given me such overwhelming reasons to go on living. But I absolutely must kiss you, now. Believe me, John – I must.'

He looked at her said, 'No, Gabrielle.'

'Oh damn, damn, damn, triple and compounded damn! Why not, John?'

'I've a feeling that I couldn't kiss you – casually. That it would very quickly get to be too much. I don't want to fall in love with you, Gabrielle. Still less to embark upon a meaningless *affaire*. So grant me that distinction, will you? The guy who *didn't* join the parade?'

She looked at him curiously. Her mouth tightened into a grimace of real pain.

'All right,' she said, 'I'll let the implied insult – that there *has* been a parade – pass, but let's sort this out, shall we? I gather that you don't want to fall in love with me, nor have an *affaire* with me, not because you find me unattractive, repugnant, repulsive or what have you; but only because I look too much like – your Simone?'

'Not too much. Exactly. But that's about the size of it.'

'John – there are some awfully good plastic surgeons in France. Even on the Côte. Perhaps especially on the Côte.'

'Gabrielle!' he said.

'I meant it. Think what great fun it would be to make love to a woman all swathed in bandages, and not even know *whom* you'd been making love to, until they took the bandages off. Because if this mug of mine stands 'twixt thee and me, I'll rip it off with pleasure! Never have liked it, anyhow. . . .'

'Gabrielle, a little while ago, you asked me not to go too fast; *not* to fall in love with you.'

'Well, I've changed my mind. A woman's privilege, isn't it?'

'No. Not really. It may be the privilege of a silly schoolgirl. But it is *not* the privilege of a woman who cheerfully admits to thirty-seven years of age; and especially not when she's dealing with a tired, pot-gutted, rapidly balding wreck of fifty-four. Then such flights of fancy, whimsy, or what have you, become plain damned silly. People our ages, my dear, don't fall in love at first sight. Not unless they're goddamned fools. And then, who'd have them? What actually do you *know* about me? And I, what do I know of you, beyond the fact that merely looking at you turns my guts to jelly – and even *that* may be a case of mistaken identity—?'

'John, stop the car. Please. I shan't hurl myself upon you with a fiendish howl. But this really *must* be sorted out. You and me.

The relationship between us – past, present and future.'

'All right,' he said and drove the Renault a little way off the road. As far as he could without going over the edge of a precipice. Which, on that road, wasn't much.

'Now,' she said, 'let me admit to having taken grossly unfair advantage of you. You asked me what do I actually *know* about you. The answer to that, John, is everything. For me, it wouldn't be love at first sight; but a – a surrender – to something – something very vital – I've been resisting – and valiantly, kind sir – for years. To set you straight from the outset, we weren't *thrown* together. I quite shamelessly begged this assignment, and the two weeks' supplementary vacation, because I had the appalling desperate feeling that if I didn't do something about you *now*, it was going to be my last chance. By which I mean that the moment it became clear that the man in the Feingold case actually was *you*, I pulled every wire in the books to get assigned to it.'

'Gabrielle!' he said, 'but why? How? Damned if I understand even a little of this!'

'You will, John, you will. But first, let's take up the things you don't know about me, because that side of the matter is shorter, simpler, and easier. I have been very *maladroite*. I jumped down your throat with the suggestion that you pry into my past, out of what is almost a conditioned reflex of your modern, *soi-disant* liberated woman – a sort of prickly, female pride. So, in self-defence, John, you *wouldn't* be joining a parade. The men in my life, since my divorce, have been very, very few. Astonishingly few – for thirteen long, long years and granting me the conditions of – of – humanity – and normality both—'

'Thank you for that, Gabrielle,' he said.

'No. *Don't* thank me. Nor give me too much credit. A good many men, y'know, would consider me an ugly little long-nosed Yid. In fact, not a few have been of that opinion. Among them – several – whom I would have gone to bed with gladly. A lack of – of opportunity – and virtue are two different things, John Farrow!'

'I grant you that. But, even so, I should still be inclined to put you on the side of the angels, Gabrielle. You've a certain look which women who aren't essentially decent just can't manage. A certain – directness. Clarity, even. And, as old-fashioned as I *am*, I don't equate virtue with virginity. I've met a good many virgins who were quite appalling whores at heart.'

'If *you* met them,' she said bitterly, 'they changed from one condition to the other with quite astounding rapidity, didn't they, John?'

'Gabrielle,' he said, 'you said you knew *everything* about me. And with that one line, you've just proved you don't.'

She bowed her head.

'No,' she said, 'what I've proved is that I can be jealous, bitchy, and unfair. I *do* know that about you. That you aren't a skirt-chaser, a Casanova, a Don Juan. That you stopped playing the field a number of years ago – probably for the same reasons that *I* did: that your taste is too finicky, and much too good – so that even normal sexual hungers – as terribly strong as they are – weren't, in the final analysis, strong enough to make wallowing with pigs appetizing.'

He looked at her, shook his head in wonder.

'You amaze me, Gabrielle,' he said, 'truly you do.'

'I know. And you'd better keep your capacity for amazement in good order. It'll get quite a workout, before I'm through!'

'Go on,' he said, 'please.'

'All right. Let me finish the dull and tiresome subject of me. I had a bad marriage. Much of it, as in every bad marriage, my fault. I honestly believe that more of it was his; but I will not enter that plea in my defence, barrister! Thereafter, I started – having affairs – to – to prove things to myself. That the fact that he'd more or less left me for a far prettier girl didn't mean I was totally unattractive. I stopped that in short order, having made the appalling discovery that most men will go to bed with – with a gila monster, or a female ape to satisfy their gross and unthinking sexual lusts – that I was proving nothing but that I was a pushover, an easy lay.'

'That is,' he said sadly, 'one of the many ways that women are better than men. Finer.'

'Don't be a fool, John! We're not. We're just more cowardly, that's all. Once the pill becomes as readily available in every pharmacy as aspirin tablets, say, we women will show men just what promiscuity means! I, for instance, am – quite highly sexed. And the reason I've had as few affairs as I've had is not because I didn't want to have more – no. That's not true. I didn't want to have *any*. The reason I've had so few even though I've lain through endless nights sick and tormented with plain and simple sexual desire is that – acceptable – partners just weren't available . . . besides, I didn't want – bed-fellows. I wanted just one – a husband. Am I frightening you, now?'

'Yes,' he laughed, 'a little!'

'But I would have accepted – partners – plural. But do you know what's available to the single woman, John? The uncounted legions of little fat, soft, anything but potent men, who *have* to believe in the great myth of female frigidity in order to comfortably escape their responsibilities, in order to avoid really having to perform, to even *last* long enough to afford a poor starved bitch a little pleasure, to control themselves, proceed with real virility, brute force combined with tenderness, or worst of all, even to learn to *like* women, actually. I mean *real* women, not playthings, dolls. . . .'

'That's true,' he said. 'That's all too terribly true.'

'So – I became more – discriminating – learned to tell almost at a glance the difference between those who probably *could*, and those who surely *couldn't*. Because to put the matter with the appalling crudity it deserves, once a girl, after months, even years at times, of enforced abstinence decides that she cannot stand it one more night, that she simply must have sex, get laid, she wants to be *laid*, not mucked about!'

'Wouldn't it,' he said quietly, 'have been much simpler just to marry again?'

'*You* didn't,' she said angrily, 'and you've been divorced only one year less than I have!'

'Good Lord!' he said, 'you *do* know an awful lot about me, don't you?'

'As I told you, *everything*. I didn't marry again, John, because I couldn't find a man I wanted to marry. You see I didn't know you in those days. I'd heard of you, of course – even in Israel, I'd heard of you – but in terms so – so extravagantly laudatory that I not only discounted them, but conceived a positive dislike for you.'

'From *whom* had you heard of me, Gabrielle?' he said.

'That I will *not* tell you, John. Not now. After our two weeks are up – perhaps. And perhaps not. That depends upon a good many things, among them how you behave towards me, how you treat me.'

'All right,' he said sadly, 'I won't press you.'

'It wouldn't do you any good if you did. I am, as you so

gallantly reminded me a while back, thirty-seven years old. A tough old bird – or rather vulture!'

He had to laugh at that one.

'Lord, Gabrielle,' he chuckled, 'the things you say!'

'All right. Let me finish this please. So that you'll have no further doubts about me. So that in the future – the exceedingly remote and nebulous future, you can never look at me in disgust and swear you were deceived; that you didn't know—'

'All right. Besides your analysis of feminine psychology fascinates me. I'm convinced you're right. What I know is that no woman has ever talked to me like this – so freely, so frankly about a subject most women don't talk about – at least to men – at all.'

'Nor do I. Not to *men*. Only to *you*. To go deeper into the subject of why I haven't married again, I know I don't have to tell you that my hand – accompanied of course by more interesting and useful portions of my anatomy – was duly asked upon several occasions. But *I* it seems had set my goals too high. For a husband I demanded a man who could keep me happy both *in* and *out* of bed. I told you that I learned to distinguish between men who could and men who couldn't. But to my shame and sorrow, I also learned what happened next—'

'And that was?' he said.

'That ten times out of ten – a figure of speech, John Farrow! There weren't anything even close to ten times! – I couldn't *talk* to him the next morning. That my beautifully muscled, gloriously performing sexual athlete was an utter *dolt*! And with the primitive methods of contraception available in those days – I'd find myself paralysed by terror at the thought that I might be pregnant by such an oaf, have let a simple, natural hunger force me to inflict that type of moronic imbecility upon my helpless child!'

'Rough!' he said sardonically. 'But wasn't the solution very simple, really? A division of labours? The gentle intellectual as husband and father? The boudoir acrobat on the side for fun and games?'

'No,' she said sadly. 'For I, at least, am incapable of dividing – *myself* – that way. So I waited – all these years – to see if there might not be one man – just *one* – with whom I shouldn't have to separate sex from love. For I swore I'd never marry again until I found him. So – thirteen years, John! During which I've learned – to calmly keep a mere physiological need – and any deeper commitment – very much apart. Oh, quite. Completely!'

He looked at her. His gaze brooded upon her face, dark – and somehow, compassionate.

'Have you? That's quite a trick,' he said.

'Oh, damn you, John! Must you be quite so perceptive? It's been all of three years now, since I've had an affair. Because my disgust – at – meaninglessness – got to be so great! And because there was no one meaningful about. And now *you* appear. Like the dark angel sent to punish all my sins! A man who not only knows what love is, but who has endured, has suffered love for twenty-eight hopeless years. I find that rather marvellous. But there's the other side: a man who looks at *me* and sees another woman! A woman who isn't *here*; who quite possibly is even – dead. Rather a bit of too much, isn't it? So now; this one last thing before I start into how, why, where, and so forth. I got to *know* you at least as well as it's possible for a woman to know a man before she's shared his bed. In spite of all the things I've said, despite the distinct, and unlovely impression of a famished female I know I've given you – a true impression, John! God knows I *am* famished for love on all its levels from mindless, bestial lust on up to the meeting and communication of like minds! – I do *not* mean to have an affair with you. I also hereby promise to keep my sweaty little hands off you as well. Agreed?'

'Agreed. But I'm beginning to see it's going to be rough keeping that agreement. For me, at least.'

'And for me. The only reason I shall be able to keep it is my fear – no, my terror – at spoiling something much more important. No! Let that pass, please! Let it go!'

'All right. Tell me what you know about me, and how you came to know it.'

'The truth is, John – that over the years we've accumulated a fair-sized dossier on you.'

'You mean – Israeli intelligence? Your famous IST?'

She nodded, said 'Yes, John. Though how you get IST out of it, I don't see – oh yes I do! Somebody translated it for you didn't they? In English *Ha Mossad L'Tafkidim Meyuhadim* would translate to Institute for Special Tasks, wouldn't it?'

'Yes,' he said grimly, 'or at least so I was told. But I still don't understand how *I* got on your list, dammit!'

'You're – ex OSS. You've made trips to Europe, notably to Paris, and to Bonn, that smelled to high heaven of previous CIA preparation. Though I must say your CIA is getting to be quite respectably professional at last. And you'd already attracted the attention of our people in New York by being, notably and quite inexplictable sympathetic towards Jewish causes in general and Israeli causes in particular. Made you stand out like a sore thumb. We couldn't understand it. By your very background – veddy, veddy U, old chap! – you should normally be, if not a rabid anti-semite, at least – indifferent to us. But you've contributed heavily, both in money, and in time without even being asked – to nearly everything Jewish. And the pattern of your friendships was astounding. Most New York Protestant liberals have Jewish friends – one is reminded of Laura Hobson's clever rejoinder to the type who defends his liberalism by protesting "Some of my best friends are Jews!".'

'I remember that: "And some of your best friends are Presbyterians, but you never think to mention it!" Go on, Gabrielle.'

'Precisely. The fact that the overwhelming majority of your friends were Jewish, was very striking, John. And for you, a Wasp, the quintessential Wasp by almost any measure—'

'That, no. Far from quintessential. My mother was French, remember.'

'True. But even so – for you to take a fledgeling Jewish lawyer into your law offices, and within three years make him a full partner—'

'What do you do with a kid like Lou Rosenstein who's got brains hanging out both ears? Put a janitor's uniform on him?'

'*You* don't. Most people of your background wouldn't either – for the very simple reason that they'd never let him inside their offices on *any* basis. All *that* struck us – very forcibly—'

'All right. But why did your people ever start investigating me in the first place?'

'Why does any intelligence service investigate a man, John? Because he is actually, or potentially an enemy – or because they think they can use him.'

'And I, I presume, fell into the latter category?'

'Right. John Kennedy sent you to Paris – to do a job. All that rather clumsy CIA pre-voyage security business alerted us at once. You came, did it, and got out. Professional as old hell. None of the fanfare that accompanies Nixon's reverse Sabbath Goy—'

He threw back his head and roared.

'So you *know* what a Sabbath Goy is?' she asked.

'Of course. The gentile servants Orthodox Jews hire to do all the things they aren't allowed to do on High Holy Days and the Sabbath. And your phrase is marvellous. It will be highly appreciated in New York—'

'If you ever get back to New York. If *I* ever let you go!'

'I might take you with me. I've been considering it, you know.'

'Have you? That's sweet of you, John. Either as a proposition or a proposal, it's still sweet.'

'Which would you rather have it be?' he said.

'We'll go into that later. Let me finish my explanation why I said so many outrageous things to you so quickly. Why I *knew* I could.'

'*D'accord*. Say on, fair lady!'

'No! Say on, fetching little piece! There's nothing ladylike about *me*, as you should know by now. Anyhow, you know our relations with the Gaullist governments have been *very* unhappy, don't you?'

'Whose *haven't*?' he said.

'But ours, worse than anybody's. In the first place old Long Charlie was a bitter anti-semite—'

'Can you *prove* that, Gabrielle?' he said.

'No. He was much too clever to be caught out on that issue. But he switched a national policy nominally friendly to us to its exact reverse, to all but supporting the people who have vowed to wipe us from the face of the earth. Embargoed all military supplies to us, including the Mystère Four parts we needed damned badly—'

'And the torpedo boats which you promptly stole,' John said solemnly.

'*After* having paid for them, my dear sir! Therefore we only took forceable delivery of what was our own. So – an anti-semite. Have you ever seen a Louis le Grand, Saint-Cyr graduate who *wasn't*? Anyhow that was where you came in. An American who is not only remarkably friendly to *us*, to our point of view, but who also has a decided *in* with the Gaullists as well, could be very useful to the State of Israel, y'know!'

'Yet,' he said, 'I have had no evidence at all that your people ever tried to so much as get in touch with me, not to mention use me in any way. . . .'

'John, you Americans are children. We are not the CIA, thank God! We – you'll just have to forgive us, my dear! – *have* used you. The position papers you brought over on your second trip, for the Johnson administration, *were written* by one of our people, a chap conveniently planted by us in your State Department some years before—'

He stared at her, and his eyes were very bleak. More. There was a cold glint of hostility in them now.

'And now,' he said, 'a beautiful woman like you, at least from my point of view – has been sent – for what, Gabrielle? To seduce me? Happy to oblige! But I must warn you, I don't talk in bed!'

She bowed her head. Looked up again.

'Another thing I already know about you, to my sorrow,' she said. 'Remember Edythe? Stunning, wasn't she, John?'

He stared at her, said: 'Good God!'

'Yes. That perfect Aryan, nordic, blonde – was an Israeli and a Sabra. We'd been informed, I suppose, judging from your wife – your ex-wife, even then – and from the girls you subsequently dated, that *that* was the type you preferred. It occurred to no one, not even to me, to ask why a man so openly and markedly friendly to Jews, *never* dated a Jewish girl. It was the one aspect of your behaviour that was inconsistent, didn't fit. I know *now*, of course.'

'And why didn't I, Gabrielle?' he said.

'Because a Jewish girl, an obviously Semitic type like me, would have reminded you too much of – Simone. And you couldn't bear it. Am I right?'

'Perfectly. You know we're going to miss lunch if we keep this up? Do you mind? I *don't*.'

'Nor I,' she said.

'All right. Then turn your face a little towards me while you talk. I want to see your mouth and your eyes.'

'So you can determine where and to what extent I'm lying, John?'

'Yes, exactly. Self-defence is no crime, Gabrielle!'

'All right. I'll even come closer. Snuggle up to you like this. Now look at me. That's it – closer! Because I'm *not* lying; and you're perceptive enough to tell. And besides, God help me! I dearly do like looking into those black and smouldering eyes of yours. . . .'

'Stop it!' he said. 'Don't shovel it all over me. It stinks, Gabrielle!'

'It's not *merde*, John; but the truth. You, sir, *wrecked* poor Edythe for us. We had to send her home finally. She had begun to waylay even the ambassador, himself, demanding to be transferred to New York, so that she could be near you. By near, she was happy to inform all and sundry she meant under, around, atop, and what have you – suitably unclothed, of course. Since she obviously would have been a danger to us in New York, we couldn't oblige. And she made such a bloody nuisance of herself in Paris, we had to send her home.'

He stared at her. She smiled at him with cool mockery, and went on.

'Just in time. *I* would have strangled her with my bare hands if I had to listen to her graphic and clinical descriptions of what a masterly lover you are, just one more time. The worst of it was I could *see* she was right. Tailing you everywhere you went in Paris, during all three of your visits, was one of my assignments and quickly became my obsession. We women generally aren't worth a damn in intelligence work, anyhow. Our hearts, sooner or later, always get ahead of our heads. . . .'

'Gabrielle, please!' he said.

'Sad truth, John. On your second trip, or rather just before your arrival, I was passing down a corridor and accidentally overheard them discussing whom they could send to be your apple turnover for tonight! So I flattened myself against a wall and eavesdropped shamelessly. The trouble was they'd already learned that a mere *tsatske* wouldn't do—'

'A what?' he said.

'A *tsatske*, pretty, brainless little thing. A play toy of a girl.'

'And why not? I didn't mind playing in those days.'

'I should say you didn't! But since the object was not merely to soften you up, but to pry some useful information out of you as to your government's intentions towards us in the near future, they couldn't risk another Edythe. And all the beautiful blondes we had on tap to keep open beds for visiting VIPs, were, like poor Edythe, rather dumb. . . .

'To my astonishment my name came up. I stood there in that hall and listened and got sicker by the minute. Sick with terror, self-loathing, shame, disgust—'

'Now you're really being complimentary, aren't you?' he said mockingly. 'If those were the emotions I inspired in you, I don't see—'

'Oh, don't be unnecessarily stupid, John Farrow! I was sick with terror because I knew I'd blot it worse than Edythe had! With self-loathing because I realized that I hadn't the simple will power to say no to that outrageously immoral proposition! That I would grab it with both hands and both feet. Shame, because just listening to them I was seized with the most abysmal, abject female lust, so much so that I stood there *hurting*, in actual pain; and disgust for feeling that way about a man who didn't know I was alive!'

'Baby,' he said, 'they should raise your salary. You *really* do a job on a guy, don't you?'

'John, you say something like that to me again, and I'll slap you! So help me!'

'Whereupon I'll paddle your delectable little derrière for you, my sweet! Go on, what happened?'

'My own boss said: "Oh no, he'd never go for a kikey little thing like Gabby!" And that was that.'

'He was a fool. With *you*, they'd have had me. I'd have spilled everything I knew to see those green eyes light up, that great big glorious mouth of yours smile. Though, frankly, what I knew wasn't much.'

'Why thank you, milord!' she said tartly. 'I suppose you *would* have gone for me, wouldn't you? For the same wrong reason I appeal to you now; because I look like your Simone.'

'Then I would have. Probably even taken you home with me – with the idiotic idea of transforming you into a replica of the angel I had lost. And made both of us as miserable as old hell. Now, I wouldn't, and I won't. Older, wiser, and more beat up, I suppose. . . .'

'About all of which, we'll have to see. Mere verbal evidence is unacceptable in this court, attorney! Anyhow – I believed everything Edythe said about you: how gentle you were, how tender. That you never displayed the slightest hint of the contempt you must have felt for a call girl brought in to entertain the visiting VIP. That within five minutes you had her feeling and acting like a bride! Besides which, by then, I'd got to know a certain Jeanne Lefèvre – the darling little creature you knew – much too well it would appear – during the war, as Marie Claire.'

'Good God!' he said, 'and where is she *now*?'

'That, dear John, is absolutely none of your business! So don't ask me for her address. I *won't* give it to you. For two reasons: First – self-defence. She's *still* lovely. Second, she's safely and happily married; but from what I've heard from her about you, but more especially from the rather excessive warmth with which she says it, I fear your reappearance might wreck a going concern.'

'I won't ask you. But not because I wouldn't love to see her.'

'She'd *love* to see you. And that's the rub. She has grown children now. But would the possession of those lovely offspring that I envy her, and the remarkably handsome and distinguished man she's married to, cause her to refrain from throwing herself into your arms? I doubt it. Sitting here in this car, this close to you, I doubt it, profoundly.'

'So,' he said coldly, 'on the basis of your having seen me on three widely separated and brief trips to Paris, I am to believe—'

'That I have developed a base biological urge for you if not a higher spiritual love? No, of course not. Although I'd been almost programmed like a computer to fall in love with you long before I'd ever laid eyes on you – by two people, one who was, I'm sure now, offering me up to you like a proprietary sacrifice for a real or fancied wrong done you long ago – but no matter! Let's say those early and maddening glimpses of you didn't help my sweet tranquillity or my peace of mind. And that the *fully fifteen trips* I've made to New York City since that time, on which I robbed time from what I was supposed to be doing to follow you around like a homeless dog, haven't made matters any easier! In fact, on my first trip to New York, you, John Farrow, almost cost me my life.'

'Now, Gabrielle!'

'God's truth! It was just after your second Paris trip, when I'd been hard put to console your tootsie for the night, who'd returned to us with her mascara running down her rosy cheeks, because you (you monster!) had put her out of your hotel room, with a smile and a most tender kiss, saying:

'Not tonight, my dear – I'm very tired; and it's scarcely diplomatic to disappoint little girls horizontally!'

'My exact words. I can see you've done your homework!'

'John, please. That's cruel. I am *not* lying. On that first trip to New York – which had absolutely nothing to do with you – I spent ten days in Mount Sinai Hospital because I'd caught pneumonia from standing outside your building in a pouring rain for hours, because I had no idea what time you'd come out and was afraid I'd miss seeing you. And, as I said, I almost died.'

'Why didn't you just come up? I'd have loved it!'

'Couldn't. That would have blown my cover all to hell. And what I was doing was important for my country, John.'

'But on the other fourteen trips?'

'Same story. I was never free – or you were all tied up with some utterly loathsome woman! God, the times you've broken my heart, you swine!'

'Gabrielle,' he said slowly, 'I wish I could believe all this, but—'

'All right, then, don't. But *do* tell me this, Mr Very-Important-Person Farrow, what connection have you with the *present* administration?'

'Apart from being pretty high up on its shit list, none.'

'All right. So why should we be interested in – using you, tricking you – even seducing you, except on a purely personal basis that last, kind sir! – *now*? Tell me that, will you please?'

'Now, you begin to convince me, Gabby,' he said.

'The proof of which is that you've called me Gabby, instead of Gabrielle for the first time since I started this. The sober truth is, John, that our embassy's interest in this case was slight. They asked Feingold to describe you over the phone. Sent me to check with the Ministry of Foreign Affairs, where your description was confirmed to a hair, just as I'd told them it would be. But since most of our people from the ambassador on down are new, they wanted a confirmation from someone else, someone less obviously prejudiced in your favour, than they could see I was. So I went. I already knew Cassière and De la Croix, of course—'

'And have had to fight both them off, on occasion, I'm sure,' he said.

She gave him a slow side-long look, so like Simone's – when she was getting ready to say something absolutely outrageous and uncalled for, with malice aforethought, and with the general intention of seeing just how angry she could get him (said intention having behind it another hidden one of the reassurance of her own doubts as to how deeply, entirely, and constantly he loved her) – that it took his breath away. Then she said, with wicked calm:

'Yes. Except that I *didn't* fight Raoul off. He's a *very* attractive man, y'know, and—'

Then she saw his eyes.

'John,' she whispered, 'I – I shouldn't have told you *that*, should I?'

'No,' he said, 'and for two reasons. First it was deliberate provocation, which I will not tolerate, Gabrielle. You may be, as you say, a liberated woman; but I am, in a good many matters, an unreconstructed male chauvinist. Secondly, quite frankly, it hurts. Vague and shadowy figures in your past are one thing; but a man I *know*, and that man a friend of mine—'

'Sorry! And so is Jeanne Lefèvre a friend of mine. And Edythe *was*. Yet I don't blame you, for either of them. My past is mine, John Farrow. I don't belong to you, *yet*. And even when, and *if* I do it will still be *mine*. I hope that's very clear.'

'What's even clearer is that those who called you a holy terror knew what they were talking about,' he said quietly. 'But there is one distinction I'd like to call your attention to. Apart from Simone's – and that was unavoidable you'll grant me – what woman's name have you heard *me* mention? I have always despised the kind of pitiful swine who boasts of his conquests. And I'd suggest to you banner-wavers of the Liberation that kissing and telling is reactionary in men and women *both*. I won't even go into what appalling taste it is. So hear this, Gabby-Gabrielle: I granted you from the outset that your past was your own. And now I very, very gently repeat: will you please, in the future, keep all names, dates and other vital statistics that you seem to have kept an awfully good record of, in a sort of diary devoted to your amatory experiences – I won't be unkind enough to call it your stud book – the goddamned hell to yourself?'

She looked at him and, for the first time, he saw tears mist her eyes.

'I've blown this haven't I, John?' she said softly. 'Ham-fisted Gabby, that's me! Oh, blast and damn! Come on. Start this thing up again, will you? Take me back down to Cannes. If you still feel like eating – which, after being told off like the silly schoolgirl I seem to have been imitating, I don't – you can have a sandwich in the hotel's snack bar. As for me, I'll go lie down. I feel sick, John; quite literally sick.'

'And if you don't eat,' he said, 'you'll feel even sicker. So now we've had our first fight. Which, I'm told, clears the air. It does, doesn't it? Only people who care about each other fight. So now, forget it. Subject's closed. I hope, forever. . . .'

He started the motor, and with one long, smooth, skilful sweep backed the little red car out on to the road.

Sitting across the table from him in the snack bar she looked at him with troubled eyes. Then suddenly she put out both her hands and took his between them.

'I beg your pardon, most humbly, John,' she said. 'I've behaved abominably. But then, I nearly always do. The one man on earth I don't *need* to defend my prickly woman's pride against, and I go and do it anyhow. I'm sorry, believe me.'

He sat there, looking at her.

'*Please* say something, John!' she said.

'All right. Do you *know* who your parents were? Or were you adopted like—'

'Changing the dangerous subject, John? Very well! I'll play along! I was adopted, just as thousands of Jewish children were in those days. By a good Catholic family. Upper bourgeoisie. No – more. From the lesser old French nobility, actually. I was brought up in their faith. Surrounded by Virgins and saints, none of which served to inoculate in me a little of your justly celebrated Christian charity! Until the day my adoptive father was informed by the nuns that I had taken part – most gleefully, you may rest assured – in tormenting one poor little ugly, Jewish child that no one had adopted. So he, that good, stern, upright godly man, proceeded to set me straight upon the matter—

'Set me so straight – by pointing out to me with the aid of a hand mirror, how obviously Semitic I was – that he made a howling schizoid of me. I grew up *hating* myself, loathing my looks, cursing God every night for having let me be born Jewish! I should have changed places and gladly with the most miserable looking little shiksa you ever saw. Every ruddy time I looked in the mirror, I could *see* this beak of mine growing! And my hair! What a mess it was! And my legs grew out of my shoulder blades. I had, I assure you, no *derrière* at all and the front of me and the back were identical! And my knees! May God give knobs like those only to my worst enemy, and may she live a thousand years to enjoy them!'

'Gabby—' he said softly.

She turned, looked at him, said:

'Oh no! Oh no! Don't tell me that she – that Simone – had a sister – a sister who'd be exactly the age I am now and—'

'Then I won't,' he said, 'if you don't want me to. Even though she did.'

'John – that's no good either, y'know.'

'Why not?'

'Gervais de la Motte, my adoptive father, didn't *know* who my real parents were. He found me in the woods. Wandering about. Eating tree bark. Roots. Berries. Mad. I mean that John. Insane. Really. The original wolf-girl, that's me!'

'And you don't know, remember?'

'No. Since I've grown up, and learned to *like* myself a little, I've tried. To remember, I mean. But it just won't come. I don't remember *anything* before one day after I'd been with Gervais and Berthe de la Motte six whole months, I suddenly became aware of them, as people – people whom I could trust, could love – and of my surroundings – that great house in the midst of La Domaine de la Motte – near Fayence. Lovely country, really.'

'It is,' he said.

'So don't you see, it makes no difference? I could be a younger sister of your Simone—'

'Why do you say younger?' he said sharply. 'I haven't told you how old she was.'

'I was nine years old in 1944, John. So she had to be older – considerably older – for your ten days in Vence to even be – physically – possible.'

'True,' he said: 'she was nineteen. Ten years older than you are. But our ten days were *not* physically possible. I got her away from the Gestapo. I spent the first six days merely trying to keep what was left of her alive. I used to lie with her in my arms, both of us stark naked – to keep her warm. Because she couldn't ever bear for a sheet to touch her back, not to mention a blanket—'

'Oh no!' she said. 'Don't tell me any more! Oh no, John, please!'

'You'll never make a gourmet of me, John,' she said, after they finished lunch. 'As you can see I'm far happier in a snack bar than in places like La Bonne Auberge. Even so, I've eaten too much, and now I'm sleepy. I should love to take a siesta. Would you like to take a siesta with me, *mon amour*?'

She pronounced those two words, *mon amour* so exactly as Simone used to that he halted in midstride.

She turned and stared at him, said sadly:

'It appears to me that, "Oh, I'm sorry, John!" is going to become the most overworked phrase in the English language. *Now* what did I say or do?'

'Nothing,' he smiled at her ruefully. 'Reminded me of Simone again. She always called me *mon amour* in that exact tone of voice.'

'You know,' she said dryly, 'I am beginning to strongly dislike this Simone!'

'Don't,' he said, 'the fault's mine, not hers. And of your parents that you look so much like her. Because I am completely convinced you are her little sister. You have to be. It isn't even necessary to prove it by papers and so forth. One day we'll drive down to Menton and I'll introduce you to Paul André Herriôt – commissioner of police there. Or rather I won't introduce you. I'll just walk into his office there with you and observe what happens. You see, he also knew Simone. . . .'

'John,' she whispered. 'Let's – don't. Please! Let me – stay me. Don't transform me into a replica of a memory – or of a ghost. It's no good, John. It really isn't.'

'Agreed,' he said. 'And you're right. Again. As always.'

'John – what are we going to do now? With the rest of the day, I mean? I'd suggest that you move me to Nice – or you to Cannes.'

'I'll move to Cannes. At least there's sand on the beaches.'

'Good! Shall I reserve you a room at the Carlton? Next to mine? With a connecting bath between them, say?'

'What are you trying to do, woman – tempt me?' he said.

'Yes,' she said gaily. 'Why yes, of course! How's your will power, today, *mon* – oh no! my love?'

'That's better. That's much better! Let's stick to English, shall we? It can be "our" language. Agreed?'

'Agreed. But have you never made love in English?'

'Never. I only got married in it – and that turned out to be a great deal less than love. Oh Christ! That reminds me! Look. Gabby, could I just drop you off at your hotel till later on? I absolutely must go back up to Grasse this evening – and before the shops close at that.'

'No,' she said, 'you may not drop me off. I'll go back up to Grasse with you – unless there's some reason why I shouldn't. Is there, John?'

'None at all. In fact, it might even be a good idea. I have to go back to the jewellery shop to pick up some presents I bought for my daughter – my grown daughter who is half a head taller than you are, my sweet – and my prospective, or by now actual, probably – son-in-law. And since Monsieur Feingold was the gentleman who got me into the unholy mess that resulted in my meeting you, it might be interesting for you to come along. Do you know him?'

'No. Of course not. We get quite a few calls like this at the embassy these days, Jean. And when the matter seems really serious, we investigate. As this case didn't really. If I hadn't insisted – for my own most selfish reasons – it would have been quietly dropped. But I did insist, even made a bloody nuisance of myself – because *you* were involved, my love! Fat lot of good it's going to do me!'

He looked at her, his gaze gliding over that trim miracle of a figure. 'My will power,' he thought bleakly, 'has been torpedoed; is down at the prow and is sinking rapidly with all hands. . . .'

Then he heard her voice; it was a trifle harsh, a little choked, warm.

'John,' she said slowly, 'I – like the way you're looking at me now. As if – you wanted me. Really wanted me. Do you?'

'Damnably,' he said.

'We – don't have to go to Grasse, today. You can phone Feingold – from – from my room—'

He shook his head, as if to clear it.

'No,' he said. 'No thank you, Gabby. But I think it better that our agreement stands.'

She stared at him. Then she laughed, took his arm, said:

'You do that beautifully! You must have had a lot of practice at it.'

'Practice at what?'

'Politely refusing ravenous females! Now come on!' she said.

By going up National 567, a much shorter, and best of all a

much flatter route than National 185, the one they'd come down by, they reached Grasse again in plenty of time. When they walked into the shop on the Rue Droit, the Feingolds looked at him a little fearfully.

'Don't worry,' John said with a smile, 'I've been acquitted. No knitting women will be spared from having to count *my* head. Incidentally, this is Madame Betrand, the lady the Israeli Embassy sent down here to investigate me.'

'Ah, so?' Madame Feingold said, 'and how do you find him, Tochter?'

'Marvellous,' Gabrielle said: 'so much so that I am going to marry him if he'll have me. Will you, John? Marry me, I mean?'

'So you can call in a Kamikaze squad to knock me off like you did poor old Betrand? Not on your life, baby!'

The Feingolds all laughed at that. That kind of gallows humour was essentially Jewish. Nearly all their jokes were the kind you make to keep from crying.

'Look, M'sieur Farrow,' Monsieur Feingold said, 'if we have caused inconvenience, we are deeply sorry. But under the circumstances, I'm sure you will understand.'

'I do,' John said, 'besides the only *real* inconvenience you caused me was to delay me long enough so that I could not avoid falling into Gabby's hot little hands. And for *that*, I shall never forgive you!'

They all laughed at that. He was happy and they could see it. There was something touching about that kind of belated, autumnal happiness. Touching and pathetic both.

'And now,' he said, 'let us complete our little transaction—'

'But the little lady,' Madame Feingold said, 'aren't you going to buy *her* a *bague*—?'

John looked at Gabrielle; grinned at her, said:

'Pick out the one you want, Gabby!'

But she was suddenly serious. And there was hurt in her eyes.

'No, John,' she said. 'No presents – yet. Go on with your business, will you?'

It was quickly done. When John had finished signing the traveller's cheques, he said, his voice grave and serious:

'I am very sorry to learn of your daughter's misfortunes, m'sieur, 'dame. Is there nothing that can be done to save – or restore her sight?'

'Quite a lot *could* be done,' Monsieur Feingold said bitterly. 'She has both retinas of her eyes – displaced, I believe the medical term is. Which requires an operation that can only be done, I'm told, in the Soviet Union, *your* country, or by one certain specialist in Barcelona. But unfortunately the operation should be done very quickly now. And I haven't been able to raise the money – for the operation, the travelling expenses, and so forth. Or are you of the opinion that *all* Jews are filthy rich, M'sieur Farrow?'

'I know better,' John said. 'Now, may I use your phone, please?'

'But, of course,' Monsieur Feingold said.

The moment they heard him say 'Opérateur International' they all stiffened. Then he said: 'Get me Plaza nine, five nine oh four, in New York. Person to person. Miss Betty Rudlege. How much wait? None? Good, things really have improved, haven't they?'

Then he was speaking, rapidly. He lost Monsieur and Madame Feingold at once, but young Feingold and Gabrielle sat there staring at him.

'Bets. Yes – it's me. Yes, I'm okay. Yes. Yes. Goddamnit, Bets, listen! Get Doctor Chen Yuan – yes, yes the Chinese eye specialist at Tom Blick's clinic in Boston. Tell him I've a patient for him. Daughter of a dear friend. An accident. Tell him I won't take no for an answer. A private room, as of—' he looked at Monsieur Feingold, hissed '*Mercredi de la semaine prochaine?*' Then went on with it: 'Wednesday of next week. Hotel rooms for two – people—' he pointed at Madame Feingold, and young Feingold 'for as long as necessary. All bills to be sent to me. I'll have them into Boston airport by Wednesday morning. Tell Tom Blick to have an ambulance there, waiting – with a good eye man aboard. That's it, Bets. You call me tomorrow at the Hotel Majestic in Cannes. That's where I'll be. Yes, yes. Now get on to it, please! Drop everything. This girl will lose *both* eyes, Bets, if we don't hop. Bless you, dear!'

Then to the operator. 'Give me the charges on that call as soon as you possibly can.' And hung up. They were all staring at him. But only Gabrielle was crying. In that same warm, wonderful way he had so often seen Simone cry.

'If I have understood—' Monsieur Feingold got out.

But his son interrupted him: 'You have understood, Papa.

M'sieur Farrow proposes to send Rebecca to Boston, Massachusetts, to a great eye specialist, accompanied by me – probably because I speak English – and Maman – and pay absolutely all our expenses. The expenses for everything. But what even *I* do not understand is – why.'

John Farrow stared at him. Then he said, slowly, sadly:

'Call it reparations. *Blutgelt.* Blood money. M'sieur Feingold, you were here in Provence during nineteen forty-three and nineteen forty-four weren't you?'

'Yes. In forty-three at Vence – thanks to the Italians. In nineteen forty-four hiding out – and starving – being kept alive by handouts from the few good Goyim – who dared. Wait! I do not blame the others! It calls for real courage to help a man and his family when you've seen other people – shot – for doing even less. Those were – bad times – terrible times, M'sieur Farrow. Why do you ask?'

'And did you, during those times hear the propaganda broadcasts of Dalton Ross?'

'*Oui. Elles étaient très vilaines.*'

'Well Ross – was a relative of mine. A very, very close relative. He practically brought me up. And as *un gosse* – I adored him. And, last of all, although none of you wanted to believe me before I fought all across this section in the same FFI group with a man named Anton Rabinowski and with – my girl. Because I'm sure you know that a good many Frenchwomen belonged to Resistance réseaux in those days. Including a number of juives françaises who had decided that the death of a cornered cat is infinitely more noble than the supine and will-less dying of a whole flock of sheep, and who proceeded to demonstrate to men just what bravery is. Like – my Simone. Who when I was wounded, stood above my unconscious carcass and fought off the whole damned Nazi army before she would let them take me. Who on another occasion, when we were being bombed and strafed from the air, threw herself across me, and took in her own tender flesh the bomb splinters that might have killed me. For whom I was going to embrace your religion in order to marry. Go to Israel with her. Then she – disappeared. I have reasons to believe that even that may have been Dalton Ross's fault. So I ask you to do me the very great favour of accepting this small and humble gesture. It will lift a great weight from off my heart.'

'Oh,' Gabrielle said, 'accept it! I, too, ask it! Accept it, please!'

'Very well,' Monsieur Feingold said with great dignity, managing that difficult feat of receiving a favour without seeming either a mendicant or servile. 'I accept it. What you do is right and just. But very rare. There are very few men like you, my friend!'

'Thank you. You, young M'sieur Feingold, will have to attend to passports and so forth. Your tickets will be waiting for you at Air France's offices in Cannes by tomorrow afternoon. When you've picked them up, come see me at the Majestic. I'll give you the necessary letters of introduction, and of credit. That's all. Now, if you'll excuse me I must—'

'No, wait!' Gabrielle said. 'John – buy me *that*.' She pointed to a heart-shaped gold locket, on a long and heavy gold chain.

'It is yours, madame!' Monsieur Feingold said, 'a present from the house.'

'*Non*,' Gabrielle said, 'it is necessary that *he* buy it for me. I could buy it, myself. But that it is a gift from *him*, from *mon* Jean, the first gift, is the whole point.'

'Then the price to you, M'sieur Farrow is ten dollars.'

'*Même pas ça*,' Gabrielle said. 'He must buy it for me, and he must pay its actual cost. Or else the occasion loses significance, M'sieur Feingold. On another occasion, you may give me something. When we invite you to the Bar Mitzvah of our first son. But not now. John, please!'

'Wrap it up,' John Farrow said.

They walked back to the car. But instead of getting into it, as he held the door open, Gabrielle stood there. Then she said in a voice that was both hushed and a little strangled:

'John, did you do that to impress me?'

He stared at her, said, 'What do *you* think, Gabrielle?'

'I think that you only call me Gabrielle when you're angry at me. And I *know* you weren't trying to impress me. You did it for – for Simone. I wasn't even *there*. And now I wonder if I'll *ever* be. John – *must* you check in at the Majestic?'

'Yes,' he said bleakly, 'until I know – and you know, what I really think; what I truly feel. Get in, will you, Gabby?'

She got into the car. But when he too got in, she took his face between two hands that were steel under velvet, and turned it to hers. Inside of thirty seconds he knew he had never been kissed like that before. Not by anyone. Not even by – Simone.

He tore his mouth from hers at last; gasped:

'My God!'

She was crying. She was smiling at him; but at the same time, she was crying.

'The agreement is off, John. As far as I'm concerned – all off. I have no intention of respecting it for one second longer. So you can stay – and fight. Or run. The choice is up to you. Which will it be?'

He looked at her, and his gaze was grave and sorrowing. She didn't know he was trying to bury or exorcize – a ghost. Not very successfully when the ghost's own face – or its exact duplicate – hung there centimetres from his own.

'I'll stay,' he said harshly, 'but on one condition, Gabrielle. I want your solemn promise that you will never mention *my* name, or boast of this conquest – if you consider it as such! – to any future lover.'

'John,' she said quietly, 'I don't believe you know what you're letting yourself in for. And that's not fair. So hear this, darling: this is *it*. There aren't going to be any more lovers. For either of us. I plan to be most disgustingly faithful. And I hope you'll have enough – consideration for me – not to – to break my heart that way. This is – for life. Legal or not. However, whatever. So if you don't think you can stand me, you'd better say so – now.'

He sat there staring at her.

'Say it!' she said. 'What *are* you thinking *now*?'

He sighed; said: 'That I'd better move you over to the Majestic. It's too late to call Betty back and switch that call over to the Carlton, now.'

He put his hand out to turn the key in the ignition; but her long, astonishingly strong fingers closed over his wrist.

'Don't,' she said. 'Not yet. Before you start this little red apple barge off, there's one thing I want of you. . . .'

'And that is?'

'Tell me – you love me. That is – if you honestly – can. If you can't, don't. But if you can't don't worry. For all that means is I'll have to work at it a little harder.'

'What do you want me to say?'

'*Meaning* it: "I love you, Gabby." '

He grinned at her; said:

'I love you, Gabby.'

'Now, repeat it. Over and over again. All the way down to

Cannes. So you'll get it straight. So you won't get mixed up. Confuse *me* with *anyone* else.'

'Don't think there's much danger of that!' he said.

'All right then, tell me: who am I?'

'Genghis Gabby. Gabby the Terrible,' he said.

15

When the phone rang the next morning at eight o'clock, and the operator said: 'Boston, Massachusetts, calling, a person to person call for Attorney John Farrow . . .' he knew it wasn't Betty calling him, but very likely Tom Blick, himself. He glanced at Gabby. She didn't move. She was sleeping so soundly that it was difficult to even see her breathe. That made him feel good. That made him feel very good. 'Creeping senility hasn't quite caught up with me yet!' he thought. He said: 'Attorney Farrow speaking. One moment, operator! I'll take the call in the next room.'

He got out of bed very carefully. Crossed to the little sitting-room, and carefully closed the double doors. Picked up the other phone, said: 'Go ahead, please. . . .'

'Here's your party, Dr Blick,' the operator said.

'John!' Tom Blick's big voice came booming over the wire just as though there weren't three thousand miles and more between them; 'What's this all about? Jesus, boy – I hate to disappoint you, but I've got 'em sleeping in the linen closets now, and—'

'Tom, will you shut up, and listen?' John Farrow said. Then he explained matters, swiftly, succinctly, clearly.

'Why the dirty, murderous bastards!' Tom Blick said. 'All right, John. You win. I'll just throw somebody out, that's all. One of these fat, rich old dames with nothing wrong but an overdeveloped imagination. They keep the joint open, really. But for a case like this – gladly. I'll have the ambulance waiting. Got the flight number, yet? No? When you have it, phone me, will you? Okay, John! Keep your nose clean, will you?'

Carefully John hung up the phone. Tiptoed back towards the

bedroom. Opened the door a crack. Gabrielle was still sleeping. She hadn't even changed her position. Quietly he crossed to the bathroom. Showered, shaved, cleaned his teeth. He slipped into a pair of swimming trunks, put on his blue terrycloth robe, stuck his feet into sandals.

As he crossed the bedroom, he paused, stared at her. The only defect she had was an appendix scar. He knew the operation had been done quite some time ago, because it was a high, lateral cut, visible, and much too long. Modern doctors made a lap incision, below bikini level. But apart from that, her body was even more of a miracle than he'd guessed it would be. She was deeply tanned all over. There were no white areas at all.

'Sun lamp?' he'd asked her.

'On my rooftop. I'm the helicopter pilots' darling,' she'd laughed: 'they hover over my place all day long!'

He stood there, wanting to wake her, to hear her voice, see her smile. But he knew enough about women to realize that waking one up at 8.30 a.m. was pure unmitigated sadism, so he went quietly through the door and to the lift, taking his briefcase with him.

Once downstairs he took advantage of one of the things that made European de luxe hotels worth what they cost you: that you can arrange nearly everything you need to without stirring beyond their grounds.

Yes, the concierge would procure him three first-class tickets – aller et retour – from Nice to Boston – a night flight out of Nice to arrive in Boston Wednesday morning, next. The return date, open. The tickets in the names of Monsieur Feingold, sa mère Madame Feingold, et sa soeur Madame Rosen. No, he didn't know the initials. The tickets to be billed to him, Attorney Farrow.

'They should be waiting at Air France's offices this afternoon for M'sieur Feingold, *fils*, to pick them up,' John Farrow said. 'Now I'm going to have breakfast beside the swimming pool. Would it be possible to send me a bilingual French-English secretary to take dictation while I'm enjoying the sun?'

'But of course, Mr Farrow!' the concierge said.

Half an hour later, he was lying beside the pool, three-quarters asleep, when a crisp British voice said:

'Attorney Farrow?'

He opened his eyes and gazed up a pair of female legs

designed by a middle-aged lecher in a fine flight of utterly salacious fancy. Above the legs was a bikini that covered, and that barely, the absolute minimum; above the bikini were unbelievable areas of sunbrowned flesh, parts of which were crowded into an accessory of the bikini – he was decidedly relieved that she hadn't worn a monokini, as many girls with this kind of a figure do on the Côte – and had overflowed. Then he saw the notepad in her hands.

'And you also type?' he said solemnly.

'Sorry, sir!' she said. 'It's the rule of the hotel. The idea is that a girl with clothes on at the poolside attracts too much attention. Arouses curiosity. Which, we presume, M'sieur le client wishes to avoid.'

'Right,' he said. 'But how is M'sieur le client ever going to remember what he started to dictate with his blood pressure soaring past the danger point . . .'

'That,' she said coolly, 'I am permitted to doubt, am I not, attorney? For last night while you were dining I had the good fortune to see – madame.'

He grinned at her, said: 'Translation?'

'That if you, Attorney Farrow, were in any danger of a stroke, or suffered from hypertension, or a heart condition, you would have been dead long since. This is not only my opinion, but is enthusiastically concurred to by the entire male staff of the hotel.'

'Thank them for me,' he said, then: 'Okay, Ma'moiselle Bombshell, let's get to work.'

It was evident at once that her looks had little to do with her getting the job. She was effortlessly professional and expert. Her long fingers made her pencil fly, taking dictation in shorthand. The only thing that broke her stride was when he switched over and began dictating translations of the letters of credit and introduction he was providing young Feingold, into French. Then she stared at him with that expression of almost pained astonishment that comes over the countenance of any French person who ever at hearing an American speak even comprehensible French, not to mention the absolute mastery of the language that John Farrow displayed. But he'd be damned if he were going to explain *that* any more. So he said quietly: 'Take that briefcase along, will you? In it, you'll find my professional stationery. Type the letters and their translations on it. Then bring them here for me to sign. If I've gone by then, leave them and the briefcase with the concierge. And thank you, very much – both for the exhibition – and the job!'

'De rien, m'sieur!' she said and left him there.

But before she had reached the lobby's door, Gabrielle came out of it. Their paths crossed. And Gabby's eyes re-invented the Laser beam. Broiled the flesh completely off her bones.

He watched Gabby's progress towards where he lay through half-closed eyes. And his feelings became curiously mixed. About three-quarters of them were unfeigned delight; but the other quarter was decided – and decidedly angry – shock.

Part of his anger was directed at himself. He had always considered himself both an urbane and a civilized man. Now Gabby was convincingly proving to him that he was neither.

'Why you primitive old bastard!' he told himself. 'Can't take it, can you? On that secretary a bikini like this was all right, better than all right, a treat for male eyes; but on *your* woman, no. You don't want all these horny old swine – and even hornier *young* swine (Ah, there's the rub, isn't it, baldy bean? There, the belt squeezes, doesn't it, potgut? That exercises your early warning system, does it not, grand-père?) gazing upon *this* much of Gabby, do you? Gazing and drooling, damn 'em! Holy Jesus! I'd have sworn it wasn't even possible to make a bikini smaller than the one my secretary for the moment had on; but this one – Lord God! This one is pure venial sin!'

Gabrielle's bikini consisted of a tiny triangle of metallic green cloth – the exact colour of her eyes – fore, and a slightly larger one aft; the two of them being held – precariously – on to Gabby by four ('Count 'em!' he raged; 'four!') elastic cords that left all of Gabby, except her exact front, and her exact rear, visible. The upper part of it cheated on the monokini, or topless concept, very, very slightly. He didn't even know what term to apply to it. To call it a brassière or a *soutien-gorge* was utterly ridiculous, for not only did it provide Gabby's small, firm breasts with absolutely no support whatsoever, but, as far as he could see, had no visible means of even supporting itself; or staying attached to the close-to microscopic areas of Gabby to which it clung, apparently by osmosis, and – theoretically – covered. It was clearly made up of two round and slight conical patches of the same green cloth as the rest of the bikini, each of them the exact size, give or take a millimetre either way, of an

American half dollar. As she came closer, he decided – correctly, it later turned out – that they had been *glued* to Gabby. The only other way she could have kept them where they were would have been to use a needle and thread to sew them to two exceptionally tender portions of her living flesh, and that he rejected at once as being impractical, not to mention hideously painful.

And he was suddenly sure – with a curious mingling of pride and anger – that no other woman he had ever known, except of course, her exact duplicate, Simone, could have worn that bikini with impunity. For, to even dare put on that species of a *cache-sexe*, G-string, loin cloth, that the lower part of it was, every single one of them, including pale blondes like Candace, would have had to shave; and to flaunt those two micro-miniature affronts to the lingering apehood in every human male that supposedly comprised its upper portion would have required their likewise being blessed with the absolutely marvellous pectoral formation, as well as those nipples smaller than an adolescent girl's that Gabby, at thirty-seven years of age, still miraculously retained.

Even to put that outfit on a body the colour of pale copper, and top it all with a mass of heavy, snow-white hair was to enter into the terrain of deliberate provocation, John Farrow realized. And to make matters worse – if worse were possible – she had placed the gold chain he had bought her yesterday, around her waist, so that the heart-shaped locket dangled down the front of her, to catch every male eye, and draw it irresistibly towards a portion of her at which every male eye was already gazing longingly.

At that moment, John Farrow would have cheerfully strangled her with his bare hands.

She dropped to her knees with boneless grace beside him; gave him quite seriously that line out of Victorian melodrama:

'Just who was that *woman*, John?'

'*Ma secrétaire*. Go put something on, damnit! Like a bikini say.'

'But this is—' she began; then she laughed, freely, gaily. 'Oh, John, how happy you have made me! You – you're jealous! You actually are!'

'Say I don't feel up to having to rescue you from a gang-bang,' he growled. 'Jesus, Gabby, you'd be more decent stark naked!'

'Then I'll take it off,' she teased, and began to tug at those elastic cords. 'And just what, may I ask, is a gang-bang, my love? That's an Americanism that eludes me.'

'Mass rape,' John supplied. 'Seriously, Gabby, this outfit's outrageous. It's wrong in the same way that keeping on a garter belt, long black stockings, and a half bra while making love is. That is, it borders on perversion.'

'Oh,' she said, 'then I'll go change it, now. I have never worn it before. I – I bought it, for you. It was to be my secret weapon. If I couldn't get you any other way, I mean. And I only put it on when I looked out our window and saw you chatting so cosily with that gorgeous naked creature!'

'She had on a hell of a lot more than you do now,' he said.

'I know. But then she's far, far younger – and *much* prettier than I am.'

'Younger, I grant you. Prettier isn't possible. To me, anyhow. That's the way I'm queer. For girls like you, I mean.'

'I thank you for that, John,' she said quietly. Her voice sounded odd. Looking up, he saw that she was crying.

'Gabby!' he said.

'Forgive me, my love. It's just that – that – wait, I'll go put on my one-piece bathing suit first, and then—'

'No,' he said, 'since everyone has already seen what you ate for supper last night, you can't shock 'em any more than you already have. Besides if you put on a one-piece they might run amok from sheer disappointment. Come lie down beside me.'

She did so, and he saw her eyes. They were both red and swollen.

'You've been crying quite a lot,' he said accusingly. 'Mind telling me why, Gabrielle? Not that girl, surely! She was just the hotel's stenographer, I asked them to send her to take some dictation. The bikini, according to her, is mandatory for poolside work.'

'No,' she whispered, 'not that girl. It did shock me to see you flirting with her at first; but then I realized that you'd never do it so openly if it meant anything. Oh – I don't know, John! I – I'm just depressed, I suppose. The morning-after blues, shall we say?'

He raised himself up on one elbow, stared at her.

'You – you're regretting – last night, Gabrielle?' he said.

'Frankly, yes. And not only – last night. I'm regretting having come down here at all, having pursued you so shamelessly and—'

His eyes went absolutely black with hurt. So black that she surged up wildly, threw both arms around his neck and kissed him in that matchless way she had, so long, and with such frank and obvious passion that a group of teenagers on the other side of the pool started to clap their hands and cheer.

'*Vive la génération plus ancienne!*' they cried.

John grinned at them, said:

'One isn't yet dead. Not entirely, anyhow.' Then he turned back to Gabby. She was crying worse than ever. He said: 'Please, Gabby – what's wrong?'

'Those kids,' she sobbed, 'they – they're so beautiful John! You realize that if we'd met when – when I was twenty, we could have – a – a son that age?'

'Or a daughter,' he said gravely. 'What's the matter? They exercise your maternal instincts?'

'Terribly. That's the one thing I've missed most out of life, John. I've all but stopped visiting Jeanne – I mean your Marie Claire – because seeing those gorgeous kids of hers hurts too much. I'm exactly the kind of woman who in other times would be always pushing a huge belly before her until she got too old; who'd be surrounded by battalions of gosses – all screaming and fighting and wrecking things – and – and d'you know what, John? I would have been so goddamned happy!'

He put out his hand and stroked her snowy hair.

'It's not too late, Gabby,' he said.

'Yes, it is. Much too late, John. No woman in her right mind starts her *first* child at thirty-seven. Her tenth, yes. But her first, no. It would kill her eight times out of ten. Any gynaecologist will tell you that. But even so I – I'd chance it, if so many *other* things weren't wrong. John – let me say – I'm sorry. That I – I apologize for the – *awful* way I behaved last night. Even – in bed – there are limits – or there should be. I'd told myself that if by some – some glorious miracle – I were ever yours – I'd be sweet – and gentle and – and tender! Instead – Oh John! – I mauled you about fearfully! Loosed the famished bitch on you! Of course it – it has been three whole years – No! it's been a whole bleak miserable lifetime, waiting for you! For *my* man. *Mon homme*. The only man in the universe, as far as I'm concerned, and I – I—'

She bent her head, and cried bitterly, terribly.

He put out his hand and stroked that snow-white hair, again.

'Now, Gabby,' he said fondly. 'I grant you that you were a trifle – athletic – at first; but I assure you it has no importance at all. When people love one another they accept variations of mood, of intensity of passion, easily enough, and—'

She looked up at him, said, sobbing the words:

'When people *love* one another, John! As I love *you*. But as you don't, and can't, and never will love me! So – when our two weeks are up, my love, I shall leave you, and live the rest of my life – upon – upon this memory! Because – she's – too strong for me. Even – dead, your Simone is too strong for me! Oh God, John, I—'

'Gabrielle,' he said sternly, 'I think you'd better explain yourself. In a way that makes sense, at that. Come on, get a grip upon yourself. Tell me.'

'All right,' she sighed. 'Last night, after I'd committed seventeen kinds of – of violation – upon you – upon your generous willingness to accommodate me – to ease me, you fell asleep. You – you looked so tired! So utterly worn out that I swore to myself I'd let you sleep – let you rest. But I couldn't. I simply couldn't. For the truth of the matter is that women are far, far sexier than men!'

'That I doubt,' he said.

'Don't, John. It's true. Men are more easily aroused; but they are even more easily satisfied. Women can *stay* – in a state of anguished desire for days and nights on end. And—'

'You're saying I disappointed you,' he said sadly.

'No! God, no! Edythe – didn't even begin – to describe what you're like. I'm not talking about – mere skill, John. Quite a few men are skilful enough, these days, I suppose. Turns *me* off. That "Look how good I am at it, darling!" business. I am not a life-sized mechanical device who needs only to have the proper buttons pushed, the indicated switches thrown, certain knobs twisted in the correct sequence to respond exactly on schedule, as desired! Nor am I a – an animal – to be ridden, goaded, whipped, spurred into a presumably ecstatic climax, you know. I'm a woman – quirky, sensitive, endlessly subjective – who responds to *you*. To the man you are. To your total personality, not just your fine, strong body. I have no doubt at all

'Oh God!' he groaned. 'Here we go again! Gabby, listen to me—!'

'No,' she said, 'I won't. You don't, you can't, you never will. So forget it. John, I'm serious about the job. I'm going to *have* to resign from mine. Something has come up. Something terrible. Two of our people – intelligence people, John, were murdered just before I left Paris. Another one – in London. So we've been ordered to retaliate. We're supposed to liquidate El Fatah's and Black September's and – a few others' agents – wherever we find them. They gave me – a gun. I'm good with a gun. And a knife. And karate – and all the rest of the bloody, futile, murderous business—'

She looked at him, went on.

'One of my incentives for pursuing you. Yes, I admit it! Motives – human motives are never unmixed. I thought I could – combine the joy of being – at least your mistress – your wife was too much to even hope for – with a neat escape from becoming – a murderess. So since I cannot be anything to you, at least help me, John. Some of your friends in London – or in California – but not New York—'

'Why not, New York, Gabrielle?' he said.

'I'd see – you – too – often. I couldn't bear it.'

He turned to her, took her face between his hands, leaned forward and kissed her mouth.

'John—' she whispered, brokenly, 'don't – torment me – it's most unkind!'

'Gabby,' he said, 'will you marry me? As soon as I can arrange it? Here in France that means twenty days, a month, but—'

She shook her head; said: 'No, John.'

He bent his head; looked up again, said:

'Then *ma 'tite maîtresse*? For the duration? As long as you care to remain with me. . . .?'

'That's – twelve days, John. All that's left of my vacation.'

He turned to her; his face tightening with real anger.

'Then we're wasting time,' he said harshly. 'Come on!'

'Come on – where, John?' she said.

'Upstairs. To our room. To bed,' he said. 'You grant me – graciously – twelve days. So I mean to make the best of them!'

He got up; put out his hand to her; said:

'Come on, damnit!'

She got up shyly, took his arm. Went with him through the lobby doors. Entered the lift. Stood there achingly apart from him, and staring up into his eyes. And hers, he saw, were big with something close to terror.

Once inside the room, she lifted that heavy locket in her hand, said:

'John – don't make me take this off, please.'

'Why not?' he said. 'Could get in the way, you know. Even – hurt!'

'Don't care. I – I swore I never would again. Until the day I die. I even bathe with it on. I tested it first, with a piece of cardboard inside, to see if it were waterproof. It is – quite. So, having robbed me of so much – my identity, my pride of womanhood, your love, let me keep at least – my relic, my souvenir. *D'accord*, John?'

'All right. But what is it? What's in it, Gabby?'

'*You*,' she said, and opened it.

He stared into his own face, nine or ten years younger; said:

'My God! Where on earth—'

'A photographer in a *boîte*. You were with Edythe. That's why – it's cut so strangely. I had to scissor her arms from around your neck. Jacques et Raoul and a couple of high-class *poules* were in it, too. I cut them off, and threw them away—'

'But how did you get Edythe to give it to you?' he said.

'Didn't. Memorized the number on the back of it, when she showed it to me – triumphantly, damn her! Went to the *boîte* and ordered a dozen from the photographer. Including a huge enlargement – with Edythe's greedy arms air-brushed out. I have that one in Paris. John—'

'Yes, Gabby?'

'Let's – don't. Not now. I – I'm too afraid. I could never understand that suicidal mania of Simone's – but now – I do – and—'

He was staring at her.

'It's really quite simple, John,' she said. 'Jeanne Lefèvre – Marie Claire – told me *all* about you two.'

'Marie Claire didn't *know* all about us two,' he said.

'More than you think. From Simone, herself – and someone else – someone who knew the whole story. John – let's go back to the pool. I'll put on my one-piece. It's black, chic – very modest, and—'

'No,' he said. 'I want you. Now.'

She bowed her head. Whispered:

'All right, John. *Ton esclave t'écoute. Et t'obéit.*'

He caught her by the shoulder. Whirled her around to face him. Said, his voice slow, quiet, almost deadly:

'*Never* imitate her, Gabrielle! Never!'

She stood looking into his eyes, said:

'Don't – abuse me, John. Don't – hurt me. You've – hurt me enough, shamed me, enough, humiliated me, enough, already. Don't – take your anger out on me – this way. I will not tolerate it.'

He didn't move. He stood there looking at her a long, slow time. Sighed. Said: 'How little you know me, Gabby!'

Then he turned, and walked over to the closet where his suits were hung. Took down a blue linen one. Went over to the bureau, opened the drawers, began to take out a shirt, socks, underwear, a handkerchief.

She said: 'John—'

'Yes, Gabby?' he said, tossing her name backwards over his shoulder.

'Are you – leaving – me?' she whispered. 'Now? Today? Is this the place the – world – stops? Where – *I* – get off?'

He turned his back to her, stripped off his swim trunks, pulled on a pair of jockey shorts, an undershirt of nylon mesh; said, still without turning: 'You figure it out, Gabrielle!'

Almost at once, he was sorry. 'I am behaving badly,' he thought. 'Like some stupid kid, who—'

But when he turned towards her, she was already gone. He heard, sharply, the bolt slam home on the inside of the bathroom door. He stood there staring at it, a little worriedly, thinking:

'Women! I hope she hasn't got some silly idea in her head. Hell, probably only wants to make pipi or –' then he heard the crash of breaking glass; heard her say: '*Mon Dieu*!'

He was before the door with one single leap. Stood there shaking. Said, snarling the words:

'Open the door, Gabrielle! Open it, goddamnit! Or else I'll break it down! You hear me, Gabrielle? I said—'

The bolt slid back. Shyly, softly. She was sitting on the edge of the bathtub. At her feet were the remains of a small bottle: a thousand slivers, pieces, bits of glass. Amid the slivers were a number of small white tablets. They were dusted all over with powdered glass. Then his trained eye hit upon the one meaningful detail: there were no bits of paper amid the glass. That bottle had no label. It had never had one.

He put out his strong, bony right hand, and caught her by the hair. Yanked powerfully. She came to her feet, her green eyes wide. He caught her by one shoulder, and by the back of the neck, and bent her brutally over the wash-basin. Took his hand off her shoulder and pushed his index and second finger into her mouth, down her throat, moved them about until she vomited.

'How many of those damned things did you take, Gabrielle?' he raged. 'Tell me! How many?'

'*Tu es une brute!*' she sobbed. '*Un lûche! Un—*'

Then she saw his face, his eyes.

She said his name. Tentatively. Not yet, or not quite daring to believe. 'John—' Drawn out. The monosyllable stretched, prolonged. Watching his mouth, his eyes. Then again: 'John!' but sharper, quicker now; having almost the quality of joy, of wonder. Then whispering the words, slowly, shyly, softly: 'John – you – you *love* me. You *really* love me. Why you – you're shaking. You – you're trembling. Oh, my love. Oh my dearest darling love!'

'I asked you a question, Gabrielle! How many—'

'None. I didn't have time.'

'Don't lie to me, Gabby!'

'Gabby!' she laughed; crying at the same time; laughing and crying, which was a wonderful thing to see; beautiful and wonderful, and – crippling; stabbing into him, robbing him of strength: 'That's better! That's much better! Oh my darling. I do love you, so!'

He peered down worriedly into that April skyscape of a face, said:

'Jesus! You scared ten whole years off the ass-end of my life!'

'Now aren't we *modest*!' she mocked him, her warm, wide mouth, tear-wet still, and salt, making that wry grimace of near despair that true women feel when the men they cannot help but love display the male human animal's almost infinite capacity for obtuseness, vanity, and folly. 'Tell me, my love, how do you keep up with your victims? All the women who *kill* themselves over you? Do you have a little *black* book? With their farewell notes arranged by alphabetical order? And pressed flowers between the pages?'

'Oh for God's sake, Gabby! You mean to tell me that these pills—'

'Aren't poisonous? Of course not, you insufferable egotist! Besides, you've been – an agent, yourself. What did *you* carry in those days?'

'A vial of potassium cyanide. The kind you put in your mouth; bite and—'

'You're dead in thirty seconds, flat. The same kind I always carry. You'd have never got a chance to ram your fingers down my throat, darling. I'd have been gone before you could have got here.'

'Still,' he said, 'you locked the door. Then I heard that bottle break, and—'

'You were quite right. I was looking for the *other*, when I knocked these over.'

'Gabrielle—'

'Oh, I'm only putting you on, my love! I shouldn't do it *that* way. I'd write a long and tragic note to all the newspapers, then cut my throat quite messily on the stairs of the American Embassy!'

'Gabrielle, I'm going to *hit* you in a minute!'

'With what? The little black book? The one with all the heartbreaking farewell notes in it, and the musty, half decayed, pressed flowers?'

'Oh Christ!' he said, 'oh God. What's the use?'

'John,' she said, 'I – I'm a little hysterical, you know. Joy does that to me. I – I was so far down. So – defeated. So whipped. Humiliated. Shamed. Then – you stood there – white as a ghost – and *shook* – because you thought *que j'avais fait une bêtise* – a stupidity. John, *never* leave me. Because I *would*. Now, I would. Now I really couldn't stand it.'

'Gabby,' he said, 'you give me that goddamned vial! Or else I'll never sleep another night!'

She looked at him, her eyes aglow, said:

'No, John. I'll keep it for the day you really decide to leave me.'

'Then you can give it to me. Or throw it away. Because you'll never need it.'

'Not even – the next time – you take this delighted – carcass in your arms – and then break its heart by calling it – Simone?'

'Get it straight, Gabby! I love *you*. I probably wouldn't even recognize Simone now. No – it's – *you* I love all right. *You*.'

'Prove it,' she said. She was smiling at him. It was a very perverse and wicked smile, alight with delighted mischief.

'Prove it how?'

'Make love to me. *Here*. On the bathroom floor. Amid the pills and powdered glass. . . .'

'Hell, no! I don't want to ruin my knees and elbows, not to mention your nice little tail. As the elderly Chinese gentleman said, "Looks like it's good for a few years yet!" Gabby, tell me: What *are* those pills, anyhow?'

'Oh,' she said airily, 'something the embassy doctor gave me – for my nerves. And to prevent – localized swelling.'

'If you've got the prescription, I'll send out for more. Those are ruined, you know. You'd never be able to get enough of that glass out of them to make them safe to take.'

'Doesn't matter,' she said softly, 'I don't need them, now. They've served their purpose. Demonstrated to me that what has to happen, is going to. If it hasn't already, as it probably has. Which would prove that I am a Levy, just as you claim. We never miss. Family trait. Or racial. Or both.'

'Gabby, you're not making much sense, you know!'

'Do I ever? But this time, yes, my love! I'm making, beautiful, beautiful sense. At last. What *were* we talking about?'

'Those pills. Those goddamned pills!'

'Oh, yes. Y'know, John, dearest – I may even have dropped them on purpose. For in some ways accidents are *never* accidents, really. They're responses to hidden compulsions. I didn't mean to drop that flask. But maybe my *hand* did. Because the – the body quite often knows more than the mind. You see, it got here first. It's older. It was prowling around – fighting, hunting, eating, making love – No! Just plain screwing – because to make love, you *need* the mind.'

'There you have a point. Go on with it, Gabby. Even when you make no sense at all, you still do, somehow. There's a curious interior logic in *everything* you say. Interior and intricate. Let's see if I can follow you.'

'I *hope* not! God how I hope you can't! But I don't need to worry, do I? You'd be the first man in history *ever* to follow female reasoning. Where was I? Oh yes! I was saying that the body was here on earth aeons ago, before what we call the mind – the higher, cerebral function that writes poetry, composes music, works mathematics, invents machinery – and decides between what's right and what's wrong – ever developed. *This* body, even. This dumb beast, ferociously female body, outraged at having its deepest instincts thwarted – by that upstart newcomer, that parvenu, arriviste, I call my mind – made my hand shake. A hand that *never* shakes! D'you know I was *the* best pistol shot of my entire promotion?'

'Trying to scare me, Gabby?' he said.

'There, you see!' she laughed delightedly. 'You *can't* follow me! Oh, John, I *do* love you so! Even when you're stupid, you're stupid in such a *nice* way!'

'Gabby, just what are you trying to tell me?'

'That I don't need these ruddy pills, that's all. They were – only a crutch anyhow. To lean on, so as not to have to stand up – and be counted among – women. Real women, I mean. The genuine, first-class article I've always wanted to be, instead of the erratic gabby fraud I am. The only real catch is that they – could even – kill me, now, John. By not existing. By not being there. But if they do – it will be a proud dying, my love! Facing my – any women's ultimate obligation. Tell me, will you cry? Will you weep for me?'

'Gabrielle!' he got out. 'Jesus H. Christ! Call Paris! Ask your doctor to mail you a copy of the prescription! If they're essential to your health, I—'

'But they're *not*, Silly One! They were supposed to be essential to my happiness, by keeping me – in a state of emotional – neutrality, say. But now, not even that's so. The only thing essential to *me*, to my life, my happiness, is *you*, John. Tell me, do you love me? Say it!'

'I love you, Gabrielle,' he said. 'You drive me out of my so-called mind, but I love you.'

'Good. Now go bring me a cardboard out of one of your shirts, will you, dearest? And a clothes brush. So I can sweep them up – glass and all. Flush them down the w.c. And good riddance for bad rubbish! Oh, don't look so worried! I'm better off without them. Truly I am!'

He brought her the clothes brush and the cardboard.

'Now,' she said, 'you go lie down. Wait for me. Take off that sexy underwear, first, though. You won't be needing it. You have to take care of – of my emotional stability, y'know.'

When she had finished sweeping up the pills and broken glass, she came back into the bedroom. He was stretched out on his stomach, face down, across the bed.

She grinned at him, said:

'Turn over! I want to *see* how much you love me!'

'Gabby, stop being outrageous, will you? I don't like it.'

She stared at him, said: 'Oh!' Her eyes darkened, became naked, uncertain, vulnerable.

'Don't look like that!' he said. 'Come. Sit down here. You've been explaining female psychology to me all morning. Turn about is fair play. And necessary. I think the first essential of male psychology is its possessiveness. Based, in the first place, before you even tell me so, on plain rut-dog sexual jealousy. And furthered by both the territorial instinct and the concept of property. If old Ugh-Bah I is going to leave his chieftain's symbols, the war club and the necklace made from the fangs of the sabre-tooth tiger, to Ugh-Bah II, he wants to make god-damned sure that Ugh-Bah II actually *is* his son. So chain the bitch to the inside doorpost, lest she stray, lest some other hairy, grunting, roaring male should mount her! Becoming a trifle more civilized, we *still* want our women to belong to us. But on a basis more flattering to our egos. *Wanting* to. Voluntarily. As you belong to me. At least I hope so. Do you?'

'Yes. But – not voluntarily. Not entirely, anyhow.'

'You mean you don't *want* to belong to me, Gabrielle?'

'As much, as fully, as hopelessly, as helplessly as I *do*; no, John. That goes beyond – love. That's a form of – of addiction; of even – slavery.'

'How can there be slavery without – a master, Gabrielle?' he said quietly. '*Mutual* enslavement adds up – to – to – no, not freedom; who wants it? – but a fortress raised against a hostile world. Not that corny expression of a few years back: "togetherness", but true union, fusion – being one. And as for being addicted to you: eyes, mouth, tits, tail, spirit, mind, joy, laughter – I'll cheerfully die of an overdose! Because there'll be no withdrawal symptoms. Not on *this* side, anyhow.'

'Nor on this,' she whispered, and kissed him. 'John, I – no. Go on with your philosophical dissertation, love!'

'All right. Apart from, and beyond mere possession, Gabby, a man has to believe what he's got is special. *Very* special. That nothing becomes him so much as his wife. A man, Gabby, *never* wants his woman to be his whore. Or even to act the part, jokingly. He wants, somehow, always – to be able to worship her. To believe *his* woman, wife – is truly his *better* half. Finer than he. Purer. Nobler.'

'And when she – *isn't*?' Gabrielle whispered.

'He does a Pygmalion job on her – or tries to.'

'Yes,' she said wryly, 'but – in reverse.'

'In reverse?'

'Yes, John – converts warm, living, panting, sweating, desirous flesh into ice-cold marble. Is *that* what you want of me: a rigid Galatea in a frozen pose, back up on that ruddy pedestal?'

'Hell no!' he laughed. 'I want you to stay – *you*. And to stay with *me* – always.'

She put out her hand and stroked his naked back, slowly, lingeringly.

'So you've really, truly decided not to leave me, John?' she said.

'Didn't have to decide. I never had any intention to – even when I was taking my clothes out of the closet. I told you I still had something to do. And since you – with a good bit of pig-headed co-operation on my part – were thoroughly spoiling my day, I'd decided to drive up to Tourette-sur-Loup. Something up there I want to see. Something that may give me a lead on – Dalton Ross.'

She put up her two hands; began to peel that caricature by gross understatement of a bikini off. Starting with the two coin-sized pieces of green metallic cloth that covered solely the nipples of her breasts. As each one came free, she made a grimace – the same kind of grimace that people make when they, or their doctors, strip off a piece of adhesive surgical tape.

'That's quite a trick,' he said. 'What do you call them, anyhow?'

'Pasties. Because they're pasted on, or rather glued. A contact glue that you have to renew every ten days or two weeks if you mean to swim, and not merely sunbathe. After testing to see whether you're allergic to it. I was to the first kind I tried. Gave me the most horrible blisters!'

She stood up, hooked her thumbs into those elastic cords, gave a brief, maddenly seductive wiggle; and the twin-linked triangles lay about her ankles.

'*Me voilà!*' she said. 'John—'

'What, Gabby?'

'Do you believe in – fate? In its inexorability, I mean?'

'Oh God!' he groaned, '*now* she wants to talk philosophy!'

'No. There's a connection. Be patient a minute, *mon amour*! And – and keep your hands off me, so I can, too. Be patient, I mean. Do you believe fate works by itself, or does one have to help it?'

'Depends. Come put your arms around me, Gabrielle!'

'No. Look, my love, I assisted fate, by pursuing you. And now – I may have assisted it even more, by something I – I forgot to do. I was out of practice, I suppose. Tell me, my love, shall we assist fate a little *more*?'

'To which end, *ma* Gabrielle?' he said.

'That we – stay together. Always. That we become – truly one. And that that one go on – in time. Shall we?'

'Yes. God, yes!' he said.

She bent and kissed him. Straightened up, her eyes aglow.

'How long is forty-eight hours, John?' she said.

'Two days – and two nights,' he said. 'Why, Gabrielle?'

'One day – and one night already gone,' she said sadly. 'But today – and tonight – and tomorrow also – as a precaution. That we stay *here*. That we don't leave this room. That we don't even get up. *D'accord*, mon Jean?'

He stared at her. Said: '*D'accord*. But *why*, Gabby? What on earth do you have in that weird and wonderful little head of yours?'

'To – make love to you. That's all. But – a marathon. Twenty-four hours – of making love. Think you can stand it, my darling?'

'Don't know,' he said, 'but I'll surely die happy trying!'

Four days past the day that Gabrielle's two weeks' vacation had been – or at least should have been – up, he was lying beside the pool, and contemplating with complacent satisfaction, the flatness of his belly. His incipient paunch had entirely disappeared. He was lean and tanned and fit, and almost indecently happy.

'I wonder what did it?' he thought, 'all the meals we managed to skip – or the fine excess of exercise? Both, likely. Now here's a new health fad, tailored to my measure! I've always known that screwing was fun; but nobody ever told me it's also good for you!'

Then he saw the boton, the page boy, coming towards him. The boy had a slate in his hands. On it had been written in white chalk: *'Attention, Mme Betrand! Communication Télèphonique de Paris.'*

He beckoned the boy closer, said to him:

'Madame is upstairs in our room, five-seventy. Tell the *standardiste* to put the call through to her up there.'

An hour later Gabrielle came down. She was wearing the new, much more discreet bikini that he had bought her. It did absolutely nothing for her figure, but, then, it didn't need to. 'Women,' he thought, 'whose bodies need compression, uplift, or support, shouldn't wear bikinis. To wear one, a girl has not only to be perfect, but to know it and be proud of it. Like my Gabby.' He looked at her face as she came towards him. 'I wonder what's eating her?' he thought.

Because that something was wrong, that she was exceedingly nervous, was immediately clear to him. In the last ten days, he had got to know her very well indeed. 'And,' he added fondly, 'the more I know her, the better I *like* her. Loving a woman's no trick. But liking them quite often is; even the ones you love. Hell, I went right on loving Candace for almost a year after I couldn't stand her!'

He put up his hand to Gabrielle; drew her down beside him; kissed her mouth.

Her lips were ice. They tasted salt. He glanced at her eyes. But if she had been crying, she had gone to some pains to conceal the fact. Used an astringent eye-wash, likely.

'What did you tell the embassy?' he said. 'To go to hell, I hope!'

She stared at him blankly, but, somehow, not quite blankly enough.

'The – embassy?' she said.

'Yes. Your call from Paris. That was the embassy, wasn't it?'

She put out her hand, let it rest on his forehead; smiled at him.

'You've been lying in the sun far too long, my love,' she said.

It was beautifully done. Smooth, practiced. But he lay there with the vile green taste of nausea rising in his throat, and all his early warning signals ringing in his gut, in that rawly sensitive area in his solar plexus that had never recovered from the war, from the damage done it by three long years of merely trying to stay alive.

Because she was lying to him. After a two-week honeymoon beyond even his capacity for dreaming, she was lying to him. Coolly. Expertly. With malice aforethought.

He lay there without moving. Even smiled at her. His insides were screaming. His guts were coming apart. But he smiled at her. He didn't argue, tell her he *knew* about the call. Because that would be to blow it, and he had no intention of blowing it. One intelligence operative was facing another now. 'I may be out of practice; but don't underestimate me, Gabrielle!' he raged inside his mind. He said, lazily: 'Thought I heard the boton paging you. Didn't come close enough for me to see his board, though. Must have been for someone else—'

'It must have been,' she agreed, only a hair too quickly. 'No one called *me*, that's for sure.' She gave, beautifully, that curiously girlish gurgle of laughter. 'I seem to have gone rather far out on a limb, for you, John, dearest. All the types in Paris who still had hopes have already scratched me off their lists, you may be sure. Especially those with honourable intentions. You've besmirched my good name beyond repair my darling! Half of Paris knows I'm a fallen woman by now . . . so tell me, what do you plan to do about it, John? About – *me*?'

'The correct, the honourable thing, of course,' he said stiffly, parodying her archaic Victorianisms. He stared at her, thinking: 'Professional? Or – personal?'

He examined the two in that order. There was, as she had already pointed out to him on the day they met, nothing that her, or any other government, could hope to pry out of him. His isolation from the current powers that be in Washington was all but complete. Nor was there any conceivable way that they could use him. In Paris, the Gaullists were slipping fast. Too many scandals – all of them financial, and hence the kind that hurt; since who was screwing whom, was, in the French capital, a theme for yawning over it – that had already made the coming to power of a Communist-Socialist coalition in the not too remote future anything but doubtful. Therefore that he still had an in – on the sous-secrétariat level, say – with the Gaullists was of steadily diminishing importance these days.

A lover, then. A lover elderly enough to be goaded into action by the threat that even a balding, fifty-four-year-old New York lawyer of, at best trifle more than comfortable means, offered his possession of Gabby; and hence, by definition an exceedingly wealthy man. Or why else should *she* be interested?

He said: 'Gabby, seriously, how could anyone know about *us* in Paris? Jacques and Raoul wouldn't talk. And I can't see *your* broadcasting any previous intentions you may have had to hop into the hay with me to your girl friends at the embassy. . . .'

'Thanks for that, John! I am not exactly a fool. But as a matter of fact it *is* known. We made last week's *France Dimanche*. I'll show you the cutting tonight. Do you care? I don't, particularly. I've done some things that were stupid, and some others that were wrong; but I don't include having sexual relations with the man I love under either category.'

'*France Dimanche*, eh?' he said, to give himself time. He knew the sheet. It was the rock bottom of yellow journalism. Its tactics were unpardonable. It printed huge headlines over stories it *knew* weren't so, and tiny back-page retractions a month later. According to it, Jacqueline Onassis had been pregnant fifty-seven times in the last two years and had had one hundred and six abortions. The Queen of England was madly in love with her chauffeur. The crowned heads of Monaco went bathing in the nude. *Not* with each other, of course. If *France Dimanche*, or its arch rival *Paris Presse*, had printed an item about people as obscure as Gabrielle and he nominally were, the story had been leaked to them. Deliberately.

He said, meaning every word of it, willing to be the perfect fool, the perfect jackass before running the absolutely insupportable risk of losing this woman:

'Gabby – marry me. Tomorrow. We can take a plane to Tangier. To Gibraltar. In both places it can be accomplished in a matter of hours. Or – Scotland. Gretna Green.'

She shook her head, said softly:

'No, John. . . .'

'Gabrielle!'

'Oh, my poor old darling! Don't sound so distressed! Of course I'll marry you! Just you try and stop me. But not tomorrow. And – not in one of those quick marriage mills. I'd like to be married in Tel Aviv. Or Jerusalem. Or New York. A – big wedding – darling. And I'll put on a flaming scarlet wedding dress to show I'm not ashamed – of a relationship we'll be legalizing, or sanctifying – or both.'

'When?' he said; his voice thick and tight with anguish.

'Two weeks. Time enough for me to be absolutely sure of what I'm practically sure of now. As I said, we Levys never miss—'

'Never miss *what?*' he said.

'The train. The boat. El Al. What have you. John, tell me something: Why do you want to find Dalton Ross? I mean now, after so many years? Wouldn't he be almost as much of an embarrassment to Washington as Pound was, say? Wouldn't it be better all round to let him *stay* lost?'

The warning signals in his gut were deafening now. This is *it!* he thought. But at the same time relief flooded him in wild sweet waves. It wasn't personal! That call *had* been from the embassy, and they—

His elation died. He couldn't believe the Israeli government, one of the most hard-headed, pragmatic groups of people in this world, would waste one pound or five minutes of time on a minor nuisance like Dalton Ross. Klaus Barbie, yes. Bormann, yes. Otto Skorzeny. Franz Stangl. Josef Mengele. Murderers. Torturers. Incredibly evil men. But a has-been of a poet, spouting antisemitic merde over the airwaves? Not bloody likely!

He said: 'My government has no interest in Ross at all. People I know in the CIA actively tried to discourage me from looking for him. You've restated their arguments, Gabby: that it would be better all round for him to stay lost.'

She turned, faced him, whispered: 'You don't agree. Why not, John?'

He said, stiffly: 'My reasons are personal, private, and my own, Gabrielle!'

He saw the sudden mist of tears blur the clear green of her eyes.

'Even from – *me,* John?' she said, 'even from – your wife?'

He went on looking into her eyes; said very, very quietly:

'Maybe especially from you, Gabrielle. Especially from my wife.'

'Oh, goddamn Simone!' she burst out. 'Will I *never* be rid of her?'

'What's – Simone got to do with *this,* Gabrielle?' he said.

'Everything, as well you know! Suppose – she – suppose she's with him, *now?* Could you take it, John Farrow?'

His gaze didn't waver.

'Is she?' he said.

'Don't know. Some woman is. Young enough. In her late forties. That would be about right, wouldn't it?'

'Yes,' he said.

'John – let's say I lead you to Dalton Ross. And that his – *maîtresse* is – *still* Simone. What would you do? Would you – kill him?'

'I,' he said, 'would turn very quietly, and walk away without a word.'

She looked at him, whispered:

'Why, John?'

'Doesn't fit the legends. Neither Oedipus, nor Orestes. Elektra – maybe. But that's her concern, not mine. Incidentally I heard that "still".'

'Still?' she said.

'As in your biting phrase "*still* his mistress". As before. As during the war. Before I met her. Before she left him for reasons having to do with those broadcasts. For your information, Gabrielle: the trust between Simone and me was absolute. She never lied to me about anything. Nor concealed anything from me. Can *you* say the same thing?'

He saw her lips go white. Then she said, quietly:

'No, John, I can't. I've lied to you about a good many things, and concealed even more from you. But always for the same two reasons: to protect you from things I wasn't sure you were strong enough to take—'

'You think I'm a weakling, Gabrielle?'

'Yes. In some ways; yes, decidedly. All men are, John. God knows what would become of you if you didn't have – women to – baby you, guide you, and protect your oh-so-vulnerable egos!'

'All right. The number one feminine myth. Let it go. Let it pass. What was the second reason you've lied to me, Gabrielle?'

'Because – I am a coward. Because I couldn't – can't – face the thought of losing you.'

'What – may I ask – is going to cause you – to lose me?'

She looked away from him, looked back again.

'Perhaps – even this – this business of Dalton Ross.'

'If the woman with him is – Simone; it won't. You can make book on that.'

'But – if she isn't? If he – can tell you *where* Simone is?'

'I'd go to see her, of course. But except for satisfying my curiosity over why she left me during the war, I'm pretty sure nothing would come of it. Before – it might have – out of a certain sense of obligation on my part mostly. Now, no.'

'Because of – me, John?'

'Because of you.'

'Thank you for *that*, my love. John, I know – or at least I *think* I do where Dalton Ross is. If you want me to, I'll take you to him.'

'Which is it?' he said harshly. 'Do you *know* or only think you know?'

'I know where a man named Benton Prescott lives. I have been informed that Benton Prescott is Dalton Ross. From the description we have of him it seems rather likely – as far as one can judge from photos taken of Ross in his fifties – twenty-eight years ago.'

'When did you receive this information, Gabrielle? This morning?'

'No. Why, no, of course not! We've known this for months. I was shown the photos – for comparison purposes, before I left Paris. They thought *I'd* be able to recognize him. I'm supposed to have seen him quite often as a child. But, of course, I can't. I was only nine years old – and besides my memory of those days is blotted out, for ever.'

'You knew this all the time, and you didn't tell me, Gabrielle?'

'No. Because I know you're only looking for Ross so that he can lead you to – Simone. I'm a proud person, John. Or I was, Almost fiercely proud. So now, you may congratulate yourself upon what *you* have done to me. Or what my loving you has. I concealed that from you – so that I could keep you, one day, one hour, one minute, more. I am – that – helpless. That abject. . . .'

'Gabrielle – do you know where Simone is?'

She bowed her head. Looked up again. Said quietly:

'Yes, John.'

'Then tell me.'

'No. I'll lead you to Ross. Let *him* tell you. I will not risk – your anger. Risk – losing you. Though I may, in any event. He's in Aix-en-Provence. We can drive down there tomorrow, if you like. In that matter, I have only one request to make of you—'

'Which is?'

'Rent a bigger car. Please? More comfortable. That's much too far to ride in your little red sardine can. I seem to have become – fragile lately. My bones ache. Old age, I guess. . . .'

He peered at her.

'You *don't* look up to par,' he said. 'Are you ill, Gabby?'

She smiled at him with great tenderness.

'Yes,' she said, 'in fact – I'm dying. I won't outlast the year.'

'Gabrielle!' he got out.

'But of such a glorious illness, John. You have given it to me. Filled me with it. Soon I shall – burst with it – and die. And the name of my illness, my quite incurable illness – is love.'

'Gabrielle,' he said, 'you're – saying something to me. In code. Something you *want* me to know; but don't want to tell. What is it?'

'John – let's get past this, first. Please? This business about Ross. If he *is* Ross. . . .'

'You're not even sure of that?'

'Of course not. How could I be? I don't remember Dalton Ross at all. I told you that.'

'Gabby – are your people – after him?'

'No. No, of course not. We've written his case off. Not worth the trouble or the expense. Besides I – we – know he was under the most extreme coercion when he made those broadcasts. If *you* don't do him in, he's safe.

'Then he's safe. But still you had photos of him—'

'From before his case was closed. From a time when we thought he was a bigger fish than he really was during the war. And our people stumbled upon his whereabouts while looking for someone else. Someone it seems this chap in Aix – Dalton or not – bears a marked resemblance to.'

'Whom were they looking for?' he said.

'Don't know,' she said, too quickly. 'I wasn't on the case—'

And again he had that sickening feeling that she was lying.

'John,' she said, 'you don't mind doing without me this afternoon, do you? I have to go out.'

She wasn't looking at him, but she must have felt his stare. Because she turned to him, and laughed, gently, gaily.

'John, darling – *please* look at me like that thrice daily, will you?' she said.

'Look at you how?'

'That black sulphuric stare of furious suspicion! It's great for my morale, dearest! *Are* you jealous of me, John? Tell me the truth – are you?'

'Yes,' he said, 'damned uncivilized of me, but it seems I am. I didn't expect – a treasure to be tossed into my arms this late in life. I'm rather acutely aware of my own limitations, of how little, really, I have to offer you. You've – made me – come alive, Gabby. You've resurrected me. So therefore I cling to you, with more desperation than perhaps is seemly. I don't believe I could do without you, my dear. I'm quite sure I don't want to try. Which is what jealousy is, really – one of the manifestations of – fear.'

'John – if you don't want me to, I won't go.'

'No – that *is* a form of slavery, Gabby. Go, if you like. But I should like you to tell me – *if* you like, of your own free will – why, and where.'

'Down the street. To the Martinez. To the beauty parlour. My hair needs trimming. And a wash. And a set. I could have it done here, but I really do like the way they do it there better. I started going to them three years ago. One of my obligations – to make myself beautiful – at least as attractive – as possible – for my man. For you.'

He put his arms around her.

'John,' she said, 'kiss me only a little, please.'

'Why?'

'Because if you kiss me a lot I won't be able to go. Not until you calm me down, cool me off. And that'll take so long I'll miss my appointment. Besides, if my hair turns out well, I'm going to have a photo made. For you. "To John, with all my love, always, Gabby." Would you like that?'

'I'd love it!' he said, and kissed her. But not a little.

'John, please!' she moaned.

He turned her loose. She leaped to her feet. Said:

'See you at supper, darling!'

And was gone.

But after she had gone, he began to see the holes in a proposition that had looked airtight. She had been shown the pictures of a man upon whom the case had already been closed, in whom her government had no further interest, just before she had come south to – identify one John Farrow. Why? Had she asked to see them? If so, why? Because she already knew that he, John Farrow was looking for Simone? And that Dalton Ross was his most direct lead to his tiny, angelic ghost?

If so, logically, she should have tried to keep him as far from Ross as possible. That is, if she, as she claimed, as she demonstrated to him with marvellously tender sensuality, or marvellously sensual tenderness both by day and by night, truly loved him. But – did she? Could it not all be a part of an intelligence operation? Intelligence operations considered by the standards that men and women as individuals are asked to abide by, hold to, were hideously immoral. You 'wasted' a dangerous opponent without a qualm. You bugged phones, planted transmitters, robbed safes, filing cabinets. You blackmailed without mercy. You provided a key embassy employee with secret, even latent, homosexual inclinations with just the right pretty boy, he couldn't possibly resist; then photographed the pair in action. A man was a rock of integrity? Bribe-proof, mistressless, a churchgoer? What about his wife? His bored restless, silly wife? Within weeks the rock has crumbled; the man of integrity is betraying his government to prevent photos of friend wife, stark naked and *in flagrante* with the Latin type, Continental smoothie of a stud you've generously provided for her, from reaching the public press. . . .

And if you were a woman you whored – in the literal sense of that ugly word – with any man your government needed to soften up, bring down, pry something out of. Say that man was Attorney John Dalton Farrow. A man of some intelligence. Of a somewhat puritanical bent. Whom your easy sluts on call could get nothing out of. You provided him with intelligence matching, or surpassing his own. With charm that could melt rocks. With the same face – plastic surgery? She – she'd mentioned that possibility, herself – you'd somehow found out he'd lived in total anguish twenty-eight years hoping to see. Supplied your glorious five-letter word with a background that even when checked would stand up. With motivation (this is not a sudden impulse/love at first sight/I've seen you before/I've followed you around like a homeless bitch for years, now!) that even a man of some caution could believe, accept, and which once convinced – being at heart a romantic – would swallow whole. And—

But – why? And it was here that his whole sickening tower of doubts collapsed of its own unsupported weight. For if intelligence operations were hideously immoral, they were even more hideously expensive. What did *he* know that warranted a small government, bent under a crushing military budget in its efforts to stay alive, spending the young fortune it would have had to in order to mount an operation of this complexity?

Try as he would, looking at the matter from every angle, the answer was always the same:

Nothing.

He lay there. 'Throw the Israeli government the hell out, John!' he told himself. 'Say her motive is – personal. What reason would she then have to lead me to Dalton Ross?'

He examined that one. Turned it over in his mind. Worried it as a dog does an exceptionally tough and stubborn bone. Came at long last to the only possible conclusion.

'She *wants* me to find Simone. To find her under condition that will forever destroy the image I have cherished so long. Mad. A drunkard. An addict. An ancient whore. And being herself, most intelligent, she refuses to lead me directly to the sickening scene and say, '*Là voilà!* There she is! That's what you've clawed your guts bloody over all these years!' She knows the ancient kings beheaded the messengers who brought them the news of defeats, shipwrecks, natural disasters. That any man hates the bearer of ill tidings. So let Dalton bear them, then; while she sweeps her skirts daintily aside, and maintains her hold on me! It would be comic, if it were not so sad. . . .

'Can you blame her, John? Yes! It's goddamned dirty fighting! Have you ever seen the female of the species fight any other way? No – never. But even that's *our* fault. We strangle their souls, if not their minds in the cast iron mould, of our conception of femininity. Still – she could leave it alone. Leave it be. She's got me. She doesn't have to compete, still less to destroy what most in life I've cherished and right tenderly. Ah! But does she *know* that? To you, she's beautiful. Others might not agree. Fuck others! That's no answer, John. Whoever has provided her with the emotional security, she needs? She sees her life with you threatened. And chiefly by your retarded adolescent romantic's absurd clinging to a dream. So – she attacks that dream. Let her! Let her destroy it if she can! For both of you – John Farrow and Gabrielle Betrand, perhaps Rachel Levy, will be much better off!'

He got up very slowly. Went back into the hotel. Upstairs to their room. Drew a tubful of hot water. Eased his body down into it.

It was all figured out, now. All decided. Only – those alarm signals in his gut kept ringing.

And he couldn't shut them off.

16

As he held open the door of the Peugeot 505 he had rented for the drive across Provence to Aix, he said, trying hard to keep the faintest hint of irony out of his voice: 'Your hair is truly lovely. They did a good job.'

She stared at him a long moment and her eyes were very wide and green and darker than they normally were, and intense and troubled. And a few other adjectives that didn't come readily to mind. Then she said: 'Thank you, my love,' and slid into the car.

It was a very good car, much bigger than the Renault. It had direct fuel injection instead of carburettors. A four-speed forward, fully synchronized gearbox. Disc brakes on all four wheels. Springing stiff enough so that you could steer it into any kind of turn whatsoever and go around it as though you were on rails. And yet its top grain calfskin bucket seats were truly comfortable. It was a real, honest-to-God automobile, of a type that Detroit wouldn't equal in the next two hundred years.

He put the Peugeot in gear, drove off; but she didn't say anything. He turned off La Croisette and drove up to the Boulevard d'Antibes, turned left into that and drove two or three blocks westward across the centre of Cannes until near the Sporting Club he found a one-way street that went directly north, which was the direction they had to go and took that one until they were facing the railroad station, and turned left again on Rue Jean Jaurès until they got to the Boulevard Carnot which formed part of National 567 itself, turned north on it and drove the four kilometres to the entrance of the Autoroute de L'Esterel, stopped at one of the toll booths, took the ticket which would show *where* they had entered the autoroute, and thus let the guard in one of the toll booths at the exit know how many kilometres they had travelled on it, and how much, therefore, to charge them; brought the Peugeot gradually and smoothly up to a hundred kilometres an hour which was fast enough, but not too fast, especially when driving a car he wasn't used to.

And all that time she hadn't said a word.

Then, finally, a full half hour after that, in a slow, soft tone of voice:

'It wasn't because of my hair, dearest; if that's what you're thinking.'

'Then why *was* it?'

Her silence lasted two kilometres. Three. Four.

'All right,' he thought. 'You win. Resisting psychological torture is *not* my speciality.' He said: 'Come on, Gabby; tell me. What's wrong? I mean not only what was wrong last night, but what's still wrong? Have you – well – fallen off the roof?'

'Oh dear!' she said. 'How quaint! How deliciously quaint! I haven't heard that expression in *years*. No, John. No, my love, my dearest, dearest love; I haven't fallen off the roof.' Then she added with an intensity, a fervour that caused him to turn and look at her: 'Thank God!'

'Why thank God?' he said. 'It's a normal enough function, isn't it?'

'Yes – I suppose so – Why, yes – of course it is – John – about last night. I – just didn't feel like it. I sometimes don't. Things – get in the way.'

'What things?' the grand inquisitor in his gut screamed at him. 'Ask her that, you fool!' But John Farrow, civilized citizen, urbane and controlled, said quietly:

'It's all right, Gabby,' Then he added, a little mockingly: 'Fact is, I needed the rest, myself!'

'You *are* a dear,' she said quietly. Then she lapsed back into that brooding silence that was strange, and troubling and out of character for a woman as normally loquacious as she – or as she had led him to believe she was.

He decided not to force the issue. He drove all the way across the autoroute to where it ended at Puget-sur-Argens a little beyond Frejus, then took National 7, past Le Muy, Le Luc, Flassans, Brignoles, and had reached St Maximin La Ste Baume, more than eighty per cent of the distance to Aix-en-Provence, before she spoke again. Then her voice come over to him strangely, high, harsh, taut, and vibrate with nerves:

'John, I know you're going to think I'm absolutely mad; but would you consider – turning back? Calling the whole thing – off?'

He looked at her almost too long for safety's sake, at the one-hundred-twenty kilometres an hour he had the Peugeot up to by then. Then he turned his eyes back to the road, said:

'I would consider it, Gabby; but you'd have to tell me why.'

'Oh,' she said.

'Oh, what?' he said..

'Oh dear. Oh hell. Oh merde. Whichever best fits the occasion. I *knew* you'd say that. And I can't tell you why. Not now. Later yes. Later, gladly. But now, no. Wouldn't you take my word for it that this is – a bad trip, to borrow a phrase from the drug culture? It is, John. Very, very bad, the worst.'

'I'd still need to know – why, Gabrielle.'

'John – even if this man, this Benton Prescott, is Dalton Ross – he *can't* lead you to Simone. He doesn't *know* where she is.'

He glanced at her briefly, said:

'Aren't you contradicting yourself, now, Gabrielle?'

'No. Not really. He could only tell you where he *thinks* she is; where actually she started out to go. He cannot tell you if she ever got there. Or if she stayed, once there. You see?'

'I see you could save me a hell of a lot of trouble if you'd simply tell me what *you* know.'

'John,' she said bleakly, 'aren't you asking a dreadful lot? That I throw away my little hold on – happiness, on hope by helping you find the one woman – who could wreck – *us*? Wreck me?'

'She couldn't,' he said. 'The only woman who could do *that* – is you, yourself, Gabrielle.'

'I—?' she whispered, 'how – John?'

'By going on doing what you have done, these last days: lying to me. Concealing things from me. Withdrawing yourself from me. Wait! I don't mean that in the physical sense, Gabrielle. At least not entirely. Your body is your own. And obligation, a sense of duty, will *never* enter into our relations if I can help it.'

'Thank you for that, John,' she said.

'But I don't like the way that – that communication has all

but broken down between us. Your reticences, your silences must have some meaning, my dear. . . .'

'They *do*,' she said sadly, 'they mean that I – I'm absolutely petrified with terror – at the risk – the quite horrible risk – I'm taking – of losing you.'

'Then why take it?' he said.

'I've already decided that I don't want to,' she said quietly, 'that keeping you – at my side, in my life; and, for life, if possible, takes precedence over everything else, even though it involves breaking my most solemn oath. And that is why, my love, I asked you – to turn back. To give up going to Aix. I ask you again: please, John, *do* turn back. Don't – force me to – to destroy myself in your eyes this way.'

He thought about that through several kilometres more. Then he said:

'You have my word, Gabrielle, that Simone will not come between us. That no matter what Dalton Ross – if this Prescott *is* – Ross – tells me, it will make no difference; *we'll* stay together. *Nothing* will separate us, my dear; nothing or nobody. . . .'

'I wish *I* could be sure of that,' she said. 'John – what's today's date?'

'September fifth,' he said, 'the fifth day of the ninth month of 1972 – our way of counting. What's that in yours?'

'To tell the truth, I don't know. Remember I wasn't brought up in the Jewish faith. Beyond that this would be the month of Sivan, if this isn't a leap year, or the month of Iyar if it is, the only thing I'm sure of is that the year is 5733. As for the day, don't ask me, we have *three* months whose days vary, instead of just one as in your Gregorian calendar. I quite shamelessly use the Catholic calendar for all my reckonings except when I'm in Israel. And there I don't have to worry: I keep a calendar hanging on the wall, or check the date by the newspapers.'

'I see,' he said: 'now tell me, why did you ask me the date?'

'To remember it. The day my life – begins – or ends.'

'Gabrielle!' he said.

'Oh no. Not that. No potassium cyanide, John. I haven't any suicidal tendencies, believe me. I shan't kill myself, no matter how – badly – you treat me. I can't afford the luxury any more.'

'Today's your day to be cryptic, isn't it?' he sighed. 'Sibylline.

All right. I won't pry into your secrets. But it seems to me no more than fair for you to tell me *why* you think *I* might treat you badly. Why do you, Gabby? And of what does this bad treatment consist?'

She bowed her head. Stared at her own shoes. Said finally:

'You know just which questions to ask, don't you? I can't answer them, John. Not now. Besides, by tomorrow or the day after, I won't even have to. They will have answered themselves. That is, if you won't turn back.'

'That's no good,' he said. 'I shouldn't like going through the rest of my life wondering just what sort of a dirty trick you've pulled off on me. I'd rather *know* what it was – and forgive you for it.'

'That's just the point,' she whispered. 'Can you, John? Can you be that *big*, my love? And if you believe you can – why not be just a trifle bigger – and forgive me without knowing? You just possibly might save my life that way. . . .'

'Gabrielle,' he said angrily, 'aren't you overdoing feminine inconsistency, now? A moment ago you just said—'

'That I shouldn't kill myself? I repeat it: I shouldn't, John. That way out is cowardly; and whatever else I may be, I am not a coward. But then, I may not *need* to lift hands against myself, my love. There could come a day – quite soon – when the mere fact of your presence, the possibility of reaching out and taking your hand – may well be the only things that would, or could, keep me alive.'

'"Men have died,"' he quoted sardonically, '"and worms have eaten them, but not for love!"'

'Who said that? Shakespeare, wasn't it? Oh yes, *Hamlet*. That time he was wrong. No, he wasn't. Because he really wasn't speaking through Hamlet; but setting his creature free to express himself. As God does, maybe. Shakespeare knew better. What did Ophelia die of, John? And how many old couples have you known who've followed one another to the grave within months, weeks, days, even hours? People die every day of – of broken hearts, my love. I sometimes think it's the commonest cause of death there is.'

He stared at her briefly; said:

'I shall never break your heart, Gabrielle. And if you have done something that you feel *this* way about, the shoe is on the other foot, isn't it?'

Go look for your Dalton Ross. Look for my – end. My finish.'

'Gabrielle,' he said. 'I don't want to see Dalton Ross – about Simone. Not any more. I want to see him for – another reason. To – to embrace him. Kiss his cheek. Tell him that I – forgive him—'

She stared at him, murmured: 'Why, John?'

'All right,' he said, 'take this – as evidence of my trust in you, ma Gabrielle; for it is a thing I've told no one else on earth: Dalton Ross was – my father. My real father. John Farrow – wasn't. He only thought he was.'

'You mean – your – your *mother* – Oh, John!'

'Yes. Just what you're thinking. My mother was a whorish bitch who strongly influenced my attitude towards women. Some of my reactions, I realize, because of her – are not realistic. I know that. I tend to put an excessive value – upon fidelity, at least. I've clung to my dream of – of Simone, so long, because my own mother – duly assisted by other women later on – taught me how exceptional she was. I think that you are as exceptional, if not more so. In spite of your efforts in the last few days to convince me that you aren't—'

She put out her hand, took his, raised it with aching tenderness to her mouth. Palm upward, the same way Simone used to. Her wide, warm, wonderful mouth quivered upon it, prayerfully. Pain slammed into his gut and all but crippled him.

'Gabrielle—' he said.

'John,' she whispered brokenly. 'I am not exceptional. Not at all. My only raison d'être – is loving you. And now, God help me, I risk even your taking *that* away from me. *Never* leave me, John – promise me?'

'I shall never leave you, Gabrielle,' he said. 'Now come on. Get dressed. Let's go find my randy old bastard of a father. . . .'

She said, sombrely: 'I wish we – didn't have to. That you'd change your mind. Let – the whole thing drop.'

'Look,' he said, 'I told you I have no intention of asking him about Simone. So you have nothing to worry about.'

'If he *is* Dalton Ross, I suppose not. But if he *isn't*; if he is who I rather think he is, I have everything to worry about, John. Even – living alone. The little time I may have left to live. Dying alone – without you.'

'Gabrielle!' he said sharply, 'that's – unreasonable. And morbid. So stop it, will you?'

'Consider it stopped, my love,' she said.

And once more, John Farrow had failed to ask the right question. Which, as it turned out, really didn't matter.

They asked the concierge how to get to the Place St Honoré. And, as they still had plenty of time, and the directions – 'straight up the Rue du Quatrième Septembre, the first intersecting street below the hotel, across the magnificent planetree-shaded Cours Mirabeau, surely one of the loveliest avenues in all the world, and into the Rue Clemenceau, at the end of which they would find the Place St Honoré – simple, they decided to walk. It was a lovely night. And since they had not turned on the radio, or even glanced at a newspaper they had no idea what was going on in Germany that same night. At Munich. At the Olympic Games.

There were several sidewalk cafés in the *place*. But John Farrow saw the right one instantly. It was called Chez Ahmad. Appropriately enough, for it was filled with North Africans. He judged from their youth that they were students at Aix-en-Provence's justly famous university.

Their swarthy complexions made the lone European among them – a big man, white haired now, who had surely been blonde before, whose age was right, the seventy-nine, or eighty-years old that Dalton would be now – stand out, even at that distance.

The age was right. But everything else, the port, the carriage, the gesticulations, or rather the lack of them, the monumental stillness, solidity – were wrong. Dead wrong. And yet all of that and even more, something undefinable, graven upon his memory, from twenty-eight years ago, from the hours he had spent tailing this man, twenty-eight years younger then, but still in his fifties, the mould already set, told John Farrow that he knew the ancient, rocklike man, knew him completely, terribly.

'Wait here, Gabby!' he said sharply. Then he crossed the square. At the big man's table, three young Arabs sat; two men, and a girl. The girl was striking: almost as dark as the Negro races to the south; but with thin, cruel lips, and a magnificent figure, except that it was somewhat exaggeratedly callipygian. The two young men were typical upper-class Arabs; high beaked, liquid eyes; all their race's matchless capacity for fanaticism; its wilful disdain, and even rejection of logic, of thought, showing in their proud and contemptuous bearing. They reminded John of Spaniards, who had inherited so much of this people's hot blood, and all their unlovely ways.

The girl saw John Farrow first. Her chin lifted. Her marvellously well-shaped nostrils flared. Her dark eyes kindled, took fire, glared at him.

'If looks could kill,' he thought, 'I'd be a dead man, now!'

But he came on, until he was close enough, until he was sure. Then he said in German: 'How are you, my colonel? Good evening, Mr Heindrich Kroll!'

That ancient dirty bread-dough face moved glacially. Those icy eyes peered through the glasses, no longer steel rimmed but mounted in heavy dark tortoise shell; that slit of a mouth opened a little, crêpey sagging jaws barely stirred. 'You are mistaken, sir,' that iron voice said calmly. 'I am Mister Albrecht Holtz. I don't know any Heindrich Kroll.'

John Farrow stood there. He was quite literally shaking with the rage that tore him. He remembered Simone – remembered what her body was like when this man and his trained sadists had finished with her, remembered how shredded, burnt, scarred, broken, reduced to so much barely alive bloody meat she had been. Then he bent his head, mastered himself. It was no good, and he knew it. He could hear her voice, whispering 'Don't kill, my love. Not even them. It is necessary to pardon – even them. One can't join them, become, like them, murderers.'

'In her name,' he thought, 'I forgive you, you bastard! Unwillingly, but I do, you murderous swine!'

'What's the matter with you, young fellow?' the man called Holtz said. 'Are you crazy? Or sick? Or – a Yid?'

John turned away. In another minute he was going to strangle this murderous old swine with his bare hands. And that would serve for nothing, except to break his word to Simone.

'After all,' he thought, 'how much longer can a man of eighty live? And what could I do to him that would not be a most tender mercy in comparison to what he did – to hundreds – to Simone?'

Then he raised his eyes and stared into Gabrielle's face. Even from where he was, he could see it was as white as her hair. Could see how her mouth was trembling, see her green gaze go blind.

Even so, it took several seconds for the realization, the peculiarly unsupportable horror to hit him. He stood there and felt his guts pull apart. Felt something inside of him dying in utter anguish. Felt the nausea rising to the back of his throat: green and vile and thick with his own blood. He swayed there, unable even to move. But he did so finally. Took one step, another, until he came to where she was. Hung there before her, trembling, shaking, tears glittering on his face.

'John!' she got out, 'don't look at me like that. I—'

'You whore,' he said softly, 'you vile, unspeakable whore. There was – nothing your government – wanted of me, was there? My connections in high places no longer exist, do they, Gabrielle? Only I forgot – the simplest precautions. I didn't ask that young type who claimed to be from the Narcotics Bureau to show me his credentials. Though he'd have had them wouldn't he? Perfect ones. Perfectly forged. So you knew – before I even got here that I could recognize, point out, finger – a certain man. And that I'd refused in New York – flatly – my cooperation. Hence, the softening up process, eh, my dearest, dearest love? Hence this marvellously expert, counterfeit – of love. I – congratulate you. In you the stage has lost a great actress, Gabrielle. And – your face. I hope the plastic surgery didn't hurt too much. Or that it didn't cost your spy master too much money to transform it into the one you knew I was incapable of resisting. Which was – a new high in refined cruelty. But no matter. Bald, stupid, sentimental old wrecks come a dime a dozen, don't they? While girls like you come higher – much higher. A hundred dollars a tumble the price used to be—'

'John!' she moaned, 'oh John!'

'Well hear this, Gabby-Gabrielle: I *do* know that man over there. He's an old friend of mine. Melvin Lipschitz, well-known manufacturer of Kashruth foods, from Milwaukee, Wisconsin. Go back and tell your spy master that, will you? Now get out of my way. I have seen all of you I ever want to. More than I ever mean to see again.'

'John,' she said quietly. 'This face is my own. Simone – was my sister, just as you guessed. And he – that man over there – killed her. Tortured her to death. Oh, I know, I know. You got her out alive. But she still died of it. Years later. In my arms. And no one paid me – to lie with you. I did that on my own.

Because – I wanted to. Wanted you. I did, still do, always will, love you, John. Like it or not. Believe it or not. Oh, dear God, what can I say? How can I prove to you that—'

'You can't,' he said; and started to lurch on past her. But she caught him by both his arms, held him with that surprising strength of hers, said:

'You can't – do this to me, John. You simply cannot. There's – so much you don't know. That I can't even tell you. Because you wouldn't believe it. . . .'

'Damned right I wouldn't,' he snarled. 'Turn me loose, whore. I'm not in the mood, nor in the market for commercial cunt. But then I never was—'

But still she clung to him with quite desperate strength. Until all the rage in him, all the hurt, all the disappointment, death of pride, roared the ancestral ape thing through his blood. He tore free of her, drew back his hand, and slapped her to the ground.

Then it left him. Cold and sick, he put out his hand to her. She wouldn't take it. She lay there sobbing. At all the cafés, the people were standing up, glaring at him. He heard the words: '*Lâche! Brute!*' float murmuring upon the air. He bent down, jerked her to her feet by main force. Pushed her ahead of him. No one interfered. In France, wife-beating is a national sport. They came back to the hotel. In the lobby the startled stares of the clients, and the hotel staff made him look at her. Her face was a mess. He'd broken her lips against her teeth, and dark streams of blood stole down out of both corners of it.

Clumsily he offered her his handkerchief. She shook her head. They went up in the lift. Came to the room. He unlocked the door. Held it open for her. She went in. Sat down on the edge of the bed, stared at him with eyes drained of everything, even hope.

He said: 'I'm sorry I hit you, Gabrielle. That was beneath me. Forgive me for that at least. You keep the room. I'll move out. They surely have others free this late. . . .'

She bowed her head. Mastered herself. Said quietly:

'John, I have very little money. I left it all, or nearly all in the Majestic's safe. Traveller's cheques. My jewellery. I haven't even enough to get back to Cannes, not to mention Paris – I didn't think I would need it.'

'Don't worry about that, Gabrielle. I've been played for a sucker – so what does a day or two more matter? I'll continue to pay all your bills till we part. I'll take you back to Cannes with me, tomorrow. In return I ask of you only one thing: that you don't talk to me. Don't try to explain. I wouldn't believe you, so why waste your time?'

'All right, John; have it your own way,' she said.

He called the desk, and asked to be moved to a single room with bath. The management, who had seen matrimonial quarrels before, put him in a single, only a little way down the hall. Clearly they were hoping that during the night this charming middle-aged couple might have wiser second thoughts, become reconciled, and hence wanted to make the matter as easy as possible for them.

'Fat chance!' he thought. He took off his jacket and his tie, kicked off his shoes, opened his shirt collar, and lay down like that across the bed. Coldly and clearly he went over the whole thing in all its revolting detail. He had absolved Gabrielle Betrand of having been sent to soften him up. Of having accepted what is essentially the role of a prostitute to achieve her government's ends, because he hadn't been able to think of a single thing he knew, or could do, that would be useful to them.

But he had forgotten the list of escaped Nazis. Of the wanted men to whom no statute of limitations applied. Of course, nowadays, the Israelis no longer kidnapped them, staged public trials. They had seen how badly, in terms of propaganda, the Eichmann case had backfired. Now they simply turned them over to the respective governments of the countries in which they had committed their crimes. Or, he suspected, in those cases where the governments in question wouldn't cooperate, liquidated them carefully and quietly, leaving not the slightest trace.

What had he, John Farrow, known that was of interest to the Israelis? The name of the maniacal sadist who had tortured hundreds, perhaps thousands of people of their religion and their race to death, sent other thousands to Chelmno, Oswiscin, Majdanek, Belzec, Sobidor, Ravensbrück, Dachau. What could he have done to benefit them? Why, point out to them one Heindrich Kroll.

Once granted those motivations, plus the knowledge that he had refused – in New York, a few scant days before he was to begin his journey to France – to cooperate with the young man who was almost surely an agent of theirs even if he were quite legitimately employed in the Federal Narcotics Bureau – a young, idealistic American Jew might find no contradiction in serving the two governments at once, would, in fact, find it easy enough to escape detection, since the goals of both usually coincided – they had dug into his, John Farrow's history (he didn't doubt for one minute Gabrielle's statement about his dossier, knowing as he did how all intelligence services operate, which was to say dirtily) until they came up with the perfect way to take him: send the image of the woman for lack of whom he was slowly dying to warm his heart, his bed.

Thinking about it more coolly now, he dismissed his theory of plastic surgery. That was Grade B movie technique, paperback thriller stuff. The truth was, it simply couldn't be done. The greatest surgeon in all of history could not make one person look as much like another, as Gabrielle looked like Simone.

Which meant that Gabrielle was actually Rachel Levy. She had confessed as much to him tonight. And, he was suddenly sure, she had been telling the truth. Granted that, what had been changed? Only her motivations, a private lust for vengeance, had – as much, or more than any spymaster's orders – impelled her to trick him, lie to him, seduce him, play the whore.

And Simone – was dead. He was surprised to find how calmly he accepted that; how peaceful, how resigned, his grief. He supposed it was due to the fact, the now doubly bitter fact, that Gabrielle had replaced her fully in his mind, his heart.

'Fool!' he cursed himself. 'Goddamned stupid *old* fool. The kind for whom there is no excuse. Experience alone should have made you able to see through her at once! My God, Candace taught you everything there is to know about female treachery! And beyond that there was Heide von Kressel and – et ta petite Maman!'

He lay there. And the rage, and some of the bitter self-contempt began to die down. Even to drain out of him very slowly. And the reason it did was his recognition of the fact that Gabrielle's behaviour simply did not fit the pattern that his mother and his ex-wife had displayed; though it did come somewhat closer to Heide's.

'For,' he laboured over the thought: 'Heide did *not* betray me. Nor lie to me for that matter. She all but confessed her past to me, except that I was too young, too inexperienced, too stupid to understand what she was trying to say. I left her once I'd been accidentally confronted with her horrendous reputation, ran like a rat, like maman's poor, hurt baby boy. . . .'

'Though, damnit all, what has that to do – with this? One thing: Gabrielle did not lie to me *all* the time. Much of it she was quite obviously, even transparently sincere. She did not force those tears shed behind my back, when I was not even with her. She didn't put pepper, say, in her eyes to make them red and swollen.

'So? So what, old fool, old goddamned sentimental fool, have you come to now in your efforts to delude your stupid self, again? That she took the job, not knowing you, really. And caught herself, at least partly, in the web she'd spun for you. She *had* repented of the dirty, dirty trick she'd played you. If you'd done what she asked, turned back, she'd be yours still—

'I don't want her!' he raged. 'Why the filthy little slut she—

'Don't lie to yourself, John Farrow. That's a coward's trick. A child's. You do want her. You'll go on wanting her until you die. You told her you'd rather *know*, so you could forgive her. Well now you know. So what are you waiting for?'

He slung his long legs down from the bed. Groped for his shoes. Heard, at that precise instant, the light, rapid knocking on his door.

With a joy he knew damned well he had no right to feel, he abandoned the search for his shoes; rushed to the door, threw back the bolt, tore the door open. Hung there. Because it wasn't Gabrielle standing there in the corridor. It was that splendid, barbaric creature he had seen in the Place St Honoré with Heindrich Kroll.

'Please!' she said in English, 'let me come in a minute. And quickly, Mr Farrow. They – they may have followed me!'

'Baby,' he said to her quietly, 'I'll admit you're gorgeous. I'll even admit you've got the finest pear-shaped ass ever hung on to a female frame. But somehow I just don't feel in the mood for being blackmailed tonight. Or drugged. Or murdered. So you go right back to Uncle Heindrich and those two Black September hotshots you're with and tell them it's no go. *Hein?* Like a nice girl? Tell them that the prospective victim just didn't want to play. . . .'

'Oh!' she said, 'you're wrong, Mr Farrow! I'm an Israeli! A Sabra! I was sent to join up – with the German – with others – so that we could stop them! Find out their plans and—'

'Baby,' John Farrow said, 'if you're a Sabra, I'm the late John Kennedy. You've got the map of Araby written all over you.'

'I know it,' she said, and he saw the tears of pure exasperation sting her eyes. 'I've suffered all my life because of my looks. My parents were from Yemen, Mr Farrow. And if you know anything at all, you know all Yemeni Jews look just like me. We're the – niggers of Israel, discriminated against, scorned. How many times have I heard "*schvartze*, go away! We don't need any blacks here, y'know—" '

That, John Farrow reflected, was true. He knew from Jewish friends who had visited Israel that the colour problem was becoming acute. Was this girl telling the truth? Did the possibility even remotely exist?

He decided it did. If Israeli intelligence wanted to infiltrate the Palestinian, Fellahin organizations, she was obviously the perfect choice. With Yemeni parents it was a near certainty she spoke Arabic. For the first time in his life, he found himself defenceless linguistically. He knew neither Hebrew nor Arabic. He only knew that they sounded rather alike.

'All right,' he said, 'come in. But before I stick my neck out too far, what proof have you that you're actually what you say you are?'

'Papers,' she whispered. 'Credentials. I know you probably can't read Hebrew, but you can tell the letters from Arabic script, can't you?'

'Yes,' he said. He could. The difference in writing, in print, between the two languages was great.

'All right,' she said, 'have the goodness to turn your back, Mr Farrow—'

'Baby, that's asking a little too much, y'know,' he said.

'Are you a gentleman, Mr Farrow?' she said acridly. 'Believe it or not, I'm a decent girl. And since to even get to my papers I have to raise my skirt to here—' she indicated a line just below her breasts, 'and even pull down my – my panties a little, I'd thank you to respect my modesty, if you will be so kind!'

'The prospect's intriguing,' he grinned at her, 'and my gentility is diminishing by the second. Go on, dark lady, show me a little flesh. I've seen some before, but yours excites me. That rich suntan you've got, maybe. . . .'

'Then—' she said angrily, 'the deal's off, Mr Farrow! I simply will not undress before a man I do not know!'

There was, he sensed, realized, a note of real sincerity in her anger. Slowly he turned his back to her. What warned him was a thing he couldn't define, or even prove the actual existence of. Except that it had saved his life several times in the past. The feeling that had made him go on by that bar near the Gare St Lazare in 1943 where he was supposed to meet Colonel Roll's men. The instinct that had made him go back to that warehouse for those two Molotov cocktails. That almost extrasensory perception that every intelligence agent either develops, or dies.

He whirled. She already had that glittering blade lifted high.

'Baby,' he said, 'they didn't train you right—'

Then he went under that high lifted blade just the way he'd been taught to do in SOE commando school, under that knife she should have held low, ripping edge up, and thrust forward and upward so fast that catching her wrist would have been a near impossibility; but twenty-nine years had gone by since then, he was older, slower, out of condition. He felt a sear along his left shoulder blade; and not knowing how little or badly he was hurt, brought his knee up into her belly with sickening force; caught her knife arm with both his hands and bent and turned and used his own still powerful back for a fulcrum, throwing her over it so that she landed across his bed, and he slammed himself down upon her, between her wildly kicking legs, and twisted her knife arm until she turned that murderous weapon loose, let it fall, and caught both her hands and pinned them to the bed, and held her down like that, until he heard Gabrielle's voice coming from the doorway, and rent and torn with the purest anguish he'd ever heard, say:

'Oh!' Then: 'Oh, my God!'

And after that, the sharp staccato clatter of her high heels running down the hall.

He turned one of the Arab girl's wrists loose. Made an expert grab for that knife. Put it against her throat. Held it there. Turned loose her other hand. Rolled away from her. Stood up. Said:

'Get out. Go quietly, and I won't call the police. Tell Uncle Heindrich not to send half-trained baby girls to do a man's job. Tell him to come himself and bring his two fellahin along. Give me the pleasure of taking all three apart.'

She smiled at him mockingly.

'We're even – after all, Mr Farrow,' she said. 'I didn't kill you, but I'll at least have the pleasure of speculating over just how you'll explain to your wife – that what she saw wasn't what she thought she saw. That we were making war – not love?'

'Baby, don't tempt me,' he said. 'Instead of wasting my breath that way, I'd just as soon use it more pleasantly by becoming guilty as charged. After all, rape's fair enough an exchange for attempted murder, isn't it?'

He took a step toward her. Another.

She stood there, staring at him – a little speculatively he thought – until he was very close. Then she said, with a purring little laugh:

'Y'know, it might even be – fun – to oblige—'

And sidestepped him neatly, and fled down the hall.

He stood there holding that knife. Went to the door. Closed it. Locked it. He put his hand and felt the cut on the back of his shoulder blade. It was plenty bad enough although he could move his left arm in all the normal ways, proving that she hadn't got down to the muscular strata. But since he had absolutely nothing else, he went to the bathroom and packed it with toilet paper to stop the bleeding. Then he came back and sat down on the bed. He knew better than to call Gabrielle, try to explain.

'For,' he thought miserably, 'if anything ever looked like a casual little quickie, *that* did. Gabby will use woman's reasoning: I was angry; I took revenge. Nothing to do but wait till tomorrow. Hope that those two fellahin don't show up with Stens. Or plasticize the joint, or—'

Slowly he undressed, threw his quite remarkably bloody shirt over the chair without even glancing at it. Crawled into bed, wearing his underwear. He was too tired to look for pyjamas. He was sure he was going to sleep soundly despite it all. But he didn't. He couldn't. And the reason he couldn't was not his nerves, but the young English couple who had registered just before him and Gabrielle. They had the room next to his. They were evidently on their honeymoon – though whether it was blessed by church or state, he wouldn't care to say.

He was already aware from previous trips that the English on the Continent underwent a marked sea-change. Their justly celebrated reticence, taciturnity vanished; they became bluff, hardy, even jolly. They struck up conversations with strangers.

But this was his first experience with the younger mod generation, who, he'd heard, were neither reserved, nor taciturn to start with. And within five minutes he was sure of two things: the little English 'bird' in the next room was quite the noisiest human female he had ever heard – or rather overheard, and that her vocabulary was distinctly limited.

In fact it consisted of one four letter medieval expletive followed by the first personal pronoun, accusative case, endlessly repeated. It was evident that she ardently desired for her young male companion to do to her the action suggested by the word in question. But from the accompanying sound effects, the squeaking of bedsprings, the snorting, gasping, pounding, it was evident that that young gentleman had complied, was complying, but all the same she went right on shrieking that choice expletive at him – as an exhortation to greater speed and vigour, John surmised, until the desired result was achieved; but not before she had proved that her vocabulary was more extensive than he'd thought. In fact it was choice, rich, and unprintable.

'Now,' he groaned, 'maybe they'll let me sleep.'

He had, he soon learned, vastly underestimated the British. Within ten minutes, they were hard at work again. And if anything, noisier than before. John pulled his pillow over his head. And, because there are limits even to youth's capacities, managed, some time later, to fall asleep.

What woke him was Gabrielle's sharp and angry rapping on his door.

Groaning, he got up and opened it.

'Has she gone?' Gabrielle demanded, in a remarkably wifely tone of outrage.

'Has who gone?' he said, stifling a yawn and a grin at the same time.

'Your little visitor. Has she?'

'Yes,' he said. 'Come in, will you?'

'All right,' Gabrielle said. 'I know it's beastly of me to wake you so early after such a strenuous night, but since I'm quite as anxious to be rid of you now, as you are of me, I thought I'd take a chance. Can't say I admire your taste, John. *Une 'tite négresse* like that one – ugh! Well I suppose you're within your rights. Noisy creature, wasn't she? Don't suppose anyone on this floor got any sleep thanks to the two of you.'

She came into the room. Then her eyes fell upon his shirt hanging on the chair. She raised them to where he'd turned and was pulling on his pants.

'John!' she said, 'you – you're hurt! You're quite badly – hurt! Why – you're all over blood!'

'I know,' he said sadly. 'My little visitor, as you call her, tried to murder me. Incidentally that wrestling match you witnessed, sexy as it may have looked, was – and I quote *her* – war not love. Look over there on the table. That's what I was trying to get away from her—'

Gabrielle walked over to the table. Picked up that knife. Whispered:

'My God! And I – I went and left you! Why she might have killed you!'

'She didn't, and that's what counts. Look Gabby, while I clean up, shave and so forth, will you run down to the nearest pharmacy and buy me a roll of gauze, some sulpha powder and adhesive tape? When I yank this wad of *papier hygiènique* out of this, it's going to start bleeding again. It's rather messy. Wouldn't do to let it stiffen up too much. I've a hell of lot of driving to do—'

'I can drive,' she said. 'All right – I'll go get the medical supplies for the wounded hero!' She started towards the door. Before she reached it, she paused; turned back to him, said, bitterly: 'But all those – noisy sessions, afterwards – what were they, John? Your way of taking vengeance? On – both of us? On her and *me*?'

'Oh that!' he said. Then crossed to the wall that separated his room from the young English couple's, pounded on it with his fist, called out:

'Hey, kids! Time's awasting! Don't tell me you're going to let the *first* night wear you out!'

Gabrielle stared at him, at that wall; then high and clear, the little English 'bird's' voice came through.

'Eric! Oh, my gawd! The – man in the next room! He – he *heard* us!'

Gabrielle stood there; then she whispered:

'I'm – sorry, John. I apologize – truly I do. Most humbly. . . .'

'It's all right, Gabby, darling,' he said. 'Go get the stuff to patch me up.'

She looked at him quizzically.

'So – it's Gabby, again now? Even "Gabby darling" I believe I heard?' she said very, very quietly.

'On the way down,' he said bleakly, 'I told you I'd rather know the truth, so that I could forgive you for it. I do, Gabby, freely. I had a long night. During it, I came to the conclusion that I'd rather – keep you. That even knowing what I know, being without you was a little too much to take. That is, of course, if you care to stay—'

'Thank you for that last question, my lord!' she said. 'Even though you only threw it in as a sop to my pride. As a matter of fact, I *don't* care to stay. I see no future in continuing any sort of relations with a man who quite honestly believes I am a whore. Who after I'd poured out the lifetime – of love – of tenderness – I seem to have somehow reserved just for him, thought it was – an act. That I was playing Mata Hari – or your typical intelligence slut – whose body – is just another instrument of warfare. No, John, I'm – flattered, and grateful, that you want to – to keep me – in spite of everything. But on that basis – no.'

He looked at her, saw the tears on her face. Crossed to her, took her in his arms. Bent and kissed her mouth. It was cold and wet and salt.

'Then on the basis of my – need for you?' he said. 'On my awful, naked, beggar's need? That I can't do without you, Gabby? That I don't even want to try? That I love you more than I ever dreamed I'd love again? Isn't that enough?'

But she shook her head.

'No, John, it isn't, I'm afraid. You see – I'd even begun to think of myself – as your wife. And wives, my dear, are not only loved – they're honoured and cherished – and even – respected, I believed. So turn me loose. I'd better go get your first-aid kit—'

'Gabby,' he said despairingly. 'You're saying – that this is the end? That you and I are finished?'

She bent her head, whispered:

'No, John. But – unless I can find some way to convince you – that I came to you because you're the only man I've ever known I'm sure I could spend a lifetime with – it will have to be. Unless I can show you that almost nothing of what you think is so; that the first day in your car coming down from Grasse to Cros de Cagnes, I told you the truth, strict, entire and whole – I can't go on. It will – perhaps literally – kill me to be without you. But to look up – a year from now, two, ten – and see your eyes go dark with questioning, with doubt, would drive me mad. And of the two, I much prefer being dead. Now, turn me loose. Perhaps I'll think of something – some way to convince you – some proof that whatever else I am, or have been in my life – suis pas putain, John! John! I am much too proud—'

He turned her loose; watched her stride away. Shook his head to clear it. Thought with aching bitterness:

'But after all, she did *know* that it was going to be Kroll at Chez Ahmad – and *not* Dalton Ross. So if she weren't sent to set me up then who the hell *was*? Oh damn it all, I—'

An hour later, they left Aix-en-Provence, started on the long drive back to Cannes. He found that he had to drive much more slowly, his arm had stiffened so. After lunch, they slept more than two hours in the car. On the autoroute he had to keep to the truck lane, since he was unable to maintain the minimum car speed. When they got back to Cannes, it was nearly night.

'John,' she said to him, 'I'm very tired – so with your permission, I'll share your bed for one more night. I promise – I shan't touch you – either gratis, or for pay, my lord! It's easier – this way than shaming each other the way you did me – in Aix by moving out—'

'All right, Gabby,' he said, 'but I'm afraid I won't be able to sleep. This damned shoulder aches – and *I* ache, internally. So I'll bunk on the sofa, so as not to disturb your rest—'

'No, don't. Here's my sleeping pills. They're quite good. Take one. Oh! Or are you afraid I'll poison you?'

'I'd rather you did than leave me, Gabrielle,' he said. 'Give me a glass of water, will you? But say – aren't you hungry? I'll phone room service, and—'

'No, don't. Not for me. I – couldn't eat, John – I – I'm much too sad—'

She was right about the sleeping pill. It put him out like a blow on the head.

What woke him was the bedside telephone. As he reached for it he saw two things; it was all of eleven o'clock in the morning of that Thursday, September seventh, and that Gabrielle had gone.

Shaking with purest terror, he picked up the phone said: 'Oui?'

'M'sieur Betrand?' a man's voice said.

The sleeping pills were great; they had left his mind entirely clear. It took him not five seconds to decided, that for all intents and purposes, he was Monsieur Betrand – and especially for *this* call he'd better be.

'This is he,' he said, calmly enough.

'I'm Doctor Gobeau, your wife's physician. Do you expect madame to return home at once?'

'I'm not sure,' John said. 'But I don't believe so. Why, doctor?'

'She just left my office not five minutes ago. And I think that it's imperative that you and I have a talk, sir. Your wife's case is serious – even grave.'

'Speak, then,' John said, trying to keep the shake out of his voice.

'Oh, no. Over the telephone, no, sir. Can you visit me this morning?

'Yes, yes certainly. Where are you doctor?'

'Seventy Boulevard Dubouchage, at Nice. At what time will you come?'

'Now!' John got out, 'as soon as it will take me to get there from Cannes!'

'Take the middle highway. It's faster. I'll wait for you, sir,' the doctor said and hung up.

As he leaped from the bed, he saw the great pile of newspapers on the chair – and on top of them the two envelopes. The first one was for him. It was in English. He read:

Dearest John –
I believe I know how to convince you at last. The other letter is to our embassy in Paris. I have written it in French instead of in Hebrew as I should have. For two reasons: my Hebrew is very bad; and because this way you will know I speak, or rather write the truth. When you have read it, mail it for me, darling. Then – if you believe me – but only *if you believe me, join me in Grasse where I have gone to visit M. Feingold to ask news of Mme Rosen – if it is not too soon for news of the results of your generosity to have arrived. The newspapers – are to show you what the people of the man you saw fit to pardon the day before yesterday do. Aided by your swarthy friends! Forgive my bitterness – but you will admit it is – a terrible thing.*

And know that – if you come to me or not – I love you. Unfortunately, it seems to be a thing I cannot help.
Yours, always,
Gabby

He read the letter to the embassy. It was a letter of resignation. The important lines were:

And when you called me on Monday, September 4th [the words underlined for his own benefit, John realized] to inform me that our man in Washington had passed on to you the information that my good friend – no, to be truthful, my fiancé, M. John Farrow, was one of the few persons living who could identify Heindrich Kroll, I don't suppose you realized you were going to wreck my life. Nor did I. It was your suggestion that I dupe M. Farrow into accompanying me to Aix since he'd already refused to cooperate with us in New York. That suggestion – spoiled things quite. M. Farrow refused to identify Kroll at all, and has broken with me, since he – quite logically – believes I was sent down here to deceive him, fool him, lead him on. Hence, my resignation. In my present state of morale, I should be of little use; and, frankly, while remaining as patriotic as ever, my distaste for the – sliminess of intelligence work has grown to the point that I don't want to continue in it any longer. I am well aware that this letter violates all security rules; but I'm afraid I do not care!
Most respectfully,
Gabrielle Betrand

He stood there. And the cool logic of her proof was inescapable. She would not write a deliberate lie to people from whom she could not conceal the truth, who knew the facts as well as she did. For her to remind them of the exact date she had been told that he, John Farrow, knew Heindrich Kroll, meant that she *hadn't* known it previously. So, up to the very moment that he, John Farrow, had directed the boton to put her call from Paris through to her in their room, she had had no motive at all for deceiving him.

It all fell into place; her obvious sincerity; the matchless tenderness with which she'd loved him. Even her deceit in the case of Kroll was understandable. The man had murdered her sister.

For though Simone had temporarily survived what had been done to her, over the years her broken body had failed, had died. . . .

Then he read the newspapers. When he had finished them he was sick. He understood the Israelis' feeling that they had no allies or friends, that for them to accept advice from anyone, to do anything except what their own hard-headed estimation of any given situation called for was suicide. Eleven innocent young men, dead in their blood, in Munich, half a continent away from Palestine, at the hands of mad fanatics who would do absolutely anything absolutely anywhere to absolutely anyone to further a cause already lost.

Then it came to him. He still had to drive to Nice to visit Dr Gobeau. And after that to Grasse. He decided that he had no time to either shower or shave. And as for breakfast, his nerves had tightened up on him so, he knew he wouldn't be able to get even a cup of coffee down.

He called the concierge, said:

'Get me the Hertz people. Tell them to send the Peugeot back again. At once. Keep it out front, somehow, anyhow, whether there's a place to park it or not. I'll be down in five minutes; no, less!'

After he left Dr Gobeau's office, he had no clear recollection of driving up to Grasse at all; but it was evident that he broke every known speed record, even those of the Rallye de Monte Carlo, getting there. He burst into Monsieur Feingold's shop like a madman, all but shouting: *'Ma femme! Madame Betrand où est-elle?'*

'Your lady – has gone, Monsieur Farrow. To Tourette-sur-Loup. She said there was a thing she had to do for you there—'

'Thank you, M'sieur Feingold!' and turned to rush out of the shop. But Monsieur Feingold caught him by the arm. John whirled, glaring at him. Then he saw the jeweller had tears in his eyes.

'My son – called this morning,' he whispered. 'From Boston. Your Chinese doctor has performed – a miracle – with Laser beams – he stitched both retinas back. It is too soon, of course, but they believe – *ma fille* will see! Not very well, but all the same – *merci,* M'sieur Farrow; *mille fois merci.*'

John stood there. The bitterness was in him very deep, and

the pain. 'Miracles!' he thought. 'Other people receive them, get them, while I – while I have everything snatched away, even her life, her life!' Then he mastered himself, said: '*Je suis heureux pour vous, M'sieur Feingold, et maintenant il faut que je m'en aille!*'

At Tourette, the first thing he saw was a little green Renault Cinq sitting in the main square. He wondered why she had chosen that type of car. He had the distinct impression she didn't like the light, tinny little things. Besides, now—

'Oh God! Oh Jesus!' he thought, and went pounding up that narrow street at the end of which Dalton Ross's house had been. She wasn't there. He went to the edge of the precipice where nearly every street in Tourette ended, looked down. Then he saw her. She was sitting at the very bottom of the gorge. She had something in her hands. It looked like a box – a little metal box of the type people keep small change in.

He went over the edge without hesitation, scrambled down those sheer rock faces to the utter ruin of his clothes and much of his hide. He pulled the cut in his shoulder blade open again, but he wasn't aware of that. He risked breaking his neck, not to mention his arms and legs, every second of that descent. He very probably also risked a heart attack considering how sedentary his life had been, and the sudden excess of exercise he was taking now.

But he got there, rushed over to where she sat, clawed her into his arms, held her against his wildly beating heart, both too moved and too exhausted to say a word.

'Turn me loose, John,' she said calmly. 'I don't want to be a widow before I am a bride. I take it you're convinced? That there's nothing – or very little – you need pardon me for? Sit down, will you? You're a bit too old for mountain-climbing, my dear!'

He sat down panting and shaking with both fear and rage. Her clothes, while dusty and ripped here and there, were in much better shape than his were. She saw his look, said,

'Oh I came down by a round-about, but much easier way. Here – I suppose *this* is what you were planning to come up here to look for, isn't it?'

He took the box from her hands, put it down on the rocks without looking at it, found both breath and voice at the same time, roared at her:

'Goddamnit, Gabby! What I'm too old for is to become a widower! Why *did* you do it? You knew it was suicide! Gobeau says you haven't the faintest chance of surviving giving birth! Your pelvis is too narrow – and too small! And if I must remind you, you're a thirty-seven-year-old woman! And yet you – you *smashed* that goddamned flask of pills, didn't you? They were *that* kind weren't they?'

'Yes, John,' she said in mock contrition, 'they were. And I didn't smash them on purpose. That was my subconscious mind taking over. Besides – when I reached for them, it suddenly occurred to me that I hadn't taken the damned things in almost three years. And that – the night before was the exact middle of the month. Between my periods, I mean. So since every Levy woman in history has always got pregnant on her wedding night, I was very likely already too late. And the most awful revulsion – against taking them at all, against stopping what I jolly well didn't want stopped – that is, having at least one child – and giving him – her – such a lovely father at the same time – made my hands shake. So I dropped them. And that's that. Are you going to marry me in time? Or shall I become the first thirty-eight-year-old unwed mother in recorded history which is almost obscenely ridiculous?'

'Gabby, I don't know whether to kiss you – or strangle you. Get up from there! I've got to get you down to civilization. And by tomorrow, on a plane – to Sweden!'

'Sweden?' she said blankly, 'why Sweden, John?'

'Because abortions are legal there, you idiot! I'll be damned if I'll stand idly by and let you die because your brains are located twenty-odd centimetres south of your navel!'

'John—' she said, 'that's no good, y'know. I won't. I simply won't. This little bastard is going to be *born*. So the first thing *you'd* better do is marry his mother.'

'Gabrielle,' he almost wept, 'will you listen to reason please? Gobeau says—'

'Gobeau is an ass. A silly ass. What does he know about *me*? Why, up until now all he's ever attended is *shiksas*. Delicate flowers. Who pipi perfume, maybe. I'm a tough, old bird, John. I won't die on you. Not if you're there to hold my hand and encourage me a little—'

'Gabby, for God's sake!'

'No, John darling – for mine and maybe even for yours,

though you're only an accessory after the fact now. Look, how'd you like to visit Israel? There's a doctor there I know – a woman. Trudy Elon. She specializes in difficult cases – which mine *isn't* really. And she brings every kid out alive, even if she has to deliver them through your left ear.'

'But,' he said, 'the mothers?'

'Most of them, too. Better than ninety per cent, I'd say.'

'*Not* good enough. I want you alive, Gabby!'

'John – if Trudy says it can't be done, I'll take – the proper steps. But if she says it can, believe me it can. So let's go to Israel, shall we? Get married there?'

He looked at her, said: 'All right, Gabby – if that's what you want.'

'It is – but d'you know why, John?'

'No. Why, Gabby?'

'So I can invite all the people who predicted I'd *never* find another husband, to our wedding! Or at least to the reception, afterwards. There'll be quite a crowd, I assure you – all those dear, sweet Tel Aviv matrons who said I was a fool to have divorced Guy, and predicted that a skinny, unattractive little *tchotchke* like me would have to remain a spinster, or rather a grass-widow, till I died. Let me exercise a little petty vindictiveness, will you, love? Display *kvell* all over the place?'

'What's *kvell*?' he said.

'In English? It's – it's something like to gloat. . . .'

'Over what – this bald-headed old *shlemiel* you've brought home with you? Or a *shlemazl* is better, isn't it? And a *Goy* to boot?'

'John, you've been associating with *Jews*, you naughty boy! You have! And besides, you're insulting me. Reflecting on my taste. Besides, I'll bet you don't even know what you're saying, really. Do you know what those words mean?'

'Sure – a *shlemiel* is a jerk who thinks he's smart, and is always getting caught in his own traps. A *shlemazl* is a type who is just plain dumb – and unlucky on top of it. That's me, all right. For if I hadn't come to France looking for Dalton Ross, look at all the grief I'd have saved myself – including getting mixed up with *you*!'

'John—' she said, 'y'know, you don't sound as if you're joking now. Not altogether, at least.'

'I'm not,' he said angrily. 'Look what I've got: a liberated woman! So damned liberated that she's got the biggest semi-frustrated maternal instincts extant, and who calmly proposes to risk her life to present me with a son. Or a daughter. Another daughter, since I've already got one!'

'John—' she said again, 'you don't *have* to marry me, y'know—'

'And if I *don't*, what?' he said.

'I'll just go back to Tel Aviv and become the oldest unmarried mother in recorded history. John, tell me something: why didn't it ever occur to you to look for her – in Israel?'

'It did occur to me. Only I knew better. Because if she were in Israel, it meant she was married to Anton. And, since I both admire Anton tremendously, and had no desire to cause him – or *her* – pain, I put Israel off limits. Was I right?'

'Perfectly,' she said. 'Another thing: couldn't we – just stay? In Israel, I mean? I love it, John. With my whole heart. And I'm sure you will too, and—'

'One moment, Gabby-Gabrielle! How'd I make a living there?'

'Practising your profession. Or teaching it in the university. You've quite a reputation as an expert in international law. We need that. In fact we need it quite badly. You'd be welcomed with open arms.'

'I'd rather be a general in the army. The women's army. From the way some of those girl-soldiers look marching by in the newsreels I've seen on TV, that's for me, Gabby!'

'John, I'm a *very* jealous woman. And an expert pistol shot. So you be careful!'

He took her in his arms, kissed her, said:

'To have and to hold. To love, honour, and cherish—' then he added, bitterly, 'but for how long? Eight more months?'

'John, I give you my word – my most solemn word – I shall *not* die on you. I swear it!'

'Well—' he said doubtfully, 'on that basis—'

'On that basis. I shall not put my – *our* – child's life before my own, which is a thing I'd ordinarily do without a second thought. Because it would be a crime and a shame to leave an absolutely helpless creature like you unprotected, and with a tiny newborn baby in his arms to boot! And in Tel Aviv! Why you'd be killed in the stampede of mothers dragging their over thirty and still unmarried daughters along behind them. All of them fairly panting to console you for your great loss!'

'Wait a minute, Gabby! That's another thing: won't it be difficult for us to get married there? I'm both a foreigner and a gentile, remember, and from all I've heard—'

'Difficult, yes. Very. But not impossible. I happen to have one *very* neat trick up my sleeve, my love. The whole trouble is that we have too many political parties, so that even quite small ones like Hapoel Hamizrahi, Agudat Israel, Herut, and Poalei Agudat Israel, when they band together can determine an election or the passage of a bill. Those parties are all composed of fanatically Orthodox religious people, John. And they, with the help of even some of our quite non-religious founders, who are now old enough to worry about dying and wonder if there may not be something in all that superstitious nonsense after all – have fouled things up for fair! Why even our *so* secular prime minister urged Knesset to define a Jew according to Talmudic law. D'you know what she said, *she* of all people! "In the twentieth century, we shall not throw away the prayer shawl and the phylacteries." '

'Gabby,' he said, 'would you like me to convert? I would, if you wanted me to.'

She stared at him. Reached up her hand and touched his cheek.

'That's sweet of you, John,' she said, 'that's very sweet – even touching. But in our case, quite unnecessary. In fact, it would make things *more* difficult, not less. For you see, John, *I* never have—'

'What!' he said, 'you mean to tell me—'

'That I'm still listed on Israeli census rolls as a Catholic? Yes, John, I don't know why, really. Except that conversion seemed too much of a bother. Especially since it also seemed much ado about nothing. I lost interest in God, anybody's God, quite sometime ago. Appears to me that if he didn't know *one* Anne Frank was already too bloody much, and went on to let them pile up six million more – witnesses – to his lack of interest in "his chosen people" – or, perhaps, looking at the matter with more rationality, more kindness – to his non-existence I could jolly well do without him. And I have. So you'll have to forgo that particular kind of high and holy ceremony – oh dear! I can just see you in a top hat under the huppah – and go confess your sins to some nice, understanding padre. Then we'll find ourselves a church – a Catholic church – Israel has a goodly number of them y'know, and—'

'Gabby, my dear; you're one hell of a Catholic, you know. We'll have to settle for a civil marriage.'

'But, John, in Israel there *isn't* any such thing. Marriage between Christians, which theoretically we both are, is quite legal. It's *mixed* marriages that are *verboten*. In such a case the gentile involved definitely *has* to convert to Judaism. And our rabbin make *that* so difficult, that most people give up in disgust.'

'Gabby, baby, you're *still* missing the boat. Where are you going to find a Catholic church that will marry *one* divorcee, not to mention *two*?'

She stared at him, whispered:

'Oh, *merde*! You know I'd quite forgotten that little detail?'

'Means marrying in Israel is out, doesn't it?'

'Definitely. Oh, John, what *shall* we do?'

'Scotland – Gretna Green. Or Gibraltar, I've heard. Or New York. Tangier's out. You look too Jewish. We might have trouble there.'

'John, would you object to – London? I mean would the fact that I got married there before bother you?'

'Not at all. You never married *me* anywhere before as I recall. And that's what counts. And afterwards, we can go to Israel for our honeymoon—'

'Oh, John! You are a dear, really.'

'But all those people you were planning to invite?'

'We'll throw a big party at the Tel Aviv Hilton. At which party I'll have a cold buffet: y'know, pickled pig's feet, hamhocks, roast pork and—'

'Oh, cut it out, Gabby,' he said. 'You won't, and you know it.'

'And won't I, just? And veal stewed in cow's milk and—'

'You won't because *I* won't let you. A decent respect for the opinions of others is part of civilization, my dear. Now come on. We've an awful lot to do.'

'Don't we, though. Tickets – and packing. Ugh! The only things I hate about travel! John!—'

'Now what?'

'You're leaving your little box. The one I've ruined my dress to get for you. D'you have any idea what's in it?'

'No. Not any more than I have the faintest idea how *you*

knew where, or even how, to look for it. How did you, Gabby?'

'Didn't, actually. You put me on with some cryptic remark of yours. And after I got here, an old, old dame pointed out to me the ruins of Ross's house. So I went to the edge, looked over the parapet – and spotted it at once. I've the eye of a vulture, y'know. Feminine curiosity did the rest. I say, aren't you going to open it, John?'

'Can't. I need a hammer and a chisel. It's locked and there's no key. Besides, my interest in its contents has become academic, if that. As you guessed – at first I was trying to find Ross in order, through him, to find Simone. Then *you* appeared, which fixed all that quite nicely. Besides, she's – dead, isn't she? I believe you told me she was. . . .'

'Yes, John. And she – died quite horribly. Don't ask me about it. I *can't* tell you about it. I mean *can't*, not *won't*. Ask Anton after we get to Tel Aviv. Though, I warn you, darling, you'll have to let me go on ahead to show him my ring and the marriage certificate first. Or else he'll *shoot* you!'

'Why should he do that, Gabby?'

'For my sake, of course. He has become quite dreadfully conservative. And I – am his sweet, little, helpless, innocent thirty-seven-year-old sister-in-law – whom you, you villain, sir! – have deflowered and—'

'Now, *that* was quite a trick!' he said.

'Well, then – not deflowered – even Anton will have to admit I *was* married once – say ruined. Do I look ruined, John? I don't feel ruined.'

'How do you feel, Gabby?' he said. 'How do you, truly?'

'Like chanting hosannahs to the Most High! And – at the same time – nervous and timid and shy – and, and afraid. Most horribly afraid!'

'But you said this lady sawbones was an ace! That she—'

'Oh, not that! Of – losing you. That something, anything, will come up at the last minute and there I'll be – with my big belly – and crying my eyes out – without you. . . .'

'You'd have to use an axe. Or your thirty-eight police special. Or something lethal. Now come on!' he said.

17

Early the next morning, leaving Gabrielle fast asleep, John Farrow went out to make the necessary arrangements for their flights to London and to Tel Aviv. From sheer force of habit, he entered Air France's offices first. And it wasn't until he came out again, a quarter of an hour later, that he remembered that Gabby had asked him to get tickets on El Al, the Israeli airline.

He hesitated a long moment, then walked on in the direction of Cook's Wagons Lit. Which airline they took couldn't matter that much, he thought. And he would have felt like the biggest fool on earth to turn around, go back into Air France's offices and ask for his money back on tickets already bought and paid for, with no valid explanation to offer, at that. . . .

At Cook's the matter took him considerably longer. He got a confirmed reservation at Claridge's from the night of Sunday September tenth onwards, for an approximate two weeks' stay; but they were unable to confirm the reservation of the Tel Aviv Sheraton for Sunday, the twenty-fourth. They assured him, however, that they would have the confirmation for the next day, Saturday, the ninth. And, since their London flight was scheduled for late Sunday afternoon, a gesture he'd made in respect for Gabby's fixed habit of sleeping till noon, or even past it – with that he had to be content.

Even when he got back to the Majestic, he did not go upstairs at once. First he put in a call to Hern, Pollock, and Ludlow, Solicitors, a London law firm he had often done business with in the past, and asked them to put one of their bright young men on the problem of obtaining whatever documents, permits, et cetera, might be necessary for a pair of non-resident foreigners to get married in a civil ceremony in London. Reassured by Derrick Hern's belief that the difficulties would be slight, he then took a chance and called Byron Graves.

By that time, of course, Byron was already en route to his own office; but his wife, Brenda, took the message with great cordiality and faithfully promised to have Byron call him at Claridge's on Sunday night.

By the time all that had been arranged it was well after eleven o'clock of that Friday morning, but even so he was surprised to find Gabrielle not only up, but dressed. She had often remarked that her idea of Utopia was a place where nobody had to get up before noon.

'Did you get them, John?' she said.

'Yes. Plane tickets and hotel reservations. We leave day after tomorrow, Sunday the tenth. Best I could do. And look, Gabby, it was stupid of me, I'll admit; but I plain forgot what you said about El Al. I booked the flights on Air France. Sheer habit, really—'

'Oh, John!' she wailed.

'Now look, Gabby,' he said, 'aren't you overdoing patriotism a little?'

'It's not – patriotism, John. It's – more nearly cowardice, actually. Most flights out of London go to Rome, first, then to Athens. And as far as Athens, they always have one or two Arabs aboard. In Athens, they have to change, or we do – because the plane that goes to Israel *can't* touch down in the Arabic countries. Once or twice I've had to fly back to Israel on lines other than our own, and I arrived literally sick from watching them, waiting for them to – to pull something, or—'

'And El Al doesn't take them?' he said.

'They don't apply. They know what we've got aboard.'

'Guards riding shotgun. Expert marksmen. I know. But do you know what a bullet going through a fuselage wall at thirty thousand feet would do, Gabby?'

'Yes. Decompress the aircraft so that the pilot would have to power-dive to get us down fast enough to where the air was breathable. But so far, it hasn't happened. For one thing, the type of ammunition our guards use is special: very low muzzle velocity. For two reasons: so it won't go through a cabin wall, and so it'll stay inside the bodies of the types they're shooting at, instead of mashing in one side and out the other with still enough force to kill someone else—'

'All right,' he said, 'I'll change the ticket in London for El Al, if you want me to, Gabby—'

'It's all right, John,' she said, 'leave them on Air France. I'm probably being silly—'

Hearing her voice, what had got into it then; perhaps what had been in it all along, he looked at her sharply, said:

'Gabrielle, what's wrong?'

'I—' she whispered, 'am – pregnant, John. Definitely. I've been throwing up all morning, ever since you left. And pregnant women are touchy and sensitive and – and vulnerable, my love. And – jealous. *More* jealous than usual. Even so, I – I've been good. Honourable. I *didn't* open the letter that she sent you. It's over there on the table.'

'The letter *who* sent me, Gabrielle.'

'Your *Schvartze*. Your Arab girl friend.'

'Now, Gabrielle!' he said.

'Yes, John. When the boton came up with it on a tray, I saw it hadn't any stamps on it. And that it was marked: "Personal. Par main." So I asked him who'd brought it. He told me that the boton of the Hôtel des Pyrénées had. D'you know it, John? It's over on the Rue de Château-neuf—'

'Never heard of it,' John said, truthfully.

'Nor had I. And since the boy who'd brought it had already gone, I – forgive me, John; but a woman has the right to – to defend her – future; hasn't she? – I looked it up in the telephone guide, and called the concierge, there. Finally, after much useless talk and too many explanations, rather, they put the little boton on. "Une femme," said he, "une très jolie femme. Nord-africaine—" I asked him to describe her. He waxed quite lyrical. But it was *she* all right. So I asked the concierge to put me through to her room with the firm intent of telling that little girl a thing or two.'

'Or three, or four, or even five,' John said solemnly.

'Yes. The wires probably would have melted. But she was no longer there. She and her two boy friends had checked out. In fact they were already in the taxi when she gave the boton that billet doux for you. That's all. There it is. Aren't you – going to open it, John?'

He crossed to the table. Picked up the letter. It was astonishingly thick and heavy. Too heavy. Even a letter with enough pages to make it this thick wouldn't weigh this much. Paper, even the stiffest, most expensive bond, simply didn't add up to this many grams. Even if she'd crowded fifty or more pages – an impossibility anyhow since the cheap flimsy envelope from the hotel's own stationery would have burst before she could have got half that into it, the letter had to weigh far less.

He put it back down, very, very carefully. Turned, said:

'Get out of this room, Gabby. Right now. This instant. You heard me, woman! Move!'

'John,' she gasped, 'you're angry at me! What did *I* do? I didn't send you that thick love letter, or even open it, or – oh! Oh, my God! You don't mean that it's—'

'I mean that if you had opened it, I'd be scraping you off the ceiling and all the walls right now. Gabby, for God's sake! You *saw* what that murderous little witch did to my back. The minute you found out it was from her, you should have called the police!'

'Oh!' she said, 'I *have* been stupid, haven't I? Y'know I never even thought of that!'

'Well think about it now. But somewhere else. Gabby, please! Take you and little Sim – and my kid out of here, will you? At once, if not sooner?'

She stood up. Came to him. Kissed his mouth. Her eyes were brilliant with tears.

'It's all right, John,' she said. 'If – it's a girl, you may call her Simone. I – I was going to suggest it – anyhow. But I won't go, unless you come with me, with us. John, I – I need you. And so does *she*.'

'Gabby, I'll be with you in a minute. But I have to take care of this damned thing. Soak it in the bathtub first, anyhow. Or else it might wreck half this floor. It may have a timer and—'

'One can see you've been out of this business a long time, my love! *Don't* soak it with water. It might well have an extra sodium or potassium compound detonator that *reacts* with water included. And since the explosive is almost surely le plastique, nitroglycerine and nitrocellulose mixed into artificial gum rubber, it will explode quite as well under water. No, better. Water has a higher specific gravity.'

He stared at her. Then he grinned.

'When you get ready to knock me off, I won't have a chance, will I? Hell of a thing being *married* to Israeli Intelligence, isn't it? Tell me Gabby – what should I do with it?'

'The sensible thing is to leave it where it is. The humane, to take it downstairs – and out into the open air. I don't believe it has a timer. So far, no letter bomb has ever had. Of course, they go on refining the technique all the time. The trouble is that any little jolt might set it off, so—'

'I'll take it downstairs. And outside. You come down – in another lift, damnit! The minute you get there tell the concierge to call the Police. The bomb disposal squad if they have one and—'

But she shook her head.

'No,' she said, 'In the *same* lift, John. With you.'

'Gabby, Goddamnit! I—'

'John, what would life mean to me, to little Simone – without you?'

'Gabby, for God's love!'

'No, mon amour – for yours. John, I'm quite sure it won't go off. To date, not one of them ever has before someone tried to open it. Let me take the chance with you. It's a quite good one. But what I will not take or even risk is the possibility of being left – thirty-seven years old, and pregnant – without you.'

'Gabby—'

'Another thing. Gobeau says that – that I'm going to have a rough delivery. John, dearest John, don't you *know* that even with Trudy Elon doing her damnedest I won't survive it unless you're there to – to hold my hand; grin at me, keep my morale high enough to bear it?'

He bowed his head. Looked up. Whispered:

'All right, Gabby. Come on!'

The elevator had an operator. And two other people – a middle-aged couple, obviously American, aboard. But John didn't hesitate. He dived into it, said:

'File, garçon! Avec les touristes. Cette lettre est sûrement une bombe. Va-t'en! Allez-y! Je ferai descendre l'ascenseur moi-même.'

The couple stared at him.

'Look, folks,' John began all over again, 'get out of this elevator, will you please? This is a bomb. I've got to get it off the premises at once. So, now, if you'll be so kind—'

'Now, see here, mister!' the male half of the couple began, 'if this is your idea of a joke—'

'Get out!' John said. 'I'm a special agent — and we don't joke, mister! Being scraped off an elevator's walls is one hell of a way to end a vacation. You heard me, scat!'

The tourist and his wife got out of the lift. The bellhop scrambled out after them. They left their hand luggage behind. But that couldn't be helped, John decided.

Going down, he held the letter against himself, so that if it did go off, Gabby would stand a reasonable chance. But she came to him, stood beside him, as he fiddled gingerly with the old-fashioned lever-operated control, trying to get the lift to operate smoothly – a thing that takes years of practice, actually. He stopped it with a horrendous jerk fifteen centimetres below floor level at the rez-de-chaussée, which is what the French call the street-level floor, the first floor being always one flight of stairs up. Eased it back up to where the doors would open. He was sweating. His shirt was soaked and sticking to his back.

The two of them crossed the lobby to the concierge's desk. John showed him the letter, told him what to do. Then he said:

'You stay here, Gabby. Please. Once I'm outside, it'll be all right.

She said crisply, coolly:

'All right, dearest. Put it down somewhere. Then move ten metres away from it. But stay there until the police come – or someone might just try to pick it up – or—'

He took it outside, put it in the shrubbery on the edge of the parking place. Stood guard over it from ten metres away until the police car came whooping and screaming up to retrieve it.

Naturally they wanted him to ride down to the Prefecture with them to make a declaration.

'With *that* aboard?' he said. 'No, thank you, messieurs les agents! You may take my declaration here and now, or come back later. My name's John Farrow. I am not leaving the hotel until Sunday.'

They looked at him. Then they shrugged. It was evident even to people as suspicious as policemen normally are that a man wouldn't mail a letter bomb to himself and then call the bomb squad to come and get it. Only incurably ill men who wanted their wives to collect their insurance by making their suicides appear accidental did things like that, in their experience. Or madmen. And this strange Frenchman in American clothing had the look of neither.

'We will come back, m'sieur,' one of them said. 'May we ask you to remain at the hotel until our return? A matter of a half an hour, no more. This is a serious matter. The cooperation of m'sieur in our investigations may well prove invaluable.'

'*Volontiers,*' John Farrow said and turning went back into the lobby.

Gabrielle was waiting for him by the concierge's desk. Her face was very white. The concierge's matched it.

'We,' John thought, 'have sure as hell worn our welcome out at the Majestic!' He said calmly:

'Any mail that comes to either of us, today, tomorrow, or after we have gone, should be delivered to the police. I shall give them carte blanche to open it, m'sieur. But I don't think there will be any. The people who sent this one have already left France, by air, this morning.'

'Oui, m'sieur!' the concierge said. *'D'accord, m'sieur! C'est fait!'*

John turned to Gabby, said:

'Come on, will you?'

'Come on – where?' she whispered.

'To the bar, baby! This is the first time in my life I've ever wanted a drink at half past ten in the morning, but now I do. Or two – or three.'

She smiled at him then.

'Y'know, darling,' she said. 'Sometimes you have *very* intelligent ideas!'

John's declaration to the police was brief and to the point. The boton from the Hôtel des Pyrénées had brought the letter. Presumably the boy had seen, and could identify, the would-be assassins. No, beyond the fact that Madame Farrow – Gabby smiled and blushed like a schoolgirl at hearing him call her that – had been informed that they were North Africans, he had no idea who they were. But when he said:

'Their motives? About that, m'sieur l'agent, your guess is as good as mine. I haven't even visited France since the mid-sixties and—'

Gabrielle cut him off.

'Now, John—' she said. 'Tell them about – Aix-en-Provence, please!'

'Aix-en-Provence?' the agent said. *'Qu'es-ce que vous êtes arrivés là-bas?'*

John glared at Gabrielle. She said, quickly:

'It's – not vengeance, John. Say, prevention, rather. They'll go on killing people. Innocent people, unless we, or somebody stops them.

'All right,' he said; then to the agent: 'We went to Aix to look for an old friend of mine. I had been informed – misinformed' – he glared at Gabby once again – 'that he lived there. But the information was – say, mistaken. The man in question was not my friend. He was an elderly German named Albrecht Holtz. Before leaving New York I was told by an agent of the Federal

Narcotics Bureau that Holtz was one of the biggest operators in the heroin trade. Whether he is or not, I don't know—'

'John—' Gabrielle began.

'Shut up, Gabby!' John said. 'All I – we – know is that he was at a place called Chez Ahmad with three North Africans. I spoke to him, calling him by name. He failed, or refused, to respond to his name. So I left. A little later, one of the North Africans – a girl, entered my room under the pretext that she had vital information to give me – and then tried to murder me. Stabbed me in the back. We believe that she is the same person who gave the boton the letter bomb to deliver to me . . . it *was* a bomb, wasn't it?'

'Bien sûr. It broke all the back windows in the Prefecture when we exploded it with pistol fire. *The* most powerful letter bomb we have ever seen. One thing more, M'sieur Farrow: you are, perhaps, CIA?'

'No,' John said, 'truly, no. During the war I was in the OSS, but afterwards I got out. I have been, on two occasions, a presidential courier, with nothing like the power or the influence that M'sieur Kissinger has today, of course. . . .'

'Then you have no idea *why* the Nord-africains wish to kill you?'

'Yes, one: they think I *know* what their connections with Holtz are. And what they are doing in France, and other European countries, I suspect. They're wrong. I don't. In fact, I haven't the faintest idea.'

'But *I* do,' Gabrielle said. 'John tell them who we think Albrecht Holtz is.'

'No,' he said, 'because I don't think anything about the gentleman, Gabrielle!'

'John,' she said softly, 'even at the risk of having you – furious at me again. I *can't* let him get away with this. They tried to kill you, *twice*. If I'd followed my natural jealous female impulses, you'd have found me, and – and your child – reduced to bloody rags when you got here. Tell me – did you mail my letter of resignation to the embassy?'

'Yes, Gabby,' he said, 'I understand your reasons. But don't. Simone wouldn't want it this way. She asked me never to—'

'I knew her *after* you did, John. She had – excellent reasons to change her mind. She died of those reasons.'

'But did she?' John said, 'specifically, in so many words, Gabrielle? *Can* you say that?'

'No. She died too quickly. But even so – even leaving Simone out of it, Kroll *has* to be stopped, John – as a preventive measure—'

'*Voulez-vous, m'sieur, 'dame,*' the agent said, '*parlez français, s'il-vous plaît?*'

'All right,' Gabrielle said. 'This M'sieur Holtz is really Heindrich Kroll. Formerly Lieutenant Colonel Kroll of the Gestapo, officer. As for the traffic in heroin, that's a false trail, or at least a useless one. He is, of course, mixed up in it; but that's impossible to prove because he is much too clever. What *is* known, first of all, is that he is now an agent of Black September. But besides that, during the war he was commander of the Villa Montefleuri here in Cannes. And he is *still* wanted by *your* government, sir, for the murder of hundreds of people, for war crimes—'

Monsieur le Agent sighed.

'*Madame est evidement – juive?*' he said, '*même, peut-être, israélienne?*'

'Yes,' Gabrielle said bitterly, 'both. Which means—?'

'That my government's policy – is not to offend the Arab countries, madame. I do not defend this policy. I merely state it. We have known what it is to be without – gasoline, without fuel oil – for weeks. So therefore if M'sieur Holtz-Kroll cannot be proven guilty of a *present* crime – *une trentaine d'années c-est – peut-être trop – maintenant, madame. Je regrette—*'

'Thirty years is too long?' Gabrielle whispered. 'And those hundreds of people, Frenchmen and women, he – he tortured to death – are best forgot? Why, m'sieur? Because they were merely – Jews?'

'*Ah, non, madame!*' the agent protested. '*C'est seulement—*'

'Forget it,' John Farrow said. 'Is there anything else you need to know?'

'No, m'sieur. I think not. Now we must go to the Hôtel des Pyrénées to talk to the people there. *Au'voir m'sieur, 'dame!*'

'*Au'voir,*' John Farrow said; then to Gabrielle: 'Gabby, I'm sorry.'

'Why?' she said morosely, 'antisemitism is one of the facts of life, John. I'll bet you three hundred Israeli pounds that they *won't* close down the Olympic games. Not over eleven murdered Yids. Oh no! And especially not under *your* Brundage who took Jews off your teams in 1936 to avoid offending Hitler!'

'He should have taken Jesse Owens off, too, then,' John said.

'Probably never occurred to him – that antisemites are usually Negrophobes, too – or else he would have,' Gabby said. Then: 'John! I just thought of something! That box! The one I found at Tourette! Couldn't they have *planted* it, there, too? Might it not be as full of *la soupe* as your letter was?'

'Don't know,' John said, 'but I don't believe so – because I spotted it, or at least a glint of metal down there long before I ever met you, Gabby. I'd been meaning to go back after it, but things kept getting in the way. . . .'

'John—' she said, drawing his name out: 'it – or a glint of metal? Any old piece of metal that they removed, and later put the box there? It's – hardly rusted at all, love. And—'

'Jesus, Gabby, they'd have to know entirely too goddamned much to pull a stunt like that! They only started after me, after us – since we came back from Aix, remember. They'd have to know I was looking for Dalton Ross, for instance, know he used to live at Tourette-sur-Loup, know—'

'John – don't open that box. Take it to the police. Please?'

'Oh, hell! I'd hate for the police to get their noses into *that*, Gabby. His diary might be inside that box, you know. Or his will. Either would probably mention a few things I damned well don't want noised abroad. His relations with – my mother, for instance. . . .'

'John, let *me* open it for you.'

'Gabrielle, you're nuts. Batty. *Folle*. Insane.'

'No, I'm not, lover. Not this time, anyhow. Let's take it up into the mountains. Not up there where we found it, but towards Puget Théniers, Valberg, Barcelonette y'know – where it's really isolated, wild. . . .'

'Then we throw it over a precipice, and scramble down after it? A *great* mountaineer like me? Or even a much better one like you, who is if I may remind her – a wee bit pregnant, just a trifle knocked up?'

'No, *mon amour*! Of course not. We simply set it up against a rock, and march twenty-five metres away from it, at which distance your delicate little bride-to-be will *shoot* the lock off it. How's that?'

'Great. Gabby – how'd you get a pistol into France?'

'Didn't. My chief gave me one when I started down here after you. Said I'd need it – to arrange my own shotgun wedding. Looks like he was right, doesn't it?'

'Absolutely. A case of rank coercion if I ever saw one. Agreed to under duress, and hence invalid. And – oh, hell, Gabby, looks like I'm stuck with you, however you slice it. So now, come on. We've got to rent a car, again.'

'John, a big one, please? Let's not scramble little Simone, or little John, jolting me all over, what?'

'Or both,' he grinned. 'Think you could manage twins, Gabby?'

She stopped still, looked at him. Her eyes filled up with mischief, with delight.

'Now wouldn't *that* be perfectly lovely!' she said and kissed him.

Riding up towards Valberg in the car, he let her hold the little box on her knees. He wasn't at all worried, because he was sure that anything that hadn't gone off when the Nazis blasted Dalton's house to rubble wasn't likely to now. And the more he considered it, the more unlikely it seemed that Kroll and playmates could have planted that box beneath a mound of debris at the bottom of the gorge at Tourette-sur-Loup. The time element was against it. And not even Kroll had known the relationship between him and Dalton Ross. The thing was too farfetched. Still, in the half worlds of terrorists, intelligence operators, international drug pushers, and spies – worlds that met, crossed, and melted together with surprising frequency these days, things even more farfetched had happened. As a matter of simple prudence, Gabby's idea of shooting the lock open from a safe distance had a hell of a lot to recommend it, he decided.

So when they reached a likely spot, a little above Valberg, one of the finest ski resorts in all of Europe, he took the chrome-plated little box and set it up against a huge boulder, holding it in place with smaller rocks so that the impact of the bullet or bullets wouldn't spin it too far away.

By the time he got back to the car, she had taken the automatic out of her handbag. It was a flat, ugly Israeli copy of the German army's Pistolle M-2. He watched her lever a bullet into the chamber expertly, thumb the safety catch off. Then she took her place, there on that mountain road with the wind whipping her snow-white hair about her face, and her skirt about her slim, beautiful legs, and held that lethal piece of bloody murder in both hands like the professional she was, rock steady, sure, and squeezed off just one shot slowly.

He let his breath out. Walked over to the box. She had hit the lock dead centre. From twenty-five metres – in a rising wind. The lid was loose, was open.

'All right!' he called out to her. 'You win! I can take a hint! I'll marry you, Gabby!'

'And love, honour, cherish, and *obey* me!' she laughed, 'as well as not even looking at another female out of the corner of one eye. C'mon – let's see what's in it!'

What was in it was a bundle wrapped in oilskin, a long, long strip cut surely from one of Dalton's raincoats. It was at least two metres long. Dalton had made damned sure that even if the little chrome-plated coin box had rusted through – which it hadn't, since the debris it was under had kept most of the rain off it – the contents of that box would still be safe. As they were.

'John – what is it?' Gabrielle said.

'Poems – mostly,' John said, 'and a letter. Addressed – to me.'

'John – may I hear it? The letter I mean? I – already know about your mother, and—'

'And what, Gabby?' he said.

'And – don't shut me out – go on – trusting me. Will you, please?'

'Yes. Why yes, of course. It isn't much of a letter really. It says: "To John Farrow II, My Son." Then: "Dear Son, If you have come here, if you find this – my only legacy to you – and, I hope, to Simone – it means that you've found out, that you know – I, not John Farrow, sired you. Do not blame your mother for this, the fault was entirely mine, mine the sin – and you, my son, for me, have been its punishment.

' "I have always been honest with you, that you know. Therefore I will not seek your pardon by telling you compassionate lies about how much I loved your mother. For truth, sad truth is that I loved her not at all. A whim, a surrender to momentary desire, *una cana tirado en aire* as the Spanish say—" '

'John,' Gabrielle said, 'I know a fair amount of Spanish. But not that much. Please?'

' "A hair tossed into the air." Or more exactly, "A grey hair tossed into the air." It's the expression Spain's legions of Don Juans use to play down a casual love affair. The whole of it is, "*No tiene más importancia que una cana tirado en aire.*" "It has no more importance than a grey hair tossed into the air." '

'John – it would – to me. If you – ever do, don't let me find it out, please. It would kill me. Quite literally.'

'Then you're going to live forever. You want to hear the rest of it?'

'Yes. Oh yes, please!'

' "It was my intention to get out of her life, leave her to the tender mercies of her legal spouse, whose name, I suppose, you must forever bear. Such a desertion, after all, involved nothing more than slow death by boredom, which is how most people die. Besides, he was a good old stick, wasn't he? I confess I rather admired him, really." '

'Enough,' Gabrielle said bitterly, 'to commit adultery with his wife!'

'You'd have to have known Dalton, Gabby,' John said. 'He was capable of compartmentalizing his emotions to that extent.' He read on:

' "Except that on a trip to Paris, when you were all of two years old, by purest accident I encountered your mother and your foster father near the Etoile, pushing you along in a pram. You were, my son, quite the most beautiful child I had ever seen, or ever was to see thereafter—" '

'Were you?' Gabrielle said.

'Don't know. Paternal pride enters in, here, I suppose. Maman said I was, but then she was hardly an unprejudiced witness, either. Let me finish it, will you? "And I knew, very suddenly, that I *couldn't* stay out of your life, John; that I simply couldn't allow that fearsome old stick to bring you up in his image!" '

'So,' Gabrielle said, '*that's* why you're so schizoid, isn't it, John? Why the side of you which appears when you're angry, say, has so little relation with the other?'

'Yes. Why, yes; you're right. Except that it's more complicated than that really. To call me schizoid is an oversimplification. Not only was I torn between three people: Dalton, "Papa" and Maman, but between two *worlds*: Europe and America. I belong nowhere. I am alien – a stranger. For instance: both Dalton and my father – oh hell, I mean John Farrow, Senior – were naturally brave. I'm not. I seem to have inherited a strong streak of cowardice, maybe from my mother. I don't know. But I came home from the war with bleeding ulcers, Gabby, that I got by forcing myself too many times to do things I simply wasn't equipped to do. To give you another example: I've inherited all my mother's sensuality; and all of Dalton's. Yet there have been long periods of time I've lived the life of a monk, because of my foster father's influence on me. I really am a sort of a puritan, you know—'

'A quality I'll gladly let you keep – for when you're *away* from home, my love! But chez-nous you'd jolly well better store it in the attic; or in the basement, or somewhere! Oh dear, I keep interrupting you, don't I? I won't again. Do go on.'

'You know the rest,' John read. ' "From that day on, I more or less remained in your life, my son; shaped you, as far as I was able, into something very fine. And to be entirely fair, John Farrow helped greatly, by keeping you from the worst of my many vices. So be it! Now since I have no time – since it has all run out on me – I leap the years to now, today. I have just this morning learned, from your good friend Pepe Gomez, that it is *you*, and not the man I thought, who now is Simone's lover.

' "I was instrumental in saving him, freeing him, so that she – the only woman in all my life whom I have *loved* – loved beyond belief, hope, and even bearing! – could have a life of sorts in the future. I fear that in this, all unknowingly, I have injured you. I hope not. I hope with all my heart you two are still together. Be that as it may, I leave to you, to her, these, my last poor efforts. You will find most of them strange; utterly unlike the *me* you know. For in this I am become as Browning's Rafael, by love transformed. If she lives – a thing I doubt – for no one could survive for many years the gentle attentions of Kroll and company, give these to her, read them to her. If not, bury them in her grave as a final offering from him who loved you both.

' "Farewell, Son. Your Father." '

'John,' Gabrielle said, 'd'you know what he meant by Browning's Rafael? For if you don't, *I* do.'

'Tell me then,' John said.

'Anton said it to me, once. In – reference to him. To Dalton Ross. He said that Dalton said it to *him*, to explain—'

'Why he'd changed from the barest, most unadorned free verse anyone ever read to – sonnets. As here. Lyrical. To anyone who knew him before, almost embarrassingly romantic. What's the reference from Browning, Gabby? Wait! Before that, tell me: Anton was the man he saved, wasn't he?'

'Yes. But he didn't trick Ross into helping him get away, John. Your father – tricked himself. He put the questions badly. He asked Anton, "Do you love Simone Levy?" Quite a different thing from asking, as he should have, "Are you Simone's lover?" Anton didn't even know *why* he asked him that until too late. Or else he'd have explained things better, instead of—'

'Answering simply and truthfully, "Yes." I see. And the Browning reference?'

> 'Raphael made a century of sonnets,
> Made and wrote them in a certain volume
> Dinted with the silver-pointed pencil
> Else he only used to draw Madonnas . . .
>
> Raphael's cheek so duteous and so loving,
> Cheek, the world was wont to hail a painter's,
> Raphael's cheek, her love had turned a poet's . . .'

'Yes,' John said, 'yes. That would apply. And it's beautiful, isn't it?'

'John, don't you find it strange that he doesn't even *mention* those broadcasts? Attempt to explain to you, to the world, *why* he made them?'

'I think he does, in the poems. There's a long one called *Apologia Pro Vita Sua*. I've only glanced at the first few lines; but it's surely an explanation. Even the title suggests that. Now come on, we'd better be getting back. We've a lot of packing to do. And on top of that, you, my sweet, are going to start resting. Taking care of yourself. Of – my future.'

'Not yet. John – read me some of them, will you. The ones he wrote for *you*, anyhow?'

'Oh hell, Gabby, we'll have all the time in the world to—'

'Please, John. Just one. Please.'

'Only one of them seems to be dedicated to me. And I wouldn't swear that even it is. Considering its title, it could be for any of fifty other little bastards. Anyhow, here it is, title and all. . . .

For the Eldest of My Carelessly,
Unlawfully, Illegitimately, But not
Unlovingly Begot Offspring . . .

You will of course imagine, being young
That before you were, no love had come to be
That no two other idiot children clung
Mouth to wild mouth in sobbing ecstasy . . .
You'll see a woman – faded, wrinkled, plain,
Halting of speech, hands trembling, vacant eyed;
And never know her lips invented pain
Or that it was of wanting her I died.
For my part, keep the arrogance of youth –
The sop's not given till you cry, "I thirst!"
Reject such useless evidence as truth
And never dream a man can hang accurst
Pierced hands and side and feet upon a tree
Nailed to his death by grief, by memory. . . .'

'He means – Simone, here; doesn't he, John?' she whispered.

'Most likely. Yes. Surely, yes.'

'Then I hope I'm *not* too much like her. I shouldn't want to hurt – a man – this much. . . .'

'Then, don't do what she did to him, to me. Stay with me, Gabby. Don't *you* hang me up there again.'

'Oh!' she said, 'I'd say that's the *last* thing on earth you need worry about! John, may I have the others now? To read on the way down? While you're driving? May I, please?'

'Of course, Gabby. Now come on,' he said.

They were almost all the way down to the Côte before she said anything. Then she said: 'He does explain it, John. In the *Apologia.* And indirectly, in some of the others. I am going to have photocopies made – of all of them. And we must keep them. So that some day, somehow we can vindicate his memory. Because he wasn't a bastard, you know. He was a good man. In the same way you are. Kind, good, tender. I *thought* that was why he made those broadcasts; but I didn't know it, before now. . . .'

John looked at her, said quietly:

'For Simone, wasn't it, Gabby? To – save her?'

'Yes. He bargained with the devil for his pound of flesh. And lost. But then, one always loses, doesn't one? He was wrong and he was right at one and the same time. But it's not only for that, that I am very grateful to him. But also for the one he wrote for *me*. Oh no! He didn't know it was for me. He thought it was for Simone—'

'Gabby, you're crazy, you know!'

'No, I'm not. Listen!' Then she read, in a voice that was low, soft, a tremble, so that he had to strain his ears to hear it:

'(For Simone, Again and Always)
Ton Peau, your skin, stretched delicately tight
Over fragile bones, dusk rose beneath old gold,
A membrane my fingers palpated between the dark and light,
Honeydripping with your tastes, your smells, sold
To my madness, for that spendthrift's price
Love: That you loved me, by which I then turned god.
You loved me and I – what? Once or twice
At first, then always, the thing no longer odd,
Learned love, a cruel, a flagellant's art
That condemns to early death, the pronoun "I,"
And flatly states two people, us, will part,
That a man, I, a woman, you, must die –
Yet *we* are eternal; what we were and are
Will people the cosmos, outlast the final star!

'Don't you see, my love, my love, my dearest love – that this – all unknowingly was for *you*, for me, for us? You're his son – you bear his blood; and I – am her sister, and her image. So – we can do *that*. Save something of both of them from extinction. In fact, we already have, haven't we? Oh John – if I could only pray! If there *were* something up there somewhere – who cared! But there isn't, is there? And – prayer's – presumptuous, isn't it? To ask him – who permitted Auschwitz, Dachau, Ravensbrück—'

'Nagasaki,' John said, 'Hiroshima. Song My. My Lai.'

'Yes. And Lod Airport. The Games – Munich, this week. To ask him – to let me live. To give you – a child. Presumptuous – and too much. So—'

'Ask him anyhow. Maybe this time the old bastard will get the wax out of his ears.'

'John!' she said.

'Don't mind me, Gabby. I'm only asking one thing, of *you* – because there's nobody else to ask it of—'

'And that is?' she whispered.

'That you stay with me, baby. That you live. Because without you, I can't. Do you promise?'

She leaned towards him, kissed his cheek.

'Yes. John, I promise,' she said.

18

Sitting there in the first-class cabin of the big Boeing 707, it came to John Farrow that he didn't feel very comfortable. And when he searched his mind for possible reasons for his discomfort, he came inescapably to the conclusion that he was afraid. That, he had to admit, was odd. He had no very strong feelings about flying one way or the other. Like any man of his social position, he had done a great deal of it over the years. His one-time reaction to it was that, generally, it bored him stiff; but today, inexplicably, he was afraid. The palms of his hands were wet; drops of perspiration beaded on his forehead.

He glanced at Gabby to see if she had noticed anything; but she had fitted – for the first time since he'd known her – a pair of huge and heavy-rimmed spectacles over her eyes, and was busily engaged in copying the poems that Dalton Ross had left as a legacy on to a ruled, folio-sized notepad, first in English, and then in Hebrew.

'That,' John said, 'is quite a trick, Gabby.'

'Oh, don't give me too much credit, darling,' she said, 'I'm only making a rough translation of their meanings, rather. In prose. I want to show them to a friend of mine, Chaim Hayle. One of our better Hebrew poets. Only he doesn't know English – even so, I'm sure he can do them justice.'

'Lord God, Gabby – why?'

'Would be quite a coup to publish them in Hebrew translation, in Israel, wouldn't it, John? The first step in – vindicating – your father. Because, after that, how could those New

York publishers you told me about last night—'

'Siegal and Hechtfield?'

'Yes. How could they then refuse? If the people of Israel are willing to accept this posthumous – apology – for the harm he did, by putting my sister's life above all else, I don't see why his former publishers can't – or won't—'

'They'd give you some damned fine business reasons, Gabby. Namely that poetry doesn't sell, never has, and never will. That apart from the lingering bad odour that Dalton's name still carries, he's a has-been; besides which he was always out of the mainstream of his times – whatever fame he formerly had was due to his unceasing efforts to shock people, my dear; both with his poetry and his life. And since, nowadays, people have become shockproof, that gimmick doesn't work any more. So—'

He unbuckled his seat belt, stood up.

'John!' she said sharply, 'where're you going? We're going to take off any minute now!'

'I know. Just want to take a gander at tourist class, Gabby. See if there's anyone *we* know aboard. . . .'

'Oh!' she whispered, then: 'Do, John!'

He was back in his seat within two minutes.

'No,' he said, 'not a familiar face. And what's more – no Arabs, as far as I can tell. So we can relax – till we get to Rome, anyhow. Because I'm quite sure we won't be bothered in England.'

'Thank God for that, darling!' Gabby said.

It seemed to him the pilot was taking an excessively long time to run in the engines. Then it came to him why: the Nice airport, called the Airport Côte d'Azur, was a scant five kilometres out of town. It was, of all the airports he knew, the one closest to the major city it served. Its defects, as an airport, were both great and incurable. For one thing it lay on a long strip of flat land, paralleling the beach, a strip so narrow that aircraft could only take off towards the city, or towards the mountains, never in the direction of the sea.

When he remembered that, his nervousness came back. What the pilot was doing was holding the big bird with the brakes while coaxing out of the jet turbines every gram of thrust possible before beginning the take-off run. The immense craft sat there and shook and bellowed. And John Farrow sat remembering all he knew about jet aircraft, which was a little too much, and shook a little harder than the plane. Because to get a plane as big as a 707 out of Nice airport at all, the pilot was going to have to pull all those tons of machinery, baggage and human flesh up into a tight climbing turn the minute he had the landing gear retracted, and pray that he had speed enough not to stall. The ground acceleration of jets, he knew, ranged from piss-poor to godawful. Every major airport in the world had had to triple the length of its runways once the jets came into service. And Nice's airport simply hadn't anywhere else to go. To make its runways any longer than they were they'd have to run them down the Promenade des Anglais.

'John,' Gabby said, 'you don't look very happy.'

'I'm not,' he said.

'Why not, darling?'

'Tell you *after* take-off,' he said. 'Well, here we go.'

The pilot did a beautiful job. His pull-off was so steep that they were rammed back into their seats by at least five Gs, and he was into that turn at once, pouring on everything he had, so that looking out and down that huge swept wing, John saw blue water below them, dropping away at an astonishing rate, the pleasure craft on it diminishing even as he stared at them. Then that wing raked skywards and the humped and bluish mountains were on the other side of them, and they, too, were dropping away, and it was all right now, it was fine.

'John—' Gabby said, 'what was wrong?'

'That goddamned airport. It always scares me spitless.'

'Why, John?' she said.

'Too small. Too short. Too close to town. Too near those fornicating mountains. Makes those poor bastards up front who already have far too much to cope with do *everything* wrong. But it's all right, now. All we have to worry about is whether Heathrow is socked in right down to ground level and those approaches to Leonardo da Vinci—'

'The Rome airport? I thought it was quite a good one, darling—'

'It is. But it's also swamped with traffic. The boys in the tower all have peptic ulcers. They average twenty-five near collisions a day—'

'John!' she laughed, merrily, 'you don't like flying very much, do you?'

'Hell, Gabby, I've never even thought about it before today.

But right now I can visualize every approach into Rome, and after that into Piraeus, and – say – how's Lod?'

'Very good, I'm told, John – are you worrying because *I'm* with you?'

'Yes,' he said, then he reached out and poked her slim middle with a tentative finger, 'and because *she* is, too.'

She laughed again, delightedly, said:

'John – if it's a boy will you be *very* disappointed, my love?'

'No. As long as the little bastard looks like you, Gabby.'

'Then *I'll* be disappointed. I want him to look like you. But anyhow, we'd better enjoy London, John, dearest! Because Tel Aviv is going to be a bit hectic, I'm afraid. Rushing about, visiting people, parties, my *big* reception—'

'No it's not,' he said grimly, 'because the *only* damn place we're going to rush to will be the hospital or clinic, or wherever it is your Dr Elon hangs out.'

'John,' she whispered, 'I – I don't want to go there first. . . .'

'Afraid she'll tell you you can't, Gabby?'

'Yes. And – and it would break my heart. You can't possibly imagine how much I *want* this child. *Our* child, John.'

'Gabby, you promised me you'd be sensible!'

'Yes – but couldn't I be sensible a little later, love? Can't I stay – happy – a little while?'

'No,' he said sadly, 'selfishly, no. Unless you *want* me to come down with bleeding ulcers.'

She smiled at him a little tearfully, said:

'All right, John.' Then she handed a sheaf of papers to him, said: 'Here, take this – read it. So you'll know why he did it. Your father, I mean. So that you can understand him, even forgive him. As I already have—'

'Lord, Gabby,' he said, 'somehow I—'

'Read it, John!' she said.

He picked up the papers. It was the *Apologia*. Sighing he began to read:

> Apologia Pro Vita Sua
> Weakness, yes.
> That's comprehensible;
> an old acquaintance, really,
> too well known, snivelling
> in the corners of all

my rooms, making
the air rank with his
halitosis, body ordure –
(Merde! Read rot mouth,
sweatstink, belchfart
shitty, puking stench
of cowardice.)
Scratching his shrivelled
balls and whining:
'It wasn't my fault! What
could I do?
They'd have killed me
if I hadn't . . .'
All the oversimplifications, the
easy answers
as if his (my) or any man's
dying, mattered.
But I can say
with some truthfulness –
say fifty-one per cent true
and hence slightly less
than half a lie –
that I'd have given my life
would have died
would have endured
(for a certain length of time
anyhow)
their tortures.

But they bypassed me there,
gave me no chance at even
cheap, bargain basement heroics,
knowing as they did I was
a romantic, and romantics never
believe in –
well, say, evil as an absolute
and men capable of it
absolutely.
Let me enumerate the choices
that they gave me;
not in self-defence, the human

condition being
by its very humanity defenceless –
but simply so you'll understand.
As if that mattered either
as if anything could matter
in
a universe emptied
of reason
order
sense
meaning.
In short, you could say –
that is, if you're religious –
bereft of God.
And those choices offered
not so much to me
as to that gesticulating ghostly
pack of semantic irrelevancies
puffed up with such specious pomposities
as now I vomit over:
my ethics, my integrity
my – dear God, dear God! – my
honour.
First, her life.
Hers, goddamn you!
If I, a person of a certain fame, of
some stature, intellectually
speaking (There were,
after all, those prizes. Few
enough, you are aware, and of
such tarnished metal, as even a
lowbrow poet could earn; one
who had better judgment
than to shun
out of pure and instinctive
distaste, let me admit it! –
the closed circle, old school
tie, properly élitist
obscurantism,
was naïve enough,
retrograde enough, sufficiently

unfashionable as to
make his meaning clear.
But those shaven bullet heads,
those technocrats of murder
were too dense to realize
that!)
would twice weekly
over the radio defend
in well chosen words
Der Führer.
Defame – cleverly, thoughtfully, not
to excess –
her people, her religion, and her
race.
Oh, they'd supply me with the rough drafts,
crafted by no less a personage
than Lord Haw-Haw, himself:
'International Jewry, the Jewrocracy,
Franklin Delano Rosenfeldt, Morgenthau
et al – you've heard it, you know
how it goes.
And seeing me stiffen, hearing
my croaking, craven, coward's whisper:
'She would not have her life of me
at such a price!'
Defining the alternatives:
The manner of her dying,
the thin steel rods stroking lightly
endlessly
the electrodes clamped to her
nipples, to the labia, to
silver-plated probes that
could be inserted
here and there until
her screams would damn my ears
forever.
Then pushing forward a chair
for me to collapse into,
offering, suavely, the
respite:

Some weeks in which to think it over,
that is, if she didn't go mad, or
even stayed alive that long
in the Feldtdirnenhaus to
which they'd send her;
branded on her
forearm and her thigh:
'Feldt Hure Nummer
Vierundfünfzig,
Field whore number fifty-four,
Reserved for officers, only!'
I have no excuse.
Love is a madness.
I did it.
Damned us both:
Me to the icy hell of
her contempt;
her, to a life become
intolerable at
the price I'd paid for
it.
Because, you see,
Love
is not enough:
the empty words must have
meaning restored to them
And God called back
from the appalling distances
when he has fled.
But – how?
I ask you that
from my dungeon
beneath the floor of hell.
How, Brother?
Tell me:
How?

He looked up, handed the pages to her. He didn't say anything for a long time. Then he said:

'Poor old fellow. Hell of a thing, wasn't it?'

'Yes,' Gabrielle said, 'the ultimate refinement of evil: this diabolic strategy of forcing their victims to embrace it. The choice that was no choice really; damned if you do; damned equally if you don't. If he had sacrificed Simone, he would never have forgiven himself; so he didn't sacrifice her; and he still couldn't forgive himself for what he was forced to do. What was worse, she couldn't forgive him either – nor herself for being alive at such a price. . . .'

'How was she – afterwards?' John said.

'Withdrawn, much of the time. Either – too talkative; too gay – or too silent. Quite often, sick. Though afterwards she'd recovered almost completely, or so we thought. When I came out to Israel with Guy – from London; that's where I met him; we were both students at London University's Central College for Foreigners – she and Anton were already settled in Tel Aviv – they had been there since forty-seven—'

'But *before* forty-seven?' he said.

'Cyprus. In an internee camp with fifty thousand other Jewish refugees. Thanks to our charming British friends, y'know. They were smuggled out of Cyprus by the Aliyan Beth – the illegal immigration organization. And into Israel in time to fight, both of them in the nineteen forty-eight war.'

John said: 'I don't need to ask how they did. I know.'

'Yes. I suppose you do. They were both decorated for bravery. Anton came out of that one as a *rav-seren*, and Simone as *segen* – in the Women's Corps. General Dayan says she was the best *chayelet* he ever saw.'

'Gabby,' he said, 'you're throwing too much Hebrew at me, you know—'

'Deliberately. The first thing I'm going to do with you is inscribe you in an *ulpan*, my boy!'

'Are you going to translate some of that, voluntarily, or do I have to belt you one?' he said.

She laughed then, freely, gaily.

'You can't, you know, my love,' she said. 'I'm just a bit – fragile these days. And since you're at least somewhat responsible for my interesting condition, you'll just have to put up with my being perfectly outrageous any time I take the notion to!'

'Which is going to be most of the time, I'll bet,' he said. 'C'mon, Gabby, what does all that mean?'

'Military ranks. A *segen*'s a lieutenant. A *rav-seren* is a major.

Chayelet's the general term for a girl soldier. And, last of all an *ulpan* is the school we send adult immigrants to, in order to make them learn Hebrew jolly fast!'

'And who's the adult immigrant, may I ask?'

'You,' she said, and kissed him.

By then the *hôtesse de l'aire* was there with the trays for lunch. She smiled at them with real pleasure.

'Votre voyage de noces, m'sieur, 'dame?' she said.

'Something like that,' John said in English: 'at least when her husband divorces her, and my wife sheds me, we'll get around to making it legal and proper. . . .'

Gabby punched him with her fist, hard.

'John, you naughty boy!' she said then to the hostess. 'Ne le croyez pas, ma'moiselle! Il—'

'He is joking. That one sees. And also that I guessed right, With a little experience one always distinguishes honeymooning couples. They – they look so happy! And never I think, have I seen a pair *as* happy as you two are. *Mes félicitations les plus sincères!'*

'Tu vois!' Gabrielle said to him.

'I see I'm *sunk*,' he groaned. 'Gabby, tell me a couple of other things: Did you *know* Simone and Anton were in Israel when you came out?'

She stared at him, and her eyes went dark with quite visible hurt.

'John,' she said quietly, 'I told you the truth: I didn't know Simone existed. Nor Anton, for that matter. I married a nice Jewish boy in London, and he persuaded me to go to Israel with him. He hadn't turned into a skirt-chaser in those days—'

'Look, Gabby, I'm only trying to fill in the gaps, that's all. Between nineteen forty-four and – fifty-five or six, wasn't it?'

'Fifty-five, John. I married Guy when I was twenty; another thing I told you before.'

'All right. In eleven years, you might have found out, mightn't you?'

'No. There really wasn't any way for me to, John. My whole family was dead – except Simone. And she was half a world away. All the people who knew us before were also dead, or scattered. I had no papers – nothing. To this day, I have no proof whatsoever that Simone Levy was my sister.'

'Except that you wear her face,' he said.

'John, if you keep this up, I'm going to a plastic surgeon so ruddy fast it'll make your head swim! Why, damn and blast! Here I am, not only in love with the creature, but quite helplessly pregnant by him, and he—'

'Loves you. Even that firecracker temper. Even, or maybe especially, the ways you're nothing like Simone.'

'You know,' she said sadly, 'it so happens that I am quite a lot like her – in too many ways. Even my falling in love with you proves it. She said I would. The first time I saw you. She – wanted me to. To – compensate you for her having run out on you, I suppose—'

'And you, like a dutiful little sister—'

'I did not! I fought against it like blazes! It wasn't until your third trip to Paris that I – really gave in, and admitted to myself how thoroughly I'd been brainwashed on the subject of one John Farrow!'

'Bless her for that,' he said.

'Yes, I do – every minute of the day and night. I suppose what you're trying to worm out of me with this not so subtle interrogation is how I got to know her, isn't it?'

'If you will be so kind. . . .'

'All right. It was pure accident, John. Guy and I were wandering about – exploring the city as it were. And we happened to pass through Dizengoff Street; that's where all the smart cafés are, y'know—'

'I didn't; but now I do. Go on, Gabby.'

'In – a little while, darling,' Gabby said.

Looking up, John saw that the stewardesses were there with the lunch. After they had been served, and by deliberately *not* drinking the champagne – because every time it went down two centimetres in their glasses their hostess was there to brim it up again – she managed to tell the rest of it.

'And so there I was, standing there with my mouth wide open and this absolutely insane little woman was embracing me and sobbing and calling "Rachi!" and "*ma petite soeur!*" and all the people were staring at us and smiling happily, because you see, darling, things like that happened quite frequently in Israel in those days. Then this tall good-looking red-haired man who was with her—'

'Anton,' John said.

'Yes, Anton – saw how astonished I was, so he said: "*Mais*

vous êtes Rachel Levy, n'est-ce pas, ma'moiselle?" And I had to admit that I didn't know *who* I was really, except that I had been brought up as Gabrielle de la Motte, and that I was now Madame Guy Betrand. So then we all sat down at a table – it was at Kassit's where all the intellectuals hang out, and as usual it was jam-packed and everyone was beaming at us fondly, and I was so bloody miserable I wanted to die!'

'Why, Gabby?' he said.

'Don't know, really. I *hate* being stared at. And they were all so – so exuberant – and so happy for us, and enjoying the touching reunion – and so ruddy *Jewish* – that I hated every minute of it!'

'Now, Gabby—' he said.

'I know, I know. I'd been brought up all wrong, dearest. I was quite your upper-class French demoiselle – and a Catholic demoiselle at that. Before I'd been there long I could yell and scream and gabble with the best of 'em – I mean of course, with the immigrants, the refugees – because the Sabras don't. They're so laconic and stiff upper-lippish and controlled they make me want to pinch 'em or tread on their toes to see if they'll jump. . . .'

'And—' John prompted.

'And, after Simone had calmed down a little, they – with the help of Guy, who kept saying, "but, Gabby, you're practically identical!" – convinced me I *had* to be the long-lost Rachel Levy. I was found near Fayence, and she was lost there—'

'At the school where the SS took away your little brother, shot two of the nuns, and put the other two in a field whorehouse. I know.'

'Yes,' Gabrielle whispered, 'but I still wouldn't believe it until Simone dragged me into the ladies' lavatory and made me look at our two faces side by side in the mirror. That did it. That evidence was too strong to deny. After that, she and Anton took us over. They moved us into their *shikun* – oh, there I go! – that's a cooperatively owned apartment building: each family owns its own flat, but the common expenses are shared; and did *everything* for us, got us jobs; taught us the most important art that anyone living in Israel has to know; *le' histader* which means exactly what *s'arranger* does in French, how to pull wires, special pleading, manoeuvring around official obstacles. . . .'

She bowed her head, whispered:

'And thereby wrecked us, for Guy became the greatest master of *le' histader* in Israel's history – especially when it came to arranging himself into other women's beds—'

'All right,' John said, 'we've both had a bad time, in that regard, Gabby, so I vote we both forget that, and concentrate on each other.'

'Yes,' she said, 'quite! That's all that counts now, isn't it? But I must tell you one more thing; that *first* night at supper, I couldn't help but stare at her horribly crippled left hand – so she explained what had happened – which brought on the subject of you. The one subject that *never* stopped. Whenever we were alone she'd – embark upon her unending paeans in praise of your virtues. One of the main reasons I switched over to the Foreign Service was to get away from that. I confess I'd got to the place where I loathed the very sound of your name. But then there was Paris and – oh look, darling! I do believe we're there!'

He gazed out the window and the mist green of England was already there below them so that he had to look backwards over the wing tip to see the rapidly receding waters of the Channel, and the big jet was whistling down a long slant of sky so that the rows of little red English houses grew and grew and there was the Thames, bright bronze in the setting sun, and the towers and spires of London until a steep bank cartwheeled earth and sky and there was Heathrow directly below them with all its criss-crossed rows of airstrips, and parking strips littered with miniature aircraft all of them growing now: hangars, buildings, streams of cars racing upwards to join them, rocking a little, then steadying ballooning up, expanding coming on. . . .

'Yes, Gabby, darling,' he said, 'it seems we are.'

Before the bellhop had even opened the door to their small suite at Claridge's, they could hear the telephone ringing insistently inside. The boy opened the door, crossed very quickly to it, picked it up; said:

'Hullo?' Then, 'yes, sir! He's here now, sir! I'll put him on directly, sir!' And handed the phone to John.

Byron's voice came crackling over the wire.

'John! I must say this is a surprise! How soon can I pick you up, old boy?'

'Well,' John said, 'give us an hour, Byron – to at least freshen up a bit. We just this minute got in. . . .'

'We?' Byron said, 'not the little creature you presented me to in New York, eh John?'

'God, no!' John said, 'suppose you just wait and see, Byron. By the way, please do bring Brenda along, will you? Right. In an hour then.'

'John,' Gabby said, 'is this Byron – the Byron Graves that Simone also mentioned quite often?'

'Yes,' John said, 'why, baby?'

'Would you mind dreadfully if I – don't come along? Tell him I've a headache. That's true. I have. And—'

'Gabrielle!' John said.

'Oh, John, dearest, I *do* hate explaining things! He'll probably think that I'm – oh, damn and blast! Why did I *ever* get mixed up with you?'

He put his arms around her, kissed her, said:

'*You* said it was because you loved me.'

'I did. I do. But – oh, I'm in a perfect blue funk that's all! Forgive me. I'll bear up. Now turn me loose – let's see if I can't make myself look at least somewhat human. . . .'

When they came downstairs she looked not only human, but to his prejudiced eyes, radiant. Even so, Byron almost spoiled things. The moment he saw her, he let out a roar:

'You found her! You actually found her! Why Simone as I live and breathe!'

Then, before anyone could say anything, he had swept Gabrielle into his arms and was kissing her with obvious delight.

'I say, John,' Brenda Graves laughed, 'even though we haven't been properly introduced, we should at least get even, don't you think?'

Brenda was a tall blonde with one of those complexions that English women invented and still hold the exclusive patent rights upon. John kissed her, said to Byron:

'Is wife-swapping permitted in England these days, Byron?'

'Don't you think you'd better marry me *first*, before swapping me?' Gabrielle said.

'You mean he *hasn't*?' Byron said, 'John, you're insane. Absolutely!'

'That's what we're here *for*,' John said. 'You two are already drafted, as witnesses. A quiet little civil ceremony – as soon as possible. I have that firm of Limey shysters I do business with working out the details.'

'I do hope they're fast workers,' Gabby said, 'or else I shall have to rush out and buy a new wedding dress. At the Pre-maman. Do you have Pre-mamans in London, Byron?'

'But, of course!' Byron said. Then he added, a trifle worriedly: 'You're pulling my leg now, what – aren't you Simone?'

'John dearest,' Gabby said, 'explain all this, will you please? Starting with the fact that I am *not* Simone?'

'Later,' John said, 'sitting down. With a drink in my hand. It's damned confusing, you know. I vote we go at it slowly. . . .'

They had dinner at Prunier's on St James's Street, the seafood restaurant. Gabby fell to, devouring oysters with such mischievous delight that John stared at her. It wasn't until later that he found out that shellfish are high on the list of the Kashruth prohibitions, which accounted for Gabby's enjoying them so much.

Between times, John explained. From time to time Gabby threw in a helpful remark. "Helpful in compounding confusion, that is," John thought.

'If I follow you, old boy, and I'm not at all sure I do,' Byron said, 'this divine and delightful little creature is *not* Simone Levy, but – perhaps, and – only perhaps – her younger sister?'

'Something like that,' John said, 'this curious little machine for ingesting oysters – Gabby, you stop it! Damnit all, you're going to be sick!' She was at the moment, signalling the waiter to bring her her fourth dozen. She grinned at him, said:

'If you can't pay the bill, you can leave me behind to wash the dishes, dearest!' And signalled to the waiter again.

'I must say I admire your capacity, my dear!' Brenda said.

'It's just that I haven't had any in so long,' Gabby said; then added, 'besides they're supposed to be a brain food, aren't they? Rich in phosphorous, or something. And since I want my son to be a *little* smarter than his father is, I'd jolly well start taking care. . . .'

'Gabby,' John said, 'shocking the English is out. They don't any more. They've joined the world.'

'I should say we have,' Brenda said, 'but just for curiosity – is she *serious?*'

'Rather,' Gabby said. 'The first day I met him, I got rid of my pills. Flushed them down the loo. How else d'you think I could have got him to propose? Oh dear! I am full – I'm afraid I can't even finish these, after all. . . .'

'John, d'you know what? I actually think she's even a trifle madder than Simone was. And it's an improvement. Charming. Oh quite!' Byron said.

Two weeks from that day, they took off from Heathrow once again. Gabby had the marriage certificate, carefully rolled up and wrapped in transparent plastic, in her hands.

'To show to Anton quickly,' she explained, 'in case we run into him by accident, before I'm prepared—'

'Come on, Gabby, you can't be that afraid of him,' John said.

'Oh yes, I am! He's the most terrible tempered man you ever did see, John! D'you know why he had to stop playing the violin? He broke his left hand on a Sabra's hard head. At the university. He was teaching a course in composition, and this blockhead of a Sabra wasn't paying attention. So Anton told him off. And the Sabra swore at him. Called him "savon", soap. That's the ultimate Sabra insult to the ex-refugees, y'know. . . .'

'Why?' John said.

'Means – that we got what we had coming to us. For – our cowardice. That we really weren't fit for anything else except to be boiled down into bars of soap—'

'And Anton hit him. Good for Anton I say!'

'Yes. There's less of that sort of friction now, John. Though more of other kinds: the colour problem, the religious problem, the siege mentality. Some people say we're becoming the Prussians of the Middle East. That's not true, of course. I suppose that what we've become is – numbed. Because in a way, the worst horror of World War Two was not the "Final Solution", but the fact that no one, no great nation, no person in power was willing to lift a hand to save us.'

'Gabby,' he said, 'aren't you exaggerating a little now?'

'I am, if anything, understating the case. *Your* State Department which ordered "an embargo" placed upon the news of the extermination camps, and deliberately withheld the reports coming in from the American press. Sir Anthony Eden who publicly refused to allow fifty thousand Bulgarian Jews to be brought to England on the score that then all the rest of the European Jews in Hitler's path would want to come. The high command of the British air force who refused to bomb Oswiscin

– or as it's probably better known to you, Auschwitz – or the railroads leading to it – as being technically too difficult, and then bombed a chemical plant three miles away – twice. And when Hagana, *our* security force, planned to parachute hundreds of young Palestinian Jews into occupied Europe to organize Jewish resistance, sabotage the death camps, that same high command refused to even hear of it.

'*Your* Secretary of State, Stettinius, who, when Dr Nahum Goldmann, President of the World Jewish Congress, pleaded with him to accept the Nazi offer to exchange Jewish lives for American or British trucks to use on the Eastern front, snapped that the generals must be left in peace to fight the war. A *truck*, John, was more important than a Jewish baby's life; more important than this little life growing inside me!

'Oh, in this business, making the world *judenfrei*, Hitler had many allies, my dear! *Your* Senate and your Congress, which both before the war refused to modify the Johnson Act even a little, expand your immigrant quotas a trifle to take in a few thousands of the millions who subsequently died, and this, even though you had, and have, whole immense states more sparsely populated than any great European city!

'The Swiss who closed their borders and turned back thousands of Jews trying to get out of occupied France. The Pope – but Pius Twelfth is not even worthy of mention – beyond reminding you, John, that he *knew*, he knew from the first what was going on and never once opened his mouth to protest. Of all the nations, *only* Sweden and Denmark behaved with courage and decency. Some of the French, which is why so many French Jews were saved. A good many of the Italians who displayed more individual compassion than any other people. For all of Eastern Europe: the Poles, the Hungarians, the Rumanians and the rest *joined* in the slaughter of my people—'

'Didn't Spain do something?' John said.

'They talked. They talked endlessly of their good intentions towards the Sephardim to whom they proposed to extend their citizenship and their protection. On February 7, 1944, three hundred sixty-seven Sephardim Jews were allowed to *pass through* Spain on their way to Palestine. That was it, John, that was all. And they have made political capital out of what they offered to do, but never complied with, ever since. . . .'

'Not to mention,' John said quietly, 'that Spain became the

number one escape hatch for the mass murderers—'

'As well as *still* providing refuge for a goodly number of them, notably your good friend Albrecht Holtz!'

'Gabby, why won't you understand that? I promised Simone—'

'Not to take vengeance on the man who murdered her. Long after, by delayed action; but murdered her just the same. Well, John, my dearest husband, *don't* promise me that. If he kills me, as he's been trying to do ever since the night he saw us together in Aix, thereby killing our baby at the same time, and you *don't* do anything about it, I shall return to *haunt* you; and that's a promise!'

He stared at her; his eyes bleak with worry.

'You think he – and his swarthy playmates – are going to keep it up, Gabby?' he said. 'Even though they've failed twice? Even over in this part of the world?'

'You don't know Ailul al Asward, John,' she said quietly. 'You and I will be safe the day that particular commando group is dead – or we are. Especially with Kroll behind them—'

'That's the main thing I don't understand, Gabby. Most of that crew of mass murderers have had sense enough to lie low, keep their mouths shut, stay out of sight. But according to you—'

'*Not* according to me. My ex-chief, Colonel Zvi Avni has a dossier on Holtz – whom you refused to help us prove is Kroll – as thick as the New York telephone book. Colonel Avni believes he went into the drug racket only to get the money to insure that Adolf Hitler should not have died in vain. In other words Kroll has dedicated his life to implementing the "Final Solution". I'm quite sure he regards his Arab friends as *Untermenschen*, as well. But, at the moment, they are the only nations officially committed to exterminating us. So Kroll embraces them. He'd embrace the Devil if the Devil were currently murdering Jews. . . .'

'He's mad!' John said.

'How could a man have been a devoted Nazi, and not have been insane, John? No. I'll retract that statement now, immediately. Say rather that all members of modern, industrial, urban civilization are mad. *All*, John – to some degree. So, therefore, the best we can do is to defend the lesser insanities against the greater: my loving you, wanting – no aching – to bear this child we've started – against – people who delight in blood and death. Oh, John, I'm so damned scared, I'm sick! I've been frightened before, but never this much! The idea that there are people who *want* to pump a whole clip of submachine-gun bullets through me *here* where *he* is, my tiny, helpless little clump of cells who is growing now, forming, becoming – you – or someone very like you – is so terrible that—'

He put his arms around her, drew her close.

'Don't be frightened, baby,' he said quietly, '*I'm* here. With you.'

'You!' she hooted, 'oh John, darling, you're so slow and out of practice, I'd probably have to take care of you, instead of the other way around. Look how that little *Schvartze* carved you up! I'd have had that knife away from her and broken her neck for her in seven seconds flat! And you—' She stopped, peered up at him, said: 'Forgive me, love. I'll *never* learn how tender male ego is. And I am glad you're here. For all kinds of reasons. Among them that you're kind and good and *not* a murderer. I wouldn't want my son to have a killer for a father.'

'Just you take care of Gabby, first,' he said. 'And after that, heaven and Dr Elon permitting, the kid – of whichever gender. Last of all, of me. I'll cope. . . .

So, in a way, he was emotionally prepared. Keyed up. Taut. Apprehensive. And that made all the difference. Between their dying and their living on.

For a little while longer, at least.

19

He spotted them even before they got on the plane at Rome. Their flight had a longish layover there: refuelling, someone's baggage lost, some few other of the two dozen various ills to which air travel is heir – and, as always, at Leonardo da Vinci Airport compounded by the general and incurable inefficiency of the Latin races – 'A part of their essential humanity,' John conceded, '*they* would never have got a Treblinka, a Ravensbrück, to even start running, no matter how hard they tried. They never get anything to work smoothly or all the time. But –

or maybe because – they retain compassion, most of them. Possess imagination. Wit enough to run when people shoot at them. And hence, an ingrained disinclination – the Sicilian Mafiosi apart, to kill the other guy. So bless 'em say I. They lose your baggage, but as a general thing, they *don't* murder you.'

He was thinking all that as he was walking with Gabrielle towards the front entrance of the Boeing. Then he broke stride, halted; stopped thinking altogether. There were three of them in the other line of passengers moving towards the rear stairs set up against the tourist-class cabin's door. Three Arabs: two men and a woman. Then he told himself: 'Relax, John. There're hundreds of thousands of good, decent North Africans who—'

But he couldn't keep his eyes off them, which was why he noticed the one tiny detail that was wrong. That was all wrong, and thereby warned him. The woman was dressed in traditional Arabic robes, her face heavily veiled; but she was walking between the two men, and clinging lovingly to the arm of one of them. He had been in most of the North African countries not once, but several times. So his brain formulated that objection slowly:

'An Arab woman who walked with her man, clung to his arm in public would be wearing a miniskirt, likely, showing not only face, but thigh. Chewing gum, too, probably. Modern as the twenty-first century. But a woman dressed like that one would walk respectfully two to five paces behind him. To which rule, there are *no* exceptions!'

He watched them start up the stairway, conscious of the fact that he was finding it difficult to breathe. That there was a knot in his solar plexus. A sharp pain in his gut. As they went up that stair, the loose robe momentarily tightened across the woman's behind. He grinned wryly. 'Two *derrières* like that one there, are damned unlikely, John, boy!' he thought. 'Natural enough. The types are new. But little Fat-ass had to be sent along to finger us. So—'

He bent close to Gabby's ear, whispered, trying hard to keep the shake out of his voice:

'You've got that cannon in your bag, baby?'

'No, John,' she said, 'I was afraid they'd X-ray us, or something. So I put it in my—' Then she saw what he was looking at, said: 'Oh! Oh my God!'

'The Black September hotshots are new,' he said, 'but that

exquisite pear-shaped ass I'd recognize anywhere. Even in that burnoose or whatever the hell they call it.'

'John!' she said, 'what are we going to do? We'd better warn the pilot! Tell the stewardess to tell him – or, John! Let's turn back! Not even get on that plane!'

It was then that he did one of the single most stupid things he had ever done in all his life. He remembered her voice hooting at him: 'John, darling you're so slow and out of practice that I'll probably have to take care of you, instead of the other way round!

'Look how that little *Schvartze* carved you up!' – and let unreasoning, atavistic male pride take over, rule him. He said, calmly enough:

'Gabby, all our baggage is already on. That's one thing. And they could be three peaceful pilgrims on their way to Mecca, or something. I vote we keep still and wait for something to pop loose. I can hardly tell the stewardess: 'Look, mamoiselle, keep an eye on that Arab lady back in tourist class; it seems to me I recognize her derrière.' How can I? If they do start something we improvise. . . .'

'John, darling, you are mad. Quite, I have my baby's life to think of now—'

He took her by the arm, propelled her firmly ahead.

'Then think about it in the middle seat. Or the window one. Leave the outside aisle seat to me, Gabby,' he said.

But the minute they were seated, he was sorry. It was a fool trick, a goddamned fool trick absolutely idiotic, and he knew it. He had no right to risk Gabby's life, risk – he turned in his seat, looked back to the curtained door between them and tourist class, thinking:

'Fool. Stupid, infantile fool. You were stung because Gabby said – telling the strict, unvarnished truth – that you're too old and too slow to handle this kind of a situation. If you've even got the nerve left any more, which I doubt. Oh Jesus, I—'

'John,' Gabby whispered, 'we've got reinforcement. That man who got on a little behind them is – one of ours. Captain Meir Yariv. One of the best. He may even be tailing them. Though I doubt that. We keep hands off whatever happens on any airline other than El Al. So he – he's probably not even armed either. We've the strictest orders never to carry a sidearm when we use foreign carriers. . . .'

'Fat lot of good he'll do us, then,' John said. 'Because they most likely *are*. Fat-ass has probably got everything lethal you ever heard of, up to and including a couple of MiG 23s under that burnoose. Gabby, I am sorry! This was stupid of me. We should have stayed off this thing, just as you said and—'

She grinned at him then, coolly; perfectly in control of herself, now, sure.

'Al tidag, my love,' she said. *'Bli panika. Yehiye b'seder.'*

And all of a sudden he *knew* what those words meant. 'Don't worry, don't panic; it's going to be all right.'

'Baby, you give me Hebrew, I'll return you Yiddish. Right now I feel like yelling *"Oy gevalt!"* ' he said.

But before he could say anything else, the take-off started. Leonardo da Vinci is a big airport with good long flight strips, though most of them are as bumpy as old hell. The pilot used up ninety-seven per cent of the one they were on before sending the big jet screaming up a steep sun, mist, smoke, fog ramp of naked air, holding it in that climb so long that John could feel the shudder of an approaching stall. Then he slammed the nose down, lifted flaps – the co-pilot had already retracted the landing gear ages ago – and poured on power. Italy careered away below them, as they slanted across the thickest part of the calf towards the Adriatic Sea.

And nothing happened. Nothing at all. They were both beginning to relax, breathe freely. The first scattering of the Greek islands were already scudding away beneath them, like the bones of skeletal fingers spread out across the wine dark sea.

'False alarm,' he said to her – or started to – for then one of the young Arabs came up the aisles pushing an all but petrified air hostess before him with the muzzle of his Sten.

'Bli panika, my love,' Gabby said.

It was beautifully worked out. The pilot's voice came over the public address system, shaking with fear, with rage. His English deserted him; not until he switched into French could they understand what he said.

'Everyone was to keep to their seats. *Messieurs* the passengers who were *not* of Jewish faith or race, would be allowed to deplane at Athens. *Messieurs les passagers juifs,* unhappily must remain aboard. He had been assured by the gentlemen of Septembre Noir that no harm would befall them; they would merely be exchanged for prisoners in Israeli, German, French and North American jails—'

'North American?' Gabby whispered.

'Sirhan, surely. The one who knocked off Robert Kennedy,' John explained.

Another of the Arabs took his place in the aisle. The air hostesses went down the aisle as directed, asking for passports, keeping some, returning others. They kept Gabby's, returned John's.

'One moment, ma'moiselle,' John said, 'you'd better keep mine, too. This lady is my wife.'

'But *you're* not—' the air hostess began.

'Jewish? The name's Cohn-Bendit, ma'moiselle. Or Mendes-France. Or Léon Blum. Or – Dreyfus. Captain Dreyfus at your service. Anyhow, I'm *not* getting off the plane.'

'John—' Gabby began.

'*Bli panika*, baby,' John Farrow said.

Then the young Arab was standing beside them in the aisle, glaring at them, and demanding in halting French what was wrong.

'*Ce m'sieur,*' the hostess faltered, '*ne veut pas descendre de l'avion, parce que madame, sa femme est juive. . . .*'

The young Septembrist rammed the muzzle of the Sten into John's belly.

'You get off, you!' he said in English.

'And you go defecate in your turban; then pull it down about your ears,' John said pleasantly. 'Now take that hardware out of my gut. It upsets me. And when I am upset I become unpredictable. I might *do* something to you. Such as breaking your back teeth out. By the long route, at that.'

'John!' Gabby moaned.

'Peeg!' the Black Septembrist said. 'American peeg!'

But by then, the girl was there. She had shed the heavy traditional robes and the veil. Under those robes she had been wearing not a miniskirt, but hot pants. On her those little pants were quite something. On her belt he could see the hooks by which the Stens had been suspended. Under that robe.

She ripped out a string of harsh Arabic gutturals. The young hotshot took the Sten away.

'Thanks, doll,' John said to her, then: 'I think I told you once that you've got the finest pear-shaped ass in all of Araby. Too bad you didn't stick around the night you carved me up. . . .'

She looked at Gabby's stricken face, and smiled with cool malice.

'I confess I was tempted to,' she said, 'but then – who knows – perhaps my chiefs will consent to turn you over to me for interrogation, Mr Farrow. I'm sure I could think of some interesting ways to get you to talk—'

'Why you little bitch!' Gabby began, but the girl swung her Sten around.

'Don't tempt me, madame!' she said. 'Killing you would be too much of a pleasure. Though truth to tell I don't need to widow him. You see he really doesn't interest me that much, or at least not for that long!'

Then, having delivered herself of what John had to admit was a hell of a good exit line, she turned on her heels to march away. As she did so, John saw the hilt of the commando knife she had strapped to her waist.

'You can't,' that sober, sensible part of his mind that he labelled, and libelled, cowardice, told him. 'You're fifty-four years old. Slow. Fat. Scared shitless. You haven't the chance of a snowball in hell to—

'Shut up!' he screamed silently at his mind. His hands, moving, blurred sight. He pulled that knife out of its scabbard so fast and smoothly she didn't even miss it; put, in one effortlessly graceful surge, his left hand into the back of her belt and yanked powerfully, jerking her off her feet so that she fell heavily across him. As she fell, her finger tightened on the trigger of the Sten, sending a good long burst up the walls and through the roof of the cabin. The air whistled out that string of holes explosively.

But by then, John Farrow had the point of the knife against her throat.

'Throw that thing down, baby,' he said.

All the other passengers were crouching between the seats by then. Except Gabby. She stared at him with luminous eyes.

'Throw that goddamned Sten down!' he said again.

The Arab girl grinned at him coolly. The muzzle of the Sten was jammed against the seat in front of them, so she couldn't swing it up to kill him.

'What is it this, John, darling,' she mocked, 'love or war?'

'War,' he said grimly, and pushed the knife point into her flesh, hard. Hot blood spurted about his hand.

She went on smiling. She could feel his guts quivering against her.

'You won't,' she said. 'You haven't got it in you.'

'You are so right,' he thought despairingly; but then a sudden surge of rage tore him.

'My wife's pregnant,' he said. 'So believe me, I *will* kill you, baby. Goddamnit, throw it down!'

Her hands came away from the Sten. He didn't hear it strike the floor. For two reasons: Gabby had it before it got there; and those long, slim night bronze hands had turned talons, raking for his eyes.

He pushed the knife in deep, slashed sidewise a full inch. Her hands came away from his face. She lay there quietly, staring at him. And bleeding.

'Call those hotshots, will you?' he grated.

'No,' she said evenly, 'I won't. You'll have to kill me.'

He moved that knife a little. His big gut knotted up on him. Nausea crawled hotly up from his middle, mounted his throat.

'It's still "no", John, darling!' she mocked him. But by then both the Septembrists were there.

Out of the corner of his eye, he saw Gabby sighting on them coolly. And despair went keening along every nerve he had. If she or they opened fire, one-hundred-thirty or forty-odd people were going to die. It was getting hard to breathe already. Up where they were at eleven or twelve thousand metres, nearly forty thousand feet, the atmosphere was too thin to sustain life. And nobody had thought, dared, or even tried to pull the oxygen masks down from the containers above the seats.

Then, at that exact moment, as if to prove that fortune favours the brave, or more truly that maniac God takes care of his idiot children, the pilot did the correct, the professional thing. He peeled off on one wing, slammed the control column all the way forward and power-dived the big jet as though it were a fighter. He was afraid those shots that had perforated the aircraft's skin were going to cause the greater air pressure inside the cabin to split the plane apart. As it was already beginning to. Cracks were running bullet hole to bullet hole, now.

The first wild lurch threw the two Arabs back against the bulkhead with sickening force. But once into the dive, the big plane steadied, went screaming down as though it were on rails.

'Throw those Stens down, boys!' John roared above the eerie whistling scream of the cabin air pouring through those rents, 'or else I'll serve you up some butchered she-goat! You heard me! Throw them down!'

They hung there glaring.

John slashed another full inch across her throat. Her hands came up, clawing; but they were all gone, feeble, fluttering like great golden autumn leaves. A scald of nausea hit the back of his throat.

'She's – dying,' he thought. 'You've killed her, you bastard! Killed a woman – no – this glorious girl-child who only wanted to—'

A piece of aluminium fully forty centimetres square tore loose from the roof with a crack like a pistol shot. John felt the outrush of the cabin air tugging at him violently.

'Hold on, Gabby!' he yelled.

Then he saw those two Stens strike the floor. And Gabby was out of her seat and scrambling across him and the inert girl and then kneeling in the aisle bracing herself, sighting on the two male Septembrists, and a stream of guttural Arabic was pouring from her lips.

John noted with half his senses that the air was no longer roaring out the hole in the roof. Instead it had reversed its direction and was screaming into it with a wail like all the damned souls in hell. They were down low enough now. And safe. If both main spars didn't give way when the pilot attempted the pull-out. If the wings didn't sheer off, go fluttering down, leaving the silver projectile of that fuselage to bury itself and them in Grecian earth, splattering bits of bones and tatters of bloody flesh for kilometres around.

The pilot knew his business. He didn't try to yank the huge plane out of that dive by main force, instead he eased it out gradually, making the angle of the dive ever shallower, ever more parallel to earth.

Even so, John felt the enormous pressure of gravity almost crush his chest. The girl was still, too still. Her mouth was open a little. Her lips were blue. Her blood was all over everything. His pants were soaked with it. The seat.

And now, at long, long last the plane steadied, came level. The jagged peaks of the Greek mountains tore by, not five full metres below them. The pilot eased up into a gentle climb. The roar of the air through the hole lessened. He could hear himself think again, now.

Gabby rapped out more Arabic, grimly. The Septembrists' left hands went to their belts; tugged at the buckles. Their pants sagged down about their ankles. Their underwear was a sight to see: purple stripes; gold stripes; red stars.

Then a short, stocky, tremendously powerful man came through the curtains from tourist class. He retrieved the two Stens from the floor. Tossed one aside; sighted with the other on the Septembrists. Grinned at Gabby. Said something to her in Hebrew. Then to John:

'Jolly good show, Captain Farrow! If you're planning to stay in Israel, come to see me. You've a job waiting, sir!'

But John was staring at the inert girl. His hand came up, clawed out his handkerchief. Clumsily he tried to bandage her throat. She was still bleeding, but less rapidly now. 'No blood left,' he thought, despairingly. Then he felt something touch his arm. Looking up he gazed into the white, strained faces of the air steward, and two of the air hostesses.

'We'll take her now,' the steward said.

John felt her weight go up and away from him. He stood up, staggered to one of the toilets, pushed the door open and bent in half, puking his guts up, vomiting noisily, terribly, throwing it all up, all his awful fear, his hatred for war and violence, his gut-deep loathing for the thing he'd been forced to do, had done; his sickening knowledge that even being right didn't excuse it; that nothing ever excused murder, that nothing ever could.

Then he felt something cool and wet, bathing his face. Gabby was there beside him, helping him, attending to him with grave and wifely tenderness. Her face was awash with tears.

'Thank you, mon amour,' she said.

'Don't thank me!' he snarled. 'I – I've killed her! Cut her throat like a pig's! You said you didn't want a murderer for—'

'She's not dead, John,' Gabby said. 'And even if she were, you wouldn't be. Even she knew that. That you couldn't. That you literally couldn't. That was what I thanked you for—'

'For what, Gabby?' he said.

'For being *you*, John. Brave enough when you have to be. Even though you have to tie your guts back together to do it. But – always kind. Never cruel—'

'Never cruel!' he got out. 'What d'you call *that*, Gabby?'

'Necessity. The one being to whom even the gods must bow. *Anagnke*, the Greeks called her. And even Zeus prostrated himself before her. Now come on. We'd better sit down somewhere. We've been circling Athens for a quarter of an hour. . . .'

They had to spend the night in Athens, at the Hotel Grande Bretagne on Constitution Square, the colonels obligingly having put a whole company of soldiers all around every hotel to which the damaged Air France plane's passengers were assigned.

But for the Farrows and Captain Meir Yariv, they outdid themselves. They gave them adjacent rooms, and put armed guards before their doors.

And John Farrow sent the clothes he had been wearing down to the furnace room to be burned.

They were coming down the stairs out of the plane El Al had sent to Athens to retrieve them, when Gabby touched his arm.

'John!' she got out; then, 'Oh, my God!'

All the waiting spaces at Lod Airport were black with people. The rooftops of the buildings. Policemen were holding back a swarm of reporters at the foot of the stairs. The flashes of the photographers blinded them. Reporters were shouting for a statement in Hebrew, English, French, German and a few other languages he couldn't even recognize now.

He did the best he could; put it in a line or two.

'It was this way, boys, I've already visited Cairo, Amman, Damascus and Beirut. Just couldn't see my first trip to Israel spoiled, that's all; and especially not since it happens to be our honeymoon. . . .'

Then the police came and took them away from there. In an office at the airport itself, the three of them, Gabby, John and Captain Yariv, went through a solid two-hour interrogation that was as correct and courteous as it was thorough. John was surprised to note that the mention of their wedding in London caused a quick, interrogatory glance to pass among the higher officials. Then one of them said it:

'Civil – or religious, sir.'

'Civil,' John said evenly, 'we're of different faiths.'

'I see,' the official said. 'Very well, Captain Farrow. You and your – lady, are free to go. And thank you very much. Splendid job, indeed!'

When they came out of that office they didn't have to go look for their baggage. It was already there in a neat row, just outside the door. It and a crowd of people who began at once to clap and cheer.

John turned to Gabby, said: 'We've sure as hell blown our cover, Gabby.' But before the words were half-way out of his mouth, a pair of soft, plump feminine arms were around his neck so hard he couldn't breathe and he was being kissed all over his face with great wet kisses that tasted salt, and a voice was babbling: '*Jean! Mon Jean! Ah mon très, très cher!*'

He pushed her a little away from him, stared down into that plump, rosy face, framed with a mass of blonde ringlets coiffed in the very latest style; opened his mouth, said:

'*Marie Claire! Mon Dieu, c'est—*'

Which was as far as he got, because she was strangling and kissing him again, and a sweet, girlish voice was saying:

'*Ah Maman! Ça c'est trop! Toute le monde est en train de nous regarder! N'as-tu pas même un peu de la honte?*'

And Gabby, in English, acridly:

'I say, Jeanne, would you mind removing your paws – or claws – from my husband, please?'

'I quite agree. Turn him loose, Jeanne,' a man's voice said.

'Anton!' John said. 'Well damn me for a sinner!'

'Which you most assuredly are,' Anton said, and put out his hand to him. They shook hands, gripping hard. 'Don't expect me to congratulate you for your heroic feat,' Anton went on, 'that was a damned fool stunt, John. Unpardonably risky and stupid. That you got away with it doesn't change that. Though, I must say, I'm glad you did. We're quite fond of *la petite* Rachel, here. . . .'

'Now, Papa,' a baritone voice came from somewhere, high in the air. 'Must you always be so rough on people? I do congratulate you, sir. What you did was jolly fine!'

John stared up into the face of a young man close to thirty years of age. He wore his reddish blond hair fashionably long. He had the equally fashionable bushy moustache. He was several inches above six feet tall and amazingly handsome. John stared from him to Anton to Marie Claire.

'*Mon fils,*' Marie Claire said with quiet pride. 'I named him Anton-Jean – after both of you. Though it should be the other way around. Anton – only made him in a careless moment. While you, mon cher Jean – kept him alive. For this bad tempered monster's bullet would have killed both of us that day. And these are – *mes filles, Jeannette, Claire, venez*—'

The two girls were utterly beautiful. They were, John guessed, all of ten and twelve years of age.

Then young Anton II was pushing forward a pretty, dark-haired young woman, hugely pregnant.

'This is my wife, Manya,' he said fondly. 'Unfortunately, being a blockhead of a Sabra, she speaks only Hebrew.'

'And – and a leetle English,' Manya said.

But Gabby had already seized her, dragged her into her arms and was kissing her and crying, and saying a couple of thousand things to her in Hebrew that sounded wondrously tender to John's ears.

'Come on, all of you,' Anton said, in his brusque way. 'We've afforded the public enough of a spectacle. I've the car outside. We'll be a bit crowded, but no matter. I'll take you home.'

'Look, Papa,' Anton II said, 'I've got my bus outside, too. So let's split up. I'll take the girls. That way it'll be only the four of you. Divide up the luggage, too. Don't think we can get all that in one trunk, can we?'

'Anton, wait!' Gabby said, 'by home, d'you mean *your* place?'

'Of course, Rachie!' Anton said. 'The girls can double up. We've enough space.'

Gabby grinned at him, said:

'Anton – I just got married, y'know.'

Anton glared at her.

'That's another subject we'll have to discuss, you little idiot!' he said. 'Now come on!'

'Anton—' Gabby protested. 'I'm *still* on my honeymoon. I am not yet – tired of my husband. Besides which I am noisy. Very. Your *shikun's* too small. Take us to the Sheraton, please? We've got reservations there.'

For a long moment John was afraid Anton was going to hit her. Then he relaxed a little, growled:

'I suppose you're old enough to know what you're doing, Rachie. All right, the Sheraton, then. But you're dining with us. We've an awful lot of damned serious talking to do! You ruddy Levy women! Every stupid one of you has got your brains between your legs!'

'Now, Anton,' John said, mildly.

'Oh, I'm not blaming you, John! But Rachel is from here, a citizen of this country. She knows perfectly well that under our law a civil marriage, contracted in a foreign country, is no marriage at all! And now here she is with a silly grin on her silly face, dragging you into one unholy mess, and, if I know her, planning to stay. Even to naturalize you if possible!'

'Isn't it?' John said. 'Possible, I mean?'

'Yes. And in the case of a foreigner with a needed skill – you qualify there, of course, not even too difficult, really. And what with that French pilot shooting his mouth off, and getting everyone's back up, public sympathy will make it easier still. The real difficulty is going to be – oh, merde! This is no place to discuss such a delicate matter. For God's sake, come on!'

When they were finally inside their room in the Sheraton – on the seaward side, away from the rumble of traffic on Hayarkon Street and circling through Independence Park – Gabby walked over to the big windows, and stood there, looking out over the sea. She stayed there so long, unmoving, almost statue-like, that finally John came over to her, and put his arms around her.

'Gabby,' he said, 'what's wrong?'

'Everything!' she wailed: 'Oh, darling, I have bitched it for you, for fair!'

'You mean Anton? Hell, Gabby, he's been a bad-tempered cuss ever since I've known him. Doesn't mean anything. Actually it's all bark, When you get right down to cases, he's one of nature's noblemen. Nobody could ever call him a diplomat, but it seems to me that he's usually fair.'

'Yes,' she said, 'he is. But I was depending on him to – to help us along, rather – and that very fairness of his; that sense of absolute rectitude, strict justice, just might become an obstacle. I thought that when I arrived and presented him with our marriage as a fait accompli, everything would be all right. Instead it seems that the fait is far from accompli! I have, John, dearest, just become the family's scarlet woman – again!'

'And I the villainous seducer?' John said.

'Oh, no! He doesn't blame you. *I* did it all. Oh, blast and damn! How am I *ever* going to tell them about – our baby now?'

He grinned at her, said:

'Don't. Just wait a couple of months, and the evidence will speak for itself.'

She stared up at him, whispered:

'No, I couldn't do that. I *have* to tell them, John. Because if some old nosey parker phones them to report I've just been seen waddling down Ben Yehuda street pushing a perfectly enormous bulge before me, Anton will never forgive us. And even Jeanne will resent my not having confided in her—'

'Jeanne? Oh Lord! I'll have to get used to people's real names, won't I? Marie Claire is Jeanne. And you're, Rachie. C'mon, Rachie, give me a kiss.'

'Not if you call me Rachie, I won't! My name is Gabrielle. Legally. There's not one iota of proof that I am Rachel Levy. And the name's hideous. I *hate* it. I can't make them stop calling me that, but don't *you* start it, John Farrow!'

'*D'accord*. Come on, Gabby-Gabrielle, kiss me. Or is the honeymoon over already?'

'Far from it!' she said, and kissed him, taking all the time in the world about it. Then she said: 'John—'

He knew what she meant when she said his name like that.

'What about that beauty parlour you were going to in order to have your hair fouled up like Marie Claire? I mean like Jeanne's?'

'Paula's? It's right downstairs. In *this* hotel, darling. And – besides – the preliminaries are unnecessary, today. Oh quite. I've been wanting to ever since we left London. No, before we left London. And last night, you—'

'I was in no mood to oblige. But, Gabby, don't you think we ought to check with that lady sawbones first to see if—'

'No. There's no danger of that. Just be – gentle with me, darling,' she said.

Anton called for them at eight o'clock. By that time they were already down in the Maccabean Room talking to a reporter from the English-language newspaper, the *Jerusalem Post*. He had called them earlier and asked for an interview. And one of the things that his career in public life had taught John Farrow was that it is never wise to offend the press.

But Anton glared at the young reporter as though he had committed a public nuisance by merely existing. Whereupon Gabby took her ex-brother-in-law by the arm, and led him to another table.

'Buy me a drink, Anton,' she said, 'let John handle the press alone. Believe me, he knows how. . . .'

But when they were outside in the car, Anton started in at once:

'You didn't tell him anything about your wedding, did you John?' he said with far more anxiety in his tone than the occasion seemed to call for. 'And especially not that you – both of you – have been married previously, and divorced?'

'No, neither,' John said. 'But why all the hassle, Anton? I've always thought that divorce and remarriage were permitted under Judaic law. Wasn't that one of the things that Jesus got into trouble with the Pharisees over?'

'Yes. Why yes, of course. But about two years ago, the Orthodox religious parties – aided, incredibly enough, by dear Golda herself – really clamped down. Fouled everything up most dirtily. Damn them, they should realize that these aren't biblical times! No public transportation on the Sabbath – which means that eighty-odd per cent of the population who have no cars have to walk. All the better hotels have had to install automatic elevators which run up and down all day long, stop automatically at every floor to let guests on and off, so that you don't even have to push a button to work 'em, since button pushing constitutes work – while walking, theoretically *only* to a synagogue, doesn't! The blithering idiots! They've pushed us back into the dark ages!'

'Anton,' John said, 'The last time I saw you, you approved of the Orthodox point of view. . . .'

'I did. But that was before they rammed a bill through Knesset officially declaring that *my* marriage to a shiksa is invalid, because it took place in France at a Mairie in a civil ceremony, and that all my children are bastards before the law. So now I am obliged to adopt my own children before a rabbinical court to make them Jews, and Jeanne has to convert so that I can marry her all over again and thus raise her out of concubinage! Before a rabbi, naturally, and under the huppah!'

'Anton—' Gabby said softly, 'sounds to me as if you are on *my* side!'

'I am. As much as it pains me to be. If they would only make conversion a little simpler! But now it takes years, under the suspicious eyes of a group of rabbin who really don't *want* to take converts in, and who – shades of the Nazis! – are concerned about preserving Jewish racial purity – just as if there were any such thing. In a country where we have jet black – but entirely Orthodox – Ethiopian Jews studying in the same Ulpans with blonde, blue-eyed Sabras, and every shade between, they talk about discouraging mixed marriages! They blaspheme against Moses, himself, who among others, took an Ethiopian wife—'

'Then, you aren't angry at me for marrying a Goy?' Gabby said wistfully.

'Of course not! John, as you should know, is one of my best friends. What I am put out about is your showing up here with him after having pulled a Grade B movie stunt aboard that aircraft which has made your entering into the country quietly and anonymously impossible. . . .'

'Couldn't be helped, Anton,' John said. 'These types weren't ordinary skyjackers. They were after *us*. After Gabby and me, specifically. I grant you we should have come in on El Al, but that was my fault and—'

'Tell me about it,' Anton said.

'No – not yet,' Gabby said. 'Anton – suppose we just go on living in sin, as sin is now defined by Israeli law. What would happen?'

'To the two of you, nothing. There must be hundreds of couples – including Jeanne and me – in the same boat. The trouble starts if you decided to have a child. Then both of you have to convert, get married all over again, and legitimize him. Or else the poor little fellow's *sunk* in Israel. Among other things he can *never* marry, since all marriage is religious, and he wouldn't be a Jew—'

'He could marry a Christian, couldn't he?' Gabby said.

'Yes. But nearly all Israeli Christians are Arabs. And I'm quite sure you wouldn't enjoy having an Arab daughter-in-law, Rachie.'

'I most certainly shouldn't!' Gabby said.

'But your son's married to a Sabra,' John pointed out.

'I adopted him. I could do that, because I *am* a Jew. I also adopted the girls. And Jeanne is suffering through conversion, right now. So my problems are almost over. Yours are just beginning. So hear me, children! Don't have any offspring. If you do, go live somewhere else. And if this damned Levy idiot of a sister-in-law of mine insists upon both living here and having children – she's still young enough, and I must say you do look fit, John! – convert. Under those circumstances you haven't any other choice—'

'Well, baby,' John said, 'looks like we'd better go look up a nice, liberal, considerate, broad-minded rabbi doesn't it?'

'There isn't any such animal!' Anton snapped. 'And I'll wager that this nitwit, being possessed of that over-developed Levy maternal instinct, is already selling you on the delights of parenthood, eh, John?'

'Well—' John began, but Gabrielle cut him off.

'Anton—' she said sweetly, 'in about seven and a half months from now, *you're* going to be a godfather, or whatever you call it over here.'

'Oh Jesus!' Anton yelped, 'that ties it! That really ties it! And don't tell me you got married a month or two ago, because I damned well won't believe you!'

'I won't tell you that, Anton, dah-link!' Gabby said, 'because we got married last week. Oh, I say! Isn't this your place?'

'It is,' Anton said grimly. 'But *before* we go upstairs, Rachie, remember that my daughters are very young. At least keep your big mouth shut until I pack them off to bed!'

To John's eyes, the apartment was austere. In the States, any skilled worker would have had a better one. He had yet to learn that in Israel an ostentatious display of wealth is considered the very worst form. Marie Claire/Jeanne came rushing to the door to kiss him all over again.

'It strikes me you do that with a little too much enthusiasm, Jeanne, dear!' Gabby said dryly.

'Oh, don't be a jealous female, Rachie!' Jeanne laughed.

'And don't call me Rachie, damnit!' Gabby said.

'I must say you've learned a lot of English,' John said, 'as well as having put on a few Israeli pounds, shall we say?'

'At one stage in her life – a woman has to decide between her face and her derrière,' Jeanne said. 'I decided to keep my face unwrinkled, and let ma derrière – extend itself, as it were. And the English – which I already spoke when I met you, mon cher – is my defence against Hebrew! Rachie and I – oh zut! All right! Gabby and I have formed the Israeli Antisemites League. Want to join?'

'I'll think about it,' John said. 'Where are those beautiful daughters of yours? I want to hold both of them on my knees.'

'Over at Anton Second's. He'll bring them over when he comes. They'll be a trifle late. Manya's not feeling too well. Natural enough in her state, I suppose. . . .'

'Is it?' Gabby drawled. 'Apart from upchucking precisely at eight o'clock *every* morning *I* feel positively ripping!'

'Don't mind her, John,' Jeanne said. 'She copied that from Simone – that trick of saying something absolutely outrageous with every second breath. Besides, ma chère Gabrielle, if you even have *that* in your mind, forget it. Thirty-seven is *far* too old to have one's first child, you know. I'm told it's quite frightfully dangerous. Safe enough to have your fifth, or your tenth at that age; but your *first* – pure insanity.'

'Jean, darling,' Gabby purred, 'John *knows* how old I am. I told him. And the insanity or whatnot of having a baby at my age – has become beside the point, rather. So before your gosses angéliques appear, get the idea through *cette tête d'âne* – I am already. *Fichée. Foutue.* Enceinte. Prrrregggnant – catch?'

'Mais non! Ce n'est pas possible!' Jeanne said.

'You mean *I* can't, or that John can't?' Gabby said. 'In the first place you may wait three months, say, and *see* how nice and round I'm going to be. Bulging out all over, what? And in the second, you'll just have to take my word for it. I jolly well don't propose to lend him to you for a trial, dear!'

'Gabby—' John groaned.

But Jeanne had taken Gabrielle in her arms and was kissing her with real tenderness.

'Ah ma chérie!' she crooned, *'comme je suis heureuse!'*

'Merci, Jeanne,' Gabby said; then, 'Trudy Elon is still practising isn't she?'

'But, of course! And you'd better see her soon. Make the appointment for your lying-in *now*. She's *that* busy. Did you know she's moved her clinic out of town? Because of the power station. The soot from that smoke stack was turning her nurses' uniforms black, not to mention the bed linen. We all agitated against their building the awful thing there – right in the heart of the residential district, John – and this was in sixty-eight when everybody'd already got excited over pollution—'

'Oh, dear!' Gabby wailed, 'don't tell me she's gone to Haifa, or Jerusalem! Or even to some kibbutz out in the middle of nowhere?'

'Not that bad, *ma chérie*. Now it's out on Israel Rokach Road, past the exhibition grounds. Nice location, green, fresh, plenty of shade trees. *Oh, zut alors!* I haven't even so much as offered John a drink! And what on earth is keeping Anton?'

'He said he was going to park the car,' John said.

'Which means he'll be all night. Isn't the traffic dreadful? What shall it be, *mon cher*? Whiskey, gin, vodka, schnapps – you name it.'

'Whiskey – with water,' John said. 'Marie Claire – I mean Jeanne – catch me up. Tell me how you and Anton got back together.'

'After you stopped him from shooting me as a Nazi spy? Did I ever tell you that story, Rach- Gabrielle?'

'Thousands of times,' Gabrielle said morosely. 'Give me a whiskey, will you? On the rocks.'

'Now, Gabby!' John said.

'Oh, I might as well pickle his brains in alcohol for him, darling,' Gabby said, 'considering the kind of world he's going to be born into. . . .'

Then the front door opened, and both Antons, father and son came in, with Manya, and the two girls.

Jeanne leaned forward quickly.

'I shall have to postpone that story for now, mon cher,' she whispered, 'Anton would be horrified if I told it before the girls.' She gave a low, throaty chuckle, and went on: 'He'd be even *more* horrified if he ever heard the stories his two little angels bring home from school every day! I encourage them to be frank with me, you know, and—'

'Stop whispering sweet nothings into John's ear, Jeanne!' Anton said mockingly, 'Rachie's not going to turn him loose; and you, my sweet, for bad and for worse, are stuck with me!'

Anton Second had his hands full of newspapers.

'Thought you'd like to see them,' he said to John, with his curiously shy and gentle smile. 'The pilot's statement has caused the regulation degree of white-hot indignation. Our latter-day Sternists and Irgunists are all for denying Air France further landing rights in Israel. It is proposed that Knesset give you a public vote of thanks at the next session—'

'Lord!' John said, then, 'tell me, son, just what did that pilot say?'

'That you had no right to endanger the aircraft the way you did for the benefit – of a minority of the passengers. That he'd been assured that no harm would befall the Jewish passengers, who would be held only temporarily until—'

'*Merde!*' Gabby said, 'he'd been assured by whom, Anton

Deux? By Ailul al Asward! Black September! After the massacre at Lod he accepts their word? After Munich? And besides, there were two people aboard that aircraft who jolly well weren't going to be exchanged, not even for Sirhan-Sirhan, say. And those two were John and me! John's got an eighteen-centimetre long scar down his back now, where they tried to knife him. And I missed being dismembered by inches, because my finicky feminine pride kept me from opening what I thought was a love letter addressed to him in a most dainty hand. Why the ruddy thing was even perfumed! But if I had opened it, you'd all be sitting in a darkened room on the floor, in torn clothes, celebrating the mourning Shiva for *me* – at least I hope you would. I hope *somebody* in this family loves me a little—'

'We do, *Tante* Rachel!' the two little girls cried, and rushed to put their arms around her.

'Papa—' Anton II said, 'that chap hanging about – outside when we came up, hein? He could be Arab, don't you think?'

'Could be, and probably was!' Anton said grimly. 'Look, John, you'd better give me the score. Damnit all, I'm going to call Meir Yariv, right now, and—'

'He knows, Anton,' Gabby said. 'He was on that plane, remember. And took part in the debriefing.'

'Then he should have already provided you with protection!' Anton roared.

'Here?' John said incredulously, 'in Tel Aviv? In the exact middle of Israel?'

'John, you mean to tell me you *still* don't know how or why Simone died?' Anton said.

'No,' Gabby whispered, 'he doesn't, Anton I – wouldn't tell him.'

'Then I will! She went off the balcony of our apartment in Haifa – seven storeys up, because a *fellah* threw three hand grenades into the schoolbus on which our son – hers and *mine* – was riding. The child for whom she'd submitted herself to five hideously painful operations in order to repair the damage to her genitalia caused by Kroll and company's electrodes and other delicate attentions. The man-child she almost died giving birth to. And *that* was in Israel, my friend!'

'Jesus!' John whispered.

'Anton—' Gabrielle said, 'that wasn't *why*. Not altogether. You *know* it wasn't.'

'No. It wasn't. The day before you – with your usual flair for the spectacular, my dear John! – dynamited your way into that stalag up above Cannes and got poor Simone out, with, I've been told, some small assistance from the Free French air force—'

'With a great deal of help from them, Anton. We wouldn't have lived three minutes if they hadn't pinned the Waffen SS down – but go on, please—'

'Heindrich Kroll and friends questioned Simone one more time. But realizing that their usual tactics would surely kill her, when added to all they'd already done—'

'Anton,' John said, 'tes filles!'

'*They* know all this! I've told them. They have to know what it means to be a Jew in a world of Goyim, John! Kroll changed his methods. They brought in a boy. A little boy – eleven, twelve years old. Strapped him into a chair. And killed him – by millimetres before her eyes. And every time they broke another bone they'd say to her: 'Speak! You can still save him! What's the matter, miss; don't you *like* children?'

John bowed his head. Stared at the floor. What he felt then, at that moment, had no name.

'Afterwards,' Anton went on, 'she spent years of spiritual agony trying to analyse why she did not speak, didn't save that child. I believe it was because she literally couldn't, was too numbed by them, too far gone, herself. But she tortured herself endlessly with the idea that she sacrificed that boy to save your life, John, and mine, and the rest of the réseau. That she had made her terrible offering to the Most High to save her people, Israel!'

John sat there. And again the world had stopped. But this time, terribly.

'So,' Anton whispered, 'on the day – our son – died, she was standing there looking at that smoking ruin of a schoolbus, converted by that murderous black bastard into – the phrase is *yours*, my friend, I got it from you! – a tripe factory, frozen there John, petrified – and some damned fool of a woman screamed at her: "Don't just stand there! Help us! *Do* something! What's the matter with you? Don't you even *like* children?" '

'Jesus!' John said again.

'She came straight home,' Anton said. 'Walked in the front door. Left it open. I wasn't there. I was downtown trying to teach a bunch of blockheads to follow a score, even so much as maintain tempo, keep time! She crossed straight through the living room. To the window. To that balcony. Without hesitation. Then over – and down – and out – of a life become unendurable to her. She – she didn't die right away. She was horribly broken, but she couldn't die. She finally – went – in Rachie's arms. And the whole time until her last breath was gone she kept whimpering: "Alors, ma'moiselle, tu n'aimes pas les enfants?" '

John stood up. Strode to the window. Stood there with his back to them, rigid as man turned to stone.

Gabrielle was out of her chair in one wild rush, crying:

'John! Oh no, John! Please! I—'

When she was close to him, she heard his voice. It was a ripple below the dead still surface of all sound.

'And I,' he said, 'I let that bastard go!'

20

Gabby was sitting on the arm of his chair. She bent down suddenly and kissed his cheek.

'There's a lot to be said for being to the manner born, my love,' she said, 'I couldn't do it.'

'Do what?' John said duly.

'Behave as beautifully as you've done all evening,' she said. 'You even ate enough of Jeanne's quite marvellous cooking to be polite. John – tell me something—'

'What, Gabby?' he said.

'Will you ever be *mine*? Will I *ever* have you?'

'Now, Gabby!' he began.

'It's – all right, darling,' she said. And looking up he saw that she was crying.

'Yehosiphat!' Anton roared, 'what's got into you now, Rachie?'

'Nothing,' Gabby said, 'sometimes things get to be too much for me. Such as living in the world with insensitive dolts! Even when one such dolt is also a great musician!'

'Now what on earth did *I* do?' Anton said.

'Nothing. Jeanne – could I go lie down a while? I – I feel bloody awful!'

'No, you don't, Gabby,' John said, 'you're being childish. Anton has done absolutely nothing to hurt your feelings, and you know it.'

'No,' Gabrielle whispered, 'he hasn't, has he? Nor have you, have you, John? Nor both of you together. Not even demonstrating to me again – that I mean much less to – to either of you – than does a memory! A ghost – oh blast and damn! Why did I *ever* fall in love with you? With a blind man? A man who can't even see me!'

Manya was evidently asking Anton II in Hebrew to explain to her what was going on. He shook his head worriedly.

'Rachie,' Anton said gently, 'whatever it is I've done, I apologize. I really didn't mean to make you cry.'

Gabrielle got up at once, went over to her brother-in-law and kissed him.

'You – dddidn't,' she got out, crying still: 'It's – just that – that the first time John saw me – called me "Simone!" and almost fainted. I – I haven't got what it takes to make a man – stay in love with me – twenty-eight whole ruddy years! We – we even agreed *not* to fall in love with one another – because – because, oh blast and damn! – I could never be sure it was *me* he was in love with – and not my resemblance to Simone. But I – but I—'

'Pauvre petite!' Jeanne said, *'on voit que tu n'es pas française!'*

'And if I were French, Jeanne?' Gabrielle said.

'You'd be more of a realist. *I*, in your place, would never stop to worry why I had John. I shouldn't turn him loose long enough to think about anything!'

'You have just earned yourself a beating, my sweet!' Anton roared in mock wrath; and some of the tension went out of the air.

'Anton,' John said, 'now that you've packed the little angels off to bed, I should really appreciate your filling in the gaps. Starting with how you and Marie Claire – *oh merde!* – I mean you and Jeanne got back together again—'

'It took *him* all of two years to accustom himself to calling me by my true name,' Jeanne said. 'You were smart to call yourself Jean, John. The transition is not so difficult.'

'You mean that Rachie hasn't even told you *that?*' Anton said.

'I told him absolutely nothing!' Gabrielle said, 'I was having a bloody rotten enough time trying to get him to realize I was *me*, without reminding him of the past. And since this is *sure* to bring on the rest of it: how you took Simone away from John, and escaped with her from France, I'm going to lie down somewhere. I don't want to hear it again. I claim a pregnant woman's privilege of being over-sensitive and jealous and bitchy and unpleasant. So excuse me, all! I—'

'No, you don't!' John said. 'Skip that part, Anton. If it makes Gabrielle unhappy, I don't want to hear it either.'

She stared at him.

'No,' she said. 'You *must* hear it, John. I want you to. I insist upon your hearing it.'

'Not behind your back,' he said. 'Not with you hiding somewhere building things in your imagination. That's no good, Gabby. I thought we'd put distrust behind us.'

'*Ma nisma?*' Manya wailed ('What's happening?')

Anton II tried to explain to her. Turned to his father in exasperation.

'Papa, you can say what you will, but it's *not* a language yet! Not fully. I think I speak it well, but I *can't* explain nuances like these – emotions – to Manya. It isn't that I lack the words, it's that there aren't any—'

'He's talking about modern Hebrew – and its deficiencies, John,' Anton explained, 'but he's got the cart before the horse. The reason modern Hebrew is so limited in the department of emotion – delicate shades of feeling – is because the Sabras were trained not to have too many emotions – lest they turn out to be cowards like us old bars of soap. Hence they've never felt the need to invent those words. The parts of a gun, yes. Every bloody piece in a bombing plane has its exact technical term in Hebrew. But the reasons and ways that poor Rachie is unhappy now have no words—'

'Nor in any language spoken of man,' Gabrielle said suddenly. 'But tell John your story, Anton. I'll stay. I'll even behave myself for a change. Because, after all, he *is* stuck with me, isn't he? And maybe one day he'll learn to love me.'

'Gabby—' John said reproachfully.

'Oh, I suppose you do – as much as you can at this stage of the game,' she said, 'and I should be quite content – if I didn't *see* what happens to you – to your face, your eyes, your mouth, every time someone mentions Simone's name. To Anton, too. But Jeanne doesn't seem to care very much. Perhaps in time I'll develop an armoured hide – and – and learn to put back together again the pieces of my heart. . . .'

'Maybe the Sabras are right,' Anton said. 'People shouldn't wear their feelings on their sleeves, Rachie.'

'Forgive me,' she whispered. 'Tonight I seem to be in a mood. Go on, Anton. Tell John about how you stole his girl!'

'Didn't. At least not intentionally. After Dalton Ross got me out of the Villa Montefleuri – I say! This puts me rather in a spot! John, do you know what relation you bear to Dalton Ross? Or at least what relation he *claimed* you bore?'

'Yes,' John said, 'and it's not "claimed", Anton. Unfortunately. I am his son.'

'That's a relief!' Anton sighed, 'that you know, I mean. It seems that the old fool was labouring under two, from my point of view, anyhow, useful misapprehensions: the first being that Simone had escaped from that prison in the general outbreak after the French bombed it without anyone specifically helping her to do it. He didn't know what a dreadful condition, physically, she was in. Nor did I. Kroll concealed that detail from both of us.'

'Why should he have?' John said. 'Don't tell me Heindrich Kroll *cared* what you thought!'

'No. Of course not. But Kroll was, and probably is, an extremely intelligent man, John. I'd expect to find his IQ close to the genius rating. . . .'

'Anton, for God's sake!' John said.

'John, all you're implying is that he was mad. Proves my point. Stupid people never go mad. They degenerate into imbecility, into moronity, but it usually takes an extremely intelligent person to go insane. Kroll, like most of the better – correction! – like most of the more efficient SS officers, was a true paranoiac. And, paranoiacs, my dear John, are the most lucid of madmen. Everything they say and do is perfectly logical, connected, clear, makes, I insist, damned good sense – if you accept their original premise, start from *their* jumping-off place. But since that jumping-off place has not the remotest connection with reality, all their towering, connected, logical structure becomes a stairway leading nowhere. Except to their victims, of course. For if you honestly believe that the Jews are the cause of all the world's ills, the "Final Solution" becomes somewhat less than unthinkable, doesn't it?'

'Jesus!' John said.

'Another paranoiac,' Anton said dryly, 'but let's not go into that now. The second misapprehension your dear illegitimate papa was labouring under was that it was *I* and not *you* who had succeeded him as Simone's lover.'

'Sure you didn't aid and abet him in that one, Anton?' John said.

'No. Quite honestly, no. Of course I *would* have if it had occurred to me; but it didn't. You see, he asked me—'

'"Do you love Simone Levy." And you said, "Yes." Which was true. But backtrack a little, Anton. Why did Kroll conceal from Dalton, and from you, that he and his trained Sipo Four sadists had tortured Simone almost to death?'

'Didn't want to get our backs up. We were still useful to him. Same principle they used then they forced the first wave of deportees to sign picture postcards showing neat, attractive bungalows with flower gardens around them, yet! – as their new places of residence, which the Nazis then sent to their relatives and friends still awaiting deportation. Sent them from such charming health resorts, John, as Oswiscin, Belzec, Majdanek, Chelmo, Treblinka!'

'I see,' John said. 'Psychological lessening of resistance. But this business of being useful? My father, all right. He *was*. At making those miserable antisemitic broadcasts—'

'In order to save Simone, John,' Anton said. 'He was fool enough to believe you could trust them—'

'I know that. But how were *you* useful, Anton?'

Anton held up his left hand. It was scarred, a trifle withered, drawn.

'Until I did *this*,' he said, 'it was my nightly duty to play the violin for that monster. A damned good violin, incidentally – an excellent, authentic, Stradivarius, *circa* 1710, stolen from God knows whom. His taste in violin music was very good. I wasn't surprised when he requested the tremolo section of the Introduction to *Die Walküre*. All Nazis of a little culture were mad over Wagner. The beginning of the Prelude to *Lohengrin*, of course. But the six Bach Partitas? The Marche Funèbre from Beethoven's *Eroica*? Das Helden Geführtm from Richard Strauss' *Life of a Hero*? The beginning of Mahler's First Symphony – and before you point out that these are all Germans, he also asked for Debussy's *Iberia*, Saint-Saëns' *Carnival of Animals*, Berlioz's Scherzo from *Romeo and Juliet*. All virtuoso violin sections, John; and that monstrous murderous madman knew them every one!'

'According to my beloved bride,' John said dryly, 'you broke that hand against a Sabra's hard head.'

'For the second time. Thus making any hope of my recovering my former skill out of the question. But the first time I smashed it, myself, with a hammer, to make damned sure I stopped being Heindrich Kroll's court musician!'

'I see,' John said. 'I take it *you* were treated well?'

'What makes you ask that, John?' Anton said angrily.

'Gabby, you know all those sonnets by heart, don't you?' John said.

'Yes, John,' Gabby said.

'Say the fifth one for Anton, will you?'

'John, I—' she faltered.

'Say it!' John said.

'John, now you're being unkind!' she said sharply.

'Say it, Rachie,' Anton said quietly. 'Let me be the judge of that.'

'All right,' Gabrielle said bitterly, 'if I must be used in your mutual war over the affections of a dead woman, here goes! It's called "Sonnet Five: For Simone, Again." '

Then very quietly, vibrantly, almost achingly, she recited it:

I offer you, in recompense, my life,
A tawdry thing, worth little, without you;
Worth something less than that, worth nothing. A knife
Across a fat pig's throat, drawn slowly through
Bristle and squeal and grease, would surely kill
A thing of greater value. At least
Pork's edible, but such swill
As I will make, such fly blown dead beast
Rotting, what good is that? What good
Was I alive? A scribbler of gaudy lies
Already forgotten, never understood –
Say then a good man's saved, a brave one dies –
No – say coward for swine, which is more nearly so.
Their gun butts smash the lock now. Good-bye. I go.

In the curiously heavy silence after she stopped speaking,

they could hear Anton II's voice going on, translating it into Hebrew for Manya's benefit. When he had finished, Manya said, venturing her heavily accented English for the first time.

'But – thees – thees ees terrible! Cruel!'

'Yes,' Anton sighed, 'but not entirely unjust. And to your question, John: yes, I was treated well. I was the valuable hostage to be exchanged for Kroll's miserable murderer's life. I thought smashing my hand would do that – reduce my value, permit me at least the privilege, the relief, of dying with my brothers. But Kroll was too smart for me; he saw at once, and told me, that as long as the world didn't *know* I was now the ex-great violinist, my value remained undiminished. He set their best military surgeons to work on my hand. It was still in a cast when Dalton came to visit me – oh, they were very sure of him, by then – with the damnedest assortment of files, and hacksaw blades you ever saw. Even – changed clothes with me, so that they would follow him, instead. . . .'

'And gave his life for yours,' Gabrielle said.

'Yes. And no. I think that Kroll wanted him alive. For he, too, had a certain value. Kroll was sure that the Americans were itching to get their hands on Dalton Ross in order to stage a spectacular show-trial before hanging him—'

'He was wrong,' John said. 'When have my people *ever* given a damn about a poet? The only thing ninety-seven per cent of them know about Pound is that he broadcast propaganda for Mussolini, not ever that he was truly a great genius. . . .'

'And for his genius I'm supposed to forgive him the *Pisan Cantos*, John?' Anton said.

'No – but for his madness, maybe,' John said.

'Then for what reason am I supposed to forgive Eliott for that line in "Sweeney Among the Nightingales" about Rachel née Rabinovitch's rapacious paws? Or such pieces of quintessential nastiness as "Burbank With a Baedeker, Bleistein With a Cigar"? Shall I quote for you? "The rats are underneath the piles. The jew—' with a lower case j, John; note it! – is underneath the lot." '

'Let's say that poetic excellence and moral bastardy go together,' John said. 'I've known that all my life. Had my nose rubbed into it from babyhood, Anton. Get on with it. So you escaped. Made your way up to Vence, persuaded Simone to run away with you. . . .'

'Didn't have to persuade. On the morning after my escape, Dalton joined up with what was left of Réseau Merle. That fact alone proves it was *not* his intention to sacrifice himself for me. You know he spoke idiomatic Spanish, didn't you?'

'Yes,' John said. 'He was responsible for my learning it.'

'And Pepe, as you know, was all for anyone who spoke his native tongue. They talked for hours. Among the things that came out in the wash, my dear John, was Pepe's telling Dalton how you got Simone out of that prison, and Dalton's telling Pepe you were his, Dalton's son.'

'So?' John said.

'Pepe passed that information on to Simone. She believed it at once, because she was able to recognize the many traits that the two of you had in common. She seems to have regarded the fact that she had had well – sexual relations with both of you, with father and son, with a primitive, superstitious kind of horror. She was convinced that her remaining with you would damn you forever. So she begged me to take her away, not the other way around.'

'And you—'

'Refused, until I saw that she was going to leave anyhow, alone and sick, she was going to. So I gave in, for which I do *not* apologize, John Farrow! – and took her with me. The only thing I regret about that decision is that it may have caused her death. Perhaps with you, somewhere else—'

'And perhaps not,' John said. 'Life seems to have its inevitability built in, doesn't it?'

'Yes. Because when Dalton Ross found out she had gone away with me, he blamed himself for having wrecked your life. By then he knew that it was you who'd been his successor! And, far from offending him, the idea pleased him. He seems to have fallen into – well, call it a curiously senile sort of stupor – at the news. He admitted to himself that he was old, tired, beaten. So he left Réseau Merle. Went back up to Tourette-sur-Loup. Let himself be seen by the rightist Milice bastards who reported everything to the Germans. The Nazis came after him. He holed up in that house, and put up the greatest one-man fight, I'm told, of the whole ruddy war. They had to bring up a Mark Four Tiger tank, and blast that house to rubble with its eight-eight millimetre before they got him.'

'Bless him,' John said. 'Anton—'

'Yes, John?'

'I'd like to be at peace with you from here on in. It doesn't seem to me that apologies, pleas for pardon, are necessary on either side. But if I have offended you in any way, you have mine, freely given. And humbly.'

'John,' Gabrielle said, 'I – I *do* love you, you know. One *has* to, doesn't one?'

'Yes,' Jeanne said, 'one has to. John is one of the only two wholly good people I have known in all my life. And Simone was the other.'

'You're wrong, Jeanne,' John said, 'about me at least, you're dead damned wrong. About Simone, I'd say you're right. And though none of you seem to be willing to give her credit for it, so is Gabrielle, here. That's the main reason I married her. . . .'

'You married me,' Gabby said sweetly, 'because that silly ass of a gynaecologist, Gobeau, called you up and told you I was pregnant. And since you're so ruddy honourable that you squeak, you just had to do right by little Nell. And that, my dearest John, is the truth of it!'

'The term that suits Aunt Rachie is what we call *ohev tzarot*, sir!' Anton II laughed. 'And that means she just loves trouble. I have never known a time when she wasn't in hot water over something or the other.'

'All I hope,' Anton mocked, 'is that the little bastard looks at least a little like you, John. With Rachie, here, one never knows!'

'Why Anton!' Gabby said, 'you're a swine, y'know! And that constitutes defamation of character and is actionable as such! Besides which, you haven't even answered John. Are – you at peace with him, too? I do *so* want you to be!'

'Quite,' Anton said. 'And I confess it's a relief. I've been carrying around a good many semi-guilty feelings too ruddy long. Peace it is. Shall we drink to it, John?'

'*Shalom!*' John said, and raised his glass.

'I say, Papa,' Anton II said, 'I'd better get this Production Project home and to bed. It's jolly late, you know—'

'And I, this one,' John said. 'Could you drop us off, son?'

'Oh no you don't, John Farrow!' Jeanne said. 'Anton Senior will take you back to the hotel. It's my turn now. I must tell you how *I* caught Anton.'

'Do, please,' John said, '*this* Production Project – I thank you for that one, son! – will sleep past noon in any event, so don't let us detain you.'

'You won't,' Anton II said. 'We really must go. *I* have to get up in the morning. I have a beastly violin class at the gymnasium for a totally tone-deaf bunch of little squeakers. I'm the only one who does have to be an early bird. Papa's work doesn't begin until late afternoon – and the women, like women everywhere these days – have got it made. What we need is a man's liberation movement it seems to me.'

'Put me down as a member when you start it,' John said.

'And there I was,' Jeanne said, 'outside this great symphony orchestra conductor's dressing room at L'Opéra, with Anton Deux beside me – and this miserable species of a flunky was determined not to let me get anywhere near him!'

'At my orders,' Anton said. 'You cannot possibly imagine, John, how many idiotic mothers with their moronic sons, each with a cheap fiddle tucked up under his arm, attempt to storm backstage at every concert. Though I must say, the boy's really quite talented. His damned paws are much too big to manage a violin properly, but he does rather well, all things considered.'

'He plays better than *you* do, Anton!' Jeanne cried. 'Admit it!'

'Since I broke my hand, yes, before, no. Get on with it, Jeanne – maternal pride is one of the world's biggest bores, y'know.'

'How did you get to see him finally?' John said.

'Started screaming like a poissonière! "*Dites-lui!*" I shrieked, "*que c'est moi, Marie Claire – qu'il a connu trop bien pendant la guerre! Et que ce garçon est son fils!*" That brought him out on the run, I can tell you. And do you know what he said when he saw me, *mon cher*? Can you imagine?'

'No,' John said.

' "Oh damn that John Farrow anyhow!" ' Jeanne said with a silvery burst of laughter.

'Why damn me – at that particular juncture?' John said, 'so far as I know I was thousands of miles away from Paris at that time and—'

'For not permitting him to *shoot* me, John!' Jeanne laughed, 'thus saving him all this si drôle of a predicament! So after that we talked all night. I was only asking him to finance Anton Deux's musical education, nothing more. But he glared at me and said: "D'accord; but on one condition, Marie Claire! That you marry me at once, and come to live with me in Israel!"'

'And that,' John said, 'was that.'

'Practically. But not quite. He had concerts at Lyon, Bruxelles, Genève and even London, while I was left alone to struggle with French bureaucracy. I was so afraid he'd change his mind meantime! But finally I had all those *drôle des papiers* and there he was scowling at me, and saying *oui* to the mayor as though he hated the very sight of me. In fact I'm sure he did, but he was willing to take me in order to get his hands on Anton Deux. Because, once you put them side by side, he had as much chance of denying my son was also his as Rachie had of denying Simone was her sister!'

'Perhaps she wasn't,' Gabrielle said. 'Unrelated people often look exactly alike. I've heard that Hitler had *eleven* doubles to take his place when he didn't want to be bothered, or if there were some danger. So—'

'That makes you act like her? Even this business of saying something outrageous with every second breath? Even to your taste in men? Have you forgotten the letter you wrote me the day after the first time you saw John in Paris?'

'She'd – brainwashed me. Simone, I mean,' Gabrielle said. 'Anton, would you please, please, please take us back to the Sheraton, now? All three of us: John, me, and the Production?'

'Yes. Why yes, of course. And, I say, Rachie, don't put off going to see Trudy Elon too long. You're rather a bit of an oldish bag, y'know and—'

'See why I *love* Tel Aviv, John, dearest? They say the *nicest* things to a girl here!' Gabby said.

But the next morning, after having permitted himself the blissful luxury of sleeping much longer than he customarily did, he woke up with the distinct and startled feeling that something was wrong.

It was: Gabrielle was nowhere to be seen.

He leaped from the bed, stood there swaying dizzily. He had taken a whiskey or two too many last night, he realized. Then he saw the folded piece of notepaper on the dresser. He opened it, read:

'Darling – Had to go out. Back in a jiffy. Love, Your Blushing, Blushing Bride!'

It was cheerful enough if scarcely explanatory. He plunged under the shower. Shaved. Dressed. Went downstairs into the restaurant, still feeling a trifle rocky and hungover, there to be confronted with an Israeli breakfast.

Now to face an Israeli breakfast when one is even in the best of form is a feat requiring something close to heroism. John sat there staring at the buffet table the waiter rolled up for his inspection. On it were piles of raw eggs waiting to be prepared according to the client's taste, several huge pitchers of various kinds of fruit juice. A vacuum coffee maker, bubbling busily over a hot plate. Sardines, sprats, herring marinated, herring creamed, herring in the rollmop style. Grated carrots. Tomatoes, cucumbers, onions, olives green and black. Milk and cream. Yogurt. A cheese plate with cheeses he didn't even know the names of. Three kinds of jam. Honey. Butter, Rolls. Loaves. Whole wheat bread. Toast. Biscuits. And stewed fruit compote.

'Grapefruit juice,' John groaned, 'coffee – black. Nothing more.'

The waiter looked at him as though he had insulted national honour.

'A little too much partying last night,' John explained. 'All that food reminds my stomach of how squeamish it feels.'

'Then you *should* put something into it,' the waiter said. 'Allow me, sir. I'll arrange you something light. . . .'

What he called light would have sunk the Israeli navy. Out of politeness, and even more out of certain residual timidity, John Farrow ate what he could. And immediately felt better. Even his head seemed to weigh a couple of tons less.

Which was why, perhaps, it came to him *where* Gabrielle probably was; and what she was almost surely doing:

'Out at Dr Elon's clinic sure as hell, selling that lady sawbones a bill of goods without me around to interfere!'

He jumped up from the table and almost ran into the lobby, rushed up to the desk, said:

'Get me a taxi, please!'

The concierge turned to a bellhop, said, '*Monit!*'

'Come with me, sir!' the bellhop said.

There were a row of taxis waiting outside.

'Now, sir, if you will tell me where you wish to go, I will tell the driver,' the bellhop said.

John told him. The boy turned to the driver and rattled off a string of Hebrew. John caught the words *Beit Kholm*. And *Rof'a Elon*. Then: *Shederot Israel Rokach*.

He tipped the boy an Israeli pound, which seemed to make the little fellow happy enough. He rode off, thinking that what with the money, the food, and the language, Israel was going to take some getting used to.

At the clinic a young nurse, pretty enough to make him feel better, even as worried as he was, greeted him with: 'Shalom. *Boker Tov, Adon*.' ('Peace. Good day, sir.')

But he'd already learned by then that most Israelis speak at least a little English, so he said:

'Good morning, I'm Attorney John Farrow. I believe my wife is here to see Dr Elon.'

'Yes, sir,' the pretty nurse said, 'they're in the office now, sir. Will you come with me?'

But before he got even close to the door, he heard Gabby's voice. She was speaking English, which meant that Dr Gertrude Elon was *not* a Sabra. Most of the European immigrants spoke the languages of their country of origin among themselves, after struggling with the really awesome difficulties of Hebrew all day long. And, as in the case of Gabby and Dr Elon at this moment, when they were from different countries, they usually fell back on English as a lingua franca.

'Trudy, for God's love!' Gabrielle was saying.

The nurse raised her hand to knock on that door. To her vast astonishment, John reached out and caught her wrist.

'Please!' he whispered, 'not yet! I want to hear this! Maybe this way I'll get at the truth, finally. . . .'

She stared at him disapprovingly, but she held her tongue.

'If you wish to kill yourself, Gabby, dahlink,' Dr Elon's rough contralto came through that door, 'you should use your gun. Shoot yourself. I do not murder idiots. Not even overaged female idiots who forget to take their pills or leave off their diaphragms!'

'But, Trudy, I can *so* have my baby!' Gabby said, hotly, 'you *know* I can!'

'Well—' Dr Elon said, and it seemed to John her voice softened, let a note of – say amused tenderness creep in, 'you want this little brat *that* much dahlink?'

'More than I've ever wanted anything in my life, Trudy,'

Gabrielle said, and he could hear the tears drowning her voice; 'except one thing—'

'And that one thing was?'

'Its father,' Gabrielle said.

He stepped quickly past the puzzled young nurse and opened the door himself.

'John!' Gabrielle said.

Dr Elon let out a booming laugh. She was about fifty years old and built on the general lines of a Sherman tank. But she had competence written all over her. 'And kindness,' John thought. It was that kindness he was afraid of now.

'They say eavesdroppers never hear good of themselves,' she said, 'but you, Attorney Farrow, break that rule. As it seems to me you have broken a good many rules already. I am glad you have come. We must talk about the case of the little Gabrielle and what there is to be done.'

'Good morning, doctor,' John said. 'But there's only one thing to be done, isn't there? You must cause her to abort.'

'Oh blast and damn!' Gabrielle said: 'John, sometimes I *hate* you, y'know!'

'I'm not too fond of you today, either,' John said, 'sneaking around behind my back to risk your life this way. Or at least to try to persuade Dr Elon to—'

'She *has* persuaded me, attorney,' Trudy Elon said. 'She can have this child. And after it perhaps one other, or maybe even two.'

'Oh, Trudy!' Gabrielle said; and embraced the doctor wildly.

'But isn't it dangerous, doctor?' John said.

'Of course. Any birth is. This one a little more than most because you – both of you – waited too long to start a family. You're . . . fifty-ish, aren't you?'

'Fifty-four,' John said.

'Men that old don't make strong babies. Usually they don't even make strong love, but—'

Gabrielle let out a delighted hoot of laughter.

'Much you know about *that*, Trudy!' she said.

Trudy Elon winked at John merrily.

'It is by such tactics that I find out the things I need to know,' she said. 'Sit down, attorney. Let us talk. First, when can *you* come in for a complete check-up?'

John stared at her, said: 'Why, doctor?'

'It takes two people to make a baby, my good sir! To determine the baby's chances I need to know all about his father's health as well. When can you?'

'Who'll do the check-up? *You*, doctor?' John said.

'How Anglo-Saxon!' Dr Elon laughed. 'But of course I shall! Or do you insist upon my bringing in a male doctor to preserve your modesty?'

'Oh John, don't be silly!' Gabby said.

'All right,' John said slowly. 'Whenever you say, doctor.'

'Next week. For all of this week. I shall be very occupied, mainly with your little wife. She must remain here. I have already assigned her a room. Number Twenty-one – at the end of the corridor. It is our best, Gabby, dahlink – away from all the noise. You, sir, may bring her tonight such few things as she will need. For knowing her of old, I shall keep her prisoner until all the tests are made!'

'I'll be good, Trudy,' Gabby said, like a child.

'It will be the first time, then!' Dr Elon said. 'But truly we gain time by starting now.'

'But, doctor,' John protested, 'are you *sure*?'

'As sure as one can be. I was testing Gabrielle when you came. Psychologically. And I am satisfied. When a woman wants her child as badly as Gabby does, she usually does damn fine, no matter how old she is. Besides Gabby is almost a Sabra. She is like the Kibbutz women. In the old days, we used to hitch 'em up alongside a camel or a mule for the ploughing. And they'd drop their brats in the furrows. Of course we always gave 'em twenty minutes rest before hitching them back up again!'

'You see, darling!' Gabby said triumphantly.

'I see you've sold the doctor a bill of goods,' John said.

Dr Elon stared at him, said:

'Tell me one thing, sir: you *don't* want this child?'

'At the cost of my wife's life, no.' John said at once.

'That's a good answer,' Dr Elon said, 'but if I assure you that within the limits of medical probabilities, the danger can be reduced to a very slight one indeed? No more than in the case of a girl of twenty-two or three, say?'

John stared at Gabrielle.

'Oh, John, please!' she said.

'All right,' he said, 'but first I must say this: I don't think I could – survive anything happening to Gabby, doctor. I honestly don't think I could.'

'That is the best of all answers!' Dr Elon said softly. 'So therefore we take all the precautions. After the tests: Rh negatives, y'know, any history of Tay Sach's disease in the family, and the rest of it, you, Gabrielle, must give me your solemn word that from the beginning of the seventh month, on, you will return here to *stay*. So that at any moment you will have essential care. At the very worst I may have to do a Caesarian. Oh don't worry – a lap incision: you can go on wearing your scandalous bikinis! And, if you obey me as to exercise, foods, and the rest, your figure should remain jolly good . . . so now it is agreed we bring this little half-Goy into the world?'

'Yes, oh yes!' Gabby said, then: 'Oh, John. Please!'

'Yes, agreed – since it means so much to you, my dear,' John said.

She came over to him shyly, took his hand, looked into his eyes said softly:

'And it *doesn't* to you, my love?'

'If it works out all right, it will be the greatest happiness I've ever known,' he said.

'Then it will work out; I promise you that, John, dearest,' she said, and kissed him.

'Good! Now you get out of here, attorney!' Trudy Elon said, 'for we, Gabby and I, have much work to do!'

He was supposed to come back to the clinic with Gabby's overnight bag and toilette case at nine o'clock that night.

But he didn't get back until after ten, which was Gabrielle's own fault. She phoned Manya, Anton's daughter-in-law, to tell her John was all alone at the hotel, thus achieving the desired result: Manya sent Anton II after him, the minute her young husband came home from the gymnasium, which was not the athletics and sports building of a high school as in the States, but the entire high school after the nineteenth century Middle-European fashion. Thus making sure – quite innocently, of course, just what Gabby had intended from the outset would take place: that is, that Jeanne Rabinowski would not be presented with the opportunity, or the temptation, to entertain John Farrow in both her, Gabby's, and Anton Senior's absence.

And by this surrender to unwarranted, irrational, and distinctly petty jealousy, Gabrielle almost wrecked her life.

But, on the other hand, by following instantly and without question, her professional instincts, she indisputably saved it.

She was lying in her bed in Room Twenty-one, resting after one really rough test. Trudy Elon had made her run at top speed for close to a quarter of an hour, upon a mechanical treadmill, or endless belt, with all the electrodes of the electrocardiograph and those of the oscilloscope taped to her body. She had passed that test with flying colours, but it had worn her out.

She was lying there fighting the temptation to call John at Anton Second's house, just to talk to him, although she really hadn't anything to tell him because the other tests, Pap's vaginal smear, blood, and urine, wouldn't be ready until late tomorrow, nor would the cell biopsy performed to detect evidence of Tay Sach's disease, a hereditary, congenital defect found only among Jews of Middle-European origin. She was not worried about the tests, nor any of the others Dr Elon would perform in the next three or four days. Though small and slight in build, the members of her family had always enjoyed robust health, the women always producing numerous sturdy babies, a tradition that only Simone and she had broken, or rather quite against their wills had been forced to break by being born at the terrible time they were.

She was also toying with the idea that if the baby were a boy and beautiful, and healthy, could she not persuade John to convert and adopt the name Levy, so that her family should not vanish from the earth. Nearly every immigrant to Israel changed his name to proud and warlike Hebrew names in order to throw off the stigma of the Diaspora. So why shouldn't an American–French Goy of no particular beliefs oblige her in this thing? That it meant that Anglo–Protestant Farrows must vanish in their stead, *tant pis*! They already had! Because John wasn't even a Farrow. Wasn't it better to be an honest and legal Levy than a bastard Ross?

The very idea was so wonderfully outrageous that it made her laugh aloud in pure delight. She also had another idea she knew she must approach more slowly. If the child were a girl she jolly well *wasn't* going to call her Simone. Rather she was going to give her the same name that Israel's first Prime Minister Ben Gurion had given *his* daughter: 'Guela.' Which meant 'Salvation.'

She was thinking all that, when quite suddenly, she looked out her window. And fear hit her in the pit of her stomach like an icy fist. Because, by now it was early evening, and the shadows were lengthening across the land of Israel. Those trees that came to within five metres of her window, and which made this wing the coolest and most desirable of the clinic, being, as it was, far away from the noise of traffic, seemed to her abruptly monstrous.

'I shall not stay here!' she said; and, picking up the phone, she called Dr Elon's office.

A quarter of an hour later, after almost hysterically rejecting all Trudy Elon's arguments about the advantages of Room Twenty-one, and the unlikelihood of Black September's even knowing where she was at the moment, she was somewhat less than comfortably installed in a cubbyhole of a room on the noisy street side, next to Dr Elon's office itself.

'I,' Trudy Elon said, only half in jest, 'have one damn fine Mauser automatic in my desk, dahlink. You hear a noise in the night, you call me!'

But Gabrielle didn't call her. Instead, worn out by what had been a really strenuous day, and the fact she'd had only four hours of sleep the night before, Gabby dozed off while still waiting somewhat worriedly now, for John.

What woke her was the shattering thunder of that satchel charge as it blew Room Twenty-one completely off the clinic; and collapsed the whole end of that wing like a house of cards.

Gabby was out of her bed in one long, beautifully graceful leap. She didn't even look in the direction of the billowing smoke, the leaping orange-red flames. Instead she dashed, barefooted, and with the backless hospital gown exposing her, fortunately panty-clad, derrière to public view, into Trudy Elon's office, tore open the desk drawer, snatched up the Mauser, sprinted out the door and around the side of the clinic. They were still there, just as she'd known they'd be, skulking under the trees enjoying the results of their work. She could see their teeth and eyes gleaming in the fire glare.

She stopped still, fell into the expert pistol marksman's crouch, held that big, heavy long-barrelled Mauser in both her slim hands, squeezed the trigger slowly.

With just two shots she killed them both.

After that she waited where she was until the police cars and fire trucks, ambulances came whooping up Israel Rokach Road. Among the police were naturally a number of secret service men. And one of them was Meir Yariv.

By then, she was sobbing hysterically, because she was sure everyone in that wing was dead. And if they were, she was the direct cause of their deaths.

'I should have told Trudy!' she stormed. 'To ask for guards! I knew they were after me! I knew it, Meir!'

'And so did we, Rachie,' Captain Yariv said. 'So if anyone failed in their duty, it was us. We should have had you and your husband tailed every step you took. Only we just didn't believe that here in Tel Aviv, of all places, for God's sake! They'd—'

He looked at where the police were examining the two dead fellahin.

'Damned good shooting, Rachie,' he said.

'No,' she whispered, 'no, it wasn't, Meir. Good shooting would have been to – to drop them before they got here. With that plastic charge still in their hands. Only I was so – tired, and I fell asleep—'

'And you're slightly pregnant, too, I hear,' he said.

'Yes,' she said softly, 'but what kind of life can he have, Meir? What kind of life can my baby have when I – when I have to – kill people – to even allow him to be born?'

'Don't think about that now, Rachie. Come on. You'd better get back inside, and to bed. The fire's out. See – there's only a little smoke left. And in that outfit you could catch pneumonia. . . .'

He put his arm around her shoulder, led her around the building. When they came in the front door, they met Dr Elon.

'Baby!' she cried, 'my God, you had me scared! When I couldn't find you, I—'

'Trudy—' Gabby whispered, 'how many—?'

'Just one. A little nurse's helper named Paula Onn. Several hurt pretty badly. But those we'll save. But poor Paula – she's – unrecognizable. Horrible thing. Her face, her head—'

Gabby bent in half then, and started vomiting. Captain Meir Yariv swept her up into his arms.

'In there!' Trudy Elon said. 'I'm going to give her a shot that'll put her out till this time tomorrow.'

'No!' Gabby shrilled, 'please, no! John! I have to call him! Tell him—'

'Baby,' Trudy Elon said, 'those bastards cut the telephone lines *first*. It'll take several hours to restore connections, so just you relax. We'll get word to him somehow. . . .'

'I'll drive in and get him. Bring him out here, if you like,' Meir Yariv said. 'You're at the Sheraton, aren't you?'

'Yes. But he may be at Anton Rabinowski's flat. The son's flat, Meir – not the father's. Do get him for me, because by now—'

'Don't worry about it, Rachie,' Meir Yariv said.

He was too late. Because when that satchel charge of plastic went off, John Farrow had already parked his rented Ford Taunus, and was walking towards the clinic. He ran in a long diagonal slant across those grounds and plunged into those flames. He had a very good idea where Room Twenty-one should have been. He tore into the wreckage at or about the spot his mental picture of the clinic's layout told him Gabby's room had to be. He dug away rubble with his bare hands until he had uncovered that pair of long slim, beautiful legs, lying there amid the debris: powdered glass, broken plaster, the twisted wreckage of the bed. He bent, caught her by the ankles, and pulled her free.

She was quite naked. The blast had blown her clothes completely off her. She was hideously burned. And she hadn't any face.

He turned: walked away from there. Very quietly. Exactly as he had in 1943 when Hélène died. He was, by any man's definition of the term, clinically insane. Coldly, completely, dangerously mad. He moved towards the car, one step after another, steady, sure. His face had become a mask, a frozen map of the hinterlands of hell. Only his eyes were alive, and they were screaming without sound. The whole of him, his pose, gait, terrible quiet, described, defined the ultimate degrees of anguish.

He reached the car. Unlocked it. Drove it with apparent calm, almost excessive care, to the hotel. Went upstairs. Packed one two-suiter flight bag. Got his passport, his money. Took that flat, ugly Pistolle M-2 automatic out of the big handbag where Gabrielle always kept it. Put it in his breast pocket. The extra clips, he put into his attaché case along with his passport, and his traveller's cheques.

He came back downstairs; checked out; paid the bill.

'But, madame?' the desk clerk said.

John looked at him. Looked through him.

'She won't be coming back,' he said flatly, quietly. 'You see – she's dead.'

Then he went outside to where he'd parked his car. Drove out to Lod Airport. Went to the ticket office of El Al, said:

'Give me a ticket to Madrid, Spain.'

'Try BOAC over there,' the ticket vendor said. 'We don't have flights to Spain, sir. . . .'

So Meir Yariv was too late. Under the circumstances, he had to be. First he had gone to Anton Rabinowski II's flat. And Anton II told him:

'He left here in a rented car, sir. He'd already hired it when I went to pick him up at the Sheraton, and insisted on bringing it along – tailing me here that is, so that I wouldn't have to drive him out to Dr Elon's clinic later on.'

'Odd that he *didn't* appear at the clinic, though. Perhaps I'd better check the hotel; Rachie's damned worried that he didn't show—' Mair Yariv said.

'Anton!' Manya said in Hebrew: 'you drive me out to the clinic! See if she's really all right—'

'She is,' Captain Yariv said, 'not a scratch. You see she'd changed rooms – on a hunch. A premonition. She was truly lucky, I'd say. . . .'

'Captain,' Anton said, 'did John Farrow *know* she'd changed rooms?'

'I don't know. Those murderous swine cut the telephone before planting that satchel charge so it's not unlikely that he didn't.'

Anton II crossed the room. Picked up the telephone.

'Give me four-five-one-one-one,' he said; then, a few seconds later: '*Malon Sheraton? Shalom. Adon John Farrow, beva kasha. Ma! Matay? Ken. Ken. Tov meod – Ken – Toda rabba.*'

He turned back to his wife, to Captain Yariv, his eyes appalled.

'They say,' he got out, 'that John's – checked out. And that Aunt Rachie – is dead!'

'Oh, no!' Manya said, and started to cry.

'She wasn't when I left her half an hour ago. Not a scratch on her. In fact, she'd polished off the characters who did the job. Damned fine operator, Rachie. Pity she's resigned. Any fool woman can make babies, but – Anton! Call that ruddy hotel back and ask them who *told* them Rachie was dead!'

Anton II did so. Turned back to them, said:

'It was John, himself, sir. They said he looked awful. As though he really didn't know what he was doing. Captain Meir, d'you think—?'

'No time to think now, son! We'd better find him – and fast. Don't you see – he must have arrived at the clinic, during all the confusion. And – why damn me for a Syrian! – a girl was killed in that wing! She was – unrecognizable. Face quite blown away. So say John Farrow *didn't* know Rachie had changed rooms! Say he saw – a mutilated female corpse. Slim enough. Shapely enough – let's go, son!'

'Yes, sir!' Anton said, 'but *where, Katsin* Yariv? Tell me *that*. Where?'

Then Manya said it:

'Go to the clinic. Ask Rachie. She'd know. She's the only one on earth who *would*.'

So Meir Yariv was too late. By the time that he, Anton II, and Gabrielle got to Lod Airport, John Farrow was twelve thousand metres in the air, in a BOAC jet screaming across the Mediterranean, at 975 kilometres an hour.

Towards Spain. Towards Madrid.

Where the man called Albrecht Holtz by now almost surely was. But where he wasn't going to be much longer. Neither there. Nor anywhere.

Except possibly – in hell.

21

He was in no hurry at all, and that in itself, gave him certain advantages. His mind functioned with a crystalline lucidity he was normally incapable of, since his own analysis of himself, of his character – that he was a romantic, a sentimentalist, and even something of a puritan – was basically correct. But Gabrielle's belief that there was much that was schizoid about him was just as correct. He could be, and very often was, the direct opposite of all the bland and foolish traits of which he accused himself. Like all puritans, he was profoundly sensual, since people who don't have strong emotions, never learn the fear and hatred of them that is puritanism's root cause. And like all sentimentalists he could be cruel. As for his romanticism, it was gone, drained out of him, along with every normal emotion, leaving only that icy lucidity that makes the crimes committed by paranoiacs the despair of criminologists, of the finest detectives, since these cold and absolutely clear madmen are marching to a different drumbeat, operating at an oblique tangent to normality's sense of motivations, cause and effect, mode of operation, even time.

The first thing he did upon leaving the Aeropuerto de Barajas was to take a taxi straight to the Castellaña Hilton on the Paseo de la Castellaña, a hotel he ordinarily wouldn't have been found dead in. For not only was it the most American of all the hotels of Madrid, but it was always filled with exactly the type of American businessmen and tourists who have greatly facilitated the spread of anti-Americanism all over the civilized world.

But that very fact, combined with his now perfect American accent in English, and his obviously (though a good bit better cut than is the norm), American clothes, would provide him with a degree of protective coloration – or to use the professional word for it, 'cover'. Of course there were Americans everywhere these days; but at the lovely old Ritz, or the Palace where normally he would have gone, he would have been just a trifle more noticeable, if only because at those hotels, as at the newer Luz Palacio only a block farther up the street, the more leisurely Continental pace with which everything was conducted gave both management and help time to notice and remember individual clients, while amid the nasal whining, flat-toned, twanging, endlessly complaining bedlam its guests turned the Hilton into, no one had time to remember even his own name.

The second thing he did, once upstairs in his room was to pick up the Madrid telephone directory. This, almost surely, no professional intelligence agent would have thought to do. Captain Meir Yariv, for instance, would have assumed, with perfect logic, that Heindrich Kroll, a wanted war criminal, would *not* be in the telephone book, even under his alias, Albrecht Holtz. But then, Captain Yariv didn't know Spain. And practically couldn't, since that country's unwavering support of the Arab bloc was monolithic.

While he, John Farrow, did. Knew that an ex-Nazi had absolutely nothing to fear in a country that had sent thousands of its youths to die in its Blue Division – 'A singularly appropriate name,' John Farrow thought, 'since that's the colour most of them were frozen into—' on the Eastern front, alongside Hitler's hordes against the Russian; and still maintained – if somewhat creakingly – the only admittedly fascist party in power anywhere in the world today.

He could have pointed out to Captain Yariv that the pages of the directory under the letter W – a letter that doesn't even exist in the Spanish alphabet – were devoted almost exclusively to German names. And that of those names a high proportion were ex-Nazis living in perfect tranquillity in a country whose government damned well was not going to permit their extradition anywhere for any reason whatsoever.

So he turned to the pages under H. There was an even chance that Albrecht Holtz might be listed there. His reasoning turned out to have been perfect. His luck, equally so. Holtz was.

Holtz had in fact two listings: a business address, the conventional export-import that so many people whose real occupations were questionable used for cover; and a home address. The business address John discarded at once; because, even if, for appearances' sake, Holtz did appear at his so-called office from time to time, he would surely do so only during normal business hours, and, worse still, the office was located in one of the busiest and most frequented parts of Madrid. There the ex-Oberstürmbannführer was as safe as a man in church.

But Holtz/Kroll's home address was much more promising. He lived in the Moraleja residential section, several kilometres north of Madrid on the old Madrid-Burgos Road. John sat there remembering what he knew about that section, which was a great deal, for, during the influx of American businesses into Spain in the middle and late sixties under the advantageous laws the Spanish government had passed to attract them, he, because of his knowledge of Spanish, had not only drawn up the contracts, but had sat in on the actual signings in Madrid of a good many of the agreements by which the new bi-national subsidiary companies were set up. As a result, he had been wined and dined by not a few of Madrid's wealthiest businessmen.

And Moraleja was where the super-wealthy lived. For it was by long odds the most luxurious residential section, or rather suburb, in the whole Provincia de Madrid. It had replaced both La Florida and Casa Quemada in that regard, just as they had, in their day, replaced the ancient and now badly run-down Puerto de Hierro section. It was even more luxurious than the newer Somosaguas, because its developers maintained a stern prohibition against dividing lots into anything smaller than a full *hectario,* ten thousand square metres, or roughly the size of two English or American acres. And their prices, as well as the only kind of houses one was permitted to build there, baronial manors with floor plans ranging from six hundred to a thousand square metres, effectively prevented any but the hardest of hard currency multimillionaires from even dreaming of attempting to live in Moraleja.

So, naturally, Albrecht Holtz/Heindrich Kroll could live there. With the kind of money there was to be made in heroin – the fortunes gained from the deliberate and total destruction of hundreds of thousands of otherwise useful lives, at the price of turning the great cities of the United States into very nearly uninhabitable asphalt jungles where mindless young addicts robbed and murdered every minute of the day and night to get the money for their next fixes – he could afford to live anywhere he pleased.

But, even granting that, it was still damned strange that he had chosen, not the section, but the city which it served, and more especially the country of which that city was the capital. For Spain was not only *not* the best place for a master pusher to have his residence; it was, John Farrow knew, pretty close to the worst. The Spanish police were indisputably the most rigorous in Europe when it came to cracking down upon drug-runners. Which was why the real professionals avoided Spain like the plague – with the sad result that Spanish jails were packed with incautious young Americans, students and hippies, for the most part, who had been caught with a couple of marijuana cigarettes, or a few ounces of 'grass' intended surely for personal use, as they crossed the frontiers into Spain, and who, as a result, were serving minimum sentences of six years.

Why, then, did Kroll risk it? The answer to that was very clear. Gabby – and so complete was John Farrow's icy, shock-bred emotional disassociation, that he could think her name calmly, without even letting the image of those naked legs, that hideously burnt female trunk, that smashed, unrecognizable mass that had been her achingly beloved face, her devilishly saucy, wise and witty head, enter his mind to disturb his implacable purpose – had been right. Clearly Kroll had retired from the active pursuit of the world's ugliest, most nefarious trade in order to implement the fulfilment of the maddest of all madmen's dreams: that he, Heindrich Kroll, could do what his late insane monster of a master, at the head of an entire great nation gone – with but the rarest of exceptions – as criminally insane as he, had tried to do, and had, by the narrowest of margins failed: that is to put into effect the Final Solution, to render not only Europe *judenrein, judenfrei,* but the entire vast circling globe, as well.

And for working out at least the beginning stages of that dream, Madrid was an excellent choice, as was Spain. First of all because, while it was true that the Spanish people probably retained less residual antisemitism than any other Western Europeans; had in fact, a marked fondness for the Sephardic Jews (a trickle of whom were steadily over the last few years returning to their mutual homeland) who had shaped so much of Spain's highest culture; even a shame-fed sympathy (born of the memories of the Inquisition) for the land of Israel – what the Spanish *people* think or feel, mattered not a damn. The Spanish government, the most autocratic west of the Iron Curtain, did what it would without let or hindrance, as Spanish governments of whatever political colouring or stripe, throughout all of that martyred country's terrible history always had, and probably always would.

As in the case of the pro-Arab policy, which had filled Madrid with embassies and consulates with the emblem of the Crescent waving overhead, many, if not most, of which busily engaged in passing El Fatah's and Ailul al Asward's activists through to the rest of Europe to set up a letter-bomb posting station in Amsterdam, say; to machine gun an El Al airliner in Geneva, to murder athletes in Munich, to present two little sex-starved and bird-brained English 'birds' in Rome with a portable phonograph chockful of explosives and tickets on an Israeli plane for Tel Aviv; to sabotage a pipeline in Trieste.

So Holtz/Kroll had come to the right place. Nowhere else in Europe could he have made better or easier contact with the first and only group of nations openly committed to a policy of avowed genocide in the whole of human history.

'For even Hitler concealed his intentions, to a degree,' John Farrow thought; 'while these types tell the world what they mean to do. Only they've stopped saying *when*, these days. And it's taken three damned rough lessons to teach them even that much caution. So to hell with them, and that. The question is what does one John Farrow do?

'First he calls for room service. Food. Loathsome thought! But necessary. Even to get this useless carcass from here to there. But not back again. One-way trip. Aller sans retour. A job to do, that's all. And afterwards? There's no afterwards. The world's stopped. So get off. But not alone. Take Kroll along for the ride, the slide. Straight down to—'

He picked up the phone.

He sat looking at the food. It wasn't bad. In fact it was pretty good food, as hotel room-service food goes. But he couldn't get it to his mouth. He couldn't. It was a simple, physical impossibility.

He pushed back his chair. Stood up. Put back on his tie, his jacket. Left his attaché case, his passport on the bed. Put the automatic in his left breast pocket. The extra clips in his hip pocket. Surveyed the effect in the bathroom mirror. They didn't show. Much.

He went downstairs into the lobby. Entered the American Express office; said to the young man behind the desk:

'You've a car rental service, haven't you?'

'Yes sir. What kind of a car would you like, sir?'

'Seat. Mil quinientos. Negro.'

'¿Entonces Usted habla español, señor?'

'Jesus!' he thought, 'I've blown it!' He had thought the make of the car in Spanish, automatically, and quite rapidly, due consideration being given to how much there was involved in the choice. For that Spanish copy of the Italian Fiat, built under licence in Spain by la Sociedad Española de Automoviles de Turismo, whose initials formed its name, was by far the most numerous car seen on Spanish streets and highways and, therefore the make least likely to attract undue attention if someone should spot it parked in some unlikely place.

But he had also had to do some fast thinking about one other factor: in a country as rigidly stratified by social classes as Spain was, he had also to consider the model. And it had cost him scarcely any reflection at all to realize that in a place like Moraleja, *nobody* would drive a 600, an 850, or even a 1430, as the other models of Seats were called from the total capacity of the cylinders of their motors in cubic centimetres. No, it had to be the top of the line: the 1500, or *mil quinientos* as it was familiarly known in Spain. And, even so, at Moraleja, such a relatively modest vehicle as *any* Seat was, would be a family's third, fourth or even fifth car, to be used by the chauffeur or the butler when running errands; that is when, as was very often the case nowadays, it didn't actually *belong* to said chauffeur or butler. In Moraleja they earned enough to afford a car. And domestic servants being everywhere the world's worst snobs, they, too, would choose the very best they could afford.

But he hadn't meant to speak Spanish, except in situations where he couldn't possibly avoid it. A pretended ignorance of a language one knew goddamned well was one of the best pieces of cover extant. The Russians had invented that one. How many times had he heard diplomats who spoke English like Oxford dons working slowly and painfully through interpreters?

So now to recover what ground he could. He said:

'*Un poquetin. Estilo Berlitz.*'

'Then,' the American Express man said, 'Berlitz have improved enormously.'

'Thank you,' John Farrow said. 'Here's my driver's licence.'

'But your passport, señor?'

'Hell, I left it upstairs on the bed. Is it really necessary? If it is, call the botones and send him up after it. It's Room three-eighty-three—'

'No, sir, it's not that important. Tomorrow you can give me the number of it, date and place of issue – or you can give them to me now, if you remember them.'

'The date and place of issue were August 4, 1970, Washington, D.C. But the number I don't remember. Does anybody?'

'Very, very few. Almost no one. And tomorrow will do just as well, Attorney Farrow. It's just one of those routine things the police makes us fill out. Much ado about nothing really, but still we have to.'

'Makes sense,' John said calmly. 'Or how else would you trace the types who forget to return your cars?'

'That risk is so small as to be practically nonexistent. I've worked here ten years without ever having had such a problem. Besides, the company is fully insured against every contingency. I suppose it really is the insurance company who obliged the police to require this form. In any event, tomorrow will do as well—'

'Tomorrow,' John thought grimly, 'you're going to have your first case of a non-return, son.' He said: 'When can I have the car?'

'In twenty minutes, sir. I'll call for it now. Please sign your name to these three forms. Thank you for your patronage, sir.'

'Think I'll go have a drink in the bar,' John said. 'When you have the keys, send them to me by the botones, will you?'

'Very well, sir,' the American Express man said.

That drink – or rather those three drinks – good, smoky Scotch on the rocks, added up to a mistake, especially since he had eaten absolutely nothing since the day before. They dimmed his perceptions, slowed his reflexes. He could only pray that driving with the windows open would clear his head.

It did, but not enough.

At the immense archlike entrance to Moraleja, a guard flagged him down.

'Should have expected this,' he thought. 'They even try to keep strangers out of La Florida now, and God knows, it's nothing great. What'll I tell him? That I've come to look the place over with a view to buying? In a Seat? Hell, I should have rented a Mercedes.'

'*¿Si señor?*' the guard said.

'*Ist bei hier – Ah, pardon! ¿Hay aquí un Señor Aleman wie heist – ah pardon otra vez! – que se llama – Albrecht Holtz? El ist mein Freund. ¡Oh diablos! ¿Cómo se dice mein Freund en Castellaño, amigo?*'

'*¡Eso!*' the guard laughed happily: '*Mi amigo. Si señor. Vaya Usted recto por cinco calles—*' (He held up his five fingers to make his meaning clear.) '*La sexta es la suya.*' He added one more finger. '*Tuerce Usted a la izquierda. Es número catorce. La última casa de la calle.*'

'*¡Gracias, amigo!*' John said.

'*Bitte schön, mein Herr!*' the guard answered him proudly.

That wasn't surprising. Thousands of Spanish workers had gone to Germany by then, attracted by the higher salaries offered. And sooner or later all of them came home again, driven by homesickness, by the abominable German weather, by their constitutional inability to learn the language, but even more by the fact that the Germans, racists to the marrow of their bones, treated them as Americans treat Blacks. No, worse.

That the guard could say, 'You're welcome, sir!' with a fair accent meant nothing. John wagered that he could also say, 'Thank you. Good morning. Good evening. Good night.' And – 'What time is it?' But nothing more than that. Even if he had been in Germany five years or more.

He followed the directions given him: drove straight past five streets, turned left on the sixth. And saw at once that Kroll had chosen the site of his magnificent Norman chateau with care. Since each house sat in the middle of a two-acre park, no house was really close to its neighbour. But number fourteen, Kroll's chateau, was at the far end of the street. Beyond it was only woodlands, an undeveloped section that John Farrow was sure didn't even belong to the Moraleja district. What's more, the house next to Kroll's, number twelve, was closed. It had metal shutters over all the windows and doors. Number ten was still under construction, which meant that no one lived there yet.

On the other, the odd-number side of the street, the *last* house was number seven. The two-acre lots for numbers nine, eleven, thirteen, and fifteen had been cleared; but no construction had started on any of them.

He drove on by Holtz/Kroll's mansion. A little beyond it, he stopped the car. It wasn't dark enough yet. He'd have to wait.

While he waited, he went over the location in his mind. As hellishly expensive as Moraleja was, it was, nevertheless, fairly well populated. None of the other streets he'd passed showed such a high incidence of vacancies, or so little construction underway. Not even this same street showed it on the other side of the main boulevard he'd driven down to get here.

'That woodland,' he thought, '*his* – sure as hell. And the shuttered house next to his chateau. The lots on the other side – not a damn one of 'em has a for-sale sign on it. Why not? Because Kroll and pals own them, that's why. The house under construction – if I looked it up, its owner's name would be something like Abdul al Hassanein. Planned isolation, brother! Why you could fight a tank battle in this set-up, and nobody you didn't want to would even hear the shots. . . .

'Why? Maybe some of his Islamic buddies bring him in a kilo of pure, uncut stuff in their diplomatic pouches. No. That no. But – explosives, say? Tricky detonators? Radios which can talk to Cairo direct? And – a quiet spot to question whatever Israeli operatives might fall into their hands? No one would hear a poor bastard screaming his guts up out here.

'But – he's played into my hands. Because I couldn't have dreamed up a better spot for a little plain or fancy liquidation than this. . . .'

When it was dark enough, he got out of the Seat and walked to the big iron gate. The house was dark. Too dark. It really wouldn't be much of a trick to climb one of the walls and do a little quiet prowling. But then, neither did it make much sense. At this time of night, the absence of lights meant that Holtz/Kroll probably was not at home. He could even be, John realized, at his flat in Barcelona. Or his villa on the Costa Brava. What was needed now was information. And to get that information he had to take a chance.

He tried the gate. It was locked, of course. But there was an opening in the ironwork big enough for you to put your arm through and touch the button of the bell.

He did that. Waited. He didn't have to wait very long.

A gorilla came to answer it. A gorilla dressed in a butler's uniform. A gorilla with an Arab's face.

'Of course,' John thought, 'three-quarters of Andalucia wears this kind of face – and precisely because the Arabs occupied it for eight hundred years. But still there is something about this gorilla—'

He used the French expression 'gorille' which is argot for bodyguard. But in this case it was singularly apt. The butler was built exactly like a gorilla. Except that he was probably a hell of a lot stronger than any gorilla born.

'*Buenas noches, señor,*' the butler said. '*¿En que puedo servirle?*'

His Spanish was very good indeed. Almost perfect. Still there was something about it . . . Then it came to John how to find out.

'Whose house is this?' he said.

'*Al Señor Holtz,*' the butler said.

'Christian, or given, name?' John said.

'El Señor Albrecht Holtz,' the butler said.

'¿Y no al Señor Heindrich Kroll?' John said sharply. It was, he decided, a reasonable risk. He was two hundred per cent sure that Kroll had never mentioned his real name to his help.

'No, señor,' the butler said.

'But you know Mr Heindrich Kroll, don't you?' John said.

'No, señor. No conozco ningún Heindrich Kroll,' the butler said. He pronounced that aspirate *H* perfectly, a thing that most Spaniards, and all Andalucian find practically impossible to do. In Spanish the letter *H* is nearly always silent. He was an Arab all right:

'Good,' John said, 'I had to make sure. Didn't want to take any risks. I'm at the right place, then. Is your employer at home?'

'No, señor,' the butler said.

'Oh, Christ!' John thought. He said, 'Could I, perhaps, wait for him?'

'No, señor,' the butler said.

'Why not?' John said.

'Because I have orders to the contrary,' the butler said. 'Besides, the sir will return very late, or perhaps tomorrow. He has gone to a party at the Syrian embassy. Sometimes when he goes to parties he stays in town. At a hotel. Understand?'

'Yes,' John said, 'I understand. In that case I'll come back tomorrow.' He turned to go. But the butler said, quickly:

'One moment, sir. Whom can I say had called?'

John hesitated barely a second.

'Digale, el Doctor Josef Mengele,' he said, and turning, walked back to his rented car.

It was a damned fool trick, to give the name of that murderous quack butcher at Oswiscin, or Auschwitz. But, then, maybe it wasn't. Mengele was believed to be hiding out in Argentina. During Kroll's years in Chile, could not the two of them have got in touch? It wasn't unlikely. Besides, it was done now, and to hell with it!

He got into the Seat, and drove off carefully, passing before the house in the direction of the big arches. But long before he got there, he turned off, doubled-back through a parallel street, passed behind the Norman chateau; crept up alongside it with the motor barely turning over. Cut the contact. Sat there in the dark. Hour after endless hour.

He felt his weariness crushing down upon him like a weight, his bones ached. With the pain of fifty-four miserable hopeless years.

'God, I'm tired!' he thought. 'I'll catch forty winks. In order to be at least a little alert when—'

He lay back against the seat. Closed his eyes. He didn't hear the soundless purr of that magnificent Mercedes 350 SL as it slid through those gates at four-thirty in the morning. He didn't hear or feel anything at all.

What waked him was the red sun glare on his eyelids. He looked at his watch. It was eight-thirty-five. And he had blown it. He had blown it all to hell. By daylight, it was impossible. He'd have to wait until it was night again.

'Come on, James Bond!' he snarled at himself, 'haul this young, iron-muscled carcass of yours back to the Hilton. To bed. So maybe tonight you can keep your eyes open. And yourself on your feet. Oh Jesus, I—'

He turned the key. The motor caught. He drove off towards the entrance to Moraleja.

Above him a triple jet BOAC Trident went whistling across the sky in the direction of Barajas Airport. Looking at it, he had a feeling of sadness at the thought that he'd never fly again. Then he pushed the Seat on through the arches, out on the road.

In the Trident he had seen, a youngish looking, attractive woman with snow-white hair peered down from an oval window.

'Is this it, Meir?' she said.

'Yes, Rachie, this is Madrid,' Captain Meir Yariv said.

22

'Now, what shall we do?' Gabrielle said, 'try calling all the hotels?'

'You know how many hotels there are in a city of well over three million people, Rachie? And the capital of the country at that?' Captain Yariv said. 'Besides, your husband impresses me as a real pro. He very likely wouldn't go to a hotel at all. Hole up in a miserable flea-bag of a pension in some obscure street—'

'He is not a pro, Meir. He's much too kind. Without me he's as helpless as a baby. But he wouldn't go to a pension. With his clothes and his looks he'd stand out like a sore thumb. And as unprofessional as he is, he's not stupid. He'd go to a hotel. A big hotel, where Americans go.'

'That's *all* the big ones, Rachie – and still too many to check by phone. Believe me, our best bet is to find Kroll first. Get there *before* John Farrow does.'

'How d'you know he hasn't found Kroll already?' Gabrielle said.

'Because if he'd found Kroll, there would have been a bit of fireworks, what? Guns going off. People falling. Some of them *not* getting up again. That sort of thing. And the papers would be full of it. And they aren't. Not a line.'

'You've only read two,' Gabrielle said.

'The two that count: *ABC* and *Ya*. What's *not* in them won't be in any of the others. So, play it my way, Rachie. Let's go find Kroll.'

'All right. But now you tell me how, huh, please?'

'Something I wouldn't do ordinarily. There's some risk that we might blow their cover, which means Colonel Avni will have to pull them out, and put in others. But since time is in *very*, short supply, baby, we'll just have to risk it. We have people here. We'll call on them.'

'Oh, Meir!' Gabrielle said, 'come on!'

'No,' he said, 'we'll go there at exactly quarter-past one – you see, the cover's a shop on the Gran Via. We go in – and you start looking at things. Buying. He closes at one-thirty. By then I'll have identified us to him. We take him out to lunch. An out-of-town, roadside place. Where we can talk. . . .'

'All right,' Gabrielle whispered. 'Meir—'

'Yes, Rachie?'

'You're thinking that – *they* might have got John – already? Killed him?'

Meir Yariv sighed.

'The possibility exists, Rachie,' he said. '*They* could, without its making the papers, until weeks from now. When they find him floating in the Manzanares, say. . . .'

'And we – we wouldn't even *know*,' Gabrielle said.

'Which means we'd better get our hands on Kroll. Alive. Teach him some modern versions of his own old tricks. With improvements. Until he sings like a canary bird.'

'Which – wouldn't – bring John – back,' Gabrielle said.

'No. But it would give us a hell of a good excuse for liquidating Kroll and company. If any further excuse is needed, that is.'

'Meir – a dead female Israeli – would be a bit of an embarrassment to our people here, wouldn't she?'

'Rachie, goddamnit, don't talk like that!'

'I won't stay alive five minutes after I know John's dead, Meir. No. Not even one.'

He poked her in the middle with a thick, powerful finger.

'And end both the Farrows – and the Levys, for ever, Rachie? You don't even have that right, now.'

'I should *hate* the little bastard!' she got out. 'Every time I look at him, I'd be reminded that—'

'A man loved you enough to die to get what he thought were your murderers. A decent man. That's very rare. A decent Goy. That's rarer still. And you are – and Simone was – pretty marvellous, Rachie. I vote that both strains be preserved. Selective breeding – in the interest of – decency. There's not a goddamned excess of it, around, y'know.'

She stared at him, said:

'You know just what to say, don't you? And you're right. I can't kill my baby, can I? And it's something to live for, isn't it? John's son—'

'Or his daughter.'

'Or his daughter. Oh, Meir, it's *so* long till one-fifteen!'

'We'll just have to wait, Rachie, that's all,' he said.

John Farrow lay face down across the bed. He'd just thrown up the lunch he had carefully and slowly eaten, masticating each morsel a conscientiously counted fifty times before swallowing it. But it had all come back up again, just the same. And when it did it was copiously mixed with blood.

He knew what that meant. His ulcer again. It hadn't acted up on him since his relations with Candace had really gone bad Twelve years ago, that had been. 'Now it has to,' he thought, 'now. When I need my strength.'

He felt too weak to even move. So weak that memory broke through and invaded him. It crawled all over him with all the tactile warmth, softness, tender ardour of her flesh. He remembered the feel, taste, smell of her; the merry mocking devilry of the things she said. Her green eyes' glow. Her voice, shaping his name. 'Johnnn—' drawing it out, into an invitation, and a caress. Her heavy, snow-white hair framing the face that had retained, held, joyously kept, its youth. The flash and flare of her lightning temper. The way she moved, walked, sat, turned, had her being. Her left hand rising to push aside her hair. Her mouth. Her mouth—

He bent his head and cried.

David Weinberg walked to the glass door of the narrow little cubby-hole of a shop on the Avenida José Antonio, or, as the people of Madrid will go on calling it for ever, despite its politically inspired change of name, la Gran Via. Carefully he shut the door, locked it, hung a little plastic sign in it.

Cerrado, Closed, the sign read.

'Now,' he said, 'I am at your disposition, my friends.' He looked at Gabrielle, and his grin widened. 'Especially at *yours*, ma'am,' he said. 'Because if they've got a few more like you out there in Israel, I'm taking the next plane!'

'Dave's the service's Don Juan, Rachie,' Meir Yariv said. 'According to him, that is. And that Yank accent's authentic. Brooklyn-boy. Came out some years back duly equipped with a master's degree in Spanish from Columbia and the University of Mexico. So we sent him here. Where he could do some good. He has, too; first rate.'

Gabrielle didn't answer. Instead she looked at all the swords and shields and engraved gold-inlaid Toledo steelwork. Some of it seemed quite good, but most of it was tourist junk of the most abysmal sort. She glanced up at the sign above the counter. It bore both the Star of David, and the word Sephardim, prominently displayed. Another had the seven-branched candlestick.

'Is that wise?' she said. 'I mean here in Spain?'

'Changing the subject, honey?' Weinberg said. 'Letting me know you're not exactly swept off your feet by my boyish charms?'

'Oh come off it, Dave,' Meir Yariv said. 'Rachie's a respectable married woman y'know.'

'And for *that* I'm supposed to lay off, Meir?' Dave quipped. 'Got news for you, boy – respectable married women are fun! They *already* know how. . . .'

Gabrielle said quietly:

'I'm no fun. Not now. You tell him why, Meir.'

Captain Yariv explained. Rapidly. Succinctly.

'I see,' Dave Weinberg sighed. 'Colonel Avni *knows* you two are here?'

'Yes. And with carte blanche to do the necessary,' Meir Yariv said.

'Then I haven't got the chance of a bishop in a whorehouse to persuade you two to do the right, the professional thing, have I?'

'If you mean by that – to call it off, no, David,' Gabrielle said.

'Thought not. Another proposition then: any chance of the two of you finding Farrow, and persuading him *not* to do something stupid? Spain's not the place to go, "Bang! Bang! You're dead!" Not with Krauts. Especially not with Krauts with Ay-rab buddies.'

'We know that. If we can find John in time, we mean to stop the action. We're not here to blow anyone's cover, Dave.'

'Mine you aren't going to be able to,' Weinberg said, 'because I'm not going to be seen in public with either of you. And when you leave here this time, do me a favour, will you? Don't come back!'

They both looked at him. A trained operative should be security conscious. But when he got to be too security conscious, he became a danger. Because it was the best of all possible signs that his nerve was going. Weinberg had been a first-class agent for a good many years now. Perhaps too many. Perhaps it was time to pull him out.

'A pity, Dave,' Meir Yariv said. 'We were planning to invite you to lunch. Some quiet spot, where—'

Dave grinned at him.

'Instead I'll invite you two,' he said. 'Upstairs in my flat. Unbugged. Where we can really talk in peace. Of course, the grub's not exactly Kosher – Helen's a shiksa, after all. . . .'

'Helen?' Gabrielle said.

'Don't worry, honey – it's legal, sort of. We did it in Gibraltar. She's a little wide-beamed Iowa piece with a special wiggle. Got addicted to it – the wiggle I mean, and decided to keep her around. And she *can* be trusted. One of those flaming, flaming liberals who have to prove it. Ex-exchange student at the University of Madrid. Hell, when I met her, she was dating a spade – *that's* how liberal she is. But I kind of think she was a little relieved when I broke that up before she had to prove her liberalisms *that* far. Good kid, Helen. Now come on.'

Helen was a big, placid Iowa farm girl. Blonde. A sweet, trusting, naïve face. Broad-beamed, just as Dave had said. And quite noticeably pregnant. Which explained Dave's security consciousness, Gabrielle thought.

'Hi,' Helen said.

'Friends of mine from Israel, baby,' Dave said. 'They're gonna take pot luck with us. So open a few more cans, will you? Helen's great with that little old can opener. They teach Yanquí broads can-opener craft in kindergarten—'

'Now, Dave, don't be mean!' Helen said.

'Another thing, baby: Mrs Farrow – she's married to a Goy, too – all this assimilation's going to be the downfall of the Jews! – and Captain Yariv are here on a job. So you can listen, but not too hard, catch? Because if some *real* bad guys catch you and start carving pretty designs into your milk-white hide, I'd just as soon you *didn't* know what they'll be trying to find out.'

'I – I'll fix lunch, and then go for a walk, if you want me to, Dave,' Helen said.

'No, don't,' Gabrielle said, 'anyone with a Botticelli face like this can be trusted, Dave. By the way, my name's Gabby, Helen. And – we seem to be in the same boat. Only I'm not showing yet. That's why we're here. To bring my baby's father back alive if possible—'

'Oh,' Helen said, 'you mean he – he's in trouble? Here in *Spain*?'

'We're trying to catch him before he gets in too deep,' Meir Yariv said, and lifted the glass Dave had put into his hand. 'Well, here's to – all two and a half of you!' he said.

'First thing you do,' Dave Weinberg said, 'is rent yourselves a car. You're going to need it.'

Gabrielle stared at him, her green eyes very wide.

'You mean – you actually *know* where Kroll lives?' she said.

'Me and everybody else in Spain who can read, honey,' Dave

said; 'that murderous old bastard is in the telephone book. That is, if there's anyone around who knows that Holtz is Kroll. And there must be. Among the German colony, anyhow. But *they're* not talking, you can bet on that.'

'In the telephone book!' Captain Yariv said. 'Now who would have ever thought of that!'

'Anybody who knows Spain, Meir,' Dave Weinberg said. 'The only ex-allies of the Nazis still in power. *You* should know the score, damnit! Has any country whatsoever succeeded in extraditing *one* fascist murderer out of here? Look, my count shows one hundred and twelve major businesses in Spain today that are headed by naturalized Germans. And you can lay down any odds you want to that not one of said company heads still bears the moniker his *Vater* hung on him. You want to know where the cash came from to start those hundred'n twelve flossy outfits in the first place? I'll tell you: my grandma's gold teeth melted down into bars that could be smuggled in easily enough. The earrings they pulled through the lobes of women's ears without bothering to unfasten 'em. Every tawdy piece of jewellery some poor little Yid had on her – before she was pushed into the gas chambers, I mean—'

'Dave,' Gabrielle said, softly, 'I suppose it *is* special pleading in a way. But he – Kroll – killed my oldest sister. Tortured her to death.'

'Oh, Dave!' Helen said, 'you've *got* to help them! You've got to! I'll never speak to you again, if you don't.'

Dave glared at Gabrielle. Then his face relaxed.

'Okay, honey, you win,' he said.

'Rachie,' Meir Yariv said, 'you've still got a *French* driver's licence, haven't you? I'd just as soon *not* show the car rental people an Israeli one.'

'Yes, Meir,' Gabrielle said.

'And your wedding certificate?'

'Yes. Don't know why, really. Just picked up my *porte-documents* with everything in it and – why Meir?'

'Not to be pessimistic – John just might get hurt, say. Or he might already be—'

'Meir, please!' Gabrielle said.

'You've got to be realistic, Mrs Farrow,' Dave said. 'You may have to get his stuff out of whatever hotel he's in. Including his passport. Lots of people have them, and their valuables, in the hotel's safe. Meir, there's one other point we'd better clear. If any of you – of us – gets hurt – and the rest can get him out, we can't even try a hospital, you know. Or a doctor. We'll have to bring him – or her, because I can see this little lady's fairly spoiling for a fight and bullets sure ain't got no home-training, honeychild! – here. To my place. I'll give you a duplicate to the street-door key, in case we get separated, or something. That way you don't have to call the *sereno*—'

'The what?' Gabrielle said.

'*Sereno*. Night watchman. He has keys to all the doors to all the buildings on a couple of blocks. People clap their hands to call him. But you *don't*, catch? Not if you've got a shot-up party on your hands.'

'But if – if John should be hurt – or Meir, or even me – why can't we call a doctor or—?'

'Gunshot wounds are a police matter. Prison hospital for the wounded. Jail for his or her chums. Seventy-two hours incognito before they even have to book you. And some of those types down at La Dirección General de Seguridad could teach the SS how it's done. And they aren't even nice to dames, Mrs Farrow. Then if it came out in the wash that you'd been making rude noises in the general direction of their Arab pals, you might get out of jail by year two-thousand and one, but I doubt it. And both of you with Israeli passports, yet! Oy!'

'So one lies on your kitchen floor and bleeds to death, then?' Gabrielle said.

'No. I'll call my sawbones. Good Joe. Loves the powers that be a little less than somewhat. Remembers what the Moorish troops that the winning side brought over in the Crusade for God and for España did to his mother. And his oldest sister. And how his papa looked sliding down a post with twelve bullets in him. He'll cooperate. But try not to get hit, will you? There's only one place a skin like yours ought to be perforated – I mean penetrated – honey!'

'Oh, Dave, *must* you be so awful?' Helen wailed.

Gabrielle looked at him.

'That's already been attended to, David,' she said.

When John Farrow came driving up that street, he had only the parking lights on the Seat on. Even so, he saw that dark bulk from three blocks away. Decided that he wasn't going to take any chances on its being what it seemed to him: a car. A dark coloured car. Probably black.

He turned the Seat into the very next street he came to. Drove down it until he came to the fifth street, parallel to the one Kroll's Norman chateau was on. Drove out that one until he was behind the back wall of Kroll's place. Stopped the car. Got out. Climbed that wall.

Inside the huge wooded plot it was very dark. But a few windows glowed in the house to show him which way to go. He started in that direction. Before he was five metres away from the wall, he felt something tug at his ankle. Hard.

And all that section of the plot was flooded with light.

He dropped to his belly behind a tree.

'A tripwire, you ass!' he told himself. 'Didn't you know this old swine would have everything in the books, and even a few the boys who write the books haven't even heard of yet? And now – the gorilla. Or the gorillas. Hope to Christ there aren't too many of them—'

But then he heard the ripping snarl of attack dogs coming on.

There were three of them. Two of them were Dobermann Pinschers, the meanest, most savage dogs on earth. The kind that go for the jugular by pure instinct; and when they've been trained the way these probably had – what they could do to a lone man had to be seen to be believed. The third was the Spanish version of the German police dog: the *perro lobo*, or wolf dog, as he is called in Spain. A good bit bigger and stronger than any wolf. By himself he was enough. He didn't even need those bone-mean Pinschers to help him shred flesh.

'I've blown it,' John thought sadly, 'before I can get anywhere near Kroll, I've—'

He took that automatic out and sighted very carefully. He knew that he was going to pin-point his position by shooting, but if those three ravenous beasts got anywhere close to him what he was going to be was dead. Messily dead. Fang slashed. Chewed to rags.

He fired, two-handing the gun. Squeezing the trigger slowly. The police dog somersaulted. Thrashed. And, smelling his hot blood, the two Pinschers tore into him with bestial fury.

John killed them in perfect leisure.

He saw the two gorillas come pounding up the path. Two. Only two. He had a chance. Then they split and began to approach his tree from two sides at once. Pros. Doing it right. The way it should be done.

From tree to tree. *Not* shooting; getting close. One of them had a submachine gun. A Schmeisser type. The other had a Mauser automatic. The kind you could turn into a machine carbine by clipping a light rifle stock into a slot built into the back of the pistol grip. One of the longest barrelled pistols made, and hence, one of the most accurate. In comparison to either weapon, Gabby's Pistolle M was a plaything, a toy.

Then he heard that heavy, quavery old man's voice bellow in German:

'Wait! I'm coming!'

And the two gorillas stopped where they were.

But one of them, the one with the Mauser, exposed himself a little too much. John squeezed off another shot from prone position, steady, sure. The gorilla spun out from behind that tree, clasping his shoulder and screaming Arabic curses.

The other one, the one with the Schmeisser ripped off a burst. A long, tearing burst. Splinters a foot long flew up from the tree behind which John Farrow was.

Then it happened. He heard a sharp, staccato 'Splat! Splat! Splat!' A quiet, almost whispered sound. Silencers, he realized. Pistols equipped with silencers. But who in the name of God—?

Then he saw the two gorillas were down. Down and unmoving.

Only Heindrich Kroll stood there, his icy old eyes glaring through his spectacles.

John came out from behind his tree. Walked towards the old man. Kroll's mouth came open. He had forgotten to put in his false teeth. His face was a sagging crêpey mass of wrinkles, visibly quivering in the floodlights. His eyes were blobs of pearl and silver rolling, wild with terror.

And John Farrow stood there, turned to stone. He was powerless to raise his arm and send a bullet through this poor old shaking bastard of a man. He forced himself to remember those slim, beautiful legs lying there in that tangled rubble of Room Twenty-one; that seared burnt black female trunk, that smashed, faceless horror that had been a woman achingly beloved. Not a woman. His woman, equal, partner, wife. Murdered at this man's orders, with his child within her womb. His Gabrielle.

It did no good. The rage he sought simply would not come.

What came, slowly, relentlessly, were other things: an emasculating kind of pity that embraced even this ancient embodiment of evil before him, an utterly crippling sorrow no longer to be borne, a bone-crushing, soul-mangling weariness with straining, back-bent and bloody-handed against Time's Sisyphean stone, the recognition that in a world drained of all meaning, as his had been when Gabby went, nothing was to be served by this senile monster's death.

He saw with a curiously calm detachment himself already at one remove from that long torture that had been his life, that trembling old hand-jerk level. But still he could not break free from that haunting siren call to blissful néant that held him. staring almost gratefully into the muzzle of Kroll's Luger. He felt a hammer blow smash into his lower belly, two centimetres below, and seven to the left of his umbilicus. Felt a white hot stab of pain.

Then with no transition he was lying on the ground and all the searchlights were torturing his eyes. He put his hand down there. Held himself carefully, delicately, so as to keep his insides together. To contain that awful molten pain. Locked his teeth together so as not to scream.

That splatting noise came again. Twice.

And someone – a woman by her voice, was screaming like a demented thing. Tearing the night apart with the shrillest, most anguished shrieks he'd ever heard. And amid the dreadful sounds she made he was sure he heard his name.

Then she was cradling his head with her two arms and great almost scalding tears were falling on to his face, and she was moaning, 'John, John, John. Oh, my darling, don't please, don't John, don't die, darling! Please I beg you! Please!'

He opened his eyes. Said:

'Gabby—' Then, 'there is – after all. There is—'

'John!' she wept, 'don't talk! You're too hurt and I—'

'There is,' he said calmly, clearly. 'And to think I didn't – believe it.'

'Didn't believe what, dearest? Oh God, how you're bleeding.'

'Heaven,' he said. 'I'm – with you. So – heaven. Evident. Has to be.'

'Meir!' she said, 'you heard that? Even – dying – he says things like that and I—'

'Rachie,' the voice came out of the light glare far above, 'hope your petticoat's clean. But anyhow, take it off. We've got to stop this bleeding somehow . . .'

That was the last thing John Farrow heard for a long, long time.

'Where's Dave?' Gabrielle said.

'Gone to cut these ruddy lights. And to call that doctor. Thank God this place is so isolated. I honestly believe that nobody heard those shots. How's he doing, Rachie?'

'Don't know. My slip's not doing much good, Meir. He's – still bleeding. It's – slower, I think. But, dear God! – what are we going to do, now?'

'Take him to my place,' Dave Weinberg said. 'Enrique will be waiting there when we get there. Come on, Meir. Let's pick him up. Easy does it! Careful, now! That's it. That's it . . .'

An hour later, Helen and Gabrielle were sitting on the living-room sofa, waiting for Dr Enrique Garcia Valverde to come out of the bedroom. Helen had her arms around Gabby, was trying to comfort her. Dave and Meir Yariv had gone to dispose of the two rented cars, before daybreak. They were going to leave both of them in outlying districts – said districts as widely separated from one another as time permitted – where it would take days for the police to find them.

Helen had the radio on, very softly. Tuned to Radio Nacional de España. Radio Nacional gave news bulletins every hour on the hour. They had heard two now, and there had been no mention of the gun battle at Moraleja, so far.

Dr Garcia came out of the bedroom just as Dave and Meir came through the door.

'Had to wash that back seat with cold water,' Dave said. 'Think I got it all. Just as well they don't connect that car with – how's he doing, Enrique?'

'Well. Better than I'd expected. Seems very strong. I've given him a half-million units of penicillin. And he's on plasma – but I can't go after that ball. Not here. It's close to a major operation, I'm afraid. Any clinic we sign him into would have to report it. So – I confess I don't know what to do—'

'Doctor,' Meir Yariv said, 'could the operation be delayed – two days, say? Three?'

'Well – yes. So much the worse for the patient. But with luck—'

'Then,' Meir said, 'we extract that bullet – in Israel.'

'Meir!' Gabby said. 'But how? How on earth could we—?'

'Get him on a plane? In a wheelchair, Rachie. With – I've got it! – his left leg in a plaster cast! And you, my dear, saying sweetly, turning on the charm: "My husband's had an accident, officer. It's not too grave, but it's very painful. So he's under heavy sedation. I'll attend to the formalities." '

'That is,' Dave said gloomily, 'if somebody doesn't find Kroll, dogs, and pals before—'

'It's a chance we have to take. Dave, can you get us three tickets to Paris? Don't worry about Israel. Just to Paris. What time does Cook's open?'

'Nine-thirty. I'll be at the door when they open. Which means at best the noon Air France Caravelle. Awful long time, Meir – for somebody not to—'

'I'm gambling on that place's isolation and Kroll's evident desire for secrecy. I'll wager his habits are so irregular that he won't be missed for days – maybe not even for weeks. . . .'

'Could be,' Dave said. 'Say, Meir – what killed Kroll really? He had a bullet in his left arm, and one in his right thigh. Neither of them fatal. Of course he was an old party, but—'

'My face,' Gabrielle said, 'my face killed him, Dave.'

'Whaaat?' Dave said.

'Assisted by a capsule of potassium cyanide. When I – bent over him, he said: "*Du! Vom Hölle zurück gekommt!*" You! Come back from hell, and bit down on the capsule. I suppose he thought – I was Simone. Was my sister, come back to haunt him. Doctor, may I—?'

'Of course, señora! He's not quite out, you know. Your presence might even help. Captain Yariv, you want me to make that plaster cast? If so I'll have to go home to get the materials.'

'Please,' Meir Yariv said. 'Rachie – see if you can get out of John *where* he was staying. We *must* have his passport, y'know. . . .'

Gabrielle went into the bedroom. Came out again almost at once. Whispered:

'At the Hilton. The Castellaña Hilton. Helen would you – sit with him? For only I can—'

'No!' Dave said sharply. 'Not before eight or nine o'clock in the morning. Even that's too soon, but granted the emergency, they'll believe that. What are you going to say, honey? You've got to have a damned good reason for your not having checked in with him. . . .'

'I – just came. He – met my plane. On the way in – we had an accident. Collision. A truck. I've been with him in – a clinic – all night. Will it do, Dave?'

'Perfectly. You don't remember the name of the clinic. You're too upset. But you know how to get there. Can direct the *taxista* to turn left, turn right and so forth. Catch? They probably won't check – especially after you've paid John's bill in full. I'll take you there. Then you take a taxi down to Cook's. I'll wait for you there. After that, here. After that—'

'What, Dave?' Gabby whispered.

'We pray, honey; we pray,' David Weinberg said.

Then it was all done. Or almost. Dr Garcia had built a most impressive cast around John's left leg.

'It's in two halves,' the doctor said. 'Held together only by these two strips of tape. As soon as you safely can, you take it off. I'll be going now. There's nothing else I can do. I've – fitted him with a catheter. For – urine. He won't be able to walk to the aircraft's WC, you know. The – other's no problem. He's empty. Main thing that saved his life. If that bullet had perforated an intestine full of fecal matter, he'd be dead by now. Feed him liquids. Soups, Juice. Water. Nothing else. God bless you, señora! You're very brave. I kiss your hand!'

'Not brave, doctor. Numb. May God bless you – eternally. To say – thank you – is so small a thing. But I do. Truly. With all my heart.'

And it worked. It all worked. Like clockwork. Like a charm. Until they got to the airport. Even there, at first there was no trouble at all. The Spanish officials bent over backwards to be helpful, sped them through customs, through passport control ahead of all the other passengers. Air France's personnel laid a ramp of boards across the stairs, sent two muscular porters to roll the less than half conscious man up into the plane.

They had John half-way or slightly less, up that ramp when, turning, Gabrielle saw a horde of grey-clad police come pouring through the gates, and start sprinting towards the plane. She turned towards Meir Yariv, her face gone white, her green eyes wide with terror.

'*Bli panika*, baby!' Meir said. 'Let me handle this.'

But he didn't have to. Because the grey-clad police with the red bands around their caps, went storming past, beneath the Caravelle's wing, straight towards a nearby Alitalia plane.

Even so, Gabrielle didn't really start to breathe until they had started their takeoff run. She sat there, cradling John's head against her shoulder, and crying a little from pure relief.

They were flying over Marseilles when the air hostess told them:

'It just came over the air. Someone – murdered – a respected German businessman. In Madrid. And two of his servants as well. Even ses chiens – his dogs. But it seems the police have known for years that this M'sieur Holtz was somehow connected with – the underworld. Even with drugs. And those two types – Sicilians – had already aroused suspicions. So they pulled them off Alitalia. And it seems they had much heroin hidden in their baggage so—'

'Ma'moiselle,' Meir Yariv said, 'could you ask the radio operator to send a message for me? It is in connection with my injured friend. We must get him to Israel as soon as possible. I'd like to ask El Al to delay their late afternoon flight. And I also need to get through to the Israeli embassy in Paris. But in that case, if it can be arranged, I should like to talk to them in Hebrew, myself. The – matter's confidential, ma'moiselle. Delicate. D'you think your operator would permit me to—'

'But of course, m'sieur!' the hostess said.

So, when they got to Orly, the El Al plane was waiting, having delayed its take-off for one full hour. The embassy's own doctor was already aboard it, with plasma bottles, antibiotics, the works. He was hopping mad. He gave Gabby and Meir hell.

'This man should be in an ambulance on his way to the American hospital in Neuilly now!' he said. 'He's an American citizen! Well known! Respected! He dies on my hands and God knows what will happen next! Nixon will divert the next batch of Phantoms to the Arabs, likely and—'

'Doctor,' Gabrielle said, 'he's *my* husband. We're going to live in Israel. He's going to take our citizenship. Convert—'

'You're dreaming, madame!' the doctor said. 'Mad and dreaming! Because long before we get to Israel, your husband will be dead!'

Meir looked at the doctor.

'See that he isn't, doctor,' he said. Like, that, very quietly.

The doctor shut up. Abruptly. Got to work. They took the arm out of a pair of seats, stretched John out, took the fake plaster cast off him. Covered him with blankets. Curtained him off from the rest of the passengers, with sheets hung on nylon lines the stewardesses strung up. The doctor hung the plasma bottle up, adjusted the drip. Took John's temperature every quarter of an hour. Injected terramycin. Sat there with grim patience. Gabrielle sat there too, or knelt beside the improvised bed. The way she was crying really was not to be borne.

'I'm sorry, Madame Farrow,' the doctor said, in a gentler tone. 'I'm doing what I can. The rest is – up to time. And God—'

'He's – sinking, isn't he, doctor?' Gabrielle said.

'Yes,' the doctor said. 'I wish I could say he wasn't, but he is. A bullet through the small intestine is an awful thing. Even if he gets there alive it will still be a race. We'll have to type his blood. Find donors whose blood-type match. Build him up even enough to stand the extensive surgery that's going to be necessary. I wish I could hold out more hope, but I can't. I honestly can't, my dear.'

'It's – not your fault, doctor,' Gabrielle said.

And then finally, the last of the blue Mediterranean was pouring backwards behind them, and the shoreline of old Joppa, a yellow haze on the water's edge, before. John Farrow hung between heaven and earth, truly in limbo until he felt her mouth on his, moving, praying:

'Don't die, John. Please don't. I need you. Our baby does. The – world does. The good – the kind – the just – are so very few. Stay with me, John. Don't – go away. Don't – empty the world. I ask you that. I beg you, please!'

His eyes came open. Glassy, unfocused. Then they cleared. His lips moved, shaping words. She had to bend until her ear touched his lips to hear them.

'Don't – worry – Gabby – I am here,' John Farrow said.

She turned, looked up at the doctor. Her eyes were imploring. Gravely the doctor nodded.

'He'll make it now,' he said.

Gabrielle caught John's hand. Held it against her left breast, against her heart.

'*We'll* make it,' she whispered fiercely. 'John, and I – and our baby. So if you don't mean to help, stay out of it, will you? Leave it to me. To Trudy Elon. But mainly to me. Because this man's going to have his son. His image. His continuation. You hear me, God?'

And the big jet went whistling steeply down a long, bright and golden slant of air.

John's eyes came open. His lips moved, shaping words. His voice was strong enough for her to hear.

'Made it. Didn't we? Home, Gabby?'

She bent her head.

'Have we?' she thought. 'Does one ever? Even after forty years – nearly that many anyhow for me; and more than that for him – of wandering in the wilderness? Without ever getting anywhere near Horeb; with no Moses to strike water from the rock? Parched with thirst? Never having known the taste of manna? Lacking both pillars – of cloud by day, of fire by night – to guide us? Can we? Have we? Does anyone, ever?'

Then she felt his gaze upon her, warm, quiet, sure, through all his awful pain. He was smiling at her. And it was all right, suddenly. Perfectly all right.

'Yes, John; our Diaspora's over. We've come home,' she said.